Anthony James Cassidy was born in Dublin, Ireland, in 1942. He joined the Royal Navy at sixteen. After demobilisation, he worked in electronics, banking, public relations, building and engineering. He spent two years in Nigeria during the Biafran War. At present he works at the Open University, designing experimental equipment for student use.

ANTHONY JAMES CASSIDY

Ceremony of Innocence

Paladin
An Imprint of HarperCollins*Publishers*

Paladin
An Imprint of HarperCollins*Publishers*
77–85 Fulham Palace Road,
Hammersmith, London W6 8JB

Published by Paladin 1992
9 8 7 6 5 4 3 2 1

First published in Great Britain by
Arlington Books (Publishers) Ltd 1989

The Author asserts the moral right to
be identified as the author of this work

ISBN 0 586 09108 4

Set in Baskerville

Printed in Great Britain by
HarperCollinsManufacturing Glasgow

Mere anarchy is loosed upon the world,
The blood-dimmed tide is loosed and everywhere
The ceremony of innocence is drowned.

W. B. YEATS 'The Second Coming'

Part One

Week One

Monday 11 June – Sunday 17 June

Mam says I must be the only boy in Dublin that doesn't know how babies happen. She keeps saying it's high time Dad told me. They had another row about it last night. Dad said, 'I will, when he's a bit older.'

Mam said, 'How much older does he have to be? Any day now he'll be shaving and wanting a pair of long trousers.' Dad kept humming and hawing, but Mam pinned him down in the end. She's worried that I don't show much interest in girls.

Dad said, 'There's no point rushing the boy.' He said he never had much interest in girls either. Mam got very cross about this remark. She said, 'And where does that leave me?'

Dad's promised her he'll have a man-to-man chat with me on my next birthday, when I'm fourteen. That's in exactly ten weeks from today. The 19th of August, 1956, Anno Domini. It's a Sunday, which is a pity. I'll have to get dressed up in my best jumper and waste a lot of the morning at Mass. Afterwards, we're all going for a picnic in the Phoenix Park, and a visit to the zoo. Dad says Dublin Zoo is famous. It's the only place in the world where they breed lions in captivity.

My ambition is to be as tall as Dad by the time I grow up. Already I'm five feet ten inches and eleven stone. I know this because I weighed myself at the vegetable shop. Mr Walsh let me use his potato scales, when I helped him clear up after two beggars tipped over his fruit display. They wanted some squishy bananas and bruised apples for nothing. Mr Walsh told them to eff off and they turned nasty.

Mam says I'm going to be brainy like my father and grandfather. I'm very pleased about this, but Mam says she hopes I make better use of my talents. I asked her what she meant but she wouldn't discuss it.

Dad came home early from work, and said he's been sacked

from his job as a bus-driver. It's because of his varicose veins. All the drivers have to take a test every year. He passed everything except the emergency stop. He couldn't stop the bus quickly enough, because his legs were too painful. Also, the Inspector didn't like him driving in slippers. He said Dad should have been wearing boots like all the other drivers. Dad lost his temper, as usual, and told the Inspector it was lucky he wasn't wearing boots. If he had been, he'd have felt tempted to take appropriate action.

This led to a row, and Dad was reported to the Chief Clerk and the Depot Superintendent. They offered him work as a conductor, with rubber stockings for his legs. Dad said no. He'd hate to spend the rest of his life running up and down stairs, breathing Woodbine fumes and trying to get fare money out of drunks and teddy boys.

There will be no money to pay the rent or buy food until Dad gets another job. He says it's God's Will and God will provide. He keeps saying we should look on the bright side. He never wanted to be a bus-driver in the first place, and he only took the job because he had no option.

Mam and I are very upset. My birthday will probably be ruined. It's not fair of God, especially after all Dad's done for Him. Mam says that after they got married, Dad gave up his worldly ambitions so he could concentrate on being holy. Mam was very disappointed about this. When she first met Dad he was planning to be a famous surgeon.

I asked him about taking up surgery again. He said it would be too difficult. His medical books are stored in the loft. He can't get them down because of his bad legs.

He says he's lost interest in the medical business anyway. Doctors nowadays are just like the general public: drunks, teddy boys and gobshites.

He's decided to work as a freelance mobile mechanic. His plan is to ride round on his motorbike, with the side-car full of tools, and do roadside repairs for broken-down motorists. He's going to use the tools Uncle Louis left here when he went to England.

Uncle Louis only emigrated in May, three weeks ago, and already he has a cushy job. He works for a middle-aged widow who owns a pub in London. It must be some sort of clerical work. Uncle Louis is a mechanic but he doesn't need his tools with him. He said in his first letter that he gets paid for spending most of his time in bed. Dad says he's an idle gombeen. Mam says Dad is too innocent for his own good.

Dad was given a week's wages and another week's payment instead of his holidays. He came home with only half the money, after spending the rest of it helping an old woman who fell off a bus. It happened in Parnell Street. The woman was standing on the platform, ready to get out at the next stop. The bus jerked and her shopping bags fell out. She jumped off to rescue them and got hit by a car. A fellow on a bicycle grabbed the shopping, tried to cycle off with it, and got hit by another car. The bags burst and everything was ruined.

Dad saw all this. He took the man and woman to Jervis Street Hospital in a taxi, then he went and bought the woman more shopping, and a new wheel for the man's bike. He said God is quite hot on the idea that we should love our enemies, and do good to them that harm us. There was a terrible row when he told Mam. She said she wished he'd spent the money on drink; at least it would show he was normal. Mam says it's very difficult living with a saint.

Dad told me afterwards, he did spend some of the money on drink. He replaced six bottles of Guinness that got smashed in the old woman's bags. I told him he should have admitted this to Mam. He said no; she might not have seen the funny side of it.

Dad asked me to stay off school tomorrow and give him a hand to do up his bike and side-car. He also wants me to help him sort out Uncle Louis' tools. They're in a terrible mess, covered with rust and cobwebs. He left them in tin boxes in the shed out the back. After he went to England most of the roof blew off in a storm. Dad tied a sheet of canvas over the boxes, but it was stolen straight away.

Dad said it probably ended up as a bed-sheet in one of the downstairs flats. I thought he was joking, but he said no, he wasn't; the sort of neighbours we have would consider it a luxury. He was sorry to lose the canvas. It was the remains of the tent he and Mam used for their honeymoon.

I'm amazed the tools weren't stolen. Dad says no one in Dublin will steal the tools of a man's trade. They're the means of his livelihood. Everyone knows the tools in the shed belong to Uncle Louis. He'll need them again if the job in England fizzles out.

I went to bed early, but I couldn't get to sleep with the racket

Mam and Dad were making. They spent most of the night quarrelling about Dad losing his job.

'It's your own fault you've been sacked!'

'What!?'

'You've never learned to accept the realities of life.'

'If the realities of life consist of tugging my forelock to some wizened little windbag behind a big desk, I'd sooner live in Fairyland!'

'It's not just this job. You've been sacked – '

'Or resigned!'

' – from loads of jobs. And always for the same reason; you're pigheaded and stubborn!'

'I call it pride, and self-respect!'

'And I call it stupidity and lack of self-control! You should have said "Yes" to that conductor's job. At the very least, it would have kept us going 'til you find something else.'

I'm glad Dad didn't take the job as a conductor. Eugene Magee's dad is a conductor, and he's always telling Eugene stories about looking up girls' skirts when they go upstairs in the buses. The latest thing is for teddy girls to go around with no knickers on. All the conductors are desperate to work the Donnycarney service. That's where most of the teddy girls come from.

Mr Magee says there's been a big increase in heart-attacks among bus crews, and that it's all Bill Haley's fault. If he hadn't come up with Rock-and-Roll, girls would still be going round in long skirts, and knicker-legs down to their knees.

I was disgusted with Eugene for repeating all this filth, so I gave him a good belting.

I woke up exhausted, through being kept awake by Mam and Dad. Then I remembered I wasn't going to school. I felt better immediately.

I got up quietly and cut myself a thick slice of bread. I spread it with dripping and Bovril, and went downstairs to sit on the front steps. It was just after six o'clock. I could tell by the chimes from the church clock in Gardiner Street. The Square was empty and peaceful, because of it being so early.

I tried to imagine what Mr Magee could see on the buses that would give him such a thrill. I don't know what causes the big interest in seeing up girls' skirts. I've seen my own sisters with no clothes on, and as far as I'm concerned, they haven't got anything worth seeing.

A fellow came round the corner from Belvedere Place, pushing a hand-cart loaded with books. He looked like Fagin in the pictures in Mam's book about Oliver Twist. She got it as a school prize when she was a girl. She won't let me read it because it's so old and valuable. The fellow stopped and grinned at me. He had hardly any teeth, and huge nostrils. I could see right up his nose. He said he was on his way down to the quays, hoping to flog a few books to the Dublin intelligentsia as they staggered from pub to pub along the length of Bachelors' Walk.

He told me I was a well set-up looking lad. I thanked him for the compliment, even though I didn't know quite what he meant. He grinned again and said, 'You have a good head on you, and a serviceable weapon, too, no doubt.' I told him I didn't need a weapon. I was good with my fists. He gave me a sarcastic look, and sniggered.

'Do you not know what I mean? About the weapon?'

'Of course I do! A weapon is a catapult, or a bow 'n' arrow, or a good thick stick.'

That set him off sniggering again. 'I'm referrin' to the weapon between your legs. The one ye'll be using in the battle of the sexes!'

I was bamboozled by all this, so I just sat and glared at him, without saying anything. He shook his head at me. 'Have ye never heard of the vomiting cobra? Or the one-eyed trouser snake?'

I thought of telling him to eff off. I'm a bit like Dad; I don't like people making me look stupid.

'What about the birds and the bees, and girls' cracks, and babies, and all that class of information?' I said I wasn't interested in that sort of dirty talk.

'That's a real shame! A real shame, that is. A fine big lump of a lad like you! You'd have no trouble getting off with the girls if you turned your mind to it.' I told him I didn't know the first thing about girls.

'Bejasus, then, I have the very book that'll do the trick! It's a book banned throughout the length and breadth of Ireland.'

'Banned?' I said. 'What does that mean?'

'It means no one's allowed to read it; that's what it means!'

'In that case, what's the point of it?'

The barrow-man got so excited, he didn't bother to answer my question. 'The very author of it, a Dublin man like yourself, was ostrich-eyed and forced to hide in a remote country called Paris! Fancy that! And all because of what he wrote into this particular book!' I told him not to be so stupid; what could there be in a book that would make a man go and hide himself?

'Aha! That'd be telling! You'll have to read it for yourself. I'll guarantee ye this; if it doesn't give you the fancy to slip one up the next girl you meet, I'll give you your money back.'

That seemed fair enough, so I went into the house and fetched a shilling I'd saved up. The fellow said it wasn't enough; he wanted one and sixpence. I said it was a shilling or nothing, because it was all I had. He soon gave in.

He told me to go straight into the house with the book, and not to show it to anyone. He warned me that if my parents saw it, they'd report him to the Authorities. He'd be arrested, taken round to the Castle Yard, put up against the wall, and shot.

I didn't know what he was talking about but it seemed a serious thing. I hid the book under my jersey and went up to my room. Mam and Dad were up by this time, still arguing. Neither of them took any notice of me.

The minute I looked at the book, I knew I'd been diddled. The cover of it said *Ulysses* by James Joyce. I could read this with no trouble, because it was written in English. Inside the book, though, it was a right cheat; it was printed in a foreign language! I flew into a rage.

I ran across to Summerhill Depot and jumped onto the first bus going to Nelson's Pillar. The driver slowed down to let me on; they all know who I am because of Dad. I stood on the platform looking out for the fellow with the hand-barrow. My plan was to catch him and get my shilling back.

Through a stroke of luck, the bus got held up by a traffic-jam at the top of O'Connell Street. I saw the very man I was looking for, poking through the rubbish bins outside the Savoy cinema. I jumped off the bus, gave him a kick, and said I wanted my money back for the book. He went white at first, and then got cheeky. He said, 'What book?' and denied he'd ever seen me before.

I said I'd tip his barrow over and break both his legs. It wasn't a very Catholic thing to say, but I hate being cheated. His memory quickly recovered.

'Ah yes, I do remember ye now. Ye had a copy of *Useless* offa me.' I said it certainly was useless, it was all in foreign writing. He said I should have expected this. 'Sure wouldn't the name of the book itself tell you? That's why it's called "Useless". No one can read it except Joyce himself, and maybe a handful of Jesuits who can make out the odd word here and there.' I told him I still wanted my money back.

'Sure I've already spent it! Look . . .' He showed me a packet of fags and a bar of chocolate. He told me to have a look through the barrow. 'See if there's anything else that takes your fancy.'

He asked me to keep an eye on the barrow while he went across the road to the Carlton. He wanted to look in the bins in the foyer. 'There's always good pickings in the Carlton rubbish. They only show the horror films, and the audiences has the fear o' God put into them. They drop sweets and bags of crisps and half-eaten sandwiches all over the floor.'

The poster over the Carlton read: *Attack of the Fifty-foot Woman!* 'Surely,' I said, 'people would only laugh at a silly film like that?'

'Oh no; the Fifty-foot Woman goes round tearing people's heads off and trampling their bodies into a bloody pulp.' He looked longingly at the picture of the woman on the poster. 'Jaysus, it's a pity she's not real! If I got the chance for a jump on a tart that size, it'd be more than just me Jack Rooney I'd have up her. The head would be in there first, hat and scarf and all, for a good sound gobble.'

He warned me not to run off with anything while he was away. He knew where I lived. He went across to the Carlton and I started rummaging through the books.

A big red-faced guard with pimples and bad teeth came along and asked me was the barrow mine. I pretended to be stupid and didn't answer. The guard got annoyed. He said barrows weren't allowed in O'Connell Street, except in transit; I'd have to move. The smell of his breath nearly made me faint.

I looked across to the Carlton, but there was no sign of the fellow who owned the barrow. I got hold of the handles and pushed it left, into Cathedral Street, and then left again at Marlborough Street. I meant to go round the block and meet up with the barrow-man at the corner of Cathal Brugha Street.

Outside the Pro-Cathedral I stopped for a rest. A man asked me if I had any 'hot stuff'. I didn't understand what he was on about, so I said no. He said he'd be interested in anything to do with art or statues or paintings. I told him to have a look for himself. If he could find anything he fancied, he was welcome to make me an offer for it. He had a good root round and discovered a Greek history book, full of pictures of gods and goddesses, mostly with no clothes on. He asked me how much I wanted for it. I chanced my arm and said, 'A shilling.'

The man said it was only worth sixpence, because of all the scribbling on the pictures. He showed me where people had drawn spectacles and hair and funny clothes on most of them. He said he'd have a hard job rubbing it all off, so I took pity on him and let him have it for eightpence.

After he went, I discovered a secret compartment under the handles, full of copies of the Joyce book. There were dozens of them! The next man that stopped at the barrow, I asked him if he'd be interested in buying a forbidden book. He went as pink as a baby pig but eventually he said yes.

I told him the yarn about being taken to the Castle Yard and put up against the wall and shot, and made him promise not to look at it until he was safely home. I began to enjoy myself, making up really ridiculous stories about the *Useless* book. Fellows were coming along in droves and paying three shillings a time for it!

One man even had two copies from me; he said the extra one was to send to his brother in the Kerry Mountains. They have a terrible time there in the winter, what with the long evenings and no sort of entertainment at all. I hope his brother doesn't mind having to learn a foreign language. At least it will give him something else to do.

A man asked me if I knew a good place to see a bit of leg in Dublin. I wasn't sure what he meant. I asked him to explain. 'A show, or a film, maybe, with music, and dancing, and girls twirling their skirts, and doin' the high kicks. Are ye with me now?'

I told him to go to the film at the Carlton. I said he'd see enough leg to satisfy him for the rest of his life. He gave me thruppence.

I ran out of the Joyce books, and thought of a new idea. I bought three dozen brown paper bags from a fellow selling fruit off a barrow, and put all the remaining books into them. As soon as anyone asked me why they were wrapped up, I said they were all banned books. If I was caught selling them, I'd be taken down to the Docks and put on a boat for Paris, and never be allowed to set foot in Ireland again.

The books disappeared like lightning. I never saw anything sell so fast. By the time the barrow-man caught up with me, all that was left was a set of books called *The Encyclopaedia of Universal Knowledge*. He was so pleased with the money I'd made, he insisted on me having the whole set. He wanted me to go into business with him. I said I'll think about it, but I won't. It'd be murder if I ran into anyone who bought the *Useless* books, or the ones wrapped up in paper bags.

When I got back the house was empty. Dad left me a note. 'I'm too fed up to bother about the bike today; we'll do it tomorrow. Gone shopping with Mam. Love, Dad.' It was cold in the house. I sat on the front steps looking through the encyclopaedias.

Two men in gangster-hats and belted raincoats came along and stood on the pavement, looking at the house. The old hag in the middle flat was leaning out of her window. She shouted down at them. 'Whadda yez want?'

They said they were newspaper reporters. 'We're looking for the knight in shining armour.'

The oul one said she couldn't manage the shining armour. 'Will yez settle for a night in a brass bedstead?' She laughed so much she had a coughing fit and spat her dentures out. They came hurtling down and smashed to bits on the pavement. I was going to pick up the pieces but Murphy's mongrel gobbled them up before I could move.

It turned out the two men were from the *Herald*. The nurses at the Hospital were impressed by Dad's kindness to the old lady who fell off the bus. They got in touch with the newspaper, who want to do an article about him.

I told them everything they wanted to know, including Dad's plan to start a mobile repair business. They said they'd make a point of mentioning it in their article; it would be useful publicity for him, and might help to bring in a bit of business to get him started. They wanted to take a photo, to go with the article. I said Dad would be back later. The man with the camera said they couldn't afford to wait; was there any chance of catching him tomorrow?

'Yes,' I said. 'We'll be working out here all day, fixing his motorbike.' They said they'd come back in the morning.

Mam came home on her own. Dad stayed in town to chat up a few people about a job. I told her about the reporters coming back tomorrow. She said not to tell Dad; he'll only get into a temper. He likes to hide his light under a bushel. I don't know what that means. Mam said it will be great if Dad does get into the papers; some Good Samaritan might offer him a proper job, or start a collection for him in the pubs.

I spent the whole evening looking through my new books. They're terrific. I can find out everything I've ever wanted to know.

Dad's motorbike and side-car have been chained to a lamp post in the Square ever since the tax ran out at Easter. The whole outfit was in a terrible state. Both tyres have been slashed, all the chrome has gone rusty, and everything that could loosen, was loose.

We took the cover off the side-car and discovered it was full of stinking water. There was a dead starling floating in it, which made us both feel sick. We had an argument about how to empty it. I wanted to bale it out with a bucket, but Dad said this would take ages.

He tried to tilt the bike and side-car, to tip the water out in one go. It was too heavy to lift, so of course Dad got into a bad temper. He's a very nice man usually, but he hates it when one of his ideas doesn't work. Unfortunately, this happens quite often.

While we were trying to heave the side-car into the air, the floor split open. The filth and water rushed out all over our shoes and Dad's trousers. At that moment the two reporters arrived. One of them had a camera. They asked me if Dad was the man they were looking for, and I said yes.

They took his photograph before he knew what they were up to. Dad got into an even worse temper, and tried to grab the camera. The reporters left, in a terrific hurry. Dad couldn't understand who they were, or why they'd taken his picture. I thought it best not to tell him, in the circumstances. He went into town to get a new tyre and certain other bits. After lunch, we finally got the bike going.

About four o'clock, we were sitting on the front steps cleaning the rust off Uncle Louis' tools. I was laughing at a joke Dad had just told me.

Suddenly, Jembo Nolan got killed in the street right in front of us. He was only eight.

There was a coal-cart parked outside the house, and Jembo was under the cart, filling his pockets with bits of loose coal. The driver was in the basement having an argument with Mr Nugent. Mr Nugent had come home a few minutes before, and found the coalman messing around with Mrs Nugent. The argument turned into a fight, and the coalman rushed up the steps with Mr Nugent after him. He jumped onto the cart and cracked his whip at the horse.

As soon as the cart moved, Jembo took fright. He tried to dart out sideways, between the wheels. This was the worst possible thing he could have done, because he got run over straight away. The cart jerked to a stop, with Jembo trapped under one of the back wheels. The coalman jumped down to see what was wrong. When he saw Jembo he was sick in the road. Everyone was screaming.

Jembo's Uncle Eamonn came cycling up the street. He had a ladder and two dead rabbits tied to his crossbar. He saw what happened. Even though he's only a little fellow he went straight up to the coalman and punched him in the mouth. He got pukey stuff all over his hand, and then he burst out crying.

Dad leaped up and pushed the cart back off Jembo. Jembo just lay quiet, with his eyes shut, and blood bubbling out of his mouth and nose.

Mrs Nolan came out of the house and started screaming. Jembo's other uncle, Dermot, rushed out of the house. He gave the coalman another wallop, and made his nose bleed. Dermot used to be a painter but now he just drinks and spends all his time writing things for the papers. I suppose he'll write about this.

Dad took charge of everything. He said the first thing was to get Jembo to hospital immediately. He stepped into the street in front of a baker's van. The van-driver blew his horn and screeched to a halt. He told Dad to eff off out of the way or he'd run him down.

This sent Eamonn and Dermot into a fury. They tried to attack the van-driver. Dad pushed them away and explained the problem to the van-driver. The van-driver blessed himself and turned out to be very decent. He cleared all his trays out of the van. Dermot and Eamonn put Jembo in the back with Mrs Nolan. Dermot got in the front with the van-driver. They begged Dad to go with them but he wouldn't. He wanted to stay and make sure the coalman didn't escape.

The van-driver left his trays on the pavement outside the house. When he drove off, everyone helped themselves to the bread and cakes from the trays. Dad said this was disgusting. He tried to stop them but no one would listen.

Mam said it wasn't worth getting himself killed for. It was only stale stuff going back to the bakery to be made into bread-pudding.

The coalman was lying on his back on the pavement, trying to stop his nose bleeding. Dad poked Eamonn's ladder through the spokes of the cart-wheels. He fastened it with the bicycle chain and padlock, so the coalman couldn't drive off. Eamonn jumped on his bike again and pedalled off, shouting that he was going to get the police. At the mention of this Dad got nervous; he said we'd have to stop working on the bike and go inside. Dad is hopeless with the police. He just can't be civil to them. He says they're all big ignorant bowsies from Kerry.

Mam told him he should stay and be a witness. Dad said no. With the whole Square as witnesses, the police would hardly be inconvenienced by his absence. I think he was worried they might ask him awkward questions about the motorbike.

Dad started his travelling mechanic business today. He got up early but didn't get away until ten o'clock. Even after all the work we did on it yesterday, the motorbike took ages to start. Mam said it was typical.

Eventually, Dad got the engine going. He went off in a terrible temper. Five minutes later, he was back. He'd forgotten his sandwiches and billycan. He skinned his ankle when he came to start the bike again.

Mam said, 'Maybe God doesn't intend you to be a travelling mechanic.' Dad went off with his face strained and muttering a prayer to St Veronica. I think she's the patron saint of patience. Mam doesn't hold out much hope for this job.

We had another letter from Uncle Louis this morning. He says his work is wearing him out. He's in danger of being sacked for sleeping on the job. Mam went into hysterics about this, but I couldn't see the joke. It sounds to me as if he needs a bit of fresh air and exercise to buck him up. I could do with some fresh air myself; I'm getting a terrible boil on the side of my jaw.

Dad never came home at the time we were expecting him. We all got worried sick about him being so late, especially on his first day working for himself. I said to Mam, 'Maybe he's made a lot of money. He could be gone shopping for presents for us.'

Mam said, 'Don't be ridiculous; we're the last people he'd think of, if he had money!' She says Dad has no idea of how to look after his family; he thinks God does everything. I'm not sure Mam is right about this; Dad is very good fun and doesn't drink or swear.

Very late, just when we were sure he must have had an accident and been killed, the Man From The Bottom Flat appeared. He said there was a policeman downstairs looking for Mam. Mam went pale, blessed herself slowly, and went down to speak to the policeman. She never said a word to the Man From The Bottom Flat. He was very annoyed; he'd crawled all the way up the stairs without his wheelchair so he could give her the message. Mam didn't even bother to thank him or invite him in. She doesn't like him; she says he's a shifty little creature.

The policeman told Mam that Dad's been arrested for stealing a lorry-load of pigs. We're all flabbergasted. We can't understand how Dad got into this situation. He has to stay in the police station overnight. We won't be able to see him till tomorrow morning.

Mam and I went to the police station this morning. The police have had to let Dad go free. No one has claimed the pigs, so they can't accuse him of stealing them. They don't seem very happy about the matter.

The lorry was in the yard at the back of the police station. The pigs were making an awful racket. The sergeant said there was a calf and two sheep in the lorry, as well as the pigs. He said it was like having Noah's Ark in the yard. I asked him, for a joke, if there was an elephant or a duck-billed platypus in the lorry. He gave me a sly crack on the ear when Mam and Dad weren't looking.

Mam asked Dad how he ended up in this predicament. When he told her, she said, 'So much for the travelling mechanic idea!' Dad had stopped to help a man broken down with a lorry. It was a typical farmer's vehicle; everything was banjaxed. He told the man it would take all day to fix, and the man got very upset.

He said his wife would be worried about him. Dad lent him his motorbike to go to a phone box while he got on with the repairs. The man never came back.

Dad had to come home in the pig-lorry, thinking the man must have had an accident. He stopped at the traffic lights in Drumcondra. One of the pigs managed to scramble over the tailboard and jump into the road, without Dad noticing.

A policeman saw it. He cycled after Dad and caught up with him at the next traffic lights. They went back and looked for the pig. It took them ages to catch it. Half the population of North Dublin got involved in helping them. The whole affair caused no end of bother. The policeman started lecturing Dad about being careless. Dad lost his temper. He told the policeman the pigs were nothing to do with him. The policeman got fed up and arrested him. Dad should have kept his mouth shut.

Anyway, Dad is safely home now, but without his motorcycle and side-car. The police say the whole caboodle has probably ended up in a bog in the middle of Ireland. I hope Uncle Louis doesn't lose his job in England and suddenly need his tools back. I'd better send him a note about the matter.

Dad was very depressed this evening. I offered to get his medical books down from the loft but he got shirty with me. He's decided to look for a place where he can start a business repairing cars. We live in a flat at the top of a four-storey building. Dad has no garden or shed to work in. The shed that had Uncle Louis' tools in it is only about three feet square. He told Mam we'd have to move. This led to a row.

'Why can't you use the spare bedroom as a workshop?'

'I'm damned if I'm going to carry motorcars up four flights of stairs!'

'Why don't you start fixing things you *can* carry up the stairs!'

'Such as what, for example?'

'Radios, or electrical things!'

'Sure I have no experience in fixing radios and electrical things!'

'Lack of experience didn't stop you trying to fix lorries! Or, for that matter, getting married.'

I spent all evening writing to Uncle Louis. I told him about the loss of the tools, and gave him some advice about exercise. I also told him about constipation; it could be why he's feeling so tired and listless. I suggested he should ask the woman to get in another man, to share the job with him.

Just as we were going to bed, there was a tremendous racket in the road down below. We could hear an engine revving, and people shouting, and the noise of animals roaring and squealing. The Man From The Bottom Flat came crawling up the stairs. He said there was a policeman at the door with a lorry for Dad. We had to carry him back down; he'd got splinters in his hands and knees. I hope he doesn't get gangrene.

The policeman told Dad they were giving the lorry back to him. No one has claimed it or reported it stolen. Dad was furious. He said he didn't want it, or the pigs. The policeman said Dad had no choice. Technically, Dad's in charge of them. The man who went off with his motorbike left the lorry in his custody.

Dad went upstairs to ask Mam's advice. The policeman ran off down the street and jumped into a car that was waiting for him. Dad came back down with Mam. She said there was no way we were keeping a lorry-load of pigs outside the house. Dad asked her, 'What am I supposed to do with them, in that case?'

The Man From The Bottom Flat bounced down the front steps on his backside. He sat on the pavement listening to us. Mam said, 'Don't sit there; it's all spit and filth.' The man got very upset. It turned out he hadn't heard her properly. He thought she said she'd spit on him if he didn't shift.

When this was sorted out, Mam asked Dad what he was going to do. Dad said he hadn't the faintest idea. The Man From The Bottom Flat said there was only one thing to do; knock up the nearest butcher and sell him the pigs as a job lot, cash in hand and no questions answered.

Dad said this was out of the question; the pigs weren't ours to sell. He wouldn't budge on the matter, even when the neighbours said he could take the money from the butcher and give it to them, as an act of charity. They accused him of keeping food from the mouths of babes. Mam agreed with Dad, but for a different reason; she said it would be keeping porter out of the mouths of men.

The Man From The Bottom Flat gave in, and said we should drive the lorry up into the mountains and let the pigs out to look after themselves. Mam said this was a brilliant idea. The man said he'd come with us and direct us to the mountains. Dad said that, being a former Dublin bus-driver, he didn't need any guidance, thank you very much. The man started blubbering, and said he only wanted to come because he never got out, through being in the wheelchair. Dad took pity on him and said he could come. This turned out to be a big mistake.

We drove down Parnell Street and Capel Street, then I lost track until we got to Harold's Cross. Dad drove out along the Tallaght Road, heading for the Wicklow Mountains. The Man From The Bottom Flat got very excited, saying he hadn't been out for years, and how it was a great pity my Mam hadn't packed us some ham and mustard sandwiches and a bottle of the 'hard stuff' against the cold.

He told us his life story, and how he came to have lost the use of his legs. 'I used to be a delivery driver for Guinness, back in the forties when they were still using th'oul horses and carts. One particular Thursday afternoon, I was down in the cellar of the Brazen Head, waiting for the next barrel to come rolling down the ramp. I'm standing there, looking up, expecting it any minute, but nothing happens, so I start wondering if yer man up top has emigrated to Bulgaria, or nipped off home for a quick gallop with the missus, or round to Joe Carthy's to put half a dollar on a horse.

'Anyway, after a few minutes pondering over the various possibilities, I took a couple of steps up the ramp, to check on the state of affairs, and what do I see only your man up on the cart, fag in hand, and him chatting down to this mot who's lounging at the side of the cart, smiling up at him with sheep's eyes and a mouthful of gleaming teeth. Well, me head ended up just about level with the bottom of her skirt, and the bottom of her skirt ended up just about level with her knees, and what with one factor and another, I found meself enjoying the privilege of inspecting her undercarriage.

'Naturally, like any other red-blooded man in the same and identical circumstances, I gave her a wolf whistle and a bit of blarney. "Would you drop them," shouts I, "if I asked you nicely?" Your man up top, of course, hears this out of the corner of one ear, and thinks I'm yelling up at him, and without thinking to check, he lets go of a barrel, pronto.

'Well, it came thundering down the ramp, aiming straight for the whites o' me eyes, and the next minute, yours truly was lying in a mangled heap on the floor, drifting in and out of consciousness, and thinking to meself, "Begod, the missus was right after all; she always said the drink would be the death of me!"'

We had to stop at three pubs for the Man From The Bottom Flat. Once for a drink, and twice for him to go to the toilet. We had to carry him in and out every time. Dad got fed up with the situation. He said the noise of the pigs was getting him down. He was all for abandoning the lorry at a pub in Terenure. 'They're such a bunch of eejits in Terenure, they won't notice the difference between a lorry-load of bellowing pigs and a charabanc of country priests up for a night out in Dublin . . .'

The Man From The Bottom Flat said this would be useless; we had to get rid of the lorry once and for all, otherwise it would turn up in the hands of the police again. Dad asked him how he proposed to get rid of the lorry; was he planning to disguise it as a motorised wheelchair?

The man started blubbering again. He said his idea was to let the pigs out, then drive the lorry to Ballyfermot and leave it under a lamp post. By tomorrow morning, gangs of thieving gurriers would have it stripped down to the last nut and bolt. There'd be nothing left but a smell of pigshit and a few oil stains on the road.

Dad said this was a great idea. He bought the man some bottled stout to drink in the lorry. This resulted in more lifting in and out, to hold him over ditches. It wasn't as bad as carrying him into pubs and putting up with remarks about 'three drunks and one of them completely legless'.

We spent a long time driving around the Wicklow mountains looking for water. The Man From The Bottom Flat said we couldn't let the pigs out without making sure they had access to a drink. Dad got even more irritable.

'Maybe we should park the whole shebang, pigs and lorry and all, under the lamp post in Ballyfermot.' He said the women there would think it was the last bus with their menfolk on board. They'd take the pigs home to bed with them and not notice the difference. Dad can be a bit cynical at times.

Eventually, we saw a sign saying 'Blessington'. Dad was delighted. 'That's where they have the reservoir that supplies Dublin with water! God must have guided us. I've often thought the water is only fit for pigs to drink!' The Man From The Bottom

Flat laughed so much, he had a choking fit. He wet himself before we could get him out of the cab.

At Blessington, we couldn't get into a field in the vicinity of the reservoir. Every gate was blocked by courting couples in cars. Dad said it was a sign of the times and further proof of the moral decay caused by radio and newspapers. The Man From The Bottom Flat said we should make a note of the car numbers and give them to the police. Dad asked him if he was born with no brains, or had he just lost them through lack of use? How would we explain what we were doing up the Wicklow mountains, spying on motorised depravity? The man said we could pretend we were birdwatching or catching rabbits, or the list could be sent in anonymously. He seemed very keen to stamp out courting in cars.

Dad had to ask him to take his trousers off. The dampness was steaming up the cab and we couldn't have the windows open with it being so cold. Needless to say we had to help him off with the trousers.

The man said he was freezing. He wanted something to wrap round himself. Dad gave him a bit of blanket that we found behind the seats. It smelt as if a dog had been sick on it, but it wasn't as bad as the trousers.

A few minutes later the lorry ran out of petrol. Luckily it happened just after we turned a corner and started to go up a hill. Dad is very good at mathematical problems to do with trajectories and angles. He worked out that we could let the lorry roll backwards and across the road at the bend. Then we'd drop the tailgate down on top of the hedge and let the animals jump off it into the field.

We rolled back down the road all right, but another problem occurred. A car came whizzing round the corner just as we were shooting across the bend at the bottom of the hill.

Dad had to brake very suddenly. He managed it perfectly, even with his bad legs. If only he'd managed to do it as well in his emergency bus-stopping test! He wouldn't have been sacked and none of this trouble would have happened.

The car managed to avoid hitting us. It had to screech up over the bank and back onto the road. It got covered in uprooted bracken and bits of hedge. The Man From The Bottom Flat wet himself again with fright. The car stopped. The driver came back to ask Dad what the Hell he was playing at.

The Man From The Bottom Flat jumped out and hopped round the front of the lorry. The blanket came off him. The car driver saw him sitting in the road, half naked, in the beam from the headlights. He gave a terrible scream and ran back to his car and drove off. Our man hopped after him begging for a lift back to Dublin but it was no use.

Dad was furious about having to stop. We'd used up most of our momentum and were still a long way from the hedge. He let the brakes off again, and we rolled back some more, slowly at first, and then a bit quicker.

Suddenly there was an almighty lurch. The lorry nearly fell to bits. The back wheels had rolled into a ditch. Dad forgot to include it in his calculations. I've never seen him in such a bad temper. I told him to pray to St Veronica for patience. He said something very rude about her.

The pigs were thundering about in the lorry, bellowing at the tops of their voices. The Man From The Bottom Flat was sitting in the road shouting that his underpants were all ripped with the tarmac and he'd be sure to get a bad attack of gravel rash. Dad was also shouting and fuming, kicking the side of the lorry and saying that we were all doomed. It would be only a matter of minutes before a police car turned up. They were never there when you wanted them and bloody vice versa.

I went round the back of the lorry. At least one bit of the plan had gone right. The tailgate had come smashing down on top of the hedge. It hadn't taken the pigs long to catch on. They were jumping off it into the field. I told Dad and he cheered up a bit. Soon, all the pigs were running around in the field enjoying themselves. The sheep and the calf were still howling in the back of the lorry. They were afraid to jump. Dad and I got in to give them a hand.

Wow, what a smell! We nearly fell over. The three animals were filthy. We had to lift them out and drop them over the hedge. We did it as gently as we could, and they ran off straight away, so they must have been all right.

We got out and stood breathing deeply, trying to get clean air into our lungs. There was a horrible grunting and roaring from inside the lorry.

'Damn it!' said Dad. 'We missed one!'

We got back in and felt around in the dark with our feet. There was another pig lying right up at the back, honking and snorting. I said 'Maybe it's injured?' but Dad had had enough of pigs by this time.

'I don't give a monkey's tit whether it's injured or not. It's going out the back of the lorry and over the hedge with the others!'

We couldn't get a proper hold of it. It was too heavy, and covered with filth and slime. We had to slide it along the floor of the lorry. Dad gave it a few crafty kicks to help it on its way. Just as we were about to roll it off the end of the tailboard the pig raised its head and shouted at us.

'Ye pair of black bastards!'

We were struck rigid with fear, even Dad, who believes animals have souls, the same as human beings. As he said afterwards, though, you don't expect a pig to suddenly call you a black bastard, especially when you're trying to do your best for it.

The Man From The Bottom Flat hopped round to the back of the lorry with a torch he'd found in the cab. He shone it on his bum. 'Look at that! Look at the state of me! Me trunks in ruins and me arse tattered and torn. There's hardly a shred of skin left on me lower parts!' Dad jumped down and grabbed the torch to shine at the pig. It turned out to be a man. He had his arms and legs tied together. Dad whispered to me, 'Say nothing to your man below about this.'

The pig started shouting again, about black bastards, and spending every penny to see that we swung for it, and how he had a brother and an uncle in the Government, and that every avenue would be explored, and how it was beyond belief that such an outrage could happen in Catholic Ireland. He also threatened to write to the Pope and have us excommunicated.

Dad and me jumped off the lorry. Dad had to give The Man From The Bottom Flat a smack in the face. He'd gone hysterical at hearing the voice. Dad tried to calm him by saying it was only a pig that had strayed into a seminary. It must have been accidentally taught a few words by the Christian Brothers. They could have mistaken it for a farmer's son with a vocation.

The Man From The Bottom Flat wouldn't take any notice of this. 'How in the name of Jesus could they teach a pig a word like "excommunication"? Sure half the Christian Brothers can't pronounce it themselves, never mind teach it to a dumb animal!

And anyway; how could a pig have a brother and an uncle in the Government?'

I expected Dad to say something really funny and sarcastic, but I was disappointed. He was too busy trying to think of a way out of the situation to waste time making jokes.

The man tied up in the lorry was listening to all this. He shouted that even if he lost the sight of his eyes, what with all the filth and germs in them, he'd still recognise us throughout the length and breadth of Ireland by our voices. Dad immediately started talking in a Scottish accent, the one he does at Christmas parties.

We went round to the front of the lorry and had a chat about the situation. Dad said it was no wonder the police hadn't had a report about the loss of a lorry-load of livestock. The poor devil who'd lost it had been in the back of the selfsame lorry the whole time. Whoever robbed the lorry in the first place must have put him in there. It's two days since the business first started with Dad getting arrested in Dublin.

I asked Dad how the man could possibly be still alive without food or drink. 'Farmers are like camels; they can live for weeks on accumulated fat.'

The Man From The Bottom Flat was impressed by this information. He asked Dad if he'd explain it all to him sometime. Dad said we'd probably have lots of further discussions on the similarities between farmers and camels, not to mention pigs, if the three of us had the misfortune to end up in the same cell in Mountjoy. Personally, he hoped this wouldn't happen, as he was now off the subject of animals for the rest of his life. He especially hoped never to see another rasher of bacon staring up at him off a plate. The Man from The Bottom Flat started whingeing. 'How are we going to get home?'

Dad said we had a bigger worry to face up to; the moral problem of whether we should release the farmer, or leave him tied up where he was?

The farmer must have had good ears. He started shouting and roaring again, saying that the minute he was free, he'd get hold of a big spanner from the tool box in the cab and beat the shite out of us. Dad was relieved to hear this. He said it solved the moral problem by converting it into a practical one; were we prepared to be belted senseless with a spanner?

The Man From The Bottom Flat seemed to be catching the

trick of logical thinking: 'How would it be if we got to the spanner first, and beat the guts out of the farmer? Then we could untie him when he'd be too far gone to be any danger to us.'

The farmer suddenly remembered he had another brother and an uncle who were in the police, as well as an aunt who worked for the Inland Revenue and a cousin who was a bishop. Dad blessed himself when he heard this, even though, as he said, the farmer was probably making it up as he went along. The Man From The Bottom Flat got very worried. 'Your man's Bishop could get a letter read out in every church in Ireland. He could command the guilty men to stand forth under pain of mortal sin and eternal damnation. Where would we all be then?'

Dad agreed it would be a tricky situation, and that each of us would have to square it with his own conscience. This solemn moment was interrupted by another car coming down the hill.

As it came round the curve, its headlights caught the lorry sticking out of the ditch. The driver slowed, and stopped. The three of us dived into the long grass. Dad was sure the police had turned up. Then we heard English accents, so we knew it was ordinary human beings.

People got out of the car and came over to have a look. We heard them talking. They were worried that someone might be lying injured in the wreckage. The farmer started to shout and bellow again.

'Oh my God!' said The Man From The Bottom Flat. 'He'll give the whole game away! Jump in the lorry and clap a hand over his mouth.'

I whispered to Dad, 'Let's tip the farmer off the tailboard and roll him down the field.'

Dad said no. He might not be found for weeks. There was a limit to how long even farmers could live on accumulated fat. Besides, there was the delicate question of how he'd manage to go to the lavatory if he was lying trussed up in a field. Dad is great at these details that most people overlook. I expect it's the medical background.

The Man From The Bottom Flat kept on at Dad to get into the lorry and keep the farmer quiet. Dad got fed up and said, 'Why don't you get in and keep him quiet?' The man said he couldn't, through not being able to use his legs. Before he could say another word, Dad lifted him and dumped him in the back of the lorry.

Within seconds there was an outbreak of thumping and screeching, and shouts of 'Poxy bastards!' and the lorry swaying and bouncing. Me and Dad decided it was pointless to stay hiding with this racket going on. We stood up. The English people got a bit of a fright. There were three of them: two men and a woman, all middle-aged. They asked us if we were all right.

'Oh, sure and begorra, yes,' said Dad, putting on a bogtrotter's accent. 'Don't pay any heed to the noise; it's only the lads arguing over who's going to fetch the tractor to pull us out.' The bad language and screaming rose to a terrible pitch. The Man From The Bottom Flat stuck his head through the hole in the side of the lorry. 'The bastard has hold of me thumb between his teeth! He's grindin' his way through to the bone!' The English people got worried. 'Would it not be a good idea to stop the argument, before there's any serious damage?' 'Oh no,' said Dad; 'sure it's the only enjoyment they get, is fighting.'

'But supposing one of them does lose his thumb?'

Dad told them about the miracles of modern surgery and how it could easily be sewn back on. He made up a long rigmarole about a friend of his who'd had his head decapitated off the top of his neck when he tried to poke his head out through a window and forgot to open it first. 'And d'ye know what he did? He made his way over to Trinity College, his head tucked under his arm, and went straight into the Medical Faculty. In ten minutes, would you believe, he had the brain-box renovated and stitched back on by a saintly medical student from the wild jungles of Borneo! Would you credit that, now?' Dad made the story as ridiculous as possible. He wanted the English people to think the whole affair was a typical Irish carry-on. He hoped they'd stop worrying and drive off.

Instead, they got very annoyed with him. The woman accused Dad of being an irresponsible drunk. This is the biggest insult you can give Dad. He doesn't mind being called irresponsible, but he is dead serious against drunkenness. He said so to this woman. In his temper he forgot the bogtrotter's accent. He slipped into his South Dublin voice. It's the one he has left over from better days. The English people immediately got suspicious and started asking awkward questions. Dad made it worse by slipping back into a disguised accent. He made another mistake, by putting on the Scottish one. That provoked even more questions.

We stood there, deadlocked, glaring at each other. I wondered if it would be any good saying I had leprosy. All of a sudden, the woman let an awful screech out of her.

We all looked round to see what she was screaming about.

It was the farmer, covered in muck and blood, with his clothes ripped to shreds. The glare from the English people's car head-lamps made him look like a monster in a horror film.

'Good Lord,' said one of the Englishmen, just like they do in books. 'I believe we've stumbled upon an attempt to murder someone!' The woman screamed again and fainted, then one of the Englishmen fainted. The farmer ripped a plank of wood off the side of the lorry and broke it in half over his knee.

The Englishman who was doing all the talking said to Dad, 'Look here, what the Devil is going on?' Before Dad could answer, the farmer hit the Englishman over the head with the lump of wood. He slumped down on top of the other two. 'Right, me bold bucko,' said the farmer to Dad. 'You're next!'

Dad asked him if he'd hang on for a minute and listen to an explanation of the whole business. This put the farmer in an even bigger rage. He came lunging at Dad. Dad swung open the cab door and the farmer crashed straight into it.

The Man From The Bottom Flat stuck his arm out through a hole in the side of the lorry. He has very strong arms, from operating his wheelchair. He grabbed the wood off the farmer and brought it down on his head with a tremendous crack. The farmer fell down in a heap, roaring and bellowing and shaking his head.

'Quick; into the car!' shouted Dad. He courageously went back for The Man From The Bottom Flat, dumped him in the passenger's seat and then jumped in himself.

'By God, this is a bit of luck!' said Dad. Our luck didn't last long. The ignition key was missing. Dad said one of the Englishmen must have the key in his pocket but there was no time to search for it. The farmer recovered and pulled himself to his feet. 'Desperate situations demand desperate solutions,' said Dad. He pulled The Man From The Bottom Flat into the driver's seat and shouted, 'Get ready to steer!' He said to me, 'Quick, give me a hand to push. If we can get this thing rolling down the mountain, we can jump in and freewheel most of the way back to Dublin.'

The Man From The Bottom Flat yelled out that he'd never steered a motor in his whole life. Dad told him to shut up;

the situation was bad enough without bringing up trivial objections.

We got the car moving. The Man From The Bottom Flat managed to steer it round the corner and along the straight bit to where the road sloped down again. The car picked up speed. Dad yelled to me to run alongside and get in quick.

We couldn't. The Man From The Bottom Flat panicked. He was weaving the car from side to side. We kept dodging at it, trying to grab the door-handles. It was no use. The car went quicker and quicker as the hill steepened. We jumped onto the back bumper, with our fingers clinging to the roof. It was frightening. Dad cursed The Man From The Bottom Flat.

'Put the bloody brake on, you bloody eejit!'

'Where is the bloody brake?'

'Down where your bloody feet are!'

'My bloody feet don't work! That's the whole bloody point in me having a bloody wheelchair!'

'If you don't stop this bloody car, there'll be more than your bloody feet not working!'

I've never heard so much cursing. It must have been the strain of the situation. We were going so fast, Dad's cap blew off. I said to him, 'Why don't we jump off ourselves?'

'No! We could break a leg. Anyway, I've had another idea.' I never found out what the idea was, or whether it would have been any good. The Man From The Bottom Flat lost control of the car. We swerved into a gateway and smashed into the back of a parked car.

Dad and I shot up over the roof of the English people's car and landed on the bonnet. By the light of the headlamps we could see into the other car. We had a glimpse of bare arms and legs waving in the air, then the back doors flew open.

A girl and a fellow leapt out. They ran off across the field, screaming and yelling. The fellow was wearing only his shirt and socks. The girl had no clothes on at all. Dad wasn't a bit surprised. He said it was no more than you expected in Catholic Ireland nowadays, with all this rock and roll music and coffee-bars springing up everywhere.

I was worried that the courting couple would get cold down in the field. I was all for going after them to apologise and explain the circumstances, but Dad stopped me. He said we must use the situation to our own advantage. God worked in mysterious ways. He never closed one door but He opened another.

He checked the courting couple's car. The ignition key was still in it. 'There you are! That's what I mean about God. We can escape after all.' 'That's fine for us,' I said, 'but what about the courting couple?' Dad had a quick think about this. 'They should be grateful to us. Our intervention saved them from committing a mortal sin.' The Man From The Bottom Flat, gasping with terror from steering the other car, said he disagreed. 'It looked to me as if they were well into it!' 'True, true . . .' said Dad, 'they may have been. But if we take the car, we'll prevent a recurrence of the offence.' He started their car up and backed it out of the gate. He pushed the English people's car out of the way as he went. I got in the front with him. The Man From The Bottom Flat got in the back.

Dad very kindly remembered the courting couple. He asked me to get their clothes out of the back, and leave them hanging on the gate. The Man From The Bottom Flat said we should keep the clothes, to teach the courting couple a lesson.

Dad asked him how he'd like to be stranded in a field in the middle of the night with no trousers on? The Man From The Bottom Flat said he already had been, not so long ago, and without the comfort of a naked hussy to make it worth while. He insisted on keeping the fellow's trousers but at least he took the wallet out of the pocket and left it. He also kept the girl's underwear. He said he was going to give them to his niece. I hung the fellow's jacket and things on the gate with the girl's dress, and put their shoes on the bonnet of the other car.

All the way back into Dublin I was a bit quiet, worrying about the courting couple. Dad said there were certain things I had to learn about life. The first thing is, if you have a farmer after you with a bit of splintered plank, you take advantage of whatever opportunities come your way. Furthermore, if we hadn't escaped, the English people would undoubtedly have reported us to the police, and we'd have been back in a huge mess over the stolen pigs. Finally, he said, and this was the central nub of the thing, God had obviously arranged the whole affair for the express purpose of saving the immortal souls of the courting couple. Our timely arrival had shown them the folly of parking in gateways in the Wicklow mountains with no clothes on. Their moral and spiritual outlook will definitely benefit from the experience. I asked what we were going to do about giving their car back. Dad said, 'The Lord giveth and the Lord taketh away, and then He giveth back.' We'd leave the car outside Clery's in O'Connell Street. It would block the traffic in the morning. The police would soon look into it, and search for the owner.

The Man From The Bottom Flat was busy struggling into the courting man's trousers. 'What about fingerprints? What are we going to do about them, eh?' Dad told him they didn't matter. None of us has a criminal record. The Man From The Bottom Flat said 'Speak for yourself' in a low voice. He was quiet for a few minutes, then he suddenly let out a terrible moan. 'Oh God, me trousers!'

Dad said it served him right if they were too tight; he should never have stolen them.

'I'm talking about me own trousers; the ones I left in the lorry!' It turned out he'd left his spot-the-ball entry, complete with name and address, in one of the pockets. Dad was livid with him. 'I've a good mind to take you back up the mountain and let the farmer murder you there and then!' 'Ye wouldn't dare!' 'Wouldn't I just!' The man said he'd tell the farmer where we lived. Dad thought about this for a minute. 'Maybe . . . maybe we should murder you ourselves. When they find your lifeless body stuffed into that poor fellow's trousers, and your pockets full of that unfortunate girl's underwear, who knows? They might think you're only a dirty little shitbag that got his just deserts.' The Man From The Bottom Flat threw the girl's things out the window. He swore he wouldn't say a word if only we'd take him home. Dad asked him what he'd say if the police came round.

'I'll tell them you gave me a pound to sleep in the lorry overnight and keep an eye on it. These two fellows kidnapped me and stole the lorry. They took me trousers so I couldn't escape.'

Dad said this was a hopeless story. 'Why would the robbers be so fond of you that they'd want to keep you?' The Man From The Bottom Flat thought about it a bit more. 'How would it be if I told the police I secretly took off me trousers, intending to throw them out the window for a clue? To let them know which way the lorry had gone . . .' Dad looked at him, a bit sceptical. 'There's a snag with that story; how the hell could you secretly take your trousers off, and you crammed into a lorry cab with two other fellows?'

Then Dad said he had the answer himself; a story that fitted all the known facts. 'When the police come round, you'll say, right enough, that I gave you a pound to sleep in the lorry and keep a watch over it. Now then; listen to this stroke of genius! There you were, sitting in the lorry, and this oul whore came tapping on the window. Flush with the pound, you let her into the cab. In accordance with the usual procedure, you took your trousers off. Afterwards, exhausted by your immoral activity, you fell asleep. The next thing you knew, these two big bowsies jumped in, threw you out into the road, and drove off with your trousers still in the cab.'

Dad was extremely pleased with himself by the time he'd finished. 'Well? What do you think of the story?' I thought it was brilliant, even though I didn't understand about the oul whore. The Man From The Bottom Flat also thought it was brilliant. He wanted to drive back and find the girl's knickers, so he could pretend they belonged to the oul one. He thought the police would be more convinced.

Dad told him not to be stupid; the police would connect him with the girl in the car straight away. It would be more convincing if he got hold of an old sack and cut two leg-holes in it. That was nearer the kind of low-class lingerie old whores would have on.

I asked Dad how he knew about these things. He said it was from watching the old flower sellers on O'Connell Bridge. There's a terrible breeze comes up off the Liffey. You can see anything you want if you can bear to look.

The Man From The Bottom Flat asked if there were ever any young ones standing in the breeze showing their attributes. Dad said no. Nowadays they're all poured into these skintight American jeans. He blames the influence of the film magazines. The Man From The Bottom Flat wanted to talk to Dad about the skintight jeans, but Dad clammed up.

After this we drove back into Dublin and up to Mountjoy Square. We didn't want to have to carry The Man From The Bottom Flat. I got out at the corner and made sure the police weren't already watching the place. We stopped outside the house and let the man out. Dad and I drove off and abandoned the car in O'Connell Street.

Dad had a serious chat with me, while we were walking back. He says the first thing we must do is go to confession. We've been involved in a lot of irregular conduct; swearing and stealing cars and mingling with unclothed females. We must make our peace with God at the first opportunity.

The reason for this, Dad says, is that if the farmer really has a cousin who's a bishop, and he does get him to issue an edict to be read out in churches, we can sit tight on our backsides, knowing that the matter has already been dealt with between our Maker and ourselves.

The second thing we have to do is get out of Mountjoy Square immediately. We need to find a safe place away from Dublin until the trouble dies down. Dad doesn't trust The Man From The Bottom Flat. He's the sort to sell his grandmother for a drink. He could easily do it to us, thinking the police would let him off lightly because of being a cripple.

Dad says it all goes to show you should never get involved with low-class ignorant goms, even if God does love them.

Dad woke me at the crack of dawn, even though we'd only been in bed a couple of hours. He'd remembered the early morning confessions for daily communicants at the Pro-Cathedral in Marlborough Street. We could get rid of our sins right away, and spend the rest of the day arranging to get out of Dublin.

We went off without even having a mug of tea, which amazed me. Dad always says he can't function without a good shot of tannin, first thing in the morning. We walked along O'Connell Street. The courting couple's car was still parked outside Clery's. Dad said it was a sign from God that we were doing the right thing. I couldn't work this out.

We had a shock at the Pro-Cathedral. There was a long queue for confession and only one priest. I was pleased to see there are so many holy people in Dublin. Dad said it was nothing to do with holiness; it was a sign of the immorality that goes on day and night around the clock since the introduction of cheap rail travel.

After a few minutes, he said he couldn't survive a long wait; he'd have to get in straight away. He said there's a tradition in the Church that if you're in a grave state of sin, you can jump the queue. He forced his way into a pew and started muttering 'Mortal sin – mortal sin!' in people's ears.

I'd never heard of this before, and I don't think anyone else had. They became very annoyed. The noise got so bad the priest had to lean out of the box and complain. Dad was standing gripping a fellow's shoulder, trying to pull him out of the way so he could get past. The fellow was struggling desperately.

The priest reminded Dad that he was in the house of the Lord, and asked him if he'd been drinking. I prayed the hardest I've ever done in my life that Dad wouldn't get in a temper again. God must have heard me. Dad let go of the fellow. He said he'd been helping him up, thinking he was a paraplegic.

The priest was sceptical about this. He told Dad God had His eye on him, and not to risk eternal damnation with any more schoolboy antics. He gave a fierce look at the fellow Dad had been struggling with, saying that the two of them were as bad as each other. I thought this was a bit hard on the second fellow. He'd been sitting there not bothering anyone until Dad got irritable with him. Anyway, they soon got friendly, Dad and the fellow. He apologised, to Dad, for the trouble! Dad said, 'Oh, that's all right. No harm done, not another word,' as if it had been the other fellow's fault.

There were a lot of black looks when the fellow got up to let Dad go into the box next. Dad didn't want to go in. The person who came out was an old tramp. He wanted to wait, in case the tramp had left fleas and germs behind.

Another racket started, with everyone hissing and booing at Dad to get on with it. They all squashed up tight in the seat to force him off the end. The priest got impatient and poked his head out of the box. When he saw Dad glaring at everyone he wasn't too pleased. He asked him if he had a bona fide reason for being in church.

Dad put on his Bob Hope expression and said he certainly had a bona to pick, but it didn't belong to Fido. He'd never steal from a dog. Dad's very fond of an audience, even though none of us knew what the joke meant.

The priest was annoyed, and asked Dad if he had any respect for the cloth. Dad said the only cloth he has any respect for is the green baize on a billiard table. This is one of Dad's problems; he never backs down to anyone. The priest pulled his head in and slammed the window.

I whispered to Dad, 'You'll be ruined if you go into the box. He'll have it in for you. You'll get a huge penance. He might even tell the police!'

Dad said, 'No, there's no chance of that. God's justice is always administered impartially.' I couldn't make any sense of this at the time. I thought he said 'administered in parsley'.

Dad was in the box for ages. Everyone got fed up waiting. They were muttering that it must be his first visit in twenty years, or that he was a politician making his annual confession. There was a shout from the priest. 'Are you having me on?' he yelled, in a squeaky Cork accent. Dad answered him in the deep voice he uses when he's being very sincere about something. The priest said, 'All right, all right, but if this turns out to be a yarn . . .'

I was so embarrassed I went to the back of the Cathedral and started looking through the Catholic Truth Society bookstall. It took me a while to read all the titles. The only decent light was when people opened the door to come in or out. I found some interesting booklets at only 3d each: *The Catholic Church and Science, Does God Really Exist?, Is Hanging Morally Justifiable?* and *The Church's Attitude to Sex.* I read bits of this by the light of the offertory candles and decided to buy it. It was 6d but there were so many fingermarks and creases in the pages I thought it was worth only half the price. I put threepence in the box. I hope God agreed with me. I had to hide the book down the front of my trousers, in case Dad saw it. He might think I'm getting dirty-minded.

I went back to the confession box. Dad was still droning away. The people in the seats were at the end of their tether. Dad had been in the box for over twenty minutes. A normal confession is five minutes at the most, and that's only if you haven't been for ages. The priest let out another yelp. 'Ah go on; no! You're pulling me leg!' After this he started to cough, and I knew he was trying to cover up a laugh. It was the sort of pretend cough we do at school when we don't want to get belted for sniggering.

The coughing from the box got really bad. Dad kept talking on in his deep voice. The priest was gasping things like 'Ah no; no! It's too much!' and 'I've never heard such a story in me whole life!' The coughing turned into a desperate hacking sound. We could hear him wheezing for breath. He opened his little window and shouted out, 'This fellah's going to be the death of me!'

The next minute, he collapsed off his chair and fell out through the door. He lay on the floor purple with choking, kicking his arms and legs in the air like a baby having a tantrum. The crowd in the pews was dumbfounded, especially as the priest had no trousers on under his surplice. I suppose he got up so early he hadn't time.

One hard-chaw shouted that the priest was choking to death. He knelt on the floor and yelled in his ear. 'Tell us, Father, before ye go; was it buggery or child molestation?'

Another man said he recognised Dad as the publican from Capel Street who'd been convicted of drowning a prostitute in a barrel of stout in 1937. A woman in a tight frock and high heels with a lot of lipstick and bright red patches on her cheeks screamed, 'Jesus Christ!' in a terrified voice, and rushed off.

The people trying to lift the priest kept falling on top of him, through pulling in different directions. Meanwhile he was recovering from the choking, even though his eyes were still streaming with tears and his body shuddering with trying to get his breath. 'Oh God . . . Oh God! I've never heard such a story! That fellah's either a lunatic or a comic genius!'

This reminded everyone of Dad. They all turned to stare at the box. The two hard-chaws said it was only right that Dad should be dragged out of the box and made to apologise to the priest. 'And after that, we'll kick him out of the Cathedral, and bounce him down the front steps on his arse!'

Three old women were all for roping Dad to the back of a cart and dragging him through the streets to the Bishop's Palace. 'Begod, sure an insult to even the humblest priest, is an insult to the Church as a whole.'

The priest got huffy. He said he wasn't that humble. 'I'm a BA in European History, for one thing!' The old ladies said this was truly wonderful. There he was, already in the History of Europe, and him not even dead!

The priest thought of something else. 'How many people d'ye know with life membership of the Portmarnock golf club! Tell me that!' The hard-chaws said that was impressive, all right. They supposed he'd be mixing with royalty and the like. Wasn't it a well-known fact that golf was the sport of kings!

The priest said it wasn't just history and golf, either. He was a well-known figure in cultural circles in Dublin. 'Sure ye must all have read me book reviews in the literary columns of the *Irish Times*!' Nobody knew what to say about this. They didn't look the sort that would have much interest in reading literary articles.

A man at the back of the crowd said it wasn't the Bishop's

40

Palace they needed. It was the President's Palace, up in the Phoenix Park, that they should be aiming for. When all was said and done, an insult to the Church was an insult to the very soul and fabric of Ireland itself.

The priest managed to stand up at last. Everyone was very respectful, brushing him down and saying 'Are you all right, now?' and 'Would you like me to pop round to Mooney's, Father, for a drop of something to steady the nerves?'

I felt a hand poking me in the back and looked round. It was Dad, crouched in a pew and looking very cross. 'I'm off,' he said. 'I'll see you outside.' He went scuttling down the side aisle on his hands and knees.

The crowd were all for dragging Dad out of the box, thinking he was still in there. The priest wouldn't let them. He said he must resume the confession. He couldn't leave a sacrament dangling in midair. They were welcome to do what they liked with Dad, once he and God had finished with him. He went back into the box and everyone settled down to wait. It seemed to me a good time to leave.

Dad was waiting outside, huddled behind the knick-knack stalls in the front porch. He asked if anyone was following me. I said no, and we went and had a pot of tea in a café in Earl Street. After this, Dad felt a lot better.

He said that the best thing was to get out of Dublin immediately, before the police and the clergy combine forces. He decided to visit his sister in Blackrock, and ask for help.

His sister is called Nana, because she's very old and jolly. Her real name is Elizabeth. She looked after Dad and her other brothers and sisters when their mam and dad died. They drowned after skidding into a frozen lake in their Rolls Royce while they were on holiday in Switzerland. That's what Nana says, anyway. No one really knows what happened to them. They just disappeared. Mam says it's more likely they fell into the Liffey after staggering out of a pub on Eden Quay. Maybe that's why Dad is so dead against drink.

On the way to the bus I asked him about the blind people and dwarfs and hunchbacks begging outside the Cathedral. I can't understand why God allows people to be born like that. It doesn't seem fair.

Dad said it's so the rest of us can feel grateful and give thanks to

Him for our own blessings. I said this still didn't seem fair; it's all very well for God to do something so the rest of us can feel grateful, but what about the poor people He's done it to? Dad says He gives them the necessary grace to bear their burden. For many of them, that burden is a precious and tangible sign of God's love for them. This sounds like absolute rubbish to me. I wonder if I'm going to be an atheist when I grow up?

We got the Blackrock bus and stood on the platform chatting to Mick Magee, the conductor. It was fun going round corners, especially when we swung round College Green. I nearly landed on the pavement outside the University gates. Mr Magee seems to have forgotten about me kicking Eamonn at school, or maybe he didn't want to say anything with Dad there. Mr Magee is very small, like Eamonn.

Dad says Blackrock is very snobby, full of politicians, schoolmasters and retired jerry-builders, the economic harlots of a capitalist society. I'll have to look up 'harlots' in the dictionary. It must be something to do with being rich and living in a big house.

Nana's house is enormous, with huge windows, and hidden in a private wood near the railway station. When we got there we went up the front steps and straight into the hall. The front door was missing. Dad said Nana probably gave it to someone with a hard-luck story. He says she's a real soft touch for beggars and tinkers and Kleeneze men.

The hall was choked with dead leaves and piles of newspapers and cardboard boxes crammed with old milk bottles full of dead slugs and insects. There was a huge tramp asleep in the corridor, wrapped in potato sacks and snoring. We couldn't get past him and had to go round to the back door.

Nana's garden is as big as a field. It's full of old trams which she bought to use as greenhouses in her business of growing plants. She was in one of them stuffing flowerpots with manure. She came out when she saw us. She ruffled her fingers through my hair. I got a shower of smelly bits down the neck of my pullover.

She took us inside to the kitchen, and told us to sit down at the table. It was piled high with papers and dirty dishes and letters and plant catalogues and balls of string and a dead hedgehog. Nana made a space for us by sweeping her arm across the table and tipping everything onto the floor. She must do this quite often. The pile of stuff behind the table is nearly as high as the table itself.

Nana rubbed her face with her hands and got streaks of manure on her cheeks. I wanted to laugh but Dad glared at me. She offered to make us tea. Dad got agitated and said no; we already had gallons of it sloshing around inside us. No wonder he's so particular about dirt and tidiness. It must be because of growing up with Nana.

Dad told her about not having a job and needing a place with a shed to start a business. Nana said we could come and live with her. Dad said that was impossible. Nana said, 'Why not? There's plenty of space here.' Dad and I gave each other a desperate look. We could hardly breathe with the smell of the dead hedgehog.

Dad thought quickly. He said Blackrock was a very snooty area. He wouldn't be able to afford posh clothes for the children. They'd spend their time being mocked at school and in the street.

Nana said this was a fair enough reason. She thought for a minute, and said she had another big place out in Kilmara. It's a seaside village, about twelve miles south of Dublin.

Nana owns a lot of property left to her by husbands. She's been married four times and all of them have died. The place in Kilmara is the middle house in a Georgian terrace right beside the sea. I sat there with my eyes shut, imagining what it would be like to smell the fresh breezes in off the sea. Dad said he knew the sort of place Nana was talking about; the summer residences of the aliens who raped our land for eight hundred years. I suppose he meant the Vikings.

It's four storeys high but there's a snag; only the basement is vacant. Dad asked was it because of the damp, or what? Nana said no, it was just that no one would stay there for long. They all said it was haunted. Dad said that wouldn't worry him. I don't think Mam will be quite so happy about the matter.

The advantage of the basement flat is that it includes a big garden with a stable in it. Nana says the stable would make an ideal workshop. Dad got all excited, rubbing his hands and grinning, but Nana was worried about him getting homesick for Dublin.

I started to explain about the pig-lorry and the police. Dad interrupted me and said he'd be glad to get out of Dublin, what with so many shysters, sharks and shit-bags walking the streets disguised as decent Catholic men and women.

Nana's not going to charge us rent for the place in Kilmara, because it's in such a terrible state. All the junk from the other flats gets thrown in the basement. I don't like the sound of it much, or the thing about it being haunted. It would be much better to have enough money to buy our own house. I wish Dad hadn't made that promise to God after he got married. I think he should have got rich first, then changed over to being holy when it was more convenient. That's what I'm going to do, if I don't become an atheist.

On the bus on the way home Dad was very thoughtful, working out how we were going to move our stuff from Mountjoy Square to Kilmara. We have no money to hire a removal lorry and anyway, he doesn't want strangers humping our stuff down four flights of stairs for all the neighbours to stare at. He says we'll move at night, as soon as he fixes up some transport.

When we got back to Dublin we stayed on the bus until the North Circular Road, then walked down Belvedere Place to get into Mountjoy Square from the back, in case the police were watching out for us.

As soon as Dad told Mam the plan, she said no. 'Why on earth would we want to move out to a place like Kilmara? It's right at the back of beyond!'

Dad didn't dare tell her the latest developments in the pig-lorry affair. She thinks we just went and dumped the lorry. She doesn't know about the farmer, and the stolen cars. Dad had to make out that Kilmara was a glorious place to start a business.

Eventually, after hours of pleading, Mam agreed to come out and look at the place. We're going there first thing in the morning.

Dad and I spent the rest of the day feeling very nervous. We were forever glancing out the window.

Dad asked me as a favour if I'd mind going round to the pawnshop with my cigarette-card collection and getting some money. I got twenty-five shillings for it. Dad bought a dozen bottles of stout and a packet of Craven A for The Man From The Bottom Flat. He wanted to get him stocious, so he couldn't go out and blab to his cronies in Mulligan's bar.

The plan worked all right, except for one thing. The Man From The Bottom Flat crawled up the stairs, drunk, and blabbed the whole story to Mam instead. She told Dad that if it wasn't for her marriage vows, she'd leave him. Dad was upset about this. He said there are times he regrets not being a drinking man.

At midnight Mam said she couldn't stand another minute of The Man From The Bottom Flat. He got tearful and stupid. He said it was a dreadful thing to be on his own. Could he not stay the night? Mam said no; absolutely not.

The man said he didn't want to go; his flat was cold and miserable. Mam said sarcastically that if it didn't suit him, he could always stay at the Gresham. The man put his arms over his head and screamed for mercy. It turned out he thought Mam said she was going to boot him, for always being in a state of aggression. As well as being a cripple, he's a bit deaf.

He wet himself with fright. We had a terrible job carting him downstairs.

We were wakened by the neighbours shouting and banging on the door. Dad is famous at last. His photo is on the front of the paper, with his name and address, and all about being sacked, and rescuing the old lady, and starting a mobile mechanic's business.

The Man From The Bottom Flat crawled up to see us. He says he's going to make a clean breast of things, the minute the police come round. Dad says it won't be just the police. It'll be the farmer and the clergy as well, and everyone from whom he's ever borrowed five bob or scrounged a packet of fags. He was all for jumping out the window, there and then. Mam told him not to be so melodramatic. It's a good word. I must look it up in the encyclopaedias.

We went straight down to O'Connell Street and caught a bus to Kilmara. We had no trouble finding Richmond Terrace. It's where the bus turns round to go back to Dublin. Mam said this was the only good thing about the place. Dad said we had no choice; it's Kilmara or the Foreign Legion, as far as he's concerned.

The terrace is very nice. It looks out over the sea, with a stone parapet along the front and steps leading down to the sea. Just along the road, there's an overgrown park, and then beyond that miles and miles of beaches and sand dunes. Out in the sea, facing the terrace, there's an island. It's about half a mile away, with a golf course on it. There's a landing stage at the bottom of the terrace, and men with boats, to row the golfers out to the island.

Number Ten, which is going to be our place, is right in the

middle of the terrace. The bus conductor told us that the first house, where the bus turns, is the village police station. It's also the sergeant's house. This got Dad very worried. He said he'd never have considered the place if he'd known.

The conductor said there was another policeman at the bottom end of the terrace, but he was retired. Dad says this is no consolation; policemen never retire, they just get wilier as they get older. I think Dad is getting a thing about policemen.

We couldn't get into the basement at first. The gate was rusted shut and the stairs were rotten. We knocked at the flat above to ask if they'd let us through the house to get in from the back. A woman shouted at us through the letterbox to go away; she never opened the door to tinkers or Jehovah's Witnesses. Dad thought up a sarcastic comment but Mam stopped him saying it. She said there was bound to be a lane at the back of the terrace. We walked round the end of the block and sure enough there was. The back of the terrace is like a small version of the front, with stables most of the way along.

The other side of the lane is one big solid wall of grey stone, like a castle wall. Exactly opposite our stable there's an enormous archway with big gates, like a castle entrance. Dad said the place must be the coal yard and gasworks for the village. He could just see the top of a gasometer sticking up above the wall. Mam said this was just charming.

The stable doors were bolted shut from the inside but there was enough space to see between them. We all had a peep through. The door into the garden from the stable was open, and the windows had no glass in them. The garden has trees in it, and stone walls separating it from the next-door gardens. The walls are about six feet high and all crumbled along the top.

Dad said it would be a doddle to go into one of the neighbouring gardens, shin over a wall, unbolt the stable doors and let us in. Mam got agitated about this, but Dad insisted. She said, 'Supposing you're caught?' Dad said he'd be all right. There was no one about, and anyway, he'd only be a matter of seconds. He tried the door of the stable on our left. It was locked, and so was the one next to it. He had to try on the right, and then even further up, before he found one unlocked. That was only because it was derelict, with the doors hanging off. Mam said to him not to be mad; he'd have to go through two gardens and across two walls, with the police station only yards away. Dad said God would look after him.

He disappeared into the first garden and got safely over the wall. As soon as we lost sight of him we went back to the stable at Number Ten. There was a long wait before we saw him again. He said afterwards he'd disturbed a woman hanging up washing. He told her he was a debt collecter trying to get at some crooks in the next house. She asked him who. He said 'The Sullivans'. This was the name on the flat we'd knocked at round the front. He said he was a bit ashamed of himself for saying this. On the other hand, they'd put us to a lot of trouble by not letting us in in the first place.

Mam and I were crouched down with our eyes to the gap between the doors all this time, thinking God must have abandoned Dad for the time being. He appeared over the wall on the right and dropped into the garden of Number Ten. Mam and I were relieved and stood up. Someone coughed gently behind us. We turned round.

It was a police sergeant. He was dressed in his cap and trousers and boots, but with only a vest and braces on top. We knew he was a sergeant, by the particular type of moustache he had. He was looking at us thoughtfully, chewing on the handle of a toothbrush.

My heart absolutely jumped. Mam went as pale as anything. There was nothing we could do to warn Dad. Dad clattered into the stable. We could hear him whistling loudly, very pleased with himself. He pulled back the bolts, shouted to us to stand back, and flung the big doors open. He looked like the hero in a cavalry film letting the wagon train into the fort.

He caught sight of the sergeant in his vest and braces. The two of them stared at each other for a minute, Dad startled and the sergeant still looking thoughtful. Their expressions both changed to amazement.

'Billie!' yelled the sergeant.

'Alex!' yelled out Dad.

Next minute the two of them were dancing around in the lane like madmen, shouting about how great it was to see each other again. Dad's coat flew over his head. He almost strangled himself getting untangled. The sergeant nearly swallowed his toothbrush before he remembered to take it out of his mouth.

It turned out that Dad and the sergeant used to be in the Irish Army together. They were great friends, and went in for all sorts of sports and dancing. They both raced motorcycles on the Isle of Man when they were young. His name is Mr Doyle, but I always think of him as the Sergeant.

The Sergeant is tall, like Dad, but heavier built, and has bushy grey hair cut very short and a grey moustache, and big, brown, thoughtful eyes.

He took us up to his house in the barracks and made us very welcome. He has fourteen children! His wife is dead. Mam said to me, 'It's hardly surprising.'

Most of the children are girls; only two of them are boys. Christie is the same age as me but very small. His brother Liam is nineteen. He's tall, like Dad and the Sergeant. Liam has a moustache which makes him look like a spiv, and dresses very neatly. Christie told me it's because he's interested in girls.

I might get interested in girls myself, after seeing Christie's sisters. One of them is called Rowena; she's fifteen, which is a bit old for me. I might think about marrying her when I'm older. She's got lovely long hair and very dreamy eyes, like a cat lying in front of a warm fire.

I'm not going to make up my mind immediately. There are a lot more girls in the family. It might be best to see how some of the others turn out before I get too serious about Rowena. Anyway, I've got too many other things to think about at the moment, with hobbies and school and all this moving business.

We had tea and bread with gooseberry jam on it, which is one of my favourites. Afterwards the Sergeant took us back to Number Ten for a look round. It was dreadful. The place is full of junk and dead birds and stray cats. It stinks to High Heaven with damp and bad air and rottenness.

The drains and guttering from the rest of the house end up in the basement. All the drain covers are choked with leaves and rubbish. The electricity isn't working and neither is the water in the scullery. Someone has hammered the lead pipe flat where it comes through the wall from outside.

There's a huge room at the front. Dad says it would have been the kitchen, when the house was owned by a rich family. There's a lift going up through the ceiling to the rest of the house, and a big old-fashioned coke-burning stove in a recess at the bottom of the chimney. Mam says she wouldn't be able to cope with this. She's too used to cooking with paraffin.

The rest of the basement is just small storerooms with no windows, except for the rooms right at the back. Outside the back door there's a row of brick sheds, full of junk, and right at the end a lavatory. This hasn't even got a light in it. It's full of huge spiders, which are the one thing I'm scared of.

The garden is terrific. You have to go up some steps outside the lavatory to get into it. It's got two huge trees in it, a sycamore and a holly. Dad told me what they are. I didn't know the names myself.

Dad got really excited about the stable. He stood in the garden looking at it for ages, smoking, with a dreamy look in his eyes. It's got two big windows downstairs, and two small ones upstairs, all with broken glass, and a big door with an old-fashioned lock on it. The key was still in it, but rusted up. Dad says he'll cure that with penetrating oil. Inside it's as big as a schoolroom, with a floor made of bricks and a stairway going up to the loft. We went up to have a look round, but we had to be careful; most of the floor is rotten with woodworm. Dad says he can get cheap planks from a demolition site and make it all right again.

There's a big skylight in the roof, covered in cobwebs, and a door in the outer wall of the loft, overlooking the lane. There's a crane bolted to the wall beside it. The Sergeant says it was for lifting bales of hay from a cart, to store in the loft. This door is just opposite the big archway into the coal yard. If you lean out you can see right up and down the lane.

I got out onto the crane and pretended I was a sailor up in the crow's nest of a sailing ship. It was quite exciting. Mam was out in the lane and saw me. When I came down she gave me a skelp on the back of the legs. She said I could have fallen off and killed myself.

Dad says that when his repair business gets going he can store spare parts in the loft. He's decided to start a car and motorcycle repair business. Mam made him promise to put some screws in the loft door so I can't open it and lean out again.

The Sergeant very kindly told Dad he'll give him a hand to get the whole place cleared up. Mam said this was just as well; she certainly doesn't intend to. Dad was a bit embarrassed. She said this right out in front of us all. He and the Sergeant looked at each other meaningfully and made queer faces.

On the bus back to Dublin, Mam told Dad that if he's determined to move to Kilmara she's going to take my sisters and stay with her parents in Mullingar until the basement has been made fit to live in. After that they didn't speak to each other.

It was late when we got back to Dublin, but still quite bright because of it being summer. It was our last day of living in Mountjoy Square. I didn't get much time to think about it.

Dad asked Mam to try and be polite to The Man From The Bottom Flat. He doesn't want her to provoke him. The man might decide to contact the police or the papers.

He grabbed my arm and we ran over to the bus depot at Summerhill. Dad took me into the canteen and bought me tea and bread and butter and sausages. He asked me to wait while he had a word with the lads in the repair shed. He said he'd be as quick as possible.

I sat there eating and reading for an hour. I'd found the booklet about the Church's attitude to sex still stuffed down the front of my trousers. I never took them off last night, through getting home so late. I had to put it away when the table filled up. I didn't want any funny comments.

Dad came back and said he'd fixed something up, but we'd have to wait until dark to put the plan into operation. We went up into the rest-room and played snooker for a couple of hours. We were playing foursomes. Even with me as his partner, and I'm useless, Dad still managed to beat everyone. He's a genius at snooker, but he really prefers billiards. He says snooker is to billiards as draughts are to chess. I don't like billiards myself. It isn't so colourful as snooker, but Dad says it's a much more skilful game.

When it got dark we went back to the repair shed. It was still busy and full of mechanics. They work all night fixing the buses. Dad had arranged with one of the mechanics, who's a friend of his, to take out a bus for a test drive. It was going to be a longer test drive than usual. The scheme was to call round to our house, load up the bus with furniture, and drive it out to Kilmara.

We drove back to Mountjoy Square, with me going first to make sure no one was waiting for us. Dad's hopes of moving house on the quiet didn't work out. Everyone in the Square was out standing under the lamps discussing the case of Jembo. He was dead when they got him to hospital. His uncles went off and got stocious drunk with sadness. Mrs Nolan had to have the doctor for her nerves. Everybody has got up a collection to pay for this, and for the funeral. Dad says he'll send a postal order as soon as we have a bit of spare money.

As it happened, it was useful having everyone around. They all helped us to carry our furniture down. Dad didn't want this. He's very proud, but everyone insisted. Only a few things were stolen. The mechanic was the best help. He's big and strong and eats well. It's because he has a steady job working for the Corporation.

Mam had already packed and gone to Mullingar by the time we got back. Dad was very sad about this. She left him a letter saying she'd join him as soon as she knew how things were working out. It's funny she didn't ask me to go with her. Maybe she realises Dad and I are good friends, and that he needs me at the moment, for company.

As soon as the bus was loaded we drove to Kilmara. Dad was worried about the mechanic being missed. He said we weren't to worry. If anyone asked him why he'd been away so long, he'd say the bus had broken down again, while he was out testing it.

We hit a snag at Kilmara, what with the front steps being rotten and no electricity for light. We'd forgotten about this, with all the worry and excitement. Dad had the idea of driving round the back to the lane and unloading everything into the stable. Luckily the doors were still unlocked. We'd forgotten that as well, in the excitement of meeting the Sergeant and his family.

The Sergeant came down while we were unloading. He said he'd been up in his bathroom, Bombing China, and happened to glance out the window. He couldn't help noticing a bloody great doubledecker bus with all its lights blazing. Normally, the only vehicles parked in the lane are courting couples with their lights out, so it made a bit of a change.

We put everything into the stable. The mechanic said goodbye. Dad thanked him and said he'd see he was all right as soon as business got going. The mechanic said, 'Not at all; forget it!' The only reward he needed was the knowledge that he'd helped one of the few decent men still operating in Ireland. Dad shook hands with him for ages when he said this.

As soon as the Sergeant realised we were intending to sleep in the stable, he offered us beds at his house for the night. Dad said we couldn't possibly accept. Where would he fit us with all his own family to think of? The Sergeant said that was no problem; Dad could sleep in one of the cells and I could bunk in with his two lads. I said I'd rather stay in the cells with Dad. The Sergeant said no; there was too much filthy writing on the walls, put there by drunks and perverts. It might give me bad ideas if I was to read it.

Dad said to me, on the quiet, that it was very strange to go to all this trouble to get away from the police in Dublin, and here he was about to spend his first night in Kilmara in a police cell. He said he hoped it didn't turn out to be a rehearsal for the real thing.

Even though it was quite late, the Sergeant's daughters insisted on getting up to look after Dad and me. They made us a big fry-up. I had to eat black pudding, which I hate, but I didn't want to make a fuss after they'd gone to so much trouble. It made my head spin, trying to keep my eye on so many people all moving around at once.

Christie and his big brother sleep in the loft. The girls take up all the bedrooms downstairs. They need proper rooms to keep all their frocks and fancy stuff. The way into the loft is by a spiral staircase. There was only Christie up there. His brother was out with a 'mot' somewhere. I didn't know what this meant. I asked him if it was short for motorcycle. He thought I was joking. He couldn't believe I didn't know that 'mot' means a girl. I told him I wasn't very knowledgeable about certain things, especially girls. I spend all my time reading and making models, and fixing radios, and visiting museums, and going for walks round the old mysterious parts of Dublin. Christie was interested in my hobbies. He said he'll teach me everything about girls if I'll be friends with him and teach him the things I know about. This seemed a useful arrangement, so I said yes.

Christie said if I gave him threepence he could start teaching me about girls straight away. I said this seemed a bit odd. I never heard of anyone charging their friends money. He said that he was giving me good value. If we weren't friends, the secret he was going to show me would have cost sixpence. He and his brothers make loads of money out of this particular thing. I hadn't got any money but I gave him the booklet about sex. He said he could sell it to his brother.

There are no beds in the loft, only mattresses on top of planks. When I gave Christie the booklet he moved his mattress, and the plank underneath, and showed me a hole he'd made in the plaster of the bathroom ceiling. I could see his sisters, but only when they were right underneath the hole. It didn't seem very interesting to me. Christie says it's quite good on a Friday night. They all have a bath and walk round with no clothes on. I said I'd like to try again, when Rowena is having a bath. He said it's a shilling to have a look through the hole on Friday nights. That's a lot of money just to look at girls. I could get a World Assortment Pack of two hundred stamps from Woolies for that.

Week Two
Monday 18 June – Sunday 24 June

We spent the morning clearing rubbish from the basement. It was mainly broken furniture and tea-chests full of junk. Dad wanted to burn it but the Sergeant said no; it was too windy. We'd put smuts all over everyone's washing.

The Sergeant sent for a man called John-Joe Maguire. Mr Maguire took everything away on a horse and cart. He's a small, neatly-built man with brown, leathery skin and clever blue eyes and one of those faces that you can't tell how old the person is. He wears an old, loose jacket with bulging pockets and a pair of smelly trousers and two different boots, one black and one brown, and neither of them with laces in.

In the summer, John-Joe earns his living selling pots of tea on the strand. He has a hut where he boils water and sells crisps and biscuits. Kilmara is popular with Dubliners wanting to spend a day at the seaside. In the winter he does odd jobs with his pony and cart. He also deals in scrap. Playing chess in Dolan's pub is his hobby. The Sergeant says Mr Maguire has a great brain in his head. He could have gone to university and had letters in front of his name but he couldn't be bothered. After Mr Maguire had taken away the junk, Dad and me swept up with big brooms the Sergeant lent us. They're the ones the police use for sweeping up after car accidents. They have very strong bristles. We started at the front of the house and did the big room first.

After lunch we started on the small rooms. There are four of them opening off the corridor that leads to the back door. None of them have any windows. They're like dungeons. We started with the first room on the left. It still smelt horrible, even after we'd cleared and swept it. Dad lit a fire of old newspapers crumpled up in a bucket. He said this was a good way to air a room. We kept bits of paper burning while we did the other three rooms. That took us quite a while. When we went back to the first room, it smelt as bad as ever. The floor was different from the other rooms. It was covered by a big sheet of plywood. The others all had stone floors. The wood was damp and rotten from moisture in the floor underneath. Dad said this was probably the cause of the smell.

The Sergeant came down to give us a hand. He said the smell reminded him of dead rats. He went away and came back with two paraffin lamps. We hung one on the back of the door and the other from a row of hooks on the opposite wall. Dad said the room must have been a meat store. The hooks were for hanging bacon and poultry.

I left quickly when they lifted the sheet of plywood. The floor came alive with spiders and insects. Hundreds of them crawled out and rushed around the place. Dad and the Sergeant dropped the plywood. They nearly fainted with the smell that came from under it.

We went to the barracks for mugs of tea and a rest. The Sergeant got out two gas masks. They were issued to the police during the War. It was in case the Germans decided to invade Kilmara. Dad says he doesn't know how we'd manage without the police. He's changed his mind about them in the last few days. When we went back the smell was even worse. It was mixed with the fumes of the paraffin lamps. We'd left them burning to help dry the room out. Dad and the Sergeant put on the gas masks and lifted out the sheet of plywood. It was so rotten it kept crumbling and falling to bits. The floor underneath turned out to be bare earth. Dad said, 'Maybe that's why the wood was laid down?' The Sergeant wasn't satisfied. He's been trained to be suspicious. He examined the floor and discovered an odd patch in one corner. It was sunk down and softer than the rest. He said someone had been digging in that corner.

Dad asked, 'Why would they do that?' The Sergeant said it could be an indoor latrine. Dad couldn't believe this. The Sergeant said it was nothing compared to some of the things he's seen. He knows people with only one pot in the house. At night they use it as Nature dictates. During the day, it's used to boil up vegetables. He said he often wonders whether they bother to empty it before they toss the spuds and carrots in.

Dad and the Sergeant decided to investigate the corner. They found two spades in the sheds, and took turns digging. During the Sergeant's turn, his spade hit something hollow. It was another piece of plywood, about a foot down in the ground and eighteen inches square.

'Well, lads,' he said, 'get ready to hold your noses. Whatever the smell is, it's under this bit of board.' He knelt down and pulled the bit of plywood out of the hole. He bent over for a moment, peering into the hole. Suddenly, he jumped upright and smashed back against the wall, ripping his gas mask off.

'Jesus Christ!' he said. 'Jesus fucking Christ . . .' His face was white, and his eyes half-shut as if he was in pain. He said to Dad, 'Get the lad out, Billie; we've got a quare one here.' He spoke in that flat voice people use when they've got to deal with something horrible. It was the voice Dad used when he carried our dog in off the road, after a tram ran over it and sliced it in half.

Dad said quietly that he and I had been through a lot together. He wasn't going to start hiding things from me now, if the Sergeant didn't mind.

The Sergeant looked at the two of us very soberly, and then at me particularly. He took the lamp off the hook on the wall. 'Come over here, then, the two of you . . .' He shone the lamp into the corner. We moved over slowly, letting our eyes get used to the light. We were dreading what we'd see in the hole.

It was the crumpled-up rotted body of a baby.

Dad was the first to speak. 'May God have mercy on its soul . . . and on the soul of whoever put it there.' The Sergeant said 'Amen,' and so did I.

'Well . . .' said the Sergeant, after a while, 'there's your smell. It looks as though I'm going to have a busy day.'

We walked along the corridor into the back garden, and sat on the steps. Dad and the Sergeant lit up cigarettes immediately. The Sergeant said he'd have to call the police doctor out from Dublin. We couldn't touch the body ourselves, for fear of disturbing evidence. Also, there might be a risk of disease. The cause of death would have to be established and a post-mortem gone into.

The rest of the day was a blur to me and Dad. The doctor came and took the body out of the hole. He wore rubber gloves and a face-mask. He said the baby was badly deformed. It had six toes on each foot and webs between its fingers like a frog. Its leg bones were bent and it hadn't got a proper nose, even before it went rotten.

The Sergeant has to trace all the previous occupants of the

basement. This will be a big problem. There have been so many and most of them have stayed only a short while. He's worried about how many years back he'll have to go. The doctor said it was difficult to say. His theory is that the baby died shortly after birth, of natural causes. It could have been buried in the basement by the mother, possibly because she wasn't married. With the baby dead, it was a logical way of covering up her guilt.

None of us could eat for the rest of the day. We spent the evening in the Sergeant's office, discussing the best thing to do. Dad said it would be a shame to give up the basement, and especially the stable. The Sergeant said that if we did give it up, someone else would eventually come and live there. If we could just get over the day's events, it might as well be us.

Dad decided to tell the Sergeant the reason why we'd come to Kilmara in the first place. He told him the story seriously, without any of the funny bits he usually adds to a story. The Sergeant listened to him carefully. He said he knew Dad well enough to know he must have been acting for the best where the pigs were concerned. He's going to forget Dad ever told him the story, so far as his official position is concerned. If ever there are any enquiries from the Dublin police, he'll fob them off.

Dad said it's a mercy Mam wasn't with us. He asked me what I think about staying on in the basement. I said I don't know at the moment. The Sergeant said he could ask his girls to come down as a clean up posse. They could brighten the place with soap and water and a couple of buckets of whitewash. He has a heap of curtains in a shed out the back of the barracks. They're from the old cinema down by the green. The owner let him have them when he closed the place down.

Dad asked what colour the curtains are. 'They're not black, by any chance?' The Sergeant said no; they're scarlet and gold, as far as he can remember. Dad went off to sleep in the cells, muttering 'Scarlet and gold; scarlet and gold . . .' over and over to himself as he went.

The Sergeant stayed in the office writing out a report of the case, and drinking whiskey from a little tin mug. I went up to bed in the loft. Christie was asleep so I didn't have to talk.

I wonder if I'll get a chance to make my own secret hole in the bathroom ceiling? I could save myself a lot of money.

* * *

Dad woke up this morning feeling positive. We went up and had breakfast in the barracks and told the Sergeant we're definitely staying.

The Sergeant outlined a scheme he'd thought up during the night. He said our best plan is to leave it all to him. Dad told him we'd be happy to do so. 'We're in God's hands, and God has chosen you as His handmaiden.' The Sergeant gave him a queer look. I think Dad should have chosen another way of putting it.

The Sergeant rang the pub and got hold of John-Joe Maguire and two of his lads. He gave them instructions to pick up four bags of cement and half a yard of sand from the builders merchant. Part of the plan is to concrete the floor in the room in Number Ten. The Sergeant has a budget for any damage or inconvenience his men cause in investigating crimes. There haven't been any recently, so he has plenty of money in the fund. He's written up the case as an official murder investigation, explaining that he had to dig up the floor and replace it. Dad says the Sergeant is a very decent stick, and one of the best.

The Sergeant says the matter of the dead child is between us and the police headquarters in Dublin. They sent a police van out from Dublin to collect the body for further investigation. We're all agreed not to say a word to another soul.

John-Joe came round with the sand and cement early on in the day. When he found he couldn't use the front steps he went away. We thought that was the last we'd see of him, but we misjudged him. He came back with a staircase he rummaged out from the junk he keeps in his yard.

The stairs are wooden, with a good strong bannister. They're painted red. They still have carpet on them, from being in someone's house. John-Joe and his men got rid of the old stairs by smashing them with big hammers. They burnt all the bits out in the back garden. Luckily, there was no washing out today. John-Joe spent the rest of the day mixing and pouring concrete. The Sergeant's daughters, those who weren't at work or school, were busy cleaning and scrubbing the basement.

Dad and I cleared out one of the back sheds, and found some half-empty tins of paint, all different colours. Christie's eldest sister, Ellen, lent us paint-brushes and turpentine. We had great fun washing down the walls and painting them different colours. Ellen says it looks quite Bohemian, like an artist's studio. I think

Mam will have a fit when she sees it. In the evening some of Christie's sisters had a bath. They were filthy from working in the basement. Rowena wasn't one of them, so I didn't bother when Christie said I could have a look for only tuppence. I haven't got any money anyway.

I'm sure it must be a sin to peep at girls in bathrooms. I wish I could find out, without giving a clue that I've been doing it. In any case, it doesn't seem right, when the Sergeant and his family are being so good to us.

Dad is worried about me missing school. He wants me to start in the village school as soon as possible. There's only a few weeks to go until the end of term, and I'm due to take my Primary Cert. this summer. If I don't pass it I've no hope of getting into the Tech. I'm going to train as a carpenter, or maybe a radio repairman. I've no interest in being a motor mechanic. I couldn't stand having greasy hands all day.

It's a pity Dad hasn't the money to send me to a Christian Brothers school. With a good education, I'd be certain of a cushy office job in England. All I'll get from the Tech is a chance to be a tradesman.

Christie says he hopes we're going to be friends. He's lonely with only his sisters and big brother to talk to. It's not the same as having friends to knock around with. I asked him why he's not in a gang. It's because his dad is a policeman. None of the other lads will trust him.

This reminded me that I'll need new friends myself. I'll have to make up a gang of my own, then I can let him into it. I suppose I'll have to forget about my friends in Dublin. The only one I'll really miss is O'Donnell.

After school Christie called for me and showed me round the village. First he took me to the overgrown park opposite the terrace. It's called the band gardens. It used to be a park for the English people who lived in the terrace in the old days.

The park is about half a mile long and quarter of a mile wide. It's very dark and mysterious. Everything has grown wild since the English left. There's a metal railing all round it, with the tops of the iron poles shaped like Roman spears, and barbed wire wound in and out among them. The gates at each end have padlocks on them, and notices saying that trespassers will be prosecuted.

Christie showed me how to get in through some bent bars halfway along the coast road, facing the sea. No one can see you getting in and out, except people in boats. Inside the park it's all huge bushes and giant clumps of brambles and enormous trees that are very climbable. Nobody's cut off the bottom branches, the way they do in parks in Dublin, to stop boys getting up them.

There's an overgrown maze, which Christie says has dead bodies in it. They're people who went in without telling anyone, and never found their way out. The village gangs use the maze when they're playing dirty with their girlfriends. The girls have to go into the maze while the fellows count to a hundred, in fives. If the fellows find them the girls have to let them have a kiss and put their hands up their knickers. The girls are always easy to find. They never go far into the maze, for fear of the dead bodies. Christie says he's never let into these games. He only spies on them. If we had our own gang we'd be all right.

The rich Protestants in the village have their tennis club right in the middle of the band gardens. It's like that story about the Sleeping Beauty, where the castle is surrounded by thick, dark forest and thorn bushes. When the prince fights his way through, he discovers this wonderful palace. The tennis club is beautiful and neat, with grass courts, and a pavilion with a verandah, where the toffs sit drinking gin and watching the games.

There's a shed for storing nets in the winter, and other sheds where they keep the lawn-mower, and the roller, and the machine for making white lines on the grass.

In the summer, according to Christie, the gangs sneak into the band gardens and hide in the bushes round the tennis courts. They look up the girls' skirts when they're whacking the balls. He says it's a fact that the poshest girls are the ones who wear the shortest skirts. They're always bending over showing their knickers. They pretend to be doing up their laces or picking daisies to put in their hair.

There's a fence made of wire netting all round the tennis court, about ten feet high, to keep the balls from escaping. It has canvas hung on it, up to about six feet, to stop people looking in. The tennis club people know about the gangs in the bushes. Christie says the canvas only makes it easier to spy on the tennis girls.

The lads hide behind it and make peep-holes with the point of a penknife.

There's a man employed to keep the gangs out. Christie says he's worse than the gangs. He has a ladder hidden in the bushes behind the pavilion. He uses it to get up on the roof and spy into the changing rooms through the skylight. Christie showed me where the man keeps the ladder.

I'm interested in all this talk about gangs. There must be plenty of adventures going on. Christie says there's a Hill gang for the new council estate at the top of the village, and a Village gang, and a Dump gang. There isn't a Terrace gang, because the families living in the terrace have only girls in them.

After the band gardens we went round to the lane at the back of the terrace. Christie took me into the gateway of the coal yard. It stinks from so many people using it as a lavatory. The men from the village collect in there after mass to play pitch-and-toss. They sometimes lose their whole week's wages in a couple of hours.

The coal yard is derelict since electricity came to the village. It's impossible to get into the yard because the doors are so big and strong. There's a rumour in the village that the yard closed down because of a tremendous explosion in the gas-making machinery. The inside of the yard is supposed to be littered with dead bodies, their eyes and brains picked out by seagulls. Christie's a right one for dead bodies!

We went down the lane to the sea and turned left onto the village green. All the lamp posts have signs on them saying a circus is coming. The green is right at the edge of the sea, with fishermen's cottages round the sides. It's a dangerous place for fun-fairs and circuses. The strong winds coming in from the sea blow the tents down.

Just by the green, the proper sea stops and turns into an estuary. It's about a mile wide, with an embankment running across it for the Dublin to Wexford railway. Right in the middle of the embankment there's a long iron bridge to let the tide in and out of the estuary.

The biggest dare among the gangs is to walk along the railway embankment to the bridge. The water rushes out at great speed when the tide is going down, and the noise is deafening, like Niagara Falls. There's barely room to stand on the bridge when a train comes. When it's coming towards you the wind from it nearly blows you off the tracks, and when it passes the suction tries to drag you along behind it.

The worst thing of all is when two express trains from different directions cross at the same time. Boys have been so frightened they've climbed down among the girders and fallen off and been drowned.

You can get to the bridge by walking along the bottom of the embankment when the tide is out. It's just as dangerous as risking being hit by a train on the top. If the tide comes in it's impossible to climb the bank, because of the steep angle and the thick nettles and thorns and barbed wire.

The water rises very quickly when the tide comes in. The embankment works like a dam and the water piles up against it, instead of rising slowly like on a beach. The bridge doesn't let all the water through quickly enough.

We walked across the green to the boat-yard. We had to be careful because you're not supposed to go into it. The boat-yard is derelict, like the coal yard, because the coal-boats don't come here any more.

It's spooky and lonely, with black hulks of old wooden ships lying around like the skeletons of prehistoric monsters. There are deserted sheds of all sizes, with doors and corrugated iron roofs that creak and groan in the slightest breeze. The whole place feels haunted. Christie says it's even scarier in the winter, and most people are too frightened to go in there.

The village dump is in the boat-yard. The bin lorries come into the yard and tip the rubbish over the remains of the harbour wall, straight into the sea. A lot of the rubbish has collected at the bottom of the wall, but most of it drifts out to sea with the tide. I think that's disgusting.

The driver sets fire to each load when he dumps it. It's supposed to help to get rid of it. The Dump gang, if they're not at school, wait until he's gone and kick the fire out. The Dump gang earns a lot of money from sorting out lemonade and beer bottles to take back to the pubs, and jam jars at a halfpenny each for Bertie Brannon the grocer. He sends them back to the jam factory. It's put me off jam, but I suppose it's no worse than milk. I'm just thinking of those bottles in Nana's hallway. I was amazed at the stuff in the dump. There were no end of radios that I could dismantle to use for scientific experiments, and lots of old prams and bikes that would be good for making carts.

Another thing is cereal packets. Kelloggs are doing a series of cut-out models of trains and railway buildings, and Weetabix do masks on theirs, including Roy Rogers and Batgirl. There are millions of these packets just scattered around. I can't understand people throwing out such useful stuff.

Christie says you can find loads of Meccano in the dump. Fellows' mothers get fed up with bits lying round on the floor, and sweep them up to throw out with the rubbish. Jeremy Lynch, the Dump gangleader, has collected so much Meccano he's almost got a Number Ten set.

There are also lots of English magazines, and the *News of the World*, which has dirty stories in it, and pictures of women in dresses you can see down the front of. Christie's favourite is Diana Dors. He says the Dump gang have a big collection of these pictures.

I asked Christie if he'd help me form a gang to fight the Dump fellows and drive them out, so we can be in charge. He said it would be impossible. The Dump gang are ferocious. If they catch fellows prowling around they light the rubbish and throw them into it from the top of the wall.

Another thing they do is to tie them up and leave them in one of the sheds in the yard. The dump is swarming with rats. Christie says this is even more frightening than being thrown into the fire. The only way you can be rescued is by your parents missing you and reporting it to the police. Sometimes it takes them all night to find a boy. By that time he's usually half out of his mind with terror.

That's made me even more determined. I'd be doing everyone a favour by taking over the dump and stamping out all this cruelty. On the other hand, it may be necessary to be cruel myself. Otherwise, how would I stop fellows helping themselves to whatever they fancy?

The answer is to beat this Jeremy Lynch and take over his gang myself, or form another gang and battle them out of the place. Just think of all the money I could be making from those bottles! I'm extremely glad we've come to live in Kilmara.

Dad went into Dublin to see Nana about a loan to get started in business. He wore his reading spectacles and my old beret pulled down over his ears. He hasn't shaved since Monday. He rubbed boot-polish into the stubble to make it seem more like a beard. I think he looks highly suspicious. I told him he'd attract less attention by being his ordinary self. He wouldn't listen. He believes everyone in Dublin will be on the look-out for him, after the newspaper article.

The Sergeant told him he's being ridiculous. Dubliners have short memories for what they read in the papers. If it doesn't involve big money, political corruption, or an illicit leg-over in genteel circles, it goes in one eye and out the other.

I spent the day having another look round the village. There's a cinema in the main street. It's called the Palace, but it's more like a flea-pit. This week's film is *Three Coins in the Fountain*. The cleaning woman was scrubbing the foyer.

I asked her if I could go in and have a look round. She said no. I told her I'd left a jumper behind, when I was last in there. She said she hadn't come across anything when she was clearing up. I smiled at her, and said please, and she let me in. I was sorry I bothered. It's as bad inside as it looks outside. The whole place stinks of cigarettes and damp. There's even a rip in the screen.

Next to the cinema there's a little sweet shop called Solly Cohen's. There's a notice in the window saying that all goods are manufactured on the premises. Dad gave me threepence to spend, so I went in. I asked the girl what the notice meant. She said there's a sweet factory in the yard behind the shop.

Another fellow came into the shop, about my age. I looked at him, wondering why he wasn't at school. He glared at me and asked me what I was staring at. I said I wasn't sure, but it could be a monkey in trousers. He got very shirty, and left. When I came out he was waiting for me. He swung a kick at me.

I've been studying ju-jitsu from articles in the *Eagle*, so I know how to protect myself. I grabbed his foot and toppled him over. He got up in a temper. The girl in the shop was looking out the window, laughing.

He started another kick with his foot, then tried to trick me by swinging his fist instead. I was ready for this. I gave him an elbow in the belly that made him gasp with pain. He stopped then and looked at me carefully. 'You're a tough bugger, all right,' he said.

I thought he'd given up, but he hadn't. He made a dive at me and knocked me down on the pavement. I fell on my back, with his hands pinning mine to the ground and him sitting on my stomach. I realised he could be useful to me, if he wasn't already in a gang.

He said he isn't in a gang. He has no mother and father. No one will talk to him, because their mothers won't let them. I told him this didn't worry me, because I have a strange family myself. My mother has gone off to Mullingar with my sisters and the police are after my Dad. I shouldn't have said this, but I wanted to make him feel better about having no parents.

He said I was a little creep, making up stories. He has no mother at all, not even one who's gone away. I didn't understand this, and asked if he'd get off my stomach, as I couldn't breathe. He said no; I was his prisoner and I'd stay that way, until such time as he got tired of it.

I thought about kneeing him in the guts and then decided not to, for the moment. I told him I'm new in the village and I'm going to form a gang. Would he like to be in it? He said he hates gangs. They just make fun of him. I couldn't understand this; he's quite tall and strong, even if he is a bit spotty.

'Anyway,' he said, 'why should it be your gang? I could start a gang myself.' I said this wouldn't suit my plans; I had to be the boss and make the decisions. He laughed and said I didn't look much of a boss, lying there at his mercy. I decided at that point I'd have to beat him up; he wouldn't see reason any other way. I gave a heave and turned us both over, then grabbed him by the hair and banged his head up and down on the pavement. I was pleased to see he was a good fighter. He struggled viciously and wouldn't give in.

A man came out from the paper shop across the road and began kicking us both. He shouted that we were behaving like a pair of wild animals and frightening decent people off the street. I let go of the fellow and grabbed the man's foot. I tipped him over with the same ju-jitsu trick. Mam says reading comics is a waste of time. If she'd seen me, she'd have realised they can be useful. On the other hand, she'd have walloped me for fighting in the street.

While the man was recovering, the two of us scrambled up and ran off along the main street. We reached the chapel, and turned right and ran down Back Street. It's an odd name for a street but it's on a wall, written in English and Irish, so it must be right.

We agreed to stop fighting and call it pax. The fellow's name is Sean Malone. He's a year older than me, nearly fifteen, and finished school last summer. He lives in Back Street with his granny and grandad. Both of them spend all their time in bed, reading and smoking pipes. The walls and ceilings and even the windows in the house are stained brown with smoke.

He has to look after himself and get his own meals and make his own bed and even wash his own clothes. Since he left school he's been running a business, repairing bicycles. When he's older he's going to move on to motorbikes and then cars. Maybe he can get a job with Dad.

He made me promise never to call him a bastard, not even in fun. I said, 'Why not; it's only a swear word?' He says it means something really hurtful to him. I've promised I won't.

He asked me if I knew what a prostitute is. I said yes, because Dad has told me. It's a woman who sells her body and risks her immortal soul for the sake of money. Sean asked if I understood what I was talking about. I had to admit I didn't. The reason he asked is because he has a place of his own. It's a cottage that belonged to a prostitute. She came to the village from Dublin and died from a dreadful disease called gone-over-here. No one else in the village will risk going near it. I asked him if her body is still in the cottage. I've had my head so full of dead bodies by Christie I wouldn't have been surprised, especially as she died of a terrible disease. Malone just snorted up his nose and spat.

He took me further down the street and across to a lane at the back of the chapel. There's a big hollow in the ground where they dug up the rock to make the chapel foundations. In the middle of this hollow there's a little cottage. It's built of stone, like the chapel, with two rooms, two windows, a door, and a roof made of corrugated iron. This is the prostitute's house.

Sean took me in and showed me round. All her furniture and her clothes are still there, even her jewellery and make-up still laid out on a fancy dressing-table. It has a tilting mirror with a gold pattern painted in zigzag lines round the edge of it.

Sean says he lives in this place because no one ever comes round bothering him when he's in there. They're afraid they might catch the disease. I asked him why he wasn't afraid of catching it himself. He says all the germs are safely dead now. Anyway, if he did catch it, he knows what to do. He'd go straight out and stick his jake up the nearest virgin. There's a chemical in virgins' love-juice that kills gone-over-here.

As well as the cottage, Sean has a goat tied up in the quarry. He gets milk from it. A tinker gave it to him in exchange for a cartload of scrap bicycles.

Sean says if I do start a gang he'll join it, but only as an equal partner in charge of the rest. I can give the orders provided I discuss them with him first. This isn't a satisfactory arrangement but I've said yes, for the moment. I haven't told him it's only for the moment. Sometime I'm going to have to beat him up once and for all, and get him to agree to me being the boss. The trouble is, he might leave the gang. That would be a pity. There's not many fellows with their own business and practically their own house.

The thing I don't like about him is that he smokes all the time, and hawks up brown spit. His fingers and nostrils are brown, too; dark brown, the colour of Dad's boots.

I asked him if he knows Christie Doyle. He said yes; he knows him well. A dirty little shit who sells his sister's knickers at the back door of the pubs on Saturday nights. The man who runs the paper shop, the one who was kicking us, is Christie's biggest customer. I asked Malone how he knows this, but I didn't get an answer.

It looks as though I'm going to have problems with rivalries in the gang. Unless, of course, I have two gangs. That might be the best idea. I could have a Terrace gang and use it to take over the Dump gang, then keep the two of them separate.

I'm a bit worried by this story about Christie and the knickers. It doesn't seem a very decent thing to do. And why should the paper shop man want them? I suppose he buys them on the cheap for his wife.

I'm feeling a bit guilty about not giving Dad much help this week. Dad says he's getting along very nicely without me. He'll have our beds set up in the basement by tonight. That's terrific news. I won't have to sleep in the Sergeant's loft any more. The spiders are really getting me down. I can see them staring down at me from the rafters.

I've got a lot on my mind. I need to get established in the village. Then I can start working on my plans. The main thing I want, is to be in charge of the dump. The quickest way to do it is to challenge this Jeremy Lynch, and take over his gang. If that doesn't work out I'll have to do it the long way. I'll form a stronger gang and drive him out.

I went round to see Sean today, and asked him about the dump. He works in his granny's garden shed, fixing the bicycles. There's a garage at the back of the house, much bigger than the shed. I asked him why he doesn't work in the garage. He said it's because there's no room. There's a car stored in it, that used to belong to his grandad. It's been given to him. He's not allowed to drive it until he's sixteen and can get a licence. He's going to take me to the dump tomorrow, to show me Jeremy Lynch.

It's Saturday, so the whole gang will be there. Malone says I'll shit myself when I find out what I'm up against. He doesn't know me very well.

We slept in the basement last night, as Dad promised. Christie was disappointed at losing my company. I was disappointed too; I haven't had a chance to look at Rowena in the bath. On the other hand, I was too relieved at getting away from the spiders to think about it for long.

I went round early to see Sean but he was busy working on bicycles. He told me I could wait in the prostitute's cottage, provided I didn't mess anything up.

I was out the back playing with the goat when a voice called me. I looked around but couldn't see anyone. The voice told me to look up. There was a priest leaning over the wall at the back of the chapel yard, grinning down at me. He has quite a young face.

He was interested to know who I was. I told him I'm new in the village. The conversation didn't last very long. We got fed up shouting at each other. He was quite high up and I couldn't see properly with the sun shining in my eyes. The goat kept jumping at me, as well, making a racket and knocking me off balance. The priest shouted at me to come and see him sometime. I said I would, even though Dad has warned me to stay away from priests.

When Sean came along I told him about the conversation. He said the priest is the only friend he has in the village. I told him he's got me as well. Sean said he'd prefer to wait and see how things work out. He's had a lot of disappointment in his life.

The bottom of Back Street leads straight down to the dump. Instead of going that way, Sean took me round to the railway station. We squeezed through the fence just opposite the signal box and crouched down behind the bushes. Sean said the best way to spy on the dump is from the top of the railway embankment. It's tricky to get along it. There's always a danger of being seen by porters or knocked down by trains.

We waited until the signalman wasn't looking. We walked casually along the path that runs alongside the railway on top of the embankment. We had to go in single file because it's so narrow. I was all for running, to get out of sight of the station. Sean said that was really stupid; didn't I know that quick movements always attract attention? He says the corners of your eye are specially made for this. He's pretty smart, but of course he's a year older than me.

We walked along until we got to where the embankment starts to run out across the estuary. I was amazed at how high up we were. Sean said you could kill yourself falling down the bank, if the nettles and brambles weren't there to slow you down.

When we got to where the embankment overlooks the dump, we crouched down and peered over the top of the wall, which is quite low. It was like looking down on a huge map of the village. I could see over the boat-yard and the green and right across to the terrace in the distance. We were nearly as high as the roof.

'See down there?' said Sean. 'That's the fellow you have to deal with. That's Jeremy Lynch.' I looked cautiously where he was pointing. I saw a little runty fellow with filthy torn clothes and hair sticking off his head in every direction. He was standing on top of the dump wall pissing into the sea.

I didn't think he'd be much trouble to beat up. Sean said not to underestimate him. He has a shrewd cunning brain and a very big gang. He knows how to make money out of the rubbish business, and can pay to keep people loyal.

'Well, how do we get down there?'

'We don't. We're only here to have a look.'

'I want to go down straight away and get started on Lynch.'

'We can't go down the bank. It's too steep. Anyway, it's covered in barbed wire and brambles and nettles. And there's a deep gully at the bottom. It's filled with water and floating rubbish.'

'You're a scaredy-cat! If I had a bit of rope I'd be down in a flash.'

Sean got irritable. 'I hope you're not going to be a big trouble to me. Why can you not have a bit of patience?'

'I'm in a hurry to take over the dump. I can't do it until I beat up this Lynch fellow.'

'You're a right one for beating people up! Do you never think of using your head? There might be a less troublesome solution.'

I explained to him that I was used to doing things by force. That's the lesson I learned in Mountjoy Square.

'Why are you so determined to take over the dump?'

'I want to get at the bicycles, and prams, and old radios, and cereal packets, and anything else that's useful.'

'In that case, why don't you just ask to join the gang, and save yourself a lot of bother? Jeremy Lynch is only interested in Meccano and bottles and scrap metal.'

'I want to take that over as well!'

'You're a right eejit! Do you know what you'll be letting yourself in for?'

Eventually, I agreed to try just talking to Jeremy Lynch, so that I can find out what he's like. We went back along the railway and round the long way to the dump. I'm sure I could have got down the bank with a bit of trying. I'm going to have to learn how to handle Sean, otherwise I'll end up being bossed around and that's no good.

As soon as he saw us coming across the boat-yard, Lynch whistled. Four fellows came out of a shed, smoking. They lined up behind us, blocking the way out. Lynch stared at me in a calculating way. 'You're the fellow who arrived in the bus the other night.' I asked him how he knew.

'I know everything that goes on.'

Sean told him I was interested in joining the Dump gang. Lynch spat on the ground in front of Sean, and made him jump. 'Don't give me any of that shit, Malone. I know what he wants. He wants to take over the dump.'

I looked at Sean in amazement, thinking he'd already betrayed me. Sean looked back at me with a sneer. 'I'd have a word with Christie, if I were you.' I saw straight away there was no point trying to be reasonable with Lynch. It would have to be a fight. I was about to grab him when Sean stopped me. 'Don't. There's too many of them, and I don't want to get involved.'

The fellows behind us were puffing madly on their cigarettes. Sean said they were getting them red-hot, ready to jab us in the faces. I had to calm down. Lynch said he'd got a useful bit of advice for me. 'Fuck off out of here and don't come back.' He said he'd let me go, this time, but that was it. I'd get one chance, and no more.

I was livid with Christie. I said goodbye to Sean and went to look for him. None of his sisters knew where he was, and I gave up after an hour. It's lucky for both of us I didn't find him. I might have committed murder. I was too cross even to be polite to Dad. He said he's had an even better idea than fixing motorbikes and cars. He'll explain it in the morning.

I asked him why he doesn't like priests. He said it's because they're a right bunch of miseries, and with good reason. They have the thankless job of loving the common people of Ireland. It's hard enough to love your own family at times, never mind having to extend this charitable outlook to the biggest bunch of bowsies ever assembled in one nation. Old priests look back and see what a waste their lives have been. Young priests look into the future and see what a waste their lives are going to be. The ones in middle age are so busy trying to get their golf handicap down to single figures, they haven't any time for the PBPs; the poor bloody parishioners.

I asked him why anyone ever bothers to become a priest. He said they don't do it of their own free will; they're forced into it by parents. There are only three good jobs in Ireland; the priesthood, the teaching profession, and running a pub. The average Irishman, landed by God and his own sexual impulses with more children than he can fend for, thinks no further than getting the first three settled in Ireland. As soon as there's a priest, a teacher and a publican in the family, the rest of them are shipped over to England.

That, said Dad, is why young men become priests; their fathers force them into it. The mothers go along with it. They like the fact that the fellows have to take a vow of celibacy. It's the women's way of avenging themselves for the indignities of enforced childbirth. They see it as a small recompense for all those years of lying on their backs, popping them out until they're reduced to haggard wrecks.

I went to Mass in the chapel for the first time. It's an enormous building for such a small village. The spire is so high it makes you dizzy looking up at it. There are special seats up at the front for posh people. They have cushions to kneel on, and their own private door, and a silver collection plate. I went down to have a look at it, but I got glared at and had to come away. There were ten-shilling notes and half-crowns in it.

There's a man standing guard over the special seats. He has a thick red rope with tassels on it, which he hooks across the aisle to stop ordinary people sitting in them. Dad was furious about this; we're all supposed to be equal in the eyes of God. There are five rows of posh seats, then a gap and the ordinary seats start. The men sit on the left of the chapel and the women on the right. This is quite handy for staring at the girls. Right at the back of the chapel there's a space with no seats. It's where the drinkers congregate, so they can get out and into the pub as soon as Mass is over.

Masses start at seven-thirty and go on every hour until half-eleven. The more holy a person is, according to Dad, the earlier the Mass they go to. I saw some of Christie's sisters at Mass but not Rowena. I hope Rowena isn't so holy that she goes to the seven-thirty Mass. I couldn't stand getting up that early on a Sunday. Me and Dad went to the half-eleven Mass, the last one. Dad was up very late playing draughts with the Sergeant. Dad would rather play chess, but the Sergeant hasn't got the right kind of brain for it.

I don't like the confession boxes. There are three compartments. The priest sits in the middle. He takes it in turns to listen to the people on either side. How can you be sure the other person isn't holding his breath, listening, when it's your turn to trot out your sins? Worse still, supposing you're confessing dirty thoughts about a girl, and she's sitting listening in the other box!

Dad was ready at communion time to rush down the aisle and tear the tasselled rope out of the way. He wanted to show his right to get to the altar. Unfortunately, when the priest had finished the consecration, he put everything away in the tabernacle and that was it. No communion at all. Just a few prayers and Mass was over.

Dad said it was scandalous; the whole thing lasted less than half an hour. He's sure the priests are in league with the publicans, to make sure Mass ends in time for the pubs opening at twelve.

On the way out I had a look in the ordinary people's collection plate, at the main door of the chapel. It's not even a plate, just the lid off a tin box of Jacob's Assorted Biscuits. It had dozens of pennies in it, a few thruppences, a rusty safety pin, and two cigarette butts.

I was desperate to find Christie after Mass but Dad said he needed to talk to me. He's going to start a shop in the stable. I think this is an awful idea. All the shopkeepers I've ever met have been miserable and mean-minded. I don't want Dad to turn out like that.

It's going to be a wholesale vegetable shop, selling sacks of potatoes and bags of onions. I'm ashamed of the whole idea. I don't care if we do need the money; Dad should be doing something more manly. I asked him why he isn't sticking to his original plan. He says he's discovered there are already two car repair businesses in other stables in the lane.

I went into the garden in a furious temper. I kicked a brick around until I realised I was ruining the toes of my shoes. I was searching among the rubbish for a tin can when a voice said 'Boy; you there!' in the tone that teachers use. I looked round and it was a man from one of the upstairs flats.

He said his name was Major Longshott, Indian Army, Retired, and that he and I would get on well so long as I bore it in mind. He stared hard at me, and breathed in deeply through his nose, making his chest bulge like a sheet on a washing line. 'Longshott,' he said again, 'Longshott with two tees.' He let the air out slowly, through pursed lips, and glared at me, as if he expected an argument about the spelling. I was in no mood to be bossed around but I thought it best to listen to him, in case I end up liking him.

He's small, with a red face, no hair, a nose bulging with purple veins, a pipe with a silver band round it, and a little white moustache that jiggles up and down when he speaks. His clothes are very clean and smart. He was wearing a shirt with short sleeves and even the sleeves had creases in them. I'm glad I was respectful to him, because he's made me a useful offer.

He needs dung for his rose-bed. He'll give me sixpence for every shovelful I bring him. I asked him what size shovel he had in mind. He showed me. It's quite big, but he says he doesn't expect it to be crammed full. What I have to do is watch out for coal and milk carts on the terrace, and scoop up anything the horses leave behind.

He can't do it himself, on account of being a retired Major. He used to go out at night but Mrs Longshott found out and stopped him. She says it's beneath his dignity. He'd be a laughing stock at the golf club if anyone caught him at it.

I said I thought the garden belonged to the basement flat. He said I was right, except that no one has bothered about it for years. He and Mrs Longshott have taken the liberty of utilizing a small area to grow roses and chrysanthemums. I'm quite interested in this, because I've never seen flowers actually growing. I've only ever seen them on sale in buckets in Moore Street.

He said I seemed a sound sort of boy, and shook hands with me. That's the first time anyone's ever done that to me, and it made me feel very manly. I went out straight away to the terrace and shovelled some dung and gave it to him as a present. He wanted to pay me for it, but I said no; he could have it for nothing because it was only old stuff. He said the old stuff was the best, and insisted on giving me sixpence for it.

I went back into the house and apologised to Dad for being in a temper with him. He said he appreciated my honest opinion. To tell the truth, he wasn't very keen on vegetables himself. He's had another idea; he's going to ask Nana if she'll let him have plants to sell. The snag is, that he hasn't got the side-car any more, for carrying stuff around.

I left him thinking about this and went off to look for Christie. I found him hiding in the bus shelter on the corner. I told him I was going to murder him. He admitted he told Jeremy Lynch about my plans. He thought Lynch would be grateful and let him into the Dump gang. Instead, Lynch called him a sneaky shit, tied his hands behind his back, stuffed a dead jellyfish down the front of his trousers, and kicked him out of the dump. I had a hard job keeping a straight face when he told me this.

I said I was going to form a gang of my own. He can be in it, but he must be loyal to me. He has to stop being a slimy little gurrier and giving away my plans. I've made him promise to stop letting everyone into his loft to look at his sisters. Everyone except me, that is.

He said he won't be able to manage without the money, so I've given him the dung-collecting job from Major Longshott. It's not really suitable for me as a gangleader, except if I'm ever desperate for money.

I haven't said anything to Christie about the knickers business that Sean mentioned to me. I'm saving it up to ask him some other time.

Dad had a letter from Mam this morning, asking how we're getting on. He's thrilled to bits. While we were reading it, Christie rushed down the front steps with a big slice of toast and marmalade in his hand. He couldn't stay long because he would be late for school.

Christie says there's a big stink going on in the barracks about black magic. Lord Carysfort, who lives in a big castle in the woods near the village, rang to say someone's been interfering with the vaults in the castle graveyard. There's blood and queer drawings on some of the gravestones, and a dead chicken with its head cut off. Christie says his dad thinks it's just hooligans larking about to frighten people.

Anyway, it gave me a great idea. We could spread a rumour among the village gangs that it was us, and get them to think we're real hard-chaws. Christie says we could end up in jail, if his dad gets hold of the story. He always has objections to everything, just like Sean Malone. He could be right, though. I'll have to think about it a bit more.

He went off to school and I decided to go down the dump for another look round. I went the way Malone showed me, through the railway station fence and along the top of the embankment. The Wexford Express came thundering along and gave me a right scare. I had to lie down on the path so as not to get sucked under the wheels.

I was determined to get down the bank, to prove it could be done, but I'd forgotten to bring a rope with me. I went back and down into the boat-yard to see if I could find anything useful. I thought all the Dump gang would be at school. They were, but they'd left a sentry.

I saw him long before he saw me. He was lying under an upturned row-boat. His feet were poking out for anyone to see.

I stuck my head under but he didn't notice me; he was too busy smoking and reading a *Picture Post* magazine. The cover had a photograph of Jane Russell in a swimsuit, kissing a stupid poodle dog with a ribbon tied round its head.

I dragged him out by the feet. He wasn't the least bit bothered, even though he was much smaller than me. He said he was Jeremy Lynch's cousin and I'd better watch out if I harmed him. It turned out there's always one of Lynch's gang guarding the dump. They take turns mitching off school to do it.

I asked him how he'd stop me if I decided to take something. He said it wasn't his job to stop me; he was there to report to Lynch. Lynch and the gang would come round to my house. They'd do me in and take back whatever I'd had from the dump. Everyone knew this, and it was only desperate loonies or new fellows like myself who gave them any bother. I asked him if he'd got any useful information, and said I'd torture him if he didn't spill the beans. He said that wasn't necessary. I could ask him anything I liked. The Dump gang is so powerful they don't have to bother being secretive.

I quizzed him about how people get into the Dump gang. He said in the early days it was quite simple; you just had to be a relative of Jeremy Lynch. Then the supply of relatives ran out. Jeremy had to invent initiation ceremonies, to make sure that outsiders would remain loyal. He wouldn't tell me what the ceremonies are. He started sniggering and said I'd shit myself if I knew. I didn't bother to try and get it out of him. I can probably find out from Sean. He seems to know everything.

I found some rope and went back up onto the embankment. The reason I'm so keen to get down the bank is that it would be a great place to launch an unexpected attack. I waited on top, peering over the wall, until the sentry crept back under the boat. I thought it would only take me a minute to get down the bank and back up. I took a chance and tied the end of the rope round the railway track. There wasn't anything else to tie it to, anyway.

I got halfway down, about twenty-five feet, and got caught up in the brambles and nettles. After I'd struggled through these, I leaned my weight on the rope and stared down into the water.

It was horrible. The tide was in and the water was slopping against the bottom of the embankment. I couldn't actually see the water because of the rubbish and filth floating on top of it.

If it hadn't been heaving slowly up and down I'd have thought it was solid enough to walk on. It was a mixture of squashed fruit and rotten vegetables and soaking wet newspapers and old clothes and horrible scummy yellow stuff that looked like vomit.

I felt sick, and started to pull myself back up the rope. Then I heard a train coming and my heart nearly stopped. I told myself not to worry; it could be on the other line and the rope would be all right. I decided to make a big effort to get back up as quickly as possible. Just as I was pulling my hardest the train came along and cut the rope.

I spun round as I fell and went into the mess face first. I was so shocked I nearly fainted. Then I panicked. I threshed about like a maniac and kept getting stuff plastered over my face so I couldn't breathe. The water was too deep to get my feet on the ground. I was sure I was going to die. I started screaming, which wasn't very brave, but I soon stopped because of stuff going in my mouth.

I managed to struggle to the bottom of the embankment and grab at a coil of rusty barbed wire tangled up in the brambles just above my head. The wire ripped the palm of my hand but I didn't care about the pain. I tried to pull myself out of the water and the wire snapped. I fell back into the stinking filth again. This time I knew I was going to drown. I was so frightened I just wanted to get it over with as quickly as possible.

A miracle happened. Malone suddenly appeared on the dump wall and threw me a rope. Afterwards, he explained that he'd seen me going past his cottage with the other rope and guessed what I was up to. I put out my hand to say thank you but he wouldn't take it. He said I was too dirty.

We went across the boat-yard to where the sea was a bit cleaner. I jumped in and out a few times and washed most of the stuff off my clothes. Malone told me to rinse my clothes in tap water, otherwise they'll never dry with all the salt in them.

I tried to tell Malone how grateful I was. He wouldn't listen. He says I'm nothing but trouble to him. The man from the newspaper shop has cancelled having his delivery bikes repaired by Malone. It's because of me tipping him over in the street when he tried to stop us fighting. Malone went back to his shed. Before he went, he said to remember I owe him something for saving my life.

I ran around for half an hour to get dry and then went home. I didn't want to think about the fact that I'd nearly drowned, so I asked Dad to tell me about black magic. He said it's just a lot of nonsense, and an excuse for dirty-minded people to prance around naked in the moonlight. This was a useful piece of information. It's just the sort of thing that appeals to Christie.

I asked Dad if he was sure about the nakedness. He got very het-up and said that wasn't the half of it. The whole business is riddled with immorality and vice of every description, including unnatural relations with animals and ceremonies to rouse Lucifer from the depths of Hell. The real hard-chaws, the ones who live in sinks of iniquity like Rumania and Birmingham, think nothing of sacrificing virgins in the woods. When they can find one, that is. They're very rare nowadays.

I asked Dad what a virgin is. He got a bit shifty and said that, generally speaking, it means a young girl. I asked him how young. He said I hadn't quite got the idea. A virgin can be a female of any age, or even a man. I was even more confused. Dad thought very hard and put on his quiet, religious voice. 'A virgin is someone who has not been seared by the fires of concupiscence.'

Later, when I went up to wait for Christie coming home from school, I asked his sister Ellen if she knew what a virgin is. She said yes, she bloody-well ought to; she's been one for thirty-seven years and it looks as if she'll go to her grave in the same state.

I told her she was lucky, considering what my Dad had said about it. She didn't seem convinced, so I told her she ought to be grateful she hadn't been seared by the fires of concupiscence. She gave me a sarcastic look and said there were worse things happened in China.

She noticed I was still damp, which Dad luckily hadn't, and insisted on me changing into some of Christie's big brother's clothes. She came into the bathroom to help me change. She started tickling me, and said she had a feeling it wouldn't be long before the flames of whatever-it-was were burning my arse off. I thought it was strange to hear a woman saying 'arse' but I suppose she only said it as a joke.

She took my clothes away to wash, and said my trunks were disgusting. It's a good thing she didn't see them before I rinsed them in the sea. Then she took me into her bedroom and put a bandage round my hand. She said I had nice warm fingers.

When Christie came home I tried to get him interested in black magic. I told him I had a plan to go up the Castle graveyard and watch these people dancing with no clothes on and sacrificing chickens and virgins. I was sure this would get him excited.

The little shit had the nerve to say he's changed since he's met me! I've made him realise what a dirty-minded sinner he is, and he's going to change his ways. What an ungrateful little bugger! I'm certain it's just that he's afraid to go up the woods at night.

The rest of the evening Christie spent running in and out to the terrace with shovels full of dung for Major Longshott. He complained to me and Dad later. The Major only gave him three shillings for the whole lot, instead of the sixpence a shovel he was expecting. The Major said he expected a discount on large quantities, whatever that means. Dad explained that it's the usual business practice; the more you buy of something, the less you pay for it. Christie said, 'Does that mean that if I shovel tons of dung, the Major will expect to pay nothing at all?'

Dad said no, that wasn't the idea at all. It was a question of diminishing unit costs on a pro rata basis. Christie went off saying 'I see, I see', but I could tell he hadn't made head or tail of the explanation. Anyway, it's not really my problem. He shouldn't be so greedy.

I spent all day helping Dad clear the ground floor of the stable. We've piled the junk out in the garden, ready to burn.

Two of Christie's sisters came down at lunchtime. They brought us mugs of soup and cheese sandwiches. It was that Primula cheese that comes in triangles wrapped in silver paper. You can never get it off properly. My sandwich still had sharp little bits of foil in it.

Dad asked them if they had any boyfriends. They went into fits of giggles and said no. He said this was surprising, considering what a bonny pair of girls they were. We tried to find out how old they were but they wouldn't say. Dad says they're about fifteen or sixteen. They're called Josie and Imelda.

They went up to have a look round the loft, even though Dad said it was dangerous. I could see quite a lot of their legs as they went up the stairs. Imelda glanced over her shoulder and saw me looking up after them. She deliberately flicked her skirt and showed me her petticoat. I went as red as anything. I was so amazed I stood there with my eyes bulging and my mouth hanging open. How can girls be so brazen?

Malone came round while they were up in the loft. I told him what happened. He said it was nothing compared to what he can see from his cottage. There's a girl in a house overlooking the hollow who sometimes undresses in her room with the light on and the curtains open. There's a regular bunch of perverts lurk in the bushes round his cottage in the hope of catching her at it. He says it's not just thick Paddy labourers; you get toffs who work in offices as well.

Malone had a message from Jeremy Lynch. Lynch is annoyed because I went to the dump after he'd warned me not to. He said to tell me there'll be trouble when he catches me. Also, there's another fellow looking for me, that I haven't even met yet. It seems Christie's been blabbing to this fellow as well, telling him about my plan to take over the village.

He's not very happy about it. His name is Bull Bowman, leader of the Hill gang. Sean says he's a brutal character, very big and fierce. He always beats up new boys to make sure they know he's the boss.

I asked Sean if it would be worth beating up Bowman, taking over his gang, and using it to take over the Dump from Lynch.

Sean looked at me as if I was a half-wit.

He said I should wait and see the size of Bowman before I get any fancy ideas. I said it sounds as if he's afraid of Bowman himself. He said I'm dead right. He is, and so will I be, when I have the misfortune to meet him.

Christie's sisters could see us through the holes in the ceiling. They kept giggling, and pretending to be worried about us seeing up their skirts. They called us upstairs, to show us something they'd found. Malone said it was a typical girls' trick to get us to take notice of them. He told me to ignore them. I went up anyway, in case it turned out to be something interesting.

They'd been looking in some cardboard boxes and found loads of old magazines. Dad said they could look through them and take away any they wanted to read. They were afraid to get them out of the boxes for fear of spiders. I was no help to them, because of being terrified of spiders myself. In the end, Malone came up and got them out for us.

There was only one spider among all the boxes. Malone made us all scream. He picked it up by one of its legs and waved it in our faces. After a while the girls got fed up and said they'd leave if he didn't get rid of it. Malone said, 'Certainly; anything to oblige.' He popped it in his mouth and swallowed it. The girls screamed and I nearly fainted. Malone said it was no different from eating any other animal. He really is a strange fellow.

He got very excited when we found a box of magazines called the *National Geographic*. He whispered to me to hide them from the girls and save them for later. They're full of pictures of native girls showing their tits and the cracks of their arses.

He got excited again when he found a box full of *Wide World* magazines. He said they're really great. They're packed with true adventure stories of man-eating tigers and shipwrecks and ghost stories. The stories are written by people who have gone all over the world ruling the British Empire. I wonder how Malone knows these things?

The ones I'm most interested in are called the *Reader's Digest*. They're small and neat, with a list on the cover telling you what's inside. All the articles are serious and stick to important subjects, not just rubbishy nonsense like *Titbits* and *Reveille*. I'm going to start reading them so I can learn things. They're much better than school-books. They've got pages of jokes and funny stuff in amongst the serious bits.

Malone kept asking the girls what their names are. They wouldn't tell him, so he left in a huff.

The weather turned really bad after lunch. It ruined our chance of lighting the bonfire. One minute the sun was shining and the next minute it was rain and thunder and lightning and crops being battered down in the fields.

The waves have been coming in so high that the gardens at the end of the terrace are covered in spray and they look like it's been snowing. Dad says it's a freak summer storm.

He's fixed the water pipe and unblocked the outside lavatory. We're able to wash and go to the toilet at long last. It's just as well, because we're getting filthy working in the stable. There's a terrible amount of dust from the hay and straw that's fallen down from the loft.

Christie came round after school. He's heard that Boozer Quinn has been swept away in the storm. He was out in a rowing boat looking at his lobster pots when the whole thing started. I don't know who Boozer Quinn is, so it didn't matter to me. Christie said he's one of the men who row golfers out to the island.

I explained to Christie that tonight would be a good time to have a look at the castle graveyard. We'd have the place to ourselves. In bad weather the police won't bother to watch the place, knowing full well the black magic people won't want to dance around getting their bums frozen. Christie said no, so I used a bit of persuasion. I told him I know about him selling his sisters' knickers to the man who owns the newspaper shop. Christie went as white as pigeon shit, and said he will come after all.

After we had this chat Christie took me into the stable at the back of the police station. It's all very posh with nice doors and windows, and loads of things with official labels on them saying when and where they were found. It's where the police keep the clues from crimes, and stuff recovered from robbers, and bicycles and motorbikes that have been stolen and not reclaimed. It's absolutely forbidden to go into this stable if you're not a policeman. Christie said it was worth the risk. He wanted to show me something that would really interest me.

We waited until his dad finished his dinner, and had snuggled down in front of the fire with the *Independent*. The Sergeant is one of those men who start at the beginning of a paper and never put it down until they've read every last word of it. He says the mind needs sustenance just as much as the body. Reading the newspaper is like giving the brain a good solid three-course dinner.

He starts off with a horse's douvrey of headlines, and then works his way though to the sports pages as a dessert, making sure to let his brain have a good chew on the facts as he works his way through. My own dad never touches a newspaper except to light a fire or give his boots a rub. He says most of the news is just scurrilous yarns invented by half-cut reporters slumped over the bar in Mooney's, with a pint in one hand and a stub of pencil in the other.

The thing that Christie showed me was a car that had caught fire in the car-park behind Dolan's pub. The driver was in it at the time, with his dog, and they both got burned to death. It's a huge American car, owned by an Englishman who came to live in Kilmara. He didn't have a proper job. He spent all his time in the pub drinking and doing deals with fellows who came out from Dublin wearing gangster hats.

This fellow used to live in a big house down the strand road, covered in ivy and with its own tennis court. He had a woman living with him but they hardly ever went out together. Christie said they were a strange couple; he was huge and she was tiny, hardly more than a girl in years and a child in size.

I said maybe she was his daughter. Christie said no; the woman who used to clean for them said they definitely lived as man and wife. No one has seen her since the man got burned, and the house has been left empty. They think she might have gone back to England.

The man often used to get too drunk to drive home from the pub. He'd fall asleep in his car, smoking, and drinking from a bottle of whiskey. The police think he must have spilt the whiskey on this particular night, and dropped a match into it accidentally. The whole car was burning furiously by the time it was reported. The remains of his body were in the front seat but not much of it was left, on account of the tremendous heat. Christie says the bones of the skeleton just crumbled up as soon as they were touched.

His dad has to keep the car until the woman comes to claim it, or until she notifies the insurance people. It's the principal clue in the whole business. His dad says he'll use it to keep chickens in, when the case is solved. Christie says that's a joke; his dad is far too idle to bother. John-Joe Maguire is also after the car, for scrap. He says there's a good twenty-five hundredweight of metal in the wreckage, just waiting to be dismantled.

Christie says it's a funny thing, but the people in the village were more sorry about the dog than they were about the man. It was a big black Alsatian.

I asked Christie if there'd be any useful bits left in the car, like tools or a radio that I could salvage valves from. We looked inside, but it was hopeless. Everything was just ashes. We had to climb through the window frames to get inside, because the doors were all seized shut. It was more like being in a railway carriage than a car. The space inside was enormous, especially with the seats burnt away. The roads in America must be huge, if all the cars are that size.

While we were fiddling about, we could hear things clinking and jangling on the floor. We started sifting the ashes through our fingers and discovered what it was; money! There was loads and loads of it, in all sorts of coins. It must have come out of the fellow's pockets. Every single one of them was half melted and twisted with the heat but you could tell what they were by the size of them.

Christie was rooting around in the back of the car. He said to me, 'Look here, what do you think these are?' He'd found a handful of little bits, like burnt twigs. I knew what they were straight away. They were bones. I know quite a lot about bones. Dad once brought home a half-size plastic skeleton from the pawnbroker. He told me the names of all the bits. Mam made him take it back and swop it for some winter woollies.

The bits that Christie was holding were exactly right for finger and toe bones. As soon as I saw them I had a great idea. We'll get a skull out of one of the castle graves and keep it in a biscuit tin at our gang headquarters. We can call ourselves the Skeleton gang. Everyone will be terrified of us.

I told Christie the bits were bones, and that we should keep them. He said he couldn't be bothered; they were only bits from the dog. He says it always lay on the back seat. I wish he hadn't told me this; it's not half so interesting as having bones that might be off the man. I put them in my pocket anyway.

We split up the money between us and agreed to meet at midnight when everyone else is asleep. Christie's going to borrow a couple of torches from the barracks. He says he knows where they're kept, because he borrows them to read in bed when he's listening to Radio Luxemburg under the blankets. It makes him laugh to hear his dad complaining about useless modern batteries that are always flat just when you need them.

I never got to the graveyard last night, for the simple reason that Christie didn't turn up. He says his dad and the other guards were up all night with accidents caused by trees blowing down on roads. He couldn't risk sneaking out of the house. He's a right little shit-bag.

Boozer Quinn has turned up. He was blown all the way along the coast to Wicklow Head. He was exhausted when he rowed back.

Dad had the priest in today, to do an exorcism for the dead child. The priest sprinkled holy water and said prayers to make its soul rest in peace. Dad had to tell the priest the story but he told him in confession. The priest can't say anything about it to another living soul, even on pain of torture or death. That's what it says in the catechism, anyway.

Dad says there won't be any danger of haunting in the basement from now on. We can safely ask Mam to come and live with us. That's very good news. Dad is a rotten cook, and we've run out of clean clothes. It won't be for a while, though. We've also run out of money. Dad's pay from the bus company has been spent.

He doesn't want to sign on the dole, in case the police and the farmer are still looking for him. If the farmer really has got hundreds of relatives in the Government, they'll trace him the minute he signs an official form.

Dad says we won't even be able to have a dog or a radio from now on, because of not being able to apply for a licence. This was news to me; we've had dogs and radios before now and never bothered about licences. Dad says it's the principle of the thing.

He's had a bit of luck with Nana, and all because Uncle Louis has lost his cushy job in London. He's been sacked for losing his temper with the woman who owns the pub. She was secretly reading the letters I sent him, and didn't like the tone of them. She accused Uncle Louis of making fun of her behind her back. Uncle Louis went upstairs and demolished a lot of furniture. Particularly, he says, the landlady's bed. He tipped it over and found another fellow hiding under it. The fellow was completely starkers. When he stood up the end of his willie was covered in fluff. It looked like a dandelion gone to seed. Now Uncle Louis has to repay the cost of the bed, and assaulting the man, and ruining the woman's wig by stuffing it into a piss-pot.

Nana has sent him money to get him out of trouble. She says it's worth every penny for the laughs he's given her. So as to be fair to Dad, she's given him the same amount of money. Dad hasn't told me how much it is, but it's set him off on a new idea. He's going to lay a concrete floor in the stable and replace the missing planks in the loft floor, then get someone in to plaster the walls and the ceiling.

When that's done, we're going in to Dublin to a place in Dame Street where they sell everything to do with billiards and snooker. Dad is going to put a deposit on a second-hand table and start a snooker club in the stable. With the money we make, he'll get another table. There's room for two, easily. Then he'll use the money from both of them to strengthen the loft floor and put two more tables upstairs. He says we'll make a fortune in no time, with Kilmara being such a popular seaside resort.

I think this is the best idea yet. The Sergeant thinks so too. He says it will be a great boon to the lads in the village, and give them an alternative to hanging round corners whistling at girls and losing their money at pitch-and-toss. We're writing to Mam about it tonight. I'm going to spend the rest of this week helping Dad, and start school next week.

The world seems to be full of opportunities for making money. There's a hand-pump outside our back door, under the stairs from the top flats. It goes down into a well in the ground. Dad said it would be interesting to get it working. We greased the leather washers in the pump with butter, and oiled the handle, and primed the pump with a bucket of water from the tap outside the toilet.

Major Longshott watched us fixing it. No sooner had we got it working than he offered me thruppence a day if I'd draw him off a jug full of water every morning. The Major says well water is clean and pure and has health-giving properties; very important to a man of his age. He says he hates drinking tap water. Hardly a week goes by without someone finding a dead dog in the local reservoir.

Dad says I'm to make sure I pump up plenty of water before I fill the Major's jug, so that it's nice and fresh and not got insects in it that might have crept down the pipe overnight. Thruppence a day is one and ninepence a week. I can buy millions of things for that.

After school Christie wanted to show me a hut in the band gardens. He thought it would make a good gang headquarters. I told him it was a stupid idea. It would be well known to everyone else. We'd spend all our time being raided and ambushed. A gang headquarters has to be absolutely secret, with a well camouflaged entrance, and a secret escape route, so that even if it's surrounded, the gang can still get away. He saw the sense of this but he was a bit huffy. He said the question of a gang headquarters is a bit pointless until we have a gang. I said I'd made a start by recruiting Malone. Christie said this was a mistake. Malone has a nasty temper and gets vicious if anyone makes fun of him. I said this was just the kind of fellow we needed in battles.

Christie reckons Malone only fights when it suits him. He has a bad name for grabbing at girls, if he thinks he can get away with it. There are quite a few men who'd like to catch Malone up a dark alley at night, and repay him for things he's supposed to have done to their daughters. Malone always denies it. Christie says he once grabbed hold of his sister Elizabeth, who's twelve, and tried to pull her down the lane in the dark. She was wearing hockey boots. She kicked him in the coconuts and escaped. I was surprised to hear all this. Malone is always saying he doesn't like girls.

We were sitting on the steps outside the Sullivans' front door. The Sullivan girls were playing in the terrace with dolls and prams. They started looking at me and sniggering. Christie said it was because they could see up the legs of my trousers. That's the trouble with my trousers; they're an old pair of Dad's with the legs cut off. They're too loose. I went red with embarrassment. I wasn't wearing any trunks. They must have been able to see my willie. Me and Dad have run out of clean things to wear.

I stood up just as a boy came whizzing round the corner of the terrace on a bicycle. As soon as he saw me he stood up on the pedals and made a big effort to get past as quickly as possible. He was so anxious that he never noticed the Sullivan girls in the road right beside him.

The bigger one, Siobhan, who's about nine, poked a stick into the front wheel of his bicycle. The bike stopped dead and the boy hurtled over the handlebars. When he stood up his hands and face were covered in bits of gravel from the road. He had tears in his eyes from the pain but he never let a cry out of him. The Sullivan girl ran into her house straight away.

I was going to help the boy, but Christie said not to; it was only Andy Barrington, a stinking English Proddy who lives at Number Twelve. I said to Christie, 'I thought you told me there are no boys our age on the terrace?' He said Barrington doesn't count, being a Proddy.

I wasn't satisfied with this. Barrington looked very brave to me, and just the sort of fellow who'd be useful in a gang. I didn't care about him being a Protestant; Dad says there's nothing much to choose between one religion and another.

I went over and asked the fellow if he was all right. He backed away from me, frightened. I asked him what was the matter. He said I knew bloody well. I was astonished to hear a Protestant swear, because they're supposed to be posh and religious.

Christie came over and said the reason Barrington was scared is that it's usual to beat up a Proddy boy when you get the chance. He'd never had a go at Andy himself, but if I held him steady he'd give him a few kicks in the belly. I was disgusted to hear this, and felt like giving Christie himself a good kicking. Barrington looked all right to me. I couldn't see why we should go lashing into him for no reason at all.

I picked up Andy's bike. He thought I was going to throw it over the terrace railings. He got all fierce and told me to leave it alone. I told him not to be such an idiot; I was a new boy in the terrace and quite willing to be friends with him. Three of the spokes in his front wheel were bent. I said I was the leader of a gang which has its own bicycle mechanic. I could easily get it fixed for him. After a bit more chat he said he wanted to join us.

The problem is, his parents are rich, even though they live in the basement of Number Twelve. Christie says it's all done up like a pub you'd see in Grafton Street in Dublin; polished wood panelling and pictures on the wall and leather furniture. They even have a telephone. He was in there once with his dad when Andy's parents were burgled.

If that's the sort of place Andy lives in, it could be a nuisance having him in the gang. He might not be allowed to get dirty, for one thing, or stay out late on adventures. That's no good if there's something important going on. Also, it turned out he's a Boy Scout. We all know what that means. They have to spend their time thinking pure thoughts, and doing good deeds, and listening to classical music on the radio.

On the other hand, his dad is an English airline pilot. He's over in Ireland for two years, working with Aer Lingus, teaching Irishmen how to fly planes. Andy says his dad could get us into the airport for a look round and possibly even take us up for a spin in an aeroplane. Just think of that!

And there's another thing: Andy gets Spangles and Mars bars and Wagon Wheels, sweets you can only buy in England. He can also get hold of fireworks, which is something else you can't buy in Ireland. We could use them to make bombs when we're at war with other gangs.

Christie was mad at me for letting Andy into the gang. He says his brother will be pleased about it, though. There's certain things Andy could get from his parents that would be useful to him. Christie's brother won't say what these things are, because it's a sin to have them and he doesn't want Christie to blab to his sisters about it. He says Andy's mam and dad probably have a drawer full of them in the bedroom. They're English, and it's not a sin for them to buy these things, the way it is for Irish people. Christie says his brother has been at him for ages to get friendly with Andy, so he can get invited round and raid the bedroom for these things. He's promised to pay Christie good money for any that he can get hold of.

While Christie was telling me this, Andy went home to wash the gravel out of his skin. The Sullivan girls, who'd been shouting stupid remarks at him through their letterbox, came out with a rope. They attached one end to the basement railings and took it in turns to skip and twirl the rope. I got the idea of looking up their skirts and shouting out the colour of their knickers, in revenge for them seeing up my trousers. I lay down on the pavement and pretended I'd discovered a trail of ants and was busy tracking them. Christie nearly ruined it by standing between me and the girls. I had to jab him out of the way.

Before I could get a good look, they ruined the whole idea themselves. They tucked their skirts up into the legs of their knickers, and we could see them anyway. Siobhan stuck her tongue out at us and said she hoped we didn't think they'd done it for our benefit. They weren't giving us a free leg-show. It was just to stop their skirts catching in the rope.

It's strange the way girls worry about their legs. One minute they'll be lying down on the beach with hardly a stitch on and their legs stretched all over the place. The next minute, they'll be cycling home desperate with worry in case the wind blows their skirt half an inch above their knees. If it does, and a fellow so much as looks at them, they're off the bike straight away, blushing furiously and yelling across at the poor devil.

While I was still lying on the pavement, a girl with a little dog on a lead came out of the house next to Andy's. She came along the pavement and told me to get out of the way or she'd set the dog on me. I thought she was joking; it was such a puny dog. I grinned up at her, thinking she'd walk round me.

She jerked the dog into the air by its lead and dropped it down on my chest. The dog sank its manky little teeth into my jersey. I grabbed the lead and pulled hard on it. The girl lurched forward and just missed stepping on my face. For a moment, I could see right up her skirt. She knew I'd seen up her. Her face went red, but not with embarrassment. It was with temper. She was furious, and tried to pull the dog off me. Its teeth were caught in my jersey.

It gave a yelp of agony. She took no notice and pulled harder, until the wool snapped.

When she'd gone I told Christie I'd seen up her skirt. He got all excited and goggle-eyed, hugging himself and asking in a queer breathless voice what colour her knickers were, and did I get a glimpse of her suspenders. He said I should have stuck my hand up her while I had the chance. I'm going to have to talk to Dad about all this; I'm the one who saw up her and I didn't feel anything, yet Christie went mad with excitement just hearing about it.

A woman came along and said she was Andy's mother; were we the boys he'd been talking to? Christie said no. He thought it was going to be trouble. I didn't say anything at all. I couldn't believe someone so beautiful could be anyone's mother. I stared and stared at her. She looked back at me with a relaxed sort of smile and her eyebrows raised, as if she was amused and puzzled at the same time. She's lovely, like a princess in a fairy story, and quite small, hardly bigger than Christie, with smooth blonde hair and smiley blue eyes and a blouse I could see her vest through.

I fell in love with her straight away and forgot all about Christie's sister Rowena. I'm definitely going to have Andy in the gang. As soon as I could speak, I admitted we were the boys Andy had been talking to. She said she was very pleased to meet us, because Andy told her he'd found some friends at last. I said he certainly had, and that I was very fond of him already, even though I'd just met him, and would be playing with him every spare minute I had from helping my Dad.

She said we were welcome to call any time, and gave us a big smile and walked off. I felt as if my heart had melted, and stood looking after her with my mouth open. Christie was disgusted with me and went home. The Sullivan girls started jeering me, thinking that Andy's mother had been ticking us off for knocking him off his bike. I went home and spent the rest of the day dreaming about her.

Dad's had a great idea. He says we've been working so hard we deserve a holiday. Now would be the best time to go, before Mam comes back from Mullingar with the girls, and before he settles down to the business of being a snooker hall proprietor. I agreed it would be smashing but how on earth could we afford it? Dad said not to worry; the Lord will provide, and you can't beat the Lord when it comes to reliability.

The Sergeant is involved as well as God; he's going to lend us one of the unclaimed motorbikes from the police stable. It's a Scott, which Dad says is the Rolls Royce of motorbikes.

I asked him what we're going to use for money. He said we won't need any. We'll be enjoying the hospitality of that foreign head of state who rules our green and pleasant island. I thought he was talking about President de Valera, who's half Spanish and half American, but Dad said no, he was referring to the Pope. We'll be staying at monasteries, as the guests of the monks. Canonical law says that monasteries have to provide travellers with free food and lodging. This is in case God decides to have a Second Coming along the same lines as the first one.

Dad says that after the scandalous business of Mary and Joseph being stuck for somewhere to sleep in Bethlehem, the Church Fathers were determined to make sure such a thing never happens again. I was a bit worried about this. 'Surely,' I said, 'we'll need a virgin with us. The monks will hardly expect either of *us* to give birth to a new Baby Jesus!' I suggested taking Christie's sister Ellen along with us, on account of her being still a virgin.

Dad gave me a startled look, and then a cross look, and asked me how I knew such a personal thing about Ellen. Before I had time to answer, he changed his mind and tried to make a joke by saying that, virgin or not, it would be impossible to take her with us; the three of us would never fit onto one motorbike.

Anyway, he said, I'd got the wrong idea, so far as the Second Coming is concerned. 'We know not the day nor the hour', nor, for that matter, the form of the Lord's next visit. It won't necessarily be Mary and Joseph again. It could be God and Jesus in person. 'And,' said Dad, 'they don't have to stick to being a Jewish carpenter and a new-born baby. They could just as easily go round posing as a man and a boy on a motorbike.' Once he told me this I was a bit more cheerful about the situation. Even so, I think the motorbike could be a problem. I said to Dad it might be worth trying to borrow a couple of camels from the zoo, and dress up in old sheets and pretend to be two of the Wise Kings. We could say we were travelling round Ireland looking for the other one, who'd gone on ahead to make sure things were properly set up for the Second Coming.

Dad said this was a ridiculous idea. We'd be pelted with bricks and rotten fruit by the sadistic savages who make up the bulk of the Irish populace. Worse still, the monks would think we were rich Arab sheikhs and rook us for every penny the minute we set foot inside the gates.

Dad said he didn't want to hear any more fanciful nonsense. We were going to get on the bike and go off for a long weekend, and that was that.

I didn't understand this business of a long weekend; surely a weekend is a weekend, and they're all the same length? Dad said no; in England, the latest fashion is to stretch the weekend from Friday afternoon to Monday morning. It's to do with the current fashion for sexual indulgence.

I asked him about this sexual indulgence. He says it means young office Jezebels going off to four-star hotels with their bosses for disgusting high jinks. It's all charged to the company expense account and paid for by the PBWs; the poor bloody workers.

Even the higher-ups in Government and Society are no better than farm animals once they've finished tucking into their Friday lunchtime caviar and champagne. They jump into the Daimler and dash off to the country for four days of unbridled lust, and woe betide the unfortunate cyclist or County Council road-sweeper who gets in their way. Dad says it's all to do with the artificial sprays and fertilisers they use on fruit and vegetables nowadays; they affect the balance of the hormones in the brain.

One of the problems about getting ready to go away is; what are we going to take with us? I'm keen to take food, in case the monks only eat dry bread and water. Dad says I needn't have any worries on that score. The distinguishing feature of the clerical boyos is the phenomenal circumferences of their bellies. He says this is only right and proper, and not a matter he'd quibble with. They're denied every other pleasure of the flesh, so it's only fair they should be allowed to stuff themselves to the hilt.

I reminded him about gluttony being one of the seven deadly sins. Dad says there are certain things which the Church, in its infinite wisdom, has the good sense to ignore.

The Sergeant came round in the afternoon with the Scott motorbike, but he didn't stay long. He had to dash off to investigate a man exposing himself in the yard behind the butcher's shop. The reason for his hurry was that there were already hordes of women standing blocking the gateway and more arriving every minute. Dad's enthusiasm about the Scott faded when he saw it. The saddle was missing, for one thing, and the front wheel was buckled. Also, needless to say, it wouldn't start. We took the wheel off and went up to the barracks to see Guard O'Rooney.

O'Rooney is the deputy sergeant and the biggest human being I've ever seen. It's hard to know whether it's fat or muscle, because O'Rooney wears a police cape the whole time, even when the sun is melting the tar on the roads. O'Rooney's eyes are very small and sunk in his head, like a rhinoceros's. In fact, he's got an expression like a rhinoceros: half bad-tempered scowl and half sly-looking grin.

He let us into the police stable to see if there was a saddle and a wheel from one of the other bikes that would fit. There wasn't, so in the end Dad swopped the Scott for a Lambretta scooter. He chose this because it was the only machine that would start. It also had a headlamp, which was another thing missing off the Scott. Dad says it's easy to see that the Sergeant hasn't got much clue about motorbikes.

We found a bit of red rubber gas-tubing and used it to syphon petrol out of the other bikes into a bucket, and then poured this into the Lambretta. A lot of it went on the floor, because we didn't have a funnel.

Guard O'Rooney came in to see how we were getting on. He lit his pipe, and casually threw the match away. The spilt petrol caught fire and an explosive flame zoomed across the floor. It set fire to the rubber tubing and the turn-ups on Dad's trousers.

Dad was pretty annoyed. He said to me that in the old days, the main qualification for being a policeman was that you only needed half a brain. Nowadays, if O'Rooney was anything to go by, the half-brain seemed to be optional. Guard O'Rooney is so thick that he thought the whole thing very amusing, especially Dad's remark about brains. He laughed so much, the pipe jumped out of his mouth and the stem broke when it hit the floor.

Dad said he could fix it temporarily by cutting a short piece off the rubber tubing and using it to join the bits. O'Rooney said, 'Certainly! By all means! Carry on with the good work! No harm was ever done by trying! You never know what's possible if you don't have a go!' I thought he was never going to stop.

Dad had his Swiss army knife with him and did the job in a

couple of seconds. O'Rooney examined the pipe and looked at us very seriously and said Dad was a genius of the type that had brought glory to the name of Ireland throughout the centuries, and the sort of fellow any man would be proud to call a pal. He filled up the pipe and lit it. Because of the rubbery bit joining the broken stem to the bowl, and O'Rooney's habit of talking with the pipe in his mouth, the pipe kept wobbling and jumping all over the place, showering sparks and ashes down the front of his uniform.

As soon as he sucked in a couple of good strong puffs, the rubber got hot and started to make a terrible smell. We stood there waiting for him to be violently sick but O'Rooney just kept on scratching his back against the door frame and said it was the best smoke he'd ever had.

Dad suggested to him sarcastically that he ought to get hold of some rubber bands and stuff them into the pipe along with the tobacco. O'Rooney took him seriously and went off to get some assorted ones he had in a cellophane packet in his desk. Dad said O'Rooney was an anthropologist's answer to prayer, because he's so clearly the living proof of Man's descent from the apes.

O'Rooney appeared in the doorway again. Someone had gone off with his packet of rubber bands but, on the other hand, he'd found a split golf ball in the back of the drawer. What would Dad say to him peeling off the skin and unwinding the rubber string inside? Would it be as good as the genuine rubber band article itself?

Dad's face went pale and his eyes glazed over. He whispered to me that he couldn't understand how a man with such an absence of grey matter could tackle even the commonplace technical challenge of lacing up his boots first thing in the morning.

O'Rooney asked Dad his opinion about the best type of rubber to go for. Had he ever smoked a lump of tractor tyre, for example? He said he might try a bit of shredded roofing felt while he was at it, in case the golf ball turned out to be too fiddly. Dad was speechless with disbelief. I jumped in and asked O'Rooney why it was that the shed was so full of unclaimed objects. Did no one ever bother to come and take their stuff away?

O'Rooney said I'd struck it in one and seen straight into the heart of the matter. I was clearly a pebble off the old boulder, with my own contribution to make to the analysis of the cultural life of Ireland, and that if I kept on with this class of quick thinking there was every chance that a vacancy would be found for me in the next generation of the Garda Siochana. He himself would count it an honour and a privilege to put his name on the bottom of my application form, all neatly written out in block letters so the lads in the recruiting office in Dublin would take full note of it.

Dad went over and leaned against the wall, shaking his head and banging it with the side of his fist, and taking no notice of the fact that his jacket was getting filthy from the dust on the brickwork.

I had to think of something else, so I asked O'Rooney why people never came and took their stuff away. O'Rooney gave me a sly grin and said that the plain and simple reason was that they didn't know it was there. What's more, the police were in no hurry to tell them. The stuff had all been stolen once already, with all the attendant trouble of investigation and recovery. Who was to say that if the owners got it back, it wouldn't be stolen again? Where would the police be then, having to go through the same business over and over in perpetuity?

Dad pulled himself together and said we'd have to go; all this intellectual stuff was too much for him. O'Rooney said that this was the difference between a policeman and your ordinary average Joe; the police were trained to cope with the strain of having to think about the wider issues over and above the ordinary routine of everyday life. He says he'll let us know how he gets on with the golf ball.

I had to push the Lambretta down the lane because Dad was so exhausted by the whole experience. I asked him how anyone could possibly be so thick and stupid as O'Rooney, but Dad said I should be very wary of taking him at face value; the Irish have a long tradition of playing the fool when it happens to suit them. He says O'Rooney is probably very shrewd and on the ball, in spite of all the nonsense and play-acting he goes in for.

I spent the rest of the day cleaning the Lambretta, which was filthy on account of the pigeons nesting in the Sergeant's shed.

The biggest trouble with living here is having to go to the outside lavatory. There's no electric light in it, and you either have to get your business done during the day, or use a candle at night. Going during the day is all right if you happen to be what Mam calls 'regular' but I'm not. It's because I don't eat properly. Some days I have huge bowls of porridge and big slices of fresh crusty bread, oozing with melting butter and covered in mashed banana or sprinkled with sugar. Other days I hardly eat anything at all, through being too busy to think about it.

I went out to the lavatory after lunch and lit the candle Dad keeps in there, with the intention of setting fire to the spiders' webs that are in all the corners. I could see the spiders staring at me with their little glistening eyes and I had to stop, for fear they'd jump at me. There's only a small hole in the door to let the light in. I suddenly imagined the wind blowing it shut, and the latch jamming, and me stuck in there with millions of spiders eating my eyes out and crawling into my ears to eat my brain. It was the worst feeling I've ever had, even worse than falling in the rubbish at the dump or the time I put my hand in the saddle-bag of my bike without looking and someone had put a skinned rabbit in it for a joke.

Christie came round after school and said that tonight would be a good time to have a look at Rowena in the bathroom. She'd got special permission to have a bath on account of having to dress up in her Irish dancing outfit to give a demonstration at school tomorrow. I didn't have any money to give him so he took some of the melted coins we found in the car. I've got to swop them back for good ones when I get some pocket-money from Dad.

We sneaked up into his loft just before she was due to have her bath. Then a friend of hers came round and they stayed downstairs talking for ages. When she did finally decide to go to the bathroom, all I could see was the top of her head when she was walking about. I told Christie I wanted my money back.

He told me he had another hole, a much bigger one, but it would cost me more to look through it. By the time we'd finished arguing about how much I should pay him, Rowena was already lying in the bath covered with soap-bubbles and reading a magazine.

While we were waiting for her to get out, Ellen came looking for Christie because he hadn't cleaned his father's boots. He wouldn't let me stay up there on my own, so once again I've had a wasted trip.

Christie came round to see me after he'd done the boots. He's very small for his age, probably because he's a secret smoker, but has quite an old-looking face. He says he's an altar-boy, which amazed me, because I know his main hobby is dirty talk and trying to see up girls' skirts.

He's told me something terrible. He went to see the parish

priest and said he was having bad thoughts, hoping the priest would get into a conversation with him about sex. Instead, the priest lent him some books about purity, and the sanctity of the body, and how to control immortal urges with girls. I asked him what on earth he meant by 'immortal urges' but he said it was too embarrassing to explain; I'd have to ask the priest for myself. One of the books had a chapter about the physical and spiritual horrors of self-abuse. He asked his brother what this meant. His brother said it's another name for mastication. Christie's brother is nineteen and has a ten-speed bike. He knows a lot about life.

Christie said he didn't understand what mastication meant. His brother said it was a posh word for 'pulling your plonker'. He also told him how to do it. I can't say any more about it. Christie wouldn't tell me. His brother says it's a mortal sin even to think about it. The thing is, Christie has actually done it. Imagine that; deliberately committing a mortal sin!

He says his sisters heard him groaning in the loft. Ellen stuck her head up the ladder and nearly caught him at it. He told her he had a terrible ache in his stomach. I don't understand why he was groaning; it must be painful. I don't understand it being a mortal sin, either. The Devil must have a hard job tempting people to commit this plonker-pulling business. I've told Christie not to come near me again until he's been to confession. God could strike the both of us dead if He hears us talking about it.

Christie said he won't be able to come to the castle graveyard with me, in case God catches us in the dark doing something else that might be a sin. He says God can see in the dark as good as in the day, because your soul shines at night. I don't know whether that's true or not, but Christie's right about one thing. It's definitely put the kibosh on going up the graveyard, at least until he's been to confession.

The sun was shining when we woke up, and there was another letter from Mam. Dad had a good idea. We'd start on our holiday straight away and call on Mam in Mullingar to tell her the news about the snooker hall. We can't stay with Mam's family; they don't like Dad.

We solved the problem of what to take with us by deciding not to take anything at all. Dad said if we tried to cater for every eventuality we'd go mad. The scooter would finish up overloaded, and we'd be sure to need just the one thing we hadn't packed, no matter how much we took. Also, if the scooter breaks down, we can stick it behind a hedge and catch a lift, without having to burden ourselves with bags and rucksacks. The only thing worrying Dad was the lack of a pair of goggles. In his youth, he rode motorbikes all the time with the wind in his eyes, and got conjunctivitis. Now he never goes out on a bike without either goggles or a windscreen. There's a screen on the scooter but it's cracked, with bits of Sellotape holding it together. Dad doesn't trust it.

New goggles are expensive, except the ones you can send off to England for. They advertise them in the back of *Motor Cycle* and *Motor Cycling*. They're genuine RAF Spitfire pilots' goggles, with leather straps and glass lenses. Dad had a pair but he lent them to the fellow who stole his motorbike.

We went up to say goodbye to the Sergeant's family and to thank them for looking after us. The girls made us a huge packet of sandwiches and two flasks of drinks; tea for Dad and cocoa for me. Dad asked the Sergeant about goggles. The two of them went off to look in the police stable.

There was a terrible smell in the house. Ellen said it was from O'Rooney's pipe, in the barracks. 'Some joker told him you can smoke shredded rubber! Now O'Rooney swears by it.' She said if she ever found out who it was, she'd do a bit of shredding herself, with a good sharp bread knife.

Rowena was in the kitchen with Ellen. I asked her why she wasn't at school. She went red in the face and went out to the back garden. Ellen said Rowena has just started 'the curse'. 'Do you know what that means?'

I said no, but I'd often heard Mam saying she'd got it. 'I suppose it must be some kind of headache.'

Ellen gave me a queer look. 'It is, in a way, but it's a useful sort of headache.' I asked her how a headache could be useful.

'It's handy if you want to keep the men off you!' Dad and the Sergeant came back. Ellen winked at me and put her finger to her lips as a sign to say no more about it.

Dad had one of the gas masks. He unscrewed the filter canister and said he was going to use the rest of the gas mask as goggles. Ellen said the Sergeant should be issuing gas masks to everyone in the house, as a protection against O'Rooney's pipe. Dad started to laugh and was going to say something. I put on a coughing fit to interrupt him. It was no use. O'Rooney came into the kitchen to get a cup of tea. Dad asked him how the rubber was going. Ellen looked at Dad very sharply.

O'Rooney said it was the grandest thing ever, and a pleasure that ought to be promulgated from every pulpit in the land. It was a man's smoke, no doubt about it. You could keep your Mick McQuaid and St Bruno for the boys from now on, and let the oul fellahs get on with the real thing.

Ellen was staring at Dad, her eyes screwed up into half their size with O'Rooney's smoke and her own bad temper. I tried her trick of winking at him and putting a finger to my lips but he was too busy being smart with O'Rooney. 'If you fancy a different brand, try smoking a bit of old sock dipped in engine oil, the next time you empty the sump on that autocycle of yours.'

O'Rooney said he would, by God. There was no doubt about it, a good smoke was better than a woman any time. The satisfaction lasted longer, there was no messing about with boots and trousers, and you didn't end up in a breathless sweat at the end of it.

By this time Ellen was certain Dad was the person who'd put O'Rooney up to his disgusting hobby. She was feeling around in the table drawer for a knife. I went into the garden and asked Rowena to go in and say there was a man at the back gate asking to see Ellen.

'Why should I?' I said I'd tell her a secret if she did. 'Go on, then. Tell me.'

I said it would have to be later. Ellen was about to murder my Dad in the kitchen. 'That's the most ridiculous thing I've ever heard!'

She wouldn't budge. I could hear all sorts of noise going on the house. I didn't waste any more time. I ran back in and said there was a man at the gate asking for Ellen. I didn't think for a second she'd believe me. She went as quiet and stiff as a statue, and blushed even redder than Rowena. The Sergeant looked very annoyed.

'So that's the game, is it!' He was all for going off down the garden himself. 'I've told you before! If I catch that fellow hanging around that gate again, I'll have him locked up!'

Ellen flew into a rage. 'If you do, I'll leave home! The whole bloody lot of you will have to get your own meals and do your own dirty washing from then on!'

The Sergeant shouted back at her, and she shouted back at the Sergeant. O'Rooney got his pipe out ready to have a smoke and enjoy the conversation. Ellen snatched it away from him and ran out the back door, with the Sergeant and O'Rooney after her.

Dad and I decided it would be best to be on our way. We went out the front and started off on our journey. We forgot the big parcel of sandwiches. Dad said it was just as well, anyway, because we had nowhere to put them. I wasn't so pleased about it. They were banana sandwiches with brown sugar, my favourites.

Dad said we were headed for Galway, and we'd be going through the Curragh, the great central plain of Ireland. I'm always hearing about this at school. I suppose there isn't much else to say about Ireland. Dad says the Curragh is a great place for training racehorses. Millionaires from all over the world send their horses here. Ireland has the best grass, the best jockeys, and the best trainers.

It's where he was based when he was in the army. We managed to find his old barracks, deserted and falling to bits since they built a new one somewhere else. The officers' mess is still there. Dad showed me a faded wooden notice on the wall, with gold letters, that had his name on it, and a list of the awards he won in competitions. He used to be a great man for sport. He was the army champion at boxing, handball, snooker and ballroom dancing. He stood in front of it for ages, reading it over and over and saying the words under his breath. I had to leave him. His cheeks were streaming with tears and his hand was gripping my shoulder so hard I was afraid of getting bruised. When he came out he couldn't speak, and we drove for half an hour before he said anything.

The thing that made him speak was that we were passed by a big BMW, a German bike. Dad said it's one of the best bikes in the world. He got a bit dissatisfied with the scooter after that. He tried to get it to go faster, but it broke down, instead. Dad was in a temper at first, but he calmed down. Everything around us was so beautiful.

The road went straight to the edge of the horizon in both directions. We were surrounded by endless miles of green grass and yellow gorse bushes. Every now and again we'd catch a flash of shimmering silver from a distant lake or river. There was a blue sky over us with nothing in it except a great yellow ball of sun. The heat was as drowsy and humid as if we were in the palm tree house at the botanical gardens.

We lay down on the bank at the side of the road and stared up at the sky, listening to larks and watching ragged bits of half-invisible cloud floating across the sky. We must have fallen asleep.

The next thing I remember was wakening up with a dog licking my face. I sat up. Everything was exactly as it was when I first lay down, except that instead of being warm and fuzzy, the scenery was crisp and clear. Even the light felt crisp.

I felt a bit of a shiver, and put my hand out to pat the dog. It walked away from me, across the road, to where a man was sitting. I looked at the man and he nodded at me. I nodded back. I noticed Dad was sitting up, staring at the man in a thoughtful sort of way.

Behind the man there was a smooth hill, that we hadn't noticed when we first lay down. Halfway up the hill there was a patch of white among the green. It was a cottage with a trail of thin grey smoke coming from the chimney.

The black and white dog ran off up the hill, followed by the man. There was no sound from the birds, and the light from the yellow sun streamed down on us without heat, like a giant torch. I saw Dad shiver, too, and move off up the hill after the man. I followed them.

At the cottage a woman in a black dress was leaning out over the half-door as we approached, holding a bunch of scarlet poppies and yellow buttercups in her hand. She moved inside the cottage, leaving the red-painted door ajar for us to come in.

The man and the dog went over to sit by the fire, a pile of dark turf glowing orange under a copper cauldron gently crowned by blue-grey wisps of vapour. The woman motioned us to sit down. Dad took off his cap and put it on a chair. The table was of scrubbed white wood, with plates of brown clay glazed shiny and smooth. The man lit an old short pipe and sat staring quietly into the fire, while the woman filled our plates from the cauldron.

We each had half-a-dozen big floury potatoes, boiled in their jackets and split open by the steam inside them. The woman gave us a wooden plate with a round slab of butter on it, and two big spoons. None of us said a word, but it was a peaceful kind of quietness. It was very still, like the quiet of a church with the sun shining through it on Easter morning.

Dad and I scooped slices from the butter with our spoons, and used the spoons to slice our potatoes, so that the golden juice melted in among the white flouriness. The woman gave us china teacups filled with milk, and a little glass dish with salt in it. When Dad and I finished eating, the man stood up. Dad put on his cap and nodded thank you to the woman. I was going to speak to her but Dad spread his hand out to tell me not to.

The man and the dog stood at the door when we came out, and the woman came and leaned on it the way she was when we arrived. The dog walked halfway down the hill with us, and stopped. I let Dad go on a few steps, and turned to wave at the people from the cottage. There was no sign of it.

When we got back to the scooter it started right away. The noise broke the quiet of the day. The sun turned warm again, and I could see larks flying overhead. We sat on the scooter for a while, with the engine running, and both of us looking up at the green hill where the cottage had been. Even the tracks of our legs through the grass had gone.

Neither of us could think of anything to say, so we drove off. The next village we came to, Dad stopped and bought me thruppence worth of sherbet bon-bons. We sat in the sun on the steps of the shop, watching a horse drinking from the water-trough.

Dad told me about another time in his life he'd been involved in a similar mystery. One drowsy summer afternoon, he was driving an empty bus along a country road from Dublin to Portmarnock. Just as he was about to go round a notorious bend in the road, a little old woman dressed in black rushed out in front of him. He jammed his brakes on and just managed to miss killing her.

She smiled and waved, and gestured that she wanted to get onto the bus. Dad pulled in to the side of the road and let her on. He looked in his mirror to make sure she was safely sitting down before he moved off.

Just as he was about to put the bus into gear, a lorry careered round the bend on the wrong side, hit the wall fifty yards in front of Dad, ricocheted off the wall back to its own side of the road, and roared off in the direction Dad had just come from.

When Dad got to Portmarnock, he said to his conductor that it was the mercy of God he'd stopped for the old lady, otherwise he'd have been right on the bend when the lorry came hurtling round on the wrong side. The conductor said he'd seen the lorry all right, but no sign of an old lady. He remembered Dad stopping, but he thought it was because he'd heard the lorry coming.

Dad said to him, 'Surely you must have seen her? I watched her get on the bus with my own eyes!' The conductor swore, from that day to this, that no old lady ever got on the bus, and the whole thing has remained a mystery to Dad ever since.

This story reminded Dad about something else. He said to remember the name Donnelly's Hollow, for when we're on our way home. It's a haunted place that we passed on the way down but he'd been so preoccupied thinking about the old army camp he'd forgotten it. He said it was probably just as well, considering we were supposed to be enjoying ourselves.

By the time we got to the first monastery we were hungry and tired. Dad's hands were filthy from working on the scooter. The place had a big wall round it, like a castle, and big gates. There was a bell with a rope attached to it, and a notice saying 'Ring for attention'. Dad wrapped his hanky round the rope so he wouldn't dirty it. A monk stuck his head through a little trapdoor in the gate and asked us what we wanted. Dad said we were weary travellers in need of rest and refreshment, and added 'in the name of God', to make sure of the matter.

The monk asked us if we'd come through the village on our way to the monastery. Dad said no, it had been a lonely road for at least twenty miles. The monk said if we carried on for about another three miles, we'd find the village and no doubt a bed for the night, if that's what we were after. Dad was amazed. 'Do you mean to say you're sending us on our way without an offer of hospitality?'

The monk said that if they took in everyone who turned up at the gates they'd be full every night. Dad refused to be put off. He said he knew his rights, and insisted that we were to be let in. The monk went away and came back with another one, a massive brute with a bald head and sandals. The veins on his feet were so thick you couldn't tell which were sandal straps and which were veins.

This second monk asked Dad if we'd made a booking in advance. Dad said charity was a virtue whose exercise shouldn't require forewarning. After this we were let in, except that the monks said they weren't partial to noisy motorbikes on the premises. Dad said that was no problem. He hid it among the bushes outside the gate. I think he was glad to see the last of it for a while.

As soon as we got inside, they made us have a bath and change into special visitors' robes. These were a horrible light brown yukky colour, like French mustard. I don't know where they put our clothes, because we never saw them again. Much worse than that, from Dad's point of view, they confiscated his cigarettes, which he practically lives on. He says he's going to be absolutely desperate if he can't get hold of a fag for the whole weekend. It's completely ruined his whole idea of the place. He says he had this image of us sitting out on the grass reading newspapers and relaxing between meals, while the monks got on which their business and let us get on with ours.

After the bath we were led off in a procession to the chapel. We had to kneel at the altar while the monks passed in front of us, one by one, and made the sign of the cross over us. Then the massive monk with the veined feet took us for a walk, quizzing us about our moral and spiritual health. After twenty minutes of this another monk came and swopped with him, and twenty minutes later another one. After an hour walking round talking holy drivel, and with our feet aching from the gravel in our sandals, they took us into the chapel again, and made us go to confession.

Supper was a disaster. We were put at a little table of our own, right in the middle of the dining-room, with the monks sitting on benches around the walls, staring at every mouthful we ate. Dad kept dropping his food, he was so self-conscious. Worse still, the monks only had a slice of bread and a bowl of soup each, while we sat in the middle, pigging ourselves on mountains of food that they kept bringing us. If we stopped chewing for a second, even just to draw breath, the two monks looking after us got anxious and bossy, whispering at us not to waste a single crumb of the Lord's bounty. Meanwhile, a tall thin monk in spectacles with a thick Kerry accent kept reading out pious thoughts from the saints. It was stuff about becoming as little lambs and thinking only of Thee, Sweet Jesus, and praying for this mortal life to end so that we can join the heavenly choir.

We might as well have been eating sawdust, for all the pleasure we got out of it. The monks finished their soup in a couple of minutes. It took us ages to get though the stuff we had. The monks couldn't get up until we were finished. This left them with nothing to do but glare at us, and shuffle their feet, and cough impatiently.

After supper it was back into the chapel for Benediction and a long session of hymns. I found this very moving, and so did Dad, once we'd relaxed from the strain of people hounding us around. The only light in the chapel was from candles on the altar. The smell of incense made the place seem exotic and mysterious, like a place in the Arabian Nights stories. The sound of the monks' voices was deep and peaceful, echoing slowly backwards and forwards among the shadowy corners of the building. There were bats flitting around up in the rafters. Sometimes one of them would dive across the light from a candle and there would be a huge dark shape outlined across the walls for a moment or two. I thought everything was lovely, and mysterious, and scary, and it made me want to become a monk. I even felt like singing along with the hymns. Luckily, these feelings only lasted until we got out of the chapel.

We had to go for another walk before they allowed us to go to bed. This walk was even worse than the first one. They took us all round the grounds, through paths among the bushes and trees, and, with only robes and sandals on us, the midges and flies had us eaten alive. I even got bitten on my jake, from not having any spare trunks with me. The monks took away the ones I'd been wearing. At ten o'clock we were allowed to go to our rooms. Dad said he'd been more comfortable sleeping in the cells in Kilmara; at least the law laid down minimum standards of comfort for prisoners, which was more than it did for guests at monasteries.

I was so tired that I fell asleep straight away. I woke up later and spent the rest of the night in a cold shiver. We only had one blanket each and there were open slits in the wall instead of windows. I kept thinking of all the spiders climbing around in the ivy outside, and creeping into the room to get me when I wasn't able to see them in the dark.

This morning I felt terrible. Dad said he felt the same. He didn't sleep well either. The monks got us up before dawn. We had to wash in a concrete trough in the yard. The water was freezing, and we hadn't got a towel. We used the skirts of our habits. While Dad was doing this I noticed he'd managed to hang on to his long johns. After the wash we were taken into the chapel for more singing, and prayers, and then Mass. It all went on for hours.

Breakfast was the same routine as dinner. We had a huge feed of sausages and fried eggs and lashings of thick bread and butter. The monks only had tea and a slice of dry toast each. I felt sorry for the monks. Dad said I needn't be. He bet me a pound to a penny they eat like pigs when there are no witnesses around. Otherwise, he said, they wouldn't be as fat as they are.

The rest of the day was the same as yesterday. The only break in the routine was when the massive monk with the veins asked us if we'd volunteer for a bit of manual labour. He said the community was a bit short-handed. They could use any help that was offered, particularly with grave digging.

At first, we were so glad to get away from the monks that we actually enjoyed it. Dad got all hearty and cheerful. He started giving me advice about a clean mind in a healthy body. This didn't last long. His veins started giving him a bad time. Also, he was soon puffed out, through being a sixty-a-day man. In two hours, we only got down about twelve inches. Dad sat down on the edge of the grave, with his elbows propped on his knees. He gave a groan of agony and despair. 'Oh God! God . . . just one cigarette . . . one puff, even . . .'

He dropped his head onto his hands and stared into the bottom of the grave. A miracle happened. A packet of Craven A flopped down between his feet. We looked at each other, then slowly raised our eyes to Heaven.

I expected to see God's hand sticking out of the clouds, or even catch a glimpse of Him looking down at us with a grin on His face. There was nothing in the sky at all, not even a cloud for God to hide behind. Dad spoke to me in a dry cracked voice, trying to make a joke of the situation. 'God clearly isn't a smoker, or he'd have thrown down some matches to go with the Craven A!'

He'd hardly finished saying this before a box of matches landed beside the cigarettes. Both of us stood up very, very slowly, and looked round the whole sky from one side to the other. There was no sign of where they could have come from.

Dad went down on his knees with his hands together. He looked as if he was about to pray. I decided I'd do the same, just to be on the safe side. Suddenly, there was a ghastly screeching sound. It was like the noise of old women at the vegetable stalls in Moore Street when they're having hysterics at a filthy joke.

'Oh my God!' said Dad. 'I should have known; it's the Oul Fellah himself, throwing fags to tempt me!' It was getting dusk by this time. The thought of being in a deserted graveyard in the dark, with the Devil for company, didn't suit either of us. We stood up and were about to dash off. I looked at the cigarettes and then at Dad. 'Why don't you take them? A fag is a fag, wherever they came from.' Dad looked at me gratefully. 'You're right. It's not as if I've promised to sell my soul, or anything like that.'

The screeching started again. It was very near. I grabbed the cigarettes and matches and we flew off through the graveyard. We found a handy wooden bench and collapsed onto it, puffing and blowing with fear and exhaustion. I had a look at the packet, to see if there was any clue as to where they came from. It turned out to be half empty. I mentioned this to Dad. 'It suggests they're not from Heaven, anyway. I'm pretty sure they're all non-smokers in that particular department.' He sat thinking for a moment. 'Mind you, to give the Devil his due, he's known for his generosity. It doesn't seem likely he'd fob us off with a half-pack, either.'

Then I noticed the Sergeant's phone number on the packet. They were Dad's own cigarettes, the ones the monks had taken off him. Dad got into a furious temper. 'Someone is trying to make an ass out of me!'

A head popped up out of the bushes. It had a face that was the spit image of a bearded rat with spectacles. The middle of the beard opened and we got a third helping of the screeching noise. Dad got such a fright he crushed the packet of cigarettes. The creature came out of the bushes. It turned out to be a skinny little monk in a filthy habit. He had cigarette ash and food stains all down his front, and globs of foamy spit dangling off his beard. When he managed to stop laughing, he asked us if we were the two lads that were digging his grave. Dad and I looked at each other not knowing what to say. The monk had another burst of hysterics before he could manage to speak again. 'Make sure you get the bottom of it nice and flat! I don't want to be rolling around down there.'

He said he was nearly ninety, and very likely he'd be the one who'd be occupying the result of our labours. He said he'd come to give us some advice. Grave digging was the trick the monks used to get rid of people, if all else failed. Dad didn't want to believe him. The monk said he must be a babe in arms to be so innocent. How did we think the place was kept free of tramps and tinkers and idle wastrels? All the religious stuff and the meals in the middle of the room and the freezing bedrooms was entirely for the purpose of putting people off. Unless, of course, they were rich Americans, likely to contribute big handfuls of dollars as a grateful gift. If we'd come in a big flashy car, wearing check shirts, and cameras round our necks, we'd have seen a different side to monastic hospitality. Dad was so disgusted he could hardly speak.

The little ratty monk said his name was Benjamin. The other monks call him Ben Gunn, after the mad castaway in *Treasure Island*. He gets his revenge on them by warning innocent travellers like ourselves. Dad said he couldn't thank him enough for his kindness. He'd thank him even more if he could get him another pack of fags for tomorrow. Benn Gunn's eyes bulged like marbles behind his bottle-bottom specs. 'Tomorrow! You're surely not planning another day in the place, after what ye've had so far?'

Dad reminded him that tomorrow was Sunday, the day of rest. Nothing could be finer than to be stretched out on a decent deck-chair, a fag in one hand and a glass of clerical lemonade in the other. The monk gasped and spluttered. 'Will ye please, like decent men, listen to me for a minute! Sunday is the day the religious treatment really gets going!' We'd be in the Chapel from dawn to dusk, singing hymns; when we weren't singing we'd be praying; when we weren't praying we'd be meditating; when we weren't singing and praying and meditating, we'd be jumping up and down doing the Stations of the Cross. 'And if that isn't enough for ye, tomorrow is the cook's day off! Ye'll be demoted to the bread and water grub-stakes, the same as the rest of the lads in the refectory.'

Dad was flabbergasted, and I nearly broke into tears. The thought of it was too much. Dad wasted no time. We'd have to escape, he said, without further ado. No messing, we were off. Then it occurred to him that we'd need our clothes if we were going to escape. He asked the monk if he knew where they were kept. 'Yes,' he said. 'They're up in a big chest in the attic.' We wouldn't be able to go up there but he could. He'd be willing to risk getting them down for us. But, he said, there was a bit of a problem. He might get caught. If we could just tip him the odd quid or two, it would be a great consolation to him. He'd be able to pay for a perpetual candle and a couple of Masses for the possibly imminent repose of his soul. 'What do ye say to that?'

Dad said quite a few things but it didn't make any difference. The little monk just kept grinning. 'It's either pay up, or stay for the rest of the weekend.' Dad caved in, and said okay, the monk could have two quid but that was it. It was all we'd got, apart from some loose change that we'd need for buying petrol. The runty rat-bag said he hoped we wouldn't mind if he helped himself to the readies before he actually handed the stuff over. Things being what they were nowadays, you never knew who you could trust.

I was all for belting him into a heap of maggot-shit. Dad said no; he whispered to me that he had a plan. We agreed to meet up with the little monk in the archway of the main gate, at eleven o'clock. He'd hand over our stuff and let us out, then shut the gate behind us so no one would be suspicious and come chasing after us. Dad asked why on earth they'd chase us; weren't they trying to get rid of us anyway? The monk said they'd be after us to get some money out of us, even though it was supposed to be free. Dad said he'd like to see any arthritic old wreck of a tonsured choirboy catch up with a Lambretta motor scooter on full throttle. I wasn't so confident, knowing Dad's bad luck with starting bikes.

The monk said 'Right, then, see you at eleven,' and ran off with another of his ear-splitting cackles.

Dad said he was going to find our clothes somehow; he was damned if he was going to give in to the demands of a little rat-faced git. For all we knew, the fellow might be working a racket of his own, and be nothing to do with the monks at all. He could be a kitchen skivvy or, more likely, the illegitimate offspring of a kitchen skivvy, helping his mother out with the odd bob or two that he could frisk from the likes of us.

I didn't think this was very likely, considering the monk had said he was nearly ninety. That would make his mother a ferocious age altogether. Dad said to think of it another way; could you believe a word he told us? I said I could believe he was ninety, because he looked it. Dad got irritable and said a hundred and ninety would be nearer the mark.

This wasn't very logical so far as the theory of the mother was concerned. Dad can get very confused in his thinking when he's in a bad temper.

We had to go in at that point. Two monks came looking for us, waving torches and going 'Yoo-hoo, yoo-hoo' like a couple of pansies trying to attract each other in Grafton Street.

We finally got to bed at quarter to eleven, after another bout of praying and singing and eating and marching round the gravel being preached at. Dad sneaked into my room as soon as they'd left us. He said a grave suspicion had begun to form in his mind, which he'd tell me about later. We made our way very quietly down to the main hallway and into the cloakroom. Dad thought it would be a logical place to keep our stuff. He didn't believe the story about the chest in the attic. He struck matches while I had a look. All we could find was black coats and hats and rows of black ankle-boots.

We heard an unmistakable cackling sound echoing along the corridor. Dad said he had a feeling his suspicion was about to be confirmed. We crept along the corridor until we came to a door. The minute I put my eye to the keyhole I knew what Dad's grave suspicion was, and that he'd been right.

It was a big room full of leather armchairs with monks sprawled in them, fags in one hand and glasses of sherry in the other. They were all in stitches listening to the little monk from the graveyard. He looked completely different. He was all spruced up, and telling them what a pair of eejits we were, waiting in the gateway at this very minute for him to arrive with our civvies.

I stood back to let Dad have a peep. He wasn't very good at it. His bad legs let him down yet again. Trying to aim his eye at the keyhole, he tipped forward and grabbed the door-handle for support. I had time for a quick look at a roomful of open-mouthed faces, then Dad heaved the door shut and sprinted off up the corridor. Dad was thinking fast, like he always does when we're in an emergency. He ran to the front door and yanked it open so hard the inside handle took chunks out of the plaster when it slammed up against the wall.

I thought we were dashing off into the night but Dad immediately turned back and hurled the two of us into the little cloakroom. The door to the cloakroom opened outwards. As soon as we got inside Dad whipped a lace out of one of the black boots and tied a brush handle to the door knob. He jammed it tight so it stayed horizontal across the door frame and held the door shut.

There was a rush of sandalled feet in the corridor, and someone yelled that we'd legged it through the front door. They all ran out after us. I said to Dad that I couldn't see the point of blocking ourselves in. We'd have to come out sometime. I couldn't see his face in the dark but I knew he was grinning. I could feel it in his voice.

'Don't worry,' he said, 'I know what I'm up to.' He lit a match and told me to choose two coats of the right length while he picked out some boots and hats. He bundled the whole lot up, tied a scarf round them, stood up on a chair, opened the little stained-glass window high up on the wall, and threw the bundle out. 'Right,' he said, 'we're on our way.'

I looked up at the window and then at the big dark bulk of Dad. He put his hand on my shoulder. 'Michael, there's only one way I'm going to squeeze through that window. If you dare to laugh, I'll leave you in here.'

I said I had no intention of taking the mick out of him. He said it wasn't only me he was worried about. It was the opinion of the outside world that also concerned him, when, and if, we escaped.

He pulled his habit off and stood in the gloom like a headless, handless ghost. All I could see of him was the white glow from his vest and long johns. 'I'll go first,' he said. 'You're the athletic one, and I want you to fiddle the window shut behind you.' With that, he was up on a chair and out the window head first. I went next, feet first. Dad put his hands up for me to stand on while I jiggled the catch shut. I dropped down beside him. He broke into a tremendous bout of bad language. The gist of it was that I'd forgotten to throw his habit out the window. He'd have to wear a coat with the legs of his long johns showing.

The monks copped on to the fact that we'd barricaded ourselves in the cloakroom. A gang of them came running out to see if we'd escaped through the window. They were thrilled to bits when they saw the window still shut.

I don't know why they were so delighted about chasing us in the first place. It was all a bit pointless and not very holy. Maybe they needed a bit of excitement in their lives. I'm not sure why we were trying so hard to escape, either. I couldn't see why we didn't just demand our clothes back and leave. Dad agreed afterwards that

I was probably right, but he says it's amazing how men can be affected by stress and excitement in the heat of battle. As far as he was concerned, we were battling to get away with our money and dignity intact. It was bad luck that we were likely to fail on both counts, but at least it wouldn't be for the want of trying.

We lay in the shadow of the building until the monks went back into the house, then grabbed the bundle of coats and belted off across the lawn towards the gatehouse. We both lost our sandals on the way, but at least we made it without being seen. We stopped for a second to get our breath back, then tried to get the gates open. They wouldn't budge, not even the little door in the left-hand one. The handles all had chains and padlocks through them. Dad said we'd have to go up the stairs in the little towers each side of the gates, and drop from a window. Just as he said this, all the outside lights came on around the main buildings. We were lit up perfectly in the gateway by a big spotlight hung at the top of the arch.

'Quick,' said Dad, 'before they come out and see us; up the stairs!'

In the excitement, he went up the stairs on one side and I went up the other. It didn't make a lot of difference in the end, but it was just typical.

I ran up my set of stairs and found myself in a little room like a chapel, with candles burning in front of a tiny altar. The only window in the room was hardly more than a slit in the wall. My heart sank immediately. I knew Dad wouldn't have the slightest chance of getting out. The only way I'd get out myself was to turn sideways and squeeze through.

I did this, to have a look out. Sure enough, there was Dad with his head stuck through the one on the other side. He looked like half a Punch and Judy show that had got tipped sideways. There was a desperate look on his face, and no wonder; he'd managed to get stuck.

I knew it was all up to me. I squeezed the rest of myself through and half fell, half scrambled down the ivy on the outside, and ran over and hammered on the gates and rang the bell like a lunatic.

'Help! Murder! Save me!'

The little flap in the gate opened immediately. I put on a thick accent and stood to one side so they couldn't see who I was.

'Are yez looking for two madmen?' I said, in a breathless excited voice.

'Yes!' said the face in the gate.

'An oul fellah and a young fellah?'

'Yes, yes!' said the face.

'They're beltin' off down the road on me faithful Raleigh bike. I got thrown off with a stick through the front wheel. The oul fellah's pedallin' and the young one's balancin' on the crossbar!' I let out a terrible sob of misery. 'The only bicycle in the family, and it shared between twelve of us!'

The flap shut with a ferocious crack. I thought, 'Ah well, that's it; I'd better surrender and give Dad a bit of company.' Next thing I heard was all the chains and padlocks being undone. The gates flew open. I dived into the ditch at the bottom of the wall and kept my face down. A whole herd of monks came galloping out. They headed down the driveway, shining torches into the bushes. They sounded as if they were having great sport.

I risked a peep up at Dad. He was still stuck in the window, clear as anything in the moonlight. I ran back inside the gateway, up the stairs, and grabbed hold of him by the feet. He let out a roar of agony.

'Oh God, mind me legs!'

The torches down the driveway all turned back in our direction. The herd of monks came galloping back, faster than they'd run out. I gave a desperate heave on Dad's feet. He came unstuck and dropped to the floor with a tremendous crash. I just had time to run down the stairs and slam the gates shut before the monks got back. They set up a fearful racket, shouting and banging on the wood with their torches.

Dad staggered down from the tower, groaning and rubbing his back. 'Quick,' I said, 'while they're still out and we're still in.'

He pulled himself together and we dashed across the floodlit lawn, round the back of the chapel, through the graveyard, and into the trees beyond. Dad was absolutely puffed out. He wanted to collapse in the grass. I said no; there was bound to be someone still inside who'd open the gates and then they'd all be after us again. Dad kept groaning and saying, 'But why, why?'

'Because they're enjoying themselves! They think it's a good laugh, chasing us.'

Dad said he meant 'why' in the philosophical sense. 'Why is this whole ghastly business happening to us?' I could have said it was

Dad's own fault for trying to get a holiday on the cheap, but I kept my mouth shut.

He got more and more puffed. 'When are we stopping, Michael?'

'When we get to the boundary wall; then it'll be a quick scramble over and away with us back to Dublin.'

There were two snags with this idea. For one thing, the wall turned out to be too high for a quick scramble. We had to go running along the inside, hoping for some sort of an opening. The second snag was that some of the monks had had the same idea. We could hear them running parallel with us on the outside.

When we found a little gate, Dad's wits came back to him. 'Quick! Put on your coat and the hat and get ready to let them in.' I asked him if he was mad. 'No! I know exactly what to do. Just keep your mouth shut and don't panic.'

The monks on the other side of the wall started rattling the gate and discussing the best way of breaking it down. Dad gave them a terrible fright by opening it suddenly and going 'Sssschh!' at them in a bad-tempered whisper. They shut up immediately. Dad spoke to them in a low voice.

'For God's sake, will you be quiet! We have them trapped in here among the trees! Come in, quick, and fan out in a search party!' The monks were so startled they did what he told them. Dad took charge, pointing at each of them as they came in. 'You; over there. You; go that way. You two; round the back of that shed.'

In a couple of seconds they were all scattered in the darkness. Dad and me shot out through the gate. We ran along a narrow path and then over a hedge into a field. Dad wanted to stop for a rest. I said no; we had to get round the front of the monastery and find the scooter before the monks remembered it and started looking for it.

We were too late. It was gone already. Dad got furious and started cursing. 'They're a bunch of black-coated bastards! They never miss a bloody trick!'

I was too depressed to say anything. We were stuck, miles from home. We had no transport, no money, no food. We had no clothes except a couple of black coats and hats. Neither of us had any footwear. Our sandals had fallen off, and we'd left the borrowed boots behind, in the rush to escape through the gate.

I can't remember the next hour. All I know is that we walked for miles, hoping for a lift, and then arrived at a village. Dad's one ambition was to find a phone box and ring the barracks in Kilmara, to ask for the Sergeant's advice. 'At least we'd hear a friendly voice in the middle of our troubles.' I didn't think this was very likely, considering it was well after midnight. Also, we'd lost the scooter, which doesn't even belong to the Sergeant. 'And anyway,' I said, 'we haven't any money to make a phone call.'

Dad said we could do it through the operator. This would also solve the problem of having lost the cigarette packet with the Sergeant's number on it. This conversation turned out to be pointless. There wasn't a phone box in the village.

Even the pub, which you'd expect to have some life in it even at that hour, was dark and deserted. There were only two lights in the whole of the village; a blue one over the police barracks door and the red sacristy lamp suspended over the altar in the chapel.

We decided to spend the night in the chapel, and make our way back to Dublin first thing in the morning. Half an hour lying full-length on the seats of the oak pews had us perished with cold and aching in every bone of our bodies.

Dad kept saying we should go into the barracks and throw ourselves on the mercy of the police. He was starving and desperate for a cigarette, and getting more and more miserable with the cold. Dad is one of those people who give up the ghost when their temperature drops below normal. Eventually he persuaded me to go along with his scheme. 'The monks will probably come swarming round the village looking for us at the crack of dawn. We'll be like the proverbial rats in the trap. Whereas, if we go to the barracks, and get the duty policeman to ring up Alex, he can vouch for us. We can ask the police to hide us in the barracks until a rescue can be organised.' I was disgusted with Dad for getting so weak and soppy, and relying on someone else to get us out of our troubles.

'It's all to do with needing a smoke and something to warm me up. A couple of Craven A and a hot sweet mug of tea, and I'd be ready to give Einstein a run for his money.'

I said I'd go to the barracks with him if we could make up some story that would explain why we were wandering round dressed like a pair of brainless idiots. After a lot of useless chat we couldn't think of a story that was even faintly believable. We got more and more irritable with each other. In the end, Dad said, 'To Hell with it!' and gave up trying; if I was that keen on thinking up a yarn, I could do it myself.

'It's your turn, anyway! I thought up the story after that pig-farmer business. You can deal with this one.'

This gave me an idea. When we were thinking up a story to explain the missing lorry, we'd used the idea of thugs stealing it away in the middle of the night. 'That's it! That's what we'll say.'

'Say what you like. I'm off. No more messing around.'

I ran after him and told him my idea. 'We're two innocent priests on a motorcycling holiday. We've been set on and robbed by a bunch of thugs, and our motorbike stolen, and most of our clothes. What do you think?'

'How would they steal our clothes, for God's sake?'

'We were camping and asleep with hardly a stitch on when they struck. We just had time to grab a coat and hat each, and disappear into the woods, before we were murdered.'

I could tell what Dad thought of this story, by the way he groaned, but by that time we'd reached the barracks. It was too late to think of anything better. We crept warily up the stone steps to the front door, our feet so cold and hard that we could feel our skin scraping like leather on the slabs. Dad was shivering with nervousness and cold, from having nothing on but his long johns and a coat and a hat. I still had the yukky brown habit on under my coat, so I wasn't too bad.

Dad tried to take a deep breath at the top of the stairs, but it turned into a wheezing cough, and we had to wait a minute until he recovered. From inside the building a clock gave a little ding-a-ling and then solemnly struck three hollow-sounding 'dongs'. 'Damn it,' said Dad. 'That sort of noise at this time of the night gives me the willies. I hope the place doesn't turn out to be haunted.'

He gave a feeble tap on the door, and then another, but there was no answer. Eventually, he put his hand out to turn the handle. Before he even touched it, the door swung silently open, as lightly as if it was made of balsa-wood instead of heavy oak planks and iron straps. The door opened directly onto a room so enormous, and so dimly lit, that the walls and corners, and even the ceiling, faded away into a fuzzy darkness.

In the centre of the room, there was the usual counter, with official forms and books and pencils laid along it very neatly, and a newspaper spread out in the centre of it. Apart from the neatness, the counter looked very queer. It was only waist-high, and very short, hardly bigger than a school desk. It looked mysterious, stuck in the middle of the room like a tiny planet drifting in outer space.

Directly over the counter, connected to the ceiling by a length of twisted flex, hung an electric bulb with one of those white enamel lampshades that look like Chinese hats. Standing under this, and so tall that he looked as if he was wearing the lightshade as a glowing halo, was the longest and thinnest man I ever saw in my life.

I was scared stiff of him immediately, but he was so fascinating I couldn't look away from him. Anyway, there was nothing else to look at. Apart from the man, and the little counter, and the lampshade, there was nothing but cool gloominess in the rest of the room.

The door continued to swing open with hardly a sound, just a low whoosh as it moved though the air. We stepped inside, and onto the polished shimmer of the wooden floor. We didn't make a sound, not even the slightest rustle or vibration. Even so, the man under the lamp knew we were there. His head tilted up just the merest fraction from studying the paper, and we felt the blackness of his eye-sockets staring at us.

We went halfway across the floor and stopped. The policeman stared at us, taking in every detail, but still not moving a muscle. The wave of air from the door wafted across the room and gave a gentle shove to the lampshade. The light swung a couple of inches to and fro, making the man look as if he were swaying gently from side to side. It gave me a horrible fright. For a few seconds, he looked as if he were dead, and hanging stiffly from the electric wire.

Dad took a half step forward and opened his mouth to speak. The policeman came to life. He cleared his throat loudly and sternly. He put up his left hand in the gesture for stopping traffic, and then a finger of his right hand to his lips as if to say 'Ssssshhh . . .'

Dad stopped dead, standing half in the middle of moving, with his mouth open and his eyes staring as though he'd been turned into a statue. The policeman stretched his arms out in front of him and gave the cuffs of his tunic a neat flick. He reached out very precisely to lift a mug in one hand and a cigarette in the other. He took a delicate sip from the mug and then a short puff from the cigarette, holding it in a curious way between the tips of his forefinger and thumb.

'In a place like this,' he said, 'cursed with constant tranquillity, I'd go mad without a routine of minor delights to while away the nocturnal hiatus.'

His voice had a low depth to it, a pleasant and soothing drone that reminded me of a man on a distant motorbike, or a cow lowing two fields away. The sound of it took away my fear immediately. I started to breathe easily and with pleasure. I noticed he had the three stripes of a sergeant on his sleeve, which made me feel even better. I knew he'd be sure to help us.

'Tea and a smoke,' he went on, 'once an hour and upon the hour. That's what keeps me sane.' He stopped for another gulp from the mug, holding it in a manly fashion with his big hand wrapped round the body of it. He stared fixedly at Dad. 'Tea and a smoke,' he repeated, 'and reading the paper closely, so that I have matters to discuss with myself.' He paused a moment. 'It keeps the brain active, you see.' He had another swig and a puff, glanced up at the clock in a calculating manner, then looked again at Dad. 'No doubt you wish to conduct business with me?'

Dad couldn't speak. He nodded.

'Police business?'

Dad nodded again, and mustered a bleak smile. The policeman tipped his head back and drained his mug. 'Proceed with your business, but before you do; would you like to finish off this fag?' Dad's eyes shone with grateful desperation. 'I'll need my hands free,' the policeman said, 'for taking notes.'

Dad took the cigarette and examined it for wetness and spit. He needn't have worried. The policeman was a very dry-looking man, a man who looked as though he'd never sweat.

Dad stood sucking the butt with long deep pulls, one after the other. The policeman stood waiting with his hands spread on the counter. He gave me a pleasant nod, and remarked that it was a fine thing that the religious life still had its appeal for the youth of Ireland. This gave Dad a good excuse to start talking. 'It's not everyone shares your opinion! In fact, it's only the mercy of God that that boy is still alive.'

The policeman tilted his head back with a kindly, interested expression. Deciding not to waste the movement, he picked up his mug and swallowed the dregs that had collected in the bottom.

Dad had a last puff from the cigarette. This made it so small there was hardly anything left to hold. He got rid of the butt by squashing it into tiny fragments between the tips of his fingers. He drew a deep breath and leaned forward, looking at the policeman with an expression of great sincerity, and shaking his head from side to side. 'I'll tell you what,' he said, 'you're never going to believe this —'

The policeman put up his hand, fingers spread in a fan, and tapped his mug three times on the counter as a request for silence. 'Wait . . .' he said, 'wait a minute.' He turned his back and walked slowly and with great precision to the back of the room. He clasped his hands behind him, and spoke solemnly to us from the far edge of the darkness.

'Tell me,' he said; 'tell me . . . is it about a motorbike?'

Dad and I were flabbergasted. The policeman took note of our amazement. He coughed gently, in a modest sort of way. 'You are from Dublin, no doubt?'

We nodded. The policeman bowed formally in the gloom. 'I can tell by the accent.' He took a few paces forward. We could see the razor-sharp creases down the front of his trousers. 'A cosmopolitan city, and a great centre of learning. No doubt about that.' Dad was still gasping over the question about the motorbike. The policeman gave him a modest smile. 'You are no doubt familiar with the methods of the famous fictional detective, Mr Sherlock Holmes?'

He took out a silver cigarette case and a lighter, and lit a cigarette, then courteously tossed them in Dad's direction. Dad was so frozen with concentration that he didn't even try to catch them. They clattered to the floor and slid away out of sight across the polished surface. The policeman studied us with a relaxed but serious manner. I could hear Dad gulping in amazement beside me. I didn't dare glance at him, in case I missed anything interesting.

'Let me put it this way,' said the policeman. He took a puff of his cigarette, looking for a moment like a Hallowe'en pumpkin. 'This evening, I discovered a motorbike . . .' He paused, searching his mind. 'Well, a class of motorbike . . .'

Dad interrupted him anxiously. 'A scooter, would you say? A foreign thing, with the name Lambretta on it?'

The policeman nodded and spread his hands in a graceful gesture of agreement. 'The very thing. This evening. Nestling in the undergrowth down beyond the road there. Mark that.' We marked it, nodding vigorously.

'A motorbike,' he repeated. 'An object not commonly found among bushes in this vicinity.' He made another gesture towards us with his hands. 'And now, not twenty-four hours later; two weary beat-up banjaxed travellers.' The policeman paced to and fro along the length of the counter, his body tense with the effort of expressing himself, cigarette smoke streaming from his mouth like a steam-engine on full throttle.

'I'm not one of your intuitive geniuses. No, I'd never claim to be that. But, and mark this –' We went through another bout of vigorous nodding. 'In a place where nothing happens, year by year, and then two things happen in the space of one day –' The policeman passed a hand over his face and clenched his jaw, thoughtfully. '. . . I'd say a man is justified in hazarding a connection.'

After this momentous statement, the policeman placed himself at the centre of the counter, spread his hands out on it, and leaned forward with an efficient air of interest. Dad told him our story. We were on a short holiday from Dublin, camped in the woods near the monastery. A gang of thugs crept up and attacked us in the middle of the night. We'd run off for fear of our lives. As soon as we were out of the way, they'd bundled our stuff up, thrown it into the back of a lorry, and driven off.

The policeman shook his head grimly. 'It's a terrible thing that two fellahs can't even kip out in the woods without getting terrorised.' He shook his head again, and walked off out of sight into the back of the room. We couldn't see him in the darkness, but we knew he was still there. We could hear him whistling softly to the tune of Frankie Laine's song about a moonlight gambler.

Dad signed to me desperately to have a look for the smokes. He continued to stare fixedly after the policeman. I groped around on the floor, found the lighter and the cigarettes, and gave them to Dad. I asked him in a whisper if the policeman was a genius or a complete nutter. Dad whispered back that policemen, as a breed, generally are complete nutters, but he couldn't make head or tail of this one. 'One thing I do know, though. We've got to get hold of that scooter at the first opportunity.' It was amazing the way a few puffs on a fag could pull Dad back together and set his brain working again.

The whistling got a bit louder and then gradually rose into a terrible banshee wail. I fully expected the policeman to come leaping at us out of the dark, his eyes gleaming and his teeth dripping blood like a werewolf. Instead, all that happened was that he suddenly appeared with a boiling kettle and asked us if we took milk with our tea. Dad and I were so relieved we started to laugh. The policeman gave us a pleasant smile and laughed along with us. Dad handed him a cigarette, and said it was a great bit of luck to have stumbled on such an oasis of cultured hospitality.

The policeman was very pleased with this, but I knew Dad was only buttering him up. He winked at me as soon as the policeman turned his back and went off to make the tea. 'A mug of tea and that's it. We'll ask him where he's keeping the scooter, and then we'll be off.' I asked him what would happen if the policeman decided to hold us for questioning.

'Why should he? What's there to question us about?'

'The story about the thugs and the robbery, for one thing. And for another, there's no tax or insurance on the scooter. He's bound to have noticed that.'

Dad said we'd have to trick him. 'You keep him talking while I drive up the road. I'll pretend I'm just giving the scooter a test drive, to make sure it's still working. As soon as I'm out of sight, you dash after me. That policeman will be no match for you as a runner. As soon as you jump on the pillion, I'll give the bike a fistful of throttle. We'll vanish into the wide blue yonder, like Tonto and the Lone Ranger escaping on the one horse.' I didn't share Dad's faith in being able to outrun the policeman. He was built like a skeleton on stilts. I could imagine him giving a giraffe a run for its money.

The policeman came back with a big wooden tray, loaded with mugs, a teapot and a plate of Jacob's Chocolate Digestives. He asked us how much sugar we wanted, and stood stirring our tea for ages. Dad got more and more desperate. When the policeman finally handed him a mug he downed it in one long swallow. Dad had another mug of tea, and another cigarette.

The policeman asked him, in a casual way, if he ever did any freelance work. Dad was busy enjoying himself with the tea and fags. He didn't take too much notice of what the policeman was

122

saying. 'I do!' he said, cheerfully. 'I do indeed!' He was referring to the travelling mechanic business, forgetting he was supposed to be a priest. I gave him a dig with my elbow, but it was too late. The policeman coughed gently, and murmured that he was embroiled in a bit of a moral dilemma, a matter on which he'd welcome a professional opinion.

Dad copped on to what the policeman was getting at. His face took on a worried look but it was too late to back out. He said, 'Certainly, certainly, by all means. I'll be only too happy to consider any problem put to me.' He didn't look too happy at all.

The policeman said he'd feel safer discussing it within the sacred framework of the confessional. 'Is there any impediment to setting up in business right here and now, or can you only operate within the four walls of a chapel?' He said he wouldn't be asking, only it was a delicate bit of business and not one he wanted to discuss with the local man, seeing as how they practically lived in each other's pockets. With Father only passing through, a clerical ship in the night, so to speak, there wouldn't be the same restraint on him. He could get the whole affair out into the open and dealt with, once and for all. He was particularly anxious to get the matter over and done with immediately. There was a third party involved, a party whose return to the village was a matter of imminent probability. Dad gave me a despairing look. I couldn't think how to help him. The policeman nodded at me politely. 'Would you mind if we had the place to ourselves for a few minutes?'

Another idea struck Dad. He asked the policeman if I could give the scooter a bit of a trial up and down the road while the two of them were chatting. The policeman said this was a good idea; we might need to be putting in a claim for criminal damage to the bike, as well as everything else. He told me to finish my tea while he went and unlocked the scooter from a shed out the back. He said he'd wheel it round the front for me.

I asked Dad if he was mad, suggesting I should try out the scooter. 'Since when do I know the first thing about riding a motorbike?'

'It's just a ruse!' He explained the rest of his new plan. He'd listen to the policeman's confession while I wheeled the bike up the road and waited for him somewhere convenient outside the village. Then, he'd give the policeman a walloping great penance, say ten Our Fathers and ten Hail Marys, to be said immediately. Once the policeman got going, Dad would excuse himself on the grounds of not wanting to smoke in the presence of a penitent. He'd light up a fag, stroll out through the door, leg it up to the top of the village and away with us for Dublin.

The first part of the plan worked out okay. I wheeled the bike up through the village, parked it at the side of a ruined shed, and waited. After half an hour I was frozen stiff. After another half hour I knew the whole thing had gone wrong. I went back to the barracks to see what had happened to Dad. He was sitting slumped and grey-faced on the counter, the floor below him littered with ground-up cigarette butts. The policeman was pacing up and down, hands behind his back, jacket off, shirt-sleeves rolled up and his braces dangling. His mouth was working away like a perpetual motion machine.

I poked my head round the edge of the doorway and hissed at Dad. He stared at me haggardly and gave a long low moan of despair. The policeman stopped pacing and said 'Pardon?' in a quiet manner. Dad grabbed his chance. He said it was time for a résumé of the story to date.

'Paring the matter to the marrow, the position is this; Garda O'Flaherty is up in Dublin on some course or other, and you're paying court to the wife while he's away.'

'Not paying court; no. No; our mutual intimacies have gone far beyond the chaste pleasantries associated with that particular word.'

'You won't be offended, then,' said Dad, 'if I call a spud a potato, and refer to this carry-on as plain straight-forward adultery?'

The policeman said no, he wouldn't be offended; at the same time, it was a severe sort of description to apply to the case. His sole motive in associating with Mrs O'Flaherty had been to make good his promise to a brother officer.

'And this promise,' said Dad, 'if I recall you right, was that you'd keep an eye on the said lady while O'Flaherty was off up in Dublin learning the basics of traffic control?'

'Yes,' said the policeman. 'The same as any decent man would do in the identical circumstances.'

'There was no understanding, then, implied or explicit, that you'd be helping to keep the bed warm for O'Flaherty?'

'No,' admitted the policeman. 'Not on the part of O'Flaherty, anyway.'

'And yet,' said Dad, 'you've been walking up and down here this past hour, cool as you like, reciting a litany of sexual shenanigans that would put a Turkish Sultan to shame!'

'Ah yes,' agreed the policeman, 'but I took no pleasure in it.'

'Damn your pleasure!' roared Dad, in a fury. 'The desire was there, and the opportunity, and the two of them culminated in you and this O'Flaherty woman indulging in acts theologically reserved for the legal occupant of the marital mattress!'

'Granted, agreed, and fully assented to,' said the policeman, 'but the truth of the matter is this . . .' He sat down in a chair and crossed his legs gracefully. 'For weeks before he went to Dublin, O'Flaherty was neglecting his conjugal duties. Night after night at home there, reading up on Belisha beacons, and the statutory signals for directing traffic left and right, and the priorities of brewers' drays over electric trams, and the penalties for parking on pavements, and memorising lists of politicians' car numbers so there'd be no tickets on the wrong windscreens, if you follow me.' He paused for a moment, to get his breath. 'Sure by the time the man set off for Dublin, his brainbox was overloaded with matters pertaining to traffic management. In fact, to tell you the honest truth, the first time we put him on the train, he came back the same day, and all through falling into a coma with fatigue. It was the mercy of God someone noticed him when the train came back through Athlone, otherwise he might have been going up and down for days.'

The policeman stopped to light a cigarette. Dad was in such a state of indignation he couldn't speak. He lit two cigarettes at once and puffed on them both together, then rubbed his hand round his face with a look of miserable disbelief. The policeman started off again.

'Everything would have been all right, if I hadn't got into the habit of dropping by for an evening of supping porter round the fire. She noticed I had a good wrist for the poker-work, and a neat way of jiggling a pile of smouldering sods into a condition of inflamed combustion. This admiration for the poker-work gave rise to conversations rife with carnal allusions, and after that one thing just led to another.'

'Are you telling me,' said Dad, 'that there's a poker involved now, as well as everything else?'

'No, no,' said the policeman. 'The poker was purely figurative.'

'Which is more than we can say about the broom-handle,' said Dad, 'and the potato-dibber, and the two skipping-ropes, and the business with the tin of treacle, and the other business with the feathers, and the bucketful of warm buttermilk, and the – the –' He waved his hand, trying to remember.

'Are you thinking of the hanky-panky with the rolled-up newspaper?' enquired the policeman, helpfully.

'No,' said Dad. 'Not that.'

'The sheet spread with bacon-fat?' Dad gestured irritably; that wasn't it either.

'Was it the trick with the spoons?'

'Wait, hold it, I remember now,' said Dad. 'The perverted misuse of the two hot water bottles!'

'Ah yes,' said the policeman. 'That.' He nodded in agreement. 'If it wasn't for the strict Catholic upbringing, I might have slipped into temptation and enjoyed that one. It was the best of the lot.'

'Or the worst!' shouted Dad.

'Agreed,' said the policeman, 'agreed. But it's like a lot of these things. Your view of the matter depends on who's getting the benefit of it; yourself or the fellah next door.'

Dad looked over at me and shook his head in shock and disbelief. He started to say something to the policeman, then jerked his head back in my direction. I was still crouched in the doorway. Dad's eyes bulged, his jaw dropped, the two cigarettes fell out of his mouth. He shouted, 'Look out, Michael! Behind you!' A bony hand grabbed me by the neck and a familiar cackle exploded in my ear. I twisted round as much as the grip allowed. There were monks looming out of the darkness from every direction.

I dropped to the ground, twisted onto my back, braced myself against the top step, and kicked out with both my feet. I got two monks right in the belly. Both tumbled backwards, knocking over the ones behind them on the steps. There were sandalled feet and bare bums sticking up all over the place.

I jumped up, dived into the barracks, and slammed the door. The policeman was mystified. Dad shouted at him that we had to get out, now, that very minute; was the back door locked? 'No,' said the policeman. 'No, it isn't, but –'

'"But", my arse!' said Dad. He yanked the policeman's trousers down to his ankles, wound his braces round them, and tied a rapid knot. The policeman was too tall to bend down and undo it. We left him standing in the gloom like a statue, afraid to move in case he tipped over. We ran out through the back door of the office, into the policeman's kitchen, through another door, and off into the night.

We didn't bother about the scooter. The monks would have heard us trying to start it. Even if we'd managed to get it going, we wouldn't have got far; neither of us had any money for petrol. We stumbled across some fields and found a hay-shed, and burrowed into the straw for the night. Dad said we'd get up and hitch a lift into Dublin the minute we woke up. It shows you how tired I was, that I went straight to sleep without giving a thought to all the spiders in the shed.

We got a lift back to Dublin on the back of a cabbage-lorry. The driver let us off at the market in Mary's Lane at eight o'clock.

The first thing Dad did was to hide behind a stack of boxes and take off his long johns. They were itching, and driving him mad. Bits of chaff had got into them during the night. It was something we didn't think of, when we burrowed into the straw. He said it was as well to get rid of them anyway; two bare shanks would attract less attention than the sight of his long johns poking down below the hem of the coat.

We were tired and filthy, and worried stiff as to how we'd get home without causing a scandal. Dad said the whole village would see us getting off the bus, with it being Sunday and everyone hanging around after Mass with nothing to do until the pubs opened. Our first priority, he said, was to get hold of a change of clobber.

We found two tramps sitting in the gutter in Arran Street. They were scraping up the remains of a basket of eggs that had fallen off a cart. Dad told them we were priests from a rich religious order, feeling guilty about being so well-dressed. He said we wanted to swop our expensive coats for the rags off a poor man's back. It didn't work. The tramps said they were perfectly satisfied with their own coats, thank you, and what sort of a pair of demented eejits were we anyway, walking round with no shoes on and getting dog-shit all over the soles of our feet?

We went to the Anglesea Market, hoping to swop our coats for something cheaper and maybe get a pair of shoes thrown into the deal. The first woman Dad spoke to agreed to give him a grey plastic raincoat and a pair of boots with no laces, but she wanted to have a good look at Dad's coat first.

He was so keen to do a deal before she changed her mind that he had it unbuttoned and half off before he remembered he'd got nothing on underneath. The screech from the woman brought half of Dublin running straight away. We had to beat it, at top speed. We could hear her yelling for ages, roaring out that Oul Nick had appeared to her in the form of a priest, and flashed his private parts at her.

Dad said we'd done her a favour. She'd never be short of a pint in a pub from now on, not with a story like that. He said it would be all over Ireland by closing-time this afternoon, elaborated and embellished by all sorts of obscene details.

We went to another secondhand clothes stall in Winetavern Street, with a man in charge. Again, he wanted to inspect the coat before he'd do a deal. He said there was every chance the lining would be missing; we weren't the first clerical customers he'd dealt with, and he was up to all the tricks. Dad was absolutely fed up by this time. 'What the hell sort of tricks could anyone possibly get up to with the lining of a coat?'

'Ah, now,' said the fellah, 'that'd be telling!' He'd say no more, but there were priests walking round Dublin, aye, and the provinces, wearing a shirt lifted wholesale from the inside of a coat with the aid of an astute razor-blade.

'A shirt?' said Dad. 'A bloody shirt?'

'Yes,' said the fellah. 'All ye need is a dog-collar at the neck of it and ye'd be togged up fancy enough for a funeral celebration at the Shelborne.'

Dad glared at him in disbelief. The fellow went on to say that some priests were fond of using coat linings as handkerchiefs, and others would rip out strips to use in emergency if they were caught out by a call of Nature and they in the middle of a walk with no convenient newspaper to hand. The chat and nonsense went on and on, but we had to stick it out. We ended up with trousers, boots and jackets for the two of us, in exchange for the coats and the yukky brown habit.

After that we hobbled round to the Kilmara bus-stop at Nassau

Street. As soon as a bus came along, Dad and I jumped aboard and went right to the front seat on the top where we wouldn't be seen by people getting on and off. Unfortunately the driver recognised Dad as he drove up to the stop. He and the conductor came upstairs looking for us, saying they had five minutes' break for a fag and a chinwag. As soon as they saw the state of Dad, and the way he was dressed, it put the mockers on everything. They kept trying to be cheerful with us, but you could see they thought Dad must have got into a terrible state since he's been sacked. The conductor never came near us again, so there was no problem about fares, even though he wasn't a man Dad knew.

Only a few people got on the bus on the way home, mainly people from farms going to mass, and a bunch of rowdies from Gavinstown looking forward to the pitch-and-toss. We waited until everyone got off before we came downstairs. The driver was waiting for us, with his hat off as if he was at a funeral.

'Billie,' he said, 'Billie, I want you to take this.' He shoved something into the top pocket of Dad's jacket, stared at Dad for a moment with tears in eyes, and then went off back to the cab, saying over his shoulder, 'It's for the kids, Billie, for the kids.'

The bus shot off in a cloud of black diesel fumes before Dad could pull himself together. When he looked in his pocket there was a pound note and a ten-shilling note rolled up tightly together into a tube like a cigarette. Dad burst into tears himself when he got it out.

We spent the rest of the day trying to get a sleep in the back room, but from about two o'clock on, somebody kept hammering on the front door. Eventually I had to answer it. It turned out to be Christie. He'd seen us coming home off the bus. We looked so ferociously browned-off he hadn't risked talking to us at the time.

I told him I was too tired to think of going out. He said he must talk to me; he had this great new scheme for making money. I said I couldn't care less at the moment. All I wanted to do was get back to sleep. He took no notice, and insisted on telling me about it. It's all to do with this fellow Christie knows at school, Mumbo Quigley.

Mumbo works as a caddy on the golf course at Rathluan, the next village along the beach. It's a famous golf course, full of rich businessmen, and he earns pots of money at the weekend. He told

Christie about this, and said he could get him in on it, hoping that Christie would be his friend.

Christie tried it for a day, but gave it up halfway through because he couldn't remember the names of the clubs. Also, the weight of the bags, and the length of them, was too much for him. Mumbo is able to manage, even though he's the same size as Christie, because he's such a tough little bugger and never feels any pain.

This was on a Saturday, two weeks ago.

Mumbo took pity on him and told him another way of making money at the golf course. You get there very early in the morning and go round all the rough grass looking for lost balls. There are always dozens of them, because by the time the last golfers finish going round on the Saturday evening it's getting dark and they can't see properly to follow the balls. And anyway, they're too keen to get into the bar to be worried about looking for them.

Mumbo said that all you had to do was get to the links early on a Sunday and go round and pick them up, then sell them back to the golfers at a shilling each. The caddies take it in turns to do this, so that they all get a chance of making extra money.

Christie got up at the crack of dawn the next day, cycled to Rathluan before any of the caddies turned up, and got a saddle-bag full of balls before anyone else had a chance to look for them.

The trouble was, that when he tried to sell them to the golfers, the caddies took them off him and beat him up. They said he had no business trying to break into their racket. He also got a belting from the boss of the club, for riding his bicycle all over the golf course. Cycling on the greens is completely forbidden, for fear of putting grooves in the ground. They worry a lot about marks of any kind, because the balls get thrown off course by them. Christie tried to deny it but they could see where he'd been by the wheelmarks in the dewy grass. He said the club steward was really savage, and accused him of being paid to mark the grass on purpose, so that people could use the grooves to cheat. There was a big competition on later that day, and they tried to make out that Christie was making secret guidelines from the edges of the greens to the holes in the middle. Christie said this was a load of shit, because he didn't know anyone at the golf club, but it was a useful idea for the future. He never misses a chance for making money.

He was going to tell me something else, something about naked girls. Dad yelled out from the back and said he'd kick him up the stairs if he didn't stop mouthing and let us get back to sleep. I went back to bed and never woke up until the following morning.

Part Two

Week Four

Monday 2 July – Sunday 6 July

I started school in the village today. The headmaster is the worst human being I've ever met. It's dreadful that he's supposed to be looking after us and teaching us to be good Catholic Irish boys.

The school is at the back of the chapel. It's built of the same type of grey stone. It's a cold building to look at and a cold building to be in. It never gets any sunlight or summer warmth, because it's always in the shadow of the chapel.

The school is in two halves, with boys in one and girls in the other. They have a separate gate and playground and different doors for going into school. It's a sin to have anything to do with the girls. Christie says the teachers give you a beating if they catch you looking at them through the fence, or trying to talk to them in the street outside the school.

He knows a way of spying on the girls when they're in the toilet. He says it's very risky and dangerous. It involves getting up on the roof of the bicycle shed, and you can easily be seen by the teachers. I can't understand Christie; what's the point in watching girls pissing?

The boys are split into three groups. I'm in the group at the top of the room. We're the oldest, and we're nearest to the fire. It's no bigger than the fireplace in an ordinary house, and there's hardly any heat from it, but at least I can see the flames. The fire is always lit, even in summer. We're allowed to bring billy-cans of cocoa to school to heat up at lunchtime.

I made sure I sat in the front row of desks. It's the best way to avoid questions. The whole point of teachers asking questions is to make a fool of boys when they can't answer. They know only brainy fellows dare to sit at the front, so they save their questions for the thick ones who try to hide at the back.

Being the oldest boys, we have the headmaster teaching us. His name is Mr Welch. He looks like a white bull terrier, with tiny

135

vicious eyes and thin snarling lips and a sloping forehead. His clothes are perfect, never a crease or chalk dust like other teachers, who always have baggy trousers and frayed ties with egg yolk and grease stains on them.

Welch is small, but smooth and impressive like a Jesuit priest. Christie says he practically is a priest, even though he's married. He has no children, and goes to Communion every morning and Devotions or Benediction every evening. I'm certain to fall out with him. He's always got a sly smile on his face.

The boys in the middle class have a scruffy teacher called Baldy Burke. He's older than Welch but much nicer towards the boys, even though he's ugly. He has a bald head covered with warty bumps. His ears are ruffled and twisted, and so are his teeth, which have got black holes in them. They're covered in brown and yellow scum from always smoking. He often has bits of bacon rind caught in the gaps, left over from his breakfast.

His breath smells, and when he laughs he snorts in air through his nose and hee-haws it out through his mouth like a donkey. His nostrils have bushes of tobacco-stained hair sticking out of them. When he blows his nose he gets globs of snot trapped in them. Christie says that in the winter the hairs are always dripping. Sometimes Baldy comes in with icicles on them. His suit is crumpled and filthy and his whole body smells of smoke and sweat and bad feet. He's not married, which is hardly surprising.

The smallest boys have a woman teacher. Her name is Miss Donovan. She's quite young but just as ugly as Baldy and Welch. She tries to make herself pretty with lipstick and powder and nice clothes, but it doesn't make any difference. Her teeth are huge and stick out so much that she can't close her mouth properly. She looks a bit like a cross between a horse and a goldfish.

She's got the same sort of eyes as Welch, small and bright like an animal. She tries to smile but it doesn't work. Her lips peel right back off her gums and her eyes crinkle up at the corners but she still looks miserable. The older boys treat her horribly. They make smart remarks about her looking like a horse, and how they wouldn't mind being a jockey and giving her a good gallop.

I feel sorry for her. She didn't ask to be born looking like that. It all comes back to how unfair God is. The youngest boys also give her a terrible time. She's forever snuffling and crying. Welch never interferes when she's being tormented. He thinks it's amusing.

He says the proper place for a woman is at home looking after the menfolk. Baldy does his best to help her but even he finds it difficult to like her.

When I first arrived, Welch waited beside his desk until we'd all sat down, then walked over slowly and pompously to where I was sitting. He stood studying me with his hands behind his back. Everyone got quieter and quieter, wondering what was going to happen.

He brought one hand round from behind his back and held it in front of him, palm up, and pointing at me. I was mystified at first, then he started to move his hand gently up and down, and I realised he was signalling to me to stand up.

He put on a weaselly smile and said it was customary to welcome boys to the school with a handshake. He'd be honoured to continue the tradition with my good self. I could see that the rest of the fellows were expecting a laugh. I didn't know what was going to happen, so I had to shake hands even though I was suspicious.

Welch put all his strength into squeezing my hand, but looking at me very relaxed as though he wasn't doing anything. Unfortunately for him, he'd picked on the wrong boy. Dad used to be handball champion of Ireland until smoking ruined his stamina. He's taught me how to strengthen my wrists and hands by squeezing rubber balls and lifting chairs by the back-rests.

The instant I felt Welch tighten his grip, I let my hand go limp. This threw him off guard; he'd been expecting me to provide him with a tensed hand to squeeze on. His eyes looked startled but he kept on smiling, relaxing his grip for a second to get a new hold on me.

In that second, I got my hand round his and clamped a ferocious grip on it. The two of us stood smiling politely at each other. All the fellows sat grinning at Welch, sucking up to him and getting ready for the moment when I'd break down and beg for mercy. Welch had a very strong hand. Christie says it's from playing golf. I just kept thinking of Dad and what he told me about never giving in to bullies. The bones in both our hands were creaking, but neither of us would submit.

The school door opened and Jeremy Lynch came in. Welch gave him a savage look and then returned to pretending to smile at me. 'We'll continue this some other time,' he said, in a vicious whisper, and pulled his hand away. He put it straight in his trousers pocket and I could see him clenching and unclenching it to get his fingers working again. Jeremy Lynch stood staring at me from the doorway. Being a shrewd little beggar he could see the half-smile still on my face and the fact that Welch was in a temper. I thought this would show Lynch I was a match for Welch, and make him think twice before sending me any more messages about beating me up.

Unfortunately Welch took his bad temper out on Lynch and made it worse for me. He strode over to Lynch, whirled him round by the shoulders, and kicked him over to the blackboard. Lynch put his hands round to protect his backside but Welch kept on kicking. I could see Lynch's knuckles bleeding from the metal toecaps on the headmaster's shiny brown leather boots.

When he'd kicked Lynch in front of the class, Welch became smug and smiling again, hands behind his back and his bull-terrier face set in an evil grin. He put up his finger to the class and said, 'Death is – ?'

Like a bunch of creeps, even Christie, they all yelled back, 'The separation of the head from the body!'

Welch put another finger up. 'And pain is – ?'

The class roared back with pitiful excitement, 'The application of the stick to the fingers!'

Lynch stood looking at everyone with a quiet defiant look. Even though I know what a rat-bag he is, I couldn't help feeling respect for him. The class started chanting, 'Get – the stick! Get – the stick! Get – the stick!'

Welch went into a small room beside the fireplace and came out with a billiard cue. He got out his handkerchief and polished the wood up and down so it shone. He motioned to Lynch to put his hand out. Lynch did, and Welch brought the stick down so hard that I could hear it whistling. Welch's feet actually left the floor with the energy he put into it.

Lynch shut his eyes and his face went white with the pain. He screwed his hand up and clutched it under his arm, swaying with the agony. I shut my eyes myself, with the shock of it. I heard Welch's voice saying, 'Come on, come on, come on . . .' in an evil purring way like the witch in *Snow White*.

Lynch put his other hand out. There was another grunt from Welch as he whacked the stick down again. He put such an effort into it that a big juicy fart escaped from his backside. Everyone heard it but no one dared smile. Welch straightened himself up and pulled down his sleeves as though nothing had happened.

Lynch stood with both hands under his armpits and his eyes shut, face as white as a sheet. I was all for getting up and belting Welch but the fellows on either side grabbed me and said, 'For Christ's sake don't move; you'll get us all belted!'

At break-time Christie said it was nothing unusual for Welch to thrash Lynch with the cane. I asked him if Welch had ever had a go at him. Christie said no; only little things like twisting his ears or making him sit on the bucket. Welch keeps a full bucket of water in the schoolyard during the winter. When the water freezes, Welch uses it for punishment. He makes fellows pull their trousers down and sit on top of the ice with their bare bums.

Christie told me that Welch has a lot of expressions he uses in school. 'Death is the separation of the head from the body' is the most common one. Welch thinks it's very amusing. It's something King Henry the Eighth of England is supposed to have said to one of his wives.

I saw Jeremy Lynch in the middle of his gang, blowing his hands and rubbing them up and down his jumper to get the feelings back. I went over and told him I thought he was very brave. He told me to eff off. I didn't take too much notice of it. He's not used to people like me.

Christie wanted to have a smoke in the bicycle shed and invited me along. I said I wasn't interested in smoking. He said it would be a good chance to meet some other fellows. I could see Welch looking at me from the door of the school in a thoughtful sort of way. I decided it would be a bad thing to join the smokers, in case he followed me and caught the rest of them puffing.

A little dwarfy fellow came up to me and started talking. I could hardly understand him, his voice was so muffled. He talks through his nose, and hardly opens his mouth at all. It turned out his name was Mumbo Quigley, the one who put Christie onto the golfing rackets. He has a brother called Kevin who's a year younger.

Quigley said Christie's been saying at school that I'm starting a gang. He wants to join it. So does his brother. I was tempted to laugh but I didn't. The two of them look like they should be members of the Seven Dwarves' gang.

This Quigley is a bit like Miss Donovan; another person that

God didn't play fair with. I can't understand it; the catechism says God made us all equal and in His own image, and yet you get people who are so rubbish they have to go begging other people to like them.

The snag is, if I let Quigley into my gang, I'll have all the other no-hopers trying to get in as well. I'll become a laughing-stock in the village, with everyone thinking I've ended up with other gangs' rejects.

I was polite to this Quigley, and told him I hadn't actually got started yet, but I'd make a note of his name. He said he'd be very grateful; none of the other gangs will give him a chance. They say he's too short and lumpy and thick. He says he has a secret weapon, which is why no one can ever beat him up. It's his head. It's very solid and doesn't feel pain. When he's attacked, he curls up in a ball on the ground. He waits until whoever is kicking him gets exhausted, then jumps up and smashes their nose with his head.

Welch was waiting for me as soon as I got back into school. He called me into the little room and said I was to stay late as a punishment for defying him. I said no, I wouldn't; school time was his time, and anything after that was my time. Welch's little eyes nearly popped out, and his voice choked into a breathless whisper.

He asked me if I realised how serious it was, refusing to obey a headmaster's orders. He has both legal and spiritual authority over me, and can do anything he likes. The classroom is a kingdom and he, the teacher, is king of it.

He picked up the billiard cue and began polishing it. I said if he tried anything on me I'd bash him, and ram the cue right up his arse. I'm not normally so vulgar but he's such a despicable bully I had to be straight with him. Welch was sick with rage. He couldn't believe I was so calm and unafraid of him.

I said it was because my Dad hates bullies, and has taught me to be the same. I also mentioned that Dad had been the middle-weight champion of the Irish Army not too many years ago.

The rest of the morning was boring, learning how to write a letter in Irish telling someone we were having a lovely holiday by the seaside.

At lunchtime Christie warned me to stay away from Quigley.

His two sisters are dirty bitches. They both had babies and had to go to England.

Christie invited me to the bicycle shed to eat my lunch; it was a good place to spy on the girls. I thought he was trying to get me up on the roof but it was something different. There are knotholes in the planks at the back of the shed. You can see into the girls' half of the school.

A lot of them sit on the front steps, talking and larking around. They don't think anyone can see them, so they don't bother to keep their knees together the way they usually do when boys are around. You can't really see much, because of the distance, and they don't sit still for long anyway. The only one I wanted to look at, a fair-haired girl with a white blouse and a red skirt, never sat down on the steps at all, so it was a waste of time for me.

Christie says Jeremy Lynch has a little pair of binoculars small enough to fit in his pocket; he found them down the dump. One of the lenses is cracked but you can look through the other one and it's as good as a telescope. Lynch lets fellows borrow them for the price of a couple of fags. Christie says he doesn't mind paying.

After he's had a good look through the binoculars, he starts a rumour that one of the girls is sitting with her legs apart and not wearing any knickers. The other fellows get desperate for a look and pay Christie more than he gave Lynch in the first place.

I asked him what happens when the fellows find out there isn't a girl flashing her fanny. Christie says that's no problem. They always pretend they can see one, so they don't look a fool to the rest of the queue. Anyway, he can always say the girl must have got up just as he was handing over the binoculars.

After lunch we had catechism for an hour, then another break, then Irish history until it was time to go home.

Welch asked Mumbo Quigley a question about Brian Boru fighting the Vikings in Ireland years ago. Mumbo was too frightened to admit he knew nothing about it. He made up a stupid answer about hearing on the radio that Boru had mown down the Vikings with a machine-gun he'd borrowed from the IRA. Welch got hold of Mumbo by the ears and lifted him up off the ground. Mumbo was squealing in agony like a pig. Everybody was laughing except me. Welch wasn't very pleased. He said I was clearly a lad bereft of a sense of humour. I'm glad I've only got three weeks to go before the end of school.

Coming home from school I came down the lane to go in through the stable. As I was passing the coal-yard gateway I got a desperate urge for a pee. I undid my buttons and was about to get my willie out when I realised there was already someone inside the archway. It turned out to be the big girl who lives beside Andy, the one whose skirt I accidentally looked up. She was standing in the shadow at the back of the archway with her dog, letting it have a shit.

I pretended I was an aeroplane taking off from a hangar and zoomed across the lane into the stable. Once I was inside I rushed upstairs and opened the top half of the hay-gate enough to peep out. She was still in the archway, because the dog hadn't finished. She was glaring at it and saying, 'Come on, you little brute,' and looking really fierce.

When it was finished, she crept to the front of the archway and poked her head out to make sure no one was coming. When she came out she tossed her head in a very snobbish way. Her hair swung out like a dark cloak all round her face and then settled down her back again. She's really beautiful.

As she walked down the lane I opened the gate a bit more and leaned out. The stupid dog heard me and whirled round jumping and barking, twisting the girl round with it. Luckily she didn't look up, and at that minute Christie came running down from the top of the lane, whistling.

She thought the dog was barking at Christie and gave it a good whack with the end of the lead. I just had time to duck my head in before she saw me. I stayed dead still for a few seconds until she went into her garden, then leaned out and whistled at Christie. He didn't hear me at first. He was in the archway, walking round in circles staring at the ground, and raking through the wind-blown rubbish with the toes of his shoes. He was concentrating so hard I had to shout. When he saw me watching him he got quite ratty. I thought it was because I'd caught him looking for cigarette butts. He said that was nonsense; he could buy his own fags, and decent ones at that. I asked him what he was looking for. He said it was his own private business.

In the end I had to threaten him. He said he was looking for money. The pitch-and-toss school meet in the archway every Sunday afternoon when the pubs shut. Most of the players are well on with drink. They drop handfuls of coins and don't notice a few missing when they pick them up. Also, when they win a big round, they only pick up the notes and leave the small change as a kitty for the next game. In the excitement the coins often get kicked around and lost among the dust and rubbish.

Christie was cross at having to tell me all this. He's worried I'll want to be in on it, or tell other people about it. I told him it's against my principles to spoil another fellow's racket, especially as we're friends and in the same gang. He was relieved to hear this. It's the first place he goes after school on a Monday. He often finds as much as five shillings in coins. Sometimes there's a ten-shilling note or a pound. Once he even found a fiver. He had to wash it, because it had dog-shit on it, but otherwise it was all right.

This reminded me of the girl and her dog. I told Christie I'd been watching her. She swings her hair about and walks along with a straight back like a film star. I said I'd fallen in love with her. Christie got snotty and said I was stupid. I should stick with his sister Rowena, because at least there's some chance with her. The girl with the dog is too old for me, and too posh. He told me all about her. Her name is Stella Rothwell, and she's eighteen. She has a cold way of looking at people, and speaks to them as if they were dirt. This annoys the shopkeepers and also the older boys in the village. They're always talking about ripping her clothes off and shagging her.

She's too classy to work and will just do nothing until she gets married, not like the rest of the girls in the village. They have to get jobs on the farms or work in Jacob's biscuit factory in Dublin or behind the counter at Woolworth's in Henry Street. I'd marry her myself if I were older.

She lives in the house beside Andy. They own their house, unlike everyone else in the terrace, who only rent theirs. Her dad is supposed to be a rich businessman but Christie doesn't believe it. He doesn't drink or smoke and he's not fat. He looks more like a doctor, very neat and clean and with good manners towards everyone. They're also the only people in the terrace with a car, and proper curtains and a polished door-knocker.

Christie says they must be brainy as well; they read the posh English newspapers. He knows this through looking in people's bins when they put them out in the lane on Fridays for emptying. He's learnt a lot about people in the terrace, particularly from reading their letters and bills. I thought this was disgusting. I asked him if he ever saw any letters from boyfriends in Stella's bin. He said no; girls always save love-letters, no matter how many they get nor how stupid the letters are. He's read loads of them belonging to his sisters.

This reminded him of Rowena. He asked me if I'm coming round on Friday to have another go at looking through the bathroom ceiling. I said no. I'm afraid of being caught in the loft. Anyway, I said, I object to paying money just to look at girls with no clothes on. Christie said I'd change my mind one of these days, when I'm older. Fellows of his brother's age go into Dublin and pay a whole week's wages for ten minutes with a mot down a dark alley. A shilling to look at his sisters is good value. At least I'd see something, which is more than you can say about the mots in the dark in Dublin.

I said maybe the fellows bring torches with them, and shine them up the girls' skirt. Christie says that's not the point at all. It's not torches the fellows put up the girls' skirts, it's their jakes.

His brother says it's great, but you can get a disease from doing it. Your jake goes rotten and drops off. I asked Christie why they bother, if this disease is so horrible? He says it's something big fellows can't help doing. You don't get the disease from ordinary girls, only these mots in Dublin that charge money for letting you do it. That's why his brother wants to get hold of the things from Andy's parents. They stop you getting the disease.

I asked Christie why his brother pays money to the mots in Dublin, when he could put his jake up ordinary girls and not get the disease? Christie says ordinary girls won't let you do it unless you marry them. This is why big fellows pull their plonkers, or pay the mots in Dublin. There's one or two girls in the village who will let fellows put their jakes up them, without paying and without marrying them, but they always end up going to England to have a baby, like Mumbo Quigley's sisters.

The minute Christie mentioned plonker-pulling I got worried about God striking us dead. I asked him if he'd been to confession and he said yes. When I asked how much penance he'd been given, he got a bit shifty and changed the subject.

Was I determined to be in love with Stella Rothwell? I said I was. How would I feel about paying money to have a look at her, then? I laughed. I can see her practically any time I like just by going out on the terrace. Christie said he meant a gawk at her with no clothes on. I looked at him in amazement. He said it would cost me two shillings, and he wanted me to think seriously before I said no. I said there was no chance of me thinking about it at all; he was a lying little shite and only making it up to annoy me. He said it would cost me three shillings now, for calling him a liar, and another sixpence for every day that I didn't believe him.

Last Saturday, cycling to the golf course in Rathluan, he met Stella cycling back along the coast road. She had a wet swimsuit draped over the front basket. The next day, trying to get to the golf club very early, he took a short-cut along the strand. At a certain place, Stella ran out across the sand and straight into the sea in front of him. She didn't see him because of the sun in her eyes. He climbed up onto the dunes to spy on her. After a while, she came out of the water and back to this certain place. Then, and Christie swore this is true, she took her swimsuit off, rubbed herself all over with oil, and lay down on the sand without a stitch on. He watched her for ages, and saw every bit of her.

When she got dressed, and this is another thing Christie swears is true, she didn't bother to put her knickers on! He says the thought of her bare arse on the saddle of her bike made him half mad with excitement, and desperate to get his plonker out. Next time he sees her bike parked in the lane, he's going to give the saddle a good sniff.

He says the fact that she was down the beach both mornings means she might be there again this weekend. I said there was no chance of me paying him three shillings, when I can go down and find her myself. Christie says that would be impossible; there's five miles of beach between here and Rathluan. It's a secret hollow in the dunes that you can only find if you know where to look. I said I could do what he did; ride down the beach and watch out for her swimming. Supposing she saw you coming, said Christie; where would you be then? She'd get dressed straight away and maybe never go there again. I told him I'd think about it, but not to hold out much hope. Three shillings is a lot of money just to look at a girl with no clothes on.

In the evening I asked Dad what 'shagging' meant. He said it was a disgusting word used by ignorant people who knew no better. Yes, I said, but what does it actually mean? Dad hummed and hawed and said it was a coarse way of referring to a very beautiful act, an act created by God to enable men and women to express their love for each other. It's an act, moreover, which enables us to share with God in the miracle of the creation of human life.

After he told me this I didn't feel too bad about the big fellows saying they'd like to shag Stella. It just means they want to express their love for her, the same as me. I also asked Dad about this disease you get from women. He says there's two of them. I can't remember exactly what he said they were, but it sounded like gone-over-here, and slipper-lips.

I asked him why fellows go round sticking their jakes into girls. He said it's to do with sexual urges and the desire to procreate. I didn't understand this. Dad put it another way; it's all to do with making babies. This worried me. Everyone has babies; does that mean everyone gets this disease? He said no, only people who have too much sex. Sex is the name for everything to do with making babies.

I asked him if the Sergeant had this disease, because he must have had a lot of sex to have so many children. Dad said no; you only got the diseases from having sex and babies with more than one person. It's God's way of protecting the sanctity of marriage.

Provided I exercise the virtue of purity and keep myself chaste until such time as I marry a clean-minded virgin girl, I'll be all right and needn't worry about disease. I asked him how I'd know if a girl was a virgin. He went a bit red and said it was recognizable by the clear light of innocence shining from her eyes. When a girl loses her virginity she loses this light in her eyes. She develops a guilty, shifty sort of expression, and can never look people straight in the eye. I'll have to go round looking out for this.

I asked him again about virginity. I don't understand the 'fires of concupiscence' thing he told me. Dad says it means a girl who has not been intimate with a man. Was this anything to do with shagging? Yes, only I wasn't to call it that, being the beautiful act that God himself had created.

Why should this beautiful act make fellow's jakes drop off and give girls a shifty look? Dad said because it was God's way of making sure they only did it within the sacrament of marriage.

When I asked him the meaning of 'purity' and 'chaste', he got impatient. It was all a bit involved and he'd sooner discuss it with me some other time. There's too much curiosity about sex, and all it leads to is dirty talk and disgusting behaviour. When he was young he was too busy enjoying himself to worry about it, what with boxing and athletics and going to dances and pictures.

He and my Mam got married knowing nothing at all about sex. It was years before they got round to having me. They lived like brother and sister for ages, and it didn't harm either of them. I was surprised to hear this. They can't have been very happy. All the brothers and sisters that I know hate each other, and spend most of their time fighting.

Dad says everything about sex is complicated, and usually sinful. The Church is hot on stopping people sinning, so the best thing is to know as little as possible about it.

I couldn't sleep last night. I kept thinking about Stella and whether it's worth seeing her with no clothes on. My problem is, I know I should be interested, but I'm not. Well, I am interested, but not in the way other fellows seem to be. It doesn't get me all excited, like Christie that time I saw up her skirt. Even Malone, who says he doesn't like girls, is always talking about doing things to them. Maybe if I forced myself to take more interest in them, I'd discover whatever it is I'm supposed to get excited about.

At school Welch came up to me and said he hoped we could make a fresh start. I said I hoped so too. He put his hand on my shoulder in a friendly way. Before I had time to pull away, he pinched the side of my neck really hard. I was in agony but I couldn't move. He had me paralysed in one of those nerve grips. They're impossible to get out of. He stood smiling at me, delighted with the look of pain on my face. He must have been really pleased to get me back for yesterday. When he let me go I was too weak to move, so I couldn't bash him.

Baldy Burke didn't turn up, so Welch had to teach the middle class. He told us to spend the morning writing an essay called 'What I'd like to be when I grow up'. Most of the fellows couldn't think of anything and just messed about. I wrote that I wanted to be a rich businessman with a Rover car, a big house, leather furniture, a cook, a butler, and a cottage in England for my holidays. It was all nonsense, but I was the only person doing any writing.

At break Mumbo Quigley said he'd noticed I'm good at writing. I told him my Mam and Dad have taught me thousands of words. He sniggered and said his mam and dad only ever said two words to him: 'Fuck off.'

He wants to send a love-letter to a girl in the school, but he doesn't know what to say. Also, he says he's useless at writing because he has sweaty hands and can't keep a grip of the pen. That's his excuse, anyway. He wants me to do the whole thing for him.

I went looking for Christie in the bicycle shed. I wanted to talk about Stella Rothwell. He was too busy smoking and looking through the planks at the girls. I had a look myself and saw the girl with the white blouse and the red skirt again. She was too far away to see if she has the light of innocence in her eyes, so I don't know whether she's a virgin or not. If I had her for a girlfriend I could ask her what girls think about.

After break Welch collected up the essays and stood at the blackboard looking through them. Everybody was quiet and dead scared, except me and Christie and the fellow who sits on the other side of me. They both copied my essay and just put in a few different words about what they wanted to be.

The other fellow is called Norman Sculley. He always wears his coat in school, with the buttons and belt done up neatly like a girl. Christie says he never takes the coat off, even at home. It makes him look like a little middle-aged businessman. He's very short and thick in the body, a bit like Mumbo, but not at all thick in the head. He's always making smart remarks about people, especially about the way they look. His eyes bulge and he irritates everyone by making a noise in his throat as if he's trying to cough up phlegm. Christie says he's a spy for Jeremy Lynch's gang, but he's not actually in it.

When Welch finished marking the essays he said there were only three that were any good. Remarkably, all three appeared to have been written under the influence of an identical creative inspiration. He gave me and Charlie and Sculley a frozen smile when he said this. Christie told me Sculley's father is the headmaster of a big technical school in Dublin, so Welch never dares to hit him. He can't hit Christie, either, with his dad being the sergeant.

Welch said that no words could describe the contents of the remaining essays. He paused to let this sink in. This was because there were no words in the essays themselves. A page headed by a name and a date was beyond the bounds of even the most liberal definition of an essay. He paused again, and asked if anyone had anything to say about this appalling display of ignorance?

I put my hand up and said I had a book at home about Winston Churchill, the most famous man in England. Churchill as a boy wanted to go to a posh school. When he took the exam to get in his mind went blank. All he wrote on his paper was his name and the date and the number of the first question.

Welch smirked at me and said this was very interesting but what was my point? 'My point,' I said, 'is that Churchill still got into the school. The headmaster was clever enough to spot that he was a genius in disguise.'

Welch came over and handed me a jotter. He asked me if I'd be kind enough to read out the name at the top of the page. The moment I looked at it I was sorry I'd opened my mouth. It was Mumbo Quigley's name. Welch asked me in a loud voice whether I would be rash enough to suggest that Quigley was a genius in disguise?

He went on to say that if Mumbo is a genius, his disguise is so perfect it's probable his talents will remain forever impenetrable to human perception. Everyone went into fits of hysterics, even though they hardly understood a word Welch said.

At lunchtime Sculley said he couldn't help noticing how my ears stick out. Before I could think of a remark, he asked me how to spell 'impenetrable'. He wanted to make a note of what Welch said about Mumbo's hidden genius. Christie told me later that Sculley always writes down teachers' sarcastic comments, so he can use them afterwards as smart remarks. Sculley's a bit hazy with words, though. I asked him if he was recording Welch's words for posterity. He looked cunning and said, 'Who's "posterity" when he hasn't got jam on his face?' I told him posterity means future generations of people. On the way home I heard him swanking away to one of the girls in a la-di-da voice. He told her he liked to jot down interesting words and phrases for prosperity. I couldn't help laughing, which annoyed Sculley.

After school I decided to ride up and down the terrace on my bike. I was hoping to see Stella, and Andy's mother. I found a wooden ruler lying in the road, that had fallen out of someone's school-bag. This gave me an idea. I rode along holding the ruler against the spokes of the front wheel. It made a really good noise, like a helicopter.

I was so busy holding the ruler against the wheel with one hand, and steering with the other, that I forgot to look where I was going. I got up to a terrific speed, whizzed to the end of the terrace, and rode straight down the steps into the sea. The tide was full in, and right up to my waist. It took me ages to struggle upright and get my balance. Then I had to poke around in the water to find the bike. Funny enough, the first thought that came into my mind was to hope that no one was watching. I felt such an eejit. I had a terrible time getting the bike out of the seaweed floating around in the water, and another terrible time wading back to the steps, carrying the bike and being bashed by the waves.

Boozer Quinn, who rows the golfers back and forwards to the island, was sitting on the steps smoking his pipe. He was surrounded by great shiny globs of brown spit, even on the toes of his boots. He said it was the first time in his life he'd seen anyone trying to teach a bicycle to swim. I was livid with embarrassment but I didn't say anything.

I was afraid someone from the terrace would see me, so I sneaked up the lane pushing my bike and went into the stable. It was warm and peaceful, with a lovely safe smell of old dry straw.

I decided to go in the loft and read until my clothes dried. I took a magazine out of the boxes that Christie's sisters found but the windows were so dirty it was hard to see what I was reading. I got a brush from downstairs and started to sweep away the cobwebs and dust and dead insects. I got a nice reward for my efforts. I could see into all the gardens along the terrace!

Christie's sister Ellen was out hanging clothes on the line. The woman next door was playing with a baby in a pram. In the other direction, I could see Andy's mother kneeling at a flower-bed, weeding. In Stella's garden, there were a pair of feet sticking out from the end of a sun-bed. I couldn't see who it was; they had a big coloured umbrella blocking my view.

While I was staring out the window a huge black spider escaped from the tangled webs on the head of the brush. It crawled up the handle right onto my hand. I nearly died with the shock of it, and was too scared to stay in the loft any more.

All the straw from the loft is downstairs in a big heap. Dad and I got it down once we'd cleared the rubbish from the ground floor. He's going to give it to John-Joe Maguire for his horse. I lay on the straw thinking about Stella, wondering if she was sunbathing in her garden with no clothes on. I was dying to cheat Christie by telling him I'd already had a look at her. I decided to go down the lane and see if I could peep through her garden gate. On the way I passed a ginger cat with only three legs, trying to jump up the wall next to our stable. I tried to give it a lift but it spat at me and slashed the back of my hand.

Stella's house doesn't have a stable, and neither does Andy's. They have a wall at the bottom of their garden, with their two gates in it, side by side.

Her gate has a keyhole but it wasn't big enough to give me a good view of the garden. I couldn't see much except the feet poking off the end of the sun-bed. I kept looking anyway, hoping the person might move and give me a better look at her. There were some knickers on the clothes-line, but I don't think they were Stella's. They were too baggy.

My back ached from bending down looking through the hole. The feet hadn't moved for ages and I felt sure Stella must be asleep. I thought it would be safe to open the gate quietly and have a quick look. I saw straight away that the person on the sun-bed wasn't Stella. It was a much older woman.

I was backing out of the gateway when a cold hard voice spoke from behind me. 'What, pray, are you up to?'

I looked round, and it was Stella. My mouth went dry and all I could do was stare at her. She had the little dog clutched in her arms, with one hand holding its mouth shut so it couldn't bark and warn me. Her face was vicious and her lips looked thin and mean. I said the first thing that came into my mind. 'I'm looking for Andy Barrington; I thought this was his house.'

'Oh . . . so you're a friend of Andy's?'

I nodded my head madly.

'It's odd that you don't even know which house he lives in.'

I gulped and took a deep breath. She took her hand off the dog's mouth and gave me a terrific slap across the face. I was too shocked to feel any pain. She stepped back to let me out of her garden. As I passed her she gave me another whack, across the back of my neck.

'The truth is, you're a loathsome little peeping Tom. You deserve a good beating.'

My head was ringing from the two whacks. I felt so miserable and ashamed I nearly burst into tears. I tried to go up the lane but she lashed out with her hand again and caught me right across the face with her nails. The pain was even worse than the whacks, so I gave up trying to escape. She pointed her arm at Andy's gate and ordered me to go in. 'Otherwise, I shall know you were lying, and go straight to the police this very minute.'

I had no choice. I had to open Andy's gate and go in. Stella slammed it behind me and held it shut. I could hear her laughing.

Andy's mother was standing quietly by a flower-bed, with a trowel in one hand and a plant in the other. She didn't seem at all surprised to see me. She smiled and said hello. My face hurt too much to speak, so I didn't say anything. She had on a white blouse, with a black swimsuit underneath it, and no shoes. Her hair was tied back with a pink ribbon, and she looked young and pretty. She put the things down and walked over to me. When she stood in front of me, I could see over the top of her head. She put her hand up to touch the scratch-marks on my cheek. It made me jerk my head. 'You look as if you've been in the wars.'

I made up the first excuse I could think of. 'I was attacked by a cat.'

She looked thoughtful. 'It must have had very large claws. Was it, by any chance, a black-haired cat?'

I said no; more a sort of orange colour. She gave me a funny smile and said it must have been a different one to the one she'd heard spitting in the lane a few minutes ago. 'Come into the house. I'll find some iodine for those scratches.' She put her hand on my arm to lead me up the garden. As soon as she felt my sleeve she looked worried. 'You're soaking wet!'

I told her I'd been saving the cat from drowning. 'I'm just on my way home to get changed.' Then I realised this didn't explain what I was doing in her garden. 'I just came in to say hallo to Andy on my way past.'

'I see. I thought perhaps you'd popped in to escape from the cat.'

'Oh no; that was ages ago!'

She gave me another funny smile and said Andy was still at school in England. 'He won't be home until the holidays.'

I was surprised about this. 'I thought Andy went to the Protestant school in the village?'

'No. He's staying on at his boarding school in England.'

Mr Barrington is only in Ireland for a while, and it wasn't worth disturbing Andy's education. This was bad news to me. I told her it was useless having a fellow in the gang if he was never around when he was needed.

She said she knew exactly what I meant. 'Being married is a bit like being in a gang.' Her voice went sad when she said this. I thought she was upset at what I'd said about Andy. I tried to make her feel better by saying I didn't mind Andy being away, so long as he swore to be faithful to us, and spent all his time with the gang when he came home.

This only made things worse. Mrs Barrington put her hand to her mouth and turned away as if she was going to cry. She pulled the ribbon out of her hair. When she turned back she had her head bowed and her hair like a golden curtain hiding her face. All I could see was the tip of her nose. There was a tear sparkling on the end of it. I tried to say I was sorry. She put her hand out and touched my lips with her fingertips, and whispered that it wasn't my fault she was upset. She gave a big sniff and took a deep breath, shook her hair back from her face and looked me straight in the eyes.

'Will you stay and have tea with me? In the garden?' I didn't know what to say about this. I made an excuse that I had to go home and change out of my wet clothes.

'And will you have tea with me then?'

I told her it wasn't the usual thing for fellows to have tea with their friends' mothers. 'Also, I'm not a very nice person. You shouldn't really have invited me.'

She was surprised at this. I explained about Stella attacking me, and how I'd been lying to her about the cat.

'Oh gosh! The iodine – I forgot.'

I said I'd got some at home myself.

'Will your mother be worried when she sees your face?'

'I haven't got a mother at present. My Dad and I have come to Kilmara to start a new life.'

'Oh . . . I'm sorry. I wouldn't have said anything if I'd known.'

'It's all right. She's not dead. She'll be coming to live with us as soon as we're settled in.'

She said 'Oh . . .' again, and then 'I see . . .' but I could tell she was a bit mystified. So am I, really. Boys never do understand mothers and fathers.

I went home and got changed, after she'd made me promise I'd come back. I had a job finding something to wear. All my clothes are filthy. I borrowed one of Dad's shirts but I had no clean trousers. I found my swimming trunks and put them on. I didn't think she'd mind, seeing as she was wearing a swimsuit herself.

While I was home I went up in the stable loft to see if Stella was in her garden. I was afraid she might hear me talking to Andy's mother and start jeering me over the wall. Luckily there was no sign of Stella, and the feet had gone from the sun-bed. I could see Mrs Barrington getting out deck-chairs, and trying to figure out how to set them up. I waited until she'd done them. I've never been able to work out deck-chairs either, and I didn't want to look stupid.

By the time I went back she'd got everything ready. There was a little table laid with plates of biscuits and cake and Wagon Wheels, which you can't buy in Ireland, and a bottle of Robinson's Barley Water with a jug of iced water beside it, just like you see in the advertisements. There was even a bowl of flowers on the table, and another bowl with nuts in it.

Mrs Barrington had her hair tied back again, with a straw hat on top to keep the sun out of her eyes. She had on a different blouse, and a yellow skirt, with a pair of sandals on her feet. As soon as I saw her I thought, 'Oh no,' and wished I hadn't worn my trunks, especially when she saw me in them and giggled. I went bright red in the face. She said she was sorry; it's just that if she'd known she wouldn't have bothered to change.

'I wish you hadn't.'

'Oh . . . really? Why is that?'

'I liked you in the swimsuit.'

She said 'Mmmmm; I see . . .' and gave me a cheeky look. 'I'd better change back into it, then!' I told her not to go to any trouble on my account.

'It's worth it. It's not every day a lady is spoken to so frankly!' Besides, she said, the sun shines so rarely in Ireland, a girl ought to take every opportunity to enjoy it.

She went in to get the teapot. When she came back she'd changed into another swimsuit, a white one with a thin red stripe down each side. She didn't have a blouse on over it. I couldn't believe how beautiful she looked. My mouth went dry and I felt a mixture of hot and cold shivers running all over me. I couldn't move, except my eyes, which kept staring at her, even though I tried to stop them doing it.

She stood at the table pouring tea. I could smell a flowery perfume from her. She handed me a cup. It took me ages to get my hand to move; she was standing right in front of me and I could see the whole shape of her body as if she had nothing on. Every part of her seems to blend with every other part. She's all smooth and curvy, like a fighter plane or a cheetah. She didn't mind me looking at her, and stood waiting for me to take my cup, smiling at me in a friendly way. I suppose when you're that beautiful you get used to people staring.

While we were having our tea she asked me why I'd come to Kilmara. I told her about Dad's motorcycling mechanic business, and the problem with the pig farmer. She laughed so much she spilt her tea all over her swimsuit. When she leaned forward to shake the tea-leaves off, I could see right down her front. She stood up and took the jug of iced water off the table. She moved away so it wouldn't splash me, and rinsed the tea off her swimsuit. 'Cold water is the best thing for preventing stains.'

When she sat down again the water had made her swimsuit practically transparent. I could see her tummy-button and the pink circles on her breasts. When she leaned back the wetness made the pink bits in the middle stick out. She didn't seem to mind, and after a while neither did I, even though at first it had a funny effect on me. The sun soon dried her, anyway, and then she was all smooth and white-looking again, except for a tiny mark where she'd squashed a greenfly while she was rubbing the tea-stain.

After we'd been talking for ages she stopped and looked at me in surprise. 'Here we are, chatting away like old friends, and I don't even know your name!' I told her it was Michael Alexander Kelly.

We had a few minutes of silence after this. Mrs Barrington leaned back in her deck-chair with her eyes closed. When she spoke again, her voice was very quiet. 'My name is Suzanne . . . most people shorten it to Suzie.'

'That's terrible!'

'What do you mean?'

'Suzanne is a lovely name for you. But not Suzie! Suzie

sounds like the name of a pretty little girl in a children's story-book.'

She sat up and looked at me with hardly any expression on her face. 'Most people seem to think that . . . that I am a pretty little girl.'

'Oh no! That's rubbish.'

Mrs Barrington kept looking at me without giving any clue to what was going on in her mind. 'You don't think I'm a pretty little girl, then?'

'No, I don't! To me, you're a beautiful grown-up lady. I could easily fall in love with you, but I know it would be ridiculous. You're already married, and you're my friend's mother, and I'm far too young for you anyway.' Once I got started, I couldn't stop; all my feelings for her came pouring out. 'I wish we lived in olden times. I could be a knight on a white horse, and wear your scarf on my shoulder, and write you love-letters and wonderful poetry, and do great deeds for you. I could fight for your honour and for your love, and protect you from anyone who tried to harm you. I'd search the world for treasures for you, and make you mistress of my castle, and queen of all my lands!' I felt pretty silly after I said this. I asked Mrs Barrington if she minded me saying all those things.

'No . . . No.' I thought she'd finished speaking. I was just going to say something but I noticed her lips trembling, so I stopped. She spoke again: 'It's probably the nicest . . . No, it *is* the nicest thing, that anyone's ever said to me.'

Mrs Barrington put her sun-glasses on and snuggled down in her deck-chair. She lay quietly with her arms by her sides and her legs stretched out in front of her. She was so quiet I didn't dare speak, for fear she'd fallen asleep. I leaned back myself for a while. I nibbled my way through two Wagon Wheels before she spoke again. 'You know so much, and yet you've got so much to learn.'

'I know that. That's why I have a plan to teach myself everything there is to know.' I told her about reading ten pages of the encyclopaedia every night, and listening to the news on the radio every morning.

She sat up again, and took her sun-glasses off, and asked me to look at her. I sat up, and saw that she'd got tears all down her face. They were quiet tears, not tears of misery, and though she looked

sad, she also looked peaceful. 'Do you know why I'm crying?'
'No.'
'Does it upset you?'
'No. You can keep on crying if you want to.'
'That's kind of you. I do want to. Not for too long – just a little while more.' When she'd had a little cry, she asked me another question. 'Most people are upset by other people crying, and want them to stop; why don't you?'

I said that when something is hurting inside your head, or in your heart, the best thing to do is let tears wash away the pain. Those aren't completely my own words; my Dad helped me to think of them. Sometimes I cried myself, but he always said not to be ashamed. Pain bottled up always goes on hurting, whereas pain released through tears helps to clear your mind, and then you can do something positive about whatever's making you unhappy.

By the end of telling her this, I was worn out with the effort of thinking. I fell back in my seat feeling exhausted and sweaty. I got a shock from her next question, and had to sit up again, tired as I was.

'Why were you fighting with Stella?' She could see I was trying to think up a story. She leaned forward and put her hand gently on my knee for a moment. 'Just tell me the truth. I'd like to know . . .'

I took a deep breath. 'Stella caught me in her garden, trying to peep at her sunbathing.'

'I see! So I'm not the only lady you like the look of!'

'Oh yes, you are. You really are!'

'And Stella?'

'Everyone says I should be interested in girls, and find out more about them.'

She smiled, and said I seemed to know quite a lot already.

'Oh no! I know hardly anything. Nothing, in fact.'

'And looking at Stella sunbathing will help, will it?'

I couldn't think of anything to say, so I kept my mouth shut. Mrs Barrington looked at me in a kind way, and asked me to try and understand that Stella's life is very difficult. She has no friends of her own age or standing, and a difficult family situation. Her parents won't let her mix with people in the village. They've brought her up to think no one is good enough for her. Stella is a very lonely girl, and loneliness is hard on a woman, as she herself knew well. It would be a nice gesture if I could forgive Stella for losing her temper with me.

After she said this, she sat looking at me for a moment, but I still couldn't think of anything to say. She suddenly jumped up out of her chair. 'That's enough of being serious for today! Do you know how to work a camera?'

I was glad to see her cheered up, so I made an effort to smile. 'Yes. I know quite a lot about cameras.'

'Good! Richard's camera is in the house but it's too complicated for me.' If I could operate it, we could take photographs of each other to send to Andy in England. She went into the house to get the camera.

I was glancing round idly when I noticed Stella looking down at me from the top window of her house. I tried to smile at her but my face froze up and my scratches hurt straight away. By the time Mrs Barrington came back, Stella had gone.

It was a smashing camera, with a complicated instruction book, but I managed to figure it out. It even had a timer thing, so you could stand in front of it and take your own photo. Mrs Barrington asked me to set it so that we could be in the photos together.

'That's if you don't mind, of course!'

I said I didn't mind at all. She smiled and said she couldn't remember the last time she'd had such a carefree day. I didn't believe her, because of the crying, but I didn't say anything.

There was a new film in the camera, with twenty-four spaces on it. We used up every single one of them. It was great fun. We hardly stopped laughing. There was quite a lot of hugging, and fooling about, and Mrs Barrington's body kept touching me. I began to feel very strange.

When I got to the last bit of film, Mrs Barrington said, 'We ought to take a photo of us kissing! That would give Andy a shock!' It was only a joke but the thought of it got me all hot and bothered. I started sweating, and my face went the colour of a beetroot. Mrs Barrington got quite worried about me, and said I'd had too much of the sun. 'Come inside. I'll cool you down with a drink, and a damp cloth.'

We went into the kitchen of her house. I was so amazed at how beautiful it was, I just stood with my mouth open. It's got loads of cupboards with glass doors, and an electric cooker, and a beautiful

158

wooden table with cane chairs round it. Everything is absolutely clean and sparkling.

She got a snow-white tea-towel out of a drawer, rinsed it in cold water, then came over and told me to bend my head so she could reach me. She moved close to me and put one hand on my shoulder and reached up with the cloth. I could smell her perfume again, and the warmth drifting up from her body. I got another attack of the hot and cold shivers. She could feel it through her hand on my shoulder, and stepped back to look at me. 'What's the matter?' she asked, in a soft, quiet voice. 'Are you afraid?'

It was a strange question and I didn't know what she meant. I told her what was wrong. 'I feel awful. I don't know why. I'm trembling with cold and heat, all mixed together.'

She said it was probably coming into the cool kitchen after being out in the sun for so long. I knew it wasn't.

'I'll get you a rug to put round your shoulders.'

'No, please don't go; I don't want you to move!' I had that desperate feeling that Christie says his brother gets. It frightened me, because I didn't know what it meant, or what to do about it. Mrs Barrington put the cloth down on the table. She took her hand off my shoulder and stood quietly in front of me like a beautiful white statue. My breath started panting and my knees were trembling and my hands were sweating. I felt more and more frightened, but not by Mrs Barrington, only by the feelings I didn't understand.

Mrs Barrington put both her hands on my shoulders and looked at me in a very loving way. 'You poor, poor boy! Would you like me to give you a hug?'

'Yes, I would. I'd like that more than anything else in the world!'

She put her arms round my neck and snuggled up close against me. I felt faint with happiness, and moved gently back to lean against the sink so I wouldn't topple over. Her hair tickled my nose and the smell of her skin went into my head and made the shivering worse and worse.

She moved closer against me, and I felt the warm curve of her tummy pressing against mine. I dared to put my arms around her, and pulled her tighter against me. My heart was beating as hard and as fast as if I'd just climbed right to the top of an enormous tree.

Mrs Barrington leaned her face against my neck. I felt the cool tickle of her lips against my neck. Then a terrible thing happened. My willie began to swell up. I was too shocked to move, because it was such a scary thing to happen. I held Mrs Barrington even tighter. This only made it worse. No matter how hard I tried to stop myself feeling terrified, I couldn't. My willie got bigger and bigger, and started to have feelings of its own. Before I could help it, I wet myself.

I pushed Mrs Barrington away so I wouldn't wet her as well. When I looked down at myself I couldn't believe it. My willie was poking up through the waistband of my trunks. It was weeing all by itself, in little spurts like a water-pistol. It wasn't like an ordinary wee. It gave me a strange feeling of throbbing pain, mixed with a lovely hot feeling of relief.

I pulled my trunks up as far as they'd go and stared at Mrs Barrington. I was in a terrible state of shock and embarrassment. She put both her hands to her mouth and stared back at me.

Suddenly I couldn't stay there any more. I rushed out of her house and down the garden, up the lane like a madman and into my own house. I threw myself on my bed, and burst into tears. I fell asleep. When I woke up my willie had gone back to its normal size.

I fell asleep again, and after that I don't remember any more.

I woke this morning still wearing my swimming trunks and Dad's shirt. This made me think of Mrs Barrington. I got a warm feeling between my legs and my willie began to swell up like yesterday. I was so scared I knelt and prayed to the Virgin Mary. The feeling went away. I'll have to be careful about hugging girls in future. I don't want to make a disgrace of myself again. It's no wonder priests are always warning boys to stay away from girls.

I must go and apologise to Mrs Barrington, but not today. I'm still too embarrassed about what happened. It was dreadful, her seeing my willie sticking up out of my trunks. The best thing for me is to unpack all my hobby materials and start working on them again. I must also get my gang started, once and for all. Once I get busy I won't have time to think about girls any more. Especially Andy's mother.

After school I went home and found a note from Dad saying he'd gone into Dublin on business. I made myself bacon sandwiches and thought about getting the gang started. There are four of us now. That's enough to make an official gang. There's me, and Christie Doyle, and Andy Barrington, and Sean Malone. It's not enough to challenge the Dump Gang but at least it's a start.

The first thing is to invent an initiation ceremony. I don't want fellows to think they can just walk into the gang. There will have to be gang rules, and a list of the things each of us is good at, for when special tasks crop up. Another thing will be a gang diary. We'll need to plan things, and make dates for battles, and for going into Dublin to museums and the pictures. There'll be a section for making notes about girls we see at school or at the pictures.

The diary will have a list of the reasons why people were allowed into the gang, and what their good and bad points are. This will be useful in case we get fed up with them and can't remember. My reason for being in the gang is that I'm big and strong and know a lot of things the others don't. I have an intelligent father, which is useful, and I've read millions of books. Also, it was my idea to have a gang in the first place, so obviously I have to be in it even if I was no good at anything.

Malone is in the gang because he's tall and strong and clever in an uneducated sort of way. He's good at seeing the snags in things. That could save us a lot of trouble. He's good at mechanical things but not electrical stuff. I'm the one for that. Malone doesn't like girls, which means he won't be sloping off with them when we've got important things to do.

Christie is in the gang because he has to be. He was the first person I met in Kilmara and he got me started, in a way. He knows everything that's going on, through listening to his dad and the other policemen. He can be useful as a scout and a messenger to other gangs. Nobody dares to touch him on account of his dad being the Sergeant. Another good thing is his sisters, although I'm not that bothered about them any more. Not since I've met Stella and Andy's mother. Christie's only interest in girls is seeing up their skirts. The rest of the time he's too busy thinking about money.

Andy is in the gang because he's got a beautiful mother. I mustn't think about her at the moment. Andy is useful because he seems to be a daredevil with no fear of anything. When I explained this to Malone he said it's because Andy's like me; too confident and too headstrong. I think Malone was just being sarcastic.

It was Andy who told me Stella sunbathes in her garden with hardly any clothes on. His dad has made a little hole through the bricks in his garden wall, specially for taking a look at Stella. It doesn't always work out; it depends on where she's lying in the garden. His dad says she's a grown-up girl, with a proper figure, and well worth looking at. Andy says his mother just laughs about it. She doesn't seem to mind. His dad is quite interested in women, and has lots of girlfriends. It's because he's a pilot, which women think is a heroic thing to be. They're always trying to get friendly with him.

That's what Andy says, anyway. I can't see why Mr Barrington would be interested in other women when he's got such a beautiful lady as Suzanne. It's a lovely name, Suzanne. I like saying it. I'm going to draw it in big letters on a piece of white cardboard and put it under my pillow.

Christie came in, whistling and looking pleased with himself. 'So!' he said. 'You're not interested in girls, eh?' I asked him what he was on about. 'Your secret pash is a secret no longer!'

'What secret pash!?'

'You and Andy's mother. It's all round the village; the two of you, larking round in her garden with hardly a stitch on.' I flew into a temper and grabbed Christie by the neck. He was terrified. 'It wasn't me who spread the story; it was Sculley!'

'How on earth could Sculley have seen us?'

Christie told me Sculley's grannies live in the last house on the terrace. Sculley was round there having tea on Tuesday. He saw me from the upstairs window. I was really annoyed when I heard this. I'll have to see Sculley tomorrow and tell him to be more careful about shooting his mouth off. Christie asked me if the story was true.

'No! It's rubbish. I was spying on Stella, and she caught me. I only ran into Andy's garden to escape.' I showed him the scratches to prove it. Christie said they could easily be love-scratches. He says his brother often gets them on his face from mots he's been shagging. They scratch and bite when the jake goes in. They can't help it. The thrill of it gets them all excited. I told him he should take less notice of his brother. If Stella is anything to go by, the mots probably scratch him because they're trying to get rid of him.

Christie said it was just as well that I don't fancy Andy's mother. 'She has a terrible name in the village. So has Andy's dad. When he comes home from flying around the world they have loads of friends to stay with them, and big parties with all sorts of dirty goings-on.'

I asked him how he knows this. He says when they have these parties, they get two women from the village in to do the cooking, and the cleaning up afterwards. The cook and the cleaner are always round drinking tea in the barracks, and telling scandalous stories about the things that go on. 'Dirty games and nakedness and people running around in the garden after each other and being sick all over the place.'

I think Christie just made this up to put me off Andy's mother. When I said I didn't believe any of it, he said she was the worst. 'Her favourite trick is getting up on the table and doing a strip-tease to music from the record-player.' I told him to shut up, but he was too carried away to take any notice.

'When she gets down to her knickers, she takes them off and throws them at the men. Whoever catches them, she goes into the bedroom with him. Do you want to know what happens then?'

'No! I bloody-well don't!'

There was no stopping Christie. 'She lets him stick his jake into her! Yee-ha, and a good giddy-up!'

I think this is the most disgusting bit of lying I've ever heard. Nobody's mother would ever dream of doing such a thing, especially one who looks like a golden-haired virgin from the *Book of Martyrs*. I've borrowed it from the shelves at the back of the chapel, even though you're not supposed to take books away. It has a picture of a particular saint who's the very image of Mrs Barrington. I'm keeping it under my pillow, to remind me of her.

I had a serious chat with Sculley today. He said he couldn't help seeing me with Andy's mother. He's always so bored at his grannies' that he goes to the top of the house and spends the time looking out into people's gardens.

He says he's particularly interested in the garden next to Andy's. The girl who lives there is often out in the garden with hardly any clothes on. I said I know her well, and that she's got a fearful temper. I showed him the scratches I got for trying to look at her.

I told him if he says any more about me and Andy's mother, I'll tell Stella about him. He says he's not bothered; she's often seen him staring at her and she seems to enjoy it. He always knows when she's seen him. She stretches her legs out and lets the straps of her swimsuit come off her shoulders. Sculley is as big a liar as Christie.

I told him I'll beat him up if I hear any more about me in Andy's garden, and any more lies about Stella. He said if I don't believe him I can come round to his grannies' sometime and have a look for myself. I said I'd have to be pretty desperate to bother but he says I might enjoy going round there. Both his grannies are mad. Their house is full of junk, and they have a pet baboon. I don't believe that either.

I've asked him to get me some information about initiation ceremonies. He's an unofficial member of Jeremy Lynch's Dump gang, which everyone says has the worst ceremony of all. It's so bad it's the one secret they're not allowed to tell anyone.

Sculley says the penalty for revealing it is to be thrown into the cesspit at the back of the deserted farmhouse out along the Gavinstown Road. That's not the end of it. Ever afterwards, the fellow's beaten up any time the Dump gang see him around the village. His life becomes a complete misery. He either has to stay in all the time, or only go out when he's with a crowd of other fellows. Sculley is a devious little creep. He says there's going to be a Dump gang initiation tomorrow, after school, in the big boat-shed at the dump.

I asked him why he was risking his life by telling me this. He said he knows I won't tell on him, and it's up to me what use I make of the information. If it was him, he'd keep well away. The penalty for spying on the initiation is the same as for giving it away.

He said the best way to find out what goes on would be to go to the shed early and climb up into the rafters where the planks used to be stored.

The subject of initiations is very important. There has to be one, otherwise there's nothing special about joining a gang. Anyone can just come along and be in it for a day or two and then go off to some other gang. Another thing is that the ceremony has to be tough enough to discourage weeds and creepy little cry-babies who'd be no use in the gang anyway.

In the *Wide World* magazines I've found loads of articles about tribal customs in Africa. The boys in the tribe have to go through initiation ceremonies to be men.

Some of the things they get up to are really frightening and horrible. They have all their front teeth pulled out, or their cheeks and noses cut and bones put through the holes, or they have to walk on red-hot ashes, or climb a tree and take the honey out of a bees' nest without crying at the hundreds of stings they get.

One of the worst initiations is for Zulu boys. They go out on their own with only a loin-cloth and a short spear, nothing else at all. They can't come back until they've managed to kill a lion, all by themselves. They have to skin it and bring the hide back to prove that they've done it. Malone says this would be a good one for us, only instead of lions we could use girls. Each of us would have to go out with a bit of rope and catch a girl and tie her up. Instead of skinning her, we'd rip her knickers off and bring them back to gang headquarters to hang up as a trophy. I can see the point of this but I'm not sure if it's fair to girls.

Malone says they'd love it; they're all same where flashing their fannies is concerned. He says we'd have to think up a different ceremony for Christie. He'd just steal a pair of knickers from one of his sisters, and pretend he'd got them off a captured girl.

I'm still not satisfied about the idea. I think we should be doing something braver than tying up girls and stealing their knickers. Anyway, it's probably a mortal sin, although Malone says there's nothing in the catechism about it.

At school, I was so busy thinking, I hardly took any notice of Welch. He took plenty of notice of me, but he didn't try any more tricks.

I decided to mitch off at lunchtime, and spy on the initiation. My big worry was whether I'd get caught by Lynch and his gang. I knew I had to risk it, even though I was scared. Once I think of something, I have to do it. Otherwise I know I'm a coward and disgust myself.

The morning went very slowly. Sculley made it worse. He kept making out to be pally with me, and winking at me, as if the two of us were up to something. I'm certain Lynch must have noticed. He's a shrewd little devil.

At lunchtime I sneaked out of the playground and went home

by the bottom road. I had a shrivelled apple and a cup of Bovril, then went out to the stable to get my bike. The minute I saw it I knew it was ruined. The shiny bits have gone rusty and the wheels look like a junk yard bike. The spokes are covered in bits of dried seaweed and the back light is missing. I never noticed that on Tuesday. When I tried to move it, the wheels screeched and the pedals went round with the back wheel. The freewheel must be jammed. I'll have to get Malone to take it to bits and get the sand out. I should have remembered to wash the salt off before it ruined everything.

I had to walk to the boat-yard instead of cycling, so I set off early. I was nervous walking down the lane, in case Stella or Andy's mother came out of their gardens. I was about to rush past their gates when I remembered what Mrs Barrington said to me about Stella. Before I could stop it, the idea came into my head of going in and apologising to her. Then of course I had to do it.

I ran back up to the stable and had a look from the loft. Unfortunately for me, Stella was in her garden. She was lying on her tummy on the grass, with a towel under her, reading a book and eating an apple. She had on a black swimsuit. It matched her hair. The horrible little dog was chasing round after flies and wasps.

I knocked on the gate, but it was loose and only rattled. She didn't take any notice. I suppose she's used to the wind banging it about. I tried the latch but it wouldn't open. I had another go at knocking. Just as I was about to go, she came and opened the gate.

'Good God!' She stared at me in amazement. 'You've got a nerve!' She drew back her hand, intending to give me a wallop. I stepped away and told her I'd only come round to say I was sorry for annoying her.

'Oh, really?' she said, with a sarcastic smile. 'Are you sure you're not up to your antics again?'

'What do you mean, antics?'

'In your case, it means being a peeping Tom.'

I told her she must be confusing me with someone else. 'My name is Michael.'

'A peeping Michael, then.'

I told her I had no intention of peeping at her. I only wanted to apologise.

'And what were you doing the other day, only peeping?'

She seemed determined to keep on about this, so I admitted about Tuesday. I said I'd never do it again.

'And I know why! You've found someone else to spy on.' I went red at that remark.

'I saw you! Staring at Mrs Barrington in her skimpy swimsuit!'

'She didn't mind. In fact she put it on specially to please me.'

'Dear me! You *were* honoured!'

I couldn't think of anything to say. The little dog came to the gate and started yapping. Stella gave it a hard kick in the side, and told it to go away. It ran off, howling. I was surprised how vicious she was, then I remembered the way she'd hit and scratched me.

'What did you say to Mrs Barrington, then?'

I said I was just chatting to her, about loads of things. Stella interrupted to say she was talking about the swimsuit. 'Did you just ask her, point-blank, to go and put it on?'

I couldn't remember the exact details, so I said yes. Stella was astonished. 'It's a wonder she didn't slap your face!'

I said I couldn't see why. I'd explained to her that I liked looking at her in her swimsuit, and she seemed to think it was quite complimentary. Stella looked at me strangely. 'This thing about swimsuits; is that why you were spying on me?'

'Yes, but I won't be spying on you any more.'

'Oh? And why not?'

'I've told you. I don't want to annoy you.'

'You haven't gone off me, then,' she said, a bit sarcastically.

'No; not at all.'

She looked as if she was going to laugh but she stopped herself. 'So you'd still like to look at me?'

'Well, yes . . .'

'In a swimsuit?'

'Especially in a swimsuit.'

'And why is that; as if I didn't know . . .' She gave me another strange look. 'I don't know whether you're a dirty-minded brat, or just too innocent for your own good.'

She bent her head and stared at her toes, wriggling them as if she was thinking about something complicated. I took the chance to look at her legs, which are long and thin, and her tummy, which is flat. Mrs Barrington's is nicer; it's round and curvy. I wondered if pressing against Stella would give me the same feeling in my willie.

Stella looked up with a queer smile. She said there was no one in the house but herself. I didn't know what to say about this. She stared at me, her eyes cold but with a sort of shiny, excited look. 'Don't you see what I'm getting at?'

I asked her if she meant she was scared, being on her own. She rolled her eyes up and said 'Oh God!' in an irritable voice, then changed back to smiling. Her eyes still had the cold, shiny look. 'Come in, and I'll explain it in words of one syllable.'

She stepped back into the garden. I hurried past her, wary that she might be going to hit me again. She smelt of sun-tan oil and perfume. It wasn't a warm smell like Mrs Barrington; more the sort of smell that you get in ice-cream parlours in the summer. She told me to follow her, and walked off. We went through the garden, down the steps to the basement, and stopped outside the back door. It was interesting watching the muscles moving in her legs. They go right up into her bottom and make it sway from side to side as she walks.

She looked up to make sure no one was leaning out of a window watching us. She put her feet apart and her hands on her waist, as if she was going to do exercises. 'Well, there you are. Have a good look.'

She tossed her hair back and took a deep breath that made her chest stick out. She turned sideways for a moment, then right round so she was facing away from me.

'Well?' she said, over her shoulder. 'Haven't you anything to say?'

I thought she was reminding me to be polite. 'Thank you very much. It's very kind of you to let me look at you.'

She turned round and stared at me, and shook her head. 'You're hopeless. "Thanks" is the last thing I wanted to hear!'

She opened the back door and stood just inside. 'Watch this . . .' She turned her back on me again, and bent forward until she was almost doubled up. I could see her face staring at me upside down from between her legs, and her hair curled on the floor like a black fur-skin. Her swimsuit tightened up and sank into the crack of her bottom. She looked as if she'd got hardly anything on. Still bent over, she stretched one of her legs up behind her until it nearly touched her back. I thought she'd tip over, but she didn't.

I felt like clapping. It was as good as the acrobat girls you see in a circus, or in magazine photos of ballet dancers. I said I was very impressed. She straightened up and said that wasn't the point. 'Did you not feel anything?'

I said no. She got ratty and said it didn't say much for her sex appeal.

'What am I supposed to feel?'

'It's a bit pointless if I have to tell you!' She said she'd give me one last chance. She moved further back in the doorway until she was in the half-dark of the room, turned her back on me, slipped the top of her swimsuit down, and turned to face me. I just had time to see her bare chest. Then she covered herself up again and came back out into the open.

I started to get a feeling at last, a sort of mysterious excitement. I began to think how nice it would be to stroke the smooth white skin on the inside of her legs. My willie began to get warm. Stella folded her arms across her chest and stared at me.

I wished she'd bend over again and let me press myself against her bottom. I could see an outline of the slit between her legs; her swimsuit was still pulled tight against her. There was a little damp patch where it cut into her. Bending over must have made her want to wee. It sometimes happens to me when I'm doing something really energetic.

I was surprised to see tiny black curly hairs sticking out of the legs of her swimsuit. I was going to ask her about this, then I realised she must have got them from playing with the dog.

Stella started breathing in quick little gasps. She looked flushed and shivery at the same time. 'No one, absolutely no one, has ever seen my top half bare.' I told her it had been very interesting.

'Interesting!' She said I should be grovelling on my knees by now, mad with desire and begging for her favours. I said I hadn't a clue what 'desire' was about.

'Desire, you stupid boy, is the name for the love-feelings that men get for women.'

'And what about "begging for your favours"? What does that mean?'

'It means wanting to make love to me.'

I told her about Christie's brother having desperate urges to slip his jake into girls. 'Is that what desire and making love is about?'

She shut her eyes and shook her head slowly. 'I must be

dreaming all this!' She said she couldn't believe she was really having this conversation, or that she'd just displayed herself so shamelessly to an ignorant great lump she didn't even know. I said I was very grateful to her, my name was Michael Kelly from the basement of Number Ten, and that I definitely had felt a bit of desire. She asked me to describe it. I told her it was a feeling of dizzy warmth and wanting to stroke her legs and rub my tummy against her bottom.

'Do you know something? I'd normally scratch a fellow's eyes out, for such a filthy remark.' In my case, I was so innocent she couldn't take offence. Anyway, she was flattered that she'd managed to stir my erotic urges. 'That's another name for desire, in case you're wondering.'

I didn't say anything about being already stirred by Mrs Barrington, in case it annoyed her, or the fact that I'm not the first person to see her bare. She might go and scratch Christie's eyes out.

'Would you like to see more of me?'

I said yes, thinking she was going to do the ballet position again. Instead, she went back inside the basement and disappeared. I stood hanging about for a minute, thinking she was coming back. She called to me to come in. 'It's quite safe. The whole of the basement is mine.'

She took me through to the front room, the one that looks up into the terrace. It was nice, full of books and paintings and with proper wallpaper instead of whitewash. I wanted to ask her about various things but she got impatient. 'We're not here for a chat! I've got more important things on my mind.' She said she wanted to see how much desire she could rouse in me. It would be very interesting to her. 'If you take off your clothes, I'll take off my swimsuit.'

'What!? Completely off?'

'Yes. I'll let you see me naked.' Saying this got her very excited; she started to breathe very quickly and dance about from foot to foot. I asked her if she'd let me feel her legs. She answered me in a curious whispery voice. 'Yes, yes . . . anything you like . . . But you'll have to be quick; my father will be home soon.' I was mad keen to see her naked. I took my jumper off.

'No, not in here; go into the bathroom.' She said it would be safer. We could lock the door in case anyone came in and caught us. She pushed me into the scullery, where the door opens into the front basement. It wasn't like our scullery, which is a cold damp place with an old stone sink and slug marks all over the walls. Hers has been made into a lovely little bathroom with a toilet and shower and wooden planks screwed to the walls, like the inside of a yacht.

She shut the door after me and called to me to get my clothes off as quickly as possible. I called back, 'What about you?' She said she'd undress in the bedroom and come in as soon as I'd got my clothes off; she felt shy about stripping in front of me. When she said the word 'stripping' I got the hot and cold shivers straight away. I was wild with excitement at the thought of seeing her with no clothes on, and stroking her legs, and maybe rubbing myself against her bare bottom. I took my clothes off as quick as I could, and called out that I was ready. Stella came to the door leading in from the bedroom, and opened it an inch. She said she was too embarrassed to walk into the room, naked, with me already in there.

Would I go out into the basement, and give her a moment to herself in the bathroom, just to get used to the situation? I wasn't very keen on this. 'Supposing someone sees me?'

'It's only for a second. You can hide under the stairs until I'm ready.' I told her I didn't fancy it. It was too risky.

'If you don't, I won't come in!' She said her swimsuit was off. 'I'm ready and waiting. It's up to you now.'

By this time I was desperate to see her. My willie was huge and in agony for a rub against her. I wasn't in the least frightened about it, now that I knew it was all to do with desire. I put my trousers back on so I wouldn't get cold, and shouted to Stella that I was going out.

She said I was to go right under the stairs, so I couldn't peek at her through the keyhole. After a few seconds, she opened the door a tiny bit and said I was cheating. 'Where are your trousers?'

She said she wasn't prepared to let me in until I took them off. I crept to the door, hoping no one would see me, and whispered that I'd take them off the minute she let me in. She said no, this wasn't fair; she'd be naked but I'd still have something on. 'I'll be dreadfully embarrassed.'

I crept up the basement stairs for a quick look round the terrace. There was no one about, so I rushed down and pulled my trousers off. I had to undo every single button on my fly, because my willie was bulging and sticking out so much.

I tapped on the door. Stella put her hand out and took the trousers, then shut the door again. She told me to wait under the stairs again, just for a minute. 'You're in for a big surprise!'

I was delighted, thinking she was going to let me rub myself against her bottom, or even put my jake inside her. I crouched under the stairs, amazed at the size of it, and wondering if it was just a story Malone and Christie made up. Judging by what I'd seen of Stella's crack, I didn't see how I'd manage to fit it into her.

Suddenly I heard a fit of giggling. I thought, 'Oh my God, it's someone up in the terrace!' The giggling turned into loud laughter. I realised it was coming from the basement. I looked across at the window of the front room, and got a terrible shock.

Stella was standing inside, staring at me and having hysterics. What's more, she hadn't taken her swimsuit off at all; she'd got dressed instead. The shock of seeing her made my willie go small straight away. Stella waved to me to come over to the window, but I shook my head and made a desperate sign to her to let me in. She laughed even harder, tears streaming down her face, and yelled at me to go away. 'You're a filthy disgusting lout! Get out of my basement this very second!'

I was nearly in tears myself; tears of shame at being so badly tricked, and having to put up with her laughing at me for having no clothes on. It was horrible to realise she'd only been pretending to be friendly, and that all the business of getting me desperate with desire was just so she could make a fool of me.

Stella went away from the window, and opened the scullery door a tiny bit. I rushed over and tried to push in, but she had a little chain that stopped it opening more than a couple of inches. I pleaded with her to let me in. 'Please, Stella! I've had enough of this joke!'

'I've got bad news for you. The joke is only starting.'

She said I could either go home as I was, or pay a forfeit and have my clothes back. I said I couldn't possibly go home without any clothes on.

'In that case, it'll have to be the forfeit!'

I said I'd do anything, anything at all, but for God's sake to hurry up before someone saw me. The forfeit, she said, was to take my hands away from my front and let her have a look at whatever I was so anxious to hide. I told her I didn't want to do this. 'Why not? You were keen enough to show it off five minutes ago!'

'Yes! It would have been fair if we both had no clothes on. This is different!'

'Yes,' she said, 'very different; you're at my mercy now.' This made me so mad with anger I told her to go and shoot herself. I was sorry the minute I said this. Her eyes screwed up into cruel slits and her voice sounded like a cat spitting at a dog. She said I was going to pay dearly for the privilege I'd had earlier on, the privilege of looking at her body. If I didn't do exactly what she wanted, she'd go straight to the barracks.

'I'll say you broke into my house, took your clothes off, and exposed yourself to me!'

I was amazed. I couldn't believe how rotten she'd turned out to be. She said I might think twice before molesting her again, especially if the police gave me a good walloping. I said they'd never believe her. She just laughed; how was I going to explain what my clothes were doing in her bathroom?

At that minute a car drove into the terrace. I knew it must be her father, because Christie said he was the only person with a car. I got absolutely desperate, and begged her with tears streaming down my face to let me have my clothes back so I could go.

I swore I'd never ever bother her again, and that I'd do anything she said if she'd only let me go. The car got nearer and nearer, and stopped right above the basement. I never felt so awful with shame and embarrassment in my whole life. Stella whispered to me that I was to turn around, bend right over, and put my head between my knees. I said, 'No, no, please, Stella. Anything but that.'

The car door opened. I could hear the springs squeaking as Mr Rothwell got out of it.

'You've got about ten seconds,' Stella said, 'before Daddy gets his case out of the boot and goes to our front door; he'll look straight down and see you.'

I gave in immediately. I had no choice. I turned round, bent over, and put my head between my legs. I could see Stella's face, upside down, looking straight at my bum and my willie. I nearly choked with the tears running back up my face from my chin and into my nostrils.

Stella opened the door and threw my clothes straight at my backside in a soaking wet bundle. I nearly screamed with the shock of the cold water hitting me. I just had time to straighten up, grab the clothes, and dash under the stairs, before Mr Rothwell finished at the car and went up his front steps. As soon as he was inside, I tried to put my clothes on but it took me ages because they were sopping wet. I was scared stiff that Stella would take it into her mind to tell her father I was under the stairs, so I only put my trousers and shirt on.

I crept up the basement stairs hoping no one would look out the window above. Just as I got to the top, Stella opened the basement door. She shouted, 'Goodbye, little boy. Do come and play again!'

I was too sickened by misery to say a word, and ran off up the terrace as quick as I could. I'll never forget the shame of having to bend over and show everything to that vicious mocking girl, and the helpless feeling of being completely at her mercy.

I cried myself to sleep, but not before I swore a mighty oath to get my revenge on Stella. I'm going to see Christie first thing in the morning about spying on her. The sooner I get to see her without any clothes on, and the sooner she knows I've seen her, the better. I won't rest now until I have the pleasure of paying her back exactly, tit for tat.

Last night I dreamt I was crawling round the village on my hands and knees. Stella was behind me, slashing me along with a thin vicious whip. She had a leather collar round my neck and a chain to choke me if I tried to escape. I was naked, and people lined the streets, sniggering, throwing buckets of water over me.

Stella had no clothes on either, but no one dared laugh at her. She looked too proud and haughty. Her bare body glistened with perfumed oil, and her eyes flashed like glass caught by the sun. She wore a beautiful feathered head-dress, and gold chains round her neck and waist and ankles. Her face was painted like an Egyptian queen.

Fellows we passed threw themselves onto the dusty road, in a frenzy of desire and sexual urges. They tore their clothes off and crawled along behind her, howling and slobbering, and begging her to let them touch her. She took no notice of them.

As soon as I woke up I went to Christie's house. His sisters said

174

he wouldn't be up for ages. He went to bed paralytic, through drinking Ellen's bottle of cooking sherry. She uses it for making trifles. They seemed to think it was very funny.

I went home and put a kettle of water on the paraffin stove to make tea for Dad. Major Longshott came down to ask what had happened about his jugs of well-water. He said he's been expecting me every morning but so far he's had no luck. I said I'd get a jugful that very minute, and bring it up to him. He said, 'Right-oh,' then winked at me. 'I trust you're none the worse for your little spot of bother yesterday?' He said it was his habit to take afternoon tea in the front window of his flat, on account of the pleasant view overlooking the estuary. And, of course, the terrace.

As soon as I realised what he was getting at, I made up a story about Stella taking pity on me not having a mother. She offered to wash my clothes for me, but was too shy to have me in the house with nothing on. 'That's why I was waiting out in the basement.'

Major Longshott said ah, yes; he could see the logic of that. 'No young gel would want to compromise herself, especially if there were a possibility of her kindness being misconstrued.'

He winked at me again and went off, pushing himself up the stairs with his stick. I was left worrying about how many other people might have seen me yesterday. At least I've thought up a good excuse for what happened. If Stella does go to the police, I'll tell them what I told the Major.

I went out to get the jug of water. I was about to start pumping when the back door to the upstairs flats opened. I stayed quiet under the stairs, thinking it might be the Sullivan girls, and I could jump out and frighten them.

I heard a match being struck, and someone making the sighing noise that smokers do when they let go of the first puff after they've lit up. I caught sight of a reflection in the window of the basement. It was Mrs Sullivan in a long dressing gown. I could only see her back view in the window. She was standing very still, smoking and looking down the garden towards the stable.

Mrs Sullivan looks like Stella, only older and sort of weary. She's tall and thin, with the same kind of straight black hair but not so long. Her face is like Stella, too, except that Stella has a cold, hard face and Mrs Sullivan's is cold but sad, as if she has a lot of worries. She's not bad-looking when she smiles, but that's not very often.

I remembered the Sullivan girls looking up the legs of my trousers and jeering me. I thought I'd get my own back by staring up their mother's dressing gown. I had a careful look at her reflection in the window, to see if it was safe to poke my head out. She was leaning against the railings at the top of the stairs, still with her back to the window. I came out a bit and had a look.

The railing held the dressing gown against the back of her legs and I could only see her ankles. I waited to see if she'd move, but she didn't. I crept back into the house and waited for her to finish her cigarette. I'm going to try it again sometime. She might come out with only a skirt or a nightie on.

I filled the Major's jug with well-water and took it up to him. He was waiting for me on his front steps. He asked me to stay and have a chat with him. Stella came cycling round the top of the terrace, coming back from her morning swim. I ran down into the basement immediately, but not before she'd seen me.

She rode up on the pavement and stopped with her foot on the railings to balance herself. She stared down at me with a terrible mocking smile, not saying a word. I told her to go away and leave me alone. I said I could see right up her skirt, even though I couldn't. She said that didn't bother her in the least. 'It's nothing compared to what I've seen of you!'

I went in and shut the door. I heard her laughing as she rode off. Dad was awake and furious with me. I'd forgotten about the kettle and it had boiled over and put the cooker out. Everything was soaked. Dad says he's going to have to dismantle the whole thing to dry it out. Stella is nothing but trouble for me. To think that I used to love her!

I spent the rest of the morning lying on my bed, reading the encyclopaedias and looking for information about tortures. I want to write a story with Stella in it, as a girl who gets captured by savages and tortured to death. I couldn't find anything useful. I asked Dad if he knew anything about torture. He said it wasn't a fit subject for a boy of my age.

Christie came round after lunch. He looked terrible. His plonker is bleeding through pulling it so much in the night. He's dead scared to go to confession. The last time he went, the priest made him swear not to do it again, and gave him a whole rosary for a penance.

He says he couldn't help doing it again. He got accidentally drunk last night, and couldn't resist temptation. The sexual urges get really fierce when you're drunk, and you can't leave yourself alone. His brother says it's even worse for girls, when they get drunk. They haven't got anything to fiddle with, so they can't relieve themselves the way fellows do. They get desperate for the feel of a jake inside them, and grab hold of the nearest fellow and rip his trousers off. No wonder the priests are so dead against drink.

Christie's in a bad position. He's committed another mortal sin and he's broken his promise to the priest, which is even worse. The trouble is, I'll have to risk God striking us both dead, otherwise I can't go down the beach with him.

I told him I've changed my mind about spying on Stella; I want to do it tomorrow morning without fail. Christie hummed and hawed and said he wasn't sure he could make it. Getting up early on Sundays doesn't suit him. It leaves him very tired for school on Mondays. It turned out he was only trying to get more money out of me. I've agreed to give him five shillings for his trouble.

I asked him if he knew anything about tortures. He said no, but his brother might. He reads American detective magazines which are true stories about murders and rapes. I don't know what rapes are, and neither does Christie. He thinks it might be something to do with attacking women.

The covers of these magazines have photos of girls with their clothes ripped and headlines saying 'Twelve-Hour Sex Ordeal Of The Carnival Beauty Queen' and 'High-School Cheerleader's Horror Weekend'.

I asked him if he could get me a loan of some of these magazines. He said it would be difficult. His brother keeps them locked in a metal army ammunition box with a padlock. It's got other things in it as well, including letters from girls and knickers with blood on them. Christie's brother says they belonged to virgins he's shagged. It sounds as if it hurts them. I ought to find out what shagging really is and do it to Stella.

Christie wanted me to go to the cinema in Dublin with him, to see *Creature from the Black Lagoon* at the Carlton. I said I couldn't. There was something else I wanted to do. As soon as he went I got a pile of the women's magazines from the loft in the stable, and some tracing paper from Dad's private tea-chest where he keeps all his writing things. He keeps saying he's going to make a desk and write humorous stories about motor-cycling and sell them to the papers like Jembo's Uncle Dermot. I don't think he ever will. He can't sit still long enough to do anything like that.

I went back out to the stable and spent the evening drawing pictures of naked women. I did this by looking for photos of women posing in swimsuits and advertisements for corsets. Then I traced the outlines of their bodies, but not the clothes. When I had six good tracings I drew in dots to stand for the pink tips on their breasts and small circles for their belly-buttons.

I finished them off by drawing a slit for their fannies. I wasn't sure how long or wide it should be, so I drew it starting just below their tummies and reaching to the tops of their legs. When I had all the tracings done I finished them off with coloured pencils. I gave them all black hair to look like Stella, and drew chains and ropes round their wrists and ankles, and drew backgrounds of castle dungeons.

I tried to draw knickers on some of them, pulled down to their knees to show off their bums and fannies, but I'm a rotten freehand drawer. I had to rub them out and retrace the legs. I had a great time pretending it was Stella, chained in a dungeon with red whipmarks all over her and cuts pouring streams of scarlet blood. I also drew words coming out of her mouth: screams and cries and sobbing pleas for mercy. It gave me a terrible frightening sense of satisfaction and a huge bulging willie. This kept me awake for ages. I couldn't lie on my tummy and get comfortable, which is the way I normally fall asleep.

I was so excited about spying on Stella I hardly slept a wink. I was up and dressed by six o'clock. Then the whole thing turned into a washout. Christie didn't turn up until well after seven. He'd been kept awake by his brother. He came home rampant, at two o'clock in the morning, and spent hours moaning about a mot he'd met at the pictures. She turned out to be a prick-teaser. He got as far as kissing her and putting his hand up her skirt and feeling her bum. When he slipped his hand inside her knickers, she sank her teeth into the end of his nose. Christie's brother had to leave the cinema with a nosebleed. He missed the end of the big picture.

I was so fed up with Christie for being late, I didn't bother to ask him what a prick-teaser was. I asked him how long it would take to get to Stella's secret place. 'About half an hour,' he said, 'but don't be too disappointed if we miss her; we can always try again.' Then he had the cheek to ask me for the money in advance!

I said I'd give him half, and the rest if we saw her. He said no; even if we didn't see her, I'd know where to go in future, and I'd probably welsh out of paying him the rest of the money. I was furious but he wouldn't budge. I had to give it to him in the end.

Christie wouldn't walk along the road or the beach, for fear of being seen. We had to make our way through the dunes. I thought I was going to die with the breathless strain of trudging along in the sand. When we got close to where Stella was supposed to be, Christie made me stop for five minutes to get my breath back. He said she'd hear me puffing and gasping, otherwise, and be dressed and on her bike before we got anywhere near her.

The place where Stella swims is right at the end of the dunes, where the beach curves inland and turns into a big circular bay, with the coast road running round the edge of it. At the far side of the bay the beach stops being sandy and the rocks begin, low and scattered at first, and then turning into massive slabs and cliffs as you get near to the golf course at Rathluan.

I can see why Stella is so fond of the place. The line of the dunes runs east to west. The seaward hollow in the flank of the last dune faces directly into the warmth of the morning sun. The beach narrows into a bank of sand, continuing out across the mouth of the bay for about quarter of a mile. It's like a sand-bridge that someone started to build across the bay, and never got round to finishing. On the seaward side of the bank there are waves and blue sea stretching to the horizon. The inside of the bay is sheltered by the sandbank; the water is warmer and smooth as a mirror.

Christie warned me about this; he said the minute I poked my head over the edge of the dune I'd be blinded. I wouldn't be able to see where Stella was at first. She might see us before we saw her, so we had to squint our eyes against the glare. He also said there was only room for one person's head at a time; the place we had to spy through is a neat hole in the grass round the edge of the dune. Christie said it was probably made by rabbits going up and down to the beach for a swim. I'll have to look this up; I've never heard of rabbits swimming.

Christie crawled up a sandy channel to have the first look, and to make sure Stella was there. He was gone for ages. I climbed up and pulled on his feet to make him come down. He shook his head and said it was a pity; Stella was just getting dressed and ready to cycle home. If we hadn't stopped so often to listen to me complaining, we'd have caught her just in time.

I said it was his fault for being late in the first place, and told him I wanted to see for myself. I was suspicious he might be lying, to keep the view of Stella to himself. I crawled up and had a peep. I squinted my eyes half-closed against the sun, and there she was, right below me in a smooth hollow of white sand facing out across the bay.

She was packing her things into the basket of her bicycle and whistling cheerfully to herself. I never knew big girls could whistle, and it surprised me. Mam says the Virgin Mary cries if she hears girls whistling. Stella is a Protestant, so perhaps the Virgin Mary isn't bothered about what she does.

Stella finished packing and hung her sandals on the handlebars of her bike and pushed it out of the hollow and onto the beach. She wheeled it across the soft dry sand until she reached the hard, wet sand at the edge of the sea, then sat herself on the saddle and cycled out of view. I felt a hand pulling my foot so I kicked backwards and said 'Piss off!' I was still bitter with Christie and fed up with being cheated out of a view of Stella. Next thing I knew there were hands on both my ankles and I came shooting down the channel in a rush, with sand spraying everywhere and getting all over me.

I shut my eyes to keep the sand out. I got a shock when I opened them. John-Joe Maguire was staring at me with a ferocious expression. There was no sign of Christie whatever. John-Joe said he strongly objected to being kicked on the jaw and told to piss off. I said I was sorry; I thought he was someone else, someone who deserved it.

He said he had a suspicion I deserved it myself, and would I kindly explain what I was up to. I kept my mouth shut. He said he knew damn well what was going on, and if he caught me ruining that girl's privacy again he'd give me a belting. He's smaller than me, so this didn't worry me too much, but I was afraid he'd tell Dad. I decided to be polite, and asked him how he knew I was there. He said the beach provides his liveli-hood; he knows every square inch of it and keeps an eye on it, morning, noon and night, even when he's busy with other matters.

I told him I was on my way down to the golf course in Rathluan for a day's caddying, and I'd heard someone whistling. I'd been practising my Indian scouting tricks by sneaking up on them as if they were an enemy tribe. He said he'd believe me, this time, but if he caught me at it again it would be a different matter, particularly as that little bugger Doyle had a hand in the affair; he'd seen him scuttling off at high speed the minute he heard the pony give a snort. When he mentioned the pony I pretended to be interested, and asked him if I could have a look at his horse and cart.

The dunes aren't very wide, and it only took us a few seconds to get onto the road where he'd parked the cart. John-Joe was going back into the village, so I asked for a lift. He got suspicious and said it was the wrong direction for the golf course. I told him I couldn't go now, not without Christie, because it was my first visit and I didn't know anyone there.

On the way home he mentioned that he keeps a particular eye on Stella. I'm not the only person who's copped on to her early morning activities, and he'd hate to see her come to any harm. There were older, less innocent eyes than mine to be found on the beach in the mornings.

I asked him who this person is. He said, 'It's persons, plural.'

'But surely,' I said, 'Stella is stupid to go there anyway; people are bound to try to spy on her.'

John-Joe got angry, and said the girl had a perfect right to enjoy God's gifts of sunlight and sweet morning air. He dropped me off at the top of the terrace. Christie was sitting on his front steps watching his sisters playing hopscotch on the pavement. The moment he saw me he disappeared into the house.

I went to Mass and then home and had a corned beef sandwich. It took me ages to make; the key on the tin broke and I had to saw it open with Dad's hacksaw. Then the bread was mouldy. By the time I sliced the green bits off, there was barely enough for two slices. Finally, there was no butter, and I had to make do with dripping scraped from the pan. Dad and I have been using the same fat for ages, so it was full of little black bits and crinkly pieces of fried egg and burnt tomato pips. I'm fed up living without a mother to look after me.

I'm not going to let John-Joe scare me off from spying on Stella because I've had a brilliant idea. If I borrow Mr Barrington's camera I can take photographs of her sunbathing, then I'll be able to look at her whenever I like. Also, I'll be able to show them to other fellows, and make a disgrace of her all round the village, the way she did to me in my nightmare. Another thing is, I can use the photos for doing torture drawings. I won't have all the trouble of tracing pictures and trying to make them look like Stella.

Dad was in the garden, clearing rubbish out of the sheds and burning it. He asked me to help him. It was horrible watching the spiders crawling out of the junk and shrivelling up in the flames. I went round the edge of the fire stamping on any that managed to escape.

Dad saw me and told me to stop. He said they were God's creatures, just as much as we were, and entitled to their lives. I asked him why he was burning them. He said, 'Mmmm; good point.' After that he gave everything a shake and a bash before he put it on the fire. The garden was littered with things crawling everywhere. I couldn't stand it and went into the stable.

I got busy doing more tracings, this time from the *National Geographic* magazines. Malone came round, and I showed him what I was doing. He said it was an interesting idea but why was I tracing pictures of native women from the jungle?

'Because it's easier than the photos in the other magazines. They have hardly any clothes on to start with. I don't have to do so much free-hand drawing putting in their chests and bums, and working out where their legs come to.'

Malone said that was his point exactly. If they don't wear any clothes to start with, they're not likely to feel any shame about being drawn naked. I couldn't see what he was getting at. I said it hardly mattered; they were only drawings, after all. Malone got a sinister look on his face and said it did matter. 'You should get hold of some posh English magazines with photographs of well-known society women in them, and do tracings of them.' Then I'd get a proper thrill out of the torture drawings, because if they knew what I was up to, they'd want to commit suicide with embarrassment. I asked him what 'society women' are.

'High-class women with money, and silk underwear, and big houses, and husbands with yachts and racehorses.' He says his ambition in life is to shag hundreds of them. He wants to do all sorts of filthy things to them; things that will wipe the snooty smiles off their faces. He says they're so high and mighty they think their shit is sweet enough to use as toothpaste. I said, 'I thought you weren't interested in girls?'

'I'm not interested in getting myself all dolled up and spending money trying to please them.'

If a girl or a woman comes his way, he'll take what he can off her, even if it means a bit of brute force, but he's damned if he's going to go chasing after them.

He started looking through my tracings.

'Why have you labelled all the drawings "Stella"?'

I said she's a girl down the terrace who fancies herself, and who's giving me a hard time. 'If ever a girl gave me a hard time, I'd give her something hard right back; in fact, right up the backside.' I asked him if he meant his jake. 'Yes. All nine inches of it!'

I asked him about 'right up the backside'. 'Is that where you're supposed to stick your jake?'

'No, definitely not; you can hurt yourself unless you give it a good coating of Vaseline or margarine.'

'Why would you want to do it, then?'

'Because,' he said, 'it's the most disgusting thing you can do to a girl, apart from putting your cock in her mouth and spurting down her throat. You ought to think about doing it to that mot who's annoying you. She'd be too embarrassed ever to look at you again.'

I suddenly remembered I'm supposed to be a holy Catholic boy. All this sort of talk is an offence against God and probably a mortal sin. I mentioned this to Malone, but he said no. 'God gave men pricks, and then He invented women, so men would have fannies to stick their pricks into.' God has only Himself to blame if fellows get carried away by dirty thoughts. He shouldn't have invented pricks in the first place. Drunkenness is definitely a sin, and so is beating children, and stealing, and murder, but not anything to do with shagging girls. Priests only tell you it is because they're not allowed to do it themselves.

I asked him why they're not allowed to. 'It's obvious! They listen to all the women's sins in confession, and know everything they get up to. They know which ones drop their knickers, and which ones don't.' If priests were allowed to get their ends away, they'd be at it all the time, and never have any time or energy to get on with God's business.

Hearing this made me feel a bit better. I'm always thinking

about girls myself just recently, and I haven't been to confession for weeks because I'm afraid of all the dirty things I'll have to tell the priest. Malone says there's no need to worry. 'You'll be doing the priest a favour by not telling him.'

He says the priests must get a terrible horn on in the confession box, sitting there in the dark listening to all the things that go on and not being able to do anything themselves.

Malone went home at tea-time because there was nothing to eat in my house. I had a look out of the loft window. Mrs Barrington was in her garden. There was no sign of Stella, so I decided to risk calling on Mrs Barrington while the going was good. I haven't set eyes on her since Tuesday. I was afraid she might throw me out for being rude, or accuse me of being ill-mannered for rushing off without saying thank you or goodbye.

When I knocked on the gate she opened it, and stood looking at me with a surprised expression for a moment. 'Michael!' she said, and her expression changed to a smile. 'How nice to see you!'

I said I'd like to speak to her about something, but not in the garden, because you never knew who was watching. She said she wasn't in the least bothered about anyone seeing us. I said I was, because it had already caused me serious problems.

She said, 'That's a pity; I'd hoped we might be friends without all the complications people normally get into.' She had on a green bathing costume, with a small towel round her neck, and smelt strongly of sun-tan oil.

We went into the house, and on the way she walked in front of me. Going down the garden steps into the basement she gave me a cheeky grin over her shoulder. 'No compliments this time? Are you not in the mood, or have you simply given up your study of women?'

At the bottom of the steps she twirled round and put one hand on her hip and the other on the back of her head. I thought of what had happened to me with Stella on Friday. It gave me a pain in my head and a tight nervous feeling in my stomach. Mrs Barrington saw the frown on my face and gave a disappointed 'Oh . . .'

I said I'd given up staring at girls in swimsuits, because it had brought me nothing but trouble. She stopped posing and carried on into the house. Her legs aren't long and skinny like Stella's, and you can't see the muscles moving separately in her bottom. Everything works much more smoothly, but I didn't want to think about it at the time. I was too worried about Stella seeing us and yelling something at me from her windows.

'Well then, Michael,' Mrs Barrington said when we got into her kitchen; 'I hope I'm not the source of your troubles?' I shook my head.

'Oh, good; that's the last thing I want to happen.' She asked me if there was something worrying me. I shook my head again.

'You don't seem to be the same light-hearted boy I met on Tuesday.'

After this she didn't seem to know what to say, and neither did I. She came and stood near me, her head bent and her hands behind her back. I don't know why, but I suddenly burst into floods of silent tears. Mrs Barrington looked at me kindly for a moment, and traced the tip of one of her fingers under both my eyes to feel the tears. 'Oh Michael, what is it . . . what's the matter? Is it something I've done?'

I had a good sniff and said no, most definitely not; she was the only person in the world I cared about besides my Mam and my Dad and my sisters, and that I was upset about something else entirely. She was relieved to hear this, and started to smile again. She said she'd been afraid she'd never see me again, after what happened the other day. I admitted I was a bit embarrassed about it. I told her it had never happened to me before, so I wasn't expecting it. She said I wasn't to worry about it; she was quite flattered by the effect she'd had on me. I said I'd try not to let it happen again. She gave me a funny sideways smile. 'If it does, we ought to make better use of the situation . . .' After this we both cheered up.

'Will you stay a while, and have something to eat?'

'Yes; I'm starving. I'd be grateful for a sandwich or a couple of biscuits.'

'I see you've got your priorities sorted out!'

I asked her what she meant but she just grinned. 'I'll get dressed and do you something to eat. Looking after your stomach might be more effective than wandering round half naked . . .'

She said she needed a quick shower to wash off the sun-tan oil before she got dressed. 'It'll take me about ten minutes. Can you survive that long?'

'Oh yes. Quite easily; I'm used to being hungry.'

That worried her. She got me a Mars bar out of a drawer, and told me to make myself at home while she got dressed. Their basement has a kitchen at the back and two big rooms inside. There's a front room like ours and a back room the same size. Both rooms are the width of the house. They have windows reaching from the ceiling to the floor, with beautiful curtains.

Mrs Barrington said the back room is called the lounge. It's where they eat when they're having proper meals, on a long polished table with silver candlesticks. There's a record-player and an enormous radio, and even a television in the corner. It's hard to get a decent signal in Ireland, so they don't really bother about it. They also have a telephone, which you normally only see in doctors' surgeries and police stations.

There are paintings and photographs all round the walls of the lounge. They're mostly of naked women standing on rocks, with the wind blowing their hair about. I didn't dare look at them too closely in case Mrs Barrington caught me. Some of the women looked a bit like her.

The wall separating the front room from the back has a carpet hanging on it, like a giant picture. This interested me. I've never seen a carpet being used anywhere except on a floor. The carpet has hundreds of pretty angels and fairies on it, all tangled up in a big pattern. I went over to see what they were doing. From close up the angels have evil faces, and the fairies have little animal heads. They look weird. Their bodies are all so beautiful and their faces so ugly. I felt a bit scary, looking at it. Then I had an even scarier thought. When you move the curtains in a room that hasn't been used for ages, you find loads of insects hiding behind them. Would there be horrible insects and great black spiders hiding on the wall behind the carpet?

I stuffed the Mars bar into my mouth in one go so I'd have both hands free, picked up a shiny brass poker from the fireplace, and slowly and nervously lifted a corner of the carpet away from the wall. I got an even bigger fright than I was expecting. Behind the carpet the wall is just one big sheet of clear glass, like an enormous shop window. Staring straight at me, stark naked and brushing her hair, was Mrs Barrington. I dropped the carpet and went as red as a beetroot. I expected her to open the door and tell me off for peeping, but she didn't. I knew she wouldn't be too cross, because she quite likes me looking at her. Even so, I thought she'd be annoyed about being seen with nothing on. I went out to the kitchen and sat down at the table to wait for her. When she came back her hair was smooth and shiny and beautiful. She never said a word about me looking behind the carpet. She'd put on pink lipstick and a white jumper and a pair of tight white trousers.

She moved round the kitchen getting things out of drawers and cupboards, chatting away to me as if nothing had happened. I tried to keep track of what she was saying but I kept getting distracted. Her trousers were made from a very fine, thin material. I could see her knickers through them. Not just the outline of the elastic, but the whole shape of them. I got a warm feeling in my tummy watching her, and began imagining her moving around with no clothes on at all.

'Nearly ready! I'll be with you in a minute . . .' She stopped momentarily and stood quietly with her back to me, staring at something she was holding. I half stood up and leaned across the table to get a last good look at her knickers before she sat down. She gave me a shock.

'Michael; that's very naughty!' I sat down quickly, wondering how she knew I'd been looking at her. She turned round with a big shiny spoon in her hand.

'Very useful things, spoons; even if they do give rather a distorted view.'

It was just the sort of ingenious idea I'd think of myself. She leaned across the table and ruffled my hair. 'I thought you'd given up that sort of thing!'

Then she bent her head and kissed me right on the lips. It was a very light kiss, like the tickle of a butterfly's wings between your palms. The feel of it made my brain go dizzy. The taste of her lipstick stayed on my mouth, and the smell of it drifted into my nostrils. My willie started struggling around in my trousers. It got caught up in the tail of my shirt and nearly strangled itself. It hurt so much I needed to go somewhere private and untangle it. I asked her if I could go to the lavatory. 'Yes, of course. There's one in Andy's room and one in mine.' I asked her where Andy slept. 'He has his own apartment out the back. The outhouses have been done up as a bedroom-cum-bathroom-cum-playroom. I'd be happy to show you if you're interested.'

I was squirming about, feeling uncomfortable. Mrs Barrington giggled and pulled me up from the table. 'You'd better go before you have an accident! Use my bathroom; it's nearer.'

Two bathrooms in one house! I was amazed. I was even more amazed when I went into her bedroom. She showed me to the door and then closed it after me. I was able to stare around without worrying. The whole of the floor is covered in a thick white fluffy carpet, with an enormous bed right in the middle. I've never seen a bed like it; it's circular, with pink sheets and a great big shaggy eiderdown over it, made of some kind of animal skins with long white fur. The most amazing thing of all is that one side of the bedroom is laid out like a Roman emperor's palace, with marble steps up to a big bath and a shower, and potted plants everywhere. I could see myself from every angle, because all the walls are covered in mirrors. I got a bit dizzy and had to sit down on the bed. I noticed the ceiling was covered in mirrors as well, and dozens of little spotlights, the sort you see in cinemas.

I got up and went over to have a look at the wall I'd been looking through earlier, the one with the carpet hanging on the other side. I could see myself quite clearly in the glass, which seemed to be a mirror, same as on all the other walls. There are big curtains at either end of the wall. I pulled them across the glass to block out the light, and got behind them. I thought maybe it was the light from the front window shining on the glass, that made it look like a mirror. The curtains didn't make any difference. I could still see myself reflected, even though it was practically dark, but I couldn't see a thing through it. I expected to see the back of the carpet. It's a mystery to me. At least I know why Mrs Barrington didn't say anything; she couldn't see me from her side.

I went and sat on the bed, feeling baffled. My willie had gone down by this time. I remembered Christie's brother and the things he wanted from Andy's dad. I was sitting in the very place he said they'd be. I got up and went over to the dressing-table; a lovely white one with gold handles. I pulled out the bottom drawer. It was full of nylons and pretty socks, but nothing else. I tried the next one up. It had Mrs Barrington's knickers in it. I knew I shouldn't look at them but temptation came over me. They were neat and lacy and delicate, and all sorts of colours, from pink and red to black and white. I got an urge to touch them, even though I knew it would look like dirty-mindedness if Mrs Barrington caught me doing it. Just as my hand was about to reach into the drawer, she knocked on the door.

'Are you all right in there?'

I got a fright, and realised I'd been gone for ages. I flushed the lavatory to pretend I'd been using it. I had a quick look through other drawers until I found Mr Barrington's clothes. In among his socks I came across some shiny packets of things I'd never seen before. I read the writing on the packet and knew they must be what Christie's brother wants. The instructions said, 'Unroll the protective over the head of the penis.' I didn't have to read any further. I've asked Dad the proper medical name for jakes and willies and he says it's 'penis'.

I put a packet in my pocket and shut the drawer. I was about to leave the room when it struck me I was stealing. Worse still, stealing from a friend. I felt disgusted with myself and put them back immediately. It just goes to show how unholy and sinful I've got recently.

When I came out Mrs Barrington was sitting at the kitchen table slicing vegetables. She handed me a plate with tomatoes and cucumber on it.

She pointed to a bowl of lettuce and a jug of celery and a plate with sliced beetroot on it.

'I hope you won't think me rude,' I said, 'but I never eat vegetables. Except only boiled cabbage.'

She was astonished, and asked me what I *did* eat.

'All I generally get for meals is sandwiches, and once a week a big fry-up of eggs, bacon, liver, kidneys and black pudding.'

'How on earth can you look so happy and healthy on a diet like that? And have such good skin and strong teeth and bright eyes?'

'Well . . . sometimes, as a treat, we get fried rabbit.'

She handed me a wooden board covered with different bits of cheese. I had to tell her I've never eaten cheese, either.

She looked at me strangely, as if she thought I was taking the mick out of her. I changed the subject by asking if she'd lend me her camera for tomorrow. 'Why?' she asked.

'I want to take photos of the basement to send to my Mam in Mullingar.'

'It's a very expensive camera. Richard will be livid if anything happens to it.'

'I'll be extremely careful.'

'That's taken for granted! I'll tell you what; how about taking me with you?' She said she'd love to see round the place and meet my Dad. She was disappointed when I said no. I made the excuse that we were in the middle of getting the place done up, and my Dad would be embarrassed at the state of everything. She said it didn't sound like a good idea to be sending photographs to my Mother, if it was that bad.

'We'll send some more later on, to show her how much work we've done.' This didn't sound convincing even to me, but Mrs Barrington didn't say any more about coming round. She made me a jam sandwich, and went off and got the camera. I washed my hands to make sure I didn't get any stickiness on it. She said this was an encouraging sign, and that she was sure I'd take good care of it.

The film needed replacing after all the photos we took on Tuesday. I asked if I could have another one, and pay for it as soon as I've saved some money. She laughed and said that was no problem.

'Richard has loads of spare film. He's very keen on photography. He does all his own developing and printing.' She asked me if I'd like to see his dark-room. I said yes. She took me through her bedroom, and out to the scullery at the front of the basement. Mrs Barrington went in first and put the light on. The front door is blocked off, and so is the window. The whole of the room is fitted with workbenches and shelves, all packed with photographic equipment. Mrs Barrington closed the door. 'It's completely light-proof in here; I'll show you.'

She told me not to move in case I knocked something over. She put the light out. The darkness took my breath away. Even at night in the middle of winter I've never known such darkness. I felt I was smothering in it. I got panicky, and asked her to put the light back on.

She looked in a box on the bench for a film, and found a new roll among some cartons that had already been opened. She said these were films that Richard took last time he was home, and hadn't had time to develop. I offered to take them in with me to Dublin and get them done when I take my film in. She said Richard preferred to do them himself. 'He can't risk losing them!'

I asked if I could stay in the dark-room, with the light off and the door open, to change the film in the camera. 'Yes. I'll leave you to it. I want to clear up in the kitchen.' She put her fingertips to her lips and kissed them, then pressed them against my lips.

She went off with her eyes sparkling, humming a tune and looking very happy.

I took out the film we'd used for our photographs, put it in a spare carton, and dropped the carton into Mr Barrington's box. After I reloaded the camera I realised I should have kept the film I'd taken of Mrs Barrington. If Mr Barrington developed it, he'd probably want the photos for himself. I looked in his film-box for the carton, but I couldn't say which was mine. It was identical to the others that were already in there. This got me quite worried. In the photos I'd taken with the automatic shutter, Mrs Barrington was very friendly with me. She'd been hugging me, and sitting on my knees with her arms round my neck, and letting me stand behind her with my arms round her tummy and practically touching her you-know-what. If Mr Barrington saw them he might not be too pleased.

In the end I decided to take all four cartons that were in the box. I knew I'd be safe until Mr Barrington came home. Mrs Barrington doesn't seem to have any interest in going in the dark-room. I didn't feel guilty, seeing as I wasn't stealing them. It would give me an excuse to pay for them as a thank you for the loan of the camera, and Mr Barrington wouldn't have so much to do when he got home.

Coming out through the bedroom I could hear Mrs Barrington singing quietly in the kitchen. It was a song called 'Little things mean a lot' which I don't like much myself. It's too slow and dreary, but Mrs Barrington has a nice voice and made it sound light and happy.

I had another try at figuring out the mystery of the window behind the carpet. I stood inside the room looking at the mirror and stretched my arm out to lift the carpet. Not a thing; I couldn't see out into the other room at all. Next, I stood outside the bedroom, lifted the carpet again, and there it was; the whole of the bedroom, as clear as if I was looking through daylight. It must be some kind of special glass. Why they've got it I can't imagine.

Mrs Barrington was keen for me to stay and have supper with her. I made an excuse that I had to go to bed early, because of getting up at dawn to help Dad before I go to school. She was disappointed, and asked me to give her a hug before I went. 'I want to whisper a secret in your ear.'

I put my arms round her. She said she liked my company

better than anyone else in the world. 'You're simple . . . and uncomplicated. You make me feel happy and relaxed.' Being with me reminded her of what it was like to be a young girl again. 'I forget all the complicated worries I normally have to cope with.'

I said I couldn't believe she has worries; she always seems so happy.

'Ah yes; that's when you're around!' I asked if there was anything I could do to help her with these complicated worries.

'No! The last thing I want is for you to be involved. It'd be the end of any hope of . . . of friendship . . . between us.' She asked me to promise that if I ever hear anything bad about her, no matter how dreadful, I'll believe in my own opinion of her, and judge her entirely by that. As I was leaving, I asked her if she was expecting Mr Barrington to be back soon. I was worried about him catching me with the camera.

'I never know when he'll be home; it all depends on his flying commitments.' He has a room at the Airport hotel, because it's more convenient for the odd hours he works. He comes home when he has two or three days off in a row. It's not far to the airport, only about twenty miles, so he sometimes pops over for the night or a couple of hours during the day.

Week Five

Monday 9 July – Sunday 15 July

I borrowed Dad's alarm clock and slept in the stable on a camp bed. I was terrified by the thought of spiders but it saved me having to explain to Dad what I was up to. I thought I'd be too excited to sleep, but it didn't work out like that. As soon as I lay down I went off, and spent the night dreaming I was the boss of a huge well-organised gang, with loads of money and plenty of time for interesting hobbies. I didn't have even the slightest thought about girls.

I set off down the beach very early, so I'd have plenty of time to get to Stella's secret place before she arrived. It was only when I was practically there that I realised I'd left a trail of footprints in the sand. I said a prayer that Stella would come by road instead of cycling along the beach.

I walked through the dunes for the last hundred yards, so she wouldn't see any footsteps near her when she went into the water. I also made sure I wasn't in the same place where John-Joe had caught me. I chose a hiding place among the grass on the opposite edge of the hollow. This gave me a good view of the road, so I could spot John-Joe if he tried to sneak up on me.

It was beautiful lying on the top of the dune, with a warm breeze blowing in off the sea and the sun coming up in a blaze of yellow. The water in the bay quivered and shone as if it was a huge cauldron of melted gold. The beach was like a picture postcard of a desert island: miles and miles of clean white sand, and blue sea, and clear sky, and no human beings to spoil the peace with shouts and rubbish and stupid games.

I waited nearly an hour before Stella appeared. My prayer wasn't wasted, either. She came by the road and stopped at the edge of the pavement to take off her sandals. She hung them on the handlebar of her bike, then made her way among the smaller dunes and into the hollow. She laid the bike down, then sat on the sand with her arms folded round her legs and her chin on her knees, staring at the sea. She sat like that for ages.

I had to keep dead still, in case I started a river of sand running down the bank. Stella would have noticed it immediately. After a while, I was in agony with pins and needles, and then the grass started tickling my nose and I had a job choking back sneezes.

Just when I thought she'd never move, Stella lay back on the sand, stretched her legs in the air so her skirt fell around her hips, hooked her fingers into the waistband of her knickers, and slipped them off. Then she stood up, undid the waistband of her skirt, dropped it round her feet, pulled her blouse over her head, unhooked her brassière and dropped it on the sand. She undid a thin gold chain from round her neck and slipped it into her saddle-bag, and, for just an instant, turned to face the sun, her eyes closed, savouring the warmth on her naked body.

I never had a chance to use the camera. One moment she was sitting quietly on the sand; seconds later, she was gone, running off down the sandbank and into the sea with hardly so much as a splash.

There was nothing I could do but wait, yet again. She was too far away to take a photograph, and I couldn't see much of her in the water anyway. I thought of going down and stealing her clothes, which would have given her a problem about getting home, and paid her back for what she did to me.

I got a tremendous feeling of excitement when I thought of this, and the bulging willie business started straight away. I got an urge to pick up her knickers and rub my face with them. Another idea that came to me, was to keep them under my pillow so I could rub them against my willie at night, and remember how I'd got my own back on her. In the end I decided not to; it would ruin the whole point of being there with the camera. The minute she saw her clothes gone, she'd be on her guard and probably run back into the water to hide herself. It was better to take as many photographs as I wanted, and then come back and steal her clothes some other morning.

After about half an hour, Stella came out of the water. All my waiting turned out to be worth while. She ran back along the bank, lightly and gracefully, like an antelope, with her wet brown body sparkling in the sun, and her long black hair streaming out behind her. I took photos as she ran towards me, then had to dodge down as she got closer, in case she noticed my head poking through the grass.

She took a big towel out of her bicycle basket and spread it on the sand, bending over with her back to me, and her legs apart. It was exactly what she'd made me do in her basement. I took photos of her in this position, and several more while she was tidying her clothes, and then again when she lay down on the towel to sunbathe. I saw every bit of her, even a little bushy patch of black hair that she has at the top of her fanny.

I screwed my mind up as hard as I could, and imagined doing all sorts of dirty things to her; spurting my willie in her face and sticking my fingers up her bum and stuffing her fanny full of sand and tying her up in ropes smeared with dog-shit.

A strange thing happened; I couldn't keep the thoughts going. I kept trying and trying, reminding myself how horrible she'd been to me, and how much I wanted to shame her to get my own back. It was no good; I couldn't keep it up. In the end I let my mind go its own way, and lay there quietly staring down at her. It made me feel peaceful and happy, just looking at her; she was so smooth and slim and creamy and still, like a statue of a young Greek goddess that I saw once, in a book.

She seemed a different person to the vicious bitch who made a mockery of me last week. After a while I forgot she was a girl with no clothes on, and just watched her as if I was looking at a beautiful painting. I even began to get a feeling of holiness and respect towards her, like you get in a chapel.

After a while, John-Joe's cart appeared in the distance, coming from the village. Stella heard it straight away. She must have good ears, or maybe she's used to him coming along at that time. She climed up the side of the hollow opposite me. It's very steep and she went up it on her hands and knees, then crawled over the rim and stayed quiet, watching John-Joe through the screen of grass. She was directly opposite me, crouched on her knees and elbows, with her bare bottom pointed straight in my direction.

It was a perfect pose but I had to force myself to use the camera. I was still in a sort of holy glow, and the last thing I wanted was to ruin my new feelings for her by taking a photograph of her bum. In the end, I did take a photograph; I didn't want to be kicking myself later on, when the magic wore off, for not taking advantage of such an opportunity. Then I slid down the dune and went home, had toast and tea for breakfast, and went to school.

I spent the rest of the day in a sort of dream. One minute I was thinking noble thoughts about Stella's beauty and how lovely it was to have seen all the most secret parts of her body. The next minute my mind would bubble up with filthy feelings of enjoyment at the thought of having photographs of her bare bum and her hairy fanny and her pink-tipped titties.

Welch made a lot of remarks about my attitude during the day. He said I might as well be asleep for all the good the lessons were doing me. If I haven't bucked up by tomorrow he'll send me home with a note of complaint to Dad.

Malone came round in the evening and we went out to the stable for a chat. He wants to know when the gang is going to be started, and whether I'm serious about it, or just messing around wasting his time. He got very shirty with me, especially when I said I couldn't concentrate on questions about the gang because I was too busy thinking beautiful thoughts about girls. He made the usual sort of comment I've come to expect from Malone where girls are concerned; 'There's only one thought worth having about girls, and that's how soon you can get their knickers down and your dick up.' I feel very sorry for him, having this attitude. He's never going to appreciate any of the world's great works of art and literature if he keeps on thinking at that level. I tried to do him a favour by getting him interested in some pictures of statues and paintings in the encyclopaedia. All he could say was that anyone who went in for looking at that sort of stuff was just as dirty-minded as he was, but at least he didn't hide it by pretending to be an art-lover.

I said he was wrong; looking at girls with no clothes on doesn't have to be a dirty-minded thing. Malone let out a burst of coarse laughter, and said, 'That's what all those professor bastards with beards and spectacles tell you, but it's just to disguise their own filthy minds.' I got annoyed and said I knew for a fact that you could look at a naked girl without thinking dirty. I'd done it myself so I knew for certain. Malone said it was no good if I was talking about seeing my sisters; sisters don't count, because you can hardly think about shagging them yourself, so there's no point using them as an example.

'All right then,' I said; 'I'll prove it.' I told him I was talking about a proper, posh, grown-up girl, dancing around in the sun without a stitch on, and me not twenty feet away. 'Go on,' said Malone, 'you're pulling my leg; where would you get the chance of a look at a mot like that, in the altogether?'

I was reluctant to tell him at first, which was a bit of a change from my plan of last week. At that time I was going to tell everyone in the village where to find Stella, but since I've been there myself I'm not so sure that's a good idea. She's so beautiful to look at that I'm coming round to the idea of keeping her to myself.

Malone started poking me with his fist in an aggravating manner, and making sarcastic comments about my imagination running away with my mouth. Then he changed his tack and said he couldn't care less anyway; if it was naked mots I was after, I could see plenty of them round at his cottage. He said he was never short of a bare arse willing to bend over the back of his sofa.

This got me so disgusted that I told him about Stella straight away. I told him about the clean sand, and the blue sea, and the golden sun, and of Stella's brown skin with the sea gleaming on it, and the shivery excitement of seeing her clothes scattered on the sand, and the holy feelings I got from watching the oiled smoothness of her naked body stretched out on the towel. Malone looked at me with a queer expression, and said I'd got the words off pat, all right, but was there any truth in them?

'Yes,' I said, and he could see for himself if he wanted to; all he had to do was get up early and hide on top of the dunes overlooking the sand bar. She was down there most mornings, as far as I could make out. 'This mot,' said Malone, 'is she a snotty-faced bitch with a bicycle and long black hair, and a small dog that looks like a pig with indigestion?'

'She's the very one,' I said. 'The one I've been drawing pictures of, for giving me a bad time.' I asked him if he knew her, and he said yes, and then I asked him if he'd ever had a chat with her.

'A chat; with her?' said Malone. 'Are you joking? A bitch like that?' He gave a sarcastic laugh, and gobbed up a mouthful of phlegm and spat it on the floor. 'No,' he said, 'I've never spoken a word to her, or she to me, and I'll tell you why; her kind wouldn't so much as glance at me, even if I was lying in the gutter with my throat cut.'

I knew he was right, so I didn't say anything. Besides, I was sorry I'd told him where to find Stella. I asked him point-blank if he was going to go and have a look at her for himself. He said, why should he; what was she to him? This cheered me up a bit. He asked me how often I'd seen her. Just the once, I said. He wanted to know if I was going again, and I said probably not, at least until the weekend. It's too much trouble during the week, because Stella goes swimming at the crack of dawn. Getting up early would leave me feeling wrecked all day and get me into trouble at school.

Malone went home, saying that if it was mots I was after, I was wasting my time on that one; her fanny would have been sewn up at birth, and the only instrument allowed to cut the stitches is a blue-blooded prick. This operation will be preceded by a church wedding, and any subsequent pain alleviated by an injection of at least two thousand quid a year. Malone is a cynical sarcastic arsehole.

Jamie Dwyer was late for school this morning. When Welch asked him why, he said he was afraid to come in on account of not doing his ecker. 'So,' said Welch, 'you're culpable on two counts, eh?' He said this was serious stuff indeed, with a very good chance of meriting at least two whacks with the cane, and possibly more. He told Jamie to stand behind the blackboard and not move a muscle until break, by which time his punishment would be decided upon. None of us could work, with the strain of worrying what was going to happen to Jamie.

By ten o'clock Jamie couldn't stand it either, and started crying. Welch ignored him for a while, and then announced that the minimum number of whacks was now definitely three; any more whingeing from behind the blackboard would be proportionally noted. This only made Jamie worse, and after a while he wet himself.

When Welch saw the pool of water on the floor he went berserk. He belted Jamie round the head and twisted handfuls of his hair until he screamed with agony. I couldn't stand it, so I stood up and stared at Welch with a dangerous look on my face. Welch stared back with the same sort of expression, and asked me if I would be kind enough to fetch the cane. I went into the little cubbyhole that he calls an office, and got the cane out of the cupboard. I felt the weight of it in my hands, and thought to myself, there's no way I'm going to let him belt little Jamie with this. I opened the window over Welch's desk and dropped the stick out quietly, then went back and told Welch I couldn't find it.

Welch looked as if his whole body was going to explode with rage. His little eyes swelled up with redness and his forehead throbbed with bulging veins. He could hardly speak for his jaw trembling and the lump in his throat going up and down like a Yo-Yo. He screamed at me that I'd defied him once too often, told me to sit down, gave Jamie a vicious whack across the back of his head, and went into the office to look for the stick himself.

As soon as he went I grabbed Jamie, rushed him over to the door, and told him to run off home out of it. Jamie didn't want to go; he said he'd only be in more trouble when he came back. I told him not to be stupid, there was only a week or so left at school, and he could mitch off for the rest of the time. He still didn't want to go. It's terrible for a boy to be so frightened of a teacher.

Welch came back while I was arguing with Jamie, and tried to grab him off me. I lost my temper and told Welch that if he laid a hand on Jamie I'd personally beat the shite out of him, and no messing. I dodged out of his way and ran out through the door, pulling Jamie behind me.

I took him home and explained to his mother what had happened. I got no thanks for my trouble. She said Jamie was nothing but a little gobshite, put her coat on, and marched him straight back to school.

I could see a bus waiting at the end of the terrace, with the driver inside having a smoke with the conductor. I ran home, took the film out of the camera, grabbed the other films that I took from Andy's house, and managed to jump on the bus just as it left for Dublin. Luckily the driver remembered me, because I'd forgotten to bring any money with me. It was the same man that Dad and I came home with on the Sunday we came back from our long weekend. He gave me a sixpenny bit when I got off at the Pillar. I didn't want to take it, but he said it was important to him, and might do him good with the Man Above.

I walked down Talbot Street looking for a photographic shop, and found a little place in a side street with a notice saying 'Passport Photos Developt and Printid on the Premasis'. The bad spelling put me off at first, until I reminded myself that Malone can hardly read and yet he's a good bicycle mechanic, so I went in anyway.

The man said he'd do the films at five shillings each, and asked me for my name and address. I didn't want to tell him who I was, or where I lived, in case he got in touch with the police when he saw the film of Stella. I told him the films were nothing to do with me; they were given to me by a man in a car who'd stopped me in the street and given me sixpence to bring them in. I showed him the sixpence the conductor gave me but he didn't seem convinced. He said I could have found it in the gutter, or stolen it.

He said he hoped there was nothing dodgy about the films; he had a legitimate business to run and he didn't want to get involved in any funny stuff with the police. I said again that I knew nothing about them; the man just gave me sixpence to bring them in and he was going to give me another sixpence when I collected them; when would they be ready?

The fellow in the shop gave me a hard stare and said, 'Saturday, barring earthquakes and other Acts of God.' He still wanted my name, so I said I was Seamus Brannigan from Eccles Street.

'Which house in Eccles Street?' he asked me.

I said the first number that came into my head. 'Number seven.'

'Are you sure that you're not making this up?' he asked, giving me a suspicious stare.

I gave him back an innocent look and said, 'No, honestly; it is number seven.'

He said it wasn't the number that worried him, it was the name of the street; in all his years in Dublin he'd never come across a road named after a teacake. He asked me where it was, and when I told him it was off Dorset Street, he said he had half a mind to walk up and check that I wasn't spoofing him. I hope he doesn't, because a lot of the houses in Eccles Street are empty and ruined. It would be just my luck if Number Seven was one of them.

Afterwards I walked up to Parnell Square and had a look round the Municipal Art Gallery. The pictures are more interesting than the ones in the National Gallery at Merrion Square. I used the sixpence to buy a bag of chips and a penny chew, and caught a bus home for nothing.

In the evening I had a long chat with Dad. He's had another letter from Mam. She says there's no chance of her coming back with the girls at the moment, because Dad still hasn't got a job or a business going, and her dad says she'd be mad to give up the home comforts of Mullingar until such time as there's money coming into the place in Kilmara.

I had problems getting to sleep, because of a row between Mr and Mrs Sullivan upstairs. He chased her out into the garden and she ran down our steps to escape from him. They were yelling at each other outside our back door for ages. I wanted Dad to go out and stop them fighting, but he said you should never interfere between husband and wife; a precept to which he fervently wishes Mam's parents would adhere.

Mrs Sullivan only had on a skirt and a brassière but I couldn't peep out at her through being in the same room as Dad. Mr Sullivan didn't seem to have any clothes on at all, except his socks, and he sounded as if he was drunk. He kept telling her that it was her bloody duty to let him have it, and she kept yelling back that it was her who would have it; another of his bloody offspring up her spout for nine months and then another mouth to feed for nine years or for ninety, all for the sake of him getting his end away for ninety seconds. I have a feeling the argument was about this sex business.

I woke up early, quaking about school. I was sure to have a row with Welch. To relax myself, I thought about calm, beautiful things. I gave my imagination a hand by looking through my nature books. I found a picture of a coral island surrounded by blue sea, with gleaming white sand and the sun shining down on it. This reminded me of Stella, on Monday. I decided to go down the beach and see if she was there. I went out the back so no one would see me. There was a red MG sports car parked down the lane. I wanted to have a good look at it, but I couldn't spare the time. I was afraid of missing Stella.

The sky was covered in grey clouds and the rain half-drizzling when I set off. I gave up hope of seeing Stella but I thought I'd go down to the hollow anyway. There was a man ahead of me on the beach, looking at the island through his binoculars. When he noticed me he walked off the beach into the dunes. Halfway to Stella's place the rain got serious and bucketed down. I went into the dunes myself, out of the wind. I came across John-Joe's hut and went in. The same man was in there. I got quite a fright. So did he. I couldn't see his face, because he whipped up the collar of his jacket. It was one of those sheepskin collars, wide and floppy.

He pushed past me without so much as an 'excuse me'. He had a funny smell, sort of perfumed.

I couldn't stay in the hut after he'd gone. I got a queer idea he might come back and murder me. By the time I got home I was soaked. I didn't dare shelter under a tree; people in Mountjoy Square used to go on about how dangerous it is living in the country, with all the bulls and poisonous insects, and getting struck by lightning through standing under trees in thunderstorms.

I couldn't be bothered to dry myself and I was freezing anyway, so I got back into bed and rolled myself up in the blankets. The walk must have tired me out; I never woke up again until ten. At least I was dry by then, which was something.

I made tea and woke Dad. He was surprised to see me still at home. I told him I'd overslept and would get a belt for going in to school late. He said, 'Fair enough, stay at home; one day more or less isn't going to affect the course of your academic life.'

Dad is going to bed later and later these nights. He stays up playing chess and discussing politics with the Sergeant and John-Joe Maguire. The Sergeant sometimes brings another man. He's called Paddy Dalton and is forever drinking whiskey. Dad doesn't mind; he says that drunk or sober, Paddy's always a gentleman. He works for the Corporation. Dad says that could mean he's anything from a dustman, right up to the director of a huge department. He has a very good accent.

After such a bad start to the day, I'd quite happily have spent the rest of the morning in bed, reading. Dad had other ideas. He said it would be a good idea to tidy the place and wash some dishes. We were saved from this by the parish priest coming down the front steps. Dad wouldn't answer the door because of the state of the place. The priest went up and called on the Sullivans instead. He's often up there, I notice. He's probably worried about Mrs Sullivan always looking so sad. He ought to cheer her up by reminding her of the heavenly bliss that God's love can bring to unhappy people. Perhaps he's already thought of this.

After not answering the door to the priest, Dad was afraid to do anything that would make a noise, in case he heard us from upstairs. I went back to my reading and Dad spent his time writing a long letter to Mam and another one to the head of

Radio Eireann, complaining about the bad language in a play he listened to last night.

I have a terrible amount of reading to catch up on. I'll never reach my target of finishing the encyclopaedia by the end of the year. I'm still working my way through 'D'. 'Dabbler' means someone who messes about, never getting seriously into anything, and 'dabster' means the opposite; an expert at anything. Strange. Sculley asked me to look up 'debentured apprentice', because he's going to be one when he leaves school. I'm glad I did; I thought it meant a young tradesman with false teeth. I could have made a right fool of myself with that one.

Dad says it's time I was into long trousers. He's going to ask Nana if she has any old suits that would fit me. Nana's had four husbands and they've all died of one thing or another. She has a big attic full of trunks of clothes. Dad is annoyed with me always wearing wellingtons. He says it's bad for my feet and can lead to a fungal disease that rots the skin and makes your toes disintegrate. This has me worried. It was Christie's idea for us to wear wellies all the time; that, and taking the mudguards off our bikes. He says it makes us look tough.

Dad went in to Dublin this afternoon. He wasn't able to leave the house until after two o'clock, because the priest was still upstairs with Mrs Sullivan. Dad was in a furious temper at having to wait so long. He said priests should start charging for their time, like doctors and dentists. He doesn't know how they put up with it; day after day, house after house, one woman after another pouring out her troubles, while Joe Husband stands in a bar telling dirty stories and pouring Guinness down his throat.

I got fed up reading, and was lying on my bed thinking, when I suddenly remembered the dead child. My heart nearly stopped with fright. It was still pouring rain outside, with a black thundery sky. The basement got darker and gloomier, and I expected to see a ghost any moment.

I went out the back to see how Dad is getting on with the sheds. He's been clearing them out, one by one. They're not really sheds; they're built of brick with proper slate roofs and plaster ceilings inside. Dad says they're really an extension of the basement, sticking out of the back of the house. There are four separate rooms, all with their own door opening into them from the outside.

The last room, as you go up the steps into the garden, is the lavatory. Dad says the other rooms were for washing and ironing and storing stuff. The basement was the servants' quarters for the rest of the house. There's a good strong table in one of the rooms. Dad's going to make it into a workbench. I lay on it for a while reading, with a big paint tin laid on its side for a pillow. The rain pelted down even harder and it got too dark for me to see my book. I was reading *The Gorilla Hunters*. It's by the man who wrote *The Coral Island*, and it tells you what happened to Ralph and Jack and Peterkin after they were rescued. They went off to Africa and discovered gorillas, at a time when no one knew they existed.

I was lying staring at the ceiling, hoping the rain would stop, when I realized there was a trapdoor right above me. I thought how interesting it would be to go up into the loft space above. I also thought of all the enormous hairy black spiders with vicious beady eyes that would be lurking up there. I started imagining what it would be like to be captured by Stella, if she ever found out about the photographs and decided to have her revenge on me. The very worst thing she could do would be to lock me in that loft, tied up with no clothes on, and leave me at the mercy of the creepy-crawlies up there. She'd have to put a gag round my mouth, otherwise I'd scream the place down and be found instantly. That's if I was lucky and there was someone around to hear me.

I got a strange feeling thinking about this. My jake began to feel warm and mysterious. My tummy muscles went tight and set my heart beating really fast. The more I thought about it the more I almost wished it would happen, which I know sounds ridiculous.

The feeling got so strong that in the end I had to try a bit of the real thing. I stood up on the table, but I was six inches too low to poke my head into the loft. I put two paint tins side by side, and stood with a foot on each of them. I could just get my head over the edge of the hole but everything was too dark to see what was up there.

Suddenly I felt that something was crawling on top of my head. I gave a tremendous jerk and knocked the tins from under me. I fell on my back on the table with such a wallop it knocked all the breath out of me. I couldn't move, and I must have fainted from shock. The next thing I knew was Dad wakening me up and saying he'd been searching everywhere for me. It was pitch dark and after half-past eleven at night!

I told Dad I'd been trying to look in the shed loft. He said I'm not to attempt it again unless he's around. He'd be quite interested to have a look up there himself; some long-dead butler or pantry maid might easily have left a suitcase or something up there, and forgotten about it.

The big news is that Stella has been attacked. She was down swimming as usual this morning. Someone waited until she was lying on her towel with no clothes on. A woman out walking a dog found her lying in the hollow, unconscious and bleeding. Her bicycle and all her clothes were missing. The police think they were thrown in the sea, to delay her going home and raising the alarm.

Christie told me all about it. He heard his dad talking to another policeman in the wash-room at the barracks. Christie was in the lavatories making notes of the dirty jokes on the wall. He kept quiet so they wouldn't know he was there. The Sergeant said that in his opinion, Stella was asking for it. I don't why anyone would ask to be attacked. Stella doesn't know who it was. The only clue is something to do with what the fellow was wearing. Christie won't tell me what it is. He wants to earn the reward money for himself.

It was lucky the woman found her; she'd never have been able to get back to the terrace with no clothes on. The woman wrapped her in a rug that she had in her car, and drove Stella home. It was very kind of her. She even went round the back lane so no one would see Stella wrapped in the rug and wonder what was going on.

Christie's sister Ellen says Stella has no hope of getting married now, for all her airs and graces; she's damaged goods and no one will want her. Ellen says Stella might as well be dead; she can't work and she can't get married. The best she can hope for, is to become a lonely old maid and spend the rest of her life looking after her parents. Ellen says Stella's parents will have to leave the village, because of the disgrace.

Christie is worried sick about the whole business. He says John-Joe Maguire is sure to tell the police about catching us spying on Stella, and we'll become the chief suspects. He thinks we should get in first, by putting the finger on John-Joe before he puts it on us. He wants to send an anonymous note to his dad saying that certain people have seen John-Joe Maguire down the beach regularly at the same time and place as Stella.

I think this would be foolish. John-Joe knows me well, and would never think I was the sort to attack a girl. If we start putting suspicions on him, he could panic, and mention our names out of desperation. I've told Christie to say nothing to anyone, and just see what happens. Meanwhile, I'll listen to John-Joe when he's talking to Dad, and make sure he has no suspicions about us.

I was saved from any trouble at school. Welch wasn't able to do anything to me, because the police spent most of the day talking to him. They wanted to find out if there were any boys that Welch thought might have attacked Stella. I don't know what he told them, but he gave me some terrible looks during the day.

Christie was round most of the evening, moaning and groaning about how worried he is. He left when John-Joe came in to talk to Dad. They had a bit of a chat about the attack but didn't seem very interested in the matter, and soon got round to their usual hobby of playing chess and smoking.

I'm going to have to be very careful about the photographs. If I'm ever caught with them, I'll be suspected of being the attacker. I'm glad I never said anything to Christie about them. I was too fed up to do anything after Christie left, so I went to bed early and lay thinking about Stella. I suppose I feel sorry for her, really. In fact, I know I do. I would have spent the evening down the beach looking for clues, except that the police have sealed off the whole area where she was attacked.

I woke up early, worried about Stella, and got up to see if she'd gone swimming. It's exactly the sort of thing she'd do, to spite whoever attacked her and show them she's not afraid. I can always tell by her bicycle if she's in or out. She never goes anywhere without it. It's chained to the railings outside her house during the day, and put away in her garden at night. I can see it from the loft in the stable.

I couldn't see any sign of it, front or back. I got dressed in a panic, thinking I ought to go and protect her from getting attacked again. Then I remembered Christie saying her bike had been thrown into the sea. I decided to go and rescue it for her. I was creeping up the front steps, quietly, so as not to waken Dad, when I met Christie coming down. He wanted to know whether John-Joe Maguire said anything to Dad last night, anything that might incriminate us.

I said no, they'd hardly shown any interest in the matter at all. Christie was quite relieved. He asked me where I was going, and when I told him he said I was an eejit; Stella's bike has already been rescued by his dad and is in the police station being examined for fingerprints. I asked Christie to make sure the bike gets a good wash in fresh water as soon as possible, otherwise it'll go like mine and seize up completely with the sand and salt. I'll have to see Malone about fixing it for her; she'll be absolutely stuck without it. They haven't found her clothes yet. The Sergeant says they've probably been washed out to sea.

A detective has been sent out from Dublin to look into the case. Christie's dad is cross about this; he says he's perfectly capable of handling the matter on his own. John-Joe says he's heard in the pub that the police in Dublin aren't too pleased with the Sergeant. He still hasn't solved the mystery of the burnt-out car, or where the man's wife has got to.

I asked Christie if he'd come down the beach with me after school to look for clues but he wouldn't; he doesn't want to be seen anywhere near the place.

Sculley is getting me a bad name at school. He's of those fellows who can do huge noisy farts whenever he wants to. Now he's got a new trick. He's able to do the farts without making a noise at all. He lets off one of these silent stinkers while we're sitting in class, then starts to cough and splutter as though he's going to be sick, and flaps his jotter in my direction as if the smell is coming from me. When Welch asks him what's wrong, Sculley says that someone not a million miles away has rotten guts. Then he stares at me. While this is going on, all the other fellows are coughing and spluttering and staring as well. I hate that sort of stupid play-acting, so I'm the only person sitting still. Naturally, Welch thinks it's me that's done the fart.

Sculley told me how he does these silent farts; he puts a rolled-up hanky between the cheeks of his bum and pulls his trunks up very tight to keep it there. It muffles the sound. Sculley is one of those people who always have to be doing something to get noticed.

Sculley is a nuisance in another way. He's always staring at me and saying, 'My God, you have got a big head.' He also says I have bulging eyes and sticking-out ears. Sculley isn't exactly an Errol Flynn himself. I think he's jealous because he's so short and I'm so tall. I know for a fact he's sent off to England for a Charles Atlas course and those shoes with secret heels in them that make you two inches taller. When he gave me back a *Hobbies Weekly* I lent him, it had bits cut out of the advertisement page. I could tell what they were; they always have the same ones every week, in exactly the same places. When I asked him about it he said they were coupons for stamps on approval, but I know that's rubbish.

I called in on Malone on the way home from school, to see if he'd come down the strand and look for clues. He was in his shed with the door locked and wouldn't let me in. 'I'm too busy to waste time talking,' was his excuse. I had to shout to him through the door. He said I must be mad; no fellow in his right mind would go anywhere near the beach, for fear of being arrested as a suspect. He says it's well-known that criminals often return to the scene of a crime, so the police will be keeping a good watch on the strand. I told him I was going to go anyway; surely no one would suspect me of being a vicious attacker? Malone got annoyed and said I never seemed to learn, and would I kindly eff off and let him get on with his work.

I went home and changed into my wellingtons, had a slice of bread with brown sauce on it, and set off down the strand. It was a dull heavy sort of afternoon; the thunder was still hanging around and the sky was ragged and black. The tide was right out, and the estuary nearly empty. The beach is very level in Kilmara, so when the tide comes in and out it has a long way to travel. I could almost walk across to the island, except for a deep channel which must have been cut to let the coal boats in and out.

I walked along the edge of the sea until I was parallel with the end of the dunes, and then straight on for a while, well beyond the point where the strand curves inland to form the bay. I was walking along thinking deeply about all sorts of things, when I suddenly realised I was right out where the sea would be when it came in. I looked towards the shore and I could just make out the sand bar that Stella runs along, and the empty bay beyond it. Down at my feet the water was swirling in along the ripples in the sand, curling round my wellingtons like little silver snakes. I got a terrible fright, and ran for the shore straight away.

I was about half a mile out when I started, and absolutely puffed when I got to the sand bar. I rested for a few minutes, then walked up and down the sand looking at Stella's footprints. I knew them because of the bare feet and the distance between each step; she always runs along the bank. They were a bit fuzzy after the heavy rain, but still quite clear if you knew what you were looking for. I was following her footprints back to the dunes when I happened to glance up and saw a policeman's hat bobbing over the edge of the dunes. 'Aha,' I thought, 'Malone was right; they *are* keeping a watch on the place.' I turned round casually and walked back along the top of the bank, right to the end, where it's submerged when the tide fills the bay. I risked a look over my shoulder and saw the policeman standing half-hidden among the long grass on top of the dunes, staring after me.

It struck me I'd be trapped if he decided to come after me; by the time I'd make it back along the sand bar to the strand, he could easily have slid down the dune and be waiting for me. I had a look at the sea, which was still a quarter of a mile out, but coming in fast, and decided to cut straight across the mouth of the empty bay while I still had the chance. It took all my self-control not to run. It was a good distance across the sand, still wet and littered with pools and rivers from the previous tide, and I could see the waves getting closer and closer on my left. I had to go slowly, so as not to get the policeman suspicious.

I've never been so relieved as when I got to the other side of that bay! It also turned out to be well worth while. It's a completely different sort of sea-shore. Rocks and cliffs and gigantic pools and mysterious caves, and enormous piles of stuff washed up on the shore; seaweed and rubbish and wood and old tyres and bits of rope and oil drums and bottles and dead fish.

I was kicking through it with my wellingtons, and jumping about to avoid the sand fleas, when I came across a seagull tangled up in a heap of seaweed. I thought at first it was dead, and pulled it out to have a look at it. It was covered in black sticky tar so I dropped it. I scraped my hands on the edge of a rock to get the stuff off. When I looked at the seagull again, it was trying to move. I felt awful straight away, with pity and disgust; it looked horrible, and must have been suffering dreadfully, stuck helpless in the middle of a great stinking heap of seaweed and rubbish.

I leaned down to look at it closely. It gave a piteous, feeble little squawk and tried to get away. It couldn't; all its feathers were jammed solid with the tarry stuff. It was too weak even to get its head off the ground. I was staring at it, wondering what to do, when a woman's voice spoke to me from over my head. 'There's nothing you can do for it,' she said. 'There's no way of getting the tar off without damaging the bird itself.'

The woman was standing on the coast road that runs above the top of the rocks. She had an Alsatian dog with her, which scared me a bit. Everyone says they attack people and drag babies out of prams and chew their heads off. I stood looking up at her, and she stood looking down at me, but I couldn't think of anything to say at first. After a second or two, I asked her what was the best thing to do about the seagull, and she said she'd come down and have a look at it with me.

I thought she'd fall coming down the rocks, being a woman and a grown-up, but she didn't. The dog had a worse time of it than she had. We both had another look at the seagull and she said that the kindest thing would be to put it out of its misery. I asked her how, and she said by wringing its neck, like you do with a chicken. I asked her if she'd ever done it, and she said, 'No. Have you?'

I hadn't, so neither of us knew what to do. She said 'wringing' must be something like what you do with washing. She picked up the bird in a sheet of old newspaper to keep her hands clean. I got hold of its head and twisted it round and round until its neck was completely screwed up. The bird struggled desperately and I had to let go. Its head untwisted like a propeller on a rubber-powered model aeroplane. We tried it again, even though both of us were disgusted by this time. Again, it didn't work. It was horrible to see the bird miserably shaking its head to get rid of the twisting pain.

We tried it one more time, and she said I'd have to give the neck a jerk as soon as I had it wound up. I didn't want to, because I was afraid the bird's head would pull off in my hands and I'd be spattered with blood and have nightmares for ages afterwards. 'Go on,' she said. 'Pull.' I shook my head and said, 'I can't. I just can't.' Her face went sad and she said we were making a mockery of our good intention; instead of putting the bird out of its misery, we were subjecting it to even worse agony.

She asked me again to give the bird's head a sudden jerk, and again I said I couldn't. All of a sudden, she tried to do it herself, by giving the body a quick yank while I still had a grip of the head. It slipped out of the newspaper straight away, and I was left holding the whole thing by the head, only now it was the body that was whirling round unwinding. I got such a fright I dropped it. I had tears in my eyes by this time, and even the dog was whining in a sympathetic way at the seagull.

'What on earth are we going to do?' the woman asked me. All I could think of was trying to drown it in a rock-pool. We tried that for a while, holding it under and then lifting it up to have a look at it. The bird's face got sadder and sadder. I'll never forget the look of pain and bewildered misery in its expression. Holding it under water didn't seem to have any effect. The woman said there was nothing else for it; we'd have to kill it by some mechanical means. I asked her what she meant and she said, 'By hitting it with a rock, for example.' I said, 'Why not leave it to die?' She said no. We'd caused it so much pain that we owed it to the creature to put it out of its misery.

We laid the seagull on a level piece of rock, and got two stones. One was a flat, thin one to put over the bird's head so we couldn't see it. The other was a huge round heavy one to smash down on top of the first one. The woman laid the flat stone gently on the seagull's head. I lifted the other one up in the air and then brought it crashing down with all my strength.

The bird's head squished into a pulp and the flat stone splintered into bits. When I let go of the big round stone it rolled aside. We could see the seagull's mashed-up head splattered on top of the rock. I vomited immediately; I couldn't help it. I nearly coughed my stomach up, because I haven't had much to eat recently. The woman patted me on the back and gave me her handkerchief to wipe my mouth. It smelt of perfume and sherbet bon-bons.

I was ashamed of myself, and apologised for being ill. She said it was all right; she'd have been sick herself, only she was a nurse in England during the War and had seen things that were a lot worse.

We went up on the road then, because we both wanted to get away from the beach. The woman said she's beginning to wonder whether she should find somewhere else to walk her dog; that's the second thing that's happened to her this week, and in the space of two days. She asked me where I lived, and said she had her car with her, if I wanted a lift back to the village. I realised she was probably the person who found Stella, but I was too miserable to ask her about it. I said no, I'd walk back along the road and try to think of happy things, to cheer myself up. It was only when she was leaving that I noticed she was a nice-looking woman. I'd been too busy to think about it up till then. Her skirt caught on the handle of the car door and I saw the backs of her legs as she got in. Before she went the dog licked my hand, and made me feel a bit better. I think it was trying to say thank you for helping another animal, even if I ended up feeling disgusted with myself.

I went home and told Dad I couldn't eat any supper, which he said was just as well, because we had no food in the house.

I asked Dad if I could have a pound back, out of the money he owes me for pawning my cigarette cards. He gave it to me, but not very graciously. He said he was going to buy food today, but now he can't. I didn't care about that; my big worry is to get the photos before the photographer fellow gets suspicious about them. Christie says there's bound to be a report about Stella in the papers this weekend, even though the Sergeant has tried to hush it up for the sake of her family. I'm scared that the photographer will see a picture of her, or read her description. He's bound to twig something, especially with them being photos of a naked girl on a beach.

Before I caught the bus into Dublin, I went round to see Malone, to ask him if he'd come up the Castle graveyard with me tonight. I'm interested to see if the witchcraft is still going on. Malone said he was too busy. He has to do a bicycle for the district nurse. It started off as just a puncture, but the bike turned out to be such a wreck he'd have to spend the whole day on it. Anyway, he says he doesn't want to be seen with me at the moment, after the business of Stella being attacked. He said someone might have seen me spying on her, and tell the police. I'd be immediately suspected and then he might get roped in as well. He already has a bad name in the village and loads of people hate him, so he doesn't want to give them any excuse to think he was involved.

The reason he's doing the nurse's bike is that he had to see her about an injury. He caught his hand between the chain and the gearwheel on a bike. He had it upside down, whizzing the pedal round to free up a three-speed hub. He hadn't got any money to pay the nurse, so he's repairing her bike free in exchange. I asked him was it a bad injury, and he showed it to me. When he unwrapped the bandage I was nearly sick. He's got huge holes dug into the side of his hand where the gearwheel caught him. It looks just like a bite from a savage animal.

The man in the photographic shop turned out to be a miserable cheating bastard. He asked me first if I had any idea what was in the photographs, and I said no; I was only collecting them for this man that I don't even know. The photographer said he'd have to speak to the man himself; the photographs were entirely unsuitable to be in the hands of children. What's more, he said, if the police caught me or anyone else with them, he'd be done for. His shop would be closed down and he'd be put in jail, for dealing in pornography.

I asked him what he was talking about, and he said I was too young to know. The only way he'd let the photos out of the shop, was if an adult came in to collect them. What was more, the price for each film had gone up from five shillings to a pound. I said he must be joking but he said no, he wasn't; he had to charge a high price for the risk involved. I said I couldn't see what risk was involved in developing photographs, but he said these were special; they're what's called in the trade 'art photos'.

He said this type of photograph was banned by the Government, and the Church. Fortunately, he was one of a number of art-loving citizens of Dublin who appreciate such items, otherwise he'd have torn them up and thrown me out of the shop.

I said I'd come back with the four pounds as soon as possible but he said, 'No, that's no good; I want to speak to the man that gave them to you, and see if he's got any more like them.' He said there was good business in that class of photograph, if you had the right contacts among art lovers. I was raging when he said this, but there was nothing I could do. I had to let him keep them. I made him promise to hang onto them until I can get something worked out. He said the only working out that's needed is for me to tell the fellow who owns the snaps that he's got to collect them personally.

I went to the Palm Grove ice-cream parlour in O'Connell Street and spent three shillings on a Knickerbocker Glory to cheer myself up. Then I went home. I sat on the back seat of the bus, at the bottom of the stairs, in case any teddy girls decided to show their bums to the conductor. I was out of luck. Only one girl went up the stairs and she had on a jive skirt padded out with loads of petticoats, so you couldn't see a thing up it.

Last night I went to bed with a hanky tied over my eyes and ears and knotted tightly at the back of my head. I was hoping it would squash my eyes a bit further into their sockets. Sculley says they bulge. The hanky has made them worse. When I took it off they were glowing red from all the little veins I've damaged. My ears seem a bit better, though. Dad says the problem with ears is that people turn over in their sleep and bend them the wrong way. I'm going to give up the hanky business, and try holding my ears back with Sellotape tonight.

We hadn't a crumb to eat in the house. I asked Dad if he'd be honest with me; were we going to have to starve until he had a bit of luck, or was there any definite hope anywhere? All my clothes are falling to ruins, and I'm even having to keep my flies done up with pins where the buttons have come off. It's dangerous, and makes me nervous when I have a pee.

Dad said the reason he hasn't been making much of an effort recently is because he's been enjoying himself doing nothing. He says that years of being a bus-driver, and watching the clock, minute-by-minute, every working day of his life, used to get him down. That's why he's so happy these days; he never has to look at the clock at all.

He says he's going to pull himself together and get back into regular habits. He's still got most of the money Nana gave him, the time she bailed Uncle Louis out of having to go to prison in England. It's in a bank in Dublin, so that we won't be tempted to use it. I asked him what's happening about the snooker business. He said he's going to get working on it again, as soon as he's certain it's the right thing to be doing. He doesn't want it to be just another wild idea, like the wholesale vegetable shop.

A curious thing happened at Mass. I went to communion, because I'd been fasting anyway, through having no food in the house. I decided not to waste the opportunity, even though I hadn't been to confession. The woman beside me at the altar-rail got the Host on her tongue, then pulled it in and shut her lips in a queer sort of way. I got my communion wafer, swallowed it,

214

and then realised that I'd not heard her making any swallowing or gulping noises. The communion wafer is quite big, and dry, and always sticks to the inside of your mouth. People have to struggle to swallow it. I walked back up the middle aisle behind her, and watched where she went. I kept an eye on her, peering through the spaces between my fingers while I said the post-communion prayer.

She did the same for a minute, kneeling with her head bent and her hands over her face. Then she took a hanky out of her pocket and wiped her mouth with it. I'm not certain, but I could almost swear she stuck her tongue out, still with the Host on it, and somehow wrapped it up in the hanky. Then she put the hanky away in her bag, and looked around innocently, as if she was just coming back to earth from a serious praying session.

I was glad she didn't see me looking at her. Handling the Host is the most enormous mortal sin anyone can commit. The woman must have sold her soul to the Devil, and be trying to buy it back. It's the only way you can get out of the arrangement, by giving him a Host in exchange.

I was excited, and also frightened. If the Devil knows that I saw what happened, he might arrange for me to be killed by lightning, or in a motor-car accident. I was glad I'd been to communion, because as long as the body of Christ is inside you, the Devil can't do you any harm. My first thought was to tell Dad what I'd seen, but I decided the safest thing would be to forget it completely, in case the Devil sneaks up on me and reads my mind when I'm not expecting it.

I saw Christie after Mass. We've had a good idea. Well, I have. My idea is to keep an eye out for Stella in the mornings. Then, if I see her going swimming, I'll call for Christie and we'll follow her, to protect her in case anyone tries to attack her again. Christie thinks it's a waste of time; Stella won't dare go swimming on her own, ever again. Christie's dad says his sisters are not to go near the beach until whoever attacked her gets caught. Stella was raped, whatever that is. Christie asked his eldest sister Ellen what it means but she just laughed and said it was something nuns were always praying for. It must be a religious thing.

I asked Christie to come round to my house this afternoon for a gang-planning session but he said he couldn't; he's too busy working on a scheme for making money out of car numbers. I said he was mad; who ever heard of making money out of a stupid thing like that? Christie said, 'There's a way of making money out of anything, if you think hard enough.' This particular idea came to him from a film he saw recently.

In the film, this postman sees a gang making their getaway in a car after robbing a bank. Next day, delivering letters, he sees the very same car parked in the driveway of a big house. He sneaks back at night and puts a notice on the windscreen saying he wants a cut of the money, and that it's to be left in the post office, marked 'to be called for'. The crooks keep a watch on the post office, to catch whoever tries to collect the money. Needless to say, the postman simply collects it without them knowing.

The chances of anyone robbing a bank in Kilmara are pretty small. There isn't a bank, to start with. Christie says that's not the point; there are lots of other things that people get up to in cars. Parked up the woods courting a mot when their wives think they're at a sodality meeting, for one thing; and being parked round at the pub when they're supposed to be at work, for another. He says he's certain he can work something out, if he just thinks hard enough. I'll be glad when Andy gets back from England. Malone and Christie spend all their time either working or thinking about money.

I went home and messed about in the stable for a while, then I had an idea for making a swing in the garden. Not one of those sissy little things people hang on hooks in doorways, but a real high one; the sort that Tarzan swings on when he's zooming through the forest. They're supposed to be giant vines, but you can see they're only ropes with leaves tied to them.

I needed a rope, so I changed into my wellingtons and went down to the dump. As soon as I got there, I was surrounded by Jeremy Lynch's men. I said I wanted to speak to Lynch. They took me round to where he was rooting through a pile of builders' rubbish. He was looking out bits of wood to start a fire, so they could burn a pile of car tyres.

Lynch was amazed to see me. I said I wasn't there to cause trouble; I just wanted permission to collect some rope to make a swing. Lynch thought about it for a moment, then he asked me a strange question; did I know how to skin an animal? He said he'd heard that I knew a lot of useful things, and that I was always reading books, not just comics like most fellows.

I said I'd never actually done it myself but I had a book at home called *The American Boy Scouts' Handbook*, which told you how the Indians skin buffaloes and deer to make tents and clothes for themselves. Four of Lynch's men were gripping onto me all this time. Lynch nodded to them to let me go. He said if I tried any funny business they'd throw me in the fire. I said I had no intention of trying anything; all I wanted was permission to look for some rope and then I'd be off. Lynch winked at his men and said it might not be that simple; I'd been warned already not to come down the dump. It was up to him whether or not I was allowed to get out alive.

I got annoyed, and said if they tried to attack me I wouldn't waste my energy fighting everyone at once. I'd pick out one fellow as a target, and stick my thumbs in his eyeballs, with no mercy. He'd be blind by the time I'd finished, even if the rest of them managed to give me a good kicking afterwards. This worried Lynch's men. They didn't know who I'd decide to go for, and all four of them backed away.

Lynch gave me a thoughtful look, and said I was a bad enemy to have, but worth ten ordinary boys to a gang that had me on its side. This didn't please some of his fellows. They started mumbling. Lynch gave them a sarcastic look and asked them if anyone would like to volunteer to have a go at me. No one did.

He took me into the big shed they use for a gang headquarters, and showed me a dead dog hanging from a rope attached to the rafters. It was a big Alsatian. Lynch said they found it tied up in a sack a couple of weeks ago. He wanted to have the skin for a rug but he didn't fancy cutting it off himself. I was surprised the dog wasn't rotten. Lynch says they hang it over a fire every day, and it's well preserved, like kippers or a side of bacon after it's been smoked.

I said it was a strange thing to find in a sack. He said yes, it was, but no stranger than what had happened to its owner. Lynch had a medal hanging from a bit of string tied round his neck. He handed it to me. 'That's real silver,' he said. 'I got it off the dog's collar.' The medal had a name on it, Prince, and an address. Lynch asked me if the address meant anything to me. I said no; I hadn't been in the village long enough to know many people. 'I'll tell you whose dog it was, then,' said Lynch. 'It was that man who got burned to death in the car.' My face went as white as a sheet. I started trembling, and my legs went wobbly like springs. 'Are you sure?' I said, barely able to whisper, 'Are you *sure* it was his dog?' 'Yes,' said Lynch, 'it was his dog all right. I'd have known it even without the name-tag.' He said he was surprised to see me so upset about a dead dog; he'd thought I was a right toughie from the way I'd been talking earlier on. I asked him again if he was sure it was the dead man's dog, and he said yes. I told him the police were certain it was burnt in the car with the man. Lynch said, 'Well, they're wrong. That's it dangling there in front of us, the very same animal.'

I asked Lynch if the man had more than one dog, and he said no; one dog that size was enough for anyone. Jesus, I thought; what are those bones I have at home? I kept trying to put a certain thought out of my mind, but it was screaming away in the back of my brain. I was in such a state that it was ages before I realised Lynch was shaking me and slapping me on the back. When I managed to focus my eyes and look at him he stepped back with a worried look on his face, half scared and half puzzled. 'What the hell's wrong with you?' he said. 'Are you going to be sick?' I pulled myself together and said no, I was all right – I'd just had a bit of a shock. 'It's not the dead dog, then,' said Lynch, shrewdly. 'It is,' I said. 'It is the dog, but I can't tell you why.'

Lynch said he wasn't accustomed to people keeping things from him. His gang braced themselves and started to gather warily round me. 'Listen,' I said, 'I don't want any trouble; it's just that I have a suspicion about that burnt-out car, and if I'm right, that dog could be a clue to something terrible.' Lynch waved his men away from me, and told them to go outside and have a smoke while we had a word in private. He asked me again about the dog. I said it could drop him in the shit if he knew what I knew, so it was better if I kept it to myself.

Lynch said he was prepared to risk it. To be honest, I was so terrified by my thoughts that I was only too glad to share them with him. I told him about finding the little bones in the back of the car. I assumed they were from the dog; Christie said it was always in the back seat. If they weren't from the dog, could they be from the woman? She's never been seen since the fire. Had she been at the pub with the man, both of them too drunk to drive home, and got into the back seat to sleep it off?

Lynch asked me if there was anything else. 'Yes,' I said.

'Supposing the fire wasn't an accident? Supposing the dog was killed and dumped, and the woman put into the car in its place, and the car set on fire deliberately, with the murderer hoping her bones would be mistaken for the dog? She was only small, after all – hardly bigger than a child.'

'Or,' said Lynch, 'a big dog.' He asked me if I knew who might want to murder them, or why. I said no; the only clue I had was Christie mentioning men in gangster hats coming out from Dublin to do business with the man in the car. 'Our best bet,' said Lynch, 'is to get rid of that dog immediately, and forget we ever saw it.'

'What about the skin?' I said. 'I thought you wanted to save it?'

'Fuck the dog-skin,' said Lynch. 'It's more important to save our own!'

This made me laugh, and I felt better. I said we should give the dog's body to the police, but Lynch said no; if I was right about the man and woman being murdered, the gangsters from Dublin would be after us straight away, for putting the police on their trail. We could end up like the dog: tied up in a sack, dead.

I knew he was right, but even so, I didn't like the idea of the murderers getting away, if they were murderers. Lynch said that getting rid of the dog made no difference; we'd all seen it and could give evidence if we were absolutely forced to. Anyway, if he hadn't preserved the body with smoke, it would have rotted ages ago and no one would have been any the wiser. Our best bet was to get rid of it, keep our mouths shut, and see what cropped up in the future.

I agreed to this. The next problem was how to get rid of the dog. Lynch was all for burying it under a heap of rubbish. I said we should burn it, and see what was left, and whether the skeleton looked anything like a small human being. Lynch said I was a morbid bastard, but I said no; I was being scientific. He said the body would give off a terrible smell but we could disguise it with the ferocious stink of burning tyres.

I had a good idea. I told his men to stack the tyres on top of each other, to make a sort of rubber barrel. We put the dog down the hole in the middle, piled the wood round the outside of the tyres, and set light to it. I told Lynch the tyres and the dog would burn up together, leaving the bones in a neat heap in the middle. They'd be easy to collect afterwards. Lynch said I was a fucking genius. I don't know whether he was being sarcastic or not. You never know with him.

Lynch was right about the burning tyres; the smell was revolting. The smoke blew over the green, and two fishermen from the cottages came over and scattered the fire with scaffolding poles. They hooked the burning tyres on the ends of the poles and dropped them over the harbour wall into the sea. The dog didn't get a chance to burn into a skeleton, but at least it was unrecognisable, so we weren't too bothered.

I went home and hid the bones from the car in the stable loft. Me and Lynch are going to keep in touch about any developments in the case.

Mumbo Quigley is pestering me to get on with the love-letter I promised I'd write for him. He says if I don't do it this week it'll be no good to him. We finish school on Friday and that'll be his last chance to give it to this girl he fancies. He's going to work full-time at the golf club as a grounds-boy, and she's going to the Tech in Dublin after the summer holidays. She wants to train as a machinist, so she can go to England and work in a clothes factory.

I told him it's pointless chasing her if she's planning to emigrate. Mumbo thinks the opposite; if she finds out someone loves her, she might change her mind. Looking at Mumbo, I'd say it will make her more determined to leave. Anyway, I told him I'll definitely make a start on it tomorrow.

After lunch the deputy head teacher, who's in charge of the girls, came round to ask Welch if she can make a collection for Baldy's leaving present. He's retiring on Friday. Welch said in a loud voice, 'No! There is no question of my authorising a fond farewell for a man who has done so much to undermine my authority and to bring the school into disrepute!' Baldy, of course, heard all this. The deputy head went scarlet with anger and embarrassment.

Dad and John-Joe Maguire are getting very friendly. They used to meet only in the evenings. Now they see each other during the day as well. They're forever sitting out on the back steps, smoking, and talking about books and politics and new ways for Dad to make money. Dad has decided not to rush ahead with the snooker hall idea. John-Joe says no one wants to be indoors bashing balls around while the weather is so hot and sunny. He thinks Dad should find a way to earn enough to keep us ticking over for the rest of the summer. Meanwhile, we can get on with doing up the stable at our leisure, ready to install the snooker tables when the bad weather starts in the autumn.

*　　*　　*

Mumbo was waiting outside school to remind me about the letter. I said he'd have to tell me who the girl was; I need to know what to say about her. Mumbo said he'd describe her, but I said that wasn't good enough. To write a love-letter I'd need to see her for myself, otherwise I wouldn't be able to put enough feeling into it. Eventually he said he'd point her out at breaktime, but he'd kill me if I told anyone else.

I asked him to tell me her name; I might know her already and could start on the letter right away. It turned out he doesn't know her name! He lives up the hill and doesn't know the names of girls who live in the village. He's asked the other fellows but they just take the mick out of him and say she's called Smelly Knickers. This didn't sound too hopeful, but Mumbo said she's the cleanest and best-looking girl in the school.

At breaktime we went out to the playground and looked though a hole in the fence. Mumbo's bum started wriggling with excitement. 'That's her,' he said. 'The one with the fair hair and the green skirt and the white sandshoes.' I had a look and nearly fell over with amazement. It's the very girl I fancy! The whole idea of Mumbo Quigley being in love with her is ridiculous. I told him he was a fool; I'd already got her marked out for myself. Mumbo got upset and said it wasn't fair; he's been in love with her for years and I've only just come across her in the last three weeks.

I thought about it for a minute, and realised it didn't matter about Mumbo sending her a letter; she'd ignore it once she knew who it was from. I also decided to make it so ridiculous that she'd have hysterics and think he was a complete eejit. Mumbo saw me smiling to myself and got into a rage and started kicking me, so I said I'd write the letter tomorrow, and he can give it to her on the way home. He said I'd better not be kidding; he wants time to hear back from her before we split up on Friday.

I went and asked Christie who she is. He had a look and said her name was Eileen and why did I want to know? I said I'd fallen in love with her. He nearly choked with laughing. When he could speak again, he said, 'For Christ's sake, give up that idea; she has a brother who'd have your balls poached and served on a slice of toast for his breakfast.' I asked him why her brother was so keen to protect her, and Christie said, 'Because she's special, that's why; she's the nicest girl in the village.' He wouldn't tell me any more about the brother; he says it's too good a joke to spoil.

I was going to spend the evening writing Mumbo's letter but I got interrupted. Christie's brother came round after he got home from work. He asked me out onto the terrace for a chat. He's heard I'm friendly with Andy. I said I will be, when he comes back from England. Christie's brother asked me when that will be. I said probably in a couple of weeks. He said, 'Shit, that'll be too late; it's my birthday next week and this mot has promised me a shag as a present.' She's going to let him put his handle in, right up to the maker's name, provided he gets hold of the readies beforehand. None of this made any sense to me. He asked me if I understood what he was getting at. I said no. 'Jesus,' he said. 'Am I dealing with a fucking ignoramus?' I told him I don't like swearing, especially when it's at me. He looked as if he was going to hit me but he changed his mind when I put my hand on his arm and gave it a good squeeze.

He gave me a sly look and said I was a powerful young bugger; maybe it was time I had a shag myself? I said maybe it was, except that I wasn't too sure what it meant. He said he'd start at the beginning and explain the whole thing to me. A shag is when you shove your jake up a mot's juicy tube and pummel your tool in and out. After a while your balls start sneezing, and squirt your penny's-worth of condensed milk up her cunt. This leaves you gasping with relief and completely fucked with exhaustion.

The trouble is, he says, that mots know they can catch an illness from a squirting prick. I said I knew that; my Dad has told me all about slip-it-up-us and gone-over-here. Christie's brother laughed and said the illness he was talking about is called morning sickness. When mots get it, they know they're pregnant. I was still puzzled. He said 'pregnant' means they're going to have a baby. I said I knew what pregnant meant, but what was it to do with jakes up mots?

Christie's brother got impatient and said he wanted to get to the point: a good shag. A good shag, he told me, is when a mot gets so desperate for jake that she doesn't give a shite about getting pregnant. This happens when you fill them up with gargle, and get them paralytic. You lay them onto the back seat of a car, tune the radio to the Top Twenty on Radio Luxemburg, slide your hand up their skirt, and work their cunt into a trembling frenzy with your fingers. 'Then,' he said, 'when you have them panting like a sweaty sheepdog, you slip their clothes off so there's nothing to get in the way. That's what I mean,' he said, 'by a good shag.'

I thanked him for his kindness in telling me all this, but he said it wasn't kindness; he was after me for a favour, and would I kindly belt up because he hadn't finished yet. His problem, said Christie's brother, is not getting hold of mots; he never has any trouble in that department. It's paying for the gargle and getting hold of a car that's the problem. By the time he gives Ellen the money for his keep, and buys his fags, and pays for a couple of rounds in Dolan's on a Friday, there's fuck all left but the price of the dance on a Saturday night. So, even when he manages to pick up a mot, the most he can hope for is that she's already downed a half-dozen Babychams at someone else's expense.

The trouble is, if they've had nothing off you to start with, and you haven't a car to impress them, they think they're doing you a favour by going outside for a grope. Then, as likely as not, you'll be surrounded by other mots with blokes trying to get up them, or fellows pissing against the wall, or people throwing up behind the nearest bush.

This puts the mot off, and keeps her on her guard. If you do manage to slip her a length, she's ready to jump off you the minute the kettle comes to the boil. That's another thing about not having a car; the mots will only do it against a wall, for fear of getting grass stains on the back of their skirts. This means they have the edge on you; they can pull away whenever they like. When you're in a car, on top of them, they can't.

He stopped for a moment to have a gloomy think about his problems, and I asked him where all this was leading. He said it was leading back to me being friendly with Andy, and the fact that Andy's dad can get hold of these things that make all the difference with mots.

If you've got one of these things on your jake, they don't have to worry about your juice swilling around in their baby-bags and making them pregnant. This means they'll let you go all the way with them; they know they don't need to push you off at the last minute. Better still, if you can get the loan of a car for the evening, you save yourself having to be satisfied with some gruesome mot who's so desperate she'll say yes to anything with a prick, a pair of boots, and a half-set of dentures. You can swan round and pick a good-looking one at your leisure. As soon as you say you have a car and a packet of the readies, they're all eager for it. Even quiet respectable mots, when they know it's safe, get into a raging sweat for the one-eyed trouser-snake, and thresh their bums up and down as good as a five-quid whore.

I asked him what he meant by a five-quid whore. He said they're the ones in Dublin who charge a lot of money but give you good value for it; they take you home and let you strip them off and spend the whole night in bed with them. You get the chance for as many shags as you can manage, and they'll do you a hand-job, or a mouth-job, and, if you want it, the finger-up-your-arse trick, which no ordinary mot will ever do. It costs a dollar extra but it's well worth it; your prick feels as if it's been struck by lightning.

They even try to make you forget you're paying for it. They tell you they're enjoying it themselves, and that your prick is the nearest thing to a cucumber they've ever had up them. It's as good as being in a car with a real mot, except for the matter of the five quid. The cheap whores, the ten and fifteen bob ones that do it in shop doorways, won't even take their knickers off; you have to do it up the leg, and as often as not the elastic scrapes your prick and makes it bleed. He said that was by no means the worst; the half-crown whores light up their fags and blow smoke in your face while you're shafting them.

Christie's brother could see I was getting restless. He said he'd get to the point in a minute, after he'd done a bit more explaining. This mot who's promised him a birthday shag is a virgin – that's a mot who's never had a dick up them. I said my Dad has told me something completely different. Christie's brother got cross and said I could take it from him, whatever I've been told. There's no plainer way of putting it; a virgin is a mot who's never been shagged. I tried to tell him about my conversation with his sister Ellen but he wasn't interested. He said she's gasping for it like the rest of them, but she's going the wrong way about getting it. She won't let a fellah touch her until she's married to him. There has to be a ring round her finger before she'll put her ring round a jake.

'Getting back to this birthday treat,' he said. 'This mot is scared shitless of getting pregnant. Also, she's teetotal, so there's no chance of lubricating her into a strong yearning for a Dr Dick's Meat Injection. She's only agreed to do it because it's my birthday.' I asked him what other presents he was getting, but he spat on the path and told me not to interrupt him with stupid questions.

'Now,' he said, 'this is where you come into the picture; I have to get hold of a packet of the proverbials.' Otherwise, this mot would freeze up on him. He'd end up getting her to grip a slit pig liver between her thighs and shafting that, instead of the real thing. This was only marginally better than persuading her to let him deliver cream to the chocolate factory. He asked me if I knew what this meant, and said it was just as well I didn't. It's illegal, as well as a mortal sin, but some mots would sooner let a fellow up the back stairs, than risk getting shagged and pregnant against their will.

I said I could ask Mrs Barrington straight out for a packet of the things he needs. I didn't mention I've already found out where they keep them. Christie's brother said no, that wasn't on. He wanted to get hold of them on the quiet. Could I not think of some excuse to go round there and have a rummage through the drawers while she wasn't watching? I said I didn't need an excuse to go round; I was already quite friendly with Mrs Barrington, and could call in any time I liked. Christie's brother gave a whistle and a moan and said I was a lucky young fucker and no doubt about it; he'd sell his soul to Oul Nick for the sake of five minutes chopper-hopping with that particular female.

I told him I'd rather he didn't make rude comments about Mrs Barrington; she's a very nice person and she and I are friends, so I don't want people thinking dirty thoughts about her.

'Jesus,' he said, 'you're a high and mighty little bastard when you get going!' He said he could tell me a few things about that same person; things that would make me sorry I was wasting my time treating her like a lady, when I could be enjoying myself instead, putting a tail between her legs. He asked me did I have a tail, at all, or had the doctor cut it off by mistake when I was born? I got angry and said it was no business of his. He gave me a jealous look and pulled a face and said it was as well not to put it up her; I'd soon be calling on the pox-doctor if I did. He put on a false smile and said he'd be interested to hear the gory details, man to man, if I ever do shag her. Is she a goer, and what sort of kisses does she go in for, and does she like a handful of fingers up the crack of her arse when she's on the job?

I nearly knocked his head off, but I stopped myself in time. I began to feel sorry for him. Christie's brother doesn't seem to have any interest in girls except getting his jake into their fannies. He doesn't seem to know anything about loving them, or liking them as friends, or sitting talking comfortably to them, or admiring the shape of their tummies, or the way their eyes sparkle when they laugh.

I asked him about this, and he gave a sarcastic laugh and said it was all right for me; I have the brains and the class to get away with it. He has no illusions about his chances of getting off with a decent bit of stuff. You need money and a good accent and clean clothes and a Christian Brother education and a father in the offices of a respectable firm. He has none of these advantages. He knows he's just a big lumpy lout, with no hope of getting anywhere. Life for him is the few short years between leaving school and getting stuck with a family. Three years at the most, he says, of drinking and shagging and a few laughs with the lads. Then he'll get some mot in the family way and have to settle for a council house in Ballyfermot and a dead-end job in some dirty old factory in the back streets of Dublin. He says I have no business criticising him for trying to enjoy himself, in the only way he knows how, and while he still has the freedom to do it.

I told him I was sorry, and I really meant it. He said it was all right, and shook hands with me; he knew I was a decent skin at the back of it all. I asked him what he meant about me having brains and class; I was only an ordinary boy from the slums of Mountjoy Square, and my dad doesn't even have a job to go to. He said he knows all about me, from his own dad, who was in the army with mine. My mam is a rich farmer's daughter and my dad used to be training to be a doctor in the army, until he took the blame for something someone else did. The other fellow didn't own up, and my dad wouldn't sneak on him, and so he had to resign.

Christie's brother said his dad managed to be friends with my dad, even though his dad was only a corporal, because my dad was a natural gentleman. He treated the ordinary soldiers as human beings, which was more than you could say for most of the officers. That's how he knew I had class, and he could see for himself that I had the brains and the good looks to get off with any mot I set my heart on, no matter how posh or la-di-da she was. He had to be satisfied with what he could get, and that was the long and the short of it.

This was all very interesting to me, especially about Mam and Dad. I've never thought about them like that before: where they came from and what they used to be before they got married and had me and my sisters. I thought we were just an ordinary family like all the other poor people in Dublin.

Christie's brother said he had to go, he was meeting a mot down the strand at eight o'clock and he wanted to have a wash and his supper first. He says if I could get hold of some of these jake things, without letting Mrs Barrington know, he'll be very grateful and he might be able to put a few things my way. Mots go round in twos, and always ask a fellow if he has a friend with him. This is so the other mot will have company, and not get jealous and squeal on them to their parents or their regular boyfriend.

The only trouble is, when mots go round in twosomes, one of them is always a cracker and the other a dog. If he was to fix me up, I'd have to have the dog-faced one. They're always grateful for a bit of interest and let you do practically anything you want. He says they're good to practise on; if you make a fool of yourself they won't tell anyone. The good-looking ones do; they know they won't have any trouble getting another fellow, so they enjoy telling everyone what a ham-fisted prick you turned out to be.

He also said he could get me a holiday job. The place he works at always takes on a couple of strong lads to help out for the summer. If I'm interested, he'll have a word with the foreman and say I'm his brother, but I'd have to be ready to start next Monday. I thanked him for both these offers, and explained that I was already booked up for the summer; I have to put all my energies into organising a gang and that doesn't leave any time for a job or girls. He said he couldn't see the point of it, himself; if the choice was up to him, he'd sooner have a few bob in his pocket and a mot on his arm, than be running round the woods playing cowboys and Indians. I said that was fair enough; he's a lot older than me, so he has different interests. He wasn't convinced; he says I'll be leaving school in a couple of weeks, so the summer won't be the usual school holiday. I should be looking for a job anyway, as soon as I break up, so what's the point of starting a gang?

When I told him it would be a normal school holiday, because I'm going to start at the Tech in Dublin in September, he got very bitter. He said he'd spent two years at Kevin Street himself, doing

228

technical drawing, and it hadn't made a blind bit of difference to his chances; he'd still ended up working in a filthy pigsty of a factory, for slave wages and fuck-all future. Then he suddenly got very depressed and went home for his supper.

When I went back inside, Dad asked me what Christie's brother wanted. I said he was just trying to be friendly. Dad warned me to be careful; fellows like that are usually up to no good, and he doesn't want to hear that I've started smoking and drinking and running round with a bad crowd. I said there was no chance of that.

Welch had to teach the middle boys, because Baldy didn't turn up. He told us to write a letter to a pen-pal in a foreign country. This gave me a chance to get on with Mumbo's love-letter. Welch said sourly that Baldy had presumably taken the day off as a foretaste of his imminent release from the rigours of the academic profession. Sculley took ages to write down Welch's remark. I had to keep repeating it for him and spelling out the words.

I put every kind of nonsense into Mumbo's letter, starting off with 'My Dearest Sweetest Darling True-love Eileen'. I wrote that I'd long worshipped her from afar; that the colour of her hair is like a field of waving corn, that her blue eyes remind me of stars twinkling in the vast depths of the Universe, and that her figure is shapely enough to make Doris Day and Jane Russell mad with jealousy. I stuck in loads of other things as well: how the sight of her makes my heart beat as loudly as a motorbike engine, how her laughter reminds me of the sound of bells tinkling in a summer breeze, and how her teeth are as shiny as pearls and her skin as smooth as sun-kissed tropical sand.

I finished up by saying that her knickers are as white as snow, and that the sight of them makes me desperate to slip my jake into her. Mumbo is one of the people who are always borrowing the opera-glasses from Christie, and he's forever saying this very thing about the girls. Later, I decided to cross out the bit about knickers. It sounded a bit rude and jokey, and I wanted her to think the letter was serious, even though it was coming from an idiot like Mumbo.

I was really pleased with the letter, and concentrating so hard on what I was doing, that I forgot all about being in school. At the very bottom I wrote, 'You are my one true everlasting desire, and the most gorgeous girl in the whole wide world.'

Just as I was about to sign it, I got a sudden cold feeling of danger. I put my pen down slowly and realised there was a deathly hush in the classroom. I looked up and Welch was standing in front of me, smiling down with a grin like the wolf in *Little Red Riding Hood*. He put his hand out for my jotter, and said he was all agog in anticipation of perusing my latest masterpiece.

I told him he couldn't have it; it was a private letter and no business of his. Welch said it was his business; I had no right to be composing private letters during school time. As far as he was concerned, my letter was school property. He tried to grab the jotter but I dodged back, tore the pages out, and ripped them into shreds. Welch looked annoyed for a minute, then he reached out and took Christie's and Sculley's jotters. They were sitting each side of me, as usual.

'Let us see,' he said, 'whether the muse has once again visited all three of you with a similar inspiration.' He looked in Christie's jotter. Christie hadn't written anything except a list of ideas for making money. Welch wasn't very pleased. Some of the ideas were to do with girls. He said he wanted to see Christie after school. The moment he looked at Sculley's jotter, Sculley sneaked.

'Please, sir, I never wrote that myself. I only copied it off Kelly!'

To my amazement, Welch didn't seem to believe him. For a moment or two, I thought I was going to get away with it. I might have known better with Welch. He was only using the letter as an excuse to make an exhibition of Sculley. He made Sculley come out in front of the class and stand in front of the blackboard. We all knew he wouldn't hit Sculley, because of his father being headmaster of the Tech in Dublin. Even so, Sculley started to blubber and gibber on about how 'Honest to God, sir, it wasn't me, it was Kelly, I swear it!'

Welch was having a great time. It's not often he gets the chance to torture fellows he can't hit. He told Sculley to shut up and stand straight, then handed him the letter and told him to read it out. Welch was hoping to make Sculley even more embarrassed, but Sculley couldn't do it. He was blubbering and sniffing so much no one could hear what he said. This ruined Welch's plan, so he grabbed the jotter off Sculley and began to read it out himself.

After clearing his throat and fiddling around straightening his tie, he started off, 'My Dearest Darling Sweetest True-Love Eileen . . .'

After a while, Welch stopped, and told Sculley to pick up the chalk and spell 'Universe' on the blackboard. Sculley said he couldn't, and Welch told him he had to try, or else. Sculley screwed his face up in desperation, stuck the tip of his tongue out, and wrote 'Unevers' on the board. Welch asked him if he'd be kind enough to have a go at 'jealousy' and 'engine' and 'gorgeous'. Sculley made a hash of them all, even though he'd only just been copying them down off me.

'I see,' said Welch. 'Upon reflection and further analysis, I am inclined to the belief that you are not, after all, the original author of this touching tribute to the fair sex.' He told Sculley to sit down and blow his nose, then walked over and stood in front of my desk. He gave me a long hard look, then put Sculley's jotter away in the cupboard in his little room.

At breaktime no one would speak to me, as if I was a leper or a sneak. Sculley stayed in school so I couldn't get at him, and even Mumbo ran off when I tried to talk to him. He said I was in dead trouble, and nobody wanted to get mixed up with me until it was over. After break people moved away from the desks beside mine, and left me marooned all on my own. At first I was worried, then I got irritable and thought, 'To Hell with them; Welch can't do me any harm, so what are they all worried about?' At lunch-break no one would speak to me.

In the afternoon, Welch said he was so taken with the poetic images of the morning's anonymous love-letter that he felt it merited a wider audience. As it was addressed to a member of the opposite sex, and contained many memorable similes and analogies in praise of their corporeal charms, he felt it only right and proper that the ladies, too, should enjoy the literary merits of the ardent author's impassioned prose.

He told Goolash O'Toole to go round to the girls' side of the school with a note to the teachers. He said it was a request that the girls be mustered in our playground five minutes before going home time. I felt sick in my stomach; I knew I was going to end up as a laughing-stock.

At five to three, sure enough, there was a big racket and a load of giggling outside. Welch got the girls organised on one side of the playground, and the boys on the other side. When we were all ready he made a speech.

A remarkable document, he said, of considerable literary merit, had come to his notice; a document, moreover, which appeared to have been not only divinely inspired, but divinely written as well, since none of his boys claimed authorship. In view of this fact, he said, it was clear that the document must be regarded as a miraculous manifestation, and one whose message he felt it incumbent upon himself to convey to the whole school, in order that all might share in attempting to probe its mysterious and obscure purpose.

All the girls put on pious-looking faces when he said this, thinking it was going to be a genuine miracle letter. One of the girls' teachers blessed herself and shouted out, 'God be praised!' The girls knelt down and put their hands together ready to listen. Welch was annoyed about this, and had to explain that he'd been speaking in a manner which is generally known as comic irony. One of the women teachers, who's very old, said this was no fit way to speak to Catholic children; if it was a comic he was going to read out, he had no business talking about it in religious terms. Welch glared at her and told the girls to get off their knees and pay attention.

Welch read the letter out slowly, stopping at the end of every line to give people a chance to laugh at what he was saying. Everyone was dead quiet at the beginning, but then one of the girls gave an astonished gasp as soon as he said, 'My dearest Sweetest Darling True-love Eileen.' The rest of them started whistling and jeering until Welch stopped them. I had a good idea who the girl was, and I felt desperately sorry for her. More sorry than for myself, in fact.

As he went through the letter, Welch started making comments about it, to show people that they could laugh again. After a while the playground sounded like the animals having a party at the zoo. Towards the end he stopped and made a big thing about having difficulty reading one of the lines; he said there was a lot of crossing out but he thought he could just make out the words 'snowy-white knickers' and how the sight of them made the author of the letter 'desperate to slip' something or other, he couldn't say what, into the object of his affection.

This bit sent the playground into hysterics, all except for the women teachers, who were yelling at the girls not to give any notice to such filthy remarks. The boys were whistling and yelling, 'Eileen! Eileen! Show us your snowy-white knickers!' The girls were even worse, because they're jealous of her for being different from the rest of them. They were saying disgusting things which I'd rather not remember. Welch stood looking very amused by the whole thing.

There was a sudden scuffle among the girls, and someone burst into tears and ran off out the gate. I was too embarrassed to turn round and look, but I knew it must be Eileen. It nearly broke my heart to think how horrible she must have felt, being made the victim of Welch's cruel sense of humour, especially when I knew he was only doing it to make a fool of me.

From what I've seen of her, she's a very pretty girl, always clean and well dressed, and with a nice straight way of walking. She doesn't slag around with her back stooped and scraping her shoes like the rest of them, and you never hear her shouting 'Eff off' when the fellows whistle at her.

Welch was so pleased with himself that when he finished he told us we could all go home, even Christie. I waited at the corner of the school wall until everyone else had gone, to save myself being annoyed by people. They all knew who wrote the letter, because Welch kept looking at me while he was reading it.

I got half-way home and came across a terrific fight going on just inside the gateway of the butcher's yard. A crowd of girls were attacking someone lying on the ground. Some boys from the Hill gang stood watching, yelling, 'Get them off, Eileen; get them off!' A pair of knickers and a sock came flying though the air. One of the Hill gang caught them and they all ran off. I realised what was happening and flew into a blind rage. I tore after them and grabbed the particular fellow so hard I ripped his shirt completely off him. The others turned back to help him. I lashed out with vicious kicks and wallops and put three of them in agony. They gave up and ran off again.

I picked up Eileen's things and ran back to the crowd of girls. They screamed at me to eff off and go for someone my own size. I was in such a temper I said I'd murder every one of them if they didn't get out of my way. I must have sounded really fierce because they ran off immediately. Eileen was sitting on the ground with her arms wrapped tightly round her body and her legs curled under her. Her clothes were in a filthy state from the cow-shit all over the floor of the yard.

She had her head down and her hair was stuck to her face with the tears she was crying. I knelt down close to her and asked her softly if she'd like to borrow my hanky. She shook her head, which was just as well because I hadn't got one. I said, 'Please, Eileen, I'm sorry.' Her shoulders started shaking and big sobs came from her. I didn't know what to do, so I tried to give her a hug. She put her hand on my chest and pushed me away; not roughly, but just enough to make me stop. I crouched in front of her for a minute and eventually she gave a big sniff and looked straight at me, even though she must have known she looked terrible.

She asked me if I was the fellow who'd written the letter. I said yes, I was, and tried not to cry when I saw the look of pain and sorrow in her face. 'But why?' she said, in a sad quiet voice. 'Why? What harm have I ever done you? What harm have I ever done anybody?'

I felt utterly loathsome, and burst into tears myself. I seem to bring nothing but sadness to girls when I have anything to do with them. Eileen reached out and took her clothes gently from my hand, and put them in her schoolbag. She suddenly noticed something behind me, and her expression went frightened. 'No!' she shouted. 'No!'

I whirled round and tried to jump up but I slipped onto my back on the cow-shit. Jeremy Lynch was right behind me, with a big stick raised over his head ready to hit me. His face was quiet and deadly with anger. Eileen said 'No' again, and stood up, holding her skirt tight around her legs.

Then she did an amazingly kind and forgiving thing. She put her hand out for me to hold, and helped me to get up without slipping again. I felt so unworthy of her that I let go the moment I was up. She gave me a hurt puzzled look, so I said thank you and told her I didn't deserve her being nice to me after I'd caused her so much misery.

She shook her head in a way I didn't understand and walked over to Jeremy. She put her hand up, took the stick away from him and threw it behind the gate. She turned him round, put her hand on his arm and led him off out of the yard. Lynch looked back at me just before they disappeared, and gave me a terrible look of hate.

As soon as I got to the terrace I called on Christie to ask him about Lynch and Eileen. He sent a message out to say he was too busy to talk to me. I went home and rinsed my clothes and put on some others that weren't so dirty. I got Dad's missal out and read some prayers, to make myself feel better. Then I said a whole rosary in penance for upsetting Eileen. I was going to say another one but Dad called out to say that Malone was in the garden looking for me. Dad is clearing the sheds looking for bits of wood. He's busy making something out of a tea-chest and two old bicycle wheels he's found.

Malone told me I'm a stupid shit with no sense whatever. The whole village has heard about my letter to Eileen, and Lynch is determined to make up for the embarrassment and shame she's had to put up with. I asked him what the hell it has to do with Lynch. Malone said it has quite a lot; Eileen is Lynch's sister. I looked at him in utter amazement and said I just couldn't believe it. Malone said, 'Why not?' I said, 'Lynch is a dirty little bugger who spends all his time down the dump, whereas Eileen is a nice-looking girl who always wears clean clothes and looks as if she comes from a decent family.'

Malone said this is typical of me; I'm always jumping to conclusions. Lynch may be a dirty little bugger to look at, but behind it all he's a shrewd fellow with a well-organised racket and a powerful gang who always do what he says; by the time he's grown up he'll have enough experience to run a proper business.

Malone had a message from Lynch; he wants to meet me to discuss what I'm going to do about restoring Eileen's honour and paying back the people who attacked her. I was surprised by the wording of the message, and asked Malone if Lynch had actually said 'restoring Eileen's honour'? Malone looked disgusted and said I'm not the only person who reads books; Lynch has a huge collection from the dump, and he makes good use of them.

Malone said he'd come with me to see Lynch. It's after school tomorrow, in the boat-house at the dump. I asked him if I was going to be beaten up and he said no; Lynch never attacks people at official meetings. He will beat me up some other time, though.

I went to bed early and spent most of the night thinking about what Malone said. He's right; I am a stupid shit, but not all the time.

Dad stayed up late again, playing chess with John-Joe Maguire in the front room. They started the game on Tuesday and have been coming back to it ever since, whenever they're not working. Dad says John-Joe has a good brain under his hat. The thing Dad's making is something to do with them going into business together.

When I got up Dad and John-Joe were asleep in their chairs in the front room. They still haven't finished the chess game. Neither of them will give in. The ashtrays were piled high with Dad's butts. John-Joe smokes a pipe.

I was quietly making tea when Christie crept down the front steps. I'm to stay away from him in school; he doesn't want to get involved in my troubles. Writing that stupid letter and making a fool of Eileen is the worst thing I could have done. Lynch is very proud of Eileen and slaughters anyone who bothers her. I told Christie I was truly sorry about it, and that I'd no idea who she was. He says I'm not likely to forget, now I do know; Lynch will make my life a misery.

I called in to see Christie's sister Ellen on the way to school. His younger sisters were coming out. They ignored me when I said hallo. Even Ellen was a bit snotty with me. She asked me what I wanted, in a very cold way. I told her Dad and I are desperate for some clean shirts and trunks. She said she hopes I don't expect her to get them snowy white. I went red, and she said she wasn't very happy about the rumour she's heard. I asked her what rumour. She said the one about my interest in women's underwear.

I felt like saying it was nothing compared to what Christie's up to, selling her knickers to the man in the newspaper shop. Luckily I remembered what Malone said, and kept my mouth shut before I caused any more trouble. Maybe there's hope for me. Instead, I told her it was all to do with a letter I'd written for someone else. I was having to take the blame, after being caught with it.

Ellen relaxed a bit when I told her this, and winked at me, and said the letter was pretty hot stuff, from what she'd heard. She said I was a cheeky young devil. She asked me if I had a girlfriend and I said no; I wasn't all that struck on girls at the moment. She came over and kissed me on the cheek and said it was a pity I wasn't a bit older; she wouldn't mind showing me a thing or two herself. I asked her what sort of things. She laughed and said, 'Aha; that would be telling!'

I went home and got some washing to give her and then went to school. There was a horrible atmosphere and no one spoke to me except Welch. Even that was only to make a sarcastic remark about yesterday. At breaktime I was worried that people would be jeering Eileen in the playground but no one did. I suppose Lynch must have put the fear of God into everyone. She was on her own in the playground, the same as me. Lynch sent one of his men over to make sure I'd got the message about going down to the boat-yard after school.

At lunchtime I went out in the road and stood outside the Girls' gate, hoping to attract Eileen's attention so I could explain everything to her. She was sitting on her own on the log-pile at the side of the girls' bicycle shed. She was writing in a jotter and didn't notice me. Another girl yelled over at her, 'Hey! Your fellah's lookin' for yeh!' She must have thought they were trying to annoy her, because she didn't look up. Then a teacher noticed me and told me to go away or she'd report me to Mr Welch, so that was that.

After lunch Welch gave a fellow called Barney a blow on the side of his head with his fist. Blood came trickling out from the inside of Barney's ear and he was in agony. Welch sent him to the district nurse but told him to remember to say he'd fallen over and hit his head on the ground. Welch looked worried, even though he was laughing and rubbing his hands together in a jolly sort of way.

After school I went round to Malone's shed. He made me a drink of tea in an old can, to steady my nerves. When I got to the bottom of the can there were bits of baked beans still in it. I spat the last mouthful all over Malone's bench, and had to dry his tools with a rag. I told him I'm not bothered what happens to me; it's what's already happened to Eileen that's upsetting me. He said I should forget it; girls are just stupid bitches and not worth worrying over. I said he was wrong; Eileen is very nice, and so is Andy's mother, and Ellen in a sort of a way.

Malone said I should watch out for those two women; one of them will do it with anyone and the other will do it with no one. He says he knows this from personal experience. Mrs Barrington came round to get Andy's bicycle fixed last week and got some oil on her skirt. Malone told her to rub it off and gave her a rag with a drop of petrol on it. She said, 'Excuse me, I hope you don't mind,' and took her skirt off. Right in front of him, in the shed! That's what he says, anyway. She had nothing on underneath it except her knickers – no petticoat or stockings.

Malone said he knew straight away what she was after. He locked the door and deliberately put an oily mark on her knickers to give her an excuse to take *them* off. 'And did she?' I asked him. My heart was pounding with excitement and disgust. Malone said she was just about to, but his granny stuck her head out the back door and told him to go to the shop for some parsnips and an ounce of shag.

I don't know whether to believe this story; Malone could have made it up just for a joke, or else he could be boasting. He showed me the very rag Mrs Barrington used to clean her skirt. I sniffed it to see if I could recognise her perfume but the smell of oil and petrol made me choke.

Four of Lynch's gang were waiting for us at the top of the lane leading into the dump. They walked behind us to make sure we couldn't escape. There were four more waiting outside the boat-shed. They didn't want to let Malone in at first, but Lynch called out that he was invited as a witness. It was quite dim inside the boat-shed, even with the big holes in the roof where the windows used to be. Lynch was sitting in an old armchair in front of a coke fire burning in a bucket with lots of holes in it.

Lynch nodded at me but didn't speak. He waved to Malone to come and sit in a big hairy armchair beside him. Two of Lynch's fellows came up behind me and pushed me in front of Lynch. I was tensed up ready to bash them but Malone gave me a hard look and told me to be sensible. He reminded me that officially invited visitors are never harmed providing they don't try to get tough. I took some deep breaths to relax myself, and waited to see what would happen.

Lynch took out a packet of cigarettes and offered me one. I said, 'Thank you, I don't smoke', so he and Malone lit up. They puffed away quietly for a few minutes, then Lynch spoke to me for the first time. Well, he asked, what had I got to say? I said I was very sorry for everything that had happened. Lynch asked me to tell him exactly what I was sorry about. I said I was sorry for the shame I'd brought to Eileen and the fact that she'd been attacked. Lynch said there was a bit more to it than that; there was the shame I'd brought him, as Eileen's brother, and the discredit I'd brought on him, for having failed to protect her. There was also his reputation as a gang-leader; if people thought they could get away with making Eileen's life a misery, they'd begin to think they could get away with other things as well. Then there was the matter of revenge against the girls who'd pulled her clothes off, and the Hill gang who'd put them up to it. Finally, Welch had to be dealt with. Lynch said that was one of the biggest things on his mind. He could put up with any amount of pain from Welch, because he knew it spoiled the evil bastard's pleasure in whacking him. It was an entirely different thing when Welch made his sister look a fool. That had to be paid for. Normally, he said, he'd have sorted these things out for himself, including the matter of beating me to a pulp and making sure that everyone knew about it. There were three reasons why he was giving me a chance. The first reason was that I'd been fearless in saving Eileen, even if it was only from a bunch of girls and Hill-gangers. The second reason was that he had me marked down as a fellow who was brave and straight and clever, even if I was a bit headstrong and stupid at times. He himself, he said with a grin, was too clever to make an enemy of me, if he could help it. I'd be nothing but trouble to him for ever after. The third reason, he said, lighting up another fag, was that it was no use just going round beating up everyone who'd been involved in tormenting his sister – they'd still take the mickey out of her whenever they thought they could get away with it. What he wanted was a plan that would take the whole thing off Eileen, and put it on someone else.

I asked him if he had any ideas and he said yes, but the first thing was to deal with me. I had to be punished somehow: he couldn't beat me up himself, because Eileen had asked for mercy on my behalf, and, as he'd already explained, he didn't want me as a personal enemy. I had the choice of joining his gang and swearing to be loyal to him from now on, or I could take on a challenge. I said I'd go for the challenge, because I wanted to have a gang of my own as soon as possible. Lynch said I wouldn't like the challenge; it was dangerous and I was likely to suffer badly. I asked him to tell Eileen how grateful I am, for her being so kind and forgiving. He stopped me in the middle of this, to say it wasn't proper gang business. If I had anything to say to Eileen I'd have to say it to her personally.

The challenge is to deal single-handedly with the Hill gang, and teach them a lesson. Malone whistled when Lynch said this, and told me I was as good as dead. Their leader, Bull Bowman, is a huge powerful fellow who's sixteen, and has a horde of wily little shits to plan things for him. Lynch said it's fair enough if I get beaten up; I deserve it. If I don't, and beat them instead, I'll have paid part of my debt to him and Eileen. I'll also be a hero, which will be useful. It will make people think twice before they make any more comments to Eileen. He wants me to put the blame for the letter on the Hill gang, and also convince people that the letter was meant for someone else. He says he'll deal with Welch himself, and get the sisters of Dump gang members to deal with the girls who attacked Eileen.

When me and Malone were walking back up the boat-yard lane, one of Lynch's gang threw a bottle after us. It smashed on the road and showered us with splinters. I looked back and Lynch had him up against the wall, kicking him. This made me determined to succeed at the challenge. Lynch seems to a be straight man, with the same kind of honour as me.

I asked Malone where Lynch lives, and he said, 'Forget it, if you're thinking of going to see Eileen.' He said I should use my head; it would only embarrass her, because all the scruffs in the street would start shouting at the two of us. I said it was unusual to hear him being worried about a girl, and he said he wasn't; he was worried about me. If Lynch came home and found a row going on, he'd blame me, and I wouldn't be safe the way I was when I was a visitor in the boat-house. Malone said to remember that Lynch is still out to get me. I said he seems to be a very reasonable fellow. Malone says that's only because Lynch is using his head; he's certain I'll get murdered by the Hill gang and that'll save him doing it. If I don't get murdered, and somehow manage to bust the Hill gang, that'll also suit Lynch. In the meantime, I'll be fooling myself if I think Lynch is being friendly just for the sake of it. Malone is a shrewd thinker. I wish I knew whether he was lying about Mrs Barrington.

Dad showed me the thing he's been making. He's finished it, except for painting the outside. It's a cart made out of a tea-chest and two bicycle wheels, with a pram-handle screwed to the front to push it by. Inside the tea-chest there's another smaller one, and the space between them is packed with clean straw. Dad got the straw from John-Joe Maguire's horse, and he also got the idea from John-Joe Maguire. John-Joe sells hot water on the beach, for visitors who want to make tea. He told Dad they're always complaining about feeling boiling hot in the sun and wishing there was some ice-cream going. The nearest ice-cream is in the newspaper shop, and people can't be bothered to walk into the village to get it. Dad's going to fill the tea-chest cart with blocks of ice-cream and wafers and walk up and down the beach selling it.

I'm not happy about this idea. It doesn't seem a very manly job for Dad to be doing. I'd rather he was still a bus-driver.

Baldy Burke retired today. Everyone except Welch will miss him. He's a kindly man who likes children and did his best for them. Welch hates him. Baldy won't dress neatly, and he ignores all Welch's silly rules. For instance, Baldy has his lunch in the pub every day. Welch says this is a terrible example to the children. We don't think so at all; Baldy hears good jokes and interesting bits of news to tell the fellows during afternoon break.

Baldy isn't married, which is why he looks so scruffy. There's no one to look after him. He says teaching has been the one great love of his life, and all the children he's taught have been his family. He told us there's a famous English book about this sort of thing, called *Goodbye Mr Chips*, which he wishes he'd written himself.

There was a strange air of tension in school all morning. It wasn't just the end-of-school exam. Welch was nervous and irritable, and Baldy was quiet and absent-minded. We had our Irish and Arithmetic papers before break, and English and Catechism after. Welch spent the morning getting the registers up to date in his little room. He asked Baldy to keep an eye on us. We were quiet and well-behaved out of respect for Baldy's last day.

At lunchtime I got hold of Sculley. I told him Lynch and me have a plan to avenge Eileen. If he doesn't co-operate we'll hang him by his feet from a tree, with a pencil up his arse, and leave him to die from lead poisoning. I know from my encyclopaedias that it's only carbon in pencils, but Sculley doesn't. He's terrified.

I told him the following plan: at breaktime I'd pretend to beat him up in the playground, for saying he got the letter off me. He'd give in, screaming for mercy, and admit he wrote it. He'd say the Hill gang made him do it, because Bowman, their leader, fancies a certain girl in the village. They know Sculley is always writing things down, so they thought he'd be good at love-letters. By the time he got round to writing the letter, he'd forgotten the girl's name. In a panic, he wrote the letter to Eileen. She's the best-looking girl in the village, and he thought this would please Bowman. When Welch snatched the letter from him he was petrified, and told everyone it was me. He's to say he was less afraid of me than he is of the Hill gang; they threatened to pour boiling water down his wellingtons if he ratted on them.

The Hill gang won't know what to make of Sculley's false confession. They'll only hear bits of it, and by the time it gets back to Bowman it will be all garbled anyway. When they try to deny it, no one will believe them; it sounds just the sort of thing they'd be up to. Sculley is very unhappy. I've told him me and Lynch's gang will protect him until the danger blows over. I looked for Lynch to tell him the plan but he was in the toilets and said he couldn't be disturbed.

Whatever he was up to, it involved everyone except me. Lynch's fellows were going round collecting boys one by one, taking them in for a few minutes, then letting them go. I thought at first he might be making them swear an oath never to mention Eileen's knickers again, but Christie said it was nothing to do with that; it was all to do with Lynch's plan to get even with Welch. He wouldn't say any more about it.

Baldy asked the other teachers if they'd come to the pub with him at lunchtime, for a farewell gargle. The women got excited and giggly, and said they couldn't really, what would people think, etc. Baldy said he'd arranged with Mr Dolan to have the loan of his back parlour, and Mrs Dolan was laying on ham sandwiches and sherry followed by sponge cake and coffee. Welch put his foot down and said no; teachers had no business going off for a shindig at lunchtime, especially in a small village where they're looked up to as the moral custodians of the community.

Baldy's face went white with anger and he stormed off, shouting, 'Jesus! Let me out before I puke all over the floor!' The women teachers put their hands to their ears but by then it was too late. Welch told them the matter wouldn't pass unnoticed; the whole incident would be recorded and passed on in writing to the National School Inspectorate in Dublin.

Baldy came back from the pub looking very tired and quiet-faced. He looked even more untidy than usual, with blobs of mustard on his chin and bits of jam sponge-cake caught in the hairs of his woolly cardigan. He never so much as looked at Welch, and Welch didn't look at him.

At afternoon break I gave Sculley a couple of good wallops to get him crying, threw him on the ground, and sat on his chest bouncing up and down. A big gang of fellows stood round us listening while Sculley spouted the story about the Hill gang. When he'd finished, I twisted his arm, and shouted at him, 'So this letter was nothing to do with Eileen?' Sculley screamed and said, 'No; nothing at all!' I twisted a bit more, and said, 'And the filthy remarks about knickers and jakes; was that to do with Eileen?' Sculley kept screaming, and saying, 'No, no; it was all a mistake! The letter was for someone else!' I got up and let him go, and said I wanted to speak to the Hill gang fellows.

They tried to run into the school but people wouldn't let them. They said it was nothing to do with them, and swore they knew nothing about the letter. I recognised them as the ones that ran off with Eileen's clothes. I didn't feel guilty, even though I knew they were telling the truth.

I kicked them black and blue, and gave them a message for Bowman; I'd go half-way up the hill after school, and he was to come half-way down to meet me. If he didn't, everyone would know he's a coward and a shit-bag. They said I was stupid; Bowman doesn't even know me, so why did I want to give him an excuse to beat me up? I said Bowman had insulted my girlfriend, and I had to get my revenge on him.

Lynch found out about this later, and said I had no business telling people Eileen is my girlfriend. If I made a balls-up of the challenge it would bring more discredit on her, and ruin the good work I've done so far. I should have given Bowman a straight challenge and left it at that. Bowman is too thick to need a reason for a fight; he likes fighting for its own sake.

When we came in after break Welch was still in his little room sorting out papers. Someone had put a drawing on the board while we were out. It was a picture of Welch with no clothes on, riding his billiard cue like a witch's broom. There was an arrow pointing to the cue, saying, 'Welch's Jake'. No one knew whether to laugh, or what to do; we knew Welch would be furious and pick on some poor bastard to beat the shite out of.

Lynch was furious about the drawing. He said in a loud whisper, 'Whoever the stupid fucker is who drew that – wipe it off!' Everyone said it wasn't them. Lynch said he didn't give a fuck who it was; someone was to get rid of it, and quick. Still no one moved. Lynch had to go to the board himself. Welch came out and caught him. He took one look at the board, one look at Lynch, and lashed out with his hand. The blow knocked Lynch to the ground. He was so dizzy he could hardly get up. 'Right!.' said Welch, 'That's it, Lynch; clear your desk and leave. You're expelled!'

There was a terrific gasp around the room. That's the worst thing that can happen to a fellow, especially on the last day of school. Lynch staggered over to his desk in a daze, sat down, opened the lid, and started to get his books out. Welch rushed over and slammed the lid down on his wrists. Lynch gave a terrible roar of agony, but before he could pull his hands out, Welch hopped up sideways and sat on the lid, trapping him. 'Right, Lynch,' he said; 'before you go, I want an apology for that filthy drawing!' Lynch put his head down, squeezed his face up tight to relieve the pain, and shouted at Welch that he could stuff his fucking cue up his fucking arse. Welch went berserk, and bounced up and down on the lid of Lynch's desk, mangling Lynch's wrists.

At that moment, Baldy strolled over to Welch's blackboard and very carefully signed his name beside the drawing: Francis W. Burke. Then he looked straight at Welch and said, 'Well? What are you going to do about that?' Welch stopped bouncing on Lynch's wrists and stared at Baldy with his mouth open, too shocked to speak. Lynch leaned forward and sank his teeth into Welch's leg, just above the knee. Welch gave a high-pitched squeal of pain and tried to jump off the desk. Lynch wouldn't let go. Welch grabbed both his ears and twisted them till they nearly split. Lynch let go of his leg, and Welch jumped off the desk. Lynch ran out the door and down the playground into the toilets. Welch grabbed his stick and ran after him, yelling like a maniac.

The next thing we heard was a terrible scream from Welch, and then a series of muffled roars. Everyone rushed into the playground. Welch came staggering out of the toilets. He had a bucket over his head, and was covered from head to foot in a slimy mixture of shit, and piss, and dirty toilet-paper, and cigarette butts, and great glistening gobs of spit. Lynch was behind him struggling to keep the bucket on his head. Welch whirled round and managed to knock Lynch over. He shook the bucket off and put his hands to his face, screaming that he was blinded and suffocating. No one made a move to help him. After a minute Baldy walked down the yard and wiped Welch's face with his handkerchief.

We all thought Baldy had gone soft, and then he said to Welch, in a quiet, menacing voice, 'I wanted you to be able to see this, Mr Welch, sir.' He swung back his arm and gave Welch a tremendous wallop in the mouth. Welch's lips split and the blood spurted down his chin, mixed with the shit and piss. Baldy turned to us and said, 'I'm sorry it had to end this way. Goodbye, boys, I shall miss you.' He walked out through the gate and that was the last everyone saw of him. We were all too shocked to move, except Sculley, who dashed over to Welch and led him into the school. The rest of us decided to go home. There didn't seem to be anything else to do. My only regret is that Lynch didn't let me add a contribution to the bucket.

I was at home telling Dad what happened, when there was a knock on the basement door. It was Christie's youngest sister, Rosemary. She said someone wanted to see me in the bus shelter at the top of the terrace. I asked her if it was someone from the Hill gang, with a message from Bowman. She said no, and ran off up the basement steps.

I rolled my socks down, wrapped two thick magazines round my legs, and pulled my socks back up to hold them tight. Then I stuffed a thin pillow down the front of my trousers, and put on two extra pullovers and Dad's leather motorcycle gloves. The gloves were in case Bowman had a knife, so I could grab it without getting my fingers sliced off. I knew I looked ridiculous, but it was better than being kicked to death.

It was Eileen in the bus shelter. Jeremy had told her about the challenge. She didn't want me to do it. She said she'd rather put up with people laughing at her, than have me risking my life to stop them. Anyway, the whole thing will have been forgotten in a week or two, so what's the point? I told her it wasn't that simple. I'd already challenged Bowman, and I couldn't back out, because I'd told Bowman's men that the fight was to avenge my girlfriend's honour.

I expected her to be impressed. Instead, she called me a fool. She wasn't anybody's girlfriend, and she didn't want to be, from what she knew about it. I said I was sorry but I couldn't waste any more time arguing about it. After this I'm not going to have any more to do with girls.

I ran off in a temper and she called me back. She wanted to give me something. I said I didn't want any more advice. She said it wasn't advice; it was a present to say 'thank-you' and to keep me safe in the fight. It was a white hanky, very clean and nicely folded, with the initial 'S' in the corner. She said it had been blessed by a bishop at Croagh Patrick, years ago, when her mother went on a pilgrimage. I asked her who the 'S' stood for. It was for Sally, her mother's name, but the hanky was hers now, because her mother is dead. That made it very precious and valuable to her, and that was why she was giving it to me. Then she kissed me on the cheek. I was so moved I nearly cried. I reminded myself I was about to be a hero and ran off to fight Bowman.

Malone and a crowd of fellows were waiting for me at the post office. As we walked up the hill, Malone asked me if I had a plan? I said yes; to beat Hell out of Bowman, so he'd be afraid to touch me ever again. Malone said this was completely the wrong approach; my best bet was to let Bowman beat me. That way, the matter would be over and done with. I'd have had a go, and no one would think badly of me for failing, because no one has ever beaten Bowman. Furthermore, Bowman would leave me alone after that, because he wouldn't have lost status. If I did manage to beat him, I'd never have any peace. He'd still have his gang, and he'd be desperate to get even.

I said I could take over the gang, once I'd beaten Bowman. Malone snorted and spat and said a gang has to be based in the area where a fellow lives. Did I really fancy walking up the hill every day, into strange territory, and trying to control a gang whose ex-leader would be plotting to overthrow me? I wouldn't be able to trust anyone, for fear of them turning on me and handing me over to Bowman.

I got into a right sweat, trying to work out the best thing to do. My instinct was to smash Bowman, but I could see the sense of what Malone was saying. I asked him if it would be any good going for a draw. Malone said no; Bowman would feel he was in a dodgy position. He has a reputation to keep up, of being unbeatable. A draw would be bad news.

Bowman was waiting for us, half-way up the hill, sitting on the wall of the Protestant school. The wall is about three feet high, and his gang were all in the playground behind him, keeping safe from the village fellows. They started yelling brave things at us, but none of them would come out.

Bowman gave me a shock. He's big, all right. In fact he's huge. No one warned me, though, how ugly he was. The spit image of a warthog. He had on a man's hat, and a huge stick balanced across his knees. His boots were well studded, and I didn't fancy a kick from them. I worked out a way to get him before he got me, then asked him what he'd say if I agreed not to attack him. I wanted to test out Malone's advice.

Bowman was very generous. He said if I knelt down and kissed his boots and begged for mercy, he'd let me off the fight. I could hardly understand him. He has a big thick tongue and rubbery lips, and speaks in an ignorant accent.

His gang had hysterics when he said about kissing his boots. Bowman asked me if Lynch was hiding behind me. I said no; he could see that he wasn't. Bowman said he meant in the back of my trousers, with his head up my arse for safety. One of Lynch's men said he'd report this. Lynch himself appeared out of the back of the crowd and said it had already been noted. He nodded at me to get on with the job. His face was a picture when I went over to the wall and knelt down in front of Bowman's dangling boots. Even Malone was astonished. So was Bowman. He thought he was in for an easy victory. Everyone booed and hissed at me.

I asked Bowman would he be satisfied if I begged for mercy? He said yes, he would be, but only for the moment. He couldn't say what he might feel like tomorrow, or even in five minutes' time. That was all I wanted to hear. I got hold of one of Bowman's boots in each hand, stood up, and heaved him backwards off the wall. I vaulted over the wall, grabbed the stick, and jammed it across Bowman's throat. He spat in my eyes, to blind me, and rolled me off him. The two of us jumped up at the same time. I wiped my eyes with my sleeve and saw Bowman lunging at me. He got me a blow right on the nose. I swung the stick with all my force and caught him on the leg. His leg broke and Bowman dropped like a bull in a slaughter-house. He didn't even moan; just lay there staring at me in terror.

There was a deathly silence. Everyone looked at me in amazement. I raised the stick, intending to break his other leg, but Malone jumped over the wall and grabbed it off me. 'Jesus!' he said. 'You've made your point; there's no need to kill him!' I was in a cold fury, which is how I always am in a fight. I only have one ambition; to make sure the other fellow never wants to try anything on me ever again. My nose was bleeding a bit. I wiped it with Eileen's hanky, before I realised what I was doing.

Lynch and Malone took me by the arms and marched me back down to the village. When we reached the crossroads they both looked at me, shook their heads, and said, 'Jesus!' at the same time. Lynch said I was a fucking terror when I got going. They told me to go home and calm down. I did, and lay on my bed staring at the ceiling until my nose stopped bleeding. Later I discovered I'd split the back of my trousers vaulting over the wall.

Dad is definitely starting his ice-cream business on the beach tomorrow. He says he knows he's going to hate it but we're flat broke. That's not counting the money in the bank in Dublin but Dad is determined not to touch it. He's hoping to fill the ice-cream cart with blocks from the newspaper shop, and get it on tick until such time as he has the money to repay the man. He asked me to come with him when he goes to the shop but I said no; as soon as the fellow saw me he'd remember me giving him the ju-jitsu kick and that'll ruin Dad's chances of getting anything on credit. He may not want to give it to him anyway.

I wonder what will happen about Bowman's leg? I suppose his father will come looking for me.

Dad got up in a terrible state of gloom. He wasn't looking forward to going round with the ice-cream cart; it's the most undignified depths to which he's ever been reduced. He had a feeling it was going to be one of the worst days of his life. It certainly started off that way. When he wheeled his cart round to the newspaper shop and asked for ice-cream on tick the man thought he was joking. Dad explained that he'd give him the money as soon as he'd sold the ice-cream. The man asked him what would happen if he didn't sell the ice-cream? Dad said it was simple; he'd bring it back. The man lost his temper with him. 'Bring it back, and it half-melted, after being wheeled round all day in a primitive wooden box!?' The only way he'd supply Dad with ice-cream, he said, was on the basis of cash in hand for goods supplied. Dad had no money, so he had to come home. He was desperate.

Christie's sister Ellen does all the housekeeping for the Sergeant's family. I went up and asked her if she could lend me some money. She said, 'Certainly; give us a kiss and I'll lend you tuppence!' I said I was serious, and she said, 'So am I.' When I told her I needed at least two pounds she said, 'Good God, you'll have to give me more than a kiss for that!' She still thought I was joking, so I had to explain about Dad and the ice-cream. She said to wait in the kitchen for a minute and she'd see what she could do.

She did manage to get two pounds for me. It was all in coins, with nothing bigger than a shilling, so I think it must have come out of a piggy bank. I was about to go when she grabbed me by the sleeve of my jersey and pulled me back. 'Come here,' she said, and kissed me right on the lips. Next thing I knew she threw her arms around me, gave me a big hug, and said she wished to God she was twenty years younger; she'd have had the trousers off me long ago. I went scarlet. Ellen put her hand up and stroked my face. She said I was lovely. That's a queer thing to say to a boy.

She asked if there was anything else she could do for me. I remembered my ripped trousers, and asked if she could sew them up for me. She told me to take them off and leave them with her. I said I couldn't; they were the only ones I had. She told me to take them off anyway, and went away to find a spare pair to lend me.

Guard O'Rooney came into the kitchen and found me waiting with only my shirt on. He said it was a fine thing to let the air get at the particulars; it was a well-known fact that oxygen is an essential nutrient, very conducive to the health of the organs of reproduction, and nowhere more so than in the case of a lad just sprouting into manhood.

Ellen came back and was annoyed with him. I changed into the pair she lent me. Guard O'Rooney said he hoped there was no question of him interrupting any impropriety; he was never a man to spoil another fellow's fun. On the other hand, he said, evidence was evidence, and he'd have to impound my trousers. He picked them up, jokingly, and Ellen yelled at him to get out. He skipped back into the barracks with Ellen chasing him, so I left.

I gave Ellen's money to Dad, and he asked me where I'd got it. I said it was from Major Longshott, for water and horse dung, and that I'd saved it up to buy new bits for my bike. He went off to the paper shop again, and this time he got on all right. He came back with twenty blocks of vanilla and a packet of wafers. I offered to go down the beach with him but he said no, not on any account; it was bad enough being reduced to wheeling a bloody tea-chest around, without having to involve his own innocent flesh and blood as well.

It was a beautiful day, with loads of excursion buses arriving at the top of the terrace and people streaming off them, looking forward to a day on the strand. I told Dad he should wait at the bus-stop and sell the ice-cream. He said he was too ashamed to do that; all our neighbours on the terrace would see him.

After Dad left, I went up to call for Christie. Ellen saw me from the front window and rushed to the front door to tell me not to say anything to Christie about the money she'd lent me; she'd got it out of one of Christie's secret hiding places. I asked her how she knew about it if it was secret. She laughed and said it wasn't the only one of Christie's secrets she knew about.

I thought of the hole in the bathroom ceiling and went scarlet again, the same as I did earlier. Ellen winked at me and said, 'Well may you blush!' I hope she was just codding me. Maybe there's other things Christie gets up to, that I don't know about, and she thinks I do. It was very embarrassing, anyway, to have Ellen hinting that I'm up to something, especially when I don't even know what she's thinking about.

Christie was too busy to come out. He's going to spend the weekend looking through his sisters' magazines for competitions he can enter. His brother took me into the garden and asked me if I'd thought any more about his offer of a job, in exchange for the anti-baby things. I said yes, I would like the job. It struck me that it would be a good thing to be out of the way for a while, in case Bowman's gang come looking for me. I also need money to pay Ellen back if Dad's ice-cream business doesn't work out. I didn't tell Christie's brother that.

He wants the things in time for his birthday next Friday. The mot who's going to let him shag her won't be available until Saturday, because that's when her parents go away, but he says he could strike lucky on Friday at the dance. One of the mots might open her legs for him if he makes a big thing about it being his birthday. He says he'll have to be careful; he's pretended it's his birthday so often that he'll get told to eff off if he tries it on a mot he's met before.

250

I'm to meet him on the seven-thirty bus on Monday morning, and go in to work with him. He'll introduce me to the foreman and after that it's up to me. I asked him if I should wear my decent clothes, and he went into hysterics; working in a factory is a filthy business, and I'd be mad if I do. It's just as well, because I haven't got any decent clothes anyway.

I'm going to have a problem keeping my side of the bargain, seeing that I'm not keen to steal from Mrs Barrington. I'll just have to try for the job and hope for the best. If the foreman takes me on I don't see how Christie's brother can get me the sack.

I went home and spent the rest of the day in the stable loft. I traced some more drawings of naked girls but I didn't do any cuts or blood or torture instruments. I drew Ellen's face on one of them and kissed it, which made me feel stupid but got my willie going, with a terrible throbbing sensation. Luckily it got too dark in the stable to keep looking at them, or I might have been tempted to rub my willie on the drawing of Ellen's bum. That wouldn't have been very nice. She's very kind to me, and would be disgusted if she knew I had thoughts like that about her.

I went into the house, and Dad had just arrived home. I asked him how he got on, and he said straight out, 'Today was an absolute bloody disaster.'

He asked me if there was a scrap of food for supper, and I had to say no. 'Right, then,' he said; 'If I can't sell the bloody stuff, at least we can eat it.' He brought in two blocks of vanilla ice-cream, and told me I could stuff myself; there were another ten blocks melting in the cart. My tummy thought it had died and gone to Heaven; a whole block of ice-cream for supper!

Dad explained the situation to me. He'd bought twenty blocks off the paper-man at two shillings each, which came to a total of forty shillings, which is two pounds. He'd sold ten blocks altogether, divided into ten portions each and sold as fourpenny wafers. This was forty pence per block, multiplied by ten, equal to four hundred pence, or thirty-three shillings and fourpence, or one pound, thirteen shillings and fourpence.

I asked him what was the point of this long explanation. He said that the point was, that no matter how you expressed it, or wriggled round the matter, or dolled it up in statistics and rigmarole, he had gone out with two pounds' worth of ice-cream and come home with one pound thirteen shillings and fourpence, plus half his stock, which was now melting away in the cart and would be leaking all over the basement by the morning.

So much, he said, for a day slaving in the hot sun, serving the scum of the earth and being polite to exactly the sort of gobshite he'd left Dublin to escape from.

After this there didn't seem much to say. Dad's legs were killing him, so he went to bed. I lay awake for ages thinking how I could earn a lot of money in a hurry. I don't know what I'm going to do about Ellen's two pounds. She'll be really upset if I can't give it back to her for ages. Thank God I've seen Christie's brother about that job. The other big worry in my mind is what the Hell I'm going to do about Mr Barrington's films.

We went to eight-thirty Mass this morning. Dad wanted to get down the beach early and have another go at his new business. He says he knows what went wrong yesterday; he overestimated the demand for ice-cream. If he'd only bought ten blocks to begin with, he'd have come out of the affair with a profit of thirteen shillings and fourpence, instead of a loss of six and eightpence. I reminded him that it was a loss of two pounds, six and eightpence, counting the money he owes me. He said I was confusing capital costs with current costs.

He says if he reduces his stock to a minimum, he can't lose; in fact he's certain to profit, providing people buy all the ice-cream he starts off with. Today he's going to buy only eight blocks to start with, sell them down the beach, then come back and get more if he runs out. He says he'll make a big killing if it's a nice day.

After he'd gone I was in a terrible mood. No matter what I thought of doing, it just didn't interest me. There was too much worry in my mind about the photographs in Dublin. I didn't dare go up to the newspaper shop and look at the headlines; I was too afraid of what I might see.

I started to tidy my bed but it was full of crumbs, the way I like it, so I didn't bother. Crumbs are supposed to be annoying but I like the feel of them. I stretch out with no clothes on and pretend I'm being tortured on the rack. It gives me a lovely strange feeling doing it. It's probably a sin but it's no worse than saints dressing up in sackcloth and ashes. It says in the catechism they did it to mortify their flesh and please God. I wonder if that's true? They might have been doing it just to get the same sort of thrill as I get from the crumbs.

Thinking about thrills made me think of Andy's mother, and I got a big urge to go round and see her. I had it in mind to make a confession about the films. There was a car parked in the lane opposite her gate, the same MG that I've seen before. I thought maybe it was Mr Barrington's but it turned out not to be.

Mrs Barrington was in the greenhouse place they call a conservatory. It's where they eat their breakfast. She was standing pouring tea into a cup for a man sitting in a chair. All she had on was a short nightie. The man was only wearing a towel, wrapped round his waist. When I said 'Hello' she looked round in surprise and forgot to stop pouring. The tea went into the man's lap. He yelled with pain and made it worse by spilling the cup into his lap.

He got into a fearful temper and shouted, 'Jesus Christ, Suzie, what are you trying to do. Boil it so it's easier to chew?' Then he asked me who the fuck I was, coming in and getting him half-gelded. I was surprised to hear someone with a swanky English accent using bad language, especially in front of Andy's mother.

I offered to make him apologise. She gave me a worried smile and shook her head. The man looked at me in astonishment and asked me again who the fuck I was. I said, 'Mrs Barrington's friend, and I don't like your language.' He jumped up in a fury and glared at me, then grabbed me by the hair and shoved me against the conservatory wall. He leaned right up against me, shouting, and began to bang my head against the wall. I brought my knee up between his legs with my utmost strength. His mouth fell open and his eyes went blank. I did it again with my other knee. His towel came off and he crumpled to the ground with hardly a sound.

A voice inside the house called out, 'Hey, you two; what's going on?' A fair-haired woman about the same age as Mrs Barrington appeared at the back door. She had a glass of something in her hand and no clothes on; not a stitch. She said, 'When are you coming back to bed?' then saw the man lying moaning on the ground. She laughed, and said, 'Jesus, Sue, what have you done? Sucked him dry?'

She laughed again and tossed her hair back, and said it was a bit selfish of Mrs Barrington; 'That's your third go; no wonder he's legless!' She noticed me and gave a startled giggle, and said, 'Who's this; the Reserves?' Mrs Barrington didn't answer, and the woman giggled again and said, 'Bags me first; it's my turn anyway!'

The man moaned and tried to get up but couldn't. Mrs Barrington bent down to help him. She had no knickers on under her nightie, so I looked away. She told the fair-haired woman to take his other arm, and they both tried to lift him but couldn't. They got him halfway up and had to let go. As he fell he clutched at the neck of Mrs Barrington's nightie and ripped it all the way down the front. Mrs Barrington asked me to help but I felt very awkward, with trying to avoid looking at their bare bodies.

The man let out a terrible groan and the fair-haired woman realised he was hurt and got scared. She said, 'What the Hell's going on? Who is this other bloke?' Mrs Barrington said she'd explain it all later. The woman gave me a frightened look, and let go of the man. She picked his towel off the ground, wrapped it round herself, and went back into the house.

I told Mrs Barrington it would be easier if I lifted the man on my own and she said, 'Yes, yes . . . of course,' in a blank tone of voice. I carried him into the house and put him sitting on the sofa. The other woman was filling her glass from a bottle on the sideboard. She jumped when I came in, dropped the bottle and glass on the floor, and ran into the bedroom. I went back to the patio.

Mrs Barrington was leaning back in a bamboo chair with her legs stretched out and her eyes shut. I sat down opposite her. She heard my chair creak and opened her eyes in fright. When she saw it was me she relaxed again, crossed her legs, and flicked the remains of her nightie over her breasts. She had long red scratches at the tops of her legs, like you get when you're picking blackberries.

She stared at me quietly for a moment, then leaned her head back with her eyes shut and said in a weary voice, 'Michael, are you any good at keeping a secret?'

I said I was, and that no one could get anything out of me if I didn't want them to. She stayed quiet for a while, then came over and knelt down in front of my chair. She looked up at me and said, 'Michael, I want you to listen to me.' I had to look up at the sky because her nightie had come open again. She put her hand up and pulled my head very gently forward so that she could

254

see my face. 'Michael,' she said, 'Michael, will you promise me
... promise me never to say anything to Andy ... about this
morning?'

The man came out of the house, dressed, and carrying a little
black leather suitcase. He went past us and limped off down the
garden with his free hand holding his stomach. When he got to
the gate he stopped and looked at Mrs Barrington with a really
mean expression. He was going to say something but I stood up
and gave him a cold stare. He slammed the gate behind him and
a few moments later we heard a car driving off.

I asked her who he was. She thought for a minute and said, 'Just
a friend.' I said he didn't seem much of a friend, the way he'd been
behaving. She burst into tears and ran into the house. I waited a
few minutes, thinking she'd gone to get a hanky, but she didn't
come back. I decided to go in and say I was sorry for upsetting
him, and would she like me to make her a cup of tea?

She was in the kitchen, standing at the sink rinsing dishes and
staring out into the garden as though she was blind. She'd put on
a dressing gown over her ripped nightie. I tried to tell her I was
sorry about what had happened but she said there was nothing
anyone could do; if you took chances you had to learn to take the
hurt as well. She said she wanted to finish tidying up the kitchen,
to get rid of the memory of anyone being there. I said I'd better
go and let her get on with it.

She said something very quietly, still staring out the window,
and I had to say 'Pardon?' because I didn't hear what it was. She
spoke again, and said, 'Don't, please don't.' I said, 'Don't what?'
She looked round at me with her eyes streaming and asked me to
stay for a while, until she felt better.

I stood for a minute not knowing what to say or do and she
asked me if I'd like a drink. I thought she meant milk or lemonade,
so I said yes. She picked up two of the glasses she'd been rinsing
at the sink and then stood still, clutching them to her chest. Then
she did an odd thing. She held her arms out straight and banged
the two glasses together. They broke into neat pieces and clattered
into the sink.

She went back into the lounge and got two more glasses, and
picked up the bottle the other woman had dropped. There wasn't
much left in it, so she got another one out of the sideboard. She
asked me whether I'd ever drunk whiskey. I said no, nor any other

alcohol, because my Dad hates it. She said 'Oh . . .' and asked me if I minded if she drank it. I said no, and that I wouldn't mind trying a bit myself, to see what it is my Dad is so dead against. She said that was a mature attitude, and the right way to come to personal decisions; try things out and see whether they suit you. Even with her eyes still wet from crying she was beautiful, like the lady in the Rob Roy film I saw at Easter.

She poured out a whole glass of whiskey for herself, and only a tiny bit for me. I was disappointed that she hadn't given me much, but she said it was just a sip to see if I liked it. I drank it off in one gulp the way cowboys do in films. I nearly died. The pain in my throat was something shocking, and I couldn't breathe. Mrs Barrington went to the sink and got me a glass of water to drink and stood behind me patting me hard on the back until I recovered.

She had a fit of giggles, then suddenly stopped and said 'Oh God . . .' in a long sad moan as though her heart was breaking. She burst out crying again and sat down, and said she was sorry; 'I'm very tired; I didn't get much sleep last night.' She put her hand to her mouth when she said this, and said 'Sorry' again. 'I shouldn't have put it like that.' She looked across the table at me for a minute through her tears, picked up the glass of whiskey and said, 'Here goes . . .'

I couldn't believe it. She drank the whole lot down in one go! I sat waiting for her to explode into coughing but she calmly filled the glass and did it again. Another whole glass! It wasn't a very big glass, but even so! She saw how astonished I was and said, 'It's easy once you get used to it.' I said, 'Could I learn to do that?' She said she hoped I never had to – it was better to be like my father.

She poured me a bit more and tipped some water from my other glass into it and said, 'Try that.' It tasted flat and smelt like wet turf but I drank it anyway, thinking it would be a good test in an initiation ceremony. When it was gone I felt a bit dizzy, and very warm in my throat and tummy, but not burned like the first time.

There was a smear of blood on my glass from where she'd cut herself breaking the other glasses. I licked it off carefully so she wouldn't notice and then moved the taste of it round the inside of my mouth with my tongue before swallowing it. It was salty, and swallowing it made me feel holy, like being at communion.

It gave me a queer feeling, knowing some of her fresh blood was inside me.

I said I'd like another drop, and Mrs Barrington poured it, half crying and half laughing and said, 'Steady on, this is definitely the last you're having!' She poured herself another glass-full but didn't drink it straight off; just stood up and said she must get on with clearing the kitchen and getting the broken glass out of the sink. Out of the blue, she said, 'My sister . . .' I was confused and looked at her blankly. She nodded at the bedroom and said, 'Caroline, my sister.' I said, 'Oh, I see,' and tried to stand up.

I nearly collapsed and had to grab hold of the table. Mrs Barrington put her hand to her mouth and started giggling again. 'God . . .' she said, 'you're in a worse state than I am!' She came over and put her glass on the table and gave me a hug. I could feel her chest wobbling against me. I hardly dared move in case I fell over. Mrs Barrington lowered me into my chair and went back to the sink. She started singing and humming. I said she sounded as if she was all right now. She shook her head and said no, it was only the whiskey, and that in a few minutes she'd be flat out.

My brain felt warm and brilliantly clever. I asked would she mind if I had a look round while she finished the kitchen and she said, 'No, not at all.' I went into her bedroom and it was a mess. The floor was covered in women's clothes and the sheets and pillows were everywhere. Mrs Barrington came in and stood swaying for a moment with her eyes shut. She said, 'Oh God . . .' and walked over to the bed, and then, 'If there's anything you want . . . food or anything . . . help yourself.' After this she collapsed onto the bed and went to sleep.

Her feet were sticking out over the edge, so I pulled her gently into the middle of the bed and put the fur blanket over her. The fair-haired woman was already asleep on the bed, still wrapped in the man's towel. A packet of the anti-baby things was lying on the floor and I picked it up. It was empty.

I thought of Christie's brother, and Mrs Barrington saying to help myself to anything I wanted. I took three packets out of the dressing table drawer and hid them down the leg of my wellingtons. I know it was a bit of a cheat, really, because they weren't what she meant. I can always give them back if I get out of doing the deal with Christie's brother.

The fair-haired woman woke and sat up, looking at me. For

something to say, I asked if she was really Mrs Barrington's sister. She said, in a very soft voice, 'Yes . . . yes, I suppose so . . .' She asked if she should be afraid of me, and I said, 'No, definitely not!' I told her I would never harm her, or let anyone else harm her. She said this was very comforting, indeed, and got out of bed and walked across the room to where the lavatory is. She unwrapped the towel and dropped it on the floor, then sat down and had a wee without closing the door. She wasn't in the least embarrassed. Neither was I, but I don't know why not. I should have been. I felt as if I was in a dream world, where nothing was unusual.

She came back and sat on the bed, naked, as though it was the most natural thing in the world, and asked me if I was staying. My mind wouldn't work, so I couldn't speak, but I felt quite relaxed. She lay down and snuggled under the cover beside Mrs Barrington, then lifted the edge of it to invite me in. I said, 'I can't; I've got my wellies on.' She gave me a sleepy look and said, 'Take them off . . .' After an enormous yawn, she shut her eyes, and seemed to fall asleep. This saved me having to explain about the smelly feet you get from wearing wellingtons. As I was leaving the room she sat up and asked me my name. 'Michael . . .' I said, 'Michael Kelly.' 'Will I see you again?' she said, putting her hand to her mouth to cover another yawn. I said I didn't know. 'So you're not staying?' I said no; I had to see how my Dad was getting on. She said that was a pity; it would have been nice to snuggle up in bed, all three of us, and see how we got on together.

Mrs Barrington woke up and said in a husky voice, 'Caro, leave the boy alone . . .' Her sister gave me a little smile and shrugged her shoulders and said, 'Oh well . . . another time, perhaps?' I left after this, but when I got home I thought about the situation, and cursed myself for being so stupid. I could have taken my wellingtons off and washed my feet in Mrs Barrington's bath.

Dad came home and interrupted my thinking. I asked him why he was home so early and he said, 'Another disastrous day, that's why!' I was too concerned with my own troubles to ask him what he meant. I kept thinking about Mrs Barrington's sister still curled up in bed, and wondering why I hadn't got in with her. I think I was afraid of making a fool of myself. Also, it was a bit disturbing to find that women like having men in bed with them. I thought they only did it reluctantly, and as a last resort, to trap men into getting married. I've never even met

Mrs Barrington's sister before today, and yet she invited me into bed with her, with no clothes on! I don't know what to make of the whole situation. I do know one thing: I'm going to stop wearing wellingtons straight away.

I asked Dad what he thought of two women in bed together. He said he didn't think anything. I said, 'What about if they'd got no clothes on?' He said he had no thoughts on that matter either. 'How about . . .' I said, 'how about if a fellow was to get into bed with the two women?' Dad said he had no interest in discussing an immoral fantasy usually associated with travelling salesmen. I tried one last question and asked him if it would be a sin for the fellow? 'A sin?' said Dad. 'A sin? Are you joking?! He'd spend an eternity in Hell, I'd imagine! And for what? I'll tell you what; a fleeting moment of what some men would call . . .' He stopped, and cleared his throat; 'Ahem . . . I was about to say "Heaven", but that would be blasphemous.'

An eternity in Hell for getting into bed with Mrs Barrington and her sister! Why? Before I could ask him, Dad went out to the garden and sat on the basement wall, rolling himself a cigarette. I followed him out, and watched him; he can do it with one hand. He lit up, and said if I had any intention of pursuing the previous conversation, to forget it. He only had one thing on his mind at that moment, and he wanted to tell me about it. The ice-cream business is a goner; absolutely ruined.

Dad had a great day to start with. He sold his first lot of ice-cream by two o'clock. He was walking back into the village to get more when a big Mercedes car drew up beside him. A bunch of fat, ugly children got out of it and demanded ice-cream. He told them he had none left. They started bawling and blubbering, and wouldn't go away.

Next thing Dad heard was the car door opening, then footsteps coming up behind him. He turned round, and who was it but the pig farmer! He recognised Dad immediately, and made a grab for him. Dad let go of the cart and ran off among the dunes, with money scattering in every direction from his jacket pockets.

His big worry was that the farmer could trace him through the cart. He had to leave it behind, and nothing is more certain than that someone will tell the farmer who it belongs to. He says if the farmer turns up on the terrace I'm not to answer the door under any circumstances. I said he'll probably smash the door down, which got Dad more worried than ever. He went and screwed planks across it, so it won't open at all, and put a pile of tea-chests full of his medical books against it as well, for good measure.

Later, when it got dark, he sneaked up to the barracks to see the Sergeant, and came home full of beans, with a big smile on his face. He says the crisis is over, due to quick thinking on the part of the Sergeant.

After Dad ran off, the pig farmer put his cart in the boot of his car and went straight to the barracks. He was cute enough to tell the Sergeant that he'd been down the strand for a drive, and seen this poor oul devil trudging along with the cart. He'd offered to take it into the village for him, and now he'd forgotten where the oul fellah had asked him to drop it off. It was somewhere fairly close, he was sure; if the Sergeant could just jog his memory, the job would be done and he'd be off home with the missus and kids.

The Sergeant was just as cute. He said he was very obliged to the farmer, but the 'poor oul devil', as he called him, was a notorious rogue whose real business was picking pockets and stealing stuff out of the backs of unlocked cars. The ice-cream cart was a complete spoof; the oul fellah used it to hide the stuff in, as fast as he nicked it. As to where he lived, the Sergeant said he'd give a pound or two to know that himself; all he could say was that the fellow came out from Dublin in a van, with the cart on board, on bank holidays and the odd Sunday here and there. When he wasn't in Kilmara, according to informed sources, he was to be found working the same racket in Bray, Skerries, Killiney . . . you name it, he'd been seen there. 'But,' said the Sergeant, 'I doubt if we'll see him out this way again for a while!'

The farmer asked the Sergeant why the oul fellah had let him drive off with the cart, if it was an essential part of his professional equipment? 'For God's sake,' said the Sergeant, 'take a look at yourself in the mirror! Aren't you the fine big figure of a man? The very spit of a plain-clothes detective superintendent, straight out from Dublin Castle, for the very purpose of arresting him! Sure no wonder he gave you the cart; it was better than letting you give him the handcuffs!' The pig farmer was so flattered by this he went off and never asked any more questions about Dad.

I went to bed asking myself a lot of questions about Mrs

Barrington. When the glow of the whiskey wore off I remembered a lot of things I'd rather have forgotten. It made me feel panicky and breathless and sick, the more I thought about it. I got my encyclopaedias out and read the E volume until I fell asleep.

I've been getting up early for over a week but there's no sign of Stella taking up swimming again. Maybe it's the weather. There's been a lot of rain recently. The only person I've seen is Mr O'Toole delivering the milk. He's not as noisy as he used to be, which is a pity in a way. I used to rely on him to wake me up. Now I have to use the alarm clock and Dad says he's fed up with the racket.

Mr O'Toole doesn't whistle any more, and he doesn't drive his cart along the terrace. He leaves it up at Christie's house and runs along the terrace dropping the bottles off. Then he rushes back collecting the empties and disappears. A lot of people suspect him of attacking Stella; he's always up at the crack of dawn and must have known about her going down the beach.

Mr O'Toole parking at the top of the terrace is handy for Christie's manure business with Major Longshott. The horse does its business in a neat pile in one place, instead of plopping it in lumps along the road.

I had a good scrub so I'd be neat and clean for my interview this morning. Christie's sister Ellen washed and ironed a shirt for me last night, and put some buttons on it. She also lent me a pair of the Sergeant's trousers. It's the first time I've ever worn long ones. I feel as if I've got curtains flapping round my legs.

I asked Ellen about my own trousers, that she's sewing up for me. O'Rooney still has them. He says they're evidence of impropriety, to be retained for nine months pending the possible outcome of the presumed offence. Ellen says O'Rooney never knows when a joke's worn thin.

I had to wear my wellingtons because I've got no shoes at the moment. I polished them with a bit of paper dipped in Dad's bottle of ink. When I tried to put them on, I couldn't get my foot into one of them. It turned out to be the anti-baby things I took from Mr Barrington's drawer. I'd forgotten all about them.

The packets stank to high Heaven. I put them under my mattress for the moment.

I got on the bus to wait for Christie's brother. After five minutes, the driver put out his fag, started the engine and took off, with no sign of him. I ran down the stairs in a panic, thinking I'd got the wrong bus. The driver slowed passing the gate of the sweet factory. I was just about to leap off when Christie's brother came flying out and jumped on the platform. He winked at me and said there was nothing like a quick shag first thing in the morning.

The rest of the way into Dublin he sat hunched up in a seat with his eyes shut, smoking and belching up phlegm. I wanted to talk about the job but he wasn't interested. He said he needed to get his strength back.

The place where I'm working is off Portland Row. The whole area stinks of cattle dung. It's the road the cattle dealers use. They drive herds of bullocks from the North Circular Road down to the quays, and load them onto ships going to England. Christie's brother says the bullocks are always running amok and savaging people. Sometimes they run into a shop and panic, and the place ends up wrecked. The drovers' trick is to dash in quick and pinch as much as they can while the shopkeeper is petrified with terror.

Christie's brother reckons the drovers send the bullocks mad deliberately. He's seen them lifting their tails and shoving bits of blackberry stalks up their bums. Only last week a priest got trampled and seriously injured trying to save a baby that got knocked over in the road in its pram. The mother was terrified by a mad bullock and let go of the handle. I asked Christie's brother if he saw it happening and he said yes. Then I asked him if he'd done anything brave and he said, 'Not fuckin' likely; I'm not paid to be a hero.' Typical.

They repair and service lorries in this place I'm working. The lorries come up from the big petrol works down at the North Wall docks. The spare parts for mending the lorries come over from England, packed in wooden boxes as big as garden sheds. There's another fellow my age who spends all his time dismantling the boxes. He has a tool that pulls the nails out. It's a clever gadget. Whoever invented it must have been quite pleased with themselves.

The box-dismantler's name is Damien de Lacey. It's a posh name, but the fellow himself is common and stupid-looking. He

263

has a cigarette going the whole time, and fancies himself as a singer. He bawls out Tommy Steele and Lonnie Donegan songs in an Elvis Presley voice. He wears his hair in a DA. He's forever combing it and eyeing himself in a little mirror he has in his wallet.

The men who fix the lorries work in gangs of six in a big building like the shed at the boat-yard. It's so high that the windows in the roof are never cleaned, so they keep the lights on all day.

The man I saw first is called Sidney. He's the foreman, a worried-looking little man with a red face and white hair and his breath stinking of whiskey. He said it was pointless giving me a proper interview; I'd only stay five minutes anyway, once I knew what the job was. This wasn't a very encouraging start, but he turned out to be right. It's no wonder they're always looking for fellows.

My job was to put grease into the lorries when the men finish repairing them. Sidney put me with a mechanic called Bat Casey, who tests the lorries before they're driven back to the owners. The first thing Casey did was ask me my name. The second thing he did was to grab the front of my trousers and give me a painful squeeze. 'Jesus!' he said. 'You're a well-hung young stud!' I was annoyed by this, which just made him worse. He started shouting to everyone that I was rigged like a rampant stallion, with balls as big as fucking coconuts.

I was given a barrel of grease, mounted on a trolley, with a tube coming out of it and a thing called a grease gun on the end of the tube. I had to go round the lorries finding grease nipples and shoot grease into them with this gun. Every now and again the grease would slow down, and I had to put more pressure into the barrel by pumping it. There's a pump affair on the top, like on a primus stove. Casey gave me a pair of greasy overalls and a big lump of rag to wipe off any grease that squeezed out around the nipples. In half an hour I was filthy, crawling around under the lorries and having to lie on the floor to reach the nipple things.

At half-past nine, Casey told me to go and start getting the tea ready for the lads, for their ten o'clock break. I said, 'Why should I?' He said, 'Because it's part of your fucking job!' I asked him who did it before I came and he said, 'Damien de-fucking-Lacey-drawers.' 'In that case,' I said, 'he can go on making it; I've no intention of doing it.' My trouble is, I can't

264

stand being anyone's servant. I get it from Dad. Casey got into a temper and said tea-making is the job of the youngest fellow in the plant, and would I kindly fucking get on with it.

I was sick and tired of the bad language by this time, so I ignored him and got on with the greasing. He came up behind me and gave me a sudden kick in the backside. I swung round meaning to give him a whack with the grease gun but he dodged away. 'By God,' he said, 'you'll be sorry for that – very fucking sorry.' He went off and shouted up at de Lacey, who was on top of a big box. 'Damien, drop your arse down out of the clouds and get that fucking tea-urn on the go.' De Lacey whinged at him that it was the new fucker's job, but Casey said I was busy finishing a rush job for him and couldn't be spared.

At tea-break I got even more sick of the bad language. It was nothing but talk about shagging women. The married men, who you'd think would have a bit of respect for them, were the worst. We were supposed to have ten minutes for our tea but Sidney never bothered us until twenty past ten. Even then, no one took any notice of him, and only got back to work at half-past. Sidney was nearly crying with anger and shame at the way they ignored him. I felt sorry for him. I was glad when the tea-break was over; I've never heard so much filth in all my life. It's no wonder Christie's brother is the way he is.

He did a disgusting thing. They were all jeering and laughing at him for saying he had it up a mot this morning, and he got into a stupid temper. 'All right, then,' he said, 'I'll fucking prove it!' He unbuttoned his flies and got his willie out, then pulled his foreskin back and said, 'There yez are – still gleamin' and steamin' with fuckin' love juice!' He went round shoving his willie in people's faces and telling them to smell it if they didn't believe him.

One of the men grabbed it and plunged it into his mug of tea. Everyone had a good laugh, except Christie's brother. He had to rush off to the toilets to cool himself down. The man finished his tea off and said it was as good as a mouthful of fanny: better, in fact, because he didn't have to spit the hairs out afterwards.

I went into the toilet to see if Christie's brother was all right. He said the fellows were such a bunch of bastards that he'd give me a warning; before the day was out they'd have my trousers off and the grease gun up my arse. He said it always happens; every time a new fellow joins the firm, he has to be initiated. He said I was lucky being a greaser; the worst thing is what they do to the boys who pump up the tyres. Once you'd had the air-line up you, it left you farting for a week and with desperate cramps in your guts.

I asked him what happened when he joined. He said he was a sweeper when he first came, going round with a big brush and a bucket of sawdust to dry up any oil that was spilt. The men put a gallon of oil in his bucket, mixed it up with the sawdust, and poured it over him from head to foot. He had to get into the degreasing tank to get the stuff off. The chemical in the tank took all the goodness out of his skin, and left him looking like a dried-up mud-patch, with cracks all over his body.

At lunchtime everyone went outside the factory to sit on the edge of the pavement and eat their sandwiches. All except Sidney; he stayed inside going round the lorries to check on how the fellows were getting on. He's so afraid of the men he never comes out of the office unless they're all outside.

I had no lunch with me, because I hadn't thought of it and anyway there was nothing in the house even if I had. The men insisted on giving me bits of their sandwiches and bites from their apples and oranges. I was nearly sick at the thought of eating food from other people's houses. Looking at the state of some of the fellows, I could just imagine what their wives and mothers must look like. I sat on the edge of the pavement with my feet over a sewer grating, and kept dropping bits down it when no one was looking. The men were amazed at how much food I got through, and nicknamed me 'Gutso'.

The factory across the road is a place where they make jam, with hundreds of girls all standing round peeling and chopping fruit and stirring it into big steam-boilers. When the lunch hooter went, dozens of the girls rushed out and sat down on the edge of the other pavement, opposite us. After that, of course, it was all dirty talk again, with fellows and girls yelling across the road to each other, and throwing rolled-up paper and butts of apples. Christie's brother told me the whole idea was to see up their skirts. He said some of them were shameless altogether; they'd pretend to be hit in the eye with a bit of orange peel and roll backwards onto the pavement with their legs in the air.

At two o'clock, Sidney came banging on the gate behind us, shouting at us to come in. No one took any notice, same as at tea-break, and he got very upset and red-faced. I took pity on him and wanted to go but Casey grabbed me and said they'd slaughter me if I broke ranks.

After lunch Sidney came creeping over to Casey to say that he'd been checking on one of the lorries in particular. The fellows repairing it were lying under it all morning, supposedly tightening up the bolts holding the axles to the springs. Sidney said he'd had a good look and none of the bolts were done up at all. He asked Casey what the fellahs were doing under there all this time. Casey said he couldn't say; it might be anything from mystic meditation to catatonic paralysis. Sidney said this was his whole point; there was no movement, and it's movement the men are paid for.

Casey grabbed Sidney, spun him round, put his hands on Sidney's shoulders and pretended to be shagging him the way dogs do. Sidney went scarlet and tried to get away but Casey had a fierce grip on him, hopping along behind him with his front waggling up against Sidney's bum. Sidney tripped over an air hose lying across the gangway. Casey fell down on top of him, still pretending to shag him. Sidney was screaming with rage and embarrassment. All the men left their lorries to look, cheering and booing at the top of their voices.

I wanted to rescue Sidney but something told me not to. The way the men were bellowing and shouting, you could tell they'd murder anyone who spoilt the fun. Sidney managed to roll out from under Casey and ran off into his office and slammed the door. Casey was in such hysterics he had to be helped up.

I asked Christie's brother how Casey and the men could get away with treating Sidney so badly, and not be sacked. 'Because,' he said, 'Sidney lives with his mother out at Donnycarney, and so do most of the lads who work here. If Sidney tried to sack anyone, they'd go round and terrorise him, and maybe give his mother a heart attack. Sidney only ever sacked one fellow, years ago, and had all the windows and headlights in his Austin Somerset car smashed, that very night. The fellow came asking for his job back the next morning, and Sidney had to give it to him.'

After the business with Sidney, I was too disgusted to be anywhere near Casey. I wheeled my grease-trolley to a lorry I knew he wasn't working on. After a while I heard him yelling for me, and the other fellows yelling like an echo. I ignored them and got right under the lorry where no one would notice me. I knew I was going to pack the job in.

I couldn't work with such a bunch of ignorant dirty-minded savages.

I was lying under the lorry, poking around with the grease gun, when I noticed it had gone dead quiet. Someone got a grip round my ankles and pulled me out. I tried to sit up and gave my forehead a ferocious bang on the bottom of the chassis. When I sat up Casey was squatted on his hunkers looking at me with a queer vicious smile. He let go my ankles and pulled out the grease gun from where I'd dropped it. Behind Casey, all the other men were standing grinning, like a crowd at the circus.

Something told me I was in for it. I decided to do the same as I did with Bull Bowman: go for Casey while he wasn't expecting it. The only difference was, I had no personal feelings against Bowman. In fact I was a bit sorry for him, being beaten up for something he didn't do. Casey was a different matter. I hated him from the minute we first met, and for the way he treats Sidney.

I put my hands on the floor, braced myself, then sprang up like a jack-in-the-box. Before Casey had a chance to get up I grabbed the cleaning rag out of my pocket, wrapped it round my knuckles, and belted him full strength in the mouth. He went over backwards with a terrible roar and bashed his head on the ground. I grabbed him by the hair, pulled him upright onto his knees, and took another swing at him. He couldn't believe it was happening, and stayed there paralysed while I took aim, his eyes bulging with disbelief. My second wallop got him in the nose, and he started choking on all the blood he was swallowing.

As soon as the rest of the men realised I was serious, they grabbed hold of me and pulled me away. Casey was doubled up on the floor, gasping for breath and spitting blood everywhere. Then he was sick. His lunch came up and spewed on the floor. The two fellows holding me relaxed their grip, saying, 'Jesus, Bat, are ye all right?' and other such useless comments. Anyone could see he wasn't all right.

I broke loose, gave Casey a tremendous kick in the guts, and darted off. The place went into an uproar. I shot along the main gangway, aiming for the front doors. One fellow managed to grab me. He slowed me enough to let others reach the sliding doors. They started pushing them shut. I gave the fellow holding me a wallop but he hung on to my overalls. I wriggled out of them and got going again.

I shot through the doors just as they closed. Someone grabbed my arm at the last second and I got my hand trapped. The doors shut on my thumb. I thought I was going to die with the pain. I nearly fainted on the spot. Casey stuck his head out the little gate in the door. This woke me up. I wrenched my hand out and never stopped running until I got to the Kilmara bus. There was one just pulling away. I jumped up on the platform and sat upstairs, tears of agony streaming down my face all the way home. I lost one of my wellingtons at the factory. It came off when I was struggling out of my overalls. It's a good thing I have strong skin on my feet, or I'd have been cut to ribbons running for the bus. The North Strand is littered with glass from broken stout bottles.

Dad was very understanding when I told him what happened, and said I'd done the best I could in the circumstances. He went out in the garden and found one of the slices of bread that Mrs Longshott throws out for the birds, poured boiling water onto it, and wrapped it round my thumb with a handkerchief. The rest of the evening I spent listening to records on Radio Luxemburg and trying to work out why I get into these situations. I hope I'm not growing into a vicious gangster.

I mentioned this to Dad and he said the world is composed of two sorts of people; the majority, who are passive and brainless, and the minority, who have energy and drive and make things happen. He says the trick is to harness the energy and drive, and use it for productive purposes. The pain in my thumb stopped me thinking deeply about this, but I was grateful to him for his efforts to cheer me up.

I couldn't sleep with the pain in my hand. The poultice came off in the night. When I looked at my thumb this morning I nearly fainted. It was totally black. My nail was swollen with blood and bulging off the end of my thumb. My whole hand was throbbing as if someone was hitting it with a hammer. Dad took me to the doctor as soon as he saw it.

The doctor turned out to be English. His name is Dr Jackson. A nice-looking girl answered the door, and said he was having his breakfast. The surgery didn't start till ten o'clock. She saw the look on my face, and said, 'Come in, anyway. I'll have a word with my father.'

I never thought of doctors having children. She asked us to

wait in the hall. It smelt of polish and medicine and was cool and peaceful. There was a grandfather clock at the end of the corridor. It was ticking in time with the throbbing in my thumb. I couldn't keep my mind off the pain. A dog came along the corridor and sniffed at me in a friendly manner. I thought it looked familiar but I was too distracted to place it.

Dr Jackson came out, wiping his mouth with a cloth, and said he'd be with us in a minute. He went across to the door marked 'Surgery'. We could hear him rattling bottles and drawers, then he called us in. He's tall and polite and handsome, like Cary Grant, but with an English accent. I was surprised by him. I thought doctors were always old, with white hair and spectacles.

Dad thanked him for seeing us, and apologised for breaking into his breakfast. The doctor said it was perfectly all right; what could he do for us? I showed him my thumb and he said, 'Ah, so you hit the wrong nail, eh?' I said no, and started to explain. Dad poked me to be quiet. The doctor took hold of my thumb and said it was a bad bash indeed; he'd have to relieve the pressure under the nail.

I had five minutes of the worst pain I've ever known. He got a thin knife with a sharp end on it, and chipped a hole in the middle of my nail. Just when I couldn't stand another second of it, he made one last twist with the knife and the throbbing blood rushed out. The relief was absolutely gorgeous. I even managed to smile at him. He smiled back, and said I was a plucky young man. Plucky must be an English word for brave.

A woman came in with a cup of tea for me. She screwed her forehead up and stared for a moment, then pointed a finger at me and said, in a quiet voice, 'Seagull . . .' I suddenly remembered where I'd seen the dog before.

She said to the doctor, 'This is the young man I met on Friday.' He said, 'Ah, yes; a great pity, that whole incident.' The woman turned out to be his wife. She's quite a pretty lady, although a bit old: about forty, I would say. She stood at the side of the desk with her arms folded, quite relaxed, and looking at me and Dad in an interested way. She had on a very nice white frock, with a pattern of little blue flowers on it.

The doctor bandaged my thumb. Dad asked him how much we owed. He looked at his wife, and she shook her head. Dad was determined to give them something. In the end they agreed to take five shillings, on the understanding it will cover me for any more visits in connection with the thumb. Dad was respectful and pleasant with the doctor. He explained later that he regards English doctors as a completely different proposition from the native breed of alcoholic pill-vendors.

On the way home I asked him where he got the five shillings to pay the doctor. He said he was desperate yesterday, after the disaster on Sunday. He went into the bank in Dublin and took out five pounds. It's to pay our business debts and see us through the rest of the week. We went shopping, and got chippolatas and black pudding and a bag of bacon off cuts and tea and sugar and brown bread and margarine. We prefer it to butter. You can fry stuff in it and still use it afterwards to spread on bread. Butter goes all black in the pan.

When we got home there was a letter addressed to me. Inside it, folded up in a page of jotter paper, were two five-pound notes. All it said on the paper was just one word – 'Thanks' – with no name or anything. I wondered if it was a mistake, but Dad said the name on the envelope was quite clear: Michael A. Kelly. He said it must be someone who knew me well, on account of knowing my middle initial. I remembered I'd written my full name and address, in block capitals, on the time-sheet at the lorry works. I guessed straight away the money must be from Sidney, the foreman.

When I told Dad he agreed with me. 'Dear God,' he said, 'dear God, that poor little man. What a life he must lead in that place . . .' He reached out his arms and gave me a hug, and said he wants me always to remember how lucky I am. Big, and strong, and with a good brain; a brain that will see me through any problems that life can throw at me. He said the worst thing in the world is to be small and weak, and at the mercy of ignorant bullying gobshites of all social classes.

I said I'd write to Sidney and say thanks. Dad said it would be better to ring him up. Casey might see my letter and make things worse for him. 'In fact,' said Dad, 'you'd better have a word with Christie's brother, and make sure he doesn't let on where you live. That's if he hasn't already; we don't want that Casey coming out here and causing trouble.'

We had a huge fry-up, with loads of meat and bread. The only thing that spoiled it was forgetting to buy eggs, which we could have had on fried bread. We both love fried eggs, especially the crinkly brown bits round the edge. We also forgot to get tomatoes. They're smashing fried in bacon fat.

When we'd stuffed ourselves we had a serious chat. Dad can't continue with the ice-cream business. The stable isn't ready as a snooker hall, but he can't think of anything else he'd rather do, so he's going to use the front room, until the stable's ready. While he was in Dublin yesterday, he went to the billiards place in Dame Street and did some measuring. We can fit a full-size table in the front room, and a bar-billiards table against the wall by the fireplace. You have to put money in the bar-billiards to get at the balls. After a while, a thing inside stops them coming out. Then you have to put more money in.

A fellow will come out from Dame Street once a week and empty it. He'll take two pounds, and Dad will get whatever's left over. You can't buy a bar-billiards table, only rent it. All the money for games on the snooker table will be Dad's completely, because he's buying it. Dad said, 'What do you think?' but I didn't answer him. I was still thinking about the doctor's house. I'd like to live in a house like that, and be respected by people. I asked Dad why we live in a mess, and what causes it, and whether we could change things so that Mam and my sisters will come back. He said it wasn't a good time for that sort of conversation; he wanted to get into Dublin and order the tables straight away.

We got the bus in to Nassau Street and walked down Grafton Street to College Green. A dwarf walked along in front of us. His trousers were too long for him. He had the end of each leg tied in a knot, with his feet inside. Dad said he probably hadn't any shoes. He was shouting at people for no reason, and singing songs in a loud hoarse voice. He stopped to cross the road at Mooney's. As we passed him I noticed he had only one eye. This upset me, but not as much as the next thing we saw. We were waiting at College Green to get across to Dame Street and heard a drunken bellowing going on. We looked round and saw a man staggering along the pavement. He was so drunk he had to hang onto the Trinity railings.

Dad glanced at him and said it was a great shame to see a fellow reduced to such a state. Although he doesn't drink himself, he's very charitable towards drunks. He says you never know what troubles might have driven them to that state.

The drunk caught Dad looking at him, and shouted, 'What are

ye staring at? Have yez never seen a fellah over the eight before?'
The minute I heard the voice I knew who it was: Baldy Burke.
I asked Dad to excuse me a minute, and went over to speak to
him. Baldy remembered me, and tried to brush dried sick off
his jacket.

He told me a very sad story. Welch sent a terrible report
about him to the Education Department, and took out a private
summons for assault. The Department agreed with Welch. All
Baldy's years of teaching are likely to go down the drain. They've
suspended his pension and his final salary payment. Now he's
waiting for the court case. If it goes against him, he'll have to
sell all his books and personal things, even the little Morris Minor
he uses to go touring at weekends. His landlady threw him out on
Sunday, because he's been stinking drunk since Friday. She won't
let him back in until he's sober.

He's sleeping in the Iveagh Hostel with the dossers and tramps.
He gave me a bit of advice; never get into a job where I have to
kow-tow to the Welches of this world. Sooner or later I'll crack up,
like him, and then the bastards will get me. I tried to give him one
of the five-pound notes Sidney sent me. He burst into tears and
said no; he'd only squander it.

Dad was waiting for me. I said goodbye to Baldy and told him
to write to me if he needs a witness in court to say what a good
teacher he was. This made him more upset than ever. He shouted
at me to go away and forget all about him. He said he was bad
news and he wanted to go to Hell on his own, without dragging
decent lads along with him.

At the billiard-table place it's very dark and poky. You'd never
believe it's the headquarters of a business that spreads over the
whole of Ireland. The man said there's hardly a pub or club in
Ireland that hasn't some of their stuff in it, and he wished to God
he could get it back. He laughed when he said this, but I didn't
get the joke. Maybe it wasn't one.

We arranged to buy a full-size slate table with big fat legs,
a second-hand cloth with a few tears that were stitched and
hardly noticeable, six cues of different lengths, chalk and spare
tips, French chalk for rubbing the cues when they get sweaty, a
short rest, a long rest and cue, a score-board, a triangle, a set of
billiard balls and a set of snooker balls. The balls are made from
ivory, which Dad says is elephants' teeth and tusks.

I wasn't very pleased when I heard this. It doesn't seem right to kill elephants for something so trivial as billiard balls. Dad didn't agree. God put the animals on earth for man's use; it says so in the Bible. I'm always amazed when Dad starts spouting things from the Bible. I think it's just a load of yarns, the same as stories about Irish heroes and leprechauns and magical happenings. Dad gets annoyed when I say this. The Bible is the indisputable Word of God, according to him. To me, it's no different from any other book of imaginative stories.

We also hired a bar-billiards table and the bits that go with it. Dad had to sign loads of papers. It took the fellow ages to add up the bill. Dad kept interrupting him with questions about looking after the equipment. We went to the bank to get out Nana's money, then back to Dame Street to hand it over. The man promised the tables will be delivered on Thursday of this week. Dad says he'll believe it when he sees them. The man says we should get in some slot-machines and pin-tables, and a juke-box if there's room. Fellows waiting for a game on the tables will spend their money, instead of jangling it in their pockets. He gave us the phone number of people who hire out slot-machines and juke-boxes. Dad got very excited; he says we could be on the brink of making a fortune.

Baldy was gone from the railings by the time we finished in Dame Street. Dad said this was a blessing. He would have felt obliged to help him in some way, and we've got enough troubles of our own at the moment.

When we got home we moved our beds and cooking things out of the front room, to make space for the billiard tables. They're not due until Thursday but Dad wants to prepare the floor. Billiard tables have to be absolutely level. They've got screws on the bottom of the legs to adjust them. Some of the stone slabs in the front room are cracked and too far gone to take any weight. Dad's going to take them up and fill the spaces with concrete.

O'Rooney came round while we were having our supper. He said he'd heard that Dad was an officer and a gentleman, and a scholar to boot. A scholar, moreover, reputed to be gifted with great insight. Insight, according to informed sources, that extended above and beyond just one or two individual classes of information. Dad began to look nervous. He can't cope with O'Rooney's antics.

The gist of the matter, according to O'Rooney, is that he wants to put in for his sergeant's stripes. Before he can do this, he has to surmount the Academic and Administrative Examinations. Would Billie, like a decent man, put him onto a few tips regarding the proper nourishment of the brain? Dad didn't follow this.

O'Rooney said he was talking about food and drink, the two substances used to build blood and muscle and bone. Was there a particular class of chow noted for its cerebral-constructing efficacy? 'Ah,' said Dad, 'I see,' and winked at me. Fish, he said, was the very thing O'Rooney needed. He asked him if he'd ever heard of Wodehouse? O'Rooney scratched his head for a minute and said yes, by God, he had; weren't they the little grey things you found crawling under bricks and bits of rotten wood in the garden? Dad had trouble keeping a straight face. He said this particular Wodehouse was a famous English author. O'Rooney said this was an amazing thing altogether. He'd heard that queer things went on across the water, right enough, but who'd have thought they could train an insect to write! It was a tribute to the British educational system, and that was a fact. Dad said this Wodehouse had a butler, Jeeves, said to be one of the brainiest men in England. This was attributed to the fact that his diet consists almost entirely of boiled haddock.

'Well,' said O'Rooney, 'would you listen to that, now! Haddock, of all things!' He said he'd get on to it straight away but there was one little point he needed to clear up first; was there any way of circumventing the stomach, in these matters? Dad stared at him blankly.

O'Rooney said he'd put it this way; chewing up bits of fish and swallowing them was one way of doing it, granted. But, said O'Rooney, tapping Dad on the knee, wasn't it the case that every molecule of the body would be clamouring for its fair share of the goodness being distributed by the belly? And what, he wanted to know, would be the proportion left over for the brain? It might be as little as one per cent, or as much as five, but certainly no more. He was no mathematician, but he'd stake five bob on that. What he wanted, he said, was a way of getting the goodness straight to his head, where it was most needed. Could he, for example, make up a poultice of mashed haddock and strap it to his forehead with a good strong lump of Elastoplast?

Dad looked at O'Rooney's head, and said he could visualise

great difficulty in getting the Elastoplast to adhere, on account of his remarkably thick and abundant hair.

O'Rooney said, 'True for you, sir'; it was a fact that he was well-endowed in the thatch department, and for this very reason he had to have his helmets specially made in the biggest size. When he finishes with them, he sends them to the St Francis' Veterinary Hostel in Gardiner Street. They use them as sleeping baskets for abandoned dogs. 'Have you ever thought,' said Dad, 'that the hair could be the root cause, no pun intended, of your mental malnourishment? That great bush on top of your head is probably sucking the goodness out of your brain, and leaving the organ crying out for proper sustenance.'

'What organ would that be?' asked O'Rooney. Dad explained that he was talking about O'Rooney's brain. 'Ah,' said O'Rooney, 'you had me baffled and banjaxed there for a minute.' He said he only knew of one item to which the term 'organ' was applied, and that item was nowhere near his skull. He was relieved to hear that the conversation hadn't taken a turn for the worse; dirty talk was the one thing he couldn't stomach, at his age.

John-Joe Maguire arrived for his chess game, and O'Rooney left. He nodded at me to come outside with him, and asked me if I'd lost anything recently. I couldn't think of anything, so I said no. O'Rooney said he wouldn't be asking, only a certain object turned up in the barracks following my recent visit. He wouldn't want me to be at a loss for it, supposing it was mine.

I hadn't a clue what he was talking about. That's the trouble with O'Rooney; you never know what he's talking about. Even when he's being serious, you wonder if he's joking, and when he's joking, you still get the feeling that there's something serious at the back of it.

Christie's sister Ellen says I ought to watch out for O'Rooney, because he's not as daft as he pretends to be. I laughed at her at the time, but I'm beginning to wonder if she might be right. It's odd that Ellen and Dad both have the same feeling about O'Rooney, and yet everyone else, including me, thinks he's a typical Irish bogtrotter.

The pain in my thumb woke me early. I mooched about in the stable loft until it was time to get up properly. Stella's bike is back in her garden. The police have finished examining it for clues. It's rusty and ruined, exactly like mine. She'll need Malone to clean and repair it.

I heard yapping in the lane, and opened the half-door for a peep out. Stella was coming down with her dog. It was pulling on the lead as usual. Instead of trying to hold it back, she was letting it drag her along. She was walking queerly, with her feet stumbling in all directions, like someone half asleep or drunk.

The dog darted into the archway for its usual shit. When the smell reached Stella she gave a loud moan and began to sway. I thought at first she was fainting. She put her hands against the wall to steady herself, and dropped her head between her shoulders as if her neck had broken. The next minute she was gasping and coughing, trying to be sick, but nothing came up. Her whole body heaved and strained with the effort. She tried to stand up straight but didn't seem to have enough strength. The dog got its lead tangled between her legs and made her lose her balance. She lurched forward and banged her forehead against the wall. I heard the crack of it, right across the lane.

She let out another long moan and staggered out of the archway, shaking her head as if she was in a dream. Her mouth was hanging open, and gurgling with pain. Spit and phlegm trickled down her chin. Her face was deathly white, except under her eyes. It was dark there, like someone had bruised her. Blood was seeping down her face, and dripping from the ends of her fingers, where she'd torn her nails by digging them into the wall to steady herself.

It was her eyes that scared me most. They were wide open, like a mad-woman, and staring blindly into space. She looked like a woman in one of those paintings you see in the backs of old prayer books, of the souls of the damned, condemned to suffer in Hell for all eternity.

Another spasm gripped her, and her eyes screwed shut with the pain. She clutched her stomach and leaned forward, retching as if her body would burst. I was frightened to watch any more, and too scared to get involved. I crept away from the loft door, down the stairs, and back into bed in the house. I've never seen anyone so sick and terrified and lonely. I wish I'd had the courage to help her. I just couldn't, that's all. It was still only six o'clock so I went back to sleep.

Dad got up early to go to the barracks. He used the Sergeant's phone to ring the people who hire out slot-machines. They turned out to be foreigners, living in Dublin. They're coming to inspect the place tomorrow, to see how many machines they can fit in.

We had the radio on at breakfast, tuned to AFN. They play the latest American records. I heard a good one called 'Hound Dog', by a fellow called Elvis Presley. I'm going to buy it next time I'm in Dublin. Dad didn't like it. He said it sounded like a hound dog was doing the singing. He's certain a fellow with a name and a voice like that has no future. If I buy the record, Dad says he'll let me borrow his gramophone, provided I don't play it anywhere near him.

Dad started repairing the floor in the front room. I was no use to him, because of my bad thumb. He got fed up with me hanging around looking miserable. I kept thinking about Stella. He asked me why I didn't go and play with Christie or Sean? I told him about the situation with Bowman, and how it's not safe for me to go out at the moment. I didn't tell him I'd broken Bowman's leg.

I decided to go in to Dublin. Dad gave me two shillings, for my fare and a visit to the cinema. He added another shilling, in case I wanted a couple of lead soldiers from Woolies. I caught the bus from the end of the terrace. Jeremy Lynch got on at the chapel. He didn't notice me for a minute; he was too busy lighting a cigarette and picking his nose. When he looked round and saw me, he changed seats and came to sit beside me.

He says Bowman's leg is in a bad state. As well as being broken, it's swollen up. He can't get his trousers on, or shoes and socks. He's telling everyone he broke it falling off the wall, and that I'm a cowardly fucker for attacking him when he couldn't fight back. He'd have polished me off with no trouble if I hadn't fought dirty. I had a good laugh at this, but Lynch told me to shut up. He says Bowman's gang believe him.

He'll be in plaster for six weeks, then I'm for it. He's going to do me in. Meanwhile, his two older brothers are looking for me, and his gang are planning to terrorise me. Lynch said not to worry about this; he'll keep an eye on the situation and give me a hand if I need it. He says next time I meet Bowman, I'm to fight him without any tricks. Otherwise, he'll go on making out that he could have beaten me if only I'd fought fair and square. Lynch says this is a right joke, considering what a cheat and a bully Bowman is.

So far, everyone believes Sculley's story that he wrote the letter to Eileen after being threatened by Bowman. Even so, Lynch doesn't trust Sculley. He's got two of his men guarding him. Sculley can't go anywhere without them. Lynch is sure Sculley will blab to people, once he realises I'm lying low for a while.

He asked me where I was going. 'Probably the pictures,' I said. 'Or, if there's nothing decent on, the natural history museum.' He said he's never been to a museum in his life; he's heard they're boring. I told him it's a good place to look at human and animal skeletons. He said, 'Ah . . . I see,' and changed the subject, in case anyone was listening to us. He's got some rope for me, if I'm still interested in making a swing. I said I am, but it would be a bit tricky collecting it. He's going to send it round sometime. Lynch got out at Gavinstown, before the conductor had time to work his way upstairs. He waited until the bus was about to stop and shot down the stairs like a bullet. God knows what he's doing in Gavinstown; there's nothing there only a chapel and a row of cottages. It could be something to do with a girl. Malone says the Gavinstown mots are mostly tinkers. They live in huge families, like rabbits, and shag like rabbits into the bargain.

At Cabinteely two girls got on the bus. One was small and pretty, with short red hair and white sandals. It was the other one I really took a fancy to. They came up the stairs and the little one said, 'Dolores, wait for me,' so at least I know her name. She had on a yellow skirt, a white blouse, and a pink cardigan. There was a badge on her bag saying 'See you later, Alligator' but she didn't look like a teddy girl. Her face was a bit plump and gormless, but her figure was terrific. They sat three seats in front of me, on the same side.

I stared at them with all my might, hoping they'd feel my brainwaves and turn round, but it didn't work. At Stillorgan a horrible old man got on. He sat in the seat behind them, smoking and spluttering and coughing. They got up and moved to the front of the bus. I was going to get out at Westland Row station but they were still on it by then, so I stayed on all the way to the terminus at the Pillar.

I waited for them to go down the stairs, so I'd be able to walk behind them and study their legs. While I was still in my seat, the old man got up and lurched after them. He had a coughing fit half-way down the stairs and had to cling on to the bannister until he got his breath back. By the time I got off the bus, Dolores and the other one had vanished.

I went to McHugh Himself and bought the Elvis Presley record. He asked me if I was interested in rock'n'roll. I said yes, so he sold me another record by a man called Little Richard. I also bought a battery for my bicycle lamp, for reading in bed, and some wire in case I ever need it.

After McHugh's I went up past the Talbot Hotel and looked in the door. The hotel belongs to Dad's sister Elizabeth, my Aunt Nana. It's one of her businesses. There was a skivvy in the hall with a tray of dirty dishes. She asked me was I looking for someone? I said yes. She asked who. I said, 'You'll do, if I can't find anything better!' I don't know what made me say this; it must be listening to Christie's brother. She threw the dregs from a slops bowl at me, and I ended up with a face-full of tea-leaves.

I went into the Pro-Cathedral and put another thruppence in the box for that book I had about sex. I've been worried in case God thought I was cheating. There wasn't a decent flick on at the Carlton or the Metropole. I couldn't be bothered to trudge round looking at the other cinemas, so I went to the natural history museum.

On the way to Merrion Square I detoured round the back of Trinity. I wanted to listen to the screams coming from the Dental Hospital. It's where the student dentists learn to pull teeth. People who can't afford a proper dentist go there because it's free. Dad went once but swore he'd never go again. He said 'Dental Infirmary' was the wrong name for it; 'Dante's Infernory' was nearer the mark. No one ever knew what he meant.

A man came out and stood spitting blood on the pavement for a few moments. The blood kept coming, so he picked up a sheet of dirty newspaper from the gutter, rolled it into a ball, and stuffed it into his mouth. I followed him round the corner to Clare Street, to see what he'd do next. He walked round to Trinity Gate and sat on the edge of the horse trough opposite Greene's bookshop. The last I saw of him he was sitting with his hands in his pockets, chewing contentedly on the mouthful of newspaper and swallowing it bit by bit.

Greene's is my favourite place for books but I left it until later. I didn't want to be carrying books round the museum. They have toilets in the museum nowadays, which is useful. I was bursting for a wee after drinking so much water this morning. It was all that salty bacon we had at breakfast. It left me parched with thirst.

Downstairs in the museum, it's just birds and rabbits and skeletons of prehistoric Irish deer. My interest is upstairs, where the African animals are. The gorillas are in a big glass case at the top of the stairs. The inside of the case is done up to look like a jungle, with tree-trunks and vines and mysterious plants and snakes. The gorillas stare at you, their eyes wide open and their teeth snarling as if they're alive. I never get tired of looking at them. It's just like in that book I'm reading.

In the winter no one goes to the museum. I have the whole of the upstairs to myself. On dark rainy days hardly any light comes through the glass dome in the roof. The attendants don't switch the electric lights on if they think there's no one up there. I creep round imagining I'm in the jungle surrounded by live animals. The best thing is going up in the galleries and pretending to stalk them from the tree-tops.

I had a look at the human skeleton and the skeleton of an Irish wolfhound. It's bigger than an Alsatian but I'm sure the bones are the same. There are quite a few bits in a dog's skeleton that could be from a human. The skull is definitely different. There's no way you could mistake them for each other.

When I came out the attendant was sitting on the grass having a smoke. I asked him if he knew anything about burning bones. He said it was a quare question for a young fellow to ask. I'd need to go to the zoo for that kind of information. They have a gas incinerator for getting rid of animals that die of diseases. The fire station in Collybrook Road was another place I could ask. They'd have plenty of experience of bodies in burning buildings.

He wanted to know why I was interested in such a morbid subject. I said I'd heard that native tribes use the bones of animals and slaughtered enemies to make ceremonial fires. I want to know if it's true; I have to write an ecker essay about tribal customs. He said I'd be better off out in the fresh air kicking a ball around, instead of filling my head with weird thoughts. The Nasties in Germany had those kinds of ideas, and look where it got us. Millions of decent people killed in the War, and for what?

I went to Greene's and bought two books. *Corduroy* by Adrian Bell, is a true story of a fellow who leaves his posh family to be a farmer's boy. There's a motorbike in it, which will interest Dad. The other one, *Youth is a Crime*, is about a rich fellow who's bored with life even though he has loads of girlfriends. I'll have to lend it to Christie's brother. I wonder if he bothers to read books? He might not have the patience.

When I got home Dad and John-Joe Maguire had just finished putting cement in the holes in the front room. They were having a noisy argument about fairies and angels. Mr Maguire believes in fairies; he says they're the young angels who got expelled from Heaven for siding with Lucifer, but God took pity on them and sent them to earth instead of condemning them to Hell. Dad doesn't agree; he says all angels are ageless and equal, and there's no excuse for pitying any creature, man or angel, who agrees with Lucifer. Mr Maguire got excited, and said we have the authority of the Bible for believing in ranks and hierarchies of angels; what about cherubims and seraphims, and all the others, right up to archangels? Dad got sweaty and bad-tempered about this, so Mr Maguire is probably right.

I made a sandwich with a fried egg, and tried to read. I couldn't get any peace, so I went out to the lavatory. The sun was shining through the slit in the door, so I'd plenty of light for reading. I had the *Corduroy* book on my knees. When I started to eat the egg sandwich the melted butter dripped out onto the pages. I put the book down, and heard a suspicious giggling outside the door. I stopped chewing so I could hear better, and noticed the latch on the door rattling. I crept over to have a peep through the slit, but I was too late. The Sullivan girls had their skipping rope tied to the door-handle. The other end was tied round a rusted stump of railing on the steps going up to the garden. The door opens inwards, so I was trapped.

I kept dead quiet, hoping they'd go away. It was useless. They put a hose on the tap outside the door and turned the water on. Before I could do anything they shoved it through the slit and had me soaked. The shock of the cold water paralysed me for a moment, then I recovered and put my hands across the slit to block it. The room was suddenly pitch dark. I went berserk with terror. I could imagine all the spiders being washed off the walls and swimming around my feet. I stamped on the floor like a maniac, screaming and yelling at the top of my voice.

The girls retreated to the top of the stairs. They kept the hose aimed at the slit in the door. I couldn't make them stop. Siobhan pulled her knickers down and waggled her backside at me. I shrieked at her to let me out. She scraped her finger along the crack of her bum and flicked it at me, the way people do with green bogeys.

Bits of plaster loosened off the ceiling and came down on my head in sloppy chunks. My book was ruined. I kept thinking of spiders; huge, black, ravenous, hairy spiders. I forced my arm out through the slit. It was agony because I've got such big muscles. I couldn't get the rope undone. It had tightened up with the wet, and the strain of me trying to pull the door open. I got my hands round the edge of the door and pulled with the strength of a raging animal. The latch-handle pulled off the door with a crack of splintering wood. The girls ran away screaming with delight. I never even stopped to turn the water off. All I wanted to do was get away from the spiders.

I went into the stable and took my clothes off. I curled up in the hay and spent half an hour crying with relief. I'll have to get my own back on the Sullivan girls as soon as possible. I wish I'd had a camera when Siobhan stuck her bum out; I'd have made a right show of her round the village.

Later on, Dad came out to go to the toilet. He let a roar out of him when he saw the state of the place. I kept quiet at the time. When he asked me about it at supper, I said the mess was nothing to do with me. This was true in a way, so I didn't mind telling a half-lie. It was better than having to admit that the Sullivan girls had made a fool of me.

We got woken up at three in the morning. There was a row going on upstairs. Mr and Mrs Sullivan again. They were thumping on the floor, and shouting at the tops of their voices. One of the back windows got smashed. Dad went out to see what was going on. A radio was lying outside our door, broken in bits, mixed up with pieces of window-pane. Dad was relieved it was only a radio; he said he was afraid it might be a human being. Major Longshott was leaning out of his window. As soon as he saw Dad he disappeared.

I woke Dad at eight o'clock to remind him the snooker tables were being delivered today. He got cross at being woken so early. 'They're *promised* for today, right enough,' he said, 'but an Irish promise is about as reliable as a weather forecast.' He drank his tea and went back to sleep.

At half-past nine a lorry drew up in the terrace with four men and the stuff from the snooker company. Dad was livid. He said you couldn't rely on anything nowadays; the country was going to the dogs with all this bloody efficiency. He was also annoyed at being caught in his nightshirt. Mam made it out of a striped dress she bought in a lost property auction at Kingsbridge Station. The dress was enormous. The auctioneer said it proved there were still giants living in Ireland.

The men wouldn't come down the front stairs in case they collapsed under the weight of the tables. They're made from enormous slabs of Welsh slate, and weigh a tremendous amount. Dad took the men round the back but they wouldn't come in that way either; they said it was too far to lug the stuff. John-Joe came round and solved the problem by sawing through the railings at the top of the basement, and then showing the men how they could lower the slates down on ropes. He took the stairs away as well, to leave a clear drop into the basement. The men did what John-Joe suggested, and then found the slates were too big to come through the scullery door. We ended up having to take the front window out, as well as the railings and the stairs. John-Joe says he'll weld the railings back on with a blowlamp.

The men had their tea-break sitting on the back of the lorry. They whistled and made comments to the women walking along the terrace. Mrs Barrington gave them a beautiful smile and said, 'Thank you, gentlemen.' This knocked them speechless with admiration. Sculley's grannies giggled and said they were an awful gang of fellows altogether. Mrs Sullivan got cross and asked them if they'd never seen a pair of legs in a skirt before. They came up with a lot of rude remarks about this, so I think she was sorry she asked them. Christie's sister Ellen came along to see what was going on in the basement. They tried to embarrass her but it didn't work. She told them she didn't play with little boys, but if they had any older brothers at home she might be interested. This shut them up for a while.

After Ellen went, Major Longshott's wife came out. Even though she's quite old it made no difference to the men. They asked her if she was going to buy a sausage for her old man, or did he already have one? Major Longshott was putting his coat on in the hall behind her. He heard this, and came out with a face like a beetroot. The two of them marched off up the terrace and went into the barracks.

A few minutes later Guard O'Rooney came strolling down puffing on his pipe. It's a new one with a metal tube up the middle. He nodded at the men and said, 'God bless the work.' They were a bit uneasy about him, and went very quiet. O'Rooney stood looking at them for a moment, and said it was a grand thing to see such a fine bunch of hardy Irish lads assembled all in the one identical place, and they enjoying themselves in the fine fresh air of a summer morning.

He said he was heartened and bucked to hear they had plenty of crack and blarney for the benefit of the indigenous female population. It was a lamentably notable fact that nowadays a lot of lads seemed to have lost the gift of the gab. Only a minute ago, up in the barracks itself, an oul one with a face like a quince and a voice like a rusty lawn-mower, had been in complaining about a bunch of bowsies mouthing obscenities at her in the street. 'Would you believe that, now,' said Guard O'Rooney, 'that fellows could be so short of a civil word that they'd go in for that class of harassment?' Then he walked off back to the barracks.

The men on the lorry never said another word to anyone on the terrace after this. Dad pulled a straight face and said it was comforting to know that our well-paid public guardians are always on the ball, ever alert, and ever ready to challenge the dark forces of iniquity.

I stayed off the terrace for fear of jeering by the Sullivan girls, but I could hear everything from the door of the scullery.

At eleven o'clock the foreigners from Dublin arrived. They're four brothers. Three were in a Mercedes car with the roof folded back, and one on a Vespa scooter. He looked like the scooter: small and greasy and bulging at the back end. While the others were talking to Dad he asked me were there any 'sure things' in the village; he's always on the look-out for good-looking girls that 'do a turn'. He says women can't resist him.

An argument broke out between the foreigners and the men assembling the tables. The men said they couldn't work with the smell of the foreigners. It was like grafting in a Turkish brothel, what with the exotic cigarettes and the whiff of hair-oil and the reek of garlic every time the foreigners opened their mouths. Eventually the foreigners went to the hotel at Bray and had their lunch, while the men got on with assembling the tables.

The one on the scooter didn't come back with the others. Later

I saw him round in the lane with one of the big girls from the hill. She was sitting on the pillion, talking and laughing. She looked as if she was having a good time. Maybe women do fancy him. I don't know why. He has a quiff that he's always combing, and a Bill Haley kiss-curl. It could be that.

Guard O'Rooney cycled down the lane while I was spying on the fellow with the scooter. He noticed me out of the corner of his eye, and came into the stable.

He said that while Mrs Longshott was in the barracks this morning, complaining about the men, she told him she'd seen me in Stella's basement with no clothes on. He wanted to know if there was any truth in the story. 'The thing is,' he said, 'there's a multitude of rules and regulations governing the public display of the private parts.' It was a terrible shock to him to hear of a young fellow prancing about, naked as a cat's arse, bollocks on show like a greyhound, and him gripping his jake as if he was a Scotsman trying to toss a caber. I told him the story about Stella washing my clothes for me.

He said he was greatly relieved to hear the true facts of the case. He wouldn't be troubling me about the matter, only for the recent nasty business down the beach. Anything appertaining to the aforesaid Stella was potential grist to the magisterial might of the law. Particularly, he said, in conjunction with various ancillary facts and fancies currently formulating themselves in the back parlour of his brain.

Lynch's men arrived with rope and a twelve-foot scaffold pole at two o'clock. The pole was to hang the rope on, in such a way that fellows wouldn't bash themselves against the trunk of the tree when they were swinging. Lynch's men had instructions to help me put it up, provided I let the Dump gang come and use it. I asked them how often they were likely to come round. They said probably never; it was just the principle of the thing.

The holly tree is no good for a swing. It's too tall and has only one main trunk going straight up. Anyway, I couldn't climb it on account of the prickles. The sycamore tree turned out to be perfect. It splits into four main branches halfway up. We tied the pole horizontally in such a way that it stuck out over the garden.

One of Lynch's men worked his way out along the pole and looped the swing rope over the end of it. When he tried to come back, he lost his nerve. He was white as a sheet and pouring with nervous sweat, too terrified to move. In the end he got down accidentally. He lost his balance on the pole and managed to grab the rope at the same time. He gripped on for dear life and slid down it. His hands got badly blistered but he said it was better than a broken neck. After all his trouble putting it up, he wasn't able to have a swing, because of his damaged hands.

The swing is terrific. The pole is about twenty-five feet up in the air. Lynch's men pushed me, and got me up to the height of the top windows in the stable! I could see right into all the gardens along the terrace. At the other end of the arc I could look in through the Sullivans' window. Mrs Sullivan waved at me, which was surprising. I thought she'd be cross. Mind you, I didn't have much time to stare in.

Lynch's other man was having a turn, with me pushing, when the rope came off the end of the pole. We'd forgotten it was only looped round it. Luckily he landed in the soft patch where Major Longshott has his flowers. It made a terrible mess of them. I suppose there'll be trouble about it. The Longshotts are away today. They went into Dublin this morning.

None of us would risk going along the pole with the rope again, so we left it until we get a safer idea for putting it up.

Lynch's men went out through the stable. A few moments later I heard a racket in the lane. They came flying back into the garden. A bunch of Bowman's men were hiding in the archway. They jumped on Lynch's men, thinking they were members of my gang. Lynch isn't going to be very happy when he hears about it. I went out to the lane but Bowman's raiders had gone. This could be serious. I'll have to be careful when I go out. I thought Bowman was only bragging when he said they'd get me.

Christie turned up while I was still in the garden. The detective from Dublin has arrived. He's been to see Stella. Now he's going to go round the village questioning fellows again. Christie is afraid I'll let on about us spying on Stella. I told him I definitely won't.

After dark I went into the garden and dug my fingers in the earth all round the Major's ruined flowers. I made it look as if an animal has been at them. If he says anything, I'll tell him a dog got into the garden and did it. The bandage on my thumb is filthy. I hope I don't get lockjaw.

I could hear the Sullivan girls larking about in their bathroom. There's no glass in the window. Mr and Mrs Sullivan broke it having one of their rows. I got up in the tree to have a look. It's better than spying on Christie's sisters; you can see the whole room. The girls were in the bath with no clothes on. I didn't stay up the tree for long. They're a bit too young to interest me. Anyway it's not the same as looking at girls that you fancy. Also, Dad came out looking for me, so I had to climb down in a hurry.

I was up late helping him get the snooker room straight. We had to iron the tables, and brush every speck of dust off them, and make sure they were absolutely level. My last job was polishing the cues. I had to sprinkle French chalk on a cloth and rub them with it. The chalk comes in a tin with holes in the top, like baby powder. It made my hands shiny and slippery. Dad says it absorbs sweat from player's hands and keeps the cue moving freely. This is important for accurate potting.

When he wasn't looking I pulled my wellies off and put chalk down them. It was like a miracle when I put them on again. My feet slipped in without jamming, and the slimy wetness in the bottom disappeared. I'm going to do them with chalk every day from now on. I know I said I was going to give up wearing wellingtons. The snag is, I haven't got anything else. Even the ones I'm wearing now are Dad's. I lost one of mine escaping from the lorry works.

The pain in my thumb is gone, but the nail is pitch black. Dad says it'll fall off and a new one will grow in its place.

He got up at five o'clock bursting for a wee. The lavatory door wouldn't open. He thought at first it was jammed. When he tried to force it, a voice said, 'Hold on a minute; it's bolted.' Mrs Sullivan came out carrying a candle and cigarettes and a library book. She had an overcoat on over her dressing gown, and a black eye, and bruises on her neck. Dad was very embarrassed by the whole business. He says she must have been in there all night. The floor was covered in cigarette butts.

The foreigners arrived in a big van with the slot-machines and juke-box and pin-tables. There was a big row straight away. They expected Dad to have benches ready along the walls for the slot-machines. Dad hadn't done anything about it; he'd forgotten. They ended up putting them on the window-sills all round the basement. There are four along the window in the front room.

Dad had also forgotten that pin-tables and the juke-box run on electricity. There are no electric sockets in the basement. He went to see John-Joe Maguire and got miles of scrap cable from him. We spent the morning running wires from the meter in the back room. They're nailed to the skirting board so people won't trip over them. We had no plugs and sockets, so we've joined the cables to the machines by twisting the wires together and wrapping them in Sellotape. Dad says the whole thing is probably illegal, especially the way we've connected up to the meter. He hammered a big nail into each of the two wires coming out of the meter, and twisted our cables onto them, using his leather gloves. We're not even sure it's our meter; there's a whole row of them, and nothing to say which one belongs to which flat.

When we got the pin-tables working, Dad gave me a handful of pennies and said I could play on them. I told him I hadn't the slightest interest in playing pin-tables and slot-machines. Dad was disappointed, and said he hopes I don't represent the attitude of the rest of the lads in the village. I wanted to play the juke-box but it takes thruppenny bits and we hadn't got any. The foreigners made it play without money when they demonstrated it. They wouldn't show Dad how to do it. They said he could be playing it all day and they'd get nothing out of it. They're coming back on Monday, to see how things have gone, and to empty the money from the machines.

Dad kept one little room at the back of the basement for a bedroom. He's worried about me being able to sleep at night, with all the noise going on. He asked me if I'd mind sleeping in the stable for a while. I was delighted with this suggestion, until I started imagining millions of spiders crawling up the legs of my bed during the night. Dad couldn't see any difference between the stable and the basement; he says there are just as many spiders in the house.

He reckons I should sleep in the loft. If we give it a good clean out, and polish the windows, and sweep the cobwebs out of the rafters, there'll be nowhere for spiders to hide and I'll be all right. He said living in the stable will be as good as having my own house, and I can have it all to myself. I asked him if I could use it as a gang headquarters, and he said, 'Yes . . . whatever you like.' I looked in my *American Boy Scouts Handbook* and found a trick to stop ants climbing up the legs of picnic tables. You dig four holes in the ground, put a big stone in the middle of each hole, stand the table legs on the stones, and fill the holes with water. I can't go digging holes in the loft floor so I'm going to fill paint tins with water and stand my bed in them.

Andy arrived back from England in the afternoon. His dad flew over to London on a training flight and gave him a lift home. He came banging on the scullery door to say hello. We went out to the garden for a chat. I asked him if his mother was pleased to see him. He said he didn't know; he hadn't been home yet. I asked him why not and he said there was no point; his parents would be at it hammer and tongs, the minute they saw each other, and he'd only be in the way. 'At it hammer and tongs?' I said. 'What do you mean?' Andy looked at me in a puzzled way and asked if I was joking. 'No,' I said. 'Honestly, I'm not.' 'Jesus,' said Andy, and shook his head. 'Giving each other a good fucking, you daft bugger!' 'Fucking?' I said. Andy nodded, and said, 'You *know* – shagging!' and smiled as if it was nothing particular. I couldn't believe it. Andy's mother! Andy got out a liquorice pipe and bit the stem off it. 'Parents do, you know.' He spat out the silver band. 'That's the whole point of being married.'

Andy's mother with someone's jake up her? And at that very moment? Somehow I'd never thought of her doing anything as disgusting as fucking. All the filthy stuff I'd heard from Christie and his brother and Malone and the men in the lorry works came surging into my brain. A thin trickle of acid sick crept up my throat. I put my arm across my mouth, and let it soak onto my sleeve. I wanted to kill Andy's father.

Andy asked me if I was all right. I said no. He asked me what was wrong. I said I didn't like the way he spoke about his parents. If he ever used that word about his mother again I'd beat him to a pulp. He said I wasn't being fair; his parents never make any secret about what they get up to. I told him to shut up; I didn't want to hear any more. He said he couldn't see what was bothering me. I said I didn't like hearing about his mother and father doing disgusting things.

Andy got cross and said there was nothing disgusting about it; they were married and could do what they liked. 'In fact,' he said, 'they like fucking so much, they even do it with other people!' He's seen them doing it. They have parties when Andy's dad is at home, and everyone gets drunk. They play stripping games, and all the men and women take turns with each other on the carpet. He used to spy on them until he got bored with it.

Dad came out and saved me. He needed help with the juke-box. He'd been and got thruppenny bits, but the needle kept sliding off the records. Dad said the machine needed levelling. He lifted the front of it while I stuck a folded cigarette packet under one of the corners. That cured it for a while. Dad wanted to play all the records to see what they were like. Eventually the weight of the machine squashed the cardboard. The needle started jumping again, so we gave up. Dad's going to put a thin sliver of wood under it to cure the problem.

Andy and Dad helped me carry my bed up to the loft. When Dad left we did the trick with the cans of water under the legs. Andy had a good idea for stopping the castors from rusting. He put small cans inside the big cans, with the legs in the small cans and the water in the big cans.

I was so busy I managed to forget the conversation we'd had. Then Andy looked out the loft window and discovered he could see into his own garden. I asked him if he was thinking of going home and he said no, not yet; his parents were still busy. He nearly said 'still at it' but he caught himself on at the last moment. I asked him how he knew. He said the curtains in the lounge were shut. I went to the window and stared at the curtained window. I knew it would hurt me to know but I couldn't help it; I asked him why they'd closed the curtains. Andy said they were probably shagging on the sofa. How can he be so casual? And about his own mother! I didn't get on to him, because it was my own fault for asking.

I lay on the bed after that, saying nothing, staring miserably at the ceiling and trying to keep my mind empty. Andy got bored and went into the house to help Dad. He didn't came back, and after a while I fell asleep in a blank state of misery and pain.

When I woke up it was getting dark. I thought of Suzanne straight away, and of Andy's father sticking his jake into her whenever he felt like it . . . Oh Jesus; maybe right that minute! I thought of the man on Sunday, and Carol saying to her, 'That's your third go this morning!' I remembered Christie telling me about her dancing on tables at parties, and throwing her knickers at men, and Andy's remark about 'taking turns on the carpet', and that story Malone told me, about her taking her skirt off in his shed; was that true after all? He said she would have taken off her knickers if his granny hadn't interrupted them. I don't want to believe it, *any* of it. And *she* doesn't want me to believe it. She said so herself; 'Whatever you may hear about me, believe what *you've* found me to be.'

I lay watching the moonlight soaking the floor of the loft with silver pools, and listening to the cries of the curlews on the estuary. In the distance a train rumbled over the viaduct. It made me feel lonelier and more unhappy than ever. I started thinking about Sunday, and the memory of the two women in bed; how young and peaceful they'd seemed, how sleepy-gentle their faces, how soft and smooth and rounded their bodies. It would have been so warm and satisfying to have snuggled up safe and cosy between them, like three Babes in the Wood. If only I hadn't been so afraid!

I got a desperate, tight ache in my stomach and my willie swelled up to an enormous size. It started throbbing as if it was going to burst. I took my trousers off and tried to ease the pain by squeezing tightly with both hands. Before I knew what was happening, I was jerking my hands up and down my jake. Once I started, I couldn't stop. I knew I was pulling my plonker, and committing a mortal sin, and that God could strike me dead with lightning any minute, but it didn't make any difference; I couldn't stop, and I wanted to die anyway.

My heart hammered in my chest and my head pounded and my mouth was so dry I couldn't move my tongue. I shut my eyes, and suddenly I was floating in the mysterious warm heaven of Suzanne's body; floating ... floating ... floating; on waves, on pulsing waves, on waves of warm wet softness ... and in that heaven I exploded, exploded inside her tummy with a shocked scream of pain and pleasure.

I woke up still holding myself, my hands stuck to my willie with the stuff I'd spurted out. I remembered the mortal sin, and wanting to die, and I thought of Mr Barrington in bed with Suzanne. What right had he to come home and *do* that? I thought of the feeling I'd had when I exploded, of imagining myself inside her. Oh God; what must the *real* feeling be? And *he* could do it whenever he wanted to! My willie swelled again, and again I pulled my plonker, and again I slept.

Four times I did it, and I didn't give a damn whether God was watching me or not. It stopped me thinking of the pain of my love for Suzanne, and the pain of the thought of her with other men, and the pain of being alone, and the pain of feelings I don't understand.

I woke slowly this morning, and very late. It took me a long, long time to get up. My mind was empty and tired, and every bit of my body limp and lifeless. I kept shivering for no reason. When I went for a pee, the pain in my willie had me groaning and clutching myself in agony.

I decided to put Mrs Barrington out of my mind. If I don't, I'll be miserable all the time. That won't be fair to Dad and everyone else who knows me. I used to be a happy person before I fell in love with her. I was even happier after I fell in love with her. It's impossible now, though. The moment I think of her my head fills with pain and mystification. How can someone look so beautiful, and so happy and pure-looking, and seem such a nice person when she's with me, and yet be doing the things she does? If they're true, that is. I hate Andy's father more than ever. If he and Andy hadn't come back everything would still be all right.

Dad was in a terrible state when I went into the house. He's got used to me waking up first and making tea. He can't get going in the morning without it. John-Joe Maguire was helping him make benches round the walls to put the slot-machines on. Dad has to get the machines off the window-sills before tonight. He needs to be able to close the wooden shutters. It's to stop the noise of the juke-box annoying people in the terrace. They're making the benches from stacks of bricks with planks laid across them. They don't look very safe to me.

Dad said Christie's brother was like a Yo-Yo up and down the front stairs last night, looking for me. He was in a terrible temper, and well on in drink. Dad didn't tell him I was out in the stable. I know what's annoying him; I forgot all about it being his birthday yesterday. I was supposed to get him the anti-baby things in time for the dance last night. He was hoping to persuade a mot to let him shag her. Maybe he should ask Mrs Barrington.

Andy came round at ten o'clock. He asked me to go to the pictures with him. I didn't really want to see him. He reminds me of all the things that hurt me. I said I had to help Dad. Dad said he'd sooner I went to the cinema; I looked as if I could do with a laugh. He insisted on me going, and even gave me the money for sweets and ice-cream. I told Andy I'd go if Christie came with us.

Andy wouldn't call for Christie on his own. I had to go with him. I was worried about getting caught by his brother. I was lucky. Ellen said Liam was still in bed. He stayed in Dolan's drinking until all hours. When he finally staggered home, he was stocious.

Christie was busy. He's starting a new racket as a boys-only barber. He says the barber in the village is a rogue. He told us why. During the week the barber has a cardboard notice in his window saying 'HAIRCUTS: MEN ONE SHILLING, BOYS SIXPENCE.' On Saturday mornings he puts a different notice up. 'HAIRCUTS. BOYS ONLY. NINEPENCE.' 'Thruppence more, you see,' said Christie. 'It's robbery! That's because he knows boys' mothers hardly see them during the week. They only notice they need a haircut when they see them on Saturday morning.'

On Saturday afternoons there's an entirely different notice in the window. It's a wooden board painted by a professional sign-writer. 'JOHN PATRICK NOLAN. TONSORIAL ARTIST. SHAVES, HAIRCUTS, ETC. ADULTS ONLY. NO BOYS OR YOUNG MEN UNDER 21.' The barber's excuse is that he wants to do a top-class job without being distracted by the hooliganism of young fellows and children.

Christie said there's more to it than that, though. The real reason boys aren't let in on Saturday afternoons is so that the men can read pin-up magazines, and buy various secret things on the quiet. Christie stopped and sat looking at us mysteriously. I asked him what these things are. He said he couldn't tell me in front of Andy, in case Andy spills the beans.

Andy got angry, and said Christie was a little shit. I asked Christie what pin-up magazines are. He said they're magazines with pictures of naked women. Andy sniffed and said, 'Huh; so what? I've got loads of them at home.' His father brings them back from England.

Christie was interested in this. He asked if he could have a look at them. Andy said no; if he wasn't good enough to trust with a secret, he wasn't good enough to borrow magazines from. Christie thought for a minute and said he'd tell him one thing the barber sells. It's a bottle of pink stuff that looks like medicine. You slip a spoonful in a girl's drink and it makes her drop her knickers. Andy said his father has some better stuff. You don't even have to put it in a drink. You rub it on your face after a shave and the women go wild. He says he'll get me some any time I want it. Christie got all friendly and smarmy and said, 'What about me?' Andy told him to drop dead.

I asked Christie what all this had to do with him starting a boys-only barber, but he ignored me; he wanted to keep on talking to Andy. I said we had to go in a minute. Christie got huffy. He said he was sorry he'd told us anything. It was secret information he'd heard in the barracks. If we let it out he'd be in dead trouble. The guards go to the barber's on a Saturday, so they're all involved. 'Even the Sergeant?' I said. 'No,' said Christie; his sister Stephanie works as a hairdresser in Marino. She does the hair-cutting in his family. I was relieved to hear this. I like the Sergeant. I told Christie to get on with his explanation.

The problem for boys getting their hair cut on Saturday mornings, he said, is that they miss the pictures. The film starts at ten-thirty, and goes on until about twelve. The worst thing for a fellow is missing the serial. It always ends with the hero about to be killed by a train, or a giant lightning machine, or a runaway planet crashing into the earth. If you miss an episode, you're left in a state of anxiety for a whole fortnight. If you ask other fellows what happened, they tell fantastic lies to get you even more worried.

Christie has this idea of setting up as a barber, cutting boys' hair before and after the pictures. I asked him what happened to the car-number blackmail business. He said some bastard reported it anonymously to the barracks. One of the guards went round to the post office to investigate. After that he gave it up. It was too dangerous to continue.

Andy and I went to the flicks on our own. It was horrible. We paid sixpence to sit in the decent seats at the back. The woman in the ticket office is a right old hag. She has a big head and humpy shoulders and enormous bloodshot eyes. Andy said she reminded him of a buffalo. I asked him if he meant a bison. He told me to piss off. Before the film started, the woman came in and told us to move down to the front, with all the other scruffs. We showed her our tickets but she said she didn't give a monkey's tit; she wanted us down the front where she could keep an eye on us.

Andy put on a posh English accent. He said he'd be much obliged for the return of our money, and that she'd be hearing from his parents. He told her his father is the Assistant Editor of the *Irish Times*. She immediately let us sit where we wanted. It's amazing the effect an English accent has on people. I asked him how he thought up the yarn so quickly. He said he has a whole string of them, ready for different situations.

The films were ruined by the people in the front benches. The benches are right in front of the screen. They kept standing up on them and putting their shadows on the screen, pretending to be in the film. Also, there was a lot of running around, and people chasing each other, and fighting going on in the corners. The old hag was kept busy.

When the lights went on for the interval I went to the lavatory. It still hurt to pee but not as much as this morning. Coming out I saw Jeremy Lynch's sister sitting on her own in the back row of benches. She was sitting with her hands on her lap and her head bent forward, trying to ignore the stupidity going on all round her. I noticed her because she was wearing a white jumper. When I got back to my seat I asked Andy if he had a girlfriend. He said no; they're not allowed to have anything to do with girls at his school in England.

He asked me if I had one. I said yes, just to see what he'd say. He wanted to know her name. For a split second, I nearly said 'Suzanne'. I caught myself in time, and said, 'Eileen.' 'Jesus!' said Andy; 'That sounds really Irish.' He asked me what she looked like. I said if he really wanted to know, she was sitting down at the back of the fourpennies.

We couldn't see Eileen because of the partition separating the benches from the proper seats. It's about four feet high and has a brass rail running along the top for decoration. The partition is a nuisance. Fellows in the benches kept chucking things at us and dodging down behind it so we couldn't get them back.

Andy got up and said he was going to find my girlfriend and say hello to her. This put the wind up me. I was sorry I'd said anything. It never occurred to me that Andy would be so daring. If Lynch heard that his sister was being chatted to by a Protestant he wouldn't like it. He'd be sure to take it out on me; he knows Andy's in my gang.

Andy asked me how he'd recognise Eileen. I told him she had black curly hair and specs. He looked at me and said, 'Specs?' I said yes. 'Specs!' said Andy. 'Jesus!' Then I said I'd been lying to him; her name is really Dolores. Andy said that was even cornier than Eileen; where did I find these girls? He went down to the partition and leaned on the brass rail. I heard him say he was looking for a girl called Dolores. If she could hear him, would she kindly raise her hand?

There was a lot of shouting and jeering. A bunch of fellows grabbed Andy by the arms and pulled him head-first over the partition. There was no sign of the woman who runs the picture-house, so I had to rescue him myself. I ran down to the partition and poked my head over to see what was going on. This was a stupid thing to do. A vicious bitch of a girl jumped up and grabbed me by the hair. I tried to jerk away but she hung on and pulled my head down. I bashed my teeth on the brass rail. God, it was awful. The two right at the front are chipped. When I breathe through my mouth, or have a drink, the teeth feel as if they're being drilled by a mad dentist.

Before I had time to rescue Andy, the lights in the cinema went on. The woman came down the aisle and said she'd stop the film and throw us all out if we didn't stop fighting. Some fellows from the Hill gang recognised me and said they'd get me as soon as the lights went out again. Andy managed to scramble free and we decided to get out while we had the chance. Andy said he'd enjoyed being pulled over the partition. He landed on top of a nice girl with fair hair and a white jumper. He said if he sees her around the village it will give him an excuse to talk to her; he can apologise for squashing her. I hope he forgets this idea.

Christie's brother was outside the cinema waiting for us. Christie told him where we were. He was livid when he saw me, then he spotted Andy and said he wanted to speak to me privately. We went down the lane to the archway, so Bowman's men wouldn't come out of the cinema and catch me. I told Christie's brother I was in agony with two broken teeth from a fight. He said I'd be lucky to have any teeth by this evening, if I don't come up with the goods. I explained that Mr Barrington had come home unexpectedly and I hadn't had a chance to get the things yet. Christie's brother said he didn't give a toss; he wanted them by tonight and that was final. The argument went on for ages. Andy got fed up hanging around and went home.

I made a deal with Christie's brother. I said I'd get the things by tonight, but I wanted something in exchange. He didn't know I'd got them already, so he was keen to make it worth my while.

He agreed the job in Dublin was a fiasco, and that he'd give me something else instead. I said I was desperate for clothes. He said he'll give me some socks and a pair of shoes. They're black, with white patches on the heels and toes, and practically new. I asked him why he was giving them away, if they were that good. He said he was too embarrassed to wear them, after a mot at a dance asked him if he'd got them off Laurel and Hardy. He says I can cover them all over with black polish. This will disguise the white bits. His feet are a size bigger than mine, but it doesn't matter. Mine are bigger than they used to be. They've spread, through wearing Dad's big wellingtons recently.

He's also going to give me two shirts, a tie, and a pair of trousers he got from his father. He can't wear them; they're police trousers and very scratchy, and bring his legs out in a rash. The one time he wore them, he nearly died with fright when he took them off. He thought he'd caught a dose of the pox. Best of all, he's going to give me a leather jacket. He's decided to go in for teddy boy drapes and bootlace ties. He says leather jackets are old-fashioned now, except with rockers and Hell's angels. I'm not bothered about fashion. A leather jacket will be just the thing to make me look tough and vicious when I get a gang going.

I went into the house to have my tea. It was packed with people playing snooker and slot-machines, and listening to the juke-box. Dad's had to move it into the back room. The girls wanted more space so they could dance to the music. He says he's amazed; he never expected girls to come into the place. He thought it would be just fellows. I watched the girls for a while. They were doing rock'n'roll, twirling round and sliding between each other's legs and showing their petticoats and suspenders. One girl couldn't dance. She had on a very tight pencil skirt. After a while she got fed up watching the others enjoying themselves and pulled it up round her hips. You could see everything, right up to the legs of her knickers. She didn't care a bit.

The fellows waiting for a game of snooker came in for a look. There was a lot of whistling and dirty talk. Dad heard it and made her pull her skirt down again. He wrote a big notice saying 'NO IMMODEST DANCING' and pinned it to the wall over the juke-box. The girls teased him, pretending they didn't know what it meant. Dad got very embarrassed and rushed back to the snooker tables. The girls took the notice down and altered it. They crossed out the 'NO' and wrote 'ONLY' after 'DANCING'. They're a bit thick, though; they spelt it 'ONEY'.

I went out to the stable to wait for Christie's brother. He said he'd see me at six o'clock at the latest. It was five o'clock when I went out. I wanted to catch up on reading the encyclopaedia. I've got as far as 'JAC to LOM'. I've been cheating a lot, by missing out anything to do with history and religion and that kind of stuff.

I was in the loft lying on my bed. A soft voice whispered, 'Michael . . .' I looked up. Mrs Barrington was standing at the top of the stairs. My face went cold and stiff with the shock of seeing her, and my heart started hammering.

She asked if she could speak to me. I had to nod; my mouth was so dry I couldn't move my tongue. She came over and sat on the end of the bed. I didn't dare move. She took a deep breath and asked me straight out if I'd taken the rolls of film from Mr Barrington's dark-room. I was too scared to lie to her, and nodded yes. She asked me if I had them now, and I shook my head. She closed her eyes and leaned her head back as if she was tired. After a few seconds of silence she said, 'Where are they, Michael?'

I told her the whole story. She didn't say anything. I asked her if she was cross with me. 'No,' she said; 'No, I'm not.' There was another silence. She asked me an unexpected question; were we still friends? I couldn't lie, so I didn't say anything. She put her hand out and moved it along the blanket until it was near mine. Her eyes looked sort of cloudy. I hadn't a clue what she was thinking or feeling. I moved my hand away from hers, and stood up on the opposite side of the bed. Her eyes followed me for a moment, then she slowly sank her teeth into her bottom lip and turned her head away. Her shoulders sagged for a moment, then she suddenly sat up straight. Without looking at me, she said she'd appreciate it if we could go into Dublin first thing on Monday morning and collect the photographs.

Christie's brother came into the stable and yelled up the stairs. 'Are you up there, Kelly, you idle fucker?' Mrs Barrington wiped the backs of her hands across her eyes and stood up. She gave me a brief glance, tried to say something and couldn't, swallowed, took a deep breath, and said she was sorry. I was too taken aback to say anything. Next moment she was gone.

Christie's brother came rushing up the stairs. He said I was a right jammy bastard, getting it Special Delivery in the comfort of my own bed. I had to get rid of him as quickly as possible. His talk made me feel sick and dirty.

The leather jacket was filthy and smelt of cigarette smoke. The rest of the clothes weren't even washed and ironed. I was so miserable I didn't care. I gave him two packets of anti-baby things, and kept one for future deals. He wanted to stay and chat but I wasn't interested.

I asked him why he wasn't rushing off to the mot who'd promised him a birthday shag. He said he was still hankering after the one I'd been stuffing. He put his hand on the bed and rubbed it slowly up and down the blanket. I asked him what he was doing. He said he was feeling for the damp patch where the tart's bum had been. He wanted a snifter of any love juice that trickled down the crack of her arse. I got fed up and left. The last I saw of him he was kneeling by the bed with his face buried in the blanket, furiously pulling his plonker.

I went to the chapel intending to make my peace with God. There was a queue for confession. I went up into the choir gallery to wait until everyone else had gone. I didn't want anyone hearing me talking to the priest. I had too many bad thoughts and deeds to confess. It was dark and peaceful in the gallery, and I fell asleep.

When I woke, it was dark. The only light in the chapel was from the sacristy lamp and a few offertory candles. I thought I was the only person in the place. I got scared, thinking I'd been locked in for the night. I sat quiet until my eyes got used to the gloom. After a while, I was able to see almost normally. A man and a woman were kneeling, side by side, in the back row of pews. They were just below me, talking so softly that I couldn't make out the words.

The woman started to cry. The man tried to comfort her. She burst into loud sobs, and her voice went from a whisper to a high-pitched wail. It was Mrs Sullivan and the priest. He tried to quiet her, but she wouldn't stop. I heard every word. She said she was at the end of her tether. She couldn't stick another day of it. He wanted it morning, noon, and night. The minute he woke up, the minute he got in from work, the minute they went to bed. She felt like a whore; worse than a whore. A whore can say no; a wife can't. If she tries to refuse him he beats her. She has no privacy, no sense of dignity, no pride, no rights over her own mind and body. She hasn't a shred of self-respect left, because he's bored with normal intimacies. She has to submit to obscene and depraved acts to satisfy his sexual appetite.

I crept down the stairs from the gallery and went home to bed. I never even bothered to say goodnight to Dad, or ask him how the business went. What is it about men and women, that they make each other so unhappy? It's all to do with this sex business. I'm glad I've given up thinking about it.

Dad was up before me this morning. He actually brought me out a mug of tea. He's thrilled to bits about yesterday; it was a big success. He opened the snooker room at twelve noon and never shut it till two o'clock this morning. He made thirty-five shillings just from the snooker table alone. The juke-box hardly stopped playing, and people were putting money into the slot-machines non-stop. The bar-billiards was the only thing that caused trouble. Everyone said the games were over too quickly. Dad's going to ask the man from Dublin to adjust the timer, so that people get better value from it.

He finished his tea and went to the window to tip the tea-leaves out. Something caught his eye and he stopped talking. He stood still for a moment, and I heard him say something under his breath. I got out of bed to see what he was staring at. Stella was in her garden, leaning forward with her face buried in a rose bush. We thought at first she was smelling the flowers, then realised she was being sick.

Her mother came out of the house and called her. Stella dropped to her knees and hid behind the bush. Dad put his arm round my shoulders and led me away from the window. 'Poor girl,' he said. 'Poor, poor girl . . .' He blinked hard a few times, and said we should remember her in our prayers. He made an attempt to smile, but it wasn't very successful. We went into the house, and he carried on telling me about yesterday.

The snooker table was a problem at first. He started by charging sixpence a game. It was too cheap. Even young boys were able to afford it. The older fellows got impatient waiting for a game. He put the price up to a shilling. This cut out the young boys. The older fellows still complained. People were spinning the games out to get good value for their shilling. Dad had to invent a new rule. If a game went over half an hour, all the balls except the black and the white were cleared off the table. The winner was whoever potted the black.

Dad was amazed at how many people squashed into the basement. He expected only fellows, but loads of girls came in, and hundreds of day trippers from the strand. John-Joe told everyone who bought tea from him. There was so much money put into the slot-machines that Dad had to put 'out of order' notices on them. He rang the foreigners and told them the machines were full. They're coming over tomorrow to empty them.

Dad can't get over our good luck. He made more money in one day than he used to get for a whole week on the buses. I reminded him he's got to share with the foreigners and the bar-billiards man. He said he'd already taken that into account. I asked him about the money he owes me. He says he'll give it to me as soon as he gets his share from the slot-machines.

Malone came round to have a look at my bike. I'd forgotten all about it. He asked me how I was getting on with organising a gang to obliterate the Hill mob. I'd forgotten about that as well. We had a long talk about warfare and fighting tactics.

He's a very cunning thinker. Most people, he said, have a stupid attitude to gang battles. They start by having a meeting with the enemy. Both sides agree on when and where they'll have the fight. Then they have a big massacre with sticks and clubs. Fellows get kicked and bruised and have black eyes and bleeding noses. Sometimes knives are involved, and bows and arrows. This causes serious injuries: stabbed arms and legs, and poked-out eyes. At the end of the battle, each side is as badly damaged as the other. It's all a waste of time and effort. The point of a fight is to win, and with the least damage to yourself. The thing to go for is the element of surprise. No meetings, no warnings, and no mercy. I agree with him completely. It's how I beat Bull Bowman in the challenge.

We drew up a set of rules about gang battles. The first rule is: never get involved in one if we can help it. The second rule is: only accept a challenge if it's a case of defending territory. The third rule is: if we can't avoid a battle, we fight with our brains as well as our bodies. This means having traps and ambushes, and sending out scouts, and taking hostages for ransom and torture. It also includes surprise attacks, and fighting at night, and ways of scaring the other gang back to their own territory. Malone suggested having a savage dog, which I think is good. We could also shoot flaming arrows and make bombs from fireworks, if Andy can sneak some back from England.

We discussed digging big holes, letting them fill with rain-water, shovelling cow-shit into them to make stinking pits, and covering them with twigs and grass. It's a good idea but we gave it up. Pits take too long to dig, and you have to hide the earth you take out. Also, someone's certain to be spying on you while you're doing it, which makes it pointless.

Malone came up with the brilliant idea of aerial warfare. We could hide in trees and drop things on our enemies when they're sneaking around below us. He says we could use the stuff they mix up in the village garage. They empty the old oil out of engines and put it in a bucket with a shovelful of sawdust. It's used to fill up gearboxes to stop them rattling. He says it's dreadful stuff. The oil stinks and is hard to get off, and the sawdust scratches like buggery. They did it to him once, when he started an apprenticeship with them. That's why he left, and began his own business. It's exactly the same thing the fellows at the lorry works did to de Lacey. It's certainly put me off ever working in the motor business again.

I suggested pouring buckets of paraffin, and dropping rolled-up balls of burning newspaper. That would really finish the enemy off. Malone said it would finish them off permanently, and I'd end up in jail for murder. I thought of using buckets of piss. I've got a pot under my bed, which I'm always forgetting to empty. After a couple of days it smells horrible. I could get the rest of the gang to save theirs, ready for emergencies. It certainly worked well for Jeremy Lynch when he did it to Welch.

Talking about trees reminded me of the swing. I asked Malone if he had any ideas for attaching the rope to the end of the pole. We went into the garden for a look at the problem. Malone said we could have saved ourselves a lot of trouble by attaching the rope to the pole before we lashed it to the tree. I said, 'Yes, but what's the answer now?' 'The answer now,' said Malone, 'is to dismantle the whole thing, start again and do it right.' I was cross that I hadn't thought of this myself; it was so obvious once Malone pointed it out. It's no wonder he treats me as if I'm thick.

Malone said he'd have to go home and change. He was still in his Mass clothes. I hadn't thought of it being Sunday. It was too late to go to Mass. I added it to my list of mortal sins.

Malone came back with scaffold clips to hold the pole to the tree and Jubilee clips to clamp the rope to the pole. He said it's essential to make it safe; a swing of that height gets up a terrific speed on the down-stroke. When we had it all fixed up, Malone went quiet and stood thinking for a couple of minutes. He said the rope looked long enough to reach the parapet round the top of the stable. I asked him what he was getting at. He told me to wait and see, then asked if it was possible to get onto the roof of the stable. I said yes; through the skylight. Malone asked me for a ball of string, picked up a brick, climbed out onto the roof, and let the string down. I tied it to the end of the rope. He pulled the rope up, tied the brick to it, and let go. The brick zoomed down and smashed into the ground. Malone shouted to me to make a note of where it hit. I was mystified. He came down and explained.

We could have the best swing in the world if we used our heads. The rope was long enough to reach the parapet, with enough left over to knot a stick through the end of it. We could get onto the roof, sit on the stick, and launch ourselves into space. Unfortunately, the rope was too long when it hit ground level, but, if we shortened it, we wouldn't be able to reach the parapet. That's what he'd been working out with the brick. The solution was to dig a trench under the swing.

We got spades and did it. It reminded me of the graveyard in the monastery. Myself and Malone were down to eighteen inches in a quarter of the time it took me and Dad. Malone is a genius. He tried the brick several times, and said we'd have to make the trench a bit deeper, because the rope would stretch in use. Then he said the trench had to be wider. People might swivel sideways on the way down. When the hole was finished, Malone tied a sack of earth to the swing, and did more experiments. Finally, he was satisfied, and said I could try it out. I said, 'Thank you; you try it first, you've done all the inventing.' He said, 'No, no, it's your swing; you're entitled to the first go.' It turned out we were both too scared to try it.

Andy turned up and said he wanted a private word with me. Malone winked and said Andy was exactly the fellow we needed; a fearless lunatic. We explained about swinging from the stable roof. Andy did it immediately. He had six swings in a row and said it was the most exciting thing he'd ever done. I said he could keep on as long as he liked. He said no, he didn't want to stop us having a go; he'd be happier if we took it in turns.

I had no choice. I had to do it or Andy would have lost respect for me. I climbed out on the roof, sat on the parapet, shut my eyes, wriggled to the edge, let out a huge roar, and pushed off. It was terrific! I've never had such a feeling of danger and enjoyment in my whole life. I loved it! It even gave me a warm excited feeling in my jake. Andy said the same; he had the feeling he gets from seeing a girl's knickers.

Malone wouldn't take a turn; he said it was a sin to work or play on the Lord's Day. This made me laugh, considering all the digging we'd done. Malone glared and said he had to go home for his tea. Before he went, he asked me where I got the leather jacket that was upstairs. I told him I'd bought it from Christie's brother. He said he hoped I hadn't paid much for it; it looked like the same jacket Lynch tried to sell him a couple of weeks ago. It came from the dump. I told Malone he could have it but he wasn't interested; he already has a leather jacket.

When Malone left, Andy said he'd got something to show me, and we went into the stable. It was a pile of magazines he's borrowed from his father's dark-room. They're full of pictures of naked girls showing off absolutely everything, and smiling at the camera as if they're enjoying themselves. I couldn't believe it. I asked Andy how they persuade girls to do this sort of thing. He said it was no trouble; the photographers just wave money at them and they take their clothes off straight away.

Part Three

Week Eight

Monday 30 July – Sunday 5 August

I woke with a feeling of doom, like a man in a condemned cell. My head ached with worry and my eyes were tense and jumpy. I thought I had flu. Then I remembered Mrs Barrington and the films. I got so anxious I had to get up and go to the lavatory straight away.

Major Longshott caught me in the garden. He's mad about the damage to his flowers. He asked me if I had anything to do with it. I said no; it was a dog a fellow let loose in the garden while he was playing snooker. The Major says if he sees it out there again he'll get his twelve-bore and shoot it. He's not very pleased about the snooker, either. He says Dad has no business running an enterprise of that nature in a domestic dwelling. He's going to take it up with the authorities.

I told Dad. He said if the business continues as well as it's begun, we'll soon have enough money to finish doing up the stable. Then he'll move the whole operation out of the basement and there'll be nothing to annoy the other tenants. I told him I'd got to go into Dublin and needed money. He asked me to wait until the foreigners emptied the machines. He'd give me my two pounds, and money to get him all the latest records. The ones on the juke-box are out of date and the girls are complaining.

I went back to the stable to wait for Mrs Barrington. Andy came round to say he was going to the airport with his dad. They were going in his dad's sports car; would I like to go with them? I said I'd love to but I had to help Dad. Andy said my father must be a right slave-driver. Every time he asks me to go somewhere with him, I say I have to help my Dad.

He wanted his magazines back. I pretended they were hidden in the house and I couldn't get them for fear of Dad catching me. They were actually under my bed in the loft. I didn't like lying to Andy, but I don't want to give them back until I've had a good look at them. Andy went off in a temper, saying I was a bore and a misery-guts. A few minutes later I heard Andy and his dad zoom off up the lane. I never knew Andy's dad had a car. Christie said Stella Rothwell's father was the only person in the terrace who had one.

As soon as the car went, Mrs Barrington appeared. She was dressed in sandals and a pale-blue frock with a thin white leather belt. Her hair was tied back in a pony-tail with a blue ribbon. She looked neat and perfect, as if she was going to a party. We were very stiff with each other. She said she was sorry to keep me waiting; she couldn't come round while Mr Barrington and Andy were still at home.

She said it would be best if we went into Dublin separately, and met up later. She didn't want anyone to see us together, in case it got back to Andy or Mr Barrington, and made them suspicious. She offered me the money for my fare. I told her coldly that I could afford to pay for myself, thank you very much. She'd been very calm up to then, but she looked at me suddenly with a desperate expression and said, 'Michael . . . please, tell me! What have I done?' She put her hand on my arm and I jerked it away. She burst into tears and said that if she'd done something to hurt me, for God's sake tell her what it was and she'd try and make it up to me.

It nearly broke my heart to see her so upset. She looked so young and innocent and pretty, and so miserable and confused. For a moment I stopped believing all the things I'd heard about her. My tough expression faded a bit. She came close and looked up into my eyes so I couldn't avoid her. 'Please, Michael . . . what is it?' She gave a huge sob and a sniff, and a big tear quivered on the end of her nose. 'Why don't you like me any more?' My brain was in a turmoil. I wanted to scream with the pain I could feel in both of us.

I ran down the stairs so she couldn't see my face, and threw myself down among the bales of straw on the stable floor. Mrs Barrington came down and knelt beside me with her hands together in her lap. My head was pounding. I put my hands over my ears so I wouldn't hear anything she said. She shook her head and gave a long sigh of misery, then collapsed forward on top of me. She put her arms round me and clung to me as if she was drowning. I could feel the warmth and softness of her, and the shudder in her body every time she sobbed. I took my hands away from my head and put them round her waist, and held her so tightly it made her gasp for breath.

A car screeched to a halt outside, scattering gravel against the door. Andy ran in and rushed over to the bottom of the stairs, thinking I was still in the loft. Mrs Barrington had her head buried in my shoulder and didn't see him come in. He shouted up the stairway. 'We've come back to give you one last chance!' As soon as Andy yelled, her head shot up and she gave a quick gasp of surprise. Andy turned round and saw us still hugging each other. 'Jesus!' he said, and stood staring at us. Mrs Barrington let go of me and tried to sit up. She said, 'Andy . . . Andy, please . . .' He gave us a disgusted look and walked out. We heard Mr Barrington saying 'Well?' and Andy saying 'No, he's still too busy' in a toneless voice. They drove off again with a terrific revving of the engine and another clatter of gravel against the door.

After this we brushed the straw off our clothes and caught the bus into Dublin. Mrs Barrington said there wasn't much point travelling separately after what had happened. We hardly spoke at first. She spent most of the journey putting on new make-up. She was very polite, and asked me if I minded. We sat in the front seat so she could see herself in the window. She said it was too bumpy to use the little mirror she had in her bag.

It was only when Mrs Barrington had to pay my fare that I remembered I hadn't seen Dad about money before I went. I told her I was supposed to buy the Top Twenty. Mrs Barrington said she'd lend me the money to get the records, so Dad wouldn't be disappointed. I said this was very nice of her. She took my hand and gave it a squeeze, and smiled at our reflections in the window. She said it was lovely to have me speaking to her again. She didn't try to keep hold of my hand. I suppose she was afraid I'd snatch it away.

I asked her about Mr Barrington's car. She said it's not really his. There are four English pilots at the airport. One of them brought it over. They share it between them. It's not worth having one each, because they work so much. I asked if it was an MG. She said she didn't know; it was a just a red sports car to her. I said I'd seen it down the lane, and once I'd noticed it parked along the coast road. I asked her if it belonged to the man I'd had the trouble with, at her house. She said no; he'd only borrowed it. I asked if he was one of the English pilots. Mrs Barrington shook her head and said she didn't want to talk about it any more.

At the photographic shop she asked me to wait along the street, and keep well out of sight. If there were any problems she'd come out and let me know. I walked up and down looking in shop windows for about ten minutes. Mrs Barrington came out and walked casually down the street as if she was on her own. I waited until she got round the corner into Abbey Street, then followed her.

The man in the shop tried to cheat her. He said she could have the photographs but not the negatives. He wanted to keep them for himself. She couldn't argue with him, because people kept coming into the shop. She arranged to go back and talk to him privately when he shut the shop for lunch at one o'clock. I asked her why she was so desperate to get the negatives back. She said they're very private photographs, of people being drunk and uninhibited. I asked her what 'uninhibited' meant. She said, 'Doing things they wouldn't normally do.'

We had two hours to waste. Mrs Barrington was quiet and thoughtful the whole time. We walked up Grafton Street and bought two small bottles of lemonade, a packet of Kraft cheese slices, and a big crusty turnover. The sun shone on Mrs Barrington's hair and made it glow. Coming out of the baker's shop I was behind her. The sunlight shone right through her dress. I could see her body outlined as if she was only wearing a thin veil. It gave me a warm cosy feeling about her.

We went to Stephen's Green and sat on a bench to have our picnic lunch. When we'd eaten as much as we wanted, Mrs Barrington got up and stood at the edge of the pond feeding the ducks. I was still sitting down. She was between me and the sun, so I couldn't help seeing through her dress again. A man passing by noticed Mrs Barrington, and sat down beside me with a big wink. He stared at her for a few minutes, and said it was as good as a front seat at the Windmill. I got annoyed at having my pleasure spoilt, and with the dirty looks he was giving her. I took her round to Merrion Square and showed her the gorillas in the natural history museum. She said they reminded her of fellows she'd known. She didn't smile when she said it.

We were late getting back to the photographic shop. The man was looking out through the window with a bad-tempered expression. Mrs Barrington was upset. She said it wasn't a good start, and she might be inside for quite a while. I borrowed five pounds from her and went down Talbot Street to McHugh's. It took me over an hour to listen to all the Top Twenty records. I wanted to make sure there weren't any soppy love songs that people wouldn't be able to dance to. Mr McHugh put them into a cardboard box and then put the box in a small sack. They were a ferocious weight. He told me I had to be very careful not to drop them. They crack with the slightest touch.

When I got back to Marlborough Street Mrs Barrington was waiting on the corner. She looked tired and irritable. She'd been waiting ages for me. I said sorry. She gave me an angry look and walked off round to O'Connell Street for the bus. I couldn't keep up with her because of the weight of the records. I was afraid if I rushed the bag would split. I noticed her belt was twisted, and the ribbon was missing from her hair.

On the bus we didn't speak at first. She got out her make-up and put on lipstick, then she took the ribbon out of her bag and tied her hair up. She looked out the window and said, 'God . . . what a horrible experience.' She started to say something about 'Your photographer friend –' but I interrupted her and said, 'He's no friend of mine.' She was going to say something else but the conductor came to collect our fares.

When he'd gone she took a deep breath and said, 'I've got the photographs, Michael.' She stopped, and shuddered. 'And the negatives.' She said she'd looked at the photographs, and couldn't see any that looked as if they belonged to me. I didn't want to admit the Stella photos were mine, so I said I'd already had my photographs, the first time I went back. 'I see,' she said. 'And what were they?' 'Pictures of the house,' I said, 'and the garden, and Dad.'

She asked me more questions. Her voice was quiet and she didn't look at me once. 'You never took any pictures of girlfriends, then?' I said no; I hadn't got a girlfriend, anyway. 'Or of girls that you fancy?' I shook my head but she couldn't see it. 'Michael?' I said no; I hadn't taken any photos of girls, except of her with me. 'So all these photographs –' she patted her handbag, 'these films – were from Richard's dark-room?' I said yes. 'And there's no possibility of any of them belonging to someone else?' I said no; not unless the photographer had mixed up someone else's films with ours. 'No,' she said. 'No. I've looked at them. They're all people I know.'

When we got off the bus she went home without saying any more to me. I went into the basement. It was packed with people playing snooker. I thought Dad would be delighted but he was sitting in the back room miserably drinking a mug of tea. He says he's been diddled. The foreigners came out and emptied the machines and said the take had been very low. They gave Dad thirty shillings. He knows for a fact he should have got more, because the crowds at the weekend had at least thirty pounds' worth of pennies off him. He was up and down to the village shops all day getting change. He says he's going to keep a strict eye on the situation from now on, especially the juke-box. It'll be easy to check what goes into it; all he has to do is make a tick on a bit of paper every time a record is played. I gave him the bag of Top Twenty records and it bucked him up. He said he'd put them into the juke-box straight away.

I went out to the stable to read Andy's magazines. They were covered in dust from being under the bed. I blew the dust off and spread them on my bed. I got an attack of sneezing. A voice said, 'Bless you!' It was Mrs Barrington. I went as red as a beetroot at being caught. She looked at the magazines and said, 'Michael, Michael, you're wasting your time. There's nothing like the real thing.' She smiled but it was a bright, brittle smile. It scared me.

She said she was feeling tense, and needed something to relax her. I asked her if she'd like to go out for a walk, and she said no. I said, 'What about a swing in the garden?' She ignored that idea and walked up close to me. I backed away against the wall. She followed me, and put her hands round my throat, pretending to strangle me. The smell of her breath was prickly with whiskey. It made my eyes water. 'You've been a very bad boy, Michael. Those photographs are going to cause me a lot of trouble.' I said I was sorry, I really was. She said that wasn't good enough; she was going to have to punish me. She let go of me and did a dance round the loft, swinging her arms in circles and making her dress swirl.

When she stopped she was flushed and dizzy. She stood at the end of my bed and stretched her arms out sideways, then let herself fall backwards. She lay giggling for a moment, then realised she was lying on the magazines. She sat up, picked a magazine from the pile, flicked through it, chose a picture, and held it open for

314

me to look at. The girl in the picture was standing naked, smiling, with an arm across her breasts and a hand covering her fanny. Mrs Barrington looked at me, and asked me what I thought. I said I didn't know how women could do such things without dying of embarrassment.

Mrs Barrington tossed her hair out of her eyes and gave me a long stare. She put the magazine down and said, 'It's easy . . .' She slid off the end of the bed and knelt on the floor. Her frock billowed for a moment, then settled into a neat circle round her legs. 'Watch . . .' She took hold of the hem with her fingertips and stood up in one smooth graceful movement, pulling her frock up and over her head as she did so. She hadn't a stitch on underneath. I shivered with the shock of it. She twirled the dress airily round her head and dropped it, then put an arm across her breasts and a hand on her tummy, her fingers spread like a fan. She put on a big pretend smile and said 'Cheeeeese!' She posed for a moment, then swept the magazines off the bed and lay down.

I asked her how she'd managed to get the negatives back from the photographer. She said, 'It's better not to ask,' and put her arms behind her head and shut her eyes. I asked her straight out if she'd had to let him shag her. Mrs Barrington curled up like a baby, hugging her knees to her chin with her arms, and laughing. I had to look away. She said that as I'd asked her a direct question, she'd give me a direct answer. No, she hadn't had to let the man shag her. I said I didn't believe her, and told her about noticing the twist in her belt. Mrs Barrington sat up and said she'd give me another direct answer. She did offer to go to bed with him, but as soon as she started to strip off he creamed his trousers. A typical DOM, she said; all talk until they get the chance, and then they can't do it.

In the end, she got away with just posing for him. I asked her what sort of poses. She laughed, and said, 'Oh, just typical family album stuff.' She stood up and said, 'You know; this sort of thing . . .' Before I could say anything she turned her back to me and bent forward to touch the floor with her fingertips. I couldn't believe it. I was sure I was in a dirty dream. She straightened up and turned round and leaned backwards with her arms and legs spread wide. I told her to stop. She said she hadn't got to the good ones yet. I told her I didn't want to see any more. She smiled and sat down on the bed. I asked her how she could possibly do it; supposing the man started spreading the pictures around? She said it didn't matter; she was going back to England soon. I was startled to hear this. I wanted to ask her about it but she said she'd got more immediate matters on her mind.

She came over and stood in front of me. I backed away. She followed me, smiling. I ended up braced against the wall, rigid with nervousness. Mrs Barrington stretched up on tiptoes to kiss me, and said, 'Try saying "Cheese", Michael.' She put her arms round my neck and lifted her feet off the floor. I hardly noticed her weight. She whispered in my ear.

'Do you like me, Michael? Do you? Do you, do you, do you?' Her breath tickled me and I couldn't help giggling. She giggled too, and stuck her tongue in my ear. My face went hot and I got shivers down my back. Mrs Barrington put her feet on the ground and leaned back, with her arms still round my neck. Her tummy pressed tight against mine and my willie swelled up instantly. She felt it, and rubbed herself from side to side against me, swinging from her arms.

At first she smiled, then her expression changed. She shut her eyes and began to moan, and her mouth fell half-open. She pressed against me even harder, and tried to force her knee between my legs. I got frightened, and said, 'Please, Mrs Barrington . . . that hurts.' Her eyes snapped open and she stared at me with a look like a cobra about to strike. Her eyes were huge and dark, and she breathed in quick panting gasps through her mouth, her teeth together and her lips wide open.

She took one arm from round my neck and said, 'Give me your hand, Michael.' I tried to say no, but she had me paralysed with fear and longing. She took my hand and put it between her legs, and groaned, and said, 'Ooooh . . . God . . . Oh God . . . '

She told me to press my fingers firmly against her, and asked me if I noticed anything. I didn't want to say it but she made me. I said her fanny was damp. 'And do you know why?' She said this in a soft breathless voice. I was so excited and scared by what was happening. I didn't know what to say; I could hardly think or speak.

She stepped back and undid my belt. 'There's something I need, Michael. I need it badly –' She dropped my belt on the floor. 'And I need it now.' I said, 'Please, Mrs Barrington . . . ' but she took no notice. She undid the buttons on my trousers and pulled them down. My willie burst out straight away, because I hadn't got any trunks on. I was dreadfully embarrassed. It stuck out for miles, all red and swollen and throbbing with desperate urges. Mrs Barrington looked at it without any shyness. She said, 'That's what I want, Michael; and then I'll be my normal sweet self again.'

She took hold of my jake with both hands. Her fingers were cool and gentle. It was so gorgeous it hurt. She rubbed the end of my jake against her tummy, and I wanted to scream with the delicious agony of it. I asked her if she was going to stick my jake up her fanny? She said yes, in a matter-of-fact voice. I said I was afraid of catching a dreadful disease through her not being a virgin. She said I needn't worry; she keeps herself safe with some medical stuff she has.

I asked her if we'd have a baby, but she told me to shut up. She put her arms round my neck again, and pulled herself up until the end of my jake slipped between her legs. She jiggled about until I was just inside her fanny, then dropped her hips down again. I felt her slide right down the length of my jake in one smooth movement. She wriggled herself until I was as far up her as I could possibly reach. Next thing I knew she lifted her feet off the ground and wrapped her legs round my waist, clinging to me the way a monkey clings to a tree, and began thrusting herself back and forwards. She told me to put my hands under her bottom, to hold her up, and to dig my fingers into her, tight. I did, and she said, 'Harder; I want it to hurt.'

I was so worried about making her angry again, I forgot I was being shagged. I just concentrated on keeping my mouth shut, and squeezing her bum as tightly as I could, and making sure I didn't lose my balance. After a couple of minutes she got into an absolute frenzy, threshing backwards and forwards as if she'd lost her senses. I got terrified, and thought she was having a fit. My arms felt as if they were going to pull out of their sockets.

Just when I couldn't bear the worry and the weight a moment longer, she flung her head back and gave a terrible groan, as if she was dying in agony. I tried to lift her off me, thinking I'd hurt her by having my jake so far up inside her. She lifted her head and screamed at me, her eyes blazing like a madwoman. 'No! No! For Christ's sake; push against me! Push! Push! Push!'

I strained my hips forward as hard as I could. She gave a long piercing scream right in my ear. At the same time, her insides began throbbing round my jake. After a while the throbbing stopped and her whole body went limp. Her legs and arms stayed wrapped round me but she stopped gripping me. I had to take her whole weight on my hands. My wrists were in terrible pain. Her face went quiet and peaceful, the wild look went from her eyes, and her mouth curled into a beautiful shy smile. She snuggled against me and felt all soft and warm and babyish. I thought how beautiful she was, and how lovely it was to hold her naked in my arms, and then without warning my willie spurted inside her.

I'm not going to say what it felt like, because I can't. I know that afterwards I felt gentle and holy and strong, like a guardian angel. I carried her over to the bed and sat down on the end of it, with her still clinging to me. She said she wanted me to stay inside her as long as possible, and told me to lie back very carefully. I did, and we fell asleep, with her lying on top of me. When we woke up she said she had a terrible headache. Her knees were bleeding where she'd scraped them against the wall. I asked her what Mr Barrington would say. She said he'd probably find the whole thing very stimulating, but she wasn't exactly planning to tell him about it. I said I was talking about her cut knees. 'Oh,' she said. 'Them? I'll say I've been kneeling too much, weeding the garden.'

She asked me what I thought of sex. I told her I hadn't enjoyed it; I was too scared of her. She apologised for being so bossy. She said there are times when she gets very wound up. The only way she can relax is to make love. I wanted to do it again, properly, without feeling scared, but she said no. I asked her why not, and she said it was part of the punishment. I didn't like this; it sounded a bit sinister. She said I ought to take her remarks less seriously; she was only teasing me. She said this jokingly, then her voice went serious. She said sex is always a mixture of pleasure and pain. The pain is often as enjoyable as the pleasure, if you know the right way to go about it.

Some people, she said, can't get any pleasure without the pain, and others just want the pain without any of the pleasure. None of this made any sense to me. She said maybe she'll show me, sometime, what she means. I said I wasn't too sure I wanted her to. She laughed, and said I was hopeless. Then she got dressed and left. I fell asleep immediately, even though it was quite early in the evening, and still light outside.

I spent the night dreaming of Mrs Barrington, and woke up with an enormous willie. I put my hand down and gripped it. A huge booming voice in my brain shouted 'Stop!' I opened my eyes and saw God's face staring down at me from the darkness at the top of the ceiling. It gave me a terrible fright. My whole life has become a sinful mess. I even skive off Mass without feeling guilty.

I got up and made my bed properly, meaning to make a fresh start. I was nearly sick when I pulled the blankets off. A big dead spider was curled up just where my feet had been. I couldn't understand how it got into the bed, after all the trouble I went to with the tins. I looked and discovered the water had all dried up. I filled them again straight away.

I made a resolution to think pure thoughts all day, and fill my time with clean boyish activities. After I made Dad's tea I asked him if he had any jobs that needed doing. We brushed the tables and swept the floors. We couldn't believe the amount of cigarette butts we collected. There were thousands of them.

The bar-billiards table is causing problems. When the balls go down certain holes they don't come back. Dad says he'll have to get the man out from Dublin right away; he can't wait until next Monday.

I asked him about sex, and whether it's a sin. Dad said yes, except within the sacred bounds of marriage. I told him Malone says it isn't, and he got cross. He said, 'Sex is the worst sin of the lot, and the one that keeps most people from leading a holy life.' I asked him if there was any way you could have sex without it being a sin, and without being married. He said yes; if it was forced on you, against your will, and provided you took no pleasure in it. It looks as if I'm all right where Mrs Barrington is concerned. My big worry was having to go to confession and tell the priest. He might make me apologise to Mr Barrington for doing sinful things with his wife.

Dad spent the rest of the morning looking through the tea-chests we packed when we moved. He has a lot of penny insurance policies. If he puts them all together they might be worth cashing in. We could put the money towards doing up the stable.

He found his old gramophone and a box of records. He gave

319

me both things. The motor in the record-player is burnt out, so it's no good. I decided to dismantle it and use the bits for experiments. There are loads of articles in *Hobbies Weekly* telling boys how to make amplifiers and crystal sets out of old radios and gramophones.

I took everything out to my work-bench in the stable and got started. Christie arrived and asked me what I was doing. When I told him, he said I was an eejit with no business sense whatever. I thanked him sarcastically and enquired as to the business use of a broken gramophone and a pile of old records?

Christie said it was simple; I should be fixing the machine instead of making it worse. Then we could set up a private dance hall in the stable, playing records and charging people money to get in. I was cross with Christie for being such a pain in the bum. He's always thinking about money. I told him no one would want to dance to Dad's records. They're all ancient things by Mario Lanza and John McCormack and Jimmy Shand and Mantovani. Christie said he sometimes wonders why he bothers with me; I don't seem to know the first thing about mots and fellows.

Dancing is only an excuse to get together for a snog and a bit of gas. Nobody would be paying any attention to the music. They'd be too busy getting their hands into each other's clothes. Especially if we only had a forty-watt bulb to light the place. Better still, he said, we could get a coloured bulb. A red one is best; red lights make girls go mad for a length of jake. His brother told him this, and he should know; he spends all his spare time going to dances.

I told Christie about the burnt-out motor. He said, 'Could we not get a new one?' I told him it would be at least two pounds and he'd have to go halves with me. This put him off right away. He suggested going down the dump to look for another record-player. It might have a good motor in it. I said I was still wary about going out, in case Bowman's gang catch me. I thought of Malone, and said we could ask him to look out for one. He's allowed into the dump. Christie said no; Malone would want a share in the business if we involved him in any way.

While we were thinking about the problem, I had a look in my boxes of experimental equipment. I found a Meccano motor which was too small and a motor out of a fridge which was too big. Christie said he'd go and get an old Hoover from his house, one that his sisters don't use since the bag split to ribbons. We could take the motor out of that. I told him it wasn't that simple. Gramophone motors are a special sort that go at exactly the right speed. Christie said I was a right knocker, and went off to get the Hoover.

While he was gone I took the turntable and motor out of the gramophone. Christie came back with the Hoover. It was in a terrible state. I dismantled the motor out of it. There was a fan on the end of the shaft, held on by a nut and a washer each side. I took it off, and discovered that the diameter of the shaft was exactly the same size as the hole in the middle of a record. This gave me an idea. I put a record on the shaft and tightened it on with the nuts and washers. Christie thought that I was daft. He said the motor was too big to go in the cabinet. I said I could soon make a new cabinet. 'The only problem,' I said, 'is that Hoover motors go at a terrific speed and records go a lot slower.' Christie wanted to know what difference this would make. It shows how ignorant he is about scientific matters. I told him the record would be going so fast the sound would be just a high-pitched whistle. He said that was no problem; we could say all the records were by Ronnie Ronalde.

Once I had the record fixed on, nothing would do him but to switch the motor on. I said no; it would be stupid until we found some way of making it go at the right speed. He got huffy and said it was his motor, and he could do what he liked with it. That was how we nearly got killed.

I took the wire and electric plug out of the remains of the Hoover, connected it to the motor terminals by the little brass screws, and switched it on. It wobbled all over the place and couldn't get up speed. I unplugged it and put it into the gramophone cabinet. We wedged it upright with books and plugged it in again. The motor and record were steady as a rock, and zoomed up to a terrific speed. The record went so fast it made a screaming noise like a siren.

Then it suddenly blew up. There was a terrific bang, and the record flew into bits. The bits went smashing into the walls of the cabinet and the cabinet itself exploded. Christie and me got walloped by mangled bits of wood with sharp slivers of record embedded in them. If the wood hadn't taken the force of the exploding record, it would have cut us to shreds, instead of wrecking the cabinet.

It gave us such a shock we both went white and nearly fainted. I was glad Dad hadn't seen us. He would have been livid with me for being so stupid. Christie was quiet for a minute, which is unusual for him, then he said, 'Jesus, do you realise what we've done?' I said yes, but God must have been watching over us, otherwise we'd be dead. Christie got impatient and said that wasn't what he was on about; he'd had a great idea.

He asked me if I had another wooden box anywhere. He spotted the orange-box I use for a bedside table. 'That'll do,' he said, and tipped everything off it. I thought he was going queer from the fright, but he said no; he wanted to try the whole thing out again. He told me to put another record on the shaft. I said no, it was too dangerous, but he insisted. He said we'd take cover behind the bed this time.

The orange-box explosion was terrific. It was much lighter wood than the record cabinet, and blew into much smaller bits, all over the room. Also, it gave a huge bang when it disintegrated.

We did it again, with a big cardboard box. This was useless. It shredded into scraps instantly and didn't make a bang. The bits of record cut through it with no trouble. They flew all over the room, and smashed the light bulb and one of the window-panes. A bit shot past the end of the bed. Christie had his leg sticking out, and it ripped through the leg of his trousers. Half an inch nearer and it would have taken a slice out of his leg.

'That's it, then,' said Christie. 'Orange-boxes are the thing. We can get loads of them from the fruit shop. Mr Talbot even pays fellows to take them away.' I asked him what he was talking about. 'A show, you daft fucker; we can put on a show and charge people to come in!' He said we'd need loads of old records from jumble sales. We could charge a penny to watch one explosion, or sixpence to watch ten. I told him it was too dangerous. 'That's exactly what's so good about it!' Christie was so excited he had spit-froth on his chin. He said fellows are always desperate for some new thing to look at. Exploding orange-boxes were just the job.

There was a hammering on the door downstairs. We looked out over the half-door. Stella was down in the lane, beating the door with the palms of her hands. She kept saying, 'Are you in there, boy?' She pronounced 'boy' with a sarcastic loudness, and dragged it out in a long drawl.

'Jesus,' said Christie, 'she's drunk.' Stella heard him and looked up. 'Ah; there you are . . .' She leaned back to see us better, and nearly fell over backwards. 'And your tiny friend!' Christie's eyes bulged. He hates people to mention his size. He told Stella he'd piss on her if she didn't go away. Stella laughed and said that was the least of her worries. I asked her what she wanted. 'I just wanted to show you . . .' she stopped and gulped as if she was about to be sick. 'I just wanted to show you . . . show you . . .' she gulped again, 'how the mighty have fallen . . .' Then she vomited all down the door, in one quick spurt of liquid. I was stunned. She looked up and wiped her mouth with her sleeve and said, 'Sorry about that . . .' Before I could move she was gone.

'God Almighty,' I said to Christie. 'Did you see that?' Christie said he could hardly miss it. He leaned out the door and looked down to where the vomit was still steaming on the bottom door and said, 'What a fucking smell!' I leaned out beside him and had a sniff. It was like someone had poured a bottle of whiskey against the door, only it didn't smell quite like whiskey. It was sweeter. Christie said it was gin. Ellen keeps a bottle in the house. He said Stella must have been round the pub again. I said, 'What do you mean, again?' Christie said she's started drinking. She goes round to Dolan's and sits by herself in a corner, drinking and staring at fellows. The publican doesn't like it. It gives the pub a bad reputation. Single women drinking on their own get taken for prostitutes.

A man came out of the archway. He had red hair and a tweed sports jacket. He looked very relaxed, with his hands in his pockets and a cigarette in his mouth. 'Jesus,' said Christie, 'I'm off!' I looked at him, puzzled. 'It's the detective! The fellow from Dublin.' My heart missed a beat, the way Christie said it. Then I realised I'd got nothing to worry about, and said, 'So what?' Christie said, 'So he's seen Stella yelling up at us; that's what! We'll be on his list of suspects!' He scrambled down the stairs. I went over to the windows and watched him run through the garden and disappear into the basement.

I went back and looked into the lane. The detective was studying the downstairs door. The smoke of his cigarette drifted up, mixed with the steam and smell from Stella's vomit. He looked up at me and nodded. 'A bad business, eh?' He asked me if I knew the girl who'd done it. I said yes. He said he'd like to come up and have a chat with me.

He came up the stairs very slowly, taking the steps one at a time in a dignified way, and stopped at the top. After a good look round, he asked me if I had an ash tray. I said no. He walked across and threw his cigarette out the half-door. He asked me what all the stuff on the table was for. I said I was an amateur scientist. 'That's a good thing to be,' he said. 'There's money in science.'

I explained about the exploding records. The detective frowned, and said it struck him as a dangerous business. He asked me to demonstrate it. When it was all set up I told him to crouch down behind the bed. He said, 'What's to stop it shooting under the bed, and cutting the legs off the pair of us?' I told him we'd be safe; I keep a lot of junk under the bed. He went over and pulled the blankets up to have a look. 'Well, well, well,' he said. 'What have we here?'

He took out Mr Barrington's camera and stared at it, then he stared at me. 'This is a quare thing to keep under the bed.' He asked me if I wasn't afraid of it getting jammed up with dust. I said I kept it hidden there so it wouldn't be stolen. Did I not know, he said, that under the bed is the first place that burglars go for? He had another look under the bed and pulled out Andy's pin-up magazines. 'Well, well, well. This is getting more interesting by the minute.' When he pulled out the dirty drawings of Stella I just wanted to die with shame. I could have killed myself for being so stupid.

After that we had a long chat. He took away the magazines and the drawings and the packet of Durex I'd been keeping for future deals with Christie's brother. He said they were illegal in Ireland. I asked him if I was going to be had up for it. He said no; he was interested in bigger matters at the moment. I spent the rest of the day in a state of sweaty fear.

Christie came back after tea. I told him the detective won't let us do the exploding record show; it's too dangerous. He said we'd have to go ahead with the dance idea. I told him I wasn't interested in dances, or anything else. I just want to die. He went off and came back with a gramophone, borrowed from the Sergeant's lost property shed. He's going to paint it a different colour in case someone recognises it and tries to claim it back.

I asked Christie what rape is. He laughed and said it's an impossibility. A woman with her skirt up can run faster than a man with his trousers down. I told him I'd kill him if he didn't give me a straight answer. He said it means being shagged against your will.

When it got dark I went down the strand for a walk. The tide was right out. I walked to the point and out along the sandbank. Stella was sitting on the end of it, staring at the moonlight shining on the wet sandy squiggles.

I stood behind her and said 'Stella . . .' in a quiet voice, so as not to frighten her. She didn't move or look round. I said, 'It's Michael.' She said she knew who it was. I sat down beside her and told her I knew how she felt; I'd been raped too. She didn't say anything for a moment, then she shrugged. 'By a woman?' I said it could hardly be by a man. Stella said she wouldn't know; I was so innocent she wouldn't put anything past me.

After a while she said I should be pleased. From what she'd heard, it was every boy's ambition to lose his virginity. I said it wasn't mine; I'd been quite happy as I was. She told me I should think myself lucky; sexual experience is supposed to turn boys into men. For girls it's different. It turns them into cheap sluts.

She asked me who raped me. I told her I'd rather not say. She asked me was it Mrs Barrington, by any chance? If it hadn't been for the dark my face would have given me away. Stella stood up and said she was going. We walked back together. Stella put her arm through mine. It made me feel very manly and grown up. When we got to the bottom of the lane she gave me a peck on the cheek and said she wasn't going home just yet. I asked her if she was going to the pub. She said she might; she had things to attend to before she went. I asked her what she meant. She put her finger to her lips and shook her head. 'There are some things it's better I shouldn't tell you.' I came home and lay on my bed thinking, for the rest of the night.

Just after midnight I heard a car coming slowly and quietly down the lane. It was the red MG. Mr Barrington was in it, with Stella beside him. I could see them quite clearly in the moonlight. Her arm was hanging out over the door and her head was tilted right back. She had her eyes shut and her mouth open. When they stopped down the lane Mr Barrington had to help her out. He propped her against the wall and held her up. I think he kissed her but I'm not sure; there's a telegraph pole that blocks my view of the wall in that part of the lane.

Dad's friend, Joe Harding, cycled out from Dublin today. Mr Harding is sixty-eight but tall and lean and healthy. He looks like a tinker in his old hat and suit. He dresses to please himself, and doesn't give a hoot what people think about him. He goes everywhere on his bicycle. It's a heavy old-fashioned ladies' model. He says it's easier to get on and off than if it had a crossbar. Mr Harding has a gammy leg, from the War. That's why he took up cycling; to exercise the leg.

He used to be in the British Army. Now he spends most of his time cycling round Europe. He likes visiting strange places and learning languages. He always has a tent rolled up on the carrier of his bike, and a big rucksack strapped to a special frame on the handlebars. He never knows when the travel bug will strike, so he likes to be ready at all times.

There was an unfortunate incident when he arrived. Mr Harding wasn't sure which house we lived in, so he walked along the terrace peering into the basements to see if he could spot us. Major Longshott was sitting upstairs, looking out of his front window. He thought Mr Harding was a knife sharpener or a pedlar. He came out and told Joe to clear off and hawk his wares somewhere else. Mr Harding is a gentleman. Instead of bashing Major Longshott on the nose he decided to try round the back.

Major Longshott came stumping down the front stairs on his stick. He told Dad about his adventure with the tramp, and how he'd jolly-well told the beggar to clear off. Dad didn't know that the Major was talking about Joe. He invited the Major in for a cup of tea. At the same moment, Joe arrived in through the back of the house. Dad was delighted to see him. He introduced him to the Major as a very old friend from Dublin.

The Major went very red in the face. He walked over to Mr Harding, stiff and bad-tempered, and put out his hand. He stretched his arm at full length, as if he wanted to keep Mr Harding as far away as possible. 'Laurence J. Longshott,' he said, in a pompous voice; 'Major, Indian Army, Retired.' He made a big thing of pronouncing 'Major', saying it as if it was in capital letters and underlined.

Mr Harding put out his hand, shook the Major's, and said,

'Delighted to meet you, old boy.' He spoke in his best English accent, the one he got from being in the army. The Major was startled. He jumped back and stared at Mr Harding for a moment, then put on a sarcastic voice and said 'I don't believe I caught the name . . .'

Mr Harding looked at Dad, and then at me, and winked. 'Joseph A. Harding,' he said to the Major, then paused for a moment and added, 'General, British Army, Retired.' Major Longshott gulped, turned pale and then red, snapped to attention, and saluted him.

Mr Harding was startled for a split second. He recovered, and saluted the Major back. Then he said, 'At ease, Major,' and shook his hand again, and said, 'Ex-Guardian of the Empire, what? A rare breed now, eh! Pleasure to meet you, sir. Absolute pleasure! Bless m'soul, yes indeed! Honoured! Believe me, sir! Honoured!'

The Major was delighted. He stuck his chest out and his eyes sparkled with pride. Dad invited him to stay and have a chat. The Major said he couldn't. He had to report back to HQ. The memsahib would have noted his absence. He marched up the stairs without using his stick.

I left Dad and Mr Harding chatting. Joe was back to his normal voice. It's a soft quiet Dublin accent. Joe is the son of a famous lord who lives in Wicklow. I can never remember the name.

I went down the lane and round to the green. I wanted to talk to Sculley. He always knows what's going on.

The red MG was in the lane. Stella was standing inside the derelict stable belonging to the bottom house. She was talking to someone. I couldn't see who it was. Stella had her back to me. She didn't notice me walking past.

Sculley was in the front room of his house. He was trying to put a ribbon in a typewriter. I watched him through the window. He hadn't a clue. His mother came to the door and asked me what I wanted. I said I was a friend of Sculley's. She gave me a funny look and said she'd see if Norman was free to speak to me. Norman! Bloody Hell! I walked off in a temper.

Sculley came running after me. He said his mother has a thing about the way fellows dress. If they're not wearing a tie and creased trousers she calls them 'scruffs'. She thought I was one of the Dump gang.

She's in a bad temper with Sculley. It's over the silent farting trick. She found a pile of dirty hankies under his bed. He got a good walloping for having filthy habits. He told her he'd had to use them to wipe his bum at school. There was never any paper in the lavatory. His mother said he should have used his homework jotter. That was all it was fit for.

Sculley was hurt by this. He puts a lot of effort into his homework. He says his mother's just jealous. She was working in a hat shop in Thomas Street when his father met her, and she knows nothing about anything.

He asked me if I was any good with typewriters. I said yes. His dad has given him a second-hand Imperial. It's from the Tech where he's a headmaster. Sculley is going to use it to write stories. He fancies being a famous writer when he grows up. He plans to specialise in Westerns. Roy Rogers is his hero.

Sculley had made a total mess of the ribbon. I got filthy putting everything right. We tipped a cupful of paraffin out of the heater in his dad's greenhouse. It took the ink off our hands with no trouble. I dipped bits of toilet-roll in the cup and cleaned the machine. I felt great afterwards. It's ages since I've done anything pure and useful.

I tested the typewriter by printing all the letters of the alphabet. Sculley said I should have done 'the quick brown fox jumps over the lazy dog'. I said my way was better. It was quicker, for one thing.

I tested the number keys by working out the formula for the weight of air pressing on the surface of the world. Baldy gave it to us at school. I've never forgotten it; he drew it in such a way that the figures make up a sketch of a toy steam-engine. Baldy was great at things like that.

Sculley stopped me before I finished typing out the final answer. He said there were too many noughts in it. He was afraid I'd wear out the ribbon.

I told Sculley I want him in my gang. Sculley was suspicious. He asked me why. I didn't tell him I want him to spy for me. I made up the excuse that I need bodyguards to protect me from Bowman's men. Sculley gave a big juicy snort and said I had an amazing cheek. He was the one who needed protection, not me. I told him he'd get it, if he joined us.

'"Us?"' he said. 'You and who else?' I had to think of something, quickly, so I told him I couldn't say at the moment; I'm keeping the membership secret until the initiation ceremony. Sculley seemed to be satisfied with this. Actually, I may never have a gang at all, ever. I haven't seen Andy since he caught me in the stable with his mother. Christie is avoiding me, for some reason. Malone, I never know about, one way or the other.

Sculley wanted to know what I'd give him if he joined. 'Give *you*?' I said. I told him it was an honour to join. He should be giving *me* something, to let him in. He wouldn't budge. I offered him my Meccano collection. He said he'd already seen it, and it was a right joke; what could he build with three base-plates, a load of wheels with the tyres missing, and dozens of rusty perforated strips? 'You haven't even got any nuts and bolts!'

I told him I'd got beyond playing with kid's stuff. He said it would be different if I was offering him a gear set, or a complete Number Five. I told him I'd throw in a pile of *Eagle* comics and a *Beano* annual.

'I never read the *Eagle*. It's a snotty, Proddy English comic.'

I said it was the best comic there is, but Sculley wasn't convinced. 'Anyway,' he said, 'I get the *Beano* annual myself, every Christmas.' I got fed up and told him I'd torture him if he didn't join. Sculley's eyes lit up. 'What will the torture be?'

I couldn't think of anything, straight off, so I told him it would be the very worst thing he could imagine. 'Will it involve being blindfolded and tied to a tree?'

'It could do . . .' I said.

'And having my trousers pulled down?' I nodded.

'And a crowd of girls jeering me and grabbing my willie?' I said he was a right pervert, but if that was what he wanted, I'd try to arrange it. Sculley was thrilled to bits.

'You can keep the comics and the Meccano. I'll definitely have the torture!'

I asked him if he knew anyone else I could ask. He said Tony Grimes would probably join, providing I offered him money. I told him Grimes is too small; he'd be no good in fights.

'Ah yeah; but you'd get two for the price of one! Wherever Grimes goes, the brother sticks with him.' It seems Grimes's brother has a bad leg, through polio. It makes him a good fighter. He has to be; he can't run away.

Sculley invited me to his grannies' for tea. That's on Saturday. I said I'll come if I'm not too busy. I'm not that keen on visiting people, especially old women. They're usually half-cracked.

His mother came in and said I'd have to leave. She was going shopping. She needed Norman to help carry her bags. Thank God I don't have a mother like that.

When I got back to the stable Mrs Barrington was waiting for me. She'd remembered her camera. She wants it back before Mr Barrington discovers it's missing. I told her the detective has it, and she flew into a terrible temper. I said I was sorry. She said being sorry was no good. She'll have to tell Mr Barrington it's been stolen.

I told her that wouldn't be sensible. He'll report it to the police. They'll say I was the thief. Then I'll have to admit she lent it to me. That'll make everything worse.

Mrs Barrington stormed off. Later she came back and apologised. She said I'm to forget about the camera for the moment, and also Mr Barrington's photographs. She was deadly serious about this. She wanted me to swear I'd forget everything that happened on Monday.

I said I'd forget everything except what happened between us. She asked me what I was talking about. I gawped at her and said I was talking about the sex.

'Oh, that?' she said. 'You can forget that, too.' As far as she was concerned, it was just something she'd needed at the time. It was no more memorable or significant than taking an aspirin to get rid of a headache. I stared at her amazed. She shook me and said, 'Listen, Michael; having sex with you means nothing to me. I can have a physical relationship with anyone. I don't even have to like the other person. I can even hate them, but still need and enjoy sex with them.' Our friendship, on the other hand, does matter to her. She feels happy with me. That's more important than sex. Sex she can get any time. Happiness with another person is rare, and much more precious.

I couldn't believe my ears. Were we not going to have any more sex? She said she didn't know. I was in danger of getting involved in something that could destroy me. She said I'd have to trust her to do what was best for both of us. I asked her to explain what she was getting at. She changed the subject. She doesn't know what to do about Andy. He won't speak to her, and he doesn't want to be friends with me any more. I said I'd go and talk to him. She said no; leave it for a few more days.

I spent the rest of the day in the loft reading the encyclopaedias. I found an article about crocodiles. They prey on other animals and swallow them whole. Antlers and bones and hooves and even whole porcupines. After a while, their insides get clogged up with rubbish. Their digestive juices absorb the meat but leave everything else. They try to vomit the stuff out. It catches on their insides and punctures their organs. Their lungs fill up and they drown in their own blood. No wonder they always look so bad-tempered in photographs.

It got towards dark and I felt fed up. I'm always on my own these days. Two cats started fighting in the lane. I don't like cats since the three-legged one scratched me. I got the pot from under my bed and crept over to open the half-door. They heard the squeak of the hinges and ran off. I heaved the contents after them anyway. Then I was sorry I'd wasted it. If I'd waited the cats might have come back.

I decided to stay quietly in the doorway and see if they would. I pretended I was a fighter pilot waiting to bomb the enemy. I thought of getting bricks from the pile in the garden but I realised they'd be covered in insects. Also, if I hit one of the cats, I'd probably kill it and be in serious trouble. I went down to the coal-shed and got a bucketful of turf. Sods are quite good for throwing but soft enough not to kill anything.

By the time I got back upstairs, it was really dark and I couldn't see a thing. The lane gets pitch black at night, except when the moon is shining. Unfortunately, it was covered in clouds. There are no street-lamps, except one right at the top, on the corner, where it meets the main street. It makes the lane very spooky at night. If anyone walks down from the top end, the lamp makes their shadow stretch for miles in front of them. The shadows look like black ghosts crawling along the ground.

After a while, my eyes got used to the dark. I could pick out the ragged bundle of feathers and bones lying at the bottom of the coal-yard wall, just opposite. They're from a pigeon that got its feet caught in the barbed wire at the top of the wall, and starved to death. It was hanging there when we first arrived, and blew down during the freak storm. I was going to keep it but Dad said it would be full of fleas and maggots. I thought it was very tragic, the pigeon dying like that.

Dad said that the same thing happened to thousands of men during the First World War. They got shot trying to break through the barbed wire in front of the enemy trenches and were left to rot. If it was any consolation to me, I could regard the pigeon as having died a hero's death. That's what everyone convinced themselves about all the soldiers who'd died in France. I could tell by the sarcastic way he said this, that Dad has very strong feelings about the matter.

I was sitting there with just the top of my head poking over the half-door when I heard the sound of a woman's high-heeled shoes coming down the lane, and then a man saying in an irritated voice, 'Be-God, but you're a quare one!' The footsteps got down level with the stable but I didn't dare poke my head out to see who it was, in case they looked up. I could tell there was trouble between them, by the tone of their voices.

Suddenly the woman's voice got louder and she said, 'All right, all right! I'll give you a quick pull.' The man said, 'Thanks a lot,' sarcastically. The woman said he'd have to put a hanky over it. The man said he didn't want to, and she said, 'I'm not having it all down the front of my skirt.' The man got into a temper and yelled, 'It wouldn't be down the front of your skirt if you let me put it where Nature intended!' Then they went into the coal-yard archway, right at the back where I couldn't see them. I thought of all the times Stella's dog has been for a shit in there, and it made me feel disgusted.

There was a bit more quiet talking and then the woman got louder again and I heard her say she was fed up with telling him the same thing over and over; 'I'm saving it for the right man and the right time!' The man answered back that there was no point in hanging on to it until she was so old that no one wanted it off her anyway. They started to argue and yell at each other after that, and I suddenly realised who the woman's voice belonged to. It was Christie's big sister Ellen.

After a while the man came out and stood in the lane, looking into the archway at Ellen. She was crying by this time, and he turned and walked off back up the way they'd come. She came out then, and called after him in a sad voice, saying, 'Pat . . . Pat . . .' and begging him to come back. He stopped, without turning round, and she said to him, 'Do you not want that pull?' He shouted back that she knew bloody well what he wanted, and he knew where he could get it if she wouldn't give it to him. Ellen gave a terrible sob of misery and said she'd let him put his hand in while she was doing it. The man shouted back and said that she might as well put her own hand in, and pull herself, while she was at it; it looked as though no one else was ever going to get the chance to do it. Then he walked off up the lane, and stopped at the corner to light a cigarette, and disappeared. Ellen burst into the worst fit of crying I ever heard from anyone. I thought she was going to choke herself with the pain of it.

I went down to comfort her. She was back inside the archway by the time I got into the lane. I could hear her but I couldn't see. I tried to peer into the darkness, and Ellen saw my outline. She gave a startled gasp and said, 'Pat?' I whispered, 'Ellen . . .' so as not to frighten her. She asked me again if I was Pat, and I said no. Ellen began screaming at the top of her voice. 'Go away! Go away, whoever you are!' She dashed out past me and ran off up the lane, still screaming. I grabbed her by the arm and she swung her handbag at me. I shouted, 'Ellen! It's me, Michael! Michael Kelly . . .' Ellen stopped screaming and struggling immediately. I let go of her arm and put my hands on her shoulders. She was trembling like a terrified animal. She gave a huge sigh of relief and said, 'Oh Christ, Michael! I thought you were the rapist!'

I was facing up the lane, so she could see my face in the light from the lamp post at the corner. A policeman came round the corner, flashing his torch and blowing a whistle, and came lumbering down the lane towards us. I told Ellen and she said, 'Oh God; that's from me screaming! We'd better get away, quick!' I wanted to stay and explain but Ellen said no. She kicked her shoes off and told me to get running. I said we could hide in the stable but she said it was too late; he'd see us going in. She took my hand and pulled me down the lane after her. I heard the policeman's boots getting nearer, and his voice yelling at us to stop. It was O'Rooney. This made Ellen more desperate than ever to escape. She said if O'Rooney caught me now, I'd be in terrible trouble. We pelted down the lane and across the green. I was worried that Ellen would cut her feet on bits of broken bottles but she was lucky. We got to the far edge of the green and jumped down the bank onto the strand.

We looked back to see whether O'Rooney had followed us. He still had his torch on, so it was easy to spot him. Ellen whispered, 'It's no wonder he never catches anyone!' O'Rooney got to the middle of the green and stopped, shining his torch in a big circle. After a few moments, he lit his pipe and plodded off in the direction of the boat-yard. Ellen was sure we'd lost him, and started to put her shoes on. They stank, and she said, 'Oh God . . . I must have stepped in something!' I wiped them on the grass for her, but I didn't bother to mention Stella's dog.

When we got back up the lane to the stable, I said 'Goodnight', thinking Ellen was going home. She said I was wrong on all three counts; firstly, it was no longer night, it was morning; secondly, it wasn't good, it was very bad; and thirdly, she wasn't going home.

She asked me why I'd come looking for her in the archway. I said I was in the loft with the door open, and I'd heard her crying. 'How did you know it was me?' I told her I'd heard her rowing with her boyfriend. She said, 'Oh . . .' and then, 'I suppose you think I'm cheap, and dirty?' I said it was her boyfriend who disgusted me. Ellen said she didn't blame him; he only wants what most men want, and what most girls nowadays seem only too willing to give. She asked me what I'd been doing, lurking in the loft. I told her I wasn't lurking; I live up there. She said, 'Good God! that's a bit primitive, isn't it?' I said no; I've got it all done up nice and tidy and cosy.

A boot scraped in the darkness further down the lane. Ellen pushed me against the wall and flattened herself beside me. 'I bet it's bloody O'Rooney,' she whispered. I said, 'Perhaps he's not as daft as he seems.' Ellen said there was a chance he hadn't seen us, and asked if we could hide in the stable until he'd gone. We slid along the wall and through the doorway. Ellen told me to lock the door after us, but I had to tell her I couldn't; Dad took the lock off to free it up and never put it back.

We crept up the stairs and peered out through the half-door. O'Rooney was in the middle of the lane, trying to stand quietly, but his boots kept creaking. I wanted to giggle, but Ellen poked me and said it was serious. If he caught the two of us together, he'd drop sly hints to her father, and her life would be even more of a misery than it is now. I felt insulted; why should the Sergeant object to her being with me? Ellen whispered that it was nothing personal; he objects to her being with any male old enough to wear long trousers.

We peeped over the door again and O'Rooney had gone. I was about to speak normally when we heard rustling noises downstairs. Ellen was scared. 'He's inside,' she whispered; 'he's determined to find us!' We could see the reflection from his torch flickering on the wall of the stairwell. Ellen told me not to move, or even breathe loudly. O'Rooney suddenly let out a startled roar. 'Glory be to Jaysus!' The sound of a woman's voice came up the stairs, but too quiet for us to pick out the words. We heard O'Rooney say, 'I'm sorry to wake ye, Ma'am. To tell the truth, I thought ye were dead.' The woman spoke again, so low that even O'Rooney had to say 'Pardon?' He listened for a moment, and said she'd be better off in her own house, whatever her reasons for hiding in the stable. He told her he was after a rapist, and that he had reason to believe that the culprit was in the near vicinity. Ellen asked me, 'Who's that downstairs?' and I said it was probably Mrs Sullivan. Ellen whispered, 'Are you sure?' I said, 'Who else could it be?' Ellen giggled and said maybe I had a girl hidden on the premises. I told her not to be so stupid.

O'Rooney told the woman he was going to check upstairs. Ellen dug her fingers into my arm. 'What are we going to do now?' I said we could brazen it out. Ellen said that wouldn't work; we'd have to hide. O'Rooney started slowly up the stairs. I said there was nowhere to hide except on the roof, and we didn't have time for that. The stairs creaked under O'Rooney's weight. He came up very slowly, checking each step with his torch to make sure it was safe. Ellen said, 'What about this door behind us?' I told her it was a long drop into the lane. She opened it and looked out. 'Quick,' she said; 'we can sit on the ledge and close it behind us.' We managed it just in time.

O'Rooney got to the top of the stairs and shone his torch around the loft. We heard him walking about, examining things, and muttering to himself. One of Ellen's shoes dropped off and fell into the lane. Ellen said 'Blast!' under her breath. O'Rooney stopped muttering and went quiet, as though he was listening. He started to walk over towards us. Ellen and I crouched down as low as we could, and huddled our heads into our shoulders. We were saved by Mrs Sullivan. She called up the stairs to O'Rooney, and distracted him. He shouted, 'There's Divil a thing up here,

Ma'am, beyond the odd ghost or two!' He went back down the stairs and came out through the bottom door and stood for a moment lighting his pipe. Ellen and I were petrified. She said afterwards that if it wasn't for the glare of the match blinding him, he'd have seen the white of her legs dangling from the ledge.

Ellen stayed with me for the rest of the night. She said she couldn't risk going home with O'Rooney still on the prowl, and she didn't want Mrs Sullivan to see her leaving. She said she'd be still awake, and sure to hear her if she tried to creep down the stairs. I said, 'What about your father?' She leaned against me with her lips touching my ear and whispered, 'To Hell with my father!' There was a time when I would have been shocked by this, but not any more. Besides, she said it in a quiet giggly tone, as if it was just a joke.

I asked her what she'd like to do for the rest of the night and she said she might as well be hung for a sheep as for a lamb. We got into my bed, very quietly, and pulled the blankets over us. We kept our clothes on. Ellen asked if she could snuggle up against me, so I lay on my back and put my arm under her head. She whispered in my ear for a while, then fell asleep. I couldn't sleep; I kept thinking of Mrs Sullivan downstairs, and worrying that she'd creep up and discover us. By the time it got light, my arm was completely numb. I heard Mrs Sullivan going through the door into the garden at about five o'clock, and then the sound of our outside toilet flushing. After that I fell asleep. When I woke up, Ellen was gone. She left me a note. 'Sorry about last night. You must think I'm daft. I'll explain when I see you. Love, Ellen.'

I lay thinking about her for a long time. I like Ellen. She's soft and gentle when she's with me, not at all like the tough bustly person she is at home. I suppose she has to be like that; she's got so much work and worry looking after everyone. It was nice being in bed with her. The only problem was her hair. She has short black curly hair that kept tickling my nose and making me want to sneeze. She also has long dark eyelashes. Before she went to sleep, I could feel them stroking my cheek every time she blinked. It was like having a butterfly landing on my face. It gave me a delicious shivery feeling. That Pat, whoever he is, is a fool. He should marry her and stop messing about. She'd be well worth having as a wife.

After all this thinking, I was too tired to get up. I pulled the blankets over my head, to block out the light and the noise from the sparrows arguing on the roof, and a few minutes later I fell asleep.

I woke up and discovered Christie beside my bed, reading Ellen's note. I grabbed it from him and told him he'd got no business reading it. He said I only had myself to blame; I shouldn't have left it lying around. He asked if he could have it back, to keep; it'd be a useful thing to hold over Ellen. I told him I'll beat the shite out of him if he ever mentions the note to anyone. He said he'll only mention it to Ellen. I said, 'Especially Ellen!'

Christie said the dance was going to be a huge success. He spent last night in our basement, telling everyone who came in. His brother did the same in the pubs.

We spent the morning cleaning up the ground floor of the stable, moving the straw bales and sweeping up the loose hay. Christie found a saucer with a candle stump in the middle and cigarette butts all round it. The butts had lipstick on them. 'Oy, oy!' he said. 'Who have you had in here?' He knew it wasn't Ellen or Stella; they don't smoke. 'Was it Andy's ma, by any chance?' I said she didn't smoke either.

'Jesus,' said Christie. 'It's someone else, then? You're a right stud!' I said it was only Mrs Sullivan, from upstairs. Christie whistled and said, 'Christ! you're shagging her as well?' I said I wasn't shagging anyone. Christie said that's not what he's heard; according to the current crack, I'm having it off with a different mot every night. I asked him who told him this. He said everyone he talks to. My nickname in the village is Mick the Prick. I wasn't too pleased with this. I told him to keep his foul talk to himself.

We shoved all the straw under the loft stairs. Christie said it would make a good snogging platform. I fixed up a lamp socket in the middle of the ceiling. I had to nail the wire up to keep it out of the way. We put in a red lamp that Christie pinched from a cell in the barracks.

He went away for his lunch. I went up to get Ellen's note. It was gone from under the pillow. I looked everywhere but there was no sign of it. Christie must have taken it. I don't know how he managed it. As far as I can remember, he didn't go upstairs on his own.

Malone came round. He wanted to know if it was true we were

having a dance. He thought it was a stupid idea. I said it was all Christie's affair. Malone said he'd come anyway, just for the laugh. He said he'd bring a bicycle chain, in case there was any trouble, and dress up in his leather rocker's outfit. It scares the teddy boys off.

Dad came out and said we were mad. No one would want to dance in a place like the stable. He said I should have asked first, anyway. 'Supposing someone threw a butt into the hay? The whole place would go up in flames!' I said I'd rig up the hose from the tap outside the lavatory. Dad stormed off.

Christie came back with a gross of Oxo cubes and a cardboard box full of tin mugs. He borrowed them from John-Joe's hut, without asking him. He also had six dozen packets of crisps. He got them cheap from the man in the newspaper shop. Mice had been at the cartons. I asked him how he'd managed to steal Ellen's note. He said he hadn't; I could search him if I didn't believe him. I didn't bother. He'd already have hidden it somewhere else.

I asked him what the Oxo cubes were for. He said he was going to run a refreshments stall, with crisps and hot drinks. I asked him what he'd do about hot water. 'I'll use an electric kettle.' I told him there's no socket downstairs. He said we'd need one for the gramophone. I said I'd be able to fix that all right, but not one for the kettle. I hadn't enough wire. He went off to borrow a Primus stove.

Andy came in with a man. He said it was his dad. I nearly fainted. Mr Barrington smiled, and said they'd heard there was a ceilidh on tonight. My mouth was so dry I could only gurgle 'Yeck.' He must have thought I was a fool. He asked if we were expecting many people. I nodded. 'Plenty of young boys and girls, eh?' I managed to say 'Yes' properly. 'Any objection to a couple of old fogies dropping in?' I said it was open to everyone. 'And what time are the festivities scheduled to kick off?' I said, 'Pardon?' and then realised what he meant. 'Eight till eleven,' I said; 'Christie doesn't want the place filling up with drunks when the pubs shut.'

Mr Barrington said he'd been in Ireland a year and hadn't realised that the pubs did shut. Andy gave him a sour grin and went out. Mr Barrington is one of those men that women go mad about. He looks like Errol Flynn. He's so handsome I like looking at him myself, even though I'm a boy. He seems really relaxed and casual, but his eyes have a cold look. You can see that he's thinking hard and noticing everything, even when he's chatting about nothing in particular.

He said he understood that Andy and I were chums. I said, 'Yes.' 'And my wife?' I was puzzled. 'Your wife?' 'Suzanne,' he said, and paused for a moment. 'She speaks highly of you.' I said I didn't know why; I hardly knew her. He put out his hand and ruffled my hair. I hate it when people do that. He felt me flinch and grinned. He said, 'Suzanne likes a little amusement now and again.' He grinned again and said, 'No hard feelings, eh?' I felt like killing him. My face was scarlet with anger and embarrassment.

Mrs Barrington came in. She said, 'Leave the boy alone, Richard.' She asked me if I'd invited Stella. Mr Barrington gave her a lazy smile. I said I hadn't invited anyone; I didn't even want to have the dance. Mrs Barrington said I ought to ask Stella; it would take her out of herself. I said I was no good at chatting to girls. Mr Barrington said he was sure Suzanne would give me a few hints on how to go about it. Mrs Barrington frowned but didn't make any comment. Guard O'Rooney came in and she said they had to go.

O'Rooney asked if he could have a private and personal word with me. I said yes, even though I was quaking. I thought it was going to be about Stella, or Ellen. O'Rooney peeped into the lane to make sure there was no one around. He said, 'Watch this,' and twisted his head quickly from side to side. I thought he'd gone mad. He asked me if I noticed anything. I shrugged my shoulders and said no. He twisted his head again and pointed up at his hat. It was wobbling about. I said, 'What am I supposed to be looking at?' O'Rooney shook his head even harder, and said, 'The hat, look at the hat!' I said it seemed to be a bit loose. He gave me a big beaming smile. 'Got it in one!' he said. 'That's the very heart and guts of the problem!' He took the hat off. His head was completely bald.

He said he'd taken Dad's sage analysis of the source of his nutritional problem to its logical and unarguable conclusion. If the hair was the cause of his brain starvation, then, by Jesus, there was nothing else for it; the hair had to go. Now he couldn't get his hat to stay on. He asked me if I had any ideas. I said no.

'How would it be,' he said, 'if I got hold of one of them little rubber tyres off a pram or a pushchair, and pulled it down round the circumference of me cranium?' Then he could jam the hat on over it, and it would take up the slack in the headband. I agreed that it might do the trick. He said there was a snag; he didn't want to be seen rooting around in the dump like a diddicoy. Was there any chance of me doing the honours on his behalf?

I said I'd have a look, sometime, but surely he needed something bigger; a tyre off the back wheel of a tricycle, or even off a small bicycle? Could he not have a look in the Unclaimed Objects shed? There were loads of bicycles in there. O'Rooney bucked up and said that sounded like the very thing. He went off up immediately to have a look.

In fact, I didn't believe a word of O'Rooney's story, because I know the real reason he's had all his hair off. The district nurse did it. It was one of the things Ellen told me last night. O'Rooney went to see the nurse, to get something to stop his head itching, and she discovered that his hair was full of nits. She tried combing them out, but O'Rooney's hair was too thick and wiry, so she insisted on shaving it all off. Even so, you never know with O'Rooney. Why did he go through all that nonsense with Dad, about nourishing his brain? Maybe he was just getting an excuse ready, in case his hat blew off accidentally.

I went round to the hardware shop to buy a plug for the gramophone. When I came out, Ellen was just going into Bertie Brannon's. I waited outside for her. She bought six turnovers and six sliced loaves and three pounds of butter. I suppose it's because there's so many of them. I told her about Christie reading her note, and stealing it. She said she'll soon get it back. She knows where Christie hides all his little oddments. I asked her if she was tired and she said no. It was one of the best night's sleep she ever had, even if it was one of the shortest.

She asked me to come into the yard at the back of the shop. I said, 'What for?' She said, 'I want to tell you something.' I said, 'Supposing someone catches us?' She laughed and said, 'It's only for a minute!' We went round the corner and stood just inside the gate. Ellen put her messages down. She told me to shut my eyes and hold out my hands and see what God would send me. I told her not to be silly but she said, 'Go on – just shut your eyes for a second.' I had a quick look round and shut them.

Ellen put her thumbs in the palms of my hands and kissed me. It was lovely: not just a little peck, but a proper kiss. Her lips are soft and warm, and taste of Turkish Delight. I opened my eyes. She pulled us gently together and gave me a friendly hug and whispered, 'Thank you for last night . . .' Then she pushed me away and shook her head and laughed. 'What a silly pair we are!'

She said I'm the first man she's ever been to bed with. I blushed and said the same about her. Ellen said I wasn't telling the truth. I suddenly remembered Mrs Barrington. I fell asleep on my bed with her after she shagged me. Anyone could have come up the stairs and seen us. I thought Ellen might be hinting about this. She laughed and told me not to look so worried; she was talking about when I was a baby. Surely I must have slept in the same bed as my mother? I was so relieved I nearly fainted.

Bertie Brannon came out through the back door of the shop with an armful of cardboard boxes and saw us in his yard. He gave us a queer look. Ellen smiled at him and said, 'We'd better go!' We came home by the green. Sculley was in his front room, typing. He opened the window and wolf-whistled at us. I was cross but Ellen whistled back at him. Sculley went red and shut the window. Ellen said he was only jealous. She walked up the lane with me, and came into the stable. She said she had something serious to tell me.

We went upstairs and sat on my bed and Ellen gave me a terrible shock; she told me O'Rooney thinks I'm the rapist. I was flabbergasted. That's why she didn't want him to catch us together last night. After hearing her screaming, O'Rooney would have been certain I'd attacked her. 'Surely,' I said, 'you could have told him it was a mistake!' Ellen said, 'No; he'd only think you frightened me into keeping my mouth shut.' The police are quite used to that. It's how fellows get away with raping girls. They threaten to do worse things to them if they tell. 'Anyway,' said Ellen, 'O'Rooney tells me everything he gets up to. He likes trying out his theories on me. If he thinks I'm pally with his chief suspect, there'll be no more cups of tea and cosy chats.'

It's all to do with that hanky Eileen gave me. O'Rooney found it in the pocket of my trousers. The minute he saw the bloodstains and the initial 'S' he was sure I was the person who attacked Stella. 'But why didn't he ask me about it?' I said. 'I could have explained the whole thing!' Ellen said O'Rooney didn't want to put me on my guard. Anyway, there's more to it than that.

He's seen me down the strand, acting suspicious, and heard rumours about me spying on Stella, and getting up to queer games with her. Someone in the terrace told him I was in her front basement with no clothes on, terrorising her, just a few days before she got raped. Then there's the various yarns about me and Mrs Barrington, and the reputation I've got, of being a sadistic, ruthless fighter. Bowman's father has been to the barracks, and so has Welch. He told O'Rooney I was the organising genius behind the attack on him at school.

'Oh Jesus,' I said. 'Does the Sergeant know all this?' Ellen said, 'No. O'Rooney keeps his mouth shut in the barracks. He's after promotion. He wants to solve this case on his own, and get the whole credit.'

I asked Ellen if she thought I'd attacked Stella. She looked at me as if I was stupid. 'Would I be standing here now?' She came closer, and put her hands on my shoulders, and said quietly, 'Would I have . . .' She tilted her head and glanced up at the loft floor, then looked me straight in the eyes. 'Well? Would I?' I asked her why she was so nice to me. She said, 'Because I like you.' I said that didn't answer the question. Why did she like me in the first place?

She said, 'Let me ask *you* a question.' She dropped her eyes for a second, and licked her lips with the tip of her tongue. 'Why didn't you try to touch me last night?' I said I had; I still had the pins and needles to prove it. She said, 'Come on, Michael. You know what I mean. You heard me in the lane with Pat.' I said, 'I just didn't think of it.' 'Supposing,' she said, 'I'd wanted you to?' I told her I knew she didn't. She laughed, and said I was right.

Last night she'd been badly hurt. She'd always be grateful for the simple comfort I'd given her. I said I hadn't done anything. She said that was the whole point. I'd made her feel safe and cared for and clean, and I hadn't tried to take advantage of her. 'But . . .' she stood on tiptoe and whispered in my ear, 'it might be more than comfort I'm looking for next time!' I told her there won't be a next time; I'm going to be pure and clean myself from now on. Ellen gave me a wicked smile and said, 'What could be purer than going to bed with a thirty-seven-year-old Catholic virgin?!'

After she'd gone I kicked myself for getting distracted. I should have asked her what I ought to do about O'Rooney, and told her about the stuff the detective took away. If O'Rooney gets hold of it he'll be even more convinced I'm guilty.

The dance turned into an utter disaster. The gramophone Christie borrowed was useless. The sound from it was so muffled you could hardly make out what record was playing. I had a look at the pick-up and it was covered with fluff. When I cleaned it off there was no needle in it! I tried putting in the needle from Dad's gramophone but it was the wrong shape. I had to swop the whole pick-up. Everyone was booing and yelling the whole time, and saying they wanted their money back. I managed to get it going eventually, but it didn't sound much better, for all my trouble.

Then there was a lot of complaints about the records. Everyone said they came out of the Ark with Moses. So much for religious knowledge in Ireland. And so much for Christie saying no one would notice. They didn't like the dim red light, either. The girls said it made them look like whiskey-faced hags, and anyway, what was the point of getting dolled up if no one could see them properly?

The Gavinstown fellows brought a case of Guinness with them. That made everyone want a drink. The village lads went round to Dolan's and came back with more crates of booze. I said there was to be no smoking because of the danger of fire but nobody took a blind bit of notice.

Christie's brother arrived at about ten o'clock, hardly able to stand. He tried to get off with Mrs Barrington. She was standing quietly in a corner with Mr Barrington. Mr Barrington asked him to go away. Christie's brother got loud and angry, yelling that toffy-nosed mots are all the same: good as gold in public, and shagging their arses off in private. He said he knew what he was talking about; he'd just been round in Dolan's with that fucking snotty bitch, Stella. And, he said, he'd heard a few things from her, all right. Oh yes, he'd heard a few things, all right. She was well on in gargle, that one, but she still had her wits about her.

Stella appeared in the doorway and stood swaying for a moment. She came in, and leaned against the wall. Christie's brother went over and stuck his face right against hers. 'Go on, then,' he yelled; 'tell them what you told me!' Stella shut her eyes and slumped down the wall until she was sitting on the floor. Her legs bent up until her knees were under her chin. Everyone could see her knickers. Mrs Barrington went over and pulled Stella's skirt so that it covered her legs.

'She knows who it was,' Christie's brother said. 'She knows the feel of him and the smell of him!' He stopped to belch, and shouted, 'I'll tell you something else! She knows . . .' There was a sudden hush, and Christie's brother stopped again. The Sergeant was standing in the doorway. He looked at Christie's brother and said quietly, 'If you open your mouth again, I'll break every tooth in your jaw.' He gave Christie's brother a long, dirty look, and turned round and walked off up the lane.

Christie's brother was terrified for a moment. He stood with his mouth open and his face gone pale. Then he shouted at the empty doorway, 'Ah, fuck off, ye silly oul fucker!' Everyone cheered, and Christie's brother went over to the door and shouted the same thing up the lane. Then he staggered over and pulled the cork out of a bottle of Guinness, and drank the whole pint without stopping. Everyone cheered again at this, and gave each other sly looks, and told him he was a right lad, the way he got the better of the Sergeant. Christie's brother didn't realise they were being sarcastic. It put him into a good mood. He started dancing on his own, in the middle of the floor. He looked a right fool.

Mrs Barrington came over and asked me, 'Who's the loud-mouth?' I told her it was Christie's brother. 'The chap who was yelling up the stairs; the first time I was round here?' I nodded. 'And Christie's your friend, the boy who organised the dance?' She said it was very nice of him to think of it. I told her it was nothing to do with niceness; it was just another of Christie's business ideas. Christie will do anything for money, and his brother is just as bad. He'll do anything to get his way with a girl. Mrs Barrington laughed and said, 'Won't they all?!' I asked her what I should do about Stella. Mrs Barrington shivered, as if she was cold, and said, 'What can anyone do?' I'm sure she didn't mean to sound unkind, but it was a queer thing to say. She had a strange faraway look in her eyes, as if she was in a dream. She went over and started to chat with Christie's brother.

I looked round to see how Stella was getting on. Mr Barrington was helping her off the floor. She was trying to kick him away. I was on my way over to help her but I got distracted by a horrible accident. Willie Wogan tried to pull the cork out of a bottle. He was too sozzled to get a good grip. Badger Moore took the bottle off him and broke the neck against the wall. He handed it back to Willie. Willie put it straight to his mouth and sliced both his lips right open. Badger thought it was a great joke.

Willie was too drunk to feel any pain. He dropped the bottle and it smashed. The stout turned into white foam, bubbling all round his feet. Willie stared down to see where the bottle had gone. The blood from his lips dripped into the foam. It looked like he'd spilt a bowl of strawberries and cream.

Willie put his hand to his mouth, and rubbed it. A piece of his top lip came away. It trickled down his chin and dropped onto the front of his shirt. Willie screamed. He pulled his hand away, and looked down at his shirt. Then he looked at his hand. It was dripping blood. It was only then he knew what had happened. The crowd he was with thought it was hilarious. Then they realised Willie could bleed to death. They stopped laughing, and began yelling for a doctor. No one did anything about fetching one.

Malone came in. He looked ridiculous. He was dressed from head to foot in black leather; boots, trousers, jacket, gloves, and even a leather cap. Worst of all was the sun-glasses. They didn't last long. Malone swaggered across the floor, but he couldn't see properly with the glasses. A Gavinstown fellow was lying paralytic right in his way. Malone stumbled and went arse over elbow. He had a job getting up again; his trousers were too tight. He put the sun-specs away and leaned against the far wall, trying to look like Marlon Brando.

There was a scuffle behind me. Someone grabbed at my arm. It was Stella. Mr Barrington was holding her in a sort of hug. She said, 'Will you tell this man to go away . . .' I didn't know what to do. I knew Mr Barrington would just laugh at me. Mr Barrington glanced over at Mrs Barrington. She was still talking to Christie's brother, with her back to us. Stella swayed and shut her eyes. Mr Barrington winked at me and kissed her. Her eyes opened immediately. She lunged at his face with her mouth. He was lucky he dodged away. Her teeth came together with a vicious click. She could have bitten his nose off. Christie's brother still has teeth-marks on his from the time that mot bit him at the pictures. Mr Barrington gave a hard sharp smile and said to her, 'Another time, perhaps . . . ?' and then, to me, 'Good thing I wasn't the other way up, eh?' He went over to talk to Mrs Barrington and Christie's brother.

Stella said, 'Who's that fellow over there?' She pointed at Malone. I asked her if she meant the fellow dressed in leather. She said yes. I told her his name. 'I want to speak to him . . .' Malone saw us looking at him. I said, 'Is it about your bicycle?' Stella looked at me and gave a hysterical giggle. 'Why in God's name would I want to talk about bicycles?' I explained about Malone's repair business. I thought she wanted to ask him to fix her bike. An attack of hiccups got hold of her. She pressed her face against my shoulder to smother them. I could feel her teeth digging into me. It scared me. When she got her breath back, she said, 'My bicycle-riding days are over.'

As soon as Stella started in his direction, Malone moved away from the wall. He tried to work his way through the crowd at the door. Everyone was crowded round Willie Wogan. He was being sick into the lane. Stella lurched away from me and grabbed Malone. He shook her off. Stella said, 'You're not much of a gentleman.' Malone said she wasn't much of a lady. Stella said, 'Whose fault is that?' Malone told her to go away and leave him alone.

She said she would, if he'd put it more politely. Malone said he left politeness to them that could afford it. Stella said she'd go away if he'd shake hands with her. Malone said he didn't shake hands with women. Stella threatened to scream if he didn't. She had a wild look in her eyes. Malone said, 'Oh Jesus . . .' Stella put out both her hands. Malone got confused. He didn't know which one to shake. Stella said it was bad manners to shake hands with gloves on. Malone wouldn't take them off. Stella wrinkled her nose and asked me, 'Is your friend a bit queer?' There was a terrible whiff of perfume off Malone. I asked him what it was. He told me to fuck off. 'And take this daft mot with you!'

Stella lashed out with her nails. She caught Malone down the side of his face. Malone swung his arm up and knocked her to the ground. He got into a panic and yelled at me. 'Can't you see what she's at, ye daft bugger?' I stared at him blankly. 'She's looking for some poor fucker to pin it on, that's what!' Stella was gripping my legs, trying to pull herself up. Her nose was bleeding.

The crowd at the doorway moved back. Ellen and Guard O'Rooney came in. They stood blinking for a minute, until their eyes got used to the dim light and the thick fog of cigarette smoke. Ellen marched over to Christie's brother. She took him by the arm and said something to him, quietly. He tried to pull away and shouted, 'Fuck my father!' Ellen stood back and gave him a fierce slap across the face. O'Rooney went over and took his other arm. He gave it a quick twist. Christie's brother screamed in agony. O'Rooney smiled innocently, and led him into the lane, and told Ellen to take him home.

Ellen went off up the lane with him. O'Rooney stayed in the doorway. I helped Stella to stand up. She was crying. Malone tried to get past O'Rooney. O'Rooney stuck his arm across the doorway and Malone stopped. Everyone went quiet, except for Willie Wogan. He was in the lane, moaning, and holding his tie against his mouth to stop the bleeding.

O'Rooney looked at us and said it was a grand thing to see young people enjoying themselves. Was it a party or a dance or what? Mr Barrington smiled sarcastically. Christie said, 'It's meant to be a dance.' O'Rooney asked him, 'Where's the music?' Christie said the gramophone had packed in. O'Rooney said, 'Bejasus, that's the trouble with all this modern electrical stuff; it always breaks down, just when things are getting lively!' Things were different in his day; fellahs and girls knew how to enjoy themselves, without all these technical gadgets. He asked us if we'd ever heard of Kiss-in-the-Dark? No one answered him, except Mr Barrington. He said he'd be interested to hear about it.

Ellen came back down the lane with a towel and held it gently against Willie's mouth. I went out and offered to help but she said no; I'd be better off in the stable keeping my eyes and ears open. She took Willie away to the doctor to have his lips stitched.

Kiss-in-the-Dark, said O'Rooney, is a grand game for livening up a party, and for lubricating social intercourse between the sexes. The girls line up along one side of the room, the boys stand in a group in the middle. The light goes out. One of the boys starts kissing his way along the line of girls. As soon as one of the girls recognises him, she shouts out and the light goes on. The fellow is disqualified. The lights go off again, and the next fellow works his way down the line. When all the fellows are out, they line up and the girls have a go.

Everyone thought it was a great idea, except Malone and Stella and the Barringtons. Mrs Barrington wouldn't play because most of the fellows were drunk. Mr Barrington couldn't play; he's too tall and would have been recognised immediately. Malone said it was a stupid game. Stella said she couldn't stand the smell of beer and cigarette smoke off fellows' breaths. To be honest, her own didn't smell too good. I hate games anyway, so I stayed with Stella.

Christie was given the job of doing the counting, and operating the light. The first round had to be stopped, because the fellows were going too slowly. O'Rooney said it was only supposed to be a quick kiss and a cuddle with each girl, not a three-course carnal canoodle. He said anyone hankering after a full-blown gala performance would have to negotiate further arrangements on a private basis. He made up a new rule, and told Christie to count to twenty each time he put out the light. If the fellow hadn't finished going down the line by the time the count was finished, he was automatically disqualified, whether he'd been recognised or not.

Even this didn't work. Fellows started going straight for the mot they fancied, and spending the whole twenty seconds with the same one. The rest of the girls complained as soon as they copped on.

O'Rooney got sweaty and desperate. He said he'd go down the line with each fellow, and make sure he kept going. Christie put the lights out and started counting for another round. There was a lot of scuffling and giggling and then O'Rooney shouted, 'Jesus, where's me hat?' Christie stopped counting and put the light on. O'Rooney was in the middle of a pack of girls, with his hands on his head trying to hide the baldness. Everyone took the mick out of him and he left. I don't know who took the hat, and I never saw it again.

Mr and Mrs Barrington left. They had a row outside before they went home. I couldn't hear much of it. There was too much noise in the stable. Mr Barrington was disgusted about something Mrs Barrington told him. He said, 'You can't be serious!' She said, 'I've had worse . . .' Her voice sounded dull and lifeless. Mr Barrington swore. I heard her say, 'He'd be good with Stella . . . Beauty and the Beast.' Mr Barrington said, 'The fellow's an ignorant slob!' Mrs Barrington said, 'I know what I'm doing . . .' Mr Barrington told her not to interfere with Stella; she was almost ready for plucking. Mrs Barrington laughed sarcastically.

Christie played a rotten trick. He said it was the last game, and made up another rule. All the fellows and girls had to line up facing each other. When the light went out, everyone could grab the person facing them and spend the whole count kissing the one person. He promised he'd give a good long count, up to thirty.

It took ages to get the two lines organised. Everyone wanted to be opposite someone they fancied. The fellows complained that there weren't enough decent-looking girls to go round. The girls said most of the fellows were too drunk to notice. Eventually Christie put the light out and counted up to five. Then he got slower and slower.

'Sixxx . . . sevennnnn . . . eeeeight . . . niiiiiine . . . tennnnnn.'

Everyone thought Christie was being a good sport, by deliberately stretching the count so they'd have plenty of time to enjoy themselves. They all decided to let themselves go, and pretty soon all you could hear was the moaning and groaning of people hugging and kissing each other. I felt someone pulling at Stella, and she let go of me and disappeared. I thought a fellow must have fancied her and dragged her away for a snog.

Christie paused after he got to eleven, started to say 'twelve', and then suddenly switched the light on when no one was expecting it.

I've never seen so many embarrassed faces. There were fellows with their hands up girls' skirts, and girls with their hands down fellows' trousers. Annie Farrell had Tom O'Donnell's fly open and his jake out, gripping it with both hands.

Maureen Kennedy was squatting at the bottom of the stairs, with her knickers down, having a piss. Mumbo Quigley was stuffing his pockets with packets of crisps off Christie's refreshment stall. Stella was lying on the floor against the end wall. Malone was standing over her, kicking her in the stomach. When the light came on he ran out and escaped down the lane.

Kevin Fogarty was on his knees with his head up Mona Furey's skirt. He was pulling furiously on his plonker. Mona had her eyes screwed shut and her hands on the back of Kevin's head, squeezing his face into her fanny. Neither of them realised the light was on. Everyone went dead quiet.

Mona was the first to notice the silence. She opened her eyes, saw everyone staring, and fainted on top of Kevin. Kevin fell backwards with his head still up her skirt, and still pulling away at himself. His head hit the ground with all Mona's weight on him. He let out a terrific roar. His juice spurted up in the air, like a fountain. Mona went home in tears. Kevin went berserk and tried to murder Christie. It took six of us to knock him on the floor and hold him down.

The door to the garden smashed open. The Major burst into the stable. His face was purple and his eyes bulged like a madman. He had a double-barrelled shotgun. He pointed it at the middle of the ceiling. There was a huge explosion. The red bulb disintegrated and the place went pitch dark. Shattered plaster and splintered wood came showering down. The girls screamed and the fellows shouted and roared.

The Major fired again. There was another shower of plaster from the ceiling. Everyone stampeded for the door into the lane. Most of them were drunk and fell over in the rush. A pile of struggling bodies blocked up the doorway. The ones on the bottom were screaming in agony. The people trampling on them took no notice. I could hear them grunting and swearing, desperate to get out.

The Major started using his gun as a club. He was lashing out at people, not caring who he hit. I didn't dare go for him. It was pitch black. I could have had my head knocked off. He was in a terrible fit of temper. He shouted that he'd been watching us through the window. We were a disgraceful pack of filthy-minded animals, and an insult to decent society.

I tried to get round behind him, to escape into the garden. I stepped on someone's head, and felt their face squishing under my foot. They screamed, and gargled up vomit, and began choking. The noise was like an animal. I couldn't even tell if it was a boy or a girl. A wave of black disgust swept over me. I let out an enormous yell, to relieve my feelings, and dashed into the garden. I climbed the sycamore and hid among the branches.

The light went on in the Sullivans' bathroom. Mrs Sullivan stumbled in, with Mr Sullivan behind her. He was gripping her by the hair. Mrs Sullivan was dressed in a jumper and skirt. Mr Sullivan only had on a shirt and his socks. He forced her to lean over the sink and then let go of her hair. Mrs Sullivan tried to straighten up. Mr Sullivan picked up a back-scrubber and walloped her with the handle. She folded her arms round her head and bent forward again, with her weight on the sink.

Mr Sullivan lifted her skirt up round her waist and pulled her knickers down to her knees and shagged her. He was like a dog gone mad. He went so fast it only took him a minute. When he finished he pulled his jake out and kicked Mrs Sullivan viciously in the bum. Mrs Sullivan collapsed onto her knees, with her head in the sink and her hands clutching the taps to stop herself falling. Mr Sullivan gave her another kick and knocked her on the floor. He went out and slammed the door and left her lying there. If I'd had the Major's gun I would have shot him.

Dad and John-Joe came out from the basement, followed by all the fellows and girls who'd been playing snooker and listening to the juke-box. The Sergeant arrived, and the detective from Dublin, and people from all over the village who'd heard the noise. I didn't dare come down from the tree. I took my jacket off and tied myself to a big branch, with the sleeves knotted together round my waist, and drifted into an uneasy sleep.

When I woke up it was light. Everyone had gone. Everything was quiet. Even the birds were silent. I was frozen stiff with cold and cramp. It took me ages to get down from the tree. I went to the lavatory, then into the stable. My heart was thumping in my ears. I didn't know what to expect. I crept in quietly, thinking there might still be people lying about, paralytic, or injured, or even dead. The floor was slimy with sick and blood. There was rubbish and cigarette butts and smashed bottles and broken records everywhere. The gramophone was mangled, and utterly ruined. It looked as if someone had deliberately jumped on it. Christie's refreshment stall was upside down, with the tin mugs scattered round the floor. Loads of them are squashed flat or have the handles broken off. John-Joe will be raging when he sees them.

I went over to the bottom of the stairs. They were covered with dust from the shattered plaster. I could see a set of footprints going up the stairs. They were made by someone with bare feet. There were no traces of any footsteps coming down. It gave me a scary feeling.

I went very carefully up the first three steps. The fourth one creaked. I stood dead still for a minute, not daring to breathe. Something floated gently past my face and landed on the stairs. It was a little splatter of cigarette ash. When I looked up, Mrs Sullivan was leaning on the guard rail at the edge of the loft floor. All she had on was a short lace nightie. I could see up it, but I was too scared to be interested. She took a long puff at her cigarette and told me to come up.

I told her I didn't want to. She knelt on the floor and leaned out under the guard rail. There are no uprights to get in the way. She put her hand down and twisted a lock of my hair round her index finger. I put my hand up and gripped her wrist. She laughed and said, 'Aha . . . what now?' I said I could easily tip her over the edge. 'You could . . .' she said, 'but you won't.' I knew she was right. I let go of her wrist.

She pulled me gently up the stairs until our heads were level, then let go of my hair. She crouched forward on her elbows, staring at me with a curious expression. Her left eye had a purple ring round it. There was a big scrape on the end of her chin. It was covered in dried blood. I could see down the front of her nightie. Her breasts swung backwards and forwards as she breathed. One of them was badly bruised. It was completely covered in great yellow-black marks. Even the pink bit in the middle was black.

Mrs Sullivan realised I'd seen it. She pulled herself up by the rail and walked over to the window. She threw the butt of her cigarette into the garden, and stood with her arms folded across her chest. I stopped being scared, and came up the rest of the stairs.

She asked me why I'd been up the tree. I told her I'd been hiding. She said she'd been watching me since it got light. Had I been up there all night? I said, 'Yes . . . most of it.' Her arms were covered in goose-pimples. I looked at her legs. They were trembling with cold. I could see her tummy though her nightie. I couldn't help it. It was very thin material. She noticed me looking, and moved over to the dark side of the loft, away from the windows. She said, 'Why was that gormless guard chasing you the other night?' I told her it was all a mistake. 'A mistake?' she said, and asked me if I'd got any cigarettes. I said no. Her dressing gown was lying on my bed, rolled up in a bundle. She shook it out and put it on. 'What do you mean, a mistake?'

I made up a story. I said I'd heard someone being attacked in the lane. I went down to rescue her. O'Rooney arrived and thought I was the rapist. The girl didn't want me to get into trouble. She made me run away with her. Mrs Sullivan asked me who the girl was. I said I didn't know. I'd never met her before. All I did was rescue her.

352

Mrs Sullivan gave me a sarcastic look. I went red. She said, 'Considering you didn't know each other, you seem to have got pretty pally . . .' I asked her what she meant. 'She stayed the night with you, didn't she?' I glared at her. Mrs Sullivan said, 'Well . . . didn't she?' She smiled at me, but it was a sad sort of smile. I said, 'She was afraid to go home, that's all.' Mrs Sullivan said, 'I know the feeling. I know it very, very, well.'

I told her nothing sinful had happened. She looked at me as if she didn't believe it. I got flustered, and blurted out the exact words Ellen used. 'What could be purer than going to bed with a thirty-seven-year-old Catholic virgin?' Mrs Sullivan thought for a moment, and said, 'I see . . .' and then, 'I think I know the lady.' She shut her eyes for a moment, and murmured, 'A housewife and mother . . . but still a maid.'

She stared into the garden. 'I suppose there's a good view from the top of that tree?' I said I didn't know; I'd never bothered to look. She said, 'It's probably just as well . . .' I remembered what Mr Sullivan had done to her, and felt guilty. I looked away. She came and stood in front of me, and put her hand under my chin, and turned my face up to look at her. 'Why are you afraid of me?' Her hand was cold and hard and bony, even though she's quite young. '*Are* you afraid of me . . . ?' I said I wasn't – not really.

'I wish . . .' she said, 'I wish I had someone to rescue *me*.' She stopped, and took her hand away, and her face crumpled for a second. I thought she was going to cry. I put my hand out to touch her. She moved away, and took a deep breath and shook her head slowly, and smiled at me.

She said she had to go. Half-way down the stairs she paused and said, 'I hope you didn't mind me coming up here. I didn't realise it was your bedroom.' I asked her why she slept in the stable, and not in her own bed. She said she hadn't got a bed of her own. I said it was like a pigsty downstairs. She said she'd sooner sleep in a sty, on her own, than have to share a bed with a pig.

At the bottom of the stairs she met Ellen, waiting to come up. They stared at each other without speaking. Ellen put out a hand and touched Mrs Sullivan's cut chin, and ran her fingertips up to the bruised eye. Mrs Sullivan put her hand up and put it over Ellen's hand, and held it to her cheek. Ellen put her other hand behind Mrs Sullivan's head and drew her closer. They hugged each other for a moment, then Mrs Sullivan sighed and said she must go.

Ellen whispered, 'You're a saint, you know that, don't you?' Mrs Sullivan said, 'Listen to who's talking.' Ellen said, 'Why in God's name don't you leave him?' Mrs Sullivan tried to smile. 'Till death, Ellen; that's what they make you promise.' She gave Ellen a good squeeze. 'And if I did . . . he'd only find some other poor skivvy to . . .' She stopped, and looked up at me, and finished the sentence softly in Ellen's ear. Ellen's eyes blazed. 'Yes!' she said. 'That's all they're good for!' She was angry and upset. Mrs Sullivan glanced up at me again. 'They're not all bad . . .' Ellen looked up at me too. She said nothing. Mrs Sullivan went.

Ellen came up the stairs and told me I was in deep trouble over last night. The Sergeant and Dad were waiting inside for me. I was going to get a good belting. Christie already had his, from the detective and O'Rooney. The Sergeant couldn't belt Christie himself; he was so angry he'd have killed him.

Four girls and three boys were injured. One of the girls lost an eye. Someone stood on her face. I went white and felt sick. 'Ellen . . .' I said, 'I hope to God that wasn't me!' Ellen said it could have been anyone. There was a mad scramble in the doorway. The girl who lost her eye was right at the bottom. Other people had teeth knocked out and a fellow had his ear ripped. One of the injured girls has a broken wrist. Willie Wogan had to be rushed in to Jervis Street hospital. His lips have been stitched shut until they heal. He has to eat through a tube up his nose.

The Major is in hospital too. He had a fit of madness. No one could control him. He ran round the village smashing windows with the stock of his gun. The doctor had to be sent for. The police held the Major down while the doctor injected him with a sleeping drug. Mrs Longshott has gone to stay with relatives in Dublin.

Everyone, even Dad and the Sergeant, blames me and Christie for what happened. Ellen said the best thing would be to go in and get it over with. I told her it wasn't fair. O'Rooney was the one who caused the trouble. If he hadn't started that game everything would have been all right. People were already fed up and leaving, because it was such a rotten dance.

Ellen burst into tears and hugged me. She cried on my shoulder for ages. She said O'Rooney only invented the game because he was hoping that Stella would play. He wanted to give her a chance to find out something. She begged me not to make things worse by trying to fight Dad and the Sergeant. They were only trying to do what they thought was right. I said, 'What about what I think?'

Ellen sobbed and sobbed. She said there are times in everybody's life when they have to give in to whatever fate decides to send them. How did I think she'd stuck it all these years? Or Mrs Sullivan? Cooking and cleaning and shopping and nursing . . . and all for what? I said it just seemed to me all the more reason to fight against things. Ellen said, 'You can't fight against your parents . . . or against the law.'

In the end, I agreed to go into the house and have my belting. Ellen said, 'Here; have this back.' She put her hand down the neck of her jumper and pulled out a piece of paper. It was the note she left me on Wednesday. She'd stolen it back from Christie. It felt warm and smooth from being against her skin. I put it in my back pocket. She said, 'If that falls out I'll be in trouble.' She wanted me to hide it in the loft. I said no; I wanted to take it with me, to give me courage. She said, 'Look what happened with that handkerchief of Eileen's.' I said her note was different. No one could think there was anything sinister about it. She said, 'That's what you think!' She made me take one of my shoes off and put the note right down inside my sock.

I went into the house. I had to lean across one of the snooker tables. The Sergeant gave me six whacks with his leather belt. Then Dad gave me another six with his razor strop. Afterwards Dad cried. He sent me back to the stable. I'm not to come in until the place is completely cleaned up. He gave me a letter to read.

I could hardly get up the stairs with the pain in my bottom and the backs of my legs. Ellen was in my bed. Her clothes were neatly folded on a sheet of newspaper on the floor. The blankets were up around her face. All I could see was the top of her head and her eyes. They were streaming with tears. She told me to jam the doors shut so no one could get in.

I hobbled down the stairs and found some bits of rope left over from the swing. I tied the handles of the two doors together, with a bit of rope stretched across the stable between them. I got halfway up the stairs and couldn't go any further. My legs just collapsed with the pain. Ellen jumped out of bed and pulled me into the loft. She had her knickers on, but nothing on her top half. Her breasts are small and neat. They don't swing about like Mrs Sullivan's.

She pulled the blankets back and helped me to lie down. The last thing I saw, before my head reached the pillow, was Mrs Sullivan. She was staring at us from her bathroom window, with a faraway look in her eyes. Ellen didn't notice her. She was too worried about me.

She took my clothes off, and then her knickers. They were navy blue, with long legs, like my Mam wears. She looked much better without them. The note in my sock was ruined with nervous sweat. She got into bed and told me to lie on top of her. I could hardly move. She wriggled underneath me. I moaned, and said she'd be squashed. She said it was what she wanted. The pink bits in the middle of her breasts were hard and tight under my chest. She reached her hand up and took something from under the pillow. Her hands moved to my back, and something cold touched me. It made me jump. Ellen said, 'Sorry . . . it's all I could find.' She said it was a little tin of Vaseline.

She smeared some on her hands and started stroking my bottom, with smooth gentle movements. At first I was stiff with pain, and anger, and misery. After a while I relaxed. Ellen kept stroking me, her hands warm and soothing. I put my arms under her shoulders, to take my weight off her, and snuggled my face into her neck. Ellen sighed, and began to move her legs apart, a little bit at a time. I had hardly any feelings in my hips, but I knew I was gradually slipping down between her thighs.

The heat and agony in my bottom changed to a warm cosy glow. The glow spread to my tummy, and my feet, and all the bits of my body in between. I drifted into a sort of half sleep. Ellen put her hand down and tried to slip it between our tummies. I raised myself a tiny bit, to give her some room. She slid her hand gently down to where I was resting between her legs. Her fingers touched my willie. It immediately swelled to an enormous size. Ellen felt it, and rubbed herself against me, slowly, like a cat. I could feel the hair round her fanny scratching my willie and crinkling under my tummy. She said, 'Do you like that?' I said yes. I asked her why she had her hand between her legs. She whispered in my ear, 'Don't worry. I'm just . . .' she wriggled slightly '. . . putting a dab of Vaseline where it might be useful.' I asked her what she meant. She said, 'It's to stop any hurt.' I said, 'What hurt?' Ellen said, 'Oh, you never know . . .' She paused for a moment, holding her breath. 'Anything might happen.' She put her hands up around my neck and lifted my head up. She looked in my eyes for a moment, then her own filled with tears. They were happy tears. She cuddled my head and whispered 'Oh Michael . . . Michael . . . Michael!'

I don't really know what happened after that. I was in a sort of trance. Ellen's hands had made my whole body feel tingly and excited, and yet relaxed and dreamy. I couldn't tell where any particular feelings were coming from. I knew my willie was swollen but not where it was or what it was doing. I could feel Ellen's body rippling under me; rippling in long, slow movements that flowed from her breasts to her hips, down and back, down and back, down and back again. I felt I was floating on a cloud, or in a bath of warm honey, or on a soft mound of new-mown grass perfumed with meadow flowers.

The waves of Ellen's warmth flowed under me, and round me, and inside me, and over me. Waves tender and yet strong; waves that drifted me, lifted me, soothed me, lapped me; up and then down, up and then down . . . up and then down . . . slowly at first, then quickening; moving in time to my breathing, and then to my heartbeat, and then faster yet, till it matched the throbbing pulse between my thighs.

My insides glowed, and tightened, and flamed. They surged, and melted and gushed. They hardened and softened and dissolved; flowed and pulsed and flowed again. I moaned, a quiet moan, and moaned again, while the flow and pulse, flow and pulse, grew stronger and more urgent. My brain and body trembled and shook as if someone was hitting me with a hammer; shook and trembled again with pulse after pulse of pain-edged pleasure. They went on and on, one after another, miniature molten explosions stabbing away inside me, flooding my body with bitter-sweet relief, dazzling my brain and the backs of my closed eyes with rainbow-coloured fireworks. I fell asleep.

Ellen woke me, whispering in my ear. She said, 'It's only two out of three, now.' I was too relaxed to speak. I said, 'Mmmmm?' Ellen started giggling. After a while she said, 'I'm still thirty-seven. And I'm still a Catholic.' She giggled again. 'Well . . . sort of.' Her legs were wrapped tightly round the backs of my thighs, and her arms curled round my neck. I said, 'I must move. I'm squashing you.' Ellen gripped me even tighter. 'No!' she said. 'No – don't move! Please – I don't want you to!'

I lay quietly, listening to her breathing. She said, 'I'm nearly three times as old as you, Michael.' She was quiet for a minute. 'I could probably be had up for this . . .' She asked me to kiss her. I did. It was a long kiss. Her hands stroked my back. My willie began to swell again. My mouth went dry and my heart started to pound. I got desperate. I had to be inside her again, or die.

I told Ellen. My voice was hoarse with the terrible longing. She said, 'It's all right, Michael; it's all right . . .' I shouted at her. 'I can't wait! I've got to do it now!' Ellen's heart started hammering against my chest. She took her arms away from my neck and flung the blankets back, then kicked them onto the floor with her feet. 'I want you too, Michael – I want you now!' She reached her mouth up to kiss me again, moaning, her eyes screwed shut. She whispered something that I couldn't hear.

My willie felt as though it was on fire. I was frantic to plunge myself into her, deep inside her, deep down in the smooth, soft comfort of her body. I heard myself making queer little cries and grunts of longing. I found the warm juicy lips between her legs, felt the slippery softness as her entrance yielded to me, felt myself slide into her with a long groan of relief. I lay still for a moment, feeling her insides mould around me, embracing me in a caressing sheath. Then my hips started to move, and after that I couldn't stop. I moved in and out of her, gently at first, then faster and faster, and deeper and deeper, until my whole body was plunging and battering against her.

Ellen began to moan, low at first, then louder, then louder and faster. I shouted, 'Am I hurting you?' She shook her head from side to side, her eyes still closed, and a lovely smile flooded across her face. I felt a wild, piercing, searing glow of love for her. My insides began to churn and tighten, ready to explode. I knew it would happen any moment. Ellen's hips started to move, just little jerks at first, then bigger movements, then heaves and plunges as savage and powerful as mine.

For a moment it seemed as though our bodies were fighting each other, then a miracle happened. As I raised myself into the air, Ellen thrust her bottom hard into the mattress. As I came down again, she pushed her hips up to meet me. I rose again, and again Ellen pressed into the mattress. Down, and her hips rose to meet me. Within a few strokes we were thrusting together again, wilder and even more forcefully than before, but no longer with a sense of struggling against one another; we'd become two bodies moving as one, perfectly in time and perfectly tuned to each other's movements. For a split second at the top and bottom of each stroke, time seemed to freeze. I was deaf and blind and oblivious to everything, everything except the joy of Ellen's body, and she of mine.

Faster and faster we went, harder and harder we thrust against one another, tighter and tighter became the grip of Ellen's legs and arms around my body, bigger and bigger that part of me inside her, more and more urgent the surging pulses deep in Ellen's body. And then – Oh God – Oh God! Total agonising bliss! Ellen screamed in my ear, and screamed again, and again, and again, and I burst inside her; burst and exploded and throbbed and gushed until my whole body melted and emptied into her.

When we woke up I told her what Mrs Sullivan had said about her. Ellen thought it was hilarious. She laughed and laughed, and made me say it again. I asked her why it was so funny. She said, 'That's the second time today!' I thought she meant someone had said the same thing to her already. 'No,' she said, 'no. It's the second time I've gone from three to two.' I was mystified. She said, 'Housewife, mother, maid.' I still didn't get it. Ellen said, 'I'm not a maid any more!' I thought she meant she'd got someone in to do the housework for her. When I said this, Ellen had hysterics. She said, 'Maid is short for maiden!' I said, 'I still don't get it!' Ellen could hardly speak for laughing. She said, 'Maiden is another word for virgin! Now do you see?' I felt a right fool.

I remembered the letter Dad gave me. We read it together. It's from Nana. Uncle Louis is in trouble again. He's been out enjoying himself with the money Nana sent him. It was supposed to pay his fines. He went to a dirty show in London. It was in the back room of a pub. There were two tables shoved together, supposed to be a stage. This girl came out and climbed on the tables. She started to do a strip-tease, dancing to music from a tape-recorder. She got too near the end of one of the tables and fell off. Uncle Louis helped her up off the floor. His hand accidentally slipped up her skirt. She screamed, and a fierce little dwarf appeared. He asked what was going on. The girl told him about Uncle Louis. The dwarf told Uncle Louis to leave. Uncle Louis had hysterics. He asked the dwarf what he'd do if he didn't leave. The dwarf said he'd make him. Uncle Louis said, 'You and whose army?' The dwarf took out his false teeth and waved them at Uncle Louis and said, 'Me and *this* army!' He put the teeth back in and bit Uncle Louis right in the crotch. Nana says if we want to write to Uncle Louis, it's care of Ward Three, St Pancras Hospital, Islington.

When we finished laughing at the letter, we made love again, but gently and slowly, and then Ellen got up to go home. She says there'll be ructions about her being missing all day. Everyone relies on her to do everything. The Sergeant won't have had any lunch or tea. She made me look away when she was getting dressed. She said she didn't want to spoil the mystique. 'What's "mystique?"' I asked her. She said women are supposed to keep a bit of romantic secrecy in their relationships with men. 'Anyway,' she said, 'seeing me in these knickers and this tatty old bra might put you off!'

I got up to untie the rope from the doors downstairs. I didn't bother to put any clothes on. While I was trying to undo the knot on the lane door Ellen started giggling. She said the first time she'd seen me with no trousers on, at the barracks, she'd said to herself, 'If ever I do have a premarital fling, that's the fellow I'd like to have it with!' She'd never thought it would actually happen, though.

I asked her why she'd changed her mind about staying a virgin. She said, 'Why does anybody change their mind about anything?' I said I'd seriously like to know. She said it was all to do with the other night. Every man she's ever met has wanted it from her. I'm the first one who didn't. So she gave it to me. It had to go sometime; why not to someone who made her feel precious and happy? She seemed to think this was perfectly straightforward.

I got the door untied. Ellen stepped into the lane. I asked her if she was sorry she wasn't a virgin any more. She said, 'Do you really want an answer to that?' I said I did. She said, 'Why?' I told her I was afraid she might go away and start regretting it, when she'd had time to think about it, and then she might end up hating me. She came back into the stable and kissed me, and took her knickers off, and lay down on the pile of straw under the stairs. 'Come on!' she said. 'Come and find out how sorry I am!' My breath started to pant and my heart went mad again.

A few minutes later, while we were lying side by side trying to catch our breath, the Sergeant stepped in through the lane door. He looked at Ellen and said quietly, 'So that's how you've turned out . . .' He opened his jacket and undid the buckle on his leather belt and pulled it slowly from around his waist. He stood staring at us, his face grey and a look of disgust in his eyes. Ellen stared back at him with a queer frozen smile on her face.

The Sergeant shouted at her to get up, and called her a cheap bloody whore. Ellen said, 'I'm worse than a cheap bloody whore, Daddy dear; I gave it away for nothing!' She stood up and smeared her palms with the sticky wetness from between her legs and walked across to the Sergeant and wiped her hands down his face.

The Sergeant drew his arm back and hit her a tremendous smack across the mouth with his open hand, and then hit her again with the belt. Ellen hurtled across the width of the stable and smashed against the wall. The Sergeant spat, and took out his handkerchief, and wiped his face. Ellen slumped to the floor, staring at him with dazed eyes. The Sergeant threw his handkerchief away and looked at me. 'As for you, you ungrateful bowsy . . .'

I stood up on top of the pile of straw, with my back against the wall. The Sergeant stared at my willie, which was still wet and shiny from being inside Ellen. He spat again and said, 'Jesus, you're a shameless bastard!' He started to move towards me, with his belt held ready to wallop me if I tried to escape. Ellen staggered to her feet and jumped between us, her mouth dripping blood. The Sergeant swung his belt and gave her another vicious smack across the face. He yelled at her to get out of the way, before he killed the two of us.

Dad came in from the garden. He worked out immediately what was going on. He didn't bother to stop and stare, or waste time asking questions. He grabbed the belt from the Sergeant and threw it into the garden. The Sergeant went berserk. He yelled at Dad to leave us alone. He knew what he had to do, and he was bloody-well going to do it. When he'd finished giving me a bloody good threshing, he'd drag Ellen home and do the same to her. It was the only way to treat a hussy and a whore, even if she was his own daughter and his closest flesh and blood.

Dad listened to him, looking sad, and then shook his head and said quietly, 'For what I am about to do, Lord, please forgive me'. The next moment, his whole body tensed, and he brought his fist up with a lightning blow under the Sergeant's jaw. The

Sergeant's eyes bulged and his tongue flopped out between his lips. He stood swaying for a moment, then dropped to the floor like a dead animal.

Dad nodded at Ellen and said, 'Find a friend, Ellen; anyone . . . someone to go to . . . somewhere until all this blows over.' Ellen picked up her knickers and screwed them into a tight ball in her hand. She tried to say something to Dad, but her mouth was full of blood and spit. It streamed down her chin when she tried to speak. She wiped it off with her knickers but more kept coming out.

Mrs Sullivan came in from the garden. Dad told me quietly to go upstairs and put some clothes on. When I came back Ellen and Mrs Sullivan were gone. Dad asked me to help him lift the Sergeant. He carried him up to the barracks across his shoulders, like a fireman. No one came near me for the rest of the day. I was too numb to think. I spent the time cleaning up the floor of the stable. I was like a zombie.

I was worried sick all night. What would happen to Ellen? Would the Sergeant beat her up as soon as he recovered? Would he beat me up? What would Dad say to me? Would I be locked up in the barracks, or sent to an approved school?

I tied the stable doors shut, in case the Sergeant tried to sneak in and hammer me. Several times in the night I heard them rattling. I didn't get up to look who it was. I was too scared to move. Later on I realised I should have. It might have been Ellen trying to escape from her father, or Mrs Sullivan looking for a place to sleep. On the other hand, it could have been just the wind.

I woke up with an enormous stiff jake. I prayed for the grace to be pure, but it didn't work. In the end, I had to pull my plonker. I couldn't help it. It's all to do with Ellen. My whole body aches for her every time I think of her. It's just what Christie's brother warned me. Once you start, you can't do without it.

My sheet is covered in blood and dried juice. It has a fishy, salty smell. Most of the blood is where Ellen's bottom was lying. There's quite a big stain. It must have come from inside her. I feel rotten about it. I bet I hurt her when we had that mad raging shag. The rest of the blood is from me. During the night, it oozed out of the scratches on my back. Ellen did them with her nails. I didn't notice the pain at the time. They do hurt now, quite a lot.

The garden door rattled. I peeped through the window. It was

Mrs Sullivan. I went down and let her in. She was dressed, for once. I thought she was going to say something about seeing me and Ellen getting into bed, but it was nothing to do with that. She had a message from Dad. He's gone to see my Mam in Mullingar. He went very early, so he can get back by tonight. He asked Mrs Sullivan to keep an eye on me.

I asked her about Ellen. She's all right, except for a cut tongue. Mrs Sullivan wanted Ellen to stay with her last night. She thought it would be safer than going home. Mr Sullivan is away in Donegal selling fire extinguishers. Ellen said it was very kind of her but she'd rather go home and face the music.

She told Mrs Sullivan she's not afraid of her father any more, and anyway, the barracks is as much her home as it is his. The Sergeant works there, but she has the job of running the place and looking after the whole family. Ellen is determined not to be bullied.

I was relieved to hear this. Even so, I was worried. Brave words are all very well, but Ellen is only a woman and the Sergeant is a big tough man. He can do what he likes with her; he's a policeman, and her father.

Mrs Sullivan went off shopping. She asked if there was anything particular I'd like for my lunch. I said I'd have a bit of fried rabbit with some chips, if it was convenient, and a slice of brown bread, if she had any.

Christie came round to see me. He didn't stay long. Since the dance, he's been told to keep away from me. He lost all the money he made on admission tickets and from his refreshments stall. Someone stole it during the kissing game.

He says there's a terrible atmosphere at the barracks. Ellen never came home all day yesterday. Then the Sergeant was found in his office unconscious. They think someone with a grudge must have come in and attacked him. He was on his own most of the day. O'Rooney and Flanagan, the other guard, were out making enquiries after Ellen. There's a rumour it was Ellen's boyfriend, Pat. It's well known that he hates the Sergeant for not letting Ellen marry him.

Christie has to help out at Mr Maguire's tea hut this weekend. It's to make up for taking the mugs without asking. All his pocket-money has to go to Mr Maguire until the mugs are replaced. They're sixpence each, from the ex-army shop in Capel

Street. That's the place where I buy my electrical bits for doing experiments.

Christie asked me if I've still got the bones from the burnt-out car. I'd forgotten all about them. He thinks that's what's bringing us so much bad luck. He wants me to put them back. I said I will.

Andy is going round trying to get pally with Eileen. He told Christie he's going back to England soon, and he wants to have it off with an Irish girl before he goes. Girls in England are no use. They always tell their mothers if a boy does anything to them. Irish girls are too afraid to say anything, in case the priest hears about it and excommunicates them.

Malone spends all his time locked in his shed, repairing bikes. He never goes out at all. He told Christie he's going to beat me up. He blames me for the trouble with Stella.

Sculley is telling everyone I'm too scared to go out. He says I've been sneaking round to his house, begging him to protect me. He's even saying I offered him all my toys and a huge amount of money. Christie says a lot of people believe him.

Bowman is planning some kind of big revenge on me. It's going to be soon. That's all Christie knows about it. He heard one of the Hill gang boasting about it to some fellows in the paper shop. They didn't know he was listening.

When Christie left I went into the house. I cleaned up the snooker room and the room where the juke-box is. The man from Dublin came during the week and unblocked the bar-billiards table. It turned out to be a wad of newspaper with a big lump of squashed shit inside. Dad couldn't believe it.

He told the man he'd give anything to catch the fellow who did it. The man said, 'What makes you think it was a fellow?' Dad told him not to be stupid. Of course it was a fellow; a girl could never stoop that low. The man laughed at this, but Dad just looked blank. He said he couldn't see any grounds for amusement.

Afterwards, the man explained to me why he found Dad's remark so funny. I'm glad he only comes here once a week. He has a vulgar attitude to women.

I had lunch with the Sullivans. Mr Sullivan is due back tonight. He's promised all the children a present. Siobhan said, 'Will he have a present for you, Mam?' Mrs Sullivan said, 'Oh yes; you may be sure of that.' She took her plate out to the kitchen and finished her meal on her own, staring out the window. She spends a lot of her time staring out of windows.

After lunch I went back to the loft. I spent the afternoon reading the encyclopaedias, looking for anything to do with sex. They weren't very helpful. It's all stuff about biology and chemistry and cells fertilising each other. That sort of stuff is no good to me; I want to know what goes on in women's minds, and what happens in their bodies, when they let a fellow inside them. I also want to know how to avoid babies and diseases.

Sculley came round at four o'clock. I didn't bother to have a row with him. I've got bigger worries on my mind at the moment. I had to laugh, anyway; he told me the same stories about Christie, as Christie told me about him.

The point of him coming round was to take me to his grannies' for tea. I'd forgotten about it. I said I didn't want to go. Sculley was upset. He said he was only going because of me. He'd be bored stiff on his own. Also, he'd already told them I was coming, and they were doing a special meal. They'd be very disappointed, and so would I; I'd miss seeing the monkey. I thought he was joking. He said no; cross his belly and hope to puke, his grannies had a monkey. He wouldn't tell me any more. I was so curious I had to go.

I hate going to other people's houses. There's always bad smells, for one thing. If it's not dirty washing or stale cooking, it's paraffin fires or cigarette smoke. Sometimes you get them all together, like round at Malone's house. There, it's mixed with the stink of sweaty mattresses and dirty pots under the bed. His gran and grandad spend their whole lives in bed, coughing and reading newspapers. Both of them smoke pipes as well.

I also hate having to eat at other people's houses. You never know what you're going to get, or who made it, or whether the kitchen will be in a terrible state. I can't stand seeing leftover food lying round in greasy plates, and bits of wet glistening slops round the sink, and patches of black mould where the wall gets wet from the taps splashing. All these things disgust me.

I have to say that Sculley's grannies' place is all right. Everything is clean and neat, even the sink. There were no bad smells, except the usual one you get off old ladies. It's a sort of sharp, acidy, pissy smell. Otherwise, their house is very nice, if only you had room to move in it. Sculley's grannies have the place stuffed with dozens of chairs and little tables. I don't know why; they never sat down for more than a couple of seconds the whole time I was there.

There are two of them. They have a habit of rushing round like a pair of spaniels. If one of them moves, even a fraction of an inch, the other one jumps up and starts lolloping round as well. They look as if they're hoping someone will throw them a ball. Also, the minute one of them starts to leave the room, the other one immediately tries to do the same. They kept getting jammed together in the doorway. I found this really irritating.

One of them has a big scabby sore on her face. Sculley says it's called a rodent ulcer. I know she can't help it, but it made me feel sick just to look at her. The other one can't keep her balance if she stands still. She has no toes on her feet. She went a bit queer once, and went out for a walk in the middle of a snowstorm. She got very cold and collapsed. By the time they found her, her toes were frostbitten. They went black and had to be cut off. She has to have her shoes specially made. They're an odd shape, and very small.

It's no wonder his grannies are so fond of Sculley, even though he's such an absolute arsehole. It's because he's the only person who'll go near them. They told me that themselves. They'd gone to a lot of trouble to do a really nice tea. There was cake, and bread and butter, and jam, and jelly, and cold hard-boiled eggs, and biscuits, and slices of cucumber and beetroot, and a big bowl of grated cheese. Sculley managed to knock the bowl off the table, so that was one thing I didn't have to worry about eating. I kept thinking about the rodent ulcer, and imagining bits of dry scab cracking off and dropping onto the food when they were getting it ready. I just couldn't bear to eat anything. I had to keep making desperate excuses.

Sculley's grannies have a dog. It's one of those little white terriers with hair in front of its eyes. When Sculley spilled the cheese it went and rolled in it. Then it ran round in circles scattering flakes of cheese all over the carpet. The grannies kept picking bits up and eating them. They said the floor was clean enough to have your dinner off. It was more than you could say about the dog.

It kept yapping at me, and trying to sniff between my legs. I had to ask them to put it out. Sculley started joking about the monkey. The grannies asked me if I'd like to see it. I said yes. It was a good way of getting away from the tea-table.

They keep it in the basement. It's a chimpanzee, and it's dead, and they've had it stuffed. They had it as a pet until two years ago. It got into their pantry and drank a whole bottle of whiskey in one night. They found it on the floor, next morning, dead drunk and unconscious. It never recovered.

They told me a weird story. They're not really Sculley's grannies; they're his aunts, and they're sisters. One of them got married, and the three of them, the two sisters and the husband, lived in the one house. Then their father died, and their mother came to live with them. The granny's husband decided to become a sailor, and they hardly saw him from then on.

After a while the mother died. The grannies wanted the husband to come back, because they were lonely without the mother. The husband wouldn't, because he'd got used to being at sea. He sent them the chimpanzee instead. He said it would help to fill the gap left by his mother-in-law. The grannies decided to treat the monkey as their child, and christened it Albert, and took it everywhere with them, until it died.

When we finished looking at the monkey, and came back upstairs, they asked me about my hobbies. I told them I like fixing things, and making electrical gadgets. They said they had the very thing for me. They got out this beautiful varnished box, about six inches square and ten inches tall. It's a rheumatism machine. I've never heard of them before. The grannies said they used to be very popular, especially with the nobility and clergy.

You put a battery in it, and it buzzes, and gives out a high-frequency voltage. Two wires plug into it. One of the wires has a strap on the end of it. You put it round your wrist or your ankle. The other wire has a thing like a small paintbrush on the end of it. The bristles are made of very fine brass wire. You set the machine going, and brush the rheumatic bits of your body. The high-frequency electricity vibrates the muscles and does them good. You can adjust the voltage from a little tingle right up to a massive stinging shock that paralyses your whole body.

The grannies asked me if I'd like to have the machine, as a present. I said, 'What about your rheumatism?' They tittered, and said they hadn't got any, thank God. It was the husband who used to get it. 'Something chronic,' said the granny who'd been married.

She used to give him a good all-over stroke with the brush, once a week. It did wonders for his vitality.

The one with no toes said she used to have to do the same for a butler, when she was in service. He used to get terrible rheumatism in his member. He'd borrow the machine from the master's room and follow her up to the attic at bedtime. After he'd been stroked for a while his member used to get swelled up with static electricity. The only way he could get rid of the swelling was by discharging the electricity into a damp hole. The granny's fanny turned out to be just the right place.

Eventually, she got pregnant. Her mistress asked her how it happened. She explained about having to let the butler earth himself after his rheumatic treatment. The mistress told her she was an ignorant and foolish girl; it was only the butler's excuse to have his way with her.

The granny told the mistress she ought to have a word with the master, in that case, because he'd developed the same rheumatic trouble as the butler, and what with the two of them taking it in turns to discharge their electricity into her, she hardly got a wink of sleep from one end of the week to the other.

When the baby was born it was put into a home and she never saw it again. The other granny never had any children. This was why they were so keen on the monkey.

This reminded me of the dead baby in our basement. I asked the grannies if they knew everyone who'd ever lived in the terrace. They said no; there were too many people. In the old days, the terrace used to be all 'quality'. Now it was just one big dosshouse from end to end, apart from the Sergeant and the Rothwells and themselves.

'The bit you're in,' they said, 'was worse than a dosshouse; it used to be a kip.' A madam from Dublin used to rent it. She was only a young woman in age but sin had put years on her. To look at, you'd think she was old enough to have one foot in the grave. During the summer months, you'd see her working the pubs and the bus queues, passing out little cards with the address of the basement on it. It was a good business.

The customers would congregate on the front steps, sitting there smoking and waiting their turn, their collars up and their hats pulled down to hide their faces. The girls would let them in, one after another, take their five bob off them, let them perform their business, and show them out the back way. It was never more than ten minutes per customer. They all had buses to catch.

On Sunday nights the bus company kept a spare bus in reserve, in case the queue at the kip was bigger than the queue for the last bus into Dublin. The drivers used to call it the BBB; the brothel backup bus. The driver and conductor were allowed to sneak in the back way for a quick one, to keep them co-operative.

Sometimes there were too many customers and not enough girls. The madam would give a bus-driver a note for her place in Dublin, asking for more girls to be sent out. The bus coming back to Kilmara with the extra girls was called the FRF; the fanny reinforcements ferry.

In the winter, when there was no day trip business, the madam locked the place and left it to the rats and mice.

The madam was a girl from the village. She became a whore when she was quite young. She started by going to England during the War, in 1940 or 1941. She said she was going over to marry an English pen-pal, but everyone suspected it was because she was pregnant. She was well-known for 'airing her attributes' with the coal-boat crews, before she went. She came back with a boy of four, and told everyone she'd been married to a soldier who got killed. No one believed her. She left the boy with her parents in Back Street and went to live in Dublin.

I hadn't been taking much notice of the story until then. I was just glad to keep them talking, so they wouldn't notice I wasn't eating. At the mention of Back Street I started to get interested.

The girl took up whoring, and must have been good at it. She soon had a place of her own, in the old Monto area of Dublin, just off Talbot Street and convenient to the main railway station. After this she opened up a second kip, the one in Kilmara. People said it was to get her revenge on the village.

After four or five years, she caught a terrible dose of the pox, and got very ill, and had to give up whoring, and abandon her business in Dublin. She lived in the basement for a while, then bought a cottage in one of the alleys off Back Street. She got it very cheap. No one would live there ever since a priest killed himself in it. He committed suicide by jumping off the wall at the end of the chapel, but he jumped too energetically. Instead of crashing onto the rocks in the quarry below, he flew out and smashed through the roof of the cottage. His head caught in the rafters and was pulled off and hung for days before anyone had the courage to take it down. By that time the seagulls had eaten his eyes out.

I asked the grannies if the madam had a baby with her when she came to live in the basement. No, they said; but there was a rumour that she was expecting. No one could tell for sure; she was fat and bloated with drink and disease. She was attacked one night, and badly beaten up, by someone she'd given the pox to, but nothing was ever done about it.

That's when she moved to the cottage. She knew no one would have the courage to come in and molest her, because it was supposed to be haunted by the priest's ghost. Even so, she still wasn't safe there. People used to get up in the chapel grounds and throw things down at her all the time. She never had any peace. Eventually she died, but no one knew for ages. In the end, it was the smell that gave it away.

By the time they found her, she was even worse than the priest's head. Rats had been at her, as well as the maggots. The police found one of her legs in the garden. They said a dog must have pulled it off and carried it away to chew on. All the dogs in the village had to be put down, for fear they had the pox.

I asked the grannies, 'When did all this happen?' They said it was about six or seven years ago. My head was spinning by this time. They'd been talking for hours. I knew Malone must be the madam's son; it was too much of a coincidence, otherwise, what with him living in the cottage and not having any parents. Also, I worked out that he's just the right age. I didn't know what to think about the dead baby.

When I was leaving, they gave me a radio and asked me if I could fix it for them. If I do, they'll give me the rheumatism machine. Sculley asked me why I wanted it. He said I seem a bit young to suffer from aches and pains. I told him not to be a fool. I want it because it will make a terrific torture machine. Sculley's little eyes lit up when I said this. He made me add it to the list of tortures I've promised him.

I spent the evening making notes of the grannies' stories and learning words from the *Reader's Digest*. They have quizzes called 'Increase your word power'. I got quite a few of them right. 'Melancholy' is my favourite new word. It sounds exactly right for the feeling it describes. I know, because it's exactly the feeling I've got.

370

I kept hoping Ellen would come round but she didn't. Dad didn't get home until very late. I saw the lights go on in the basement. He went straight to bed.

I'm glad I went round to see Sculley's grannies. It took my mind off my troubles.

I stayed awake most of the night, learning new words and listening to AFN on the radio. It was dawn by the time I fell asleep. Dad woke me. He was banging on the stable doors, trying to get in. I had them both roped up, same as last night. I jumped out of bed and dropped into the lane from the loft door. I was already dressed. As soon as I felt the cold I was dying for a piss. I went into the archway, pulling my jake out, and still half asleep.

Stella was lying bundled in the corner. All she had on was a nightie. There was an empty gin bottle beside her, and an empty Aspro bottle, and she'd been sick all down her front. I couldn't see her face; her hair was covering it. Her hands and feet were filthy dirty. I went over and gently lifted her into a sitting position against the wall. She was so floppy I thought she was dead. I got such a fright I let go of her. Then I remembered reading that dead people go stiff. I propped her up again and put my hand against her heart. It was still beating.

Dad came down the lane and tried to open the stable doors. He gave up, and stood back to look at the loft door. He took a few steps backwards, took a run forward, jumped, and got his hands on the ledge. Dad is very athletic, apart from his bad legs. He heaved himself up onto the ledge and went into the loft. I said a prayer that he wouldn't notice us. He didn't.

He had a quick look round the loft, and came back to the door. He peered up and down the lane with a puzzled look, then went away. I waited a few minutes and went across to peer through the cracks in the bottom door. Dad was unroping the door into the garden. He went back into the house.

I lifted Stella and put her arm round my shoulder. She was as limp as a banana skin. I half carried and half dragged her down the lane to her garden gate. There was no one about. I opened the gate quietly, hoping the dog wasn't about. It was. It came down the garden yapping at the top of its voice. I left Stella sitting on the step and ran off.

I wanted to escape to somewhere where no one could harm me.

The only place I could think of was the chapel. The half-ten Mass had just started. There were no seats on the men's side, so I squashed in beside Catherine Healy right at the back of the women's seats. She glared at me at first, then started giggling. She poked some other girls, and they stared at me and started giggling. Christie's sister Rowena was in front of me. She looked round to see what was going on. Her face broke into a big smile. I thought she was pleased to see me. I smiled back at her. She turned away and put her hands over her face. Her shoulders were heaving as if she was trying to smother a cough.

Catherine Healy leaned towards me and said, 'Are you having trouble keeping them on?' I just looked at her. I didn't know what she was on about. She whispered, 'Can you hear me all right?' I said yes. She said, 'I thought maybe you couldn't.' She stared at the side of my head and had another fit of giggles, and said, 'Tell me, is it to stop your brain leaking out?' I suddenly realised what she was laughing at. I've started putting Sellotape on my ears again. With all the rushing round I'd forgotten to take it off.

I felt a right idiot. It would have to be Catherine Healy! I nicknamed her brother 'Rabbit' because of the way his ears stick out. He hates me for this. They're a lot bigger than mine. He'll be delighted when she tells him about me and the Sellotape. I'll never hear the end of it.

Eddie Butler says Catherine goes courting in the back of fellows' cars after the pictures. He says she has more fingerprints on her fanny than they have in Scotland Yard. She's only a year older than me and in the Legion of Mary, which is supposed to be all about purity.

Dad was waiting for me when I got home. He went to see Mam, to see if I could go and live in Mullingar for a while. Her dad said no; I have too much to say for myself. He thinks boys should do what they're told and not argue with their elders. He doesn't like me. Dad says it's because I remind him of him. He doesn't like Dad either.

Dad asked me if I'd been to confession. I said no. He said, when I do, he'll say no more about me and Ellen. He wanted me to swear I'll have nothing more to do with her. She's a frustrated spinster, and a danger to young fellows like myself. I got angry and said it was none of his business. He got even angrier, and said it was. 'Supposing the woman got pregnant? Where would you be then?' I never thought of this. It went completely out of my mind at the time.

'More to the point,' said Dad, 'what about your immortal soul?' Did I not realise I was in a grave state of sin, the worst possible state of sin, in fact? Sins of the flesh are a direct slap in the face, so far as God is concerned. I told him I love Ellen. Dad was furious. He shouted that I love the idea of getting my end away.

Someone started banging on the front door. Dad went through to the snooker room to see what they wanted. It was Christie's youngest sister, Rosemary. She had a message from the Sergeant. He wanted to talk to Dad, in the barracks. Dad said he'd see me later, and that I'm not to lock the stable doors, ever again. He went off with a grim face.

I went out to the stable. Christie came round, banging on the lane door. I leaned out of the loft to see what he wanted. He said he was just off down the strand to work with John-Joe Maguire for the day. He wasn't looking forward to it. Mr Maguire keeps smacking him on the back of the head.

He says things at the barracks are getting worse. Ellen and the Sergeant aren't speaking to each other. The Sergeant won't even come into the house. He has his meals sent into the office. He won't eat anything Ellen cooks; it has to be done by one of his other daughters. At night, he sleeps in the cells. Christie says they're all desperate with worry. No one knows what's caused the trouble between Ellen and his dad, and neither of them will tell.

A car came down the lane. We looked out. It stopped at Stella's gate. Christie said it was the doctor's car. I told him about finding Stella in the archway. He said I should have left her there. I could have got into terrible trouble if anyone had seen me with her.

I said he was a selfish little shit; I couldn't leave Stella lying in a filthy corner, freezing to death. Someone had to help her. Christie said the only way to help Stella now, is to marry her and take her far away, where no one knows her. She's going to have a baby. I didn't believe him. He said I must be the thickest fucker he's ever met; everyone else in the village knows about it. Whoever raped her, started the baby. That's why she's been getting drunk. She's trying to get rid of it.

Christie said it's a well-known thing. If a girl has one up the spout, the best way to get rid of it is to drink gin. It loosens up their insides and makes them shit the baby out. I was heart-broken.

Stella – pregnant! I felt so bitter and angry I could have killed Christie for telling me. I told him he'd better go. He said there was no point getting ratty with him; it was the fellow who raped her I should be mad at.

I was utterly miserable after he left. He's right. Why haven't I tried to find the fellow who did it? I've been too selfish and involved with my own problems to spare any thought for Stella's. Come to think of it, why aren't the police doing something about it? Christie says they have no clues. Stella couldn't tell them anything. The fellow sneaked up and put his jacket over her head when he raped her. All she knows is that it had a leathery feel, and a sweet sort of smell. It could be anyone. Leather jackets are very popular since teds and rockers started. The smell was probably hair-oil.

I looked at myself in the mirror. My face is getting tired-looking. I used to have sparkly eyes. They don't sparkle any more. I've got a big boil on my neck, and another one starting on my jaw. Dad says it's because we're not eating properly. I went into the house and got a needle, then came back to the loft.

I stuck the needle in the boil on my jaw. A gush of horrible white creamy stuff came out, then watery stuff, then blood. Ellen came up and caught me doing it. She asked me if I'd sterilised the needle. I hadn't. I should have held it in front of the spout of a steaming kettle. She said I was extremely careless. I could get blood poisoning or lockjaw. I said I was too miserable to think about it.

She asked me what was worrying me. I said I'd just heard about Stella being pregnant. I asked her if she was pregnant. She shook her head and said no. I asked her how she knew she wasn't. She said she was safe at the moment. I didn't ask her to explain. I'd been so looking forward to seeing her again. Now that she was there, I froze up. All the loving feelings I had for her shrivelled up. I felt awkward and ill at ease with her.

She sat on the edge of the bed. There was nowhere else to sit. She patted the bed beside her. I pretended not to notice. She asked me what was wrong. I said I was full of bad feelings; everything in my head was going round and round. My brain felt as if it was going to explode. I turned my back on her and pressed my hands into my eyes. I pressed so hard I nearly burst them.

Ellen murmered something in a quiet voice. I said, 'What do

you want?' She said, 'Would you like to lock the doors?' I turned round. She was undoing the waistband of her skirt. She stopped when she saw me watching her. We stared at one another for a moment. I felt like screaming, for no reason. Ellen dropped her skirt on the floor, and then her petticoat. She had on knickers like Mrs Barrington's; tight skimpy little white ones with no legs and lace all round the edges. I stared at them hard, like a dog glaring at a cat. Ellen was embarrassed. Her eyes flickered, and she blushed.

She tried to make a joke. She said, 'I bought them for my bottom drawer . . . just in case.' I still didn't say anything. She walked over to me and said, 'I'm sorry. I thought . . . I thought it might help.' I was frozen stiff with wild feelings of misery and despair. Ellen stretched out her arms to hug me. Something snapped in my brain. My whole body trembled with explosive energy. I gave her a vicious push. She went flying backwards onto the bed and landed with her legs sprawled apart.

The moment I saw all the bare white skin, I went mad. My willie swelled up to an enormous size. I opened my buttons and it jumped out. I threw myself on my knees on the bed, between her legs. Ellen tried to sit up. I pushed her down, and tried to rip her knickers off. I put my hand into the waistband and pulled as hard as I could. They cut into her and left a red mark round her waist. She screamed, and said I was hurting her. I put both hands on the waistband and slid backwards off the bed, pulling them with me. Again Ellen tried to sit up, and again I pushed her down. I forced my way between her legs, trying to push my willie into her. It wouldn't go. Ellen screamed again. 'No, Michael, wait! You can't do it like that!'

I put my hands on her tummy to hold her down, and kept on pushing and thrusting. She spat on her hands and wiped the spit on my willie and round the lips of her fanny. Bit by bit I got further inside her, and down to where she was juicy inside. Ellen stopped struggling, and lay with her arms stretched out as if she was being crucified. She stared up at me with no expression on her face. I shut my eyes and kept shagging.

It was no good. I couldn't get my willie to spurt. I felt like a machine, cold and dead. There was no happiness in my mind, and no pleasure or excitement in my body. All the wild badness in my mind faded away. My willie started to shrivel. I went faster and faster, but it still kept going down. In the end it just popped out. I had to give up. When I realised what I'd done I was so sick and ashamed I wanted to die. I rolled off the bed onto the floor and hugged Ellen's skirt against my face.

I lay there for ages, trying not to sniffle and sob. Ellen put her hand down and stroked my head. I got up on my knees beside the bed and buried my face in my hands. Ellen put her arm round my shoulders. I told her I was sorry. She said it was as much her fault as mine; she shouldn't have been so obvious. I said I had no business going for her like that. She said if I hadn't, she might have gone for me. Not so roughly, perhaps, but that's only because she's not as big and strong as I am. She wanted me just as much as I wanted her.

I told her I was never going to do it again, ever. 'What?' she said. 'Never?' 'Never,' I said; I'd brought her nothing but trouble. I was going to give up shagging. She said, very softly, she'd be pleased if I gave up using the word 'shagging', but she didn't want me to give up making love to her. I said I never wanted to do it again, whatever she called it. I was too ashamed of myself.

She said, 'Supposing I want you to?' I said she couldn't possibly, not after the way I treated her. Ellen breathed in my ear. She said, 'I do. I do want you to.' She sat up and took the rest of her clothes off. 'Go and jam the doors, Michael, and come to bed with me.' She nuzzled her hair into my face. It smelt clean and perfumey. She said, 'Don't be afraid, Michael; I just want you to relax and cuddle up with me.'

I locked the doors and took my clothes off and got into bed with her. She put her arms around me and said, 'There, that's better, isn't it?' It was. It was lovely. She told me what's happened since I last saw her.

The Sergeant says she's got to go on a retreat, at a convent near Terenure. It's a place that specialises in fallen women. He's written off to book it up on her behalf. While she's there, she's got to make a full confession and take a lay vow of chastity. If she doesn't agree to go, he'll throw her out on the street. He says that's where she belongs. Meanwhile, the Sergeant is refusing to have anything to do with her. He says she's a harlot. He won't even come into the house while she's there. Ellen says she doesn't mind about that; it's more inconvenient for him than it is for her. She's going to leave home, but not for a while, though. Her dad looks on her as a skivvy, and thinks he can treat her accordingly. She's going to show him otherwise. She's looked after them all for ten years, ever since her mother died. They're old enough to look after themselves now.

'Where will you go?' I asked her. She said she'd like to go back to the hotel and catering business. She wants to work hard and save money, and some day run a hotel or restaurant of her own.

'In Dublin?' I said.

'Good Heavens, no! London, or Birmingham, or better still, Paris.'

'Paris!' I was amazed. That's where the barrow-man said the Joyce fellow is hiding. I had to ask Ellen where it is. She said it's the capital of France, the same as Dublin is the capital of Ireland. She was surprised that I didn't know already. I had to explain to her that I've never had much interest in geography. I asked her if she wouldn't be scared stiff working in a foreign country with a lot of strangers.

'No, not at all,' she said. 'Paris is where I was working when my mother died. I had a lovely job as a hotel receptionist, looking after English-speaking tourists.'

I was astonished to hear this. 'How did you manage to speak to the French people?'

'By speaking French, of course! I taught myself from a set of records while I was at Marino Tech.'

It seems there are a lot of things I don't know about Ellen. I'm beginning to realise that she's not just pretty, she's intelligent as well. Maybe even more intelligent than me.

She said she'd had enough of talking. She put my right hand between her legs and showed me how to stroke her fanny so that it opened up and got juicy. I had to give up after a while. My hand went numb and fumbly. It's because I'm left-handed. When I told her, she rolled over me and lay on my other side. After a while, she said she wanted to feel me inside her. I tried, but I couldn't manage it; my willie was all limp and floppy, and didn't feel as if it belonged to me. Ellen told me to relax. She stroked my willie for a while, but it was no use. I was still too disgusted with myself from earlier on.

Ellen said it was a pity. Today is the last day she's definitely safe. She explained all about it. I told her I had some anti-baby things, but she said she didn't fancy the idea of using them. It would be like paddling with wellingtons on. Anyway, she says she likes the feeling of me spurting inside her. She says the juice is good for a woman, provided she doesn't get pregnant. It gets into her blood and makes her eyes shine and keeps her skin soft.

I had to explain why I had the anti-baby things. I didn't tell her I'd got them for her brother. I said the foreigners had given them to me, for a joke. Ellen wanted to see them, so I had to tell her the detective had taken them. I didn't tell her about the rest of the stuff he took away. Eventually, Ellen got up and dressed, and said 'Maybe I'll have to find another fellow to keep me satisfied!' She was only joking, but it made me feel rotten, and I burst into tears as soon as she went down the stairs.

A few minutes later, Dad came back from the barracks. He says the Sergeant isn't well. He's got pains in his stomach, and fierce headaches. His appearance has aged twenty years in the last couple of days. He looks like a tired old man. Dad blames me. He didn't have time to say any more. There was a crowd of fellows and girls banging at the basement door and knocking on the windows. They were impatient to get at the snooker tables and the juke-box. Dad told me to stay and make a note of how many records were played.

I listened to the girls chatting. There's a new rumour going round about Stella. Everyone's saying she was having it off on the sly with a man from the tennis club, and that she wasn't raped at all. She only made it up, when she realised she was pregnant. It was to save the man from getting into trouble with his wife.

The girls are mad at her. She's thrown suspicion on all the fellows in the village, and they don't like it. They say she should own up, and get the police off the fellows' backs. They were so busy talking they hardly bothered to play the juke-box. Dad said I could go.

I went out to the stable and fixed Sculley's grannies' radio. It was simple. The wires were loose in the mains plug. An idiot could have mended it.

I had a big surprise when I switched it on. The 'Down your way' programme was on, with Frank Linengleman. I think that's his name. He was in a village in Suffolk, in England. One of the people he interviewed was Adrian Bell. He's the very man who wrote that book I bought a few weeks ago, *Corduroy*, about a fellow who bought a motorbike and rode off to be a farmer's boy. Mr Bell is grown up now, and a farmer himself. Frank asked him what record he'd like, and he chose a song called 'The Foggy Foggy Dew', sung by Burl Ives.

I took the radio round to the grannies. They wanted me to come in and have tea with them. I said I couldn't; I had to go home and have a bath, and write a letter to my mother, and read a chapter of the Bible. They said I was a credit to my generation, and to the Catholic faith.

When I asked about the rheumatism machine they said Sculley had it. He'd asked if he could borrow it to play with. I was livid when I heard this, and went round to see him straight away. Sculley was typing in his front room, but he disappeared as soon as he caught sight of me. I banged on the door and his dad came and opened it. He asked me if my name was Kelly. I said yes. He said he'd heard a lot about me, and none of it was any good. Before I could say anything, he slammed the door in my face.

I went back to the stable in a fearful temper. It started to pour with rain, so I had to stay in. I read the *Reader's Digests* for a while, and learnt some more useful words. 'Aficionado' is really impressive, but I can't see myself having much opportunity to use it; certainly not in the kind of conversation you get in this village. Christie came round, soaking wet. Mr Maguire let him go home early, because no one was buying tea. The crowds on the strand went off for the buses as soon as the rain settled in.

Christie had a horrible experience down the strand. A man came to John-Joe's stall for a mug of tea, and asked Christie to carry it back to his deck-chair for him. He said he was afraid he'd spill it if he carried it himself. The man's excuse was that he wasn't too good on his legs, especially walking on sand.

When they got to where the man was sitting, he asked Christie to do him a favour. He wanted his boots taken off, to give his feet some sea air. Christie undid the laces and tried to pull the boots off. They wouldn't budge. The man said there was only one way to do it, and got Christie to stand in front of him with the boots under his armpits and his hands gripping the man's ankles.

Christie gave a terrific heave. The boots came away, and he fell over backwards. He heard the man say, 'Jeezes, you're a strong little bugger!' When Christie got up off the sand, he saw the legs of the man's trousers hanging down limp at the front of the deck-chair. The man said, 'You've pulled me bloody legs off!' Christie looked at the boots, and the man was right. His feet and the bottom half of his legs were still in the boots, sticking out from under Christie's arms. Christie got such a shock he nearly puked. He couldn't believe it. The man was leaning back in the chair having hysterics.

It turned out to be a trick. The man had artificial legs. As soon as Christie pulled, he let go the catches and they came off. He lost his real legs in the War. He told Christie he's always fooling people. One of the things he does is to bet people in pubs that he's the shortest man in the room. He puts down a big bet, pretending to be drunk and stupid. People think they can't lose. When they put their money down, he gets the barman to look after it. Then he goes to the toilet, takes off his legs, and wobbles back into the bar on his stumps.

I told Christie about Sculley. I asked him if he'd call round and invite him out for a chat, so I could get hold of him. Christie said he didn't have time. He had to go home for his tea and then to Benediction. Him and Sculley were the two altar-boys for this evening. He said if I went to the chapel, I could get hold of Sculley afterwards.

I said no; Benediction is too boring, and the smell of the incense makes me feel dizzy. I said I'd wait outside the chapel. Christie said I might as well go in. There was a Holy Ghost Father coming tonight, looking for boys with a vocation. He'd be speaking after Benediction.

Christie has his name down for the priesthood already. Loads of the fellows have. I thought he was joking, but he was deadly serious. He says you get a really good education at the seminary. I asked him what use that is, if you're condemned to spend the rest of your life as a priest.

Christie said it's simple; you get the education, then you say you've lost your vocation. They can't make you stay if you don't want to. After that, you write off to England and get a job as a teacher. They're desperate for teachers over there. They pay your boat fare, and find you digs, and even give you a grant to go to university, if you spin them a good enough yarn.

Once you get to England, you're made. If you get fed up with teaching, you can swop over to something interesting, like being a car salesman, or a businessman, or a comedian. English people think Irish comedians are hilarious. They laugh the minute you open your mouth. You don't even have to tell jokes.

Just putting on a Tipperary accent sends them into hysterics.

I went along to the chapel to see what would happen. When the priest and Sculley and Christie cleared up after Benediction, the Holy Ghost Father stood up in the middle of the altar. 'My dear boys,' he said. 'My dear, dear boys!'

He looked at us piously. All the village lads were there, including the lowest of the low. A right bunch, we were.

'An aspirant to the priesthood must have a clear idea of the horror of sin.'

Everyone shuffled about, smirking and coughing. He waited until the noise died down, and then continued.

'Sin, my dear boys, even the most venial of sins, is so abhorrent to God, that, given the choice between committing one minute offence against His awesome majesty, or saving the whole world and everyone in it from certain annihilation, it were better that the world should perish – better, my dear boys, better that the entire *universe* should be abolished from the infinite immensity of space – than that you should deliberately and knowingly commit that one small offence against the Divine Ruler of Heaven and earth!'

The priest paused, and gave us time to think about this.

'How much more so, then, when the sin is of a mortal or grievous nature? Can you imagine, my dear boys, can you imagine for a moment, the agony and the anguish in God's heart, when He sees a pure Catholic girl, at the cinema, for example, casting a flirtatious sidelong glance at some Brylcreemed teddy boy with a cigarette dangling between his lips? Or the grief and torment in God's mind when He catches sight of a strong, manly, upright Catholic boy, descending to the level of the beasts of the field, by allowing himself hot-blooded lustful thoughts at the sight of some innocent girl, in a perhaps overly scanty swimsuit, sunning her God-given body on the clean sands of the Bull Island!'

The priest's mouth went dry after he said this, and he had to stop for a minute, and bless himself. He stared at us, and said he would observe a few moments' silence, in order to allow time for the horror of these impure thoughts to sink into our minds. Fellows began to sit up and take notice. They thought the sermon was going to lead on to stuff about sex and girls. It didn't; the priest went back to venial sins.

He told us that sin extends even to the cross words between brother and sister when one or other of them happens to take the last piece of bread and jam from the plate. I hate this kind of stuff. If God is the sort of person who worries about such trivial things as that, He can't be as intelligent as priests say He is. Fancy having the whole universe to think about, and letting yourself get annoyed by what children get up to! I was so disgusted I got up and walked out.

I managed to catch Sculley coming out of the sacristy. He screamed and howled and said he hasn't got the rheumatism machine any more; he's given it to Bowman. I asked him how this came about, and he said it was practically my fault. He told the Hill gang about me saying it would make a good torture instrument, and they made him get it and give it to them. They're going to use it on me when they catch me. That's what *they* think!

I pushed Sculley up against the wall of the chapel with my hand round his throat, and held him till his face went purple. Then I dropped him on the ground and went home.

Mrs Barrington was waiting for me downstairs in the stable. She had that tense, nervous look in her eyes, and kept licking her lips while she was talking to me. She wanted to go upstairs with me, but I wouldn't let her. I said at first I was too tired, and she said, 'I'm not surprised . . .' I asked her what she meant, and she said she'd been round earlier on in the day, but I'd been too busy to notice. She gave me a cold look and said it was nice to know I wasn't missing her too much. I went as red as a beetroot when she said this. She tried the trick of pulling her dress up and showing me she had nothing on underneath, but I just looked away and thought about the Virgin Mary. She got very cross and said I might have reason to be sorry, one of these days; she's a woman who doesn't take kindly to being spurned. I told her I've had too many worries recently, and I don't want to have any more involvement with women.

Before she left, she tried to force me to promise, on my honour, that I won't say anything about Mr Barrington's photographs. I kept telling her, 'I *can't* say anything about them; I've never seen them!' and eventually she left. I ached to grab her and give her a hug, but I controlled myself. Later, my willie started wanting her, and I had to pull my plonker. That stopped me feeling hot and breathless, but I still couldn't sleep, thinking of her. I love her just as much as when I first saw her, which makes it even worse, now that I know it's dangerous for us to be friends.

Week Nine

Monday 6 August – Sunday 12 August

The sun was blazing in my eyes when I woke. It blinded me for a few seconds. I stepped out of bed straight onto Mrs Sullivan. She was lying on the floor with my eiderdown wrapped round her. I wasn't too surprised; there was another big row between her and Mr Sullivan in the garden last night.

Mrs Sullivan sat up and yawned. She looked terrible; like a worn-out old woman. She must have guessed what I was thinking, because she asked me if I had any idea how old she was. I said no. She told me she's twenty-five. My eyes must have been out on stalks.

She stared at me and said, 'You'd never believe it, would you?' I shook my head. 'It shows what four kids and a bag-of-shite with a prick can do to you.' She asked me if I enjoyed running a hostel for deprived females. 'Or should I say, "depraved"? Maybe it's you that's depraved. Or are you being depraved?' I didn't understand a word of this. She lit a cigarette and sat staring at me, breathing smoke in thin trickles from her nostrils.

'What does your father think about it?'

'About what?'

'You and these women you have up here.'

I said it was nothing to do with my Dad.

'Is there a waiting list?' She paused for a moment. 'I could do with a bit of comforting myself.'

I got dressed and went into the house and left her sitting there. I know it was rude, but I can't cope with any more problems to do with sex and women. Besides, Mr Sullivan is dangerous. Bad-tempered little drunks always are. Dad and I had toast and tea together. We hardly spoke. John-Joe Maguire came round. He hardly spoke either. We all sat and drank tea and listened to the news on the BBC.

The foreigners arrived to empty the machines. They gave Dad

six pounds and the usual guff about how little business he's doing. Dad lost his temper. He told them he knew for a fact there was at least twenty pounds in the slot machines, and that wasn't counting the juke-box.

The foreigners asked him if he was calling them liars. Dad said, 'Yes!' in a very definite voice. One of them went to the door and whistled. Two big fellows got out of the van in the terrace and came down the steps.

The foreigners asked Dad again if was calling them liars. Dad said he wasn't *calling* them liars; they *were* liars. Mr Maguire slipped out through the back of the house.

The two big fellows took hold of Dad's arms. I jumped on the back of one of them and gave his neck a vicious twist. He gave a roar of agony and flung me off. With his free arm, Dad smashed the other one's head against the wall. The three foreigners ran up the steps.

The two big fellows shook their heads and had another go at me and Dad. Dad gave me a big grin, and shouted, 'This is more like it!' One of the big fellows swung his fist at Dad. Dad grabbed his arm and gave a tremendous heave. He spun him round and swung him straight at the wall. The fellow's back hit a cue-rack, and the clips dug into him with terrific force.

The other fellow picked up a cue and tried to hit me with it. He missed with the first swing. The second time, I grabbed it and pulled him forward. He lost his balance and fell face-down on the floor. I jumped in the air and landed on his back, feet first, with all my weight. There was a cracking noise. I think I broke some of his ribs. John-Joe came down the front steps with the Sergeant, and the two big fellows left. They had to help each other up the stairs. I went out for a walk.

Christie's sister Rowena was sitting on the steps at the end of the terrace. I sat down to chat to her. She got up and walked off. A squashed cigarette butt was stuck to the back of her skirt. I was going to tell her about it but it dropped off after a few steps.

Sculley's grannies' dog came down the steps behind me. It stuck its teeth into the back of my jumper. I tried to whack it away but I couldn't reach. Rowena stopped and looked back. I stood up and tried to shake the dog off. The bloody thing had its eyes shut and its jaws clamped tight. I had to take my jumper off in the end. The dog ran off with it. Rowena gave me a frosty smile and said it served me right. I asked her what she meant. She just turned her back and went away.

The tide was out, and I went for a walk along the strand. Stella was sitting down at the point, huddled up inside a thick winter coat. I said, 'Are you not boiling?' She said no; she's always cold nowadays. I asked her why she'd been lying in the archway. 'Was it you that found me?' I said yes, and explained about carrying her down to her own garden, and the dog yapping. It attracted her parents' attention, and they sent for the doctor. 'You should have left me where I was.' She said she'd tried to kill herself with a mixture of gin and aspirins. If she hadn't been sick, it would have worked. She particularly wanted to die in the archway. When the fellows arrived for pitch-and-toss, they'd have found her body. It would have been some small revenge on the one who raped her. The memory of her lying there, dead, would haunt him for the rest of his life. It might even force him to confess.

'What makes you think he'd be there?'

She shrugged her shoulders. 'Why not? All the fellows in this village play pitch-and-toss. What else is there to do? Apart from . . .' She stopped and didn't say any more for a while. I told her O'Rooney thinks I'm the rapist. She laughed. I was puzzled. 'How do you know I'm not?' She said, 'Show me your hands.' I held them out, and she examined them carefully. 'It can't have been you.' When the fellow raped her, he put his jacket over her head. She started screaming, and he panicked, and tried to strangle her. Everything went black. The last thing she remembers, was sinking her teeth into his hand. They went right through his flesh, and she felt them grinding against his bones. Then she went unconscious.

She hasn't told the police about the bite. Her mind was blank, at first, and she couldn't remember what had happened. It was too horrible to think about. When the details came back to her, she kept it to herself. She wanted to find the fellow on her own.

'But why?' I said. 'Surely it's easier for the police to find him?'

'Yes. And then they'd lock him up.'

'Isn't that what you want?'

'And have him safely behind bars where I couldn't get at him? No fear! I wanted him for myself . . .' I asked her if she was still trying to find him. 'No. It doesn't matter any more.' I was amazed when she said this. I started to ask her what she meant, but she interrupted me. 'Did you know I'm probably going to have a baby?'

I nodded. She asked me if I knew about periods. I said I did, a bit. 'I've missed one, so far. The doctor says it could be just . . . just shock. I'm due again, this weekend. If I miss again . . . well, that's it.'

I couldn't believe how calm she seemed. She said she's not; not really, not inside. That's why she tried to kill herself. She can't stand the hurt any more. And the loneliness. Even her parents ignore her. They can't cope with the shame. They've had filthy notes in their letterbox. I said I'd help her. She said it was kind of me, but what could I do? Her face was expressionless, even though her eyes were streaming with tears. She said she cries all the time. She doesn't even notice she's doing it.

I told her about Malone saying he'd caught his hand in a bicycle chain. All she said was, 'Maybe he did . . .' I said, 'I've seen the cut myself. It could easily be teeth-marks!' I asked her why she didn't seem interested. She said she wasn't in the mood. 'But supposing it was him?' Stella shut her eyes and leaned her head on her knees. I couldn't think of any more to say. A dog came running up and tried to be friendly. We both ignored it. It started digging madly in the sand, barking and smiling at us. I shouted at it to go away. It bent over and had a shit right beside us. The smell was horrible. We had to get up and go. I hate dogs. Stella went home on her own. I walked all the way to Rathluan, and back. By the time I got home it was dark. I was too miserable to be hungry.

I got up early to go to the lavatory. Mrs Sullivan was sitting on the steps outside it, smoking. I had to be careful not to make windy noises. I didn't want her laughing at me.

When I came out she asked me if I'd like a piece of chocolate. She took the remains of a bar out of her dressing gown pocket. It was in a piece of crumpled silver paper. The outside wrapper was missing. She broke the chocolate into individual pieces, brushed the step clean with her sleeve, and laid them out neatly between us. 'Help yourself,' she said.

I only ate one bit. It tasted of cigarettes, from her fingers, so I didn't have any more. Mrs Sullivan ate all the rest. There wasn't that much of it.

She said she'd had a good sleep. 'The Lord and Master was

away again.' She told me she was talking to Dad last night. She went out to get the washing off the line, just before dark, and he was sitting outside our back door, smoking. He offered her a cigarette, and she went down and had a cup of tea with him. He's very worried about my involvement with Ellen. Mrs Sullivan said she felt a right hypocrite, listening to him saying how disgusted he was at what was going on between us. I asked her why she should feel hypocritical. She looked at me and smiled and shook her head.

Out of the blue, she said, 'I saw you with Stella yesterday.' I went red and said I'd bumped into her accidentally. 'I'm not saying you didn't.' She wet the tip of a finger and dabbed it among the chocolate crumbs. 'What's the latest news?' I was annoyed. She made it sound as if Stella's problems were just a bit of interesting gossip. She saw my expression, and said she was sorry. 'I didn't mean to sound casual. It's just my way.' She licked the last tiny crumb of chocolate from her finger and lit a cigarette. 'You know you're getting out of your depth, don't you?' The cigarette smoke made me cough. There was no breeze to blow it away. It's very sheltered on the steps. She said she'd like to give me a piece of advice. She nodded towards the back of the terrace.

'That little beast I married. Do you know how that happened?' I said I supposed she was once in love with him. 'No,' she said. 'I was once in love with his friend. Or at least, I thought I was.'

They went round in a foursome, her and her girlfriend, and the two fellows. She was sixteen at the time. She got pregnant, and the fellow went to England as soon as he knew.

When she told her parents, her father went berserk. He said she'd have to get married. She said the fellow had gone to England. Her father said, 'We'll have to get someone else, then!' She said she didn't know anyone else, except the fellow's friend, the one who was going with her girlfriend.

Her parents invited the other fellow round to the house. They got him blind drunk and locked her in the front room with him, and told him he could do anything he liked with her. She thought, at the time, it was the worst night of her life, but now, looking back, it was Heaven compared to what came after. The following morning, her father went to see the fellow's parents and told them their son had raped his daughter, under his very own roof; what were they going to do about it? The two sets of parents got together and made a deal, and she and the fellow were forced to marry, soon after. Her husband has never forgiven her.

I said I wasn't surprised. Mrs Sullivan said it was justice, of a sort. He'd already got her girlfriend pregnant. I asked her what happened to her girlfriend. 'She went to Glasgow, lost the baby, took to the streets, and died of drink. She was nineteen when they buried her.' I didn't get the chance to find out what she was leading up to. Siobhan came out and said the baby was yelling for its breakfast.

I spent most of the day down the strand, hoping to see Stella again. I gave up at six o'clock, and went home to the stable. There was a lot of screaming and shouting going on in the garden. I peeped out the window, and saw the Sullivan girls and some of Christie's younger sisters playing on the swing. I was annoyed about this. It's supposed to be my garden, and it's definitely my swing. I decided to go down and tell them off.

While I was thinking of what to say, Mrs Sullivan came out and called them in for their tea. They started moaning and groaning and saying they were enjoying themselves. She said the sooner they came in and ate their bread and jam, the sooner they'd get back out. Christie's young sisters didn't want to go home. They said they might not be let out again. Mrs Sullivan said they could stay. She was sure she could find a few extra slices of bread.

As soon as they went, I had an idea. I've never paid the Sullivan girls back for soaking me in the lavatory. Now was my chance. I went downstairs and got a bucket from the shed. I filled it with earth that me and Malone dug out from the trench under the swing.

I tied a length of string to the handle and climbed the tree. I pulled the bucket up, and hung it on a branch. I made sure no one saw me. By the time the girls came back, I had another bucket and six paint tins full of earth, ready to pour over them.

They all stood at the bottom of the rope, arguing about whose turn it was to have a swing. I tipped the first bucketful right on top of them. The earth was very dry and dusty. It made a terrific racket falling through the leaves. When it hit the ground it was like an explosion. A huge cloud of dust billowed up and swirled round the garden. I thought the girls would be furious. They weren't. After they got over the surprise, they loved it.

I poured the other bucket, as soon as the dust from the first one had settled. The girls heard it coming and ran to get under it. They shouted, 'More! More!' I emptied two of the tins over them.

Mrs Sullivan heard the racket. She came out, and saw the girls were covered in dirt. I thought she'd lose her temper, but she didn't. She could see they were enjoying themselves. She stood under the tree herself, and peered up at me. 'Go on, then,' she said, 'I dare you!' I threw another tin-full down. Mrs Sullivan shrieked when the stuff hit her. She jumped up and down and shook her head. I tipped a second tin over her. She ran out from under the tree and gave herself a good shake. She looked up at me, and shouted, 'I'll get you for that!' She was laughing. It's the first time I've ever seen her not looking miserable.

The girls yelled for more. Mrs Sullivan shouted, 'Wait a minute!' She took her cardigan off, and ran under the next tin-full. When the dust settled, she asked me, 'How much more have you got?' I said I was down to my last two tins. They were all disappointed. They asked me to throw down the buckets and tins. They'd fill them and pass them back up to me. I said I'd think about it, but I was a bit peeved. They weren't supposed to be enjoying it. I emptied the last two tins together. Mrs Sullivan called up, 'Is that it?' I said yes.

She ran down the steps to the lavatory and connected the hose to the outside tap, and aimed it at me. The water had no trouble reaching me. I climbed the tree to where the leaves were thicker.

Mrs Sullivan turned the hose on the girls. They ran round the garden screaming with delight. Siobhan was sitting on the stick at the bottom of the swing. She was soaked. She put up her hand to keep the water off her face. The jet caught her hand and twisted her round. Mrs Sullivan gave her a push and got her swinging. Every time Siobhan passed the end of the hose, she got the full force of the water.

All the girls wanted a turn, and the trench began to fill with water. The girls started to make splashes when their bottoms hit the water. Mrs Sullivan deliberately filled it right to the top.

The girls swung higher and higher, and the splashes got bigger and bigger. The water showered all over the garden. The dust turned to mud. Everyone got utterly filthy. They were screeching with delight.

Mrs Sullivan decided to have a go on the swing. She gave the hose to Siobhan. She tried to get onto the stick. She couldn't, because her skirt was soaked, and sticking to her legs. She glanced up at me, and then at the girls and said, 'What the Hell!' She took her skirt off, and sat on the stick.

The girls tried to push her, but they weren't strong enough. As soon as she hit the water, she came to a stop. She looked up at me again, and pushed her hair back from her face. I couldn't believe how nice she looked. Her whole face was completely different. She looked like a young girl at a birthday party. She smiled at me, with a smile as bright as a lighthouse, and said, 'Come on, you! We need a big strong man down here!'

I couldn't help showing off. I climbed down to where the pole stuck out, went along it hand over hand, and slid down the rope. Mrs Sullivan gave a startled yell and said, 'You'll have me off!' I was going too fast to stop, and I squashed right down on top of her. She let go of the rope and fell backwards into the water. I fell in on top of her. Siobhan sprayed us with the hose. Mrs Sullivan scooped up a handful of mud and slapped it on top of my head.

I pushed her under the water. All the girls threw mud at me. Mrs Sullivan jumped up and said, 'Right! You're going to be sorry!' She gave me a shove, and I went under the water. When I stood up and shook the water from my face, I saw Ellen standing at the stable door, with her arms folded. She said, 'I see!' in a severe voice, but I could tell she wanted to laugh.

Mrs Sullivan grabbed the hose from Siobhan and turned it on Ellen. Ellen darted into the stable. Mrs Sullivan shouted, 'Come out!' Ellen shouted back that she couldn't. She had her second-best skirt on.

Dad came out to see what was going on. Mrs Sullivan squirted the hose at him. Dad hates to be made a fool of. He rushed back into the house.

A crowd of girls were playing the juke-box in the back room. Two of them came out. They said, 'God Almighty, what's going on?' Mrs Sullivan said it was water sports. One of the girls asked if she could join in. Before she could change her mind, Mrs Sullivan soaked her, and told her to get on the swing.

The girl hitched her skirt up and got on. I gave her a terrific push. She went zooming though the water and up in the air on the other side. Down she came, with another huge splash, and I gave her another push. She swung to and fro, screaming with excitement. The rest of the girls came out from the basement.

390

The fellows playing snooker wanted to come out and watch. Dad wouldn't let them. They all crowded into the back room and stared out the window. By this time it was getting twilighty. They couldn't see much from that distance.

The girls from the basement crowded on the steps, giggling. They were dying to join in but they were afraid of getting their clothes dirty.

The girl on the swing let go and dropped straight into the trench. She jumped up and down in the water, enjoying herself. You couldn't see her face for mud.

Mrs Sullivan yelled over at the girls on the steps. 'Come on, you lot! Who's next?' She shot the hose against the wall, beside them. They screeched and giggled with fright and excitement.

Someone gave me a tremendous shove in the back and I went face first into the water. I scrambled out and discovered it was Ellen. She was in hysterics. I ran at her and slipped in the mud. By the time I got up, she'd dashed back into the stable. I went in after her and said, 'Right; you've had it!' I told her she was going into the water. Ellen gave a yell and said, 'No! My second-best skirt!' She was laughing, and pressing herself up against the wall. I went over with my arms out. I said, 'I'm going to grab you!' Ellen shut her eyes and grinned. She said, 'All right! All right! I give in.'

She put her hand on my chest and pushed me back. 'Just give me a minute!' She went over to the straw under the stairs and took everything off except her brassière and her knickers. They were the dark blue ones with long legs. It was quite dim in the stable, but even so, I thought she looked ridiculous. She thought so, too. She looked down at herself and said, 'Oh God!'

Mrs Sullivan shouted from the garden. 'Hurry up, in there! We need our swing-pusher back!' I said to Ellen, 'Your minute's up. I'm coming to get you!' She laughed and said, 'I can't go out there looking like this!' She grabbed her clothes up in a bundle and held them in front of her. Then she said, 'Oh, sod it! You're only young once!' She threw her clothes down and took the rest of her things off. I was startled. I thought it might be rude to grab her with no clothes on. While I was wondering, Ellen escaped.

She dashed out into the garden. There was a chorus of amazed yells when she appeared. She has such white skin, everyone could see her quite clearly. Mrs Sullivan turned the hose on her. Ellen scraped up a double handful of mud and threw it at her. Mrs Sullivan dropped the hose and ran at her. Ellen gave an excited yell and jumped into the trench. Mrs Sullivan pushed her onto her back in the water. When Ellen stood up, she was black all over. You could hardly see her.

The girls from the basement were hopping up and down with excitement. They were desperate to join in. The Sullivan children decided to take their clothes off. So did Christie's young sisters. Mrs Sullivan took hers off, absolutely everything, and flung them all over the garden. It didn't make a bit of difference. She was so covered in mud you couldn't tell she was naked. The girl who'd been swinging took her clothes off. She threw mud at the children. They threw mud at her. Ellen threw mud at all of them. Mrs Sullivan was plunging up and down in the water, splashing it at everyone. They were all delirious with the fun of it.

The girls from the basement couldn't resist any longer. First one, then two, then three, then all of them, rushed into the stable and took their clothes off, and came out laughing like delighted children. Some of them jumped into the water. Others sprayed themselves with the hose. One girl slipped onto her back and couldn't get up for laughing. Another girl tried to help her up, and fell on top of her. They started rolling round in the mud, shouting that it was gorgeous.

In a moment, they were all doing it. I joined in. A girl jumped on me and rubbed mud on my chest. She suddenly realised I wasn't one of the girls. Up to then, no one had noticed. I was so dirty you couldn't tell. She screamed and said, 'Jesus; it's a fellah!' Mrs Sullivan heard her. She told her to shut up and enjoy herself. She said, 'He's all right. He's one of us.' I was pleased she said this. It made me feel I belonged.

All the other girls jumped on me. I ended up inches thick in mud. Ellen had to rescue me. She wanted a push on the swing. I ended up pushing them all. It got really dark after a while, then the moon came out and made it light enough to see quite well. I had a lovely time, pushing bare bottoms to and fro. I was worn out by the time they all had a turn.

Eventually, when everyone was exhausted, Mrs Sullivan asked me if I'd mind leaving. She said the girls might feel a bit embarrassed, once the excitement wore off. She hosed me down before I went. All the girls were booing and whistling, thinking they were going to see me with no clothes on. They were cheated. I still had my trousers on, under the mud.

I went up to the loft and had one last little peep through the window. I had to laugh; the gardens on both sides had rows of fellows hanging by their fingertips from the tops of the walls, trying to get a look in.

I felt so fortunate, and so tired and happy, that I went to bed and fell asleep in five minutes. The last thing I heard was the girls laughing and shouting as they washed themselves off with the hose.

I woke up feeling completely happy. It's the first time for weeks. The sun was blazing through the windows, just like yesterday. I pushed the blankets off and enjoyed the warmth.

Someone came into the stable, whistling. I pulled the sheet over me. Mrs Sullivan ran up the stairs with a tray. I hardly recognised her. She looked like a younger sister of herself. She said, 'Shift yourself!' and put the tray on the end of the bed and sat down beside me. 'I've brought you up some breakfast. It's a thank-you.'

Her dark hair gleamed in the sunlight. It shimmered and flashed with colours, like a starling's wing. She had on lipstick, and perfume, and a white summer dress. Her eyes looked shiny and alive and twice as big as usual. She'd even cut the long black hairs that grow from the mole on her cheek.

She looked at me, all happy, and said, 'Well? What do you think?' I told her she looked lovely. She smiled and said, 'That's what a bit of fun does for you!' She jumped up, looked in my mirror, made a cheeky face at herself, and sat down again. She gave me a poke with her elbow. 'Come on. Eat up, before it freezes!'

Breakfast was a mug of tea, and a boiled egg, and toast and marmalade. I left the egg. I'm very fond of fried eggs, but I can't eat them boiled. When I see them still in their shells, it reminds me that they came out of a chicken's bottom.

Mrs Sullivan was excited and happy. She kept bouncing on the bed and making me slop my tea. She said she was going to try being nice to Mr Sullivan tonight. It's because of something I said. It made her think. She showed me her shoes. They're dance shoes, so she hardly ever wears them. She doesn't get the chance to. They've got very low heels, because Mr Sullivan is quite short.

I asked her why she'd made me breakfast. She said, 'I've told you; it's a "thank you" breakfast!' What was the 'thank-you' for? 'It's for . . .' She paused. 'Let me think. It's for . . . no; it's not for anything. Don't ask me.' I had to give my opinion of her hair. She said the shine came from being plastered with mud. It's good for the skin as well.

She showed me her nylons, as far as her knees, and the hem of her petticoat. It's white, like her dress. It's made of silk. It's the only really good bit of clothing she has, and her most precious possession, apart from her children. She made me feel it; it was smooth and shiny and slippery, like a cat's fur. She said she'd like to have shown me the rest of her underwear but she felt too shy. 'Isn't that ridiculous, when you think of last night!'

She said it was even more ridiculous, when she thought of last week. I'd seen a lot more than her underwear. She didn't care, then. She was too miserable. She was being used as a whore in her own home. When you're treated as a whore, you begin to act like a whore. She'd felt cheap and filthy and vulnerable. I could have told her to take off every stitch and parade round the loft, and she'd have done it. This week, though, was different. She felt like a real lady today, and she was going to behave like a lady, and see if Mr Sullivan treated her accordingly.

She warned me that Dad was in a terrible temper. He came to see her this morning. He apologised for the mess I made of her children, and of the garden. He didn't realise Mrs Sullivan was involved. He hadn't recognised her, covered in mud. She tried to tell him it was as much her fault as mine, but he wouldn't listen. He said it was inconceivable that she was in any way responsible.

That's one of Dad's problems. He thinks all wives and mothers, and all single women over thirty, are holy and pure. He treats them as if they were saints, incapable of doing wrong. He doesn't regard them as real human beings, at all.

Mrs Sullivan didn't stay long. Mr Sullivan was due back early from a business trip. She wanted to change into her usual clothes and give the flat a good going over before he arrived. She had a nice lunch planned, to get him in a good mood for tonight. 'I'm going to get him to take me out for a walk, and show me off!' She'd only got dressed up to ask me what I thought of her outfit, and to make sure everything still fitted. She gave me a hug and a kiss and skipped off down the stairs.

When I went into the house, Dad was walking up and down the corridor, smoking furiously. The moment he saw me, he lost his temper. He said he's never witnessed anything so disgusting in his whole life. His own son! Cavorting intimately with God knows how many naked females! He says I've plumbed the lowest depths of depravity. God will have wept tears of blood over what went on in the garden last night. Only He can know how many other souls I've brought to the brink of ruin by my actions.

I tried to tell him how simple and happy it had been; how free and clean and open we'd all felt, and what a lovely, innocent game it had been for everyone involved.

'Innocent?' roared Dad. 'Clean? Mauling each other's bare bodies with filthy hands! You call that clean? You call that innocent?'

'Yes!' I said. 'Yes!'

'Innocent? By God, I've heard some rot in my time but that takes the biscuit! Innocent, my foot! Shameless!'

I tried to tell him that that had been the whole joy of it, to be bare and filthy and boisterous, and yet still feel innocent and unashamed, but I couldn't convince him. He went on and on, shouting me down. I've never known him so unreasonable. I had to leave.

I went down to Stella's house and knocked on her front door. I didn't care if anyone saw me. Her mother answered. I asked her if Stella was at home. 'Are you the boy . . . Michael, isn't it? Are you the boy she talks to?' I nodded. 'She's downstairs. I don't know if she wants to see anyone.'

I looked into the basement. Stella was standing by the window, looking up at me. She shook her head and moved away. I went down and knocked on the door. Her mother leaned over the railings, watching me. Her face was sad. Stella opened the door. I glanced up at her mother. She looked down at me for a moment, and went into the house. Stella waited until she heard the upper door close.

'What do you want?' Her voice was flat and dull. I asked her if she'd like to go for a walk. No, she said, she wouldn't. It's horrible when she goes out. People used to ignore her. Now they've begun saying things to her, shouting at her, spitting words at her – horrible words, hurtful words. She's beginning to feel that she's the criminal, rather than the person who raped her.

She's been attacked again. By a group of girls, this time. The very people from whom she'd expected understanding and support. It happened last night. They were outside the pub, waiting for her. She was punched and kicked to the ground, and then they tried to rip her clothes off. They were going to throw her into the horse trough outside the butcher's, but a passing commercial traveller rescued her and bundled her into his car. He took her home, and now she's afraid to go out again.

I told her the story that's going round, about her being pregnant by a man from the tennis club. 'God! So that's it! Who thinks these things up? What sort of minds have they got? Why do they hate me so?' I was pleased to hear some life in her voice. 'I never go near the tennis club! And I certainly don't know any married men! None that I'm carrying on with, anyway.' She sounded more like the old Stella, the one with the temper, and the ice-cold eyes, and the arrogant voice. I asked her if she'd like to go round to the pub for a drink. She said she would, but she couldn't. They'd only get her again.

'I'll go with you,' I said, 'and protect you.' She looked at me in astonishment. 'You? Protect me?' I asked her what was so surprising about that. 'But you're only a – a boy!' I told her she'd be safe with me. 'If anyone dared touch you, I'd . . . I'd . . .' She looked me straight in the eyes and said, 'Yes?' I told her I'd kill them. She put her hands behind her back, and stared at me for a long time. When she spoke again, her voice was very quiet. 'Take me for a walk, first, and then we'll have a drink.'

We walked for miles along the strand. Stella explained why she started going to the pubs. She hoped the rapist would give himself away, by trying to follow her again. She wanted the chance to tear his eyes out and mark him for life, as he'd done to her.

When she realised she might be pregnant, she drank for its own sake. To blot out the past, and to blur the future. It didn't work. Self-pity turned to self-loathing. She tried to kill herself; more than once. Men did begin to follow her, and she gave herself to them, but she made sure they paid for it, with pain. She put a mixture of honey and coarse sugar inside herself. For most men it was agony, but some didn't notice. They were like brutes, with no feelings. She found other ways to hurt them.

She plunged a hat-pin through one man's penis. He was still bloated at the time, and his blood jetted everywhere. Another she slashed with the neck of a broken bottle. She put it on the end of her finger like a ring and twisted the sharp edges into his scrotum.

Usually, the men collapsed, shrieking and paralysed with pain. It gave her the chance to escape. Sometimes, though, she didn't manage to hurt them enough. They were able to grab her and pay her back. One man in particular gave her a dreadful beating, and then smeared his penis with her blood and forced it up her bottom. She was bleeding for days afterwards. I was too shocked to say anything.

Stella asked me about Malone. She'd been thinking about what I said. 'Could it have been him?' I was too confused to give her a sensible answer.

We walked back to the terrace. It was nearly twelve o'clock. Stella asked me if I still wanted to take her to the pub. I said yes.

'Even after what I've told you?' I gave her a hug, and said yes, and we both laughed, and walked back through the village, arm in arm. There was hardly anyone about. The sun was baking hot, and the road was covered in tar bubbles. All the shop windows had their blinds down. The Sergeant was standing at the crossroads, smoking a cigarette. His hat was on the back of his head, and his jacket slung over the railing of the post office. He turned his back when he saw us.

It was cool and dark in the pub. We stood for a moment to let our eyes get used to it. It's the first time I've ever been in a pub, apart from the time when we went up the mountains with the pig-lorry.

There were three people in the bar. The bartender, and Mr Sullivan, and a fellow he was talking to. When Mr Sullivan saw us, his eyes nearly popped out. 'By Jesus! By fucking Jesus! You've got a fucking nerve!' I thought he meant Stella. We both ignored him. The bartender, a boy hardly older than myself, asked me what I wanted. I don't know anything about drinks. On the spur of the moment, I said, 'Whiskey, please.' The boy asked me how old I was. 'Old enough,' I said.

The boy went away through a door and into a room at the back of the pub. Mr Sullivan was glaring at me. I could see him in the mirror behind the bar. He shouted at me. 'And what, pray, brings you in here?' I didn't answer him. Stella said we should go. I said no. She walked towards the door. Mr Sullivan jumped off his stool and blocked her way. The other man laughed. Stella stopped. Mr Sullivan stood in front of her, trembling with anger. He looked like a bad-tempered terrier. His moustache was coated with beer foam. When he spoke it blew off in little puffs of white. The boy came back with a man. The man looked at me. 'Michael Kelly, is it?' I said yes. He glared at me. 'Get out.' He nodded towards Stella, and then back at me. 'And take that bitch with you.'

Mr Sullivan said, 'Whoa there; steady on! I want a word with you, you bastard!' He pushed Stella aside and staggered over to me. 'By Jesus, I ought to fucking kill you!' He looked at the man behind the bar. 'And d'ye know what? If I did – if I did kill him – there isn't a court in the fucking land that would convict me!' He turned back to me, and spat in my face. Stella took my arm. Mr Sullivan spat in her face. 'No! Not a fucking hope of a conviction! And I'll tell you why! Because the sanctity of fucking marriage still means something in this fucking country. That's why!'

My body got ready to smash him. Stella felt my muscles tensing. 'Don't, Michael. Don't make it worse.' Mr Sullivan asked me if we'd come in deliberately to mock him. I said I didn't know what he was talking about. 'He doesn't know what I'm talking about! Jesus! Do you hear that?' He turned to the man he'd been drinking with. 'And him the bastard responsible for me shame!' He picked up his glass and took a huge swallow of stout. 'I go away – grafting, like every other decent man – to keep a roof over me family and food in their bellies. I come back – back to the bosom of that same family – and what do I hear?'

The man behind the bar told us to settle our differences outside. Mr Sullivan said no; what he had to say, he wanted to say in front of witnesses. 'I come back and I find that you – you, you bastard – you and my missus – the two of you – stark bollock naked – fucking around in the garden in front of half the – half the fucking village –' He began to gasp, and splutter, and gave up trying to find words. He pulled his arm back, and screwed his face into a ferocious expression of anger. 'Right, ye bastard; stand by to collect your fucking chips!'

He looked so ridiculous I had to laugh. Even Stella smiled, though her face was strained. Mr Sullivan flew into a frenzy. He aimed his little fist at me, with all his might. I turned sideways and dodged it. As it went by, I grabbed his wrist. As soon as his arm slackened, I brought it up and then down as if I was gripping a hammer, with his wrist as the handle and his hand the head. The top of the bar is a marble slab, solid as steel, and I smashed his hand down onto it, as hard as I could.

He squealed in agony and his face went white. I brought my knee up into his stomach. His eyes rolled upward until all I could see was the whites. His face looked like a hallowe'en mask: pale and dead and ghostly.

The man behind the bar shouted at me. He put a huge hand on the bar and vaulted over. While he was still in the air I grabbed a high stool, turned it upside down, and put it on the floor below him. His eyes bulged in horror. He could see what was going to happen but there was no way he could avoid it.

Stella screamed and covered her eyes. There was a screech of tearing cloth and the crack of splintering wood. The man gave a great sobbing gasp of pain. He was wedged upright, his legs twisted under him, impaled on the remains of the stool. His face was rigid with shock and disbelief. Blood spurted from his legs and soaked into the sawdust.

Mr Sullivan's friend tried to stop us leaving. He ran to the door to block our way. I looked at him and shook my head. I nodded at the other two, and spoke to him, gently. 'It's not worth it,' I said. The man gave me a nervous smile, then grinned with relief. 'No. No, you're right. It's not. You're dead right! Absolutely.' He opened the door for us, and ushered us out with a bow and a wave of his arm. 'Good day to ye both!'

We walked round to the lane. I didn't say a word the whole way. When we got to Stella's gate my anger went away. I felt sorry for putting the stool under the man. It was a vicious thing to do. I told Stella how I felt. She hung her head for a moment, and said, in a faraway voice, 'He was the one that . . . the one who . . .' She didn't finish the sentence, but a warm shiver of satisfaction surged through me.

Stella didn't want to go home. She wanted to stay with me. We went into the stable and up to the loft. Mrs Sullivan was lying on her back on my bed, smoking. Her white dress was stained and crumpled, and her eyes were red and puffy from crying. Her silk petticoat was lying on the floor, torn into strips, from the hem to the waistband. I picked it up, and looked at her. She said, 'Remember it? Remember how beautiful it was . . .'

She sat up and stubbed her cigarette on the floor. Her legs were bruised, and her hair sticky and matted with liquid. It looked like blood. It was all down the front of her dress. She said 'It's not as bad as it looks. Not yet, anyway. It's only tomato sauce.' She smiled wearily. 'So much for romance.'

She told us the facts. Mr Sullivan came home at ten o'clock this morning. He was in a good mood, to start with. The girls started telling him about the fun they'd had in the garden. At first, he thought it was just them, then he realised there were other people involved. He made them tell him everything about it.

He blew up, and bashed Mrs Sullivan, and poured a bottle of sauce over her, and tore her petticoat into strips. Afterwards, he went looking for me. He wanted to murder me. I wasn't in the stable, so he went roaring round the village, asking if anyone had seen me. He heard wilder and wilder versions of the story from everyone he met. He came home and bashed her again, then went to the pub. He told her that when he got back, he planned to give her a threshing she'd never forget.

Stella sat down on the bed beside Mrs Sullivan. I said I'd go and find him. I'd make sure he was in no state to harm her. Mrs Sullivan shook her head and said no. 'Let me deal with him in my own way.' I said I wouldn't be able to put up with it; if I heard her screaming, I'd have to do something about it. 'You won't hear me scream. You won't hear a sound from me. Neither will he . . .'

She asked me to promise to keep out of Mr Sullivan's way. 'Supposing he won't keep out of mine?' Mrs Sullivan sat for a long time looking at the floor. Stella cried quietly. Mrs Sullivan took her hand. She looked up at me. 'Please. Let me cope with today. Tomorrow . . . tomorrow . . . I don't know.'

She put an arm round Stella's shoulder, and drew her gently towards her. 'You poor, sad, girl. Come to me. Come, put your head on my shoulder . . . there, that's better, isn't it . . .' She sat stroking Stella's head for a while. Stella went to sleep. Mrs

Sullivan asked me to help her move. I took Stella's weight off her. Mrs Sullivan stood up quietly and I laid Stella gently back on the bed.

Mrs Sullivan kissed me with a touch as soft as a feather. 'Please,' she said, 'promise me. No heroics – not tonight.' I wouldn't promise. I couldn't. She went into the house, and I sat in the loft doorway until it got dark, watching for Mr Sullivan passing the end of the lane on his way home. I didn't see him.

When it got dark, I lifted Stella from the bed and carried her home in my arms. She didn't waken, not even when the little dog yapped. I took her into the basement and laid her on her own bed. When I came out Mrs Rothwell was at the top of the back stairs. I said, 'It's all right. She's just sleepy.' Mrs Rothwell didn't know what to say. I suppose it was strange for her.

Mr Sullivan came home very late. He had to be carried. I was desperate to make sure he didn't hurt Mrs Sullivan again, so I climbed the sycamore tree and hid among the thickest bunches of leaves. I could see into their rooms without them seeing me. After I'd been up the tree a while, Mrs Sullivan came into the bathroom. Mr Sullivan staggered in behind her, and collapsed on the floor. I was very relieved. He was too drunk to attack her.

Mrs Sullivan leaned over the bath and put the plug in. She turned the taps on. Mr Sullivan sat up. He fell over again almost immediately. Mrs Sullivan folded her arms and walked over to the broken window. She stood looking out for quite a while, glancing every now and then at the tree. I knew she couldn't see me, because it was dark, and I was well hidden. Even so, I felt nervous.

When the bath was full she turned off the taps. She came to the window again, and looked out at the tree, and then switched the bathroom light off. I stayed in the tree for hours, but nothing else happened.

Dad woke me while it was still dark. Mrs Sullivan had just woken him, to say there'd been a tragic accident upstairs. She told Dad that Mr Sullivan came home very late, after he'd been in the pub all day. He was drunk and stinking of vomit, and insisted on having a bath. Mrs Sullivan tried to help him, but he kicked her out of the bathroom. She waited in bed for him, and fell asleep.

When she woke up, he was still in the bathroom.

Mrs Sullivan got worried. She knocked on the bathroom door. The light was on but there was no answer. She went in, and Mr Sullivan was lying dead in the bath. He was so drunk he'd drowned.

Mrs Sullivan came down and woke Dad. She wanted Mr Sullivan out of the bath before the children got up. Dad told her it would be best to get him out of the flat altogether. She agreed, and said that was exactly what she wanted. Dad needed me to help him. It wasn't a woman's job to carry a corpse.

I got dressed, with my mind in a complete daze, and we went up to the Sullivans' flat. Mrs Sullivan was in the bathroom, leaning against the wall. She was smoking, and staring at Mr Sullivan. He was floating face up in the bath. There was melted shit and foamy vomit floating on the surface of the water.

Mr Sullivan had a white ribbon round his willie, tied with a double bow. I undid the bow and pulled it off him. The ribbon was a torn strip of cloth. I knew where it had come from. I could tell by the shiny smoothness of it. Dad didn't ask about it. He wouldn't.

Mrs Sullivan got a blanket and laid it on the floor in the middle of the bathroom. We tried to lift Mr Sullivan out of the bath. I took his feet and Dad took his head. He was slippery with water and filthy scum. Dad lost his grip, and Mr Sullivan dropped back into the water. He lay bobbing up and down, and for a moment, he looked as if he'd come back to life. It was quite scary. Mrs Sullivan went out and stood on the landing.

We tried again, and succeeded. We laid Mr Sullivan on the blanket and folded it over him. Dad took one end and I took the other. We carried him down the stairs from the flat, and down the outside stairs into the garden, and then into the stable. It was just starting to get light. We put Mr Sullivan on the pile of straw under the stairs. Dad said tea would be a good idea. He went in to make it. He asked me to go up and fetch Mrs Sullivan.

She was standing in the bathroom again, staring out the window. She spoke without turning round. 'Michael . . .' She paused, and said, 'You know, don't you . . .' It wasn't a question, and I didn't answer.

We had tea downstairs. Dad asked Mrs Sullivan if there was anything else she needed. She said she couldn't think of anything. He told her she was taking it very well. It must have been a terrible shock to her. Mrs Sullivan said she'd never realised how easily someone could drown in a bath. Dad blessed himself.

He went off to inform the barracks and the doctor. Mrs Sullivan went up to get the children's breakfasts. I went out to the stable and found Stella in the loft, looking through my encyclopaedias. She'd been out for an early walk and just came in on the off chance of seeing me. I took her downstairs and showed her Mr Sullivan. I told her he came home drunk and drowned in the bath. Stella stared at him for ages. I didn't say any more. When she spoke, her voice was low and scared. 'Is there a curse on all of us, Michael?'

I put the blanket back over Mr Sullivan. Mrs Sullivan came into the stable. She took Stella's hand and led her over to the loft stairs. They sat on the stairs together. Mrs Sullivan hugged Stella. Stella trembled and began to sob. Mrs Sullivan comforted her. She murmured something in Stella's ear. Stella raised her head and looked at her, her eyes wide. 'For both of us?' Mrs Sullivan nodded.

A car arrived outside the stable. The doctor came in, followed by Dad and the Sergeant. I went out for a walk and a think. I sat on the edge of the green, staring at the sea. Christie was on the landing stage, fishing for crabs. He showed me how to do it. It was so easy, it soon got boring. You find a cockle or mussel, take it out of its shell, tie it to a bit of string, and drop it in the water. The crabs go mad for it. They grab the cockle and won't let go. It's just a matter of pulling them up and dropping the cockle back in the water.

Christie had two buckets. One was already full of crabs. The ones on top kept running round the edge of the bucket. Their claws made a horrible scraping noise against the metal. In half an hour the other bucket was full. The estuary is a great place for crabs. They're scavengers, like seagulls and tinkers. The rubbish from the dump floats in and out with the tides. The crabs migrate in and out with it.

Christie told me to lie down on the stage and put my face in the water. I did. The water was only about two feet deep. The sand at the bottom seemed to be moving about. I thought at first it was the sunlight flickering down through the ripples on the surface. Then I realised what I was looking at: a solid mass of crabs, covering the sand like a green carpet. It gave me a horrible shock. I had to get off the landing stage immediately. It would have been ghastly to slip and fall in.

I asked Christie what he was going to do with the crabs. He wouldn't tell me. 'Are you going to sell them to the fish shop?' He told me not to be stupid. You can't eat green crabs. Proper 'eaters' are big and red and live under rocks in deep water. They never come near the shore.

I went up the stairs to the terrace and hid behind the balustrade, to keep an eye on him. Christie went down the coast road with the buckets. He went into the band gardens through the bent railings. I rushed down and followed him. He left the crabs in a little hut behind the tennis pavilion. Then he went home. So did I.

Dad and Mr Maguire and the Sergeant and O'Rooney were having a meeting in the basement. None of them feel sad about Mr Sullivan. It's the children and Mrs Sullivan they're worried about. One good thing about the accident is that it's brought Dad and the Sergeant together again. They've shaken hands and made it up. Both of them cried at the time, and John-Joe had to go out and leave them on their own.

Dad was all for giving Mrs Sullivan whatever money he earns this week. I hope he doesn't. We're in enough trouble ourselves. We've got to get the stable ready before the Major makes a big stink about snooker in the basement. That's if he ever gets out of hospital, of course.

Maguire came up with the idea of making a collection in the basement. There'll be loads of people round this weekend. Dad's running a snooker competition, starting tomorrow. The final is on Saturday.

O'Rooney had another idea. He said he'd run a book on the competitors, with himself against all comers, and the final proceeds to go to Mrs Sullivan. Dad and John-Joe got very excited about this. Mr Maguire said we could pull in big money. All the lads love betting. The Sergeant said we were fooling ourselves. We'd lose it all in the finals because Jay-dee Cullen is sure to win. He's the local champ and everyone know's he's a killer. They won't bet on anyone else. His real name is Dezzy; Jay-dee is only his nick-name. It stands for Joe Davis, because he's so good at snooker. His mother has loads of money and spoils him. Jay-dee spends all day in Dublin playing snooker and all night in Kilmara drinking.

O'Rooney said we'd have to find some way of barring Jay-dee from the competition. The Sergeant said the locals would lynch us if we tried to.

Mr Maguire came up with another idea. He said we'd have to find a dark horse, good enough to beat Jay-dee at the last minute. I expected Dad to volunteer, but he didn't. I was surprised, because he's a champion himself, and I'm sure he could beat Jay-dee.

He said he'd ring a couple of the old hands in Dublin. They're good players, and decent skins into the bargain. They'd come out if they knew it was a good cause. One of them might be good enough to beat Jay-dee. I kept trying to catch his eye, but he wouldn't look at me. Dad and John-Joe spent the rest of the afternoon making lists of players, and drawing up rules for the competition.

Ellen spent most of the day upstairs, looking after Mrs Sullivan's children. Mrs Sullivan went into Dublin to go to confession.

Jeremy Lynch came round at seven o'clock. He was in an ice-cold temper. He said Sculley called at his house at five o'clock. Lynch wasn't there, but Eileen was. So was his younger brother. That's how Lynch knows what happened. Sculley told Eileen I wanted to see her urgently. She went off, and didn't come back for her tea.

I told Lynch it was all a lie. I hadn't been out all day, or seen anything of Eileen. He believed me, and we both went looking for Sculley. There was no sign of him anywhere. His mother said she hadn't seen him since four o'clock. Two fellows called for him and he went out. Lynch's temper got even colder. He was sure it was something to do with Bowman. He left two fellows guarding Sculley's house in case he tried to sneak home.

He went off to organise his gang for an assault on the Hill gang. He wanted me to go with him. I didn't want to go; I was determined to find Eileen on my own. I made up an excuse, by saying that I'd collect Christie and Andy and meet him later.

Lynch said I was bluffing. Andy and his parents are in England. I didn't know that, but Lynch didn't believe me. I said I'd been laying low for weeks, and hiding away from people. Lynch said he'd give me the benefit of the doubt. I told him I wanted to go home and get a weapon. He sent two of his men with me. I gave them the slip easily enough. I left them in the stable and went out through the basement.

Dad said there was a fellow waiting to see me. Sculley was lurking under the front stairs. He grabbed me as soon as I appeared. Bowman's gang had captured Eileen. They made him give her a message, saying I wanted to meet her down by the band gardens. It's me they're really after. They know I'll try to rescue her.

I asked him where they'd taken her. He said they had her in the pavilion. They were going to torture her. I grabbed Sculley's hair and banged his head against the wall until he collapsed.

I should have gone and got Lynch, but I was in too much of a rage. I rushed over to the band gardens. There were faint screams coming out of the pavilion. I got the groundsman's ladder out of the bushes and climbed onto the roof. As I got near the skylight, I could hear the screams getting louder. I pulled myself up and looked in.

The lights were on. Eileen was stretched on a table in the middle of the room. Her wrists and ankles were tied to the legs of the table. Her skirt was up round her waist. She had no knickers on.

The rheumatism machine was on the table. A girl was stroking the metal brush up and down between Eileen's legs. Eileen had her eyes and mouth screwed shut. The terrible screams kept on. I looked at the rheumatism machine. There were no batteries in it. Eileen's mouth never opened. The girl stroking her was doing the screaming. I realised I was in a trap.

I slid down the roof and discovered the ladder was gone. I put my feet over the edge, ready to jump down. Someone slipped a noose round my ankles and pulled it tight. I was yanked off the roof and fell on my back. I got such a wallop I blacked out. When I woke up I was hanging by my hands from a beam. There was a cloth stuffed in my mouth, and another one tied round my head to stop me spitting it out. My ankles and knees were tied together. All I had on was my shirt.

Bowman's gang were gathered round the table. Bowman was leaning over Eileen. He had his face between her legs, licking her, and making slurping noises. The gang were all cheering him.

I started to kick and struggle. Bowman came over and spat in my face. He asked me if I could smell the fanny juice. His gang had hysterics. He said I should be able to taste it as well; I had Eileen's knickers in my mouth.

One of the girls in the gang took her knickers off and put them over my head. She twisted them round till I could see through a leg-hole. She said I looked very pretty. The others girls did the same. I was nearly sick with the warm steamy smells. I tried to hold my breath and shake the knickers off. I couldn't; in fact I only made it worse. They twisted round and covered my nose, so I could hardly breathe. I nearly passed out again.

Bowman made a hole for me to look out. He said he wanted me to see what was happening. Two of his gang came over with a big rough sack. They put it under my feet and pulled it up to my waist. It had bits of string knotted to the top. They put the string over my shoulders, like braces, to hold the sack up.

Bowman went out and came back with two buckets. They were the ones Christie had hidden, full of crabs. He tipped one of the buckets into the sack. The crabs fell to the bottom and then startled crawling round the inside of the sack. They had no trouble getting a grip. I went mad with fear and disgust. He took some crabs out of the other bucket. He put them inside the knickers on my head. He tied string round the waist of my shirt and dropped crabs down the collar. I screamed so hard I nearly burst my heart and lungs.

Just when I thought I was going to die with terror, the back door flew open. Lynch rushed in with a hurley stick, and smashed Bowman on the back of his head. Bowman collapsed. Lynch's gang came streaming in, and Bowman's gang tried to run out the front. Lynch's men had the place surrounded. Bowman's gang surrendered, all except the girls. There were five of them. They fought like tigers, and two of them managed to escape. One of them was the one who was pretending to torture Eileen. The three who were left were locked in the hut out the back. Their clothes were ripped off, to discourage them from trying to escape again.

Lynch undid the cords holding Eileen, and lifted her off the table. She was so ashamed she couldn't look at anyone. Lynch put her sitting in a corner with a guard round her.

Lynch's men lifted Bowman onto the table. They tied him down exactly the way Eileen had been, but with extra cords. He was still unconscious. The rest of Bowman's gang were tied up with cords round their ankles and wrists. Lynch had brought plenty of string with him. Bowman's men were forced to stand in a line round the walls. Most of them were crying.

Lynch came over and looked at me. I tried to scream at him to let me free. I was writhing in despair and agony. The rope holding me up was practically cutting through my wrists. He took the knickers off my head. The crabs fell out, and Lynch stepped on them, as casually as if he was crushing a cigarette butt. He undid the rope round my waist, and the crabs in my shirt fell down into the sack. Lynch undid the sack and threw it out the back door.

He reached up with a penknife and cut the rope I was dangling from. I fell in a heap on the floor. Lynch kicked me in the stomach and said I was a very lucky fucker. He'd caught Sculley sneaking home after I'd talked to him, and asked him what was going on. Sculley wouldn't talk, because he was afraid Bowman would kill him if he found out. Lynch's men had to throw Sculley into the sea twelve times before he told them everything they wanted to know.

My face was on one of the crabs he'd crushed. It was still alive. I could feel its legs trembling under my cheek. I rolled away from it, my mind whirling with nausea.

Lynch slapped Bowman's face until he woke up, then used his knife to slit Bowman's clothes to ribbons. When Bowman was naked, Lynch got a crab out of the bucket and shoved it between Bowman's legs. The crab sank its claws into Bowman's bollocks. Lynch got more crabs, and did the same with Bowman's jake, and his ears, and his lips. Bowman heaved and screamed like a madman.

Eileen tried to make Lynch stop but he wouldn't listen to her. He put a crab on Bowman's chest, and smashed it with the palm of his hand and the next time Bowman screamed, Lynch forced a handful of the quivering mess into his mouth. Bowman spat desperately, and choked, and vomited, and begged Lynch to stop but Lynch kept on smashing crabs and forcing them into his mouth until Bowman was almost unconscious with terror and exhaustion, and then he smeared squashed crab over Bowman's face and into his eyes and stuffed blobs of it into Bowman's ears and rubbed it in his hair.

Lynch's men threw the Hill gang on the floor, one by one, and kicked them until they screamed for mercy. They kept on kicking them, until the screams turned to feeble sobs. Then they untied them and let them go. I tried to undo the rope round my wrists with my teeth but Lynch saw me and gave me another kick and warned his gang to keep an eye on me, so I gave up trying. He told his men to get the girls from the hut, and said they could do what they liked with them, and then he took Eileen home. Neither of them looked at me as they left.

The girls were dragged in, naked, and dazed with fear. They were told they were going to be shagged, and that they could either lie quiet and have it easy, or they could put up a struggle and have it rough. All three of them burst into tears and begged to be let go, but it was no good; Lynch's men all took their trousers off and held the girls spreadeagled on the floor, and queued up and raped each girl in turn, one fellow after another, and all the while the girls screamed and heaved and threshed about, frantic with pain and terror and shame, and the more they tried to resist, the more the fellows enjoyed it, and the more they abused them.

My body went so numb from the ropes that I lost all feeling and drifted off into a half sleep, and when I woke up everyone was gone. I used my teeth again, trying to get free. I was so weak it took me ages. The pain from pins and needles was too much. I sat on the floor crying my heart out.

When I could use my hands, I undid the ropes round my legs. I had to go through the same agony again, as soon as the blood started to flow.

A bucket of crabs was still on the floor. It was half full. I took it with me and staggered back to the terrace. I poured most of them through Sculley's grannies' letterbox. I felt so bitter I had to get back at someone, and they were the people who started it. They should never have shown me the rheumatism machine.

I didn't dare sleep. I expected the parents of the Hill gang to come looking for me and Lynch, as soon as they knew what his gang had done. I spent the whole night peering out the loft door, shivering with pain and anxiety. I kept watch until eight o'clock. I was exhausted by that time, but still nothing happened.

My wrists were in agony. The top layer of skin is torn off, all the way round. I could hardly move my arms. All the muscles are stretched and aching.

Someone whistled from the bottom of the stairs. I peeped down, quaking. It was a small neat fellow in a black hat and a well-pressed grey suit, with a white shirt and a red tie. He had a cigarette in his mouth and his hands in his pockets. He looked jaunty and pleased with himself. I didn't recognise him. I thought maybe it was another detective. He came up the stairs, and it was only then I realised it was Jeremy Lynch. I couldn't believe it. He smiled at me and said, 'I'm off in to Dublin for an interview.' I gawped at him. 'An interview?' 'Yeah,' he said. 'A job interview.'

'But what about last night?'

'What about it?'

'All those fellows who got smashed up! And the girls, after you left –'

Lynch gave me a look of disgust. 'People got damaged at your dance, didn't they?'

'Yes, but –'

'You never heard any more about *that*, did you?'

I had to admit I hadn't. Lynch spat, and said most of the villagers are no better than animals; thick bloody animals. When something good happens, they're too thick to get much joy out of it. When something bad happens, like last night or my dance, they're too thick to feel much pain. Not for long, anyway.

'But those girls! Your gang – they raped them! Over and over!'

Lynch did a long brown spit, and wiped his mouth with the back of his hand. 'They'll get over it.'

'What about their fathers? They'll come down and –'

Lynch interrupted me with an angry shout. 'To Hell with their fathers!'

He said he didn't want to hear any more about last night. He was bored talking about the past; he wanted to talk about the future. He asked me if I'd like to take over the Dump gang. He's had enough of it, and his uncle, who works in Pim's, has a job lined up for him, as a junior clerk in the despatch department.

'Well, do you want it?' I was too tired to keep up with him.

'Do I want what?' 'My gang, you dozy fucker. Say the word, and it's yours; simple as that.' His men are prepared to swear loyalty to me. None of them want the trouble of being boss. None of them are capable of it, anyway; they're too thick. But they are brave and ruthless, and they don't give a shit about anyone but themselves and their leader. If I don't take over the Dump gang, there'll be an outbreak of gang war. Loads of other gangs will fancy their chances of moving in when he pulls out. His men won't know how to defend it, not without a leader. They'll need someone to plan and organise.

He says they want me to take over. They respect me. They know

I'm clever, and tough. But not quite tough enough; I've got to be ruthless, if I'm serious about running a gang. It's no business for young gentlemen. There's only one rule for staying on top. Hate thine enemies; slaughter those who would slaughter you.

Lynch went off to catch a bus. His interview was in George's Street, at ten o'clock. He said he'd see me when he got back.

I jammed the lane door shut and spent the rest of the day trying to sleep. I couldn't manage it. I was too nervous. I kept expecting the door to be battered in.

Dad came out to see me at five o'clock. He was in a terrible temper. He said he'd just heard a sickening story; some heartless wretch has been terrorising the old ladies who live at the end of the terrace, by dropping dozens of crabs through their letterbox. The two old ladies are hysterical with fear and shock. It's one of the lowest, vilest, cowardliest things he'd ever heard of. He wanted me to find out who it was.

Lynch appeared outside. I let him in. Dad grabbed him and asked him if he knew anything about the crabs. Lynch swore he didn't. Dad told us he won't rest until he gets hold of whoever did it. He went back into the house to get ready for the first night of the snooker competition.

Lynch said we had a problem. It looks as if he was wrong about last night. The bus was packed, coming home from Dublin. Everyone was talking about what happened in the band gardens. The Hill parents have been to the police. Even the village parents are shocked. Normally, they don't give a shit about Hill people. Now they're saying things have gone too far. If the Dump gang are allowed to get away with this latest outrage, they'll be uncontrollable. No one will be safe anywhere.

Lynch said he'd never heard such shit in his life. No one recognised him on the bus. He was huddled in the back seat with his hat over his face. When he got home, there was a crowd of men outside, shouting for him, and throwing bricks at the windows. He came straight round to see me.

I asked him what he was going to do. He said we need a big diversion, to take people's minds off last night. Setting fire to the cinema would probably do the trick. Even better, we could sneak into the chapel and shit on the altar steps. It would be sacrilege, but worth risking our souls for the sake of saving our bodies. There would be ructions. The Bishop would come out from Dublin and put a mortal sin on the whole village. He'd bring a gang of Redemptorist Fathers with him, to root out the culprit. People would stay in their houses, for fear of being interrogated. The Redemptorists give massive penances, even for venial sins. Needless to say, we'd have to find a way of putting the blame on the Hill gang. Otherwise, we'd only make it worse for ourselves.

I was sick and tired of Lynch's wild ideas. I said I wasn't willing to get involved in any more trouble. Lynch said he'd tell Dad that it was me that put the crabs through the old ladies' door. I asked him how he knew it was me. He winked, and said I'd just told him myself.

There was a tremendous racket in the lane. John-Joe Maguire sprang into the stable. He slammed the door after him. People on the outside tried to force it open. Mr Maguire shouted at us. 'Give me a hand with this bloody door!' He was desperate. Lynch grabbed a plank and jammed it between the door and the floor. John-Joe glared at him. 'You little bastard! I'll deal with you later!' He went into the basement. I asked Lynch what was going on. He grinned and said he'd tell me some other time.

We went into the basement and spent the rest of the day watching the snooker. Dad and Mr Maguire had all the no-hopers playing off against each other. They've saved the good players for tomorrow. John-Joe put a bucket near the door for contributions. He had a cardboard notice tied round it, saying 'For Mrs Sullivan'. The last game didn't finish till after two in the morning. Dad counted the money in the bucket. There was nearly seven pounds in it.

When I went to bed I saw lights in the Barringtons' house. They must be back from England.

After the first night of the competition, Dad and Mr Maguire were too excited to sleep. They sat up talking until five o'clock, then made themselves a huge breakfast. When this was finished they got back to talking, and practising famous chess moves. They still had the front window shutters closed, so they hadn't a clue what was going on outside.

At eight o'clock exactly, the foreigners kicked in the scullery door and crowded into the basement. They said they'd come to take their machines away. Dad said they could do what they liked, providing they emptied his money out first. The foreigners told him to drop dead, and started to carry the machines out through the door.

When Dad and Mr Maguire tried to stop them, they whistled up the stairs. Another bunch of foreigners jumped out of a van parked in the terrace, threw Dad and Mr Maguire into the back room, and jammed the door shut with a snooker cue through the handle.

I woke up just after eight, had my usual look out the window, then a visit to the lavatory and a quick rinse under the tap. I was about to go into the house when I saw Dad waving furiously at me from the back window. They couldn't escape, because the window was jammed with old paint and rotting mould. They broke some panes but the holes were too small to get through.

Dad told me to rush up to the barracks and get the Sergeant. I ran out through the stable and up the lane. Right on the corner I met the two fellows who work for Mr Maguire. They were coming round on the cart to look for him. I told them the story. They turned the cart round and galloped off to fetch more help. The Sergeant was in the middle of shaving but he came straight away. Guard O'Rooney came with him.

Two of the foreigners' bodyguards were standing at the top of the basement steps. They got confused when they saw the policemen, and made a half-hearted effort to stop them. Guard O'Rooney curled up like a rugby player and charged sideways against one of the bodyguards. The man fell back against the railings, with O'Rooney's weight squashing him. O'Rooney straightened up and caught him a terrific crack under the chin with his shoulder. The fellow started to topple forward. O'Rooney grabbed him as if he was a scarecrow and hooked his jacket shoulders over the spikes on top of the railings. The railings gave way, and fell onto the pavement, with the fellow underneath them. Mr Maguire hadn't done a very good job of mending them with his blowlamp. The other bodyguard jumped into the van.

The Sergeant went down the stairs into the basement. O'Rooney came half-way down the stairs and waited, swinging his truncheon. He had a big grin on his face. The foreigners were coming out of the scullery, laden with slot-machines. The first fellow who saw us panicked and dropped the one he was carrying. It smashed to bits on the stone slabs. The jackpot money poured out and jangled everywhere. The fellow spun round to rush back into the house but he slipped on the coins. He fell forward and knocked over a fellow who was just coming out. Another machine crashed to the ground and exploded into bits.

The foreigners tried to escape. There were about a dozen of them. They rushed up the stairs but the sun was in their eyes and they didn't see O'Rooney until it was too late. He hit the first two fellows over the head with his truncheon. They fell back on top of the rest and the whole crowd toppled into a heap at the bottom of the stairs. They got up and rushed along the side of the stairs and tried to grab O'Rooney's ankles. O'Rooney whacked their hands with his truncheon.

Guard Daniels and Guard MacMahon arrived. They both had truncheons. They came thundering down the stairs to help O'Rooney. The stairs collapsed, and the three policemen tumbled down on top of the foreigners. There was a lot of whacking and shouting and kicking. At the end of it, the only people standing were the three policemen. They lit cigarettes and waited for the Sergeant's orders.

The Sergeant released Dad and Mr Maguire. He asked Dad what he wanted to do about the situation. Dad said he'd be pleased to see the back of the foreigners, and their machines. First, though, he wanted his cut from the takings. The foreigners got excited and said he had no right to any money. They'd had all the trouble of delivering the machines, and collecting them. They were entitled to recover their expenses.

Dad pointed out that he hadn't asked them to take the machines away. That was their own decision. All he wanted was his fair split of the profits. The foreigners said no. They didn't like being called cheats and liars, and being assaulted by Irish savages. They were terminating their agreement with Dad and that was it.

Out in the basement, one of the bodyguards moved round behind Guard O'Rooney. O'Rooney casually dropped backwards and squashed him against the wall. The fellow put his arms round O'Rooney's neck to choke him. O'Rooney's elbow smashed into him like a battering ram. The fellow went ghostly white and let go immediately. O'Rooney looked at me and shook his head sadly. 'This bloody temper of mine . . .' he said. 'I'll be the death of someone yet.' I had a terrible job keeping a straight face.

Mr Maguire's two men jumped into the basement with some other fellows, and the four Macarty brothers came running in from the back garden. The foreigners tried to escape by climbing up the remains of the stairs. A huge fight broke out. Dad tried to stop it; he said the money wasn't worth the trouble. No one took any notice of him.

The Sergeant stood in the middle of the room, saying, 'Now then, lads; steady on there . . . we don't want any trouble,' but he didn't actually do anything to stop the fighting. More village fellows kept arriving every minute. The foreigners got quite a bashing.

Afterwards, the Sergeant made them empty the machines and split the money with Dad. He wanted Dad to have all of it, to make up for previous weeks but Dad was depressed by the fighting and said no; he'd only take what was due to him.

The foreigners were finally allowed to carry away the machines. They had to wait while Mr Maguire went and got planks to prop up the stairs. Someone had let down the tyres of their cars and vans. They had to push them all the way round to the garage, fully loaded, to get them pumped up again. They were mad with anger. They said we hadn't heard the last of them. When they'd gone, Dad remembered he'd left all his Top Twenty records in their juke-box.

A strange thing happened. The Macarty brothers tried to beat up Mr Maguire. The Sergeant had to save him. It turned out that the Macartys have cousins living up the Hill. Bowman himself is related to them, and so is one of the girls in his gang. I asked Lynch why the Macartys wanted to beat up Mr Maguire.

He said, 'They hold him responsible for last night.'

'Why? What's it to do with John-Joe?'

Lynch gave me a funny look, and lit a cigarette. 'Maguire . . . well, he's not exactly me dad . . . but as good as . . .' I couldn't believe it! I asked Lynch why he never told me. He said I never asked. Everyone else knows. Lynch is the son of Mr Maguire's dead brother. Maguire and his dead brother's wife live together. Mr Maguire is Eileen's father! I was so amazed I could hardly concentrate for the rest of the day.

The Sergeant and O'Rooney walked Mr Maguire home, to make sure he was safe. The Macartys are determined to get him. They say they're not the only ones. Maguire has let Lynch run wild for years, and a lot of people think it's time Maguire was paid back.

Dad had a chat with the Macartys. They were all listed to play in the finals of the championship and so is Mr Maguire. Dad said he didn't want anything to spoil the games. They were in a good cause. He reminded them about raising money for Mrs Sullivan. The Macartys are fierce fighters but they're decent at heart. They promised they wouldn't make any trouble until the championship was over. They said they won't let anyone else make trouble, either.

The eldest one had a word with me. He said that they have it in for me, as well, and warned me to stay clear of them, because I'm in their black book. If it wasn't for the fact that they like my dad, they'd have had me already. This really put the wind up me.

The snooker started as soon as we'd cleared up after the foreigners. There were a lot of people to get through, before the finals in the evening. Lynch and myself were very relieved. It stopped people thinking about us. We squashed up in a corner, on one of the benches where the machines had been, and kept quiet. We knew no one would dare touch us while Dad was around. All the lads respect him. They're also afraid of him. He doesn't stand for any nonsense.

The basement was packed. Fellows were squashed on top of each other. I could hardly see or breathe. The air was cloudy with cigarette smoke, and stank with the smell of drink and sweat.

Jay-dee Cullen refused to play in the elimination rounds. He said it would be a waste of everyone's time, and, most particularly, of his. He'd win anyway, so what was the point? Mr Maguire got angry and said he wouldn't be allowed to play in the finals. Cullen said he had no intention of playing in the finals, plural. The final, singular, yes. Him, against whoever, for the title.

Mr Maguire called him an arrogant arsehole and crossed his name off the list. This was brave of Mr Maguire. Cullen is huge, and wears enormous boots. Cullen said, 'Suit yourself; it doesn't bother me.' He left, and the crowd got angry. They said there was no point in having the finals if Jay-dee wasn't playing.

Mr Maguire couldn't understand it. With Cullen out of the running, one of them could win. Were they not glad of the chance? No, they said; they fucking-well weren't. What was the point if they couldn't have a crack at the champ? Mr Maguire stared at them in amazement. Did they like having their faces rubbed in shit, or what? They shouted back that there was always the chance of a fluke win. Jay-dee might be half-pissed, or off his stroke, or his mother could have just given him a telling-off. That always upsets him. She's the only person he's afraid of.

Dad had a quiet word with Mr Maguire. Mr Maguire sent one of his lads out after Cullen. The two of them came back immediately. Cullen had been waiting up in the terrace. He came in with a big smirk on his face. Dad said he'd be quite happy for Jay-dee to play in the final, without any qualifying rounds; he knew his form from previous experience. Mr Maguire was disgusted, and so was I, but the lads were delighted. Even so, they were a bit disappointed at the easy way Dad gave in. They were muttering about him going soft. No one realised what he was up to.

Dad's first match was at four o'clock. He was drawn against one of his friends from Dublin, a carpenter called Tom Hagerty. Tom is a bit younger than Dad. He said, 'Age before beauty, Billie. You break.' Dad seemed nervous. 'Oh. Right then. Eh . . . let's see.' It took him ages to chalk his cue, and ages to shoot. Then he miscued. The white trickled down the table and kissed the pink. He was quite embarrassed. 'Oh dear, oh dear. That's not a very good start . . .' Mr Maguire was working the score-board. 'Foul shot. Six away to Hagerty.' Tom shook his head at Mr Maguire and told him to hang on. 'It's all right. Take it again, Billie.'

The rest of the game was a disaster. Fellows were limp with gasping over how badly Dad played. Tom potted the last red, and most of the colours. The final score was eighty-odd to sixteen. Dad hardly knew where to look. 'Well,' he said, 'you managed to give me a bit of a threshing there, Tom!' Tom excused himself. He said it was more luck than skill. Dad said he'd have to pull himself together.

'Let's see how the next one goes, eh? Your break, Tom.' Tom gave the balls a good smack. Dad was delighted. 'Oh, lovely! Very nice, Tom . . . you've left me a cert right on that bottom pocket.' Tom looked at Dad in amazement. 'What?' Dad bent down and lined up the white. Tom hissed at him. 'Hold on, Bill!' Dad played the shot. Tom groaned. 'Oh Jesus! Too late . . .' Mr Maguire flicked the score up. 'Foul shot. Four away to Hagerty.' Dad was confused. He stared at Mr Maguire.

'Foul shot?'

'That was the brown you walloped into the pocket, Bill.'

'Oh Lord . . .'

Dad lost the second frame, eighty-four to forty. They were playing for the best of three, so Dad was out. Cullen was delighted. He's a bit wary of Dad. He's seen how well he can play, on a good day. Mr Maguire was bitterly disappointed. Tom was embarrassed. He came over to where I was sitting.

'Sorry about that. Your oul fellah didn't do too well, eh?' I was too upset to answer him. 'I remember the time he'd knock up a hundred while you'd be rolling a fag.'

I took a deep breath and said, 'That must have been a long time ago.'

O'Rooney came in with a big notebook. He nodded at Mr Maguire, and at Dad. 'How's it going, lads?' Mr Maguire said 'Oh . . . fair.' O'Rooney asked him what were the odds on Dad. 'A million to one –' O'Rooney's eyes opened wide. '– against.' O'Rooney stared at Dad. Dad smiled at him sadly.

'Anno Domini, I'm afraid.' O'Rooney didn't understand. 'Any dominos? What d'ye want with dominos, and you playing snooker?' Mr Maguire said that Dad might as well be playing dominos, for all the good he was tonight. Dad said he had to agree with him. O'Rooney tried to cheer them up. He said they were both wrong.

'Sure it's only a question of rusty joints! You'll soon loosen up. And anyway, isn't snooker like cycling? Once you learn it, you never lose the knack.'

Mr Maguire said it was all over for today, as far as Dad was concerned. O'Rooney got anxious. 'This book I'm supposed to be running – is Cullen still the favourite?' Dad said yes.

'And these fellahs you were supposed to be gettin' out from Dublin? Are they here? Are they any good?' Dad told him not to worry. They were here. They were good. And, apart from Tom, they hadn't played yet. O'Rooney could still get good odds on them. 'Bejaysus, I hope so! It's my own money I'll be putting up!'

Dad told O'Rooney that he wanted him to take straight bets on Cullen, at the highest odds he could get. Mr Maguire said O'Rooney would be an idiot if he listened to Dad. He'd also end up completely skint. Dad said no; they must have faith. We needed big odds to make a big killing.

'And who's going to kill Jay-dee?' O'Rooney's face was purple.

Dad just smiled, and said not to worry. O'Rooney took over the score-board while Mr Maguire went out the back to make tea. The games went on.

Mr Maguire came back with a tray of mugs for himself and Dad and O'Rooney. 'Tea up, lads!' Dad took his mug off the tray and sipped it. He grinned at Mr Maguire. 'Ah; the elixir of life! Hot, sweet and sticky.' O'Rooney heard him, and yelled over from the score-board. 'Like a farmer's daughter on top of a haystack!' The crowd roared with laughter. O'Rooney looked pleased with himself.

The evening wore on, and it was very late before the semi-final was over. One of Dad's friends from Dublin was the winner. O'Rooney made quite a bit of money, because the crowd were all betting on the local man, out of loyalty. They didn't mind losing. They knew they'd get it back when Cullen won the final.

Dad had been very quiet all evening, sitting smoking and watching the games with hardly a word out of him. Cullen was swaggering round the table, joking with the crowd. Mr Maguire was setting the balls up. Suddenly, Dad stood up and challenged Cullen. Cullen was startled. He asked Dad what the Hell he was talking about.

Dad said, 'I'm saying, I'll play you for the best of three, and the title.' Cullen thought Dad was joking. 'Jaysus, Billie; you haven't even qualified!' Dad smiled at him. 'Neither have you, Dezzy, neither have you . . .' Cullen couldn't say another word.

Dad asked his friend from Dublin if he'd mind stepping down. His friend said no. Dad asked the crowd if they had any objections. At first, they didn't know what to think. Then they said he might as well. Jay-dee would win, whoever was wielding the opposite cue.

O'Rooney went as white as a sheet. He rushed over and tried to get Dad to change his mind. So did Mr Maguire. Dad smiled at them both. He told O'Rooney to keep on taking the bets. Dad and Cullen tossed for the break. Cullen lost. Dad went in off the pink. A couple of shots later he hit the white too hard. It shot off the table. Cullen picked it up with a sneer. 'We're supposed to be playing snooker, Bill, not bowls.' Dad lost the first frame.

Cullen's face nearly cracked from smiling. I was heartbroken. O'Rooney's whole body was shivering with nerves. He told Dad he couldn't go on. He was in for over a hundred quid.

Mr Maguire set the balls up again. His face was blank with misery. Dad said he was going to the lavatory. O'Rooney rushed after him. Mr Maguire called out, 'Don't be too long, Bill.' He stared at Cullen bitterly. 'We don't want to waste any of Jay-dee's valuable time.'

Dad and O'Rooney came back. O'Rooney was shaking his head. He cleared his throat. He could hardly speak with tension. 'The book closes on the first shot. Is there any of yez want to put a last bet on?' No one did. They'd already forked out everything they had, on Cullen. O'Rooney's pockets were bulging.

Dad stood at the end of the table, trying to look casual and relaxed. He picked up the white ball and gave it a rub on his sleeve, then walked slowly round the table, chalking his cue and looking thoughtful. When he got back to the top cushion, he took out a cigarette, lit it, and drew a slow and deliberate lungful of smoke. He had another slow walk round the table, stopping now and again to examine a ball, or to flick a piece of ash from the cloth.

Once again, he came back to the baulk end. He leaned forward with his cue on the table, and took a few gentle aiming strokes. I stared at him. I couldn't understand what he was at. I thought he was afraid to get started, in case he made a mess of another game. He put down his cigarette, and stood scratching his chin for a moment. He looked very worried. He bent forward again, lined up his cue, and then slowly, ever so slowly, raised his head and gave O'Rooney an enormous, roguish wink.

He lowered his head, drew back the cue, and broke. Wham! A red rocketed into the bottom pocket. Wham! The black disappeared after the red. Dad stood up with a mocking smile and shook his head at Mr Maguire. Mr Maguire was in a trance.

'Come on, John-Joe; you'll have to be quicker than that!' Mr Maguire darted at the pocket. 'Jesus, Billie; I'm sorry! You caught me on the hop!' He respotted the black. Wham! Another red disappeared. Wham! The black went down again. Mr Maguire leapt to retrieve it. Wham! Another two reds, this time with one shot. Wham! The black again. Wham! Another red.

No one dared breathe, or move, or blink. Four . . . five . . . eight . . . thirteen times, Dad banged in a red and slammed a black after it. He only stopped once, to chalk his cue and have a puff from his cigarette. He demolished the colours, one by one, until he got to the black. He stood up and gave Cullen an enquiring glance. Cullen threw his cue on the table and walked out. The room went mad.

Dad disappeared under a crowd of fellows all trying to hug him and shake his hand. None of them minded losing their money. It was worth every penny, to be in on a game like that! 'A game in a million!' they were shouting. 'The game of a lifetime!'

O'Rooney threw his hat on the ground and danced on it. He kept shouting, 'Jesus! Sweet Blessed Jesus!' over and over at the top of his voice. He counted the bet money. A hundred and twenty-six pounds! Dad was delighted. Mr Maguire called him a deceitful bugger. O'Rooney shook his hand for ages. Everyone wanted to play snooker with him, even Cullen.

After he walked out, he went round to Dolan's and spent the evening drinking. When the pub shut, just after twelve, he came back to the basement. Everyone froze and started to quake. They thought there was going to be trouble. Dad was in the middle of a shot. He stood up and stared at Cullen. Cullen put on a really grim face and marched over to Dad.

Dad put his cue down and got ready to defend himself. At the last second, Cullen stopped. He gave Dad a big smile. 'Jaysus, Billie, you're a devious oul devil!' He stuck out his hand, and shook his head, and said, 'I don't know what to say to you!' Dad looked at him for a moment. His face was still as grim as Cullen's had been.

'I'll tell you what you *could* say, Dezzy . . .' Everyone tensed up, thinking Dad was going to make Cullen apologise. Even Cullen looked worried but Dad suddenly smiled, and said, 'You *could* say, "What about another game, Bill?"' There was a tremendous cheer, and Dad and Cullen shook hands as if they were life-long pals.

Cullen said he was sorry for walking off. Dad said he was sorry for playing the trick on him. Everyone said Dad was a gentleman and a bloody good sport. Dad said Cullen wasn't too bad, either, when it came down to it. They played seven games together. Cullen won three, and Dad won three.

In one game, Dad didn't even get a shot. Cullen potted every ball, and got the maximum break; a hundred and forty-seven. The crowd nearly brought the ceiling down. Cullen was thrilled to bits. It made up for earlier on.

The last game they played finished on the black ball. It was Dad's shot. He put his cue down and said he'd prefer to call it a draw. Cullen wouldn't have it. Dad was the champ, he was entitled to take the black.

Dad said, 'Fair enough. If that's how you want it . . .' He winked at Cullen, and miscued. Cullen got seven. He miscued, and gave Dad seven. Dad miscued, and Cullen got another seven. Mr Maguire stopped the game. He said it was illegal, the way they were playing. He declared the game a draw, once and for all. Cullen didn't agree. As far as he was concerned, Dad had beaten him fair and square. Everyone gave him a big cheer, for being a good loser.

I didn't get to bed until two o'clock. Someone was lurching about in the lane. I looked out through the loft door. There was a fellow slumped against the stable wall. I asked him if he was all right. He said yes. It was Christie's brother. He pushed himself away from the wall and tried to look up at me. He swayed, and fell into a sitting position in the middle of the lane.

He said he was totally paralytic, and totally shagged. If he was to die that minute and go to Hell, he wouldn't give a shit. He was totally fucking happy, and fuck everyone else. I didn't bother listening to any more. He was so drunk it was hard to make out what he was saying.

I went to half-eleven Mass, because it's the shortest, and the most packed with people. I hoped no one would try to beat me up, with so many witnesses around.

When I came out, three of the foreigners were parked right in the middle of the village. They were in a big American car with red leather seats and the roof folded down. The car radio was blaring music. You could hear it all round the village.

The foreigners were dressed in white suits and white hats and sunglasses, and smoking long black cigarettes. There was a huge crowd of girls round the car. Some of them were sitting on the bonnet and the boot. They were all giggling, and looking flushed and flirty. One girl was actually sitting in the car. The foreigners had their arms round her. One of them had his hand on her knee.

The village lads were annoyed. They didn't like the girls sucking up to the foreigners. They told the foreigners to get lost, but the girls stuck up for them. They said it was their own business who they talked to. The foreigners were very pleased with this. They sat in the car grinning, and smoking, and making grabs at the girls' legs. The girls seemed to love it.

About quarter-past twelve, a big white yacht arrived in the estuary. A rowing boat came ashore with more foreigners in it. When the fellows in the car saw them, they drove down to the landing stage with as many girls as they could squash into the car. The rest of the girls rushed after them, screaming and yelling like a gang of excited children. Most of the village fellows were in the pubs or playing pitch-and-toss by this time. They didn't know what was going on.

I walked down to the end of the terrace to see what would happen next. Stella was sitting on the bank above the landing stage. She waved, and beckoned me to come and sit beside her.

The foreigners tried to persuade the girls to come out to the yacht with them. They said they'd take them for a cruise around the bay. The girls kept laughing and making stupid remarks. 'What would I be doin' on a yacht!' 'Sure none of us can swim!' 'Whaddye do when ye want to spend a penny out there?' 'Are yez any good at steerin' that yoke?' 'Supposin' me Mam an' Dad heard about it!' 'If yez hit a rock, we'd all be drown-ded!' The foreigners told them they'd be quite safe. They've never had an accident yet. They told the girls they'd put on a big party, if they came on board. The yacht was stuffed with food and drink. There were crates of booze, and wine, and spirits, and no end of cooked meats, and crisps, and boxes of chocolates.

The girls started to weaken. Two of them got into the rowing boat. The boat wobbled. They sat down quickly and nearly fell over backwards. Their legs shot up in the air, and the foreigners saw up their skirts. They whistled, and made grunting noises, and rude gestures with their fists. The girls went scarlet, and pretended to be offended. They jumped out of the boat, and said the foreigners were disgusting. They stood clutching each other on the landing stage, giggling. Then they got back in.

Two more girls got in. The ones already in the boat wobbled it deliberately. The two who'd just got in tipped right back over the seats. They showed a lot more than just their legs. The more they tried to get up, the more the other two rocked the boat. It took them ages to get decent. The rest of the girls started jeering them. The ones in the boat said they didn't care.

One of them stood and hitched her skirt up. She turned and poked her bum at the girls on the bank. The boat wobbled, and the girl nearly fell out. Two of the foreigners waded into the water with their shoes on. They grabbed her by the bare legs. They had their hands right up at the top of her thighs. The girl screeched, but you could tell she was enjoying it.

Some village fellows had followed the girls down to the boat. They rushed into the water and pushed the foreigners over. The water was barely deep enough to keep the boat afloat, so there was no danger of anyone drowning. The foreigners sat in the water, afraid to get up. I suppose they thought they'd be knocked over again.

The village fellows untied the boat from the landing stage and pulled it up on the strand. They made the girls get out. The girls got angry with the fellows. They said they had no right to spoil their fun. The fellows said, 'If your idea of fun is going out in a boat with a load of greasy foreigners, you can forget it.' They stood round the boat so the girls couldn't get back into it.

The foreigners in the water stood up and pleaded with the girls to come with them. The girls said they couldn't; the fellows wouldn't let them. The fellows got even bossier. They told the girls to go home. Some of the girls at the back of the crowd started to drift away.

Stella stood up and strode along the top of the bank and down the steps to the boat. Cool as anything, she walked up to the fellows guarding the boat. She waved them aside. 'Excuse me,' she said, in a very cold, posh accent. The fellows didn't know what to do. They moved away. Stella gestured to the foreigners in the water. They stood up and pulled the boat back into the water. Stella turned and looked up at the girls.

'What a bunch of tame little skivvies you are!' She turned back to the fellows. 'I'm going to get into that boat in a moment.' She put her hand out slowly and gently, and touched the face of the nearest fellow. He stood like a statue, paralysed by the fierce look in Stella's eyes. 'Are you going to try and stop me?'

She spoke very softly, as if she were talking to a baby. The fellow gulped, and tried to move his hand up to grasp her wrist. Stella swept her nails viciously down his jaw and across the front of his neck. The fellow's eyes nearly popped out with the shock and pain of it. She stepped in front of another fellow and asked him the same question. 'Would you like to stop me?' All the fellows stepped back and huddled together in a group. Stella looked up at the girls again. 'See? It's easy.' She walked along the landing stage and got into the boat. She stepped in and sat down as gracefully as a queen getting into a carriage. There wasn't the slightest glimpse of her legs or underwear. The boat didn't even sway.

The foreigners were so impressed that they cheered and clapped. Stella sat in the boat with her hands folded neatly on her lap. She looked up at the girls. 'Well, who else is coming?' There was a rush for the boat. The foreigners had to make several trips out to the yacht. When there were about twenty girls on board, they said they couldn't take any more. The girls who were left got very bitter and disappointed.

One of the men who'd been rowing came up the steps and got into the car. I recognised him. It was the one O'Rooney hung on the railings. He said he had to drive the car back to Dublin. Would any of them like to go along for the ride? It wasn't as good as a yacht trip but he'd try and think of something to make up for it. Eight of the girls squashed in with him. He went roaring off through the village with his hand pressed on the horn-button. The girls were showing off, yelling and waving at everyone.

The foreigners untied the yacht from the buoy in the middle of the estuary and started the engine and sailed out towards the open sea. I was worried about Stella. I could imagine the girls attacking her, or egging the foreigners on to rape her. I ran along the strand, keeping parallel with the yacht. It got to where the mouth of the estuary narrows. That's at the end of the dunes, where Stella used to swim. The island bulges out and nearly connects with the sandbank.

All the girls were on deck, leaning on the railing and watching me running along. I could see Stella quite clearly. She was the only one in a white dress. The yacht went through the narrows and turned north, away from me. I watched it with tears in my eyes. I couldn't understand what had made Stella go.

I threw myself down on the sand and lay on my back and shut my eyes. I said a prayer asking God to look after her. I didn't have much hope that it would work. He seems to have had it in for her recently. I don't know how long I lay there, but after a while I felt something tickling my face. I opened my eyes, and it was

Stella's hair. She was kneeling beside me, dripping with water. She smiled at me.

'Well,' she said, 'that's my good deed for today!' She seemed very pleased with herself. I was cross. 'What possessed you to do such a thing?' She laughed. 'As soon as I realised none of them could swim . . .' She stopped, and lay down beside me. I asked her how she managed to get away. 'Easy. I just slipped over the side.' Neither of us said any more about it. After a while, Stella started talking again, half to herself and half to me.

'It's more or less definite now . . . but I'm not going to kill myself . . . not any more . . . oh no! That's something I've learned from Mrs Sullivan. Why should I? It's other people who deserve to die, not me . . . not any more. I'm going to do something about it, if I can – about being pregnant, I mean. Then I'm definitely going to do something about the other business . . . about your friend Malone. I don't know what, yet. Then I'm going away . . . far, far, far, away . . . as far away as I can possibly go . . .'

I sat up to watch the yacht. It became a tiny dot on the horizon, and then disappeared. We went up to the top of the dunes, to see if we could peer over the horizon. We lay side by side on our tummies, gazing out over the sea. Stella gave me a blade of grass to chew. We turned over on our backs and fell asleep. When we woke up we were holding hands. It was nearly dark. The strand was deserted.

We went back to the stable and lay down on my bed. We hadn't said a word all the way home. Stella put her arms round my neck. I put my arms round her waist. She pressed herself lightly against me. I could feel her heart beating gently against mine. We drifted off to sleep again. It was the most peaceful and most beautiful experience I've ever had in my whole life.

Christie woke us up, banging on the stable door. It was ten o'clock at night. He was amazed to see Stella. 'Everyone thinks you're on the boat!' He said people are calling her the Devil's Piper, and blaming her for luring the girls away. Stella told him this was rubbish. She wanted to stay on the yacht, but the other girls wouldn't let her. They threw her overboard. Christie told her to keep her hair on. He was only repeating what he'd heard. The yacht never came back. None of the girls have come home, not even the ones who went into Dublin in the car. The girls' parents and boyfriends are in a terrible state. They're all in the barracks, shouting at the Sergeant to do something.

A rumour is going round that the foreigners have kidnapped the girls to sell them into white slavery. Nobody knows quite what to make of this. Some people say it means being sold to an Irish farmer as a child bride. Others say it means working as a skivvy in a Dublin hotel. Guard O'Rooney thinks it might be something to do with joining a Carmelite nunnery.

The Sergeant keeps telling people not to panic. The girls have just gone off for a joyride on the yacht. They'll all be back safe and sound any minute.

Christie went back to the barracks. I jammed the door after him. Before he went, he asked me if I've done anything about the bones. He says there's definitely a curse on the village. That's the second person who's said that to me. I promised him I'll bury them tomorrow. I asked him where would be the best place. He said, 'The deserted graveyard out at Ashford.' It's a Protestant graveyard, but that shouldn't matter. He told me how to get there, but he won't come with me. He's too scared.

Stella was worried, after Christie left. He was sure to say he'd seen her. People would come looking for her. I said she could stay with me, and I'd protect her. She said no – I couldn't take on the whole village on my own. She went into Mrs Sullivan's flat. She was sure no one would think of looking for her there. She asked me to run down the lane and tell her parents she was all right. I did. Mrs Rothwell hugged me and cried on my shoulder for a few minutes, then she apologised and went back into the house.

Coming out of Stella's gate, I heard someone coming down the lane. I ducked back in, I don't know why. The person stopped next door, at the Barringtons' gate, and went in. I ran across Stella's garden and peered over the wall. I could just make out the shape of a man. He stopped to take a long puff at his cigarette. The glow lit up his face. It was Christie's brother.

I went back to the stable. My mind was in a whirl. A terrible suspicion came over me, but I blotted it out. I didn't want anything to spoil the memory of lying peacefully with Stella.

Hardly anybody in the village went to bed. Dad kept the snooker going all night, and let people play for nothing. It gave them something to take their minds off the missing girls. The Sergeant kept the barracks open in case of any developments. The first news was a phone call from Dublin, just after midnight. The Sergeant came down and told Dad what he'd heard. The girls who went off in the car are in Store Street police station. They were found huddled in a front basement in Henrietta Street. None of them had any clothes on. They were hysterical with fear and shame. The Dublin police hadn't any further details. They were still working on leads to trace the other two girls who were in the car.

At dawn, the Sergeant appeared again. The snooker room was crowded with people. They were staggering round, half asleep, hardly able to see the balls. The Sergeant asked Dad to come up onto the terrace, casually, as if he was going for a breath of air. I went with them.

The Sergeant was tense. His hands trembled and a muscle in his cheek twitched every time he swallowed. Boozer Quinn was standing on the pavement at the top of the stairs. He was muttering 'Jesus Christ' over and over. He looked as if he'd seen a ghost. The Sergeant said Boozer had just come to see him, with a terrible story. Boozer was out just before dawn, emptying lobster pots in the estuary. At first light, he was over near the island. He saw what seemed to be bodies lying on the sand. He rowed back to shore and rushed up to the barracks.

Dad didn't say a word. We all walked down to the end of the terrace and stared across to the island. Dad has good long-distance vision. The Sergeant wears glasses and my eyesight is ruined, from reading under the blankets. The Sergeant asked Dad what he could see.

'It's the girls, Alex . . .' He paused. The Sergeant said quietly,

'Go on, Billie.' Dad couldn't speak for a moment. He had to take several deep breaths. He was shivering, but it wasn't just the bleak morning air that was causing it.

'It's bad, Alex; very bad . . .' Boozer Quinn put his hands to his stomach and began to moan. The Sergeant asked Dad to go on. 'They're sprawled all over the place . . .'

Boozer Quinn shoved his face right against the Sergeant's face, and shouted at him. 'They're lyin' there like a bunch of new-born bloody babes!' Boozer's voice was cracked and hoarse. His breath misted in the cold dawn light. 'And not a bloody stitch between the lot of them!' The Sergeant looked at Dad. Dad nodded. 'He's right. And listen, Alex, they're either . . . they're either asleep . . . or they're dead.'

The Sergeant said, 'Jesus Christ Almighty . . .' He looked old and tired and crumpled. He took a small bottle out of his tunic pocket. He had a long swig from it and handed it to Boozer. He told Boozer to go down and clear everything out of his boat.

Then he turned to Dad and said, 'Billie, I want you to go over there with me.' Dad said he would, if the Sergeant wanted him to, but was it not a matter solely for the police? The Sergeant said no; Dad was a medical man, and a former military officer. More important than anything, he was his oldest friend. Dad and the Sergeant shook hands with great feeling. Dad said he'd help in any way he could.

The Sergeant asked us to come back to the barracks with him. He rang the doctor and asked him to stand by with medical help, then he woke Ellen and asked her to get all the cells laid out with spare beds, as many as she could fit in.

The three of us collected armfuls of blankets from the emergency store and staggered down to the boat as fast as we could go. Boozer pulled us over to the island with quick powerful strokes. We were across in less than ten minutes.

Boozer couldn't see as we approached, through facing backwards in the boat. He refused to look when we got there. He said he'd been a bachelor all his life. It wouldn't be right for him to set eyes on the poor naked creatures, be they dead or alive.

The Sergeant didn't make any comment about me sticking with Dad. All he said to me was, 'Thank God Billie's here; if ever I needed that man, it's now.'

The girls were lying in a tangled heap at the bottom of the dunes overlooking the estuary. The island is very narrow at that point. They'd been landed on the blind side, dragged across the sand, and thrown from the top of the dunes.

They weren't dead. When we tried to move them they moaned and shuddered with pain and cramp. Even so, we couldn't get any of them to waken up. We wrapped them all in blankets. Boozer had to row back to the barracks for more.

At first, Dad thought the girls were unconscious from exposure to the cold. When he looked at them closely he saw that most of them were streaked with a sticky red vomit. It had a horrible sweet smell. Dad pulled back their eyelids, and smelt their breaths. He said he knew what was wrong with them. They were all, literally, paralytically drunk. Probably, he guessed, as a result of drinking red wine. The Sergeant shut his eyes and said, 'Those fucking foreigners . . .'

It took us ages to ferry the girls back from the island. We could only fit two at a time in the bottom of Boozer's rowing boat. A huge silent crowd gathered at the steps down to the landing stage. Other men wanted to row their boats across and help us bring back the girls, but the Sergeant wouldn't let them. He wanted everything done in an orderly way, under his personal supervision. He wouldn't even let the parents touch the girls. At the barracks, the doctor examined the girls as they arrived. Ellen and her sisters washed them and put them to bed in the cells.

Two police cars arrived from Dublin with the girls found in Henrietta Street. They were allowed to go home, after they'd made a statement. They weren't drunk and they hadn't been sexually abused. They told the Sergeant that the foreigner they drove off with took them to a derelict house in Dublin. There was another fellow waiting for them. He told the girls there was a surprise party in the basement. The girls went down, but it was just a stinking cellar, full of rubbish. The men wouldn't let them back up the stairs. They poured a tin of petrol down the stairs, and ordered the girls to strip off. They threatened to throw a ball of burning newspaper into the cellar if they didn't. The girls were terrified. They had no choice; they had to take their clothes off and throw them up the stairs. The foreigners collected everything into a big bundle, threw it into the boot of their car, forced the girls back into the cellar, locked the door, and drove off.

The doctor said all the girls from the island showed evidence of sexual abuse, some of it of a brutal nature.

A deputation of men came to see Dad. They wanted the address of the foreigners. Dad wouldn't give it to them. The Sergeant had told him not to; it was police business. The men got violent, and started to smash up the snooker equipment. The police heard the racket and came down from the barracks and drove them out. The men took all the balls and cues with them. They threw the balls at the windows of Stella's house, and smashed them. Her parents were terrified. O'Rooney had to rescue them. He whacked a lot of people with his truncheon.

By six o'clock the excitement had died down. Everyone was exhausted from being up all night. The Sergeant released the island girls into the care of their parents. Everyone went home. Dad went into the terrace and collected a few snooker balls and cues that were lying around. I stayed out in the garden, keeping watch for people coming over the walls. Dad thought we might be attacked again. People are saying it's all his fault, for bringing the foreigners into the village in the first place.

Stella came down the steps from the Sullivans' flat. She was very nervous and jumpy. She didn't want to talk to me. She said she had to meet someone. I asked her who, but she wouldn't tell me. I was hurt and disappointed. After yesterday, I thought we were close friends.

Dad and the Sergeant appeared at the back door. It was just light enough for them to see us. The Sergeant was startled when he saw Stella. He'd been trying to find her all afternoon. He shouted that he wanted to talk to her. Stella ran out through the stable. The Sergeant told me to go after her. He wanted to know if she went home.

Stella went down the lane and over the bank onto the strand. I kept to the path on top of the bank. I had no trouble following her. I could hear her feet scrunching on the gravel. The noise stopped, and I thought she'd got to where the sand starts. I was afraid I'd lose her. I lay on the bank and peeped down. The moon, almost full, was coming up over the edge of the sea. I could see quite clearly.

Below me was an old iron sewer pipe, coming out from the base of the bank and running down to the sea. Stella was sitting on it, talking to Mr Barrington. He was angry. 'But it's all arranged!'

431

Stella shook her head. 'I've got money, now.'

'I'm doing it for nothing!'

'*You* may think it's nothing . . .'

'It's nothing compared to what you've already been through! Christ, girl –'

Stella stood up. 'I've got the money, and I'm going into Dublin tomorrow.' She sounded quite definite. Mr Barrington lit a cigarette, and puffed at it quietly for a moment. When he spoke again, he was quite calm.

'If you change your mind –'

Stella interrupted him. 'I won't.'

'If you do . . . it's still on for tomorrow. It's the last one before we go.'

Stella said she was getting cold. She wanted to go. Mr Barrington's voice became harsh and urgent. 'I've always wanted you, Stella – always! From the first moment I saw you. And I'm going to have you!'

Stella shivered. 'How do I know you haven't?'

Mr Barrington laughed. It was a horrible sound. 'I want you with more than your legs open! I want to see your eyes! I want you looking at me when I have you! I want to see right into those eyes – into those cold, clear, oh-so-haughty eyes!'

Stella turned away. She put her hands over her ears. 'Stop it! Stop it! I don't want to hear any more!'

Mr Barrington threw away his cigarette and raised his voice. 'But first – first I want to make them come alive! I want to see those eyes blaze – blaze with hatred and loathing of me!' He stopped for a moment and took a deep breath. 'I want to feel your body under mine – feel its wanton urges betray that loathing – watch you as that blaze of hate becomes a flame of lust!' He stood in front of Stella and clenched his fists and began to shout. 'I want to see those eyes staring into mine – wild, wild with desperate need! I want to hear you beg – plead – howl for release!'

Stella started to beat against his chest with her hands and then suddenly froze, like a statue. Mr Barrington put his hands gently on either side of her face and stroked his fingers round her eyes. 'Staring, staring into mine . . . blind with desperate need . . .'

He put his arms around her, and pulled her against him. She began to moan. 'Oh God . . . oh God! Please . . . stop . . .'

Mr Barrington pulled her head onto his shoulder. His voice

became low and gentle. 'I want to watch them melt . . . melt . . . melt, and submit, and cloud with shame, and close in final surrender . . .'

Stella began to sob and moan. Strange sounds came from her. She was like an animal in pain. She lifted her face up to Mr Barrington, her eyes closed and streaming tears. She tried to kiss him. He pushed her away. Stella put out her arms and tried to hug him. He threw her on the sand. She crawled towards him and put her hands on his shoes. He knelt down and grabbed her hair. He pulled her head up and back. I could see the moonlight shining on her tear-soaked face. She looked like a blind sick creature from another world. I didn't know what to do. I couldn't understand what was happening.

Mr Barrington looked at her for a moment, then let her go. Stella crumpled onto the sand. Mr Barrington climbed the bank and went round the corner of the band gardens. A few moments later, I heard a car driving away.

I slid back off the top of the bank and stood up. I was going to leave, and then Stella started to wail; long, piercing heart-breaking cries of sheer misery. I went down and tried to pick her up. She told me to go away. I said, 'It's Michael, Stella.' She said she didn't care who it was. 'Just leave me alone!'

I said I'd find Mr Barrington and pay him back. Stella went mad. She pushed me onto my back and knelt across my tummy, her knees either side of my waist. Her hands tried to scrape my face. She screamed at me. 'Pay him back for what?' I grabbed her wrists and yelled back at her. 'For all that filthy talk!'

Stella leaned down and spat in my face and screamed at me again. 'At least he wants me! That's something, isn't it?' She struggled to get her wrists free, and tried to bite my hands. I bucked my hips, to throw her off. She lay flat on top of me and stretched her legs out either side of mine, to keep her balance.

I pulled my right leg up between hers, and forced my knee between her thighs. She gasped, and stared down at me. I pressed harder, trying to lift her off. She began to pant, and thrust back against my leg. I straightened it and let it drop.

'No, no . . . come back!' She raised herself on her knees, and begged me to let her hands free. I said no. She yelled at me. 'My skirt's in the way!' I let go of one her wrists. She scrabbled at her skirt, and dropped back on top of me. 'Put your leg up again!'

I did. 'Higher! Press harder!' She pulled herself backwards until my knee was jammed between her thighs, and began pounding against it.

I was scared Mr Barrington would come back and catch us. I asked her to let me go. She shook her head wildly and put her full weight on my chest. The sound of her panting breath in my ear was deafening. She screamed and said, 'Oh God, it's no good! You're not doing it right!' She rolled off me, and lay on her back, and put her hands down the front of her knickers and rubbed herself madly.

Suddenly, her body began to jerk and twitch, and she rolled over onto her side and curled up into a ball, with her hands still between her legs. She let out a long low moan, and a series of little yelps, and then lay quiet.

After a few minutes, she opened her eyes and looked at me, without seeing, and said, in a barely audible whisper, 'No one else wants me . . . no one . . . no one . . .' She sat up, and shuffled across to me on her knees, her hands still down the front of her knickers, and looked down at me.

I was crying. I knew Stella was in misery, and that I couldn't do anything for her. She took her hands away from herself, and stroked my cheeks with the tips of her fingers, and kissed me.

I took her hands and gently licked her fingers clean. I don't know what made me do it. It was lovely. The taste of her juice was warm and clean and creamy. She asked me if I'd like some more, and I said yes.

She lay back into the shadow at the base of the bank and took her knickers off. I wriggled over and knelt beside her. I waited for her to put more juice on her fingers. She sighed, and said, 'Oh Michael – you're hopeless!' Her body shivered. '*I'm* waiting for *you*!'

I said, 'Oh . . .' and put my hand between her legs. I rubbed my fingers against her, and licked them. Stella moaned. Her voice became urgent. 'No! Not like that . . . with your tongue!' She pulled me forward. 'Kiss me. Kiss me . . . down there . . .' She drew her knees up and spread her legs apart. I knelt between them and bent my head forward. The smell of her creaminess made my head spin. My jake grew enormous, the first time for ages.

Stella whispered something. I said, 'Pardon?' She said, 'Say hello to the baby for me . . .' I sat up. Stella put her knees together and curled up. She began to cry. 'Oh God, I'm sorry. I don't know what made me say that.'

I sat beside her and gave her a cuddle. We sat for about an hour, with Stella crying quietly on my shoulder. When we tried to move we discovered we were stiff with cold. I took Stella home. She wanted to go to bed early. She's going in to Dublin in the morning with Mrs Sullivan. Ellen is going to look after the children while Mrs Sullivan is away.

I couldn't sleep at first. I spent hours smelling my fingers and pulling my plonker. Just after midnight, I remembered Stella had left her knickers down the strand. I went down and got them. I slept with them on the pillow beside me. They had a perfumy smell. It soothed me to sleep. By that time I was exhausted, anyway.

The village was swarming with police all day. They came out from Dublin to interview everyone. Dad kept out of their way. He spent the day playing chess with Mr Maguire. There was nothing else to do, because no one can play snooker; most of the balls and cues are missing. Dad says he'll get another lot from Dublin when the trouble blows over.

I hid in the stable loft all morning, reading the encyclopaedias. I was too scared to go out. Stella came up to see me. She was in a funny mood, half crying and half laughing. She said she had a terrible secret to tell me; a secret that I must never tell anyone. She was going into Dublin, with Mrs Sullivan, to have an operation to get rid of the baby. Mrs Sullivan knows where to find a doctor who'll do it. It's an illegal thing to do, and very expensive, but Mrs Sullivan is going to pay for it. She told Stella she owes it to her. They're going to use the money Dad gave Mrs Sullivan, the money he raised from the snooker competition.

Ellen came round to look after the Sullivan children while Mrs Sullivan and Stella were in Dublin. In the afternoon she let the girls out to play in the garden and came up to see me. She has a ticket booked for England. I asked her when she was going. 'Friday night,' she said. 'Will you miss me?' She tried to sound jokey but her eyes were sad. When I didn't answer, she said, 'Aren't you going to say yes?' I had to swallow hard before I could speak. I said yes, I would miss her. And I meant it.

Her eyes went misty. When she spoke again her voice was

husky. 'Will you let me spend a night with you ... before I go?' Before I could answer, she put her hand on my arm. 'No – don't say anything. I shouldn't have asked. I've brought you enough trouble.' She burst into tears and ran down the stairs and into the house.

As soon as she'd gone, I burst into tears myself, and cried myself to sleep. When I woke up, it was late in the evening, and Stella was sitting on the side of my bed, staring out through the window. Even in the twilight, I could see that she looked dreadful. I sat up, and she told me a terrible story.

Mrs Sullivan took her into Dublin, and they went to a pub near the Medical University. They paid the barman five pounds to tell them the name of a certain doctor. He said the doctor usually came in at lunchtime. They asked how they'd recognise him, and the barman charged them another two pounds, just for pointing him out to them.

They waited all day, but the doctor didn't turn up until five o'clock. He was young, and fat, with black oily hair and a mouth like a goldfish. He took them into a filthy back room. Stella had to lie on a table and be examined. The bar staff kept popping their heads through the door, for a look. She was so ashamed, she nearly vomited.

The doctor made them pay fifty pounds in advance. He said it would be another fifty when he did the operation. Mrs Sullivan called him a barefaced robber, for charging so much. He said Stella was obviously a cut above the skivvies he usually dealt with, and her parents presumably weren't short of a few bob. It was a hundred pounds or not at all. They had to go along with it.

He gave them another address, and told them to be there at eight o'clock. This third place was a chemist's shop off Lomas Street. The chemist was expecting them. He was a tall thin old man with bleary eyes and loose, wet, purple lips. He took them into a storeroom at the back of the shop. There was a bed in one corner, behind a pile of boxes. There were no blankets or pillows on the bed, just a stained mattress with a square of rubber sheet on it.

The chemist made Stella take her skirt and knickers off. He brought in a basin of hot water and put it on the floor. She had to squat over it and give herself a thorough wash. The chemist watched her every move. He said he had to be sure she was properly clean, and ready for the doctor. Mrs Sullivan tried to stop him watching Stella, but he told her to mind her own business. He said Stella might as well get used to him then as later. He'd be helping the doctor.

The doctor arrived. He was absolutely stocious drunk, and could hardly walk. His face was red and blotchy, and he was sweating like a pig. The chemist had to help him in through the door. He told Mrs Sullivan to hand over the other fifty pounds, and gave it to the chemist, who locked it away in a small safe under the counter of the shop.

The doctor collapsed into a chair, and told Stella to lie on the bed with her legs apart. The chemist got a shaving brush, and soap, and a razor, and shaved between her legs. Mrs Sullivan wanted to do it but the chemist said no. It was one of the perks of his job.

The doctor started to take his clothes off. Mrs Sullivan thought at first he was getting ready to have a good wash. When he got down to his trunks and socks, she asked him what the hell was going on. The doctor told her not to be so innocent. He was going to 'have it off' with Stella. It was accepted practice in his line of business. A fuck, he said, was part of the fee.

Mrs Sullivan was livid. She started to argue with the doctor. Stella begged her to stop and let him have his way. She felt so humiliated she just wanted to get it all over with. The chemist watched the doctor violating Stella. He kept licking his lips and stroking the front of his trousers.

Mrs Sullivan knelt by the bed holding Stella's hand, and prayed for her. When the doctor finished, the chemist took his trousers off. Mrs Sullivan couldn't believe it. The chemist said it was his turn now. She tried to stop him. The doctor said it was both of them, or nothing. As his assistant, the chemist was entitled to the same benefits as himself.

The chemist spent ages enjoying himself with Stella. He kept grinning at Mrs Sullivan while he was doing it. When the chemist finished with Stella, the doctor had another go. He poked himself into her and started to jog up and down. Suddenly, he gave a tremendous burp and was sick all over her. Then he passed out.

Stella was nearly smothered by his weight. She tried to struggle free but couldn't. Mrs Sullivan rolled the doctor off her. He fell off the bed and crashed onto the floor. Mrs Sullivan tried everything

437

to waken him up. She couldn't. He was so drunk, when he first arrived, he could hardly stand. The sex finished him off.

Mrs Sullivan wanted her money back. The chemist wouldn't give it to her. She threatened to go to the police. The chemist laughed in their faces. Getting rid of a baby is a serious crime. They'd be sorry if they went to the police. Mrs Sullivan was determined to get back at them in some way. Stella was too sick with shame to care what happened.

The chemist said he'd do the operation. He knew as much about it as the doctor. Mrs Sullivan asked Stella what she felt about this. The chemist said it wasn't up to Stella. It was up to Mrs Sullivan. He'd have to charge a personal fee for taking over. The personal fee involved 'having it off' with Mrs Sullivan.

He tried to pull her skirt off. Mrs Sullivan couldn't stand any more of it. She rammed her thumbs into his eyes. He fell on the floor, blinded, and threshing about in agony. She looked for something to knock him out with. The doctor had a walking stick with a heavy silver knob for a handle. She used that. When the chemist was still, Mrs Sullivan tied his ankles together and then his wrists.

She went into the shop and closed all the shutters. Then she put the light on. She searched for bottles of iodine and poured them over the chemist. Every inch of him was bright purple. It will last for weeks.

The doctor woke up. He was lying on his back. He looked repulsive with no clothes on. He shouted for a drink. Mrs Sullivan got bottles of laxative and poured them into his mouth. He had to swallow, or choke. She poured the rest of the iodine bottles over him. He passed out again, and she tied him up and rolled him onto the floor beside the chemist.

She kept going into the shop for more bottles. Anything that was liquid, she poured over them. As she emptied the bottles, she smashed them on the floor all round the two men. By the time Mrs Sullivan finished, they were completely surrounded by jagged glass. If they tried to move, they'd roll onto it. The doctor, particularly, would cut himself to bits. The chemist still had his clothes on. Mrs Sullivan was cross that she hadn't thought of taking them off. By that time, it was too late. She was afraid she'd be poisoned if she touched him.

Mrs Sullivan looked everywhere for the keys to the safe, but she couldn't find them. She tried to take the safe with her, but it was too heavy, so she tipped it on its back and poured a bottle of battery acid through the keyhole. Before they left, she turned on all the taps she could find, upstairs as well as down, and put the plugs in all the sinks.

It was eleven o'clock by the time Stella finished telling me this story. I asked her what she was going to do about the baby. She said she knew someone else who could do it. He's not a doctor but he has all the equipment. He's done it for other women. I was heartbroken. I guessed she must be talking about Mr Barrington. I pleaded with her not to go near him. She said she had no choice. He's going back to England very soon. He was over there with Mrs Barrington, last week, getting their house ready. I asked her why she was so keen to get rid of the baby. She said she wants to go to England herself, and start a new life. She's planning to ask Ellen if she can go with her.

A car came down the lane. Stella said she had to go, and rushed off. I watched her from the loft door. The moon was big and round. It filled the lane with a clear cool light. The car was the red MG. Stella got into the car, which was parked outside her gate. I thought it was going to drive off but it didn't. The hood was down and I could see Stella talking to the driver. It was Mrs Barrington.

I ran downstairs and vaulted over the wall into Number Eleven's garden. It took me only a few seconds to cross the others and then the wall into Stella's garden. I crept to the inside of her gate and listened. I could hear perfectly.

Mrs Barrington was telling Stella to go in and have a good bath, dress herself in a white nightdress or a dance frock or a full-length slip, 'anything you like, so long as it's long and white,' and then to be ready to leave for Ashford within half an hour.

I was startled. Ashford! It's where I was supposed to bury the bones. Stella asked Mrs Barrington what would happen when they got there, but she didn't answer. She got out of the car and told Stella she'd have to hurry. Everyone else was already there, ready and waiting for them.

When Stella came into her garden I tried to persuade her not to go. She said she had to. She'd been very lucky; Mrs Barrington had offered her one last chance. She couldn't turn it down. I threatened to kidnap her and lock her in the stable. She said she'd scream her head off if I didn't leave her alone.

Mrs Barrington came into the garden. She walked up to me, and said she'd telephone the barracks if I didn't go. Her eyes were huge and gleaming. Her face had the same wild look that came over her when she made me have sex with her. I asked her what she was going to do with Stella. She said it was none of my business. They both told me to go, or it would be the worse for me. Stella was shivering and sobbing. Mrs Barrington was quiet and fierce.

I ran round to the pub and stole a bicycle from the yard and cycled to Ashford. The church is on its own, on the side of a hill. The village nearby is empty and in ruins. The track up to the church had half a dozen cars parked along it. I left the bicycle hidden and crept along it, watching out for anybody guarding the track. It was deserted. I reached the church without any trouble.

It's a small derelict building with a square tower at one end. The roof is missing but the doors and windows are still attached. I could see lights flickering inside. I went to the end of the church and found a door at the bottom of the tower. It was chained up. There was a small window high on the wall beside it. The glass was missing. I put my foot on the door-chain and managed to lift myself high enough to grab the window ledge. It was just too small for me to get through. The chain snapped and I came tumbling down. There was plenty of grass and weeds, so I didn't make any noise.

I pulled the broken chain out of the latch on the door and pushed against it. The bottom of the tower was filled with rubbish and I had a job getting the door to open. Eventually I managed to squeeze through. The stairs inside the tower had collapsed but there were plenty of holes in the brickwork. I climbed up to the remains of the belfry and looked down through a slit in the stonework.

The moon was shining into the church. There were candles everywhere. The floor was covered with red and white stone slabs, faded but clean. There was no rubbish or furniture anywhere. The remains of the altar was right below me. All that's left is a great stone slab mounted on side pillars, about three feet high. There were dozens of candles burning behind it, mounted on stones jutting from the wall.

Six men and five women were lying naked on mats on the floor. They were on their backs, with their arms and legs stretched out, and their feet pointing towards the altar. There wasn't a sound from any of them. They all had black hoods covering their heads. I thought at first they were dead. It gave me a horrible fright.

One of them said something, in a low voice. They all began singing, quietly. I couldn't make out the words. It sounded like a sort of humming noise.

A little door in the side of the church opened. Two women came in. They both had the black hoods over their head. One of them was naked. The other had on a long white dress of some kind. Even if I hadn't been expecting them, I'd have known it was Mrs Barrington and Stella. Stella's long dark hair was unmistakable, and I knew the shape of Mrs Barrington's body. The people on the mats stood up and crowded round them. I could make out Mr Barrington, because of his height, but I wasn't sure of anyone else. They led Stella to the altar. One of the women, very old and horribly flabby, spread a black cloth over the stone slab. They helped Stella up onto it, and told her to lie quietly.

Mr Barrington picked up a box from beside the altar. He took everything out, and put it beside Stella. They were exactly the same things a priest uses at mass; a silver chalice, and goblets, and cloths to go over them, and a big book that looked like a missal.

They did a ceremony that was like a Mass. I couldn't watch. I knew it was to do with the Devil. I put my fingers in my ears and shut my eyes. It went on for ages. I had to keep peeping to make sure they were still there.

When the ceremony was finished, the six women went down on their hands and knees with their bottoms pointing at the altar. The six men knelt behind them and shagged them, even the horrible old flabby one. Mr Barrington was the one who did it to her.

They all stood up and moved into a semicircle in front of the altar. Stella got scared. She tried to sit up. One of the men put his hand on her chest and pushed her down. He told her to lie still. Another man took hold of the hem of the long white dress she was wearing, and tore it open all the way up to the neck. I heard Stella give a muffled scream, and saw her clench her fingers.

Mr Barrington picked up a bottle and poured some of the contents into a silver goblet. He drank from it, and passed it round. When it was empty, he filled it again. Two of the women took hold of Stella's feet and held her legs apart. Mr Barrington poured the liquid over her tummy and between her thighs. Stella gasped, and shuddered. Mr Barrington lifted the

441

cloth covering the chalice, and took out a small white disc. I knew immediately what it was; a communion wafer. I blessed myself and prayed that the wafer had never been consecrated. I was scared stiff that God would strike us all dead for committing sacrilege. Mr Barrington came down from the altar holding the communion wafer. Everyone turned their backs and bent over with their fingers touching the ground. Mr Barrington went along and touched each of their bottoms with the wafer.

They all stood upright and turned back to the altar. Mr Barrington got up and knelt between Stella's legs. He poured more of the liquid over her, and pressed the white disc into her fanny. His penis swelled up to an enormous length. He leaned forward and put his hands on top of Stella's, to hold her down. Using his penis, he slowly pushed the wafer deep into her body. For a while, he was very gentle, moving in and out with long slow strokes. Stella lay as still as though she were asleep.

Mr Barrington began to go faster, and more roughly. Stella's body began to stir. Her breasts tightened into hard little mounds. The pink tips stuck out like tiny fingers.

The people standing watching got very excited, and started squealing and moaning, and clutching at each other. A man standing behind Mrs Barrington knelt down and began kissing and licking her bum. She lay down on a mat, flat on her tummy and the man shagged her. The others lay down and did the same, but all in different positions.

Mr Barrington was hammering savagely in and out of Stella, and I could tell that she was responding to him, because her whole body was knotted with tension, and bucking and heaving in time with his movements. Her mouth was open, and her head was rolling from side to side, and I could hear her giving little cries and moans; whether of pain or pleasure I couldn't tell. The one thing she wouldn't do was open her eyes. Mr Barrington got into a terrible rage over this, and leaned all his weight on one hand and began slapping her hard across the face with the other. 'Open your eyes, you bitch; open them! Open them, do you hear me; open them! It's your soul I want to see! Your soul – your naked soul!' He screamed at her, again and again, to open her eyes, but Stella wouldn't. His voice rose to a hoarse desperate roar and he shouted, 'I'm coming! I'm coming! Open your eyes, damn you! I'm coming! I want you – body *and* soul – together – naked – naked – naked!

Suddenly, his body arched backwards and a long anguished scream of frustration poured from his mouth. He fell forward on top of Stella, and his teeth bit into her throat. He lay quietly for a while, and then raised himself on his hands again. He looked down into Stella's face, and slowly and carefully began hitting her again with the flat of his hand. Stella lay as if she were dead, her eyes closed and her face totally expressionless. Mr Barrington hit her once, then twice, then three times, then four and five and six, and then he stopped. Stella lay moaning with pain for a moment, and then, slowly, when she realised he'd stopped, her face relaxed, and she took a long slow breath, and then her eyes opened, and she looked straight up into Mr Barrington's face, and her lips curved into a slow, mocking, triumphant smile.

Mr Barrington didn't know what to do. He made as if to hit her again, and Stella raised her hand in a gesture that stopped him. He sat back on his heels, pulling his penis from inside her. It was limp, but still enormous. He stood up, and Stella looked at his penis, and said, in a low voice, 'So much, and yet so little . . .'

She sat up, and then came to a kneeling position in front of Mr Barrington, and began gently stroking his penis. She looked up at him and said, 'You promised to cure me of being pregnant . . .' Mr Barrington looked down at her with a look of baffled hatred, and said nothing. Stella said, 'You promised . . . you said if I gave myself to you . . .' Mr Barrington slapped her across the face and said, 'And you didn't – so we're quits.'

His penis began to swell, and Stella moved her head so that she could caress it with her lips. She stopped, and looked up at him again, and said, 'I've been a fool, haven't I?' Mr Barrington's penis was enormous again.

Suddenly, he must have realised what was in Stella's mind. He grabbed the long hair at the back of her head and wrapped it round his hand. He tried to jerk her head away but it was too late. Stella sank her teeth into his penis and her nails into the base of his scrotum.

Mr Barrington gave a long piercing scream, like a man falling from the top of a cliff. It faded away into a horrified whimper as Stella released him, and then his whole body crumpled into a shapeless heap and rolled from the altar onto the cold tiled floor of the church.

After a moment of shock, Mrs Barrington rushed to help him,

and the other people in the church ran up the altar steps to attack Stella. I took a huge breath and made a trumpet from my hands and gave a long, ghostly banshee wail that echoed piercingly round and round inside the walls of the church. I did it again and again and again, and when everyone had left, I climbed down and wrapped Stella in one of the abandoned mats and wheeled her carefully home on the saddle of the stolen bicycle.

I woke up to find Stella shaking me. She looked awful, like a ghost, or a person who'd just spent a night in a haunted house. She had a silk scarf round her neck, to hide the bruise where Mr Barrington bit her.

She gave me an envelope, with Malone's name on it, and asked me to give it to him. When I asked her what was in the envelope, she said, 'Don't question me, Michael, please. Don't question me – just give it to him.' She asked me to take it round straight away, and said she'd wait for me.

Malone was out in his shed, smoking, and reading a Mickey Spillane book. I handed him the envelope, and said it was from Stella. He ripped it open and pulled out a note. He read it, and his face broke into a sly dirty grin. 'Jesus,' he said. 'Women are the limit!'

He put the note in his pocket and said, 'She wants me to meet her. Tomorrow night!' He took a puff from his cigarette, and coughed. '"At the usual place," she says.' 'But why?' I said. Malone sniggered. 'For the usual reason, I hope.' 'What usual reason?' I asked him. Malone told me not to be so stupid. 'She wants her chimney swept, you daft bastard!'

I couldn't believe my ears. 'You mean she wants to have sex with you?' 'That's what it looks like,' said Malone. 'Dead of night, down in the dunes. What else could it be?' I stared at him in amazement. 'You're not going to go, are you?' He said, 'You can bet your Sunday boots I am! I'm not the man to look a gift horse in the mouth.'

He took the note from his pocket and rubbed it up and down the front of his trousers, his eyes mocking me. 'She says in here, "This will be our last chance to meet, so please don't let me down." Signed, S.R.'

'But what about the police?' I said. 'Supposing they catch you with . . . catch you down there?' Malone said I was living in the past; all that business is dead and gone, weeks ago. The police have given up watching the beach. 'Have you not heard the story? She was never raped at all; it's some married bloke she's trying to cover up for.'

I went back to the stable and asked Stella point-blank if she was going to have sex with Malone. She said she wasn't.

'But he thinks you are!'

'That's his mistake, then.'

'He says he's meeting you down the strand, tomorrow night!'

'Yes. He is. But not for sex.'

'Supposing he turns nasty?'

'I hope he does . . .'

I begged her not to go ahead with such a stupid idea, and pleaded with her to tell me why she wanted to meet Malone anyway, and especially in such a stupidly dangerous situation. She just kept looking at me, with a queer little smile on her sad, tired face, and then she suddenly got up and left, without saying another word to me. No sooner had she left than Ellen arrived. She had a little suitcase with her, and I said, 'Oh no; you're not going away already!' Ellen said, 'No, no; I've got some things here for you.' I was mystified, but she said not to think about it for a minute; she wanted to tell me something, first. The detective, the one sent to find the man who raped Stella, is going back to Dublin. He's finished his investigations, and will be submitting a report to Police Headquarters in the Phoenix Park. I was scared stiff when I heard this. 'But he thinks it was me! I'm sure he does!'

Ellen put her hand on my arm and said, 'I know; he told me.' I went white and faint with fear, and had to sit down on the bed in case I collapsed. Ellen sat down beside me, and said I'd no need to worry about it any more. 'Whatever he may think, privately, his official opinion is that "there is insufficient evidence on which to continue the search for her assailant".'

'But Ellen; I had a whole lot of stuff under my bed! He took it away – Christie says it's enough to hang me!'

Ellen lifted the little suitcase onto the bed and opened it. 'Is this what you're worried about?' Inside the suitcase she had Mr Barrington's camera, and the pin-up magazines Andy lent me, and the dirty drawings I'd done of Stella and herself. My whole body shook with relief, and my brain went dizzy trying to work out what had happened.

'Why has he given you this stuff?'

'He didn't exactly give it to me . . .' Ellen paused for a moment, 'I had to pay for it.'

'You paid him for it? Paid him? I don't understand . . .'

'He thought he was getting a . . . a pearl of great price.' Ellen looked away, and said softly, so softly I barely heard her, 'I didn't tell him the oyster had already been opened.' I was sick in my soul when I realised what she meant. She stood up and said, 'Don't worry; I made sure I was all right . . .' She put her hand in the pocket of her cardigan and took something out and threw it on the bed beside me. It was the packet of Durex I'd been keeping for future deals with Christie's brother. I looked at her, and my eyes filled with tears. 'How did you find these?'

'A couple of weeks ago . . . I came up to take away your sheets for washing. The . . . the things . . . were under the mattress. Last night, I . . . well, you weren't here, and I needed them. I . . . I just took them.' I looked in the packet, and there were only seven left. Five of them, gone! I couldn't believe it. Ellen gave me a wry smile, and said, 'I've had a pretty sleepless night, I can tell you . . .'

My head felt as if it was going to explode with pain and anger and shame. Ellen looked at my face and suddenly became very businesslike and brisk. She emptied the suitcase onto my bed, snapped it shut, and said she was leaving, before I had a chance to lecture her.

'Why?' I screamed at her. 'Why did you have to show me this?' I picked up the Durex packet and flung it at her. 'Why couldn't you have made up a story? You could have pretended you'd stolen the stuff! Or that he'd given it to you because he doesn't really believe it was me!'

'But he does believe it was you! That's why the price was so . . .' She stopped, and turned away, and walked to the top of the stairs. I put my hands to my ears and shouted 'I don't want to hear any more! Why the Hell did you tell me anything at all?'

Ellen stood looking at me for a moment, still as a statue, and said, 'I hoped you'd understand. I wanted you to know how much I . . .' She stopped, and went down the stairs, and I didn't see her again.

I lay on my bed until dark, my head pounding and my body racked with tension and misery. About ten o'clock, I heard a drunk staggering down the lane, singing to himself. I looked out and it was Christie's brother. I knew immediately where he was going, and all the white-hot rage and pain in me came boiling to the surface.

I waited for half an hour, and then went down to the Barringtons' house and walked straight in through the back door without knocking. The wall carpet covering the one-way mirror between the lounge and the bedroom was drawn back, and I could see Christie's brother on the bed with Mrs Barrington and the woman she said was her sister. None of them had any clothes on, and they were all tangled up together in a writhing heap.

Mr Barrington was sitting naked in a chair, smoking, with his legs crossed and a bandage round his penis, casually watching the three people in the bedroom. Another man, with only his trunks on, was looking through the viewfinder of a cine camera and filming everything that was going on.

I walked over, pushed him aside, picked up the camera and its tripod, and hurled it through the glass and into the bedroom. Then I walked out and went back to the stable.

Later, Mrs Barrington came to see me. I told her I know everything that's going on, and that I'm convinced Mr Barrington is the man who raped Stella, and that I was going straight to the police in the morning. She did everything she could to change my mind, but I didn't give in. She said I'd be sorry, and left. I went to sleep feeling sick and miserable.

I woke up dreaming I was shipwrecked in a storm at sea, with the wind howling, and the rain battering down on my head. I opened my eyes, and the wind and rain turned out to be real. It was howling and hammering on the roof. I immediately started bursting for a pee and got up to get my pot from under the bed. There was another banging noise downstairs, as though the stable door was blowing to and fro in the wind.

I stumbled down the stairs, half asleep, and saw Stella lying in the middle of the floor, unconscious, with Mrs Barrington kneeling over her. Mrs Barrington was soaked, with her hair streaming down all over her face, and her dress completely stuck to her body. She was tearing at Stella's clothes, as though she was trying to undress her.

Stella looked terrible. She had on a white dress with a blue cardigan and a plastic raincoat. She was sopping wet and her

447

clothes were filthy, as if she'd been rolling in dirt. I shouted over to Mrs Barrington and asked her what was going on.

The moment she heard me, she whirled round with a face like a wild animal. She shot to her feet, and stretched her hands out like claws, ready to attack me. Her eyes were wild with fury, and she was breathing deeply as if she was going to explode.

She screamed at me. 'Why? What is it about you? Why do you always have to come along and ruin everything?' I ran halfway up the stairs and turned, ready to defend myself. I thought she was going to come after me and scratch my eyes out, but she suddenly let out an enormous sigh and slumped back into a kneeling position. In a calm, lifeless voice, she told me she'd looked into the lane earlier on, and seen Stella lying in the gutter outside my stable. She'd rushed up and dragged her in out of the rain.

She stopped talking and waited for me to say something. I came back down the stairs and knelt beside her, staring down at Stella. Mrs Barrington had pulled Stella's dress up around her waist, and I could see that the front of her knickers were soaked with blood. 'Oh my God,' I said. 'She's been attacked again!'

I told Mrs Barrington I was going to fetch the police. She said, 'I'd think carefully about that, if I were you.' I asked her what she meant. She said, 'It won't look too good for you, will it?' I stared at her, with a horrible suspicion dawning in my mind. Mrs Barrington looked at me coldly and said, 'Especially if I say I heard screams and rushed in here and found you trying to rip her clothes off.'

I was so stunned I could hardly speak. I started to say, 'You couldn't possibly –' but she interrupted me. 'Oh yes, I could. It's pretty much what I was going to say, as a matter of fact.' She continued looking at me for a moment, and said, 'If I were you, I'd forget about last night, as well. And any threats about going to the police with stories about Richard.' She suddenly brightened up and said, 'Well, that's that settled, then! Perhaps things haven't turned out too badly, after all!' She stood up and crossed her arms and began pacing the floor, looking very thoughtful. 'The only problem is,' she said, 'if it wasn't you who attacked Stella – this time, I mean – then who else shall I choose?'

I asked her what the Hell she was talking about, and she laughed, and said that I'd spoiled her plans, just a tiny bit, and that I'd have to help her with an alternative. She began again trying to undress Stella, and told me to run to the doctor's and fetch his wife. I was confused and asked, did she mean both of them? Mrs Barrington said no, not the doctor, only Mrs Jackson, and to make sure I asked her to bring dry clothes for Stella. I said I could get some from Stella's mother. Mrs Barrington told me not to be so stupid; the last thing she wanted was to involve Stella's parents.

The rain was still lashing down and I hadn't a raincoat. I put on the leather jacket Christie's brother gave me. Guard O'Rooney was sheltering in the doorway of the newspaper shop. He asked me if I knew what time it was, and I said no. 'Half-past six o'clock A.M. in the morning,' he said. 'Where are you off to at such an ungodly hour?' I said I had an urgent message for the doctor's wife. He told me to hold my horses for a minute, and said it was a fine class of a jacket I was wearing; where exactly did I get it? I was in too much of a hurry to explain it to him, and said I'd had it for ages. He asked me if he could have a closer perusal and examination of it, sometime. I said yes, certainly, but would he mind if I dashed off and got on with my message? He said no, not at all, but he'd be grateful for one small word or two from me before I went; what was the nature and purpose of my visit to the doctor's wife?

I told him Stella had fainted in the lane, and Mrs Barrington had rescued her, and sent me up to get medical help. O'Rooney said he wouldn't swop places with me, even for the contents of a farmer's wallet; anything to do with women's ailments was bad news. At the first hint of any such malarkey in the vicinity of his own hearth and home, he puts the paper away and goes off down the garden for a bit of boot-scraping or wheelbarrow repair work.

'Anyway,' he said, 'off you go and forget you met me; I don't want to get dragged into the affair.' It was definitely women's work and he couldn't think of two better women than Mrs Barrington and Mrs Jackson, bearing in mind the class of job it was. He got out his notebook and pencil and I ran off.

When I got back with Mrs Jackson, Mrs Barrington had Stella's wet clothes rolled up in a bundle and was busy rubbing her all over with my towel. I was ashamed because it was so dirty, but Mrs Barrington said it was perfect for the job: stiff and rough and just the thing for getting the circulation going. Stella's wrists had strange swellings on them, like huge blisters. Round her tummy and her fanny and the tops of her legs she was covered in a red rash, criss-crossed with deep scratches. Mrs Jackson was surprised at Mrs Barrington letting me see Stella with no clothes on, but Mrs Barrington smiled and said there was little I hadn't seen already, and not just of Stella. She asked if there was any chance of me making a hot cup of tea for Stella. I went into the house and made tea as quietly as I could, so as not to waken Dad.

Stella was awake when I came back with the tea. She looked at me for a moment with dazed eyes, then her face took on a horrified look and she screamed, 'No – no!' Mrs Barrington hugged her and stroked her forehead and said it was all right; no one was going to hurt her. Stella closed her eyes and hid her face against Mrs Barrington's chest.

I went upstairs out of the way. I could hear Stella crying, and the women soothing her and saying, 'It was only Michael; we won't let him harm you.' I was annoyed by this; they had no business giving Stella the impression they were keeping her safe from me.

Mrs Barrington came up to say that Stella ought to stay downstairs until she was fully recovered. I said, 'Wouldn't it be better if we took her home?' Mrs Barrington said no; she didn't want Stella's parents to see her in such a state; they had enough to worry about already.

I asked her why Stella seemed so scared of me; she said, 'Maybe it's something to do with what you're wearing . . .' She came up close to me and whispered, 'Remember, Michael; you're right in the firing line. So keep your mouth shut, until you hear from me again.' She kissed me, with ice-cold lips, and took a blanket from my bed, to wrap round Stella, and then she and the doctor's wife left.

I sat upstairs thinking for a while but I couldn't see any way out of the situation. I'd have to do what Mrs Barrington wanted, at least for the moment. My head was thumping like an enormous drum.

I went down and asked Stella if she'd like more tea. She said she was sorry she'd screamed at me. I said it was all right; I understood. She stared at me thoughtfully and said, 'You don't, you know; you haven't the faintest idea what's going on . . .' This made me feel very uncomfortable and stupid.

I asked her why she'd been lying in the lane. She said

she had no idea. One minute, she'd been standing talking to Mrs Barrington; the next, she woke up in the stable. I said, 'Talking to Mrs Barrington?' Stella said, 'Yes.' I said, 'That's not what she told me! She said she found you lying there, unconscious.' Stella shrugged her shoulders under the blanket and said, 'What does it matter?'

I said, 'It matters a lot to me! Mrs Barrington is trying to make out that I attacked you and dragged you in here to rape you!' Stella shrugged again and said, 'So? Maybe you did.'

I was heartbroken. I shouted at her. 'Stella; how could you say that? I thought we were friends! I thought you cared about me?' Stella's eyes flared, and she shouted at me, 'Michael, I'm dead! Do you hear me? Dead! Dead, inside and out. I don't care about you, or myself, or anybody. Nothing, absolutely nothing, matters to me any more!'

She took her arms from under the blanket and thrust them at me, palms upwards. She told me to look at the blisters on her wrists. 'Do you know how I did that, Michael? I'll tell you. With a candle. That's how I did it. I held my wrists over a lighted candle, Michael, and burned them deliberately.' She stopped, and looked up at me, her eyes shiny with tears. 'Shall I tell you why?' I was too horrified to speak. All I could do was nod my head.

'To get me through the night, Michael; to see if the physical pain would blot out the pain in my mind . . .' She paused again, and put her arms back under the blankets. 'It didn't, Michael, and nothing can, now. Nothing but . . . nothing but what I'm going to do tonight.'

She threw off the blanket and pointed to her stomach and said, 'I suppose you've seen this as well?' I nodded, and she sat up. 'I've scrubbed myself raw – trying to get rid of filthy memories.' She pulled her knees up and wrapped her arms round them and tipped her head forward so that her hair fell round her like a dark cloak. 'That didn't help me, either.'

We sat in silence for a while. I hardly dared breathe. She asked me what had happened to her clothes. I said one of the women must have taken them away to wash. I handed her the little bundle of clean things the doctor's wife had brought. She stood up and got dressed in front of me, and said, 'Thank you for looking after me,' and then she left.

I spent the rest of the day in a state of torment. I knew

something dreadful was going to happen, but I couldn't imagine what it would be, or what I could do about it, even if I knew. All I did know was that I had to protect Stella from whatever was going to happen tonight, even if it was something she wanted to happen.

I spent the rest of the day hiding in the band gardens, waiting for her to go down the strand for her meeting with Malone. She didn't leave her house until half-past eleven. I followed her down the beach and watched her go into what used to be her favourite place, at the end of the dunes. The rain had cleared away and the moon came out, colouring the world with a bright, cold, sad, silver light.

I crawled to the top of the bank and looked into the hollow. Stella took her clothes off, and spread a towel on the sand, just as she did the first time I'd seen her there. I watched her take something from a small bag, and saw the glint of moonlight on shiny metal. Stella caressed the knife for a moment, and slid it under the towel, and lay flat, her legs together and her arms straight down by her sides.

Malone arrived, dressed in his ridiculous leather outfit. He took a last puff from his cigarette, threw it away, and pulled down his trousers and underpants. Stella spread her legs apart, and folded her arms under her head. Malone knelt down between her thighs, and took his penis in his hand, and guided it into her, and then thrust forward and lay on top of her. Neither of them spoke. Malone began moving in and out of her, and I could hear him start to pant and grunt as his movements became faster and rougher.

I nearly missed the flash of silver as Stella reached under the towel and brought out the knife. It was only as she raised it behind Malone's back that I realised what she was going to do. I shouted to Malone, 'Look out!' He twisted upward to see where the shout had come from, and the blade skidded harmlessly down the back of his jacket. Stella raised the knife again, and Malone saw it, and rolled off her just as she plunged it down. It went deep into her stomach.

Malone jumped up and stood looking at her in horror. I slid down the bank and rushed over to Stella, and knelt beside her. She looked up at me and smiled and said, 'Hallo, Michael. I knew you'd be somewhere around, in my hour of need . . .'

I put out my hand to pull the knife from her stomach, and she said, 'No! No! Let me do it.' She struggled to her feet, and pulled the knife out and dropped it on the sand, and said, 'Goodbye, Michael . . .' She started to run along the beach and towards the sandbank, her hands clasped across her stomach.

I shouted, 'No, Stella, no! I've got to get you to a doctor!' I jumped to my feet and ran after her, and she stopped, and picked up a handful of sand, and threw it in my eyes. By the time I could see again, she was just a dot at the apex of a long silvery wake, swimming slowly out to sea.

I yelled at Malone to swim after her but he said he couldn't swim. I shouted, 'Neither can I!' and ran back along the beach. Malone pulled up his trousers and ran after me.

'Where the hell are you going?'

'To get a boat!'

'You're a fool! It's miles to the nearest boat!'

'I've got to do something! I've got to try and save her!'

Malone jumped on my back and threw me down on the sand. 'She doesn't want to be saved!'

I struggled fiercely, yelling, 'I've got to try, I've got to try!' He put his hands round my throat and squeezed like a madman, until I blacked out.

When I came to, Malone was sitting beside me, smoking. He said, 'You'd better forget that all this happened.' I told him I couldn't; I'd have to go to the police. 'If you do,' he said, 'they'll probably have me for murder . . . and they'll try and pin the rape on me, as well.'

'And why not?' I said. 'You did it; you started all this! You're the reason she's dead!' Malone laughed, a cold hard laugh, and said I was as guilty as he was. 'And for what it's worth, I never did rape Stella.' He said he knew I thought it was him, but I was wrong, and now it didn't matter any more. All that mattered was that I should keep my mouth shut, and give him time to get a bit of money together, and go to England, and forget that he'd ever heard of Kilmara, or me, or Stella, or anybody. He reminded me that I owed him a life, a life in exchange for mine, for the time he saved me from drowning at the dump. 'And finally,' he said, 'remember this: if it came to the worst, it'd be only your word against mine, and I'm prepared to commit perjury to save my skin. Are you?'

I knew Malone was right. I couldn't fight him and win, any

more than I could fight and win against the Barringtons. I felt sick in my heart and my soul and my mind. Stella was dead, and I'd been no help to her when she was alive; now I couldn't help her even when she was dead.

I stood up and told Malone I was going back to the hollow. He said, 'Why?' I told him I wanted to collect Stella's things. 'Forget it,' he said; 'they're much better off where they are.' He said I still hadn't learned to use my head, in spite of all the good example he'd given me. I stared at him, baffled.

'Listen,' he said, 'if that stuff stays exactly where it is, we're in the clear.' He paused. 'Think about it.' He lit another cigarette, and said, 'A pregnant mot, desperate, returns to the place where her troubles started. She takes off her clothes, sits for a while praying for courage, gets out a knife, stabs herself, staggers along the beach, and swims off to die in the bosom of her beloved ocean.' He paused to take a long pull on his cigarette. 'Simple, isn't it? And all we have to do, is to leave well alone.' He put a hand on my shoulder and dug his fingers into me. 'And, remember this; hers are the only fingerprints on that knife.' He paused again, and spat on the sand, and said, 'That's why she wouldn't let you pull it out. A smart girl, that Stella – a very smart girl indeed.'

I couldn't take any more. I blacked out again, and when I woke up, it was morning, and I was lying on the floor of the stable, surrounded by Malone's cigarette butts. He must have dragged me home, and stayed to make sure I didn't go back down the beach.

Stella's clothes were found early this morning, and then the knife, covered in blood and sand, and then, later in the day, her body, washed up by the afternoon tide.

Everyone agreed straight away that it was a clear case of suicide – everyone, that is, except O'Rooney. O'Rooney had a different view of the situation.

It rained hard all day yesterday, and the sand, even high on the foreshore and among the dunes, was wet; wet enough to retain the marks of everything that happened last night.

O'Rooney, thick, slow, plodding O'Rooney, spent the whole morning sitting on the highest point of the bank above the hollow, and pieced together, from footprints and disturbances in the sand, a story that was very near the truth.

The deceased, he said, for reasons at present unknown, had gone to the hollow, removed her garments, and lain down on her towel. Two men had followed her there; one by the beach, the other by the path among the dunes. She had with her a knife, a Gurkha blade belonging to her father, and presumably intended as a protective weapon.

The man who came by the beach route was apparently known to, and on terms of intimacy with, the deceased. On joining her, he immediately adopted a position consistent with an act of carnal intercourse. The other man, the one who'd come through the dunes, also entered the hollow, and either disturbed, or attempted to prevent, the completion of this act.

A struggle followed, during which the deceased was stabbed with the knife. She ran along the beach in an attempt to escape, was pursued by one of the men, stopped to grab up a handful of sand, presumably to throw in her pursuer's face, and then, in desperation, swam out to sea and died. Following this, there was evidence of an altercation between the two men, and then a long conversation, evidenced by the remains of numerous cigarettes.

What we're looking for, said O'Rooney, is two men, or well-built young fellows, who had a known interest in, and knowledge of, Stella and her movements. Only one of them smokes, to judge by the distribution of cigarettes during their conversation. He also, he said, knew a certain amount about their clothing. One of them, the non-smoker, was wearing corduroy trousers; the lines of the material were still clear in the sand, where he'd been sitting. He knew a few other things, too, but he wanted to keep them to himself, for the moment.

O'Rooney immediately became the most unpopular man in the village. It suited everyone to regard Stella's death as suicide, and to regard it as the end of a sordid episode which had cast suspicion on every man in the community. O'Rooney was advised to keep his mouth shut, and his fanciful stories to himself.

Nonetheless, the moment the story got out, Christie went to pieces. He ran down the lane, hysterical, and burst into the stable, and told me all the details, word for word. I listened to him in silence, and when he'd finished, I said, 'What are you worried about? What's it to do with you?'

'It's not just me, you fool! "Two fellows, with a known interest in, and knowledge of, Stella and her movements." That's us – you and me! Maguire will shop us straight away!' I told him to keep calm, and everything would be all right.

'It won't! Maguire's only got to open his mouth, and O'Rooney'll come down on us like a ton of bricks!'

Christie went off round the village and told everyone that Mr Maguire was notorious for spying on Stella, and that the two fellows O'Rooney had in mind were Maguire himself, and his bastard nephew, Jeremy Lynch.

There was still such an element of bad feeling against Mr Maguire and Lynch, after the business of Lynch torturing and raping Bowman's gang, that this story caught on straight away. Within half an hour, it was regarded as gospel truth.

Christie met the four Macarty brothers coming out of Dolan's pub. He told them the lie about Mr Maguire, and got them into a tremendous drunken rage. They went down the beach looking for him, knowing he'd be working in his tea hut. Mr Maguire saw them coming and escaped, so the Macarty brothers wrecked the hut. They pushed the roof off and demolished the walls and then smashed up the floor.

In a hollow under the hut they found a bundle of girl's clothes, and took them to the police barracks. The clothes were torn and bloody, and in no time at all, everyone was saying they were the clothes that went missing when Stella was raped, five weeks ago.

Mr Maguire was immediately named as the rapist, and everyone agreed that it was obvious all along that it must have been him. All that was needed was a bit of evidence, and now there it was, found right under his own hut. They conveniently ignored the fact that they'd already decided that Stella had faked the rape, and that she herself could easily have hidden the clothes under John-Joe's hut.

A mob gathered round the barracks, yelling that the Sergeant should go and arrest Mr Maguire straight away. The Sergeant refused, saying that there was no hard evidence against him. Anyone could have shoved the clothes under the hut, either to hide them, or to put the blame on John-Joe. 'As for the rumour about him spying on Stella,' the Sergeant said, 'you can forget that. A more decent and honourable man never drew breath!'

This didn't satisfy the mob, and they surged down and began stoning Mr Maguire's house, and smashing his windows, and trying to break down the front door. The Sergeant and three policemen had to go down and rescue him, and bring him back to the barracks for his own safety.

While the police were away rescuing Mr Maguire, Christie dashed down in a great state of excitement and said he wanted to show me the evidence. Stella's clothes were in a drawer in the Sergeant's desk, waiting for the detective to come out from Dublin and take them away for tests.

By that time I was beginning to think like Stella; I didn't care if I lived or died. Christie persuaded me in the end, by saying that it would be like paying my last respects to her. I could hold her clothes in my hand and say a prayer for the repose of her soul. He said he'd done it himself, and it had given him a terrible swollen plonker, even though he was saying a prayer. He said he couldn't help thinking of what had happened to her, and it got him all excited, even though he felt sorry for her. He's a loathsome little beast.

We went into the barracks through the back door, and Christie got the clothes out of the Sergeant's drawer and handed them to me. Apart from socks and underwear, there was a white bloodstained dress, and a blue cardigan, and a thin plastic raincoat, and everything was damp.

My throat went dry with shock, and I had to force my words out. I asked Christie if he was absolutely and completely certain that these were the things found under Mr Maguire's hut. Christie said he was; there was no doubt about it at all.

I asked him if it had occurred to anyone to wonder why everything was so wet, seeing that it was supposed to have been safely under the floor of John-Joe's hut for five weeks. Christie said he had no idea, and anyway, what did it matter?

I said, 'I'll tell you why it matters; these are the very clothes that Stella was wearing when I last spoke to her, yesterday morning.'

I said I'd have to tell the Sergeant that the clothes were nothing to do with the rape, and that they were nothing to do with John-Joe, either. Christie said his father would murder us both, if he found out we'd been interfering with the evidence. Then I remembered Mrs Barrington's threats, and how easy it would be for her to convince the police that I'd taken the clothes, and hidden them under John-Joe's hut.

I went down to the Barringtons' house, to tell Mrs Barrington that an innocent man was being blamed for Stella's death, and to beg her to tell the truth, but there was no one at home. The house was locked up and all the curtains drawn.

Mr Maguire spent the rest of the day in the barracks, with a mob howling outside until quite late. It wasn't until two o'clock in the morning that it was safe for him to sneak home. I heard him come out the back of the barracks and down the lane, with O'Rooney for an escort. I was still waiting up, in the hope that the Barringtons would come home.

John-Joe Maguire was found dead in his stable this morning, with his head battered in. The story going round is that he was tacking up his horse, and something must have frightened it. The horse went mad and knocked him onto the floor and kicked him to death.

Mrs Sullivan came to say goodbye to me. She's off to live as a housekeeper to her brother on his farm in Sligo. I couldn't talk to her for crying. It's all I've done all day.

She gave me a parcel, done up in brown paper and string, and well knotted up so I couldn't see into it. I thought it was for my birthday, but she said no; it's some things she found in Mr Sullivan's big commercial traveller's bag. She made me promise to put it away unopened, and not think about it any more, because it's of no use to me at the moment. The only point in opening it, she said, would be if I ever develop an unhealthy sense of guilt about a certain matter known only to the two of us. The contents of the parcel will go a long way towards easing my mind.

She said Ellen got off safely to England last night. Her last words, after she'd kissed everyone goodbye and stepped onto the train, were that she hoped never to come back. Mrs Sullivan says she feels exactly the same; she can't wait to get out of Kilmara. She left to do the children's midday meal, and handed me two letters just before she went: one from Ellen, and one from herself. She asked me not to read either of them until she was safely on the train.

After lunch, Dad and myself carried her suitcases up to the station, and waved goodbye to her and the children, and watched for a long while as the train disappeared into the distance. Dad and I didn't say a word to each other the whole time, and we walked back through the village separately. All the shops are shut, because of the two deaths. The parish priest insisted on it.

As I was coming down the lane, Mrs Barrington drove past me in the MG. She was on her own. As soon as she passed me, she screeched to a halt and said, 'Michael, I was hoping I'd find you!' She said she needed to talk to me. I said she'd have to listen to me, first, and told her about the terrible mix-up with Stella's clothes, and how Mr Maguire had been blamed for Stella's death, and now he was dead, and how I knew it was all her fault, because she must have arranged it deliberately. She looked at me blankly, and said she didn't know what I was talking about.

'Stella's clothes!' I said. 'The ones you took off her yesterday! They were found under Mr Maguire's hut –'

She said she couldn't recall having anything to do with Stella's clothes, either yesterday or any other day. I told her it was no good lying; the doctor's wife would remember the whole thing.

Mrs Barrington looked round to make sure no one was listening, and smiled at me, and said, 'I wouldn't put too much faith in the doctor's wife, Michael.'

I couldn't take any more. I shouted at her that I was going to tell the Sergeant everything I knew, and that she could do what she liked; I didn't care what happened to me, now that Stella and John-Joe were dead.

She stopped smiling, and said that I was becoming too emotional. 'It's your birthday soon, isn't it?'

I said yes, tomorrow.

She said, 'How would you like a present – a present of the truth?' I didn't answer, because I didn't trust her.

'Think about it, Michael,' she said. 'You could spend the rest of your life wondering how much you're to blame for Stella's death.'

I still didn't answer, and she said she had to go in and finish packing. Richard and Andy had already returned to England, and she'd be going as soon as she sorted things out with me. Out of the blue, she said, 'Will you meet me down the beach tomorrow, Michael, and show me where Stella . . . where she found her peace?' She paused, and said, 'Maybe *we* could find some peace . . . between the two of *us*.'

I stared at her, and remembered how much I used to love her, and how much unhappiness she'd caused me, and how I'd have to live with that unhappiness for ever, and how much worse it would be if I didn't give her one last chance to explain things to me.

Mrs Barrington looked at me, and saw the tears in my eyes, and the longing in my soul, and said, 'Early, Michael, we'll meet early! While the world is still fresh and new, and anything and everything seems possible!' She gave me a smile like sunshine breaking through summer clouds, and hugged me, and whispered, 'I'll meet you down the strand at seven. Don't be late!' And then she was gone.

I went home and read the letters from Ellen and Mrs Sullivan. Ellen is going to write to me from England, as soon as she's settled, and send me her address. Both of them wrote some very nice things to me, and about me, and thanked me for the love and strength I'd given them. I was grateful for the letters, because as far as I'm concerned, all I ever gave them was trouble and worry.

There were special prayers in the chapel all evening, and a full Benediction, asking God to bring harmony and love back to the village. I wonder if He was listening?

I couldn't sleep, through thinking of Mrs Barrington alone in her house, and wondering what she'd do if I went down and said I wanted to sleep with her, and wondering whether, if I did, I'd find her already in bed with someone else.

I sat up until dawn, thinking. The day started off misty, with a light rain. I didn't think Mrs Barrington would turn up, but I decided to go anyway. At six-thirty I left the stable. The rain had stopped by six, but I wore my leather jacket, in case it started again.

The red MG car was in the lane, with suitcases already packed on the boot rack.

The tide was fully out and the strand looked dreary and bleak. The mist and drizzle made everything pale and ghostly and sad. I lay on top of the dunes, shivering, and watching out for Mrs Barrington. She arrived just after seven, walking along the sand with her head bowed and her hands huddled up in the pockets of a heavy sheepskin coat. She walked to the point, and looked about her, and took a comb from her pocket and ran it through her hair.

I slid down the slope behind her, and she turned, without surprise, and said, 'Good morning, Michael. Happy birthday.'

I'd forgotten. She leaned sideways and kissed my cheek, and said 'Where is the place?' I pointed, and she took my arm, and we walked to the hollow.

We sat down, and I asked her what she wanted to talk to me about. She rested her chin on her knees and stared out to sea. It was a long time before she spoke again. When she looked at me her eyes were sad.

'Once upon a time, Michael . . . we didn't have to talk about anything . . .' She looked away and said, 'Ah well . . . times change.'

After a while, she asked me if I was still going to the police about Mr Barrington.

'I have to –'

'Have to?'

'I have to clear Mr Maguire.'

'Ah yes – Mr Maguire. And what about Mr Barrington?'

'He's gone to England.'

'The law, Michael; remember the long, long arm of the law.' I said I didn't think the Irish police could bother him if he was in England. 'It wasn't the police who bothered Mr Maguire.' I asked her what she meant.

'The Irish are a fierce race, Michael. A wild-tempered race, with a simple morality and long memories. And England isn't so very far away. If you persist with your story –' She shivered, and turned up the collar of her coat. 'It wouldn't be too hard to find us.' She took a white envelope from her pocket, and said, 'Would you believe me if I said that my husband had nothing to do with the attack on Stella?'

I shook my head and said, 'No, I wouldn't believe you,' and then I remembered something. I asked her if Mr Barrington had a cut on his hand – a deep cut, like a bite from an animal.

Mrs Barrington looked at me for a while, thinking, and bowed her head, and said, 'I see . . . I didn't know about that.' She was quiet again for a few moments and said, 'Richard is a seducer, Michael; he waits for his victims to offer themselves. I can't imagine him –' She stopped, and tapped her lips with the white envelope, and held it out to me.

'And yet, Michael, there are these. I don't know quite *what* to think.' I took the envelope and opened it. There was a set of photographs inside. I took them out and my heart nearly

461

stopped. They were the ones I took of Stella. I put them back into the envelope, my fingers stiff with shock, and forced myself to look at Mrs Barrington.

She stared back at me, and said, 'Clearly, he knew where to find her.' She took the envelope from me, and got out the photographs again, and sorted through them until she found the one of Stella lying naked on her towel. She glanced around the hollow, imagining what it must have been like on that sunny summer morning, and said again, 'Yes. He certainly knew where to find her . . .' She looked through the photographs again, and passed me the one of Stella crouching on her hands and knees at the top of the dune. 'And seeing her like that . . . I suppose it's just possible –'

She stopped, and took the photograph from me, and put them all back into the envelope. I forced myself to speak, even though I was fearful my voice would crack and sob. 'What are you going to do with them – the photographs?' She said she wanted me to have them. 'What?' I couldn't believe my ears.

'They're all that's left of Stella, now. Stella as she was – Stella as she ought to be remembered.'

I told her she was mad. I could go to the police with the photographs, and they'd know immediately that Mr Barrington had been spying on Stella. Mrs Barrington just looked at me calmly. 'And how would they know that, Michael? There's no connection, you know; no connection at all.' I said I didn't want the photographs. Stella was dead, and I just wanted to put her out of my mind until the pain and hurt had time to fade.

Mrs Barrington stood up and pulled me to my feet. She slid open the zip of my jacket and put the packet of photographs in my inside pocket. I moved my hand to get them out. Mrs Barrington put a hand to each side of my face and scraped her nails hard and fast all the way down to my chest. I put my hands to my face to squeeze the pain away, and stood paralysed for a moment.

Mrs Barrington undid the buckle of my belt and with a quick heave ripped open the front of my trousers. I put my hands down to grasp her wrists and she began to scream; long wild piercing screams, with deep breaths between them.

For the second time in moments, I was paralysed with shock. Mrs Barrington jumped backwards, out of my reach, and un-buttoned her long sheepskin coat. She tore open her blouse and brassière to expose her breasts and threw herself backwards onto the sand, hitching her skirt up around her hips as she fell.

The last thing I remember of her is her slim bare legs, wide-spread, and her lovely sad blue eyes, brimming with tears, and her velvet-soft lips twisted in a hideous scream, and then I ran forward to stop her, and my trousers fell around my ankles and my body toppled onto hers, and I looked up, as if in a dream, to see O'Rooney sliding down the long slope of the dune, his face set in a grim smile of satisfaction, and his truncheon held triumphantly at the ready.